CONFLICT RESOLUTION

The captain's grin broadened. "But I'm a sporting man!" he said cheerfully, staring at his young opponent—who still had his dirk only half-drawn. "So let's have no talk of gun play. Knives you want, knives it is." And with that he brushed back the right side of his coat and drew out his own—

Knife? The thing was grotesque! It reminded Eva, more than anything else, of paintings she'd seen of old Roman gladii.

"We call this a Bowie," said the captain, as cheerfully as ever.

The young tough's face was now very pale. It had finally dawned on the fellow that the man he confronted was not only much better armed than he but also more experienced in real mayhem—and quite obviously willing to prove it.

Eva glanced at Litsa but saw there would be no help coming from her. Litsa had gone from excessive brashness to frightened paralysis.

"Please!" Eva exclaimed. "There's no need for this!" She stepped forward, interposing herself between the two might-be combatants.

The key to resolving the conflict without bloodshed, she decided, was to appeal to the newly arrived American officer. The CoC men were too angry and confused to be able to react intelligently.

"You have the advantage of me, Captain. I am Eva Katherine von Anhalt-Dessau. And you are . . . ?"

He shifted the grin to her and made a slight bow. Just enough to be polite, not enough to lose sight of his possible antagonist. "Captain Harry Lefferts, at your service."

Litsa lapsed into blasphemy. "Oh, dear God!" she exclaimed, her hand now going up toward her throat. "You're . . . real?"

Eva almost laughed. Truth be told, she'd thought herself that the "Captain Harry Lefferts" of current folklore was mostly nonsense. Seeing the man in the flesh, however . . .

Maybe not.

—From "Scarface" by Eric Flint

ERIC FLINT'S BEST-SELLING RING OF FIRE SERIES

For a complete list of Eric Flint books, please go to www.baen.com.

RING OF FIRE IV

EDITED BY
ERIC FLINT

Ring of Fire IV

This is a work of fiction. All the characters and events portrayed in this book are fictional, and any resemblance to real people or incidents is purely coincidental.

Copyright © 2016 by Eric Flint

A Baen Books Original

Baen Publishing Enterprises
P.O. Box 1403
Riverdale, NY 10471
www.baen.com

ISBN: 978-1-4814-8238-7

Cover art by Tom Kidd
Maps by Michael Knopp

First Baen paperback printing, March 2017

Distributed by Simon & Schuster
1230 Avenue of the Americas
New York, NY 10020

Pages by Joy Freeman (www.pagesbyjoy.com)
Printed in the United States of America

To Don Hodges

Contents

RING OF FIRE IV

Preface

Eric Flint

In February of last year, I received an email from David Brin telling me that, moved by a sudden impulse, he'd just written a story set in my 1632 universe. The novelette, titled "71," was attached to the email. He hoped it would fit within the series and could be published in one of the venues associated with it.

The submission came as a complete surprise to me. David and I have been friends for a number of years, and I knew that he followed the 1632 series quite closely. (For the record, I've been a fan of David's work since reading *Startide Rising* more than thirty years ago.) But I'd had no idea that David was considering writing for the 1632 series himself.

My reaction was … mixed, to be honest. On the one hand, I was delighted—ecstatic wouldn't be too strong a term—to get a submission from David Brin. David's been at the top of the science fiction field for a very long time and there are few if any authors as well known and respected as he is. Leaving aside

1

such intangible issues as prestige-by-association, I'm a professional author and as such never take my eye for very long off the commercial aspects of my trade. Having a story by David Brin in one of the 1632 anthologies was bound to boost sales for it.

On the other hand...

Writing stories that are set in another author's universe is easy to do. Witness the ongoing popularity and voluminous output associated with so-called "fan fiction." But it's very hard to do *well*. Writing in a universe you didn't create yourself does not eliminate the need to tell a story that works on its own terms. It just adds the difficulty of making sure the story works within the terms of the established setting as well.

That problem is compounded by the nature of the 1632 series itself. By now, fifteen years after the series was launched with my novel *1632*, the series—also known as the Ring of Fire series—has generated seventeen novels, fourteen anthologies of short fiction (counting this one) and sixty-five issues of a professional magazine devoted to the series, the *Grantville Gazette*. Since I hadn't done it in several years, I took the time while writing this preface to add up what that all came to currently in terms of word count. (Professionals in publishing generally use word counts to calculate length, not number of pages. That's because words are fixed whereas pages are extremely variable depending on such things as the margins, font type used, font size, etc.)

It came to the following, rounded off to the nearest thousand. Novels: 2,895,000 words; print anthologies: 2,193,000 words; electronic books and magazine: 5,673,000 words. Allowing for the fact that a little over one million words in the magazine were reissued in paper editions and should be subtracted to determine a net amount, the total count for the series as a whole comes to around 9,674,000 words.

If you're wondering what that number translates into in Reader Terms, think of it this way: The total word count for Tolkien's *Lord of the Rings* trilogy is about 455,000 words; that of Tolstoy's *War and Peace*, a little over 587,000 words. In other words, as of today the 1632 series is twenty-one times longer than *Lord of the Rings* and more than sixteen times the length of *War and Peace*.

It's not just a question of numbers, either. The multitude of stories in the 1632 series constantly intercept each other, overlap both in chronology and characters, and have plots whose elements are determined or at least shaped by the plots of other stories.

And...that was the setting into which one David Brin, jaunty *raconteur*, chose to place a story.

What could go wrong?

Mind you, I wasn't concerned that David's story wouldn't work on its own terms. There's a reason David has the status he does. I was no more worried that he'd tell a poor story than I'd be of a top-ranked major league pitcher not being able to reach the plate. My concern was that however good the story might be, it would fit so poorly within the framework of my series that I'd be confronted with the awkward necessity of explaining to an author who's a lot more famous than I am, has sold a hell of a lot more books, has a ton of awards where mine can be weighed in ounces if not grams—not to mention that he appears on television quite frequently whereas my relationship with the device is to sit in front of it with a bowl of popcorn in my lap—that his story either needed to be scrapped or at the very least completely rewritten.

Gah. Most authors in the 1632 series—of which there are now almost one hundred and fifty—start as fans of the series and learn to write fiction *within* that universe. That's true of most of my coauthors of novels, too, not just short fiction. Andrew Dennis, Virginia DeMarce, Gorg Huff, Paula Goodlett, David Carrico, Griffin Barber (forthcoming), Iver Cooper (forthcoming), Mark Huston (forthcoming)—all of them began as fans writing for the magazine or one or another anthology, before they went on to work with me on novel-length stories. That same trajectory is true as well of authors who've produced books of their own in the series: Virginia DeMarce (*1635: The Tangled Web*), Iver Cooper (*1636: Seas of Fortune*), Herbert Sakalaucks (*The Danish Scheme*), Kerryn Offord and Rick Boatright (*1636: The Chronicles of Dr. Gribbleflotz*—forthcoming August 2016), Anette Pedersen, *The Wars on the Rhine* (forthcoming), Robert Waters (title-to-be-determined, forthcoming) and it will be true of others as well.

Only six established professional authors have worked regularly within the series. Those are David Weber, Mercedes Lackey, Dave Freer, K.D. Wentworth, Charles H. Gannon and Walter H. Hunt. But the first four of them are long-time collaborators of mine, in other settings as well as my own. I've coauthored five novels (so far) with David Weber, two of them in the 1632 universe and three in his own Honor Harrington universe. I've coauthored five novels (so far) with Misty Lackey, none of them in the 1632 setting. I've coauthored no fewer than *ten* novels with Dave Freer, in five separate settings. I coauthored two novels with Kathy Wentworth in our Jao Empire setting before her untimely death cut that partnership short. (David Carrico, who emerged in the 1632 series, is my coauthor on the third book in the series, *The Span of Empire,* which is coming out this September.)

The point being that these were all authors with whom I'd collaborated many times and with whom I had a well-established, tried and tested working relationship. And when Chuck Gannon and Walter Hunt came into the universe, they came in full-bore. Both of them have works and settings of their own—three of Chuck's novels have been nominated for the Nebula award—but for both of them the 1632 series is an integral part of their unfolding careers.

I had no such relationship with David Brin. We're friends, yes, and we like and admire each other's work. But that's not the same thing—trust me, it really isn't—as being able to call Chuck or Walter on the phone and tell them their latest chapter isn't fit for anything except to be torn up for kitty litter and listen to them explain to me that the chapters were fine and the problem is entirely on my end because I'm too dumb to know good writing when I see it.

Happily, my worries proved groundless. David did a brilliant job of figuring out how he could couch his own uniquely Briniac story (of course the word exists—I just used it, didn't I?) in the 1632 series by going all the way back to the very root of the series and tweaking what we might call its cosmological constant. This is no small feat, given that the same cosmological constant applies to (so far) two other connected universes—that of the novels *Time Spike*, which I coauthored with Marilyn Kosmatka, and the forthcoming *The Alexander Inheritance*, coauthored with Paula Goodlett and Gorg Huff.

But, he managed to do it. David's speculation on the possible implications of the Ring of Fire are fascinating on their own terms without causing any problem for the established premises of the series. And the story he told on that speculative basis fits nicely within the series itself, advances it in certain directions—and, most important of all, is a lot of fun to read. You will enjoy it.

I normally use my preface to encapsulate most of the stories in these *Ring of Fire* anthologies. But this preface has grown overlong, so I'll only talk a little about my own story.

Scarface has several purposes. The first—always the basic one for any story—is to entertain the reader. This I believe it does; in fact, does quite well—but you will be the judge of that yourself.

The other two purposes belong to the series as a whole. One of them is to bring back on stage two characters who were at the center of one novel in the 1632 series—those being Ron Stone and Missy Jenkins from *1635: The Dreeson Incident*—and, in the case of Ron Stone, he is also an integral part of the Stone family which has figured so prominently in the 1632 series since Mercedes Lackey introduced them in the very first *Ring of Fire* anthology in her story "To Dye For." In one way or another, one or another—usually more than one—of the Stones has appeared and had an impact on several other novels:

1634: The Galileo Affair; 1635: The Cannon Law and *1635: The Papal Stakes*.

They will continue to do so, and hence I felt it would be valuable to bring Ron and Missy (and to a lesser extent Gerry Stone) back onto the center court of the series.

The final purpose was even more important to me. I first introduced Harry Lefferts in the founding novel of the series, *1632*. He's a vivid character, but a rather one-dimensional one. He retained that basic nature in the next two mainline novels of the series, *1633* and *1634: The Baltic War*. He was a prominent character in both novels—more than he was in *1632*, certainly—but still remained quite similar to the character as he first appeared.

You can only go so far with characters like that. After a while, you either have to drop them, allow them to quietly fade away, or you have to develop them. I don't like to drop characters I've put that much work into, unless it's really necessary—and I didn't think it was with Harry.

There was this, as well. His best friend, Darryl McCarthy, was very similar in type. But because of his situation, Darryl, who came into his own in *1633*, *1634: The Baltic War* and *1635: A Parcel of Rogues*, had no choice but to evolve and mature. Wouldn't it be interesting, I thought, to continue that friendship?—but with the friends now separated and each undergoing his own evolution.

That was a large part of the thinking that lay behind the first novel I wrote with Chuck Cannon, *1635: The Papal Stakes*. There, for the first time in his life, the brash and overly self-confident Harry Lefferts gets knocked down. Hammered flat, in fact. By the end of the novel he's recovered a great deal of his poise, but he'll obviously never be the same again.

So, what happens to Harry next? Well, you're about to find out.

Eric Flint
February 23, 2016

71

David Brin

As deeply roiled and troubled as we all have been, ever since the Ring of Fire brought disruption to our time, sending all fixed notions a-tumble, how seldom have we pondered the greater picture—the "context" of it all, as up-timers so concisely put it?

I refer to the event itself, the very act of carving a town out of twentieth-century America and dropping it into the Germanies, three hundred and sixty-nine years earlier. Engrossed as we have been, in the consequential aftermath, we have tended to wave away the act itself! We beg the question, calling it simply an Act of God.

Indeed, as a Lutheran layman, I am inclined to accept that basic explanation. The event's sheer magnitude can only have had divine originating power. Take that as given.

As to the purpose of it all? That, too, remains opaque. And yet, one aspect by now seems clear to most down-timers. By winning an unbroken chain of successive victories, the Americans and their allies

9

have at minimum forced a burden of proof upon those potentates who condemn up-timers as satanic beings. To many deeply religious folk, there is a rising sense of vindication, even blessing about them.

A consensus is growing that "America" was not named for some Italian map-maker, after all, but rather for "himmel-reich," or heavenly country. Or so goes the well-beloved rumor, nowadays, spread especially by the Committees of Correspondence.

And yet, be that as it may, "the Will of God" leaves so many other matters darkly unexamined, even by speculation! Indeed, these appear to be ignored by the Grantvillers themselves.

Among those neglected questions, one has burned— especially harsh and bright—in the mind of this humble observer.

What happened to the village of Milda, nestled in a bend of the small river Leutra in Thuringia, when it was erased from our time and reckoning by the Ring of Fire, replaced by fabulous Grantville?

To many, the answer would seem obvious—that it was a simple trade.

A swap!

And hence, the bemused neighbors of Grantville— West Virginians of the United States of America, in the year 2000—received, in exchange for their departed metropolis, a few bewildered, terrified seventeenth-century Germans, hopelessly archaic and primitive, of no practical use at all, except as recipients of kindness and largesse until—amid the welcoming spirit of that blissful nation, they would merge, adapt and transform into boring-but-content citizens. Of little import, other than as curiosities.

A trade? A swap? Oh, perhaps it was so.

Only, dear reader, let me endeavor to persuade you that—in the immortal words of the up-time bard and balladeer Ira Gershwin—it ain't necessarily so.

Kurt, Baron von Wolfschild, stared down upon a long column of refugees.

For that, clearly, they were, hundreds of them, shambling with meager possessions balanced atop heads or strapped upon backs. And, alongside the road, for as far as he could see with his foggy spyglass, many articles the migrants had abandoned, so that children might ride shoulders, instead. Those scattered discards were punctuated by an occasional old man or woman, shrilly insistent to be left behind, so that a family might live.

Such telltales were all too familiar to a knight whose own demesne suffered this very same fate, not so long ago.

People ... my tenants, villagers and farmers ... who counted on my brothers and me, to protect them. Cut down like wheat, or else scattered to the wind.

These fugitives were a grimy lot, as clouds of dust hovered in both winding directions along the bone-dry road. *In a bone-dry land,* he pondered, rising on his stirrups to scan every unfamiliar horizon. This hilly countryside wasn't exactly a desert—Kurt had seen the real thing, guarding a Genoese diplomatic mission to Egypt, almost a decade ago. Here, trees and shrubs dotted every slope. Indeed, some distance below, through a southern haze, he could make out green and fertile fields. *At least, I think that's south.* And far beyond, the shoreline of some lake or small sea.

Still, the scouts had not been drunk or lying. This was clearly not the green-forested dampness of central Germany. Nor were these Germans, shambling below on open-toed sandals. Both women and men wore robelike garments and cloth headdresses, scarves, or turbans—it was rare to spot exposed hair, except among the weary-looking children.

Now, some of the more alert refugees appeared to take notice, pointing uphill toward Kurt and his men—twenty *Landsknecht* cavalry in battered helmets and cuirasses, with two dozen pikemen and ten arquebusiers marching up from behind. Murmurs of worry arose from the dusty migrants.

Not that Kurt could blame them. His own company of mercenary guardsmen had a pretty clean record, protecting merchants through the hellscape that recently stretched from Alps to Baltic. But no civilian who still had any grip upon reality would be placid at the sight of armed and armored men.

"What's that language they're gabbling?" complained the young adventurer, Samuel Burns, from his over-sized charger to Kurt's left.

The Hollander sergeant, Lucas Kuipers, shrugged broad shoulders, looking to his commander for orders.

Kurt listened carefully for a moment. "It . . . sounds a bit like Hebrew . . . or Arabic . . . and neither. Perhaps something in between. I can't speak either of them well enough to tell. You'd better send a rider back to fetch Father Braun."

"Hebrew? So many Jews?" Burns shook his head.

"Braun won't want to come," Sergeant Kuipers said. "The villagers are terrified, since we all passed through the Mouth of Hell."

A good name for it, Kurt thought. Just over an hour ago, it had seemed that Milda and its surroundings were, indeed, being swallowed by some fiery gullet, amid a shaking, noise and painful brilliance that just had to be infernal.

"They think that it's the end time," Kuipers went on, in thickly accented Low German. "Especially after hearing what happened to Magdeburg. Half of the peasants seem bent on setting fire to their hovels, then throwing themselves on the flames."

Kurt shrugged. It was all right for the sergeant to raise a point. But a commander's silence should speak for itself. And so, with hardly a pause, Kuipers turned in his saddle to shout for a courier. *Two,* since one horse would be needed to bring the priest, if the Jesuit was wanted in such a hurry.

"*Gut.*" Kurt nodded. A sergeant who thinks is worth his weight in coppers. Maybe even silver.

Watching the riders depart, he only half listened as Kuipers began shouting at the infantry, arraying them in some kind of presentable order. Of course, the pikemen and arquebusiers weren't part of Kurt's *landsknecht* company, which had only been passing through Milda, escorting a small commercial caravan, when the calamity struck. These footmen were a motley assortment of local militia and grizzled veterans, augmented by deserters—from both Tilly's Catholic army and Protestant Magdeburgers—fleeing the atrocities to Milda's north. That siege, according to breathless reports, had come to an end as forces of the Austrian emperor and the Roman Church performed a feat of butchery surpassing the massacre of Cathars at Beziers in 1209. Perhaps even matching horror stories from the Crusades.

*Hell's mouth, indeed. What more do we deserve,
for allowing such things to happen, and murderers
to enrich themselves?*

The new infantry recruits seemed grateful to have
found employment with Kurt's company, not the richest guard unit, by any means, but one that seemed at
least free of taint from this latest soul-killing crime.
Moreover, Kurt, Baron von Wolfschild had forbidden
any man to ask religious questions of any other. There
would be none of that.

Kurt watched the couriers gallop across a broad
pasture, then ascend a rough, recently blazed trail
over a shrubby hill, disappearing beyond the crest
to where...

The terrain beyond that point was stark in Kurt's
mind, if just out of sight. There, a new, shiny-smooth
ridgeline jutted a few feet above the natural topog-
raphy. A perfect circle, it seemed, a couple of imperial miles across, centered half a mile west of little
Milda. Within, the pines and birches of Thuringia still
trembled from recent disruption, in stark contrast to
these slopes of cedar, cypress and scrub oak.

*Now that I think on it. This does resemble the
Levant...*

From here, he could see the true extant of Milda's
plug, taken fiercely out of Germany. A large hill or
small mountain loomed on the other side. There, the
circle's shiny-sheer boundary loomed *above* the plug,
and even seemed to arc a little over one of Milda's
hamlets, surrounding the local mill.

*We'll have to survey water sources, not only for
drinking but to reestablish the pond and millrace,* he
pondered, then shook his head over the strangeness

of such thoughts. Clearly, he was keeping a shocked mind busy with pragmatic fantasies, rather than grappling with what's obvious...

...for example, that the refugees below could only be another group of damned beings, like the hapless Germans who had come to join them, through Hell's Mouth. This outer circle did not much resemble the description in Dante's *Inferno*. But then, Kurt's Latin had been rudimentary when he read it.

At a cry, he turned his head to see young Samuel pointing south, not at the refugees but upslope-east a way, where clusters of figures—several score, at least—were descending rapidly from a rocky passage, perhaps a narrow pass through the hills. An ideal lair for bandits, he realized.

Metal flashed in the sun. A woman screamed. Then another. And then several terrified men.

My heart. Should it be racing like this, if I am already dead? How could a corpse or damned soul feel this familiar mixture—of fear, loathing and exhilaration—that sweeps over me, before combat?

Hell or not, this situation offered a clear enough choice. Pure evil was afoot, and Kurt, Baron von Wolfschild had means at his disposal to deal with it. Indeed, he reckoned it unlikely that there was anything better to do.

"Sergeant. Please get the infantry moving. Cavalry on me.

"Then have the bugler announce us."

#

"Wow," John Dennis Flannery said as he turned a page, and noted the hash or pound symbol "#" denoting a minor scene break, at exactly the right moment in this story. His left-hand prosthetic slipped and the sheet went floating off his desk...to be caught by the author, who gently placed it atop the pile, face down.

"Wow," John repeated. "It's even better on second reading. The rhythms, the beat and tempo of prose. They're...very modern."

"Modern, truly? Like fictions of the twentieth century? I am so glad. I tried to break so many down-time habits of what you call 'flowery prose,' concentrating instead upon the main character's *point of view*."

"Right. The hardest thing for a novice to grok, even back in America. Point of view. Show us the world, the situation through your protagonist's thoughts and senses. And especially through his *assumptions*. Things he takes for granted. Heinlein was the master of that technique."

"Yes, I studied and copied many of his story openings, until the method became clear to me."

"Only next you segue..." John used his right-hand claw to shift five more pages to the other pile... "into a seriously cool *battle scene,* during which the baron character coordinates his *landsknecht* cavalry and the Milda militia to defeat bandits bent on rape and murder. Thereby winning devotion from a few of the most important refugees. Of course anyone will recognize your inspiration."

"Of course. From the way Michael Stearns rallied his West Virginian mine workers to defeat a horde of Tilly's raiders, thus earning the admiration of his future wife. Do...do you think the *homage* is too blatant?"

"Who cares!" John shrugged. "It's seriously good action!"

"I am so relieved that you think so. I know that I

can still be prolix and garrulous. For example in my prologue—"

"Oh, don't worry about that." John waved away the author's concern. "Prologues are supposed to be like that. Heck, it will help prove that the creator was an authentic down-timer, and not Jason Glazer or me, ghost-writing it.

"Still, what I want to know is *how* you picked up these techniques for point of view and action so quickly. How did you learn it all so fast?"

John's left hook clanked against his spectacles as he pushed them back a bit. They kept sliding down his nose and he wanted to see this fellow, who could be everything he and his partners were looking for.

Don't get your hopes up too high.

"The boardinghouse here in Grantville where I am staying...the landlord has a complete collection of *Analog* magazine, which he guards like a wolfhound! But I talked him into letting me read selected stories. Eventually, he warmed to me and began enthusiastically choosing—even explaining—the best ones for me."

"Old Homer Snider, yeah. He makes me wear gloves when I come over to copy a story for the zine. He must really like you."

The author wasn't wearing clerical garb, today. Just a down-time shirt and trousers, modeled on up-time jeans and a pullover.

"I believe he sees me as a...convert."

"To science fiction?" John laughed. "Yeah. I guess there's always been an aspect of proselytizing religion to—"

He cut off abruptly with a sharp hiss, as pain lanced up his arms from the stumps at both ends.

Vision blurred for a few seconds, till he found his visitor leaning over him.

"Mein herr... Mr. Flannery. Shall I go for a doctor?"

John shook his head. "No, just... give me a second. It always passes."

The author returned to his seat and pretended to be busy with papers from a leather valise, till John finally shifted in his chair with a sigh.

"You can see why we're subsidized by the state, and by the USE Veterans' Foundation. A man who loses his legs can still do skilled tasks like machinery assembly. But a man without hands?" He lifted both arms, letting the question hang.

"Intellectual pursuits, of course." The visitor had a choked tightness in his throat.

"It's busy work."

"I beg to differ, Herr Flannery! What you are accomplishing, with your zine, is so much more than giving war amputees something to do!"

He gestured past John's office, piled high with manuscripts and proofs, toward the main workroom, where a dozen men and several women bustled about the tasks of a publishing house, one of just a few that had not moved from Grantville to the modern, bustling, capital city of Magdeburg. All but two of the staff bore major disabilities, yet hurried busily to meet deadlines.

"Well, my own disaster wasn't from battle, but a freak industrial..."

"Perhaps, as an up-timer, you underestimate the powerful effects that this literature is having, across Europe and beyond. Except in countries where it has been banned, for the insidious, underlying assumption of science fiction, that *change* is a permanent fact of life! And that any child, of no matter what mean background, can become an agent of change. No, Herr Flannery. You are still potent. Your 'hands' now guide minds upward, gently pushing them to ponder how things might be different than they are!"

"Well, that can be dangerous in these times. There are many out there, in both low and high places, who consider science fiction to be heretical, blasphemous, and radically revolutionary."

"Making you popular with the Committees of Correspondence, of course."

John shrugged. "A connection we don't publicly encourage. We get more than enough death threats. And, only last month, a crude pipe bomb. Fortunately, we discovered it in time. Still, I try to open all the packages myself since, as you can see, I have little left to lose."

He lifted both prosthetics into the light.

"Ah, but we shall soon put a stop to that!" commented a youthful voice from behind John. He turned to see Hercule Savinien casting a lanky shadow through the doorway. The sixteen-year-old editorial apprentice had survived Charles de La Porte's futile infantry advance at the Battle of Ahrensbök, with only a severe limp, thanks to twentieth-century field medicine. He now flourished a *poignard* dagger of considerable heft.

"An elegant blade like this may be obsolete for matters of honor," the young man said, in thickly accented English. "But it still can suffice as a letter-opener!"

John frowned, pretending more anger than he felt.

"Hercule, go stick that prodigious proboscis of yours into someone else's business. Unless you have some good reason to be bothering us?"

The boy's eyes flashed briefly with a mix of warning and fierce intelligence . . . but that heat swiftly lapsed into a tolerant grin.

"Jason and Jean-Baptiste have galleys for the next issue ready, when *monsieur l'editeur* will deign to look them over."

"Hm. And I assume *you* already have?"

"But of course." A gallic shrug. "The usual mix of TwenCen reprints and hack melodramas from my fellow primitives of this benighted era, who could not emulate Delaney or Verne, if their very lives depended on a *soupcon* of creative verve. If *you* had any *real* taste, you might look closer to home. Possibly in-house, for—"

"Your time will come. That is, if you drop some of your own preening pretentiousness. If you focus. Learn patience and craft, as the deacon here has done." John gestured toward his guest. "Now get out!"

Hercule Savinien's grin only widened as he delivered a flourished bow that would have served in any royal court—though conveying a shameless touch of wry sarcasm—and departed. John stared after the apprentice for an instant, then shook his head. Turning back to the visitor, he carefully used the artificial gripper of his right-hand prosthetic to shift, then pluck up the next page of the manuscript, having to clear his throat, before he spoke.

"Now, where were we? Ah, yes. What is . . . what's so cool about this story of yours—unlike so much of the 'sci-fi' we get submitted here—is that you've taken a speculative premise based upon our own shocking and strangely transformed world, *extrapolating* it into a plausible thought experiment of your very own.

"This notion, for example, that the Ring of Fire wasn't a simple *swap* of two land-plugs, one of them shifting *backward* to become powerful and destiny-changing, while the other one, shifted forward to the year 2000, would be inherently harmless, pathetically unimportant... I never realized how *smug* that image was. How self-important and based on unwarranted assumptions.

"In other words, how very *American*!" John laughed ruefully. "But you point out that it may not have been a swap, at all! It could instead be a *chain*. A sequence, shuttling a series of spheres of space-time ever-backward, one following the other, like—"

He shook his head, unable to come up with a metaphor. The visitor nodded, though with some reticence.

"At the Grantville high school, I never fail to attend Demonstration Tuesday. They once showed us a *laser*, whose magical medium is capped, at both ends, by inward facing mirrors. At the time, I was struck that perhaps the Ring of Fire was like such a device, only with *destiny* as the active medium..."

"Whoa. What a way-cool idea!" John reached for his pencil with the special grip-end.

"Only then, later the same night, it came to me in a dream... a dream that was so much more than..."

The author paused, staring into space, then shook himself in order to resume. "Well, it came to me that perhaps there might be mirror *after* mirror, after mirror...."

His voice trailed off again, as John scribbled.

"Huh. Of course the implicit paradoxes abound. We've assumed that either Grantville's arrival *changed* the former timeline, erasing and replacing the one we came from, or else it started a new, *branching* timestream that leaves the original one in place. The new one that received Grantville will gain advantages and get many boosts and head starts as a result, but also some losses. Either way, Grantville is making a huge difference.

"In contrast, Milda Village would have very little impact, arriving in the year 2000—at most a few hundred confused villagers and traders, farmers and soldiers with antique weapons and antiquated technologies...

"On the other hand, if Milda instead bounced *further back* in time, say another thousand years—"

"More like fifteen centuries."

"Yeah, in your story, more than fifteen hundred years...then it implies branching after branching of *multiple* timelines! Each one offering a technological boost to more-primitive ancestors...no offense?"

"None taken, Herr Flannery."

"In fact, why stop there? If you squint, you can envision *another* story about—"

John felt a tingle in his spine. A sense, soft but familiar, that he had just missed something important. He lifted his head from the notepad sketch that he had begun, depicting a trellis of possible histories. Now he looked, yet again at the author.

At his very distant facial expression.

John played back the conversation a bit. Then he twisted his hand-hook to put the pencil down.

"Tell me about your dream," he said.

Kurt had been pleased, day before yesterday, to find a market fair in this part of Thuringia. His troopers murmured happily as the small *landsknecht* company rode into Milda, escorting three cargo wagons and two carriages of merchant dignitaries. Perhaps, this close to Jena, the locals felt some normality, especially with a university town between them and the fighting.

It was a small fair—three or four tents where locals compared garden produce and bragged over samples of their winter piecework, while tapping barrels of home brew and betting on wrestling matches—plus a "theater" consisting of a painted backdrop behind a rickety stage, for pantomimes and palmers, preaching repentance while lacing songs and bawdy jokes amid stern morality plays.

The illusion was brave, but threadbare, and it lasted only till a breathless rider came racing though, panting news of Magdeburg.

At least thirty thousand dead and the whole city burned to the ground, with detachments of Tilly's killers now spreading even this way.

Half of the merchants wanted to turn around. The rest urged hurrying on to Jena. Their argument had raged on for hours, while a troupe of dispirited jugglers tried to herd everyone back to the little fairground for the midday highlight—a march of the local militia, with burnished pikes and laughably archaic matchlock muskets. Kurt's frantic employers made the local inn so depressing that his *Landsknechte* took their beers outside, perching on a fence to heckle as pot-bellied volunteers high stepped, trying to look martially impressive in review.

Well there's no laughing at them anymore, he now thought, watching by firelight as two of the farmer-soldiers got stitched by a pair of midwives. Beyond the circle of light, barely in view, were two more forms, shrouded and still—a tanner's apprentice and the miller's youngest son—who had been less lucky during the brief, nasty battle.

It's my fault, of course, he thought. *If only I'd ordered my cavalry to use their pistols sooner. But who knew so many bandits would be terrified by a little gunfire?*

At least none of his *Landsknechte* had been killed or injured. They now mingled freely with the militia men, who had fought a pitched battle with unexpected bravery. Still, the mercenary guardsmen were in a foul mood. The robbers had nothing of value to pillage, beyond short swords of questionable value, and most of the refugees had scattered in all directions, leaving only a couple of dozen to be collared and prodded uphill, past the Hell Mouth ring, all the way back to Milda, for questioning by Father Braun.

And our special guests, he added, peering past the coals at a cluster of people seated along the edge of the pantomime stage, where all the assembled Germans could see them. Two middle-aged men, three women and four children—all of them apparently of the same family—dressed better than the average refugee...plus an elderly fellow with gnarled hands and piercing eyes, to whom everyone deferred, as if he were an abbot or bishop.

Hours ago, during the bandit attack, both of the younger men and one woman had tried valiantly to rally other émigrés and prepare a defense—*it would have been futile, of course,* but at least they tried—when the robbers' attention had been drawn away by a phalanx of approaching Milda pikemen.

The foe never saw Kurt's cavalry till it was too late. Unlike the involuntary ones, who huddled under the half-tent behind them, this family had required no urging to ascend toward Milda, eagerly and gratefully following the pikemen while helping the wounded. Without displaying any dread, they had crossed the Hell Mouth boundary, staring at the transplanted disk of Germany as afternoon waned and Kurt rode about swiftly, inspecting the perimeter, setting things in order for nightfall.

Now, the family sat, cross-legged but erect, apparently more curious than fearful. When offered food, they spurned all meats and sniffed at the boiled potatoes, till the youngest woman smiled—an expression like sunlight—then nodded gratefully and placed a bowl before the old man, who murmured a few words of blessing, then began to eat with slow care. Gently urging the frightened ones, she got first children and then other adults to join in.

A noblewoman of some kind, Kurt realized. Or at least a natural leader, as well as something of a beauty...if you ignored a deep scar that ran from her left ear down to the line of her jaw. At one point, her gaze briefly locked with Kurt's—as it had after the battle—measuring, as if *she* were the one here with real power. Then she went back to watching intently—whispering now and then into the old fellow's ear—as Father Braun reported, at tedious length, what he had learned.

"...and so, after this extensive philological comparison, I finally concluded that they speak *Aramaic,* a tongue quite similar to Hebrew, and hence confirming that most of the denizens of this region appear to be *Jews,* plus some Samaritans, Syrians..."

The rest of the cleric's recitation was drowned out

by a mutter of consternation from those seated on
makeshift benches and crowding in from all sides—a
motley assortment of Milda residents, travelers, soldiers, teamsters, palmers, and shabby entertainers,
almost all of those who were trapped here when the
Hell Mouth snapped around Milda. Far too many to
congregate within the small village inn.

Kurt frowned at the reaction. Not all of the murmurs were actively hateful. He figured most were
only shocked to learn that a despised minority now
apparently surrounded them, in great numbers. And
at least some of these Jews were armed.

During his travels, Kurt had learned how most
prejudices were as useful as a hymnal in a privy.
Anyway, we don't have time for this. He stepped into
the light, clearing his throat. Those nearby swiftly
took the hint—from a nobleman and commander of
their little army—to settle down. Certainly, the village
headman and masters, seated on a front row bench,
seemed happy to defer.

"What about our other guests?" Kurt pointed to
a trio of grimy men who were clearly soldiers, staring fixedly at the coals, with bound wrists. Though
clean-shaven—unlike most of the local males—they
appeared to be in shock. As Kurt had felt earlier,
when he inspected their confiscated weapons . . . short,
gladius-style swords and skirted leather armor, of a
type that looked so familiar.

"I was unable to gather much from those three,"
Braun said. "They were found wandering just outside
the Hell Mouth, having apparently taken the brunt of
it, near what seems to have been the outermost wall
of some fortification."

Kurt had examined the wall in question, just before nightfall. Most of the stronghold must have been sliced away by the Hell Mouth, vanishing completely when Milda's plug of Thuringia displaced whatever had been here, before.

I wonder where that plug of land wound up, with its garrison of armed men. Perhaps they are now back where we came from?

If so, they would stand little chance against Tilly's raiders. From what he could tell, these locals had never heard of gunpowder.

"Well, never mind them. What else did you learn from the refugees?"

Braun nodded. "My smattering of Hebrew might not have sufficed. Certainly I doubted the testimony of my ears ... until this young woman made my task much easier by speaking to me, at last, in rather good Latin."

The beauty with the scar. Kurt stepped forward and switched from German.

"Est quod verum? Tu loqueris? You speak Latin? Why did you not say so before?"

She whispered in the old man's ear. He nodded permission, and she met Kurt's gaze with confident serenity.

"Et non petisti," she replied to his question. *You did not ask.*

Kurt's initial flare at her impertinence quickly tempered. Courage was acceptable coin, and he liked women who made eye-contact. So he nodded, with the faintest upturn at one corner of his mouth ... then turned and motioned for the priest to continue.

Braun sighed, as if he dreaded coming to this part.

"With her help, I questioned every person about the *name* of this region, into which we find ourselves plunged. They all replied with great assurance and consistency."

"It's hell!" screamed one high-pitched voice, possibly a hysterical man.

The Jesuit shook his head.

"Nay, it is Judea."

Kurt nodded. He had already suspected as much, from the terrain, foliage, and much else. Around him, Catholics told their rosaries while other voices spoke in hushed tones of the Holy Land.

"Then it's *worse* than hell," cried the same pessimist. "Tomorrow we'll face a thousand Turks!"

Father Braun raised a hand.

"That might have been true, had a mere shift in *location* been the only aspect of what happened to us, today. Only there is more, far more shocking than that.

"It appears, my dear children, that—by some great wonder achievable only by divine will—we have also been transported through *time.*"

This brought on silence so deep that only the crackling logs spoke. Indeed, it seemed that most of the villagers and travelers and soldiers merely blinked, assuming that the priest had shifted to some non-germanic tongue.

Kurt stepped closer to the firelight. *Someone* had to look and sound confident at this point, though his own calm was more a matter of numbness than *noblesse*. Anyway, he already had guessed the answer to his next question.

"What is the date then, Father?"

"Ahem. Well. There are discrepancies of calendar

to take into account. It's difficult to narrow down precisely. That is..."

"Priest—" Kurt gave him the full-on baron-look.

The Jesuit threw his shoulders back, as if defying fate even to utter it aloud. In so doing, he revealed a build that must have once—in a former life—been that of a soldier.

"The date is seventy, or seventy-one, or two or three, or perhaps seventy-four years... after the birth of our lord. We stand above the valley where he dwelled as a child, within sight of the sea where he preached and fished for souls."

Kurt nodded, accepting the finality of a diagnosis, already known.

"And the poor people who we see, shambling along these roads in despair? What calamity do they flee?"

He was envisioning Magdeburg, only much, much worse.

Father Braun met his eyes.

"It is as you suppose, Baron von Wolfschild. They are escaping the wrath of the Roman emperor-to-be, Titus, who has, of late, burned the holy Temple itself. And the city of Jerusalem."

Jason was having none of it.

"Come on, Johnny. It's a great story! The fellow clearly studied Piper and de Camp, in all those *Analog* zines he read. He's a natural. Anyway, weren't we looking hard for some down-timers with talent?"

Before John could answer, Sister Maria Celeste emitted a curt cough. She had been adjusting the pads on Jason's wheelchair, which kept bunching up, he fidgeted so.

"And what am I, *signore?* Chopped kidney? I have submitted to you several fine *fantasies aeronatical dei mondi qui sopra,* based upon discoveries made by my father. Yet, all you have seen fit to publish of my work are a few short poems. While you endlessly encourage *those* two rascals to believe they hold promise, as writers!"

She nodded toward the front door of the Literary Home for Wounded Veterans...where a pair of figures dressed in black tried to seem innocuous, failing to conceal daggers at their hips. A nightly charade. Caught in the act, thirteen-year-old Jean-Baptiste murmured—"We're just goin' out for a—for some air, messieurs."

The older boy, Hercule Savinien, simply grinned, as if daring anyone to make something of their evening ritual. Again, the flourished bow.

"Macht die Tür zu!" one of the other vets shouted, unnecessarily, as the lads slammed the door behind them.

"Traps and snares and trip-wires." The nun shook her head. "Romantic dolts! They should be working for *Spy Magazine,* and not *Galaxy.*" She turned her attentions to John, helping him to remove his prosthetics.

"Oh, what's the harm?" Jason said. "They think they're protecting us from assassins. And the wires are always gone, by morning. Anyway, now that your father has also moved to Grantville, won't you be too busy—"

"For writing? Typical man! Your condescension is insulting, as if a woman cannot develop her art while caring for others. I am tempted to report you to Gretchen Richter. Or, better yet, perhaps I will start up my *own* magazine. One dedicated to truly fabulous tales, unrestrained by your confining Rules of Extrapolative Storytelling!"

Despite her bellicose words, Maria Celeste's tone was as gentle as her caring touch, as she rubbed each of John's stumps, in turn.

"I . . ." he sighed. "I'll be your first investor."

Jason snorted. "Softie!"

Fortunately, conversation became impossible for a while, as the sixth member of their little commune— Vaclav Klimov—performed his own nightly ritual, cranking up the scratchy old stereo system with "Up on Cripple Creek," by The Band.

Jason muttered. "I swear I'll strangle Klimov, one of these days." Still, he tapped the armrest of his chair, keeping time to the song. And if this home for reclaimed lives were to have a nickname and an anthem, well, John figured they could do worse.

Sister Maria Celeste moved on, tending to the other fellows—efficiently, so she could return to the small cottage next to Grantville's new college, where her elderly father now both studied and taught. While Vaclav played DJ, swapping disks though a selection of blood-rousing tunes, John watched the door. And when the boys returned—pretending to be sneaky—he gave Hercule an eye roll.

I know what you're doing. And I know that you know that I know.

Almost lost under those eyebrows and behind that nose, Hercule's left eye winked. Then with a sweep, he was gone with his young friend. Leaving John to muse.

But do you know that I know your real secret, my young friend?

Caught up in a manhunt ordered by Cardinal Richelieu, just one year after Grantville arrived to upset Europe's teetering balance, scores of French subjects—mostly-bewildered—had found themselves drafted into the army that Richelieu sent marching toward the Baltic. For the youngest of these involuntary recruits, like Jean-Baptiste, the duties of a drummer boy meant no lessening of hardship or danger. Indeed, the generals were under orders. These special levees were to be given places of honor. In the front ranks.

Given what a slaughterhouse Ahrensbök became, it was fortunate that Hercule and Jean Baptiste . . . and Jason on the other side . . . got out with their lives. So many did not.

Fortunately for Jason's prospects of staying out of prison, Klimov only had the stamina to play DJ each night for half an hour or so. The evening serenade ended with another upbeat ode—"Joy to the World." After which peaceful quiet ensued. Soon, beyond the crackling fire, John was able to imagine no Grantville . . . no Germany roiling in change . . . no world wracked with upheaval. Only the universe, spinning on and on.

Or, rather . . . universes.

At last, Jason resumed where he had left off.

"It's one helluva yarn. That big battle at the edge of the Hell Mouth had my heart pounding! Roman siege ladders and catapults against pikes and matchlock muskets? That girl, hurrying back in the nick of time after fetching a *prince* and his men. A descendant of Judah freaking Macabee? Who would expect a seventeenth-century German writer to even know about that guy?"

"Well, in fact, even medieval Christians spoke of Macabee as one of the Nine Worthies," John said. "But I admit, it's solid stuff."

"Okay then. I say we publish it as a serial. As-is." John sighed.

"No way. Not without removing some of the explicit names. And changing the afterword. And even, so, we'd better brace for trouble."

"You're that afraid of fundamentalist terrorists? Screw 'em! We'll be doing our bit for freedom of speech."

"It's not that so much. Though this could unite both Protestant and Catholic extremists in fury." He shook his head. "No. What concerns me is how *sincere* this fellow seems to be. When he told me about his . . . dream . . . I could tell he was holding back. *Vision* might be the word he really meant."

John sat up and leaned toward his partner. "Look, I agree, he could be the first great down-timer science fiction author! I'd like nothing better. But we have to be careful, Jason. He needs guidance, and I don't just mean editorial."

"Because he thinks it may have been *more* than just a daydream? That it all really happened? Huh. It wouldn't be the first time."

"Exactly. Even in our own cynical, materialistic and scientific age, folks were human. And human beings tend to give great credence to their subjective imaginings. *Delusion* is our greatest talent! It can be among our finest gifts, when imagination takes us on grand journeys, that still leave us rooted in reality.

"But it's also been a curse. All of history was warped by *sincere* men and women, convinced that a delusion was real."

"Hmph. Yeah, well, science helps."

"Yes. Science teaches us to say the mantra of maturity—*I might be wrong*. But half of our citizens couldn't grasp that concept, even back in 2000. Picture how hard it is where we find ourselves. Here. Now.

"In fact, I do think this fellow gets it. He's hungry for knowledge and I've talked him into enrolling at the college. With any luck, we may squeak by and he'll become this generation's Asimov or Clarke, a creator of stirring thought-experiments. Instead of..."

John let his implication trail off. But, after a long pause, his partner finished the sentence for him.

"Instead of a prophet."

Lucilius Bassus was a canny old soldier. Kurt knew the type. The man wanted, above all, to achieve his assigned mission—the final pacification of Judea—with as little further fuss as possible. Bald, clean-shaven and a bit shriveled, wearing a white toga with red trim, the general eyed Kurt carefully while introducing his second in command, Lucius Flavius Silva, then offering Kurt a seat in his command tent.

Bassus raised an eyebrow but said nothing when Kurt motioned for Sarah to sit beside him on another camp stool. The rest of the Milda party remained outside, under a flag of truce, watching the highly ordered busy-ness of a disciplined Roman camp. Scowling, Lucius Flavius Silva remained standing in full leather armor, as his commander seated himself on a cushioned bench.

"I was told that your factotum would be a male priest," Bassus said, as servants mixed wine with water and served goblets. Sarah refused, with a soft smile.

"Father Braun is no longer with us," Kurt answered. While his Latin was improving, he still glanced at Sarah. She gave a slight nod. No correction needed, so far. "Our priest left suddenly, hurrying north, to Ephesus. This noblewoman has consented to help you..." he stumbled over the words. The correct grammar.

Sarah finished for him. "To help you, great Lucilius Bassus, to communicate with your loyal German auxiliaries," she said, gesturing an open hand toward Kurt.

That was the story the two of them had concocted, yesterday, after word came that the general had arrived in the Galilee with six fresh cohorts. The core of his legion, ready to advance and wipe out this infestation of strange barbarians. Only the messenger brought a codicil, that Bassus was willing to talk, first.

It's all one big misunderstanding, went the fabulous lie that Sarah translated into flawless Latin.

These aren't enemies. They are fierce German mercenaries who were attached to the Fifth Legion and left behind to garrison this area, when the Fifth returned to Macedonia. Apparently without properly informing the mighty Tenth.

It's not our fault that your centurion, Sextus Callus, attacked us, killing our Roman liaison officer and forcing us to defend ourselves!

Kurt left it to Sarah to spin out an elaborated version, while he tried to convey a best impression upon Bassus—that of a tough and wily, though semi-literate, soldier who cared, above all, about sparing his men further bloodshed, and getting them back to a distant homeland someday, with honor and pay.

Exactly like you, old man.

In terms of casualties, the Judean Revolt had been

the worst war in Roman history. Moreover, while plunder from the Temple was being paraded before Vespasian and Titus, back home in the Forum, only the battered Tenth Legion *Fulminata* remained to do mopping up—eliminating half a dozen holdout fortresses still held by Jewish zealots. Saving the toughest nut—Masada—for last.

Kurt had feared the worst. A vengeful commander, prideful and overflowing with fury over the defeats that his subordinates suffered in these northern hills, starting with the small garrison that formerly resided where Milda now stood—charged with preparing a thousand slaves for transport to the wharves of Akko— all taken away by the Mouth of Hell.

Deprived of that expected income, Sextus Callus had come aggressively, ruthlessly, and obstinately— responding to every failure with double strength. The final loss, two weeks ago, cost Rome almost two entire cohorts, assailing the smooth walls of the Hell Mouth with siege ladders, arbalests, and catapults, in the face of pikes and limited gunfire. And better cavalry than they ever saw. Though far too few guns and horses to make the hardened, stubborn enemy flee.

Tough bastards, Sergeant Kuipers finally acknowledged, with soldierly respect, after the Sadducee prince Ezra and his band slammed upon the Roman rear, just in the nick of time, leaving only a handful of legionaries alive. Ezra had wasted no time, directing his Galilean recruits to arm themselves with captured weapons and armor.

Even victories stink to high heaven, wretched and odious to any decent person's senses. Only this time, while bodies were gathered for burning, with respect to Roman custom, Kurt's thoughts had roiled around how little gunpowder remained, a mere volley or two, with production slowed to a crawl as the new dam filled too slowly, behind Milda's rebuilt water mill.

There was so much to do, like expanding the smithie enough to make cannon ... even recasting a church bell into a single two-pounder would be better than nothing, *which is what we now have*. If they could find one—he wasn't sure if church bells even existed in this day and age.

Or training locals to hold a pike without flinching and letting down the man next to you. Plus planning how to feed Milda's expanding population of ragged refugees. Teaching local farmers advanced, seventeenth-century technologies like the mold board plow, the horse collar, the wheelbarrow, could double production and eliminate any excuse for slavery—that is, if war could be kept off their backs.

And there were expeditions to send forth. Samuel Burns—now perhaps the only native English speaker on the planet—led a wagon and some guards to trade for sulfur, by the shores of the Dead Sea. Georg Stahl, the bravest merchant, volunteered to head east and find the Parthian trade route, seeking copper for a new distillery. While mad Johann Blisterfeld yammered about making a printing press and taking it (someday) to Alexandria, of all crazy ideas.

Finally, as if Kurt had too little cause to fret, there was Braun, raving that he had to run off. To Ephesus, of all places! Pursuing an angry old man who Braun deemed to be *more dangerous than all the world's legions*.

"All I did was read to him from the Epistles. And

some of Revelations," the priest said, coming to realize
what he had done, two full days after Sarah's uncle
and brother departed on stolen horses.

The implications only dawned on Kurt himself some
days after Braun departed. In fact, they made his head
spin so fast that he pushed the entire matter out of
his mind. Survival first. Survival first.

Now Kurt watched the Roman general's eyes, while
Sarah spun their contrived tale. How the Fifth Legion
must have neglected to inform the Tenth that German
auxiliaries were holding these hills for Rome. (Shame-
ful!) And how all their records and documentation had
burned in the fighting. And that (alas, regrettably) Kurt
had always left to others the tedious details of business—
others who were now dead. And how he counted on
Roman honor to live up to the mercenary's contract anyway! And how his men had not been paid in months, and
would the general kindly see to making up the arrears?

What a ridiculously bold fabrication! And yet, on
the plus side, what alternative explanation could there
be, for a small army of Germans to appear in this far
land? The savage folk who had destroyed the legions
of Quinctillius Varus in the Teutoburg Forest, a few
decades before. And hence Rome's most respected
source of fierce auxiliaries?

He's not buying it, Kurt realized, watching the old
general's face.

On the other hand, he is weighing the costs.

*So, Lucilius Bassus, what are your options? You can
bring the whole legion against us, an entrenched force
of uncertain size, with weapons rumored to include
hurled thunderbolts. And risk losing so many men
that the Jewish Revolt might reignite across this land.*

Or you could decide to be pragmatic. Accept a way to save face and salvage something from all this.

Sarah finished. In the ensuing silence, Kurt saw Lucius Flavius Silva scowling—even seething—exactly what Kurt would have expected of the man, whose infamy came down fifteen hundred years. But Silva wasn't the one who mattered. Not while Lucilius Bassus lived.

That figure sat completely still. At least a minute stretched. And another.

Finally, the general stood up and took a step forward, with outstretched arm.

"Dear comrade, please accept my deep regrets over the rash mistakes of Sextus Callus and his foolish centurions. This was entirely my fault. I should have sent Silva here, who can count his toes without referring to a wax board and who can tell a foe from an ally. Isn't that right, Silva?"

The younger officer blinked, then nodded. Though Kurt thought he could hear the grinding of teeth.

"Yes, General."

Kurt took the offered hand of Lucilius Bassus, not palm to palm but each gripping the other's forearm, bringing both men close to each other. Almost eye-to-eye. And the old man's grip was like iron. Only Sarah's presence, just behind him, gave Kurt the strength he needed to maintain that gaze contact . . . till Lucilius Bassus grunted, nodded, and let go.

"And now," the general asked. "I would appreciate your advice, Baron von Wolfschild, as to how I can turn my back upon the Galilee while duty calls my legion south."

❖   ❖   ❖

"*C'est tout la? Mais il n'est pas complet!*" Jean-Baptiste complained after finishing the last page of the manuscript. "How can it end there? This will infuriate everyone, across the continent, demanding to know what happens next!"

Hercule nodded.

"I think, *mon cher ami,* that is the desired result.".

The thirteen-year-old—though a veteran of war and privation—still had innocent eyes that now widened in delighted realization.

"Ah. The work of a devil, indeed. Readers will champ eagerly to buy the next issue. And some will fantasize stories of their own, that diverge, like the branchings of a river delta. Perhaps some will even write them, following the young Englishman to the Dead Sea, for example. Or Father Braun to Turkey and Greece, chasing after that mysterious old man. Do you have a clue who it might be?"

"I have suspicions. But I will leave that for you to divine. Or the author to reveal for himself."

"Bastard," Jean-Baptiste sallied. An accusation that Hercule accepted with a nod. In fact, though, he had read an earlier draft. The original version that contained some more details.

James, had been the elderly Jew's name. A Jew . . . and a Christian . . . and a powder keg. Omitting that name was one of just a few places where John Flannery had put his foot down, demanding that vagueness replace specificity, for survival's sake.

Discretion, Hercule thought. *In my other life, I apparently had none. Though I should not be ashamed of it. My modest fame on that timeline was colorful, at least. But here, with this second chance, I must school myself, if my work is to achieve real importance.*

He blew out the candle, plunging their tiny attic room into darkness. Beyond the little window, he could see by moonlight the mighty towers of Grantville, one of them four stories high, and in his minds-eye he envisioned the sky city of Manhattan. The fabulous Paris of Zola and Rostand and Bardot.

There were muted, rustling sounds as the gay couple in the apartment below settled down for the night. Here in Grantville, that didn't seem to be a problem. And it drew Hercule to ponder the accounts told by his own biographers, so varied, so contradictory. *I cannot have been all of those things. Some must be mistaken. Anyway, I do like girls. Though, I also hate whenever anyone says don't-do-that.*

He shook his head. Life was open before him. Only that mattered. Stay bold! But maybe act less out of reflex. Make fewer mistakes.

From the pallet nearby, a soft voice asked:

"Have you read any of your own plays, yet?"

Exasperation.

"We agreed not to do that."

A long pause.

"I went and read one of yours," Jean-Baptiste admitted. *"L'Autre Monde.* The one about visiting the Moon? It's really good! I guess you always had it in you to be a science fiction author."

Such admiration in his voice. Oh, the irony.

"I also tried to read one of mine," the boy went on.

"Bien? Alors then, what did you think?"

"It was all manners and people playing tricks on

each other in drawing rooms and trying to get sex. No action at all. I didn't understand or like it much."

"Well, you're just a kid. Your balls probably haven't dropped yet."

"You're only three years older!"

"But I was a soldier."

"So was I!"

"Drummer boy."

"Yeah? Well you have a great big—"

"Don't say it," Hercule warned, with a flash of the old, cold rage.

"I'm sorry," Jean Baptiste murmured in a small voice. And Hercule remembered his oath, never to let the lad come to harm.

"Forget-about-it," he growled, in English. "Anyway, I agree with you."

"About what?"

"That we can both do better, this time around. Write better. Aim higher."

"I thought you said you weren't gonna read what we—"

"Well, I lied. I read it all."

Silence, then, in hushed tones . . .

"Is it true, then? Did you *invent* science fiction?"

"Invent . . . Nah. That other me wrote silly stuff, mostly."

Hercule stared at the ceiling, envisioning a very different moon and sun and planets, all aswarm with fanciful creatures.

"But fun," he added in a very low voice. "Way, way fun."

He turned his head toward Jean-Baptiste. To that dim

shadow across the little room, he almost said: *"You have far more talent with words and drama and characters than I'll ever have. While I'm crazy enough to imagine or dare anything. Just think of what we could write together, combining your strengths with mine."*

But the words went unspoken.

Instead he commanded, gruffly, like a big brother. *"Allez dormir."* Go to sleep.

Silence reigned for a time. Though the quiet had texture, as electric music played softly, somewhere across town. There were motor sounds, a brief glimmer of headlights passing in the night. Far distant, he thought there might be the drone of an aeroplane. Miracles, brought to this gritty, hopeless world from a marvelous future. A future now bound to change.

"Good night, Cyrano," his young friend whispered, breaking open their secret, for an instant.

And—also for a moment—he answered in kind.

"Sleep tight, Molière."

Kinderspiel

Charles E. Gannon

[The author wishes to express his profound gratitude to that tireless and peerless researcher, Virginia DeMarce, to whom this story owes the largest measure of its authenticity.]

April 1635, south of Ulm, Swabia

"Colonel, riders coming."

Thomas North, one of the two colonels of the Hibernian Mercenary Battalion, turned in his saddle and squinted.

Sure enough, just as his batman Finan had reported, two mounted figures were catching up with them, following along the same route: south on the Swabian Jakobsweg—arguably the most reliable way south from Ulm to Biberach, even though it wasn't a road. Or more accurately, because it was now mid-April, the Jakobsweg was the most reliable path *because* it wasn't a road. Leaving Ulm yesterday, North and his rump platoon had witnessed three wagons hopelessly mired in the spring mud, the struggling teamsters up to their hips in the brown ooze.

North's senior lieutenant, Hastings, leaned closer. "Orders, sir?"

"Take a fire team into the brush on the left. And don't get bloody eager, Lieutenant: these two aren't trouble."

"Too few of them?"

"Too obvious. But you never know when wolves might be shadowing unsuspecting sheep. Off with you, now."

Hastings tossed his reins to Finan, dismounted, and gathered his fire team from the front of the formation, ensuring that his actions were unobservable by the oncoming riders. The hastily assembled group disappeared into the sparse undergrowth.

Several of the other Hibernians saw Hastings' small screening force vanishing and hefted their .40-.72 black-powder Winchesters higher into a ready cradle posture.

"Easy, men," said Thomas in a gruff but even tone that was, for him, a soothing croon.

That was the same moment that the taller and wider-shouldered of the two riders stopped and put up a hand, whether in greeting or invitation to parley, North couldn't be sure.

But the larger of the two resumed his approach without waiting for Thomas' gesture to do so, making the rider clearly suicidal. Or insane.

Shortly thereafter, North discovered that insanity was indeed the cause of the unbeckoned approach and that the oncoming rider had no hope of ever recovering his wits. By dint of his origins, his madness was endemic and permanent.

In short, he was an American.

And not just any American. As soon as the rider called a greeting, "Hello, Colonel North," Thomas knew who it was: Larry Quinn. Now Major Larry Quinn, if recent scuttlebutt was to be believed.

North waved at the bushes to his right; Lieutenant Hastings and his men emerged.

Quinn approached, riding up along the short column of North's men, exchanging nods of recognition with those he had met when he accompanied the Hibernians to retrieve a Mughal princeling from Austria two years ago. The men had seemed to like Larry well enough then, and the smiles now were genuine and lingered after he passed.

North rested his hands on his saddle horn—riding with a Western saddle had been another up-time habit he had happily acquired—and studied the slightly younger man. Immediately after the mission to Austria, he had seen a fair amount of Quinn: the powers that had then guided the fate of the State of Thuringia-Franconia—Mike Stearns and Ed Piazza—had made him the regular liaison to the Hibernians.

But then, Quinn all but disappeared. He was rarely seen even in Grantville's favorite watering hole, the Thuringen Gardens. Word had it that he had shifted away from his military duties and become a scholar, studying law with an elderly up-timer whose name seemed especially appropriate to an educator of jurisprudence: Riddle.

Thomas had been puzzled and a bit disappointed by Quinn's choice; although the Englishman had been unwilling to admit it openly, the up-timer had promise as a soldier. And if twentieth-century assumptions of what soldiering meant had hindered him a bit at first,

Larry had shed those misperceptions shortly after the jaunt to Austria. North expected that with that leavening experience, Quinn's up-time military service with the West Virginia National Guard would stand him in good stead. Indeed, as the Hibernian Company expanded into the Hibernian Battalion and made the acquisition of near-up-time capabilities its hallmark characteristic, North had more than once wished that Quinn would become a regular at the Gardens, once again . . . for professional reasons. Although North had infinitely more field experience, Quinn had been trained to use rapid-firing weapons at both short and long ranges. The relevant tactics that had been drilled into the American by rote were unknown in this world—and Thomas' evolving unit had urgent need of such knowledge. Far more than the Englishman was able to acquire from his assiduous viewing of—not to say addiction to—the movies that the up-timers had brought with them.

Quinn drew up to North and extended a hand. "It's good to see you again, Colonel."

"It won't be if you insist on being so bloody formal, Larry."

Quinn smiled. "Okay, Thomas. So, you're on your way to Biberach."

"Evidently you can read a copy of my orders as well as I can. Which means you also know that I'm to see to the safe establishment of the first airship ground facility there."

"Which you just finished doing in Nuremburg."

"Yes. Dull work. Indeed, the only noteworthy event since leaving Grantville is finding you riding around in the same patch of country we are. Pure coincidence, I'm sure."

"There's no fooling you, is there, Thomas?"

"No, Larry, there isn't." North smiled. The excessively earnest and often anxious young man of two years ago had grown up a great deal: he was as easy in his banter as he was in his saddle. "And although your appearance here is a mystery, I suspect I can be sure of one thing: that I'm not going to like the reason for it."

Larry grinned crookedly and urged his horse to resume its shambling progress toward Biberach, pulling ahead of the formation. He cast a meaningful glance at Thomas.

Who thought, *Great. Just great.*

The reason for Larry's decision to precede the column at a confidentiality-ensuring distance revealed itself soon enough. And it also explained why the pace he was setting was a leisurely one: according to the latest news, Biberach's town fathers had suddenly reversed their decision of three months ago and were now refusing to host the aerodrome.

"And how did you hear about this problem when even I haven't?" North asked.

Larry hooked his thumb back at the smaller rider who had been with him, and who was now trailing behind Hastings. "That guy, Kurzman, arrived in Nuremburg about three days after you left. I got there a day later and heard the news from him. He was the USE factor for establishing the aerodrome in Biberach."

"And what reason did the burghers give him for changing their minds?"

"That's part of the problem: they didn't. He had been staying down there, doing the groundwork, gathering the necessary supplies and fuel—"

"Some of which we need to take on to Chur in the Alps, I suppose you know."

Quinn nodded. "Yep. And then, about six weeks ago, the regular confabs with the big shots ceased. No sign of a problem; Kurzman just figured they had pretty much ironed out the last of the wrinkles and were in a holding pattern until you arrived. Then ten days ago, the burgers show up at his inn and tell him that unfortunately, the arrangements must be rescinded. No timetable for resuming discussions, no reason. Just the implication that Kurzman had no further reason to remain in Biberach and therefore, shouldn't."

"My," observed Thomas, "such friendly people. I suspect they'll be welcoming us with garlands. Of slip-knotted hemp."

"Doubtful, but not impossible."

"Larry, you were not supposed to agree with me. As the sunny-dispositioned American, your role is to dissuade me from my excessive pessimisms and ensure me that Everything Is Going To Be Just Fine."

"Sorry."

"Yes. Well, I wouldn't have believed you anyway. So Kurzman went up to the aerodrome in Nuremburg?"

"Right. Figured they'd have a radio. Ran into me the day after he arrived, told me his sad story, and here we are."

Thomas considered the American from the corner of his eye. "And why were you in Nuremburg to begin with, Larry? Rather far from Grantville."

"Well, yes. About that. I'm actually preparing to travel even farther from Grantville. Much farther."

"About which you can say no more." Larry's response to Thomas' jocularity was a somber nod, causing the

Englishman to reassess: *so Larry is down here for some other reason, found out about this snag, was retasked to handle it. Probably via radio in Nuremburg. Which means that Larry has become a confidential agent for Stearns, or Piazza, or both. Poor sod.* Aloud: "So fate redirected you to me."

Larry looked at Thomas. "No: I was coming down here to find you, already."

To find me? *Well, this is becoming far too personal for comfort.* "And to what do I owe the honor of your undisclosable interest?"

"Well, I can disclose some of it: I'm interested in hiring four of the men in this unit. For a little job I have."

North raised an eyebrow. "I'm always interested in new business contracts—but not pertaining to men already in the field. Take up the matter of appropriate staffing with my business partner, Liam Donovan."

"I already have—and with Ed Piazza. From what I understand, you'd be quite pleased at the deal they struck."

North stared at him, appalled. "You're going to take the men from me. While I'm in the middle of an operation."

Larry stared at the fleecy clouds overhead. "Now would I do that?"

"Of course you would."

To which Larry had no rebuttal other than a sheepish smile.

When they stopped to water the horses, take a brief meal and rest, North's temper was even enough to resume the conversation.

"Which four of my men are you taking, Larry?"

Quinn answered around a mouthful of bread. "Templeton, Volker, Winkelmann, and Wright."

How nice: cherry-picking the very best among the regulars. Which means Larry had detailed advice from—"Donovan made the recommendations?"

Quinn chewed, nodded.

"So why are you still riding with us, then? Why not depart with your human loot, you pirate?"

"Because—as you no doubt suspect—I've also been asked to help resolve the situation in Biberach. And that will give me a chance to see the four men in action."

Thomas' eyebrows rose. "'In action'? Do you suspect it was foreign influence that undermined Biberach's commitment to the aerodrome?"

Quinn shook his head, gnawed on a small wedge of cheese. "Nope. Stearns and Piazza have pretty much ruled that out. The likely culprits lack sufficient motivation to go to the trouble of trying to sow dissension in our ranks. Bavaria's preoccupied with internal post-war problems, Austria has adopted a posture of cordial entente, and it's hard to see what the French would stand to gain. Besides, if there was an attempt at subornation by a foreign power, it would probably be aimed at the disgruntled Catholic population of Biberach. But Kurzman reports that all the *burgermeisters*—both Protestant and RC—were in lock-step about rescinding the aerodrome deal."

"But you're still expecting that our men might see some 'action'?"

"Well, given how they tossed Kurzman out on his ear, there's no knowing just how unfriendly a reception we're going to get." Quinn popped the last morsel of cheese into his mouth. "And besides, if the town fathers won't reconsider their decision, it's not like we've got a lot of options regarding what we have to do next. Biberach has been using *our* seed money to gather the oil and ethanol that's needed farther south at the aerodrome you'll be establishing in Chur. And Biberach itself is at the transport sweet-spot the airships need. It's less than one hundred miles to Chur, and not much more to Nuremburg. That makes it the essential hub between the two, given the airship's operational range."

North frowned. "Essential? What about other nearby towns? It's not as though the region is sparsely settled. Quite the contrary."

Quinn shook his head, moistened his finger, and ran it around the paper that the cheese had been wrapped in. "Other locations have already been considered. Ulm isn't stable enough, either economically or politically; they didn't get spared by the Thirty Years' War the way Biberach did just after Grantville fell out of the future into Germany. And Buchau and Schussenried are too far south."

"What? Just another ten miles or so—"

"Thomas, these blimps have really tight range limits. Biberach is already a little too far from the Nuremburg aerodrome—by about five miles or so. So pushing the aerodrome farther south would endanger the airships. A bad alpine headwind pushing against you could mean a forced landing in a field—or worse. And if Biberach is actually a little closer than it needs to be to Chur—only eighty miles—well, let's just say the place you want the most margin for error is when you're actually entering or leaving the Alps. Far more surprises there than in flat-land flying. Or so I'm told."

Thomas shrugged. "Well, I suppose that ties it, then. And since Biberach has the safest market south of Nuremburg, it's the logical cachement hub for the fuels these airships need."

Larry nodded. "It's also the best town in terms of being receptive to our polydenominational culture. Although there's no love lost between Catholic and Protestant, they've managed to maintain a joint government. Not always with perfect equity, of course. Three years ago, the Swedes gave the Protestants the upper hand—a position they've used to beat up on the Catholics a bit. But it's still a joint government, say what you will. That's a hell of a lot better than most other places."

"Well, Larry, I suppose Biberach is the pearl of great price, then—particularly given recent news."

If Quinn heard the leading tone, he didn't let on. "Oh? What news?"

"The news coming out of Italy. That the Spanish cardinals are getting singularly restive. That Naples seems to be an armed camp squatting upon an incipient rebellion."

Quinn checked the belly straps on his saddle. "And your point would be?"

"Well, I'm sure Mssrs. Stearns and Piazza might find it somewhat reassuring to be able to initiate a fast transalpine connection to Italy in such tense times. Given all the up-time friends they have down there."

Larry turned to face North and smiled. "Let's ride, Thomas."

An hour later, they drew within sight of Biberach's walls, but on the advice of Kurzman, stayed on the west bank of the river Riss. Larry Quinn looked at the narrow ribbon of water and made a remark about creeks being promoted to the status of rivers in Germany.

Kurzman nodded, but stuck doggedly to sharing his recommendations. "Herr Quinn, you should choose only a few men to go into Biberach. A large number will not be welcome. Nor will I."

Thomas raised an eyebrow. "So we are to expect the singular joys of bivouacking in the delightfully moist fields of early spring?"

"*Nein*, Herr North. You vill go to Ringschnaitt. It is the little village just to the west, beneath the walls of Biberach. A farm village; a garden and dairy market for the town, *ja*?"

"And do you particularly recommend any of Ringschnaitt's fine establishments for our custom?"

"What?"

Thomas slowed his Amideutsch, pruned out the idioms of his youth. "Will we be more welcome in some barns than others?"

"If you haff money, you vill be welcome."

"Ah, well that simplifies matters. Hastings?"

"Sir?"

"You will procure lodgings for our men. Rations, as well. Double-guard, and everyone stays within the perimeter."

"Are we expecting trouble, sir?"

"No, but we do not want to be surprised by it, either."

Larry cocked an eye at North. "And where will you be, during all of this?"

"Why, with you, of course," North scoffed. "You don't think I'm going to trust you to the tender mercies of the locals on your own, do you?"

"Or let me have the sole enjoyment of a warm taproom and hot food?"

"That, too."

After having settled the detachment in Ringschnaitt and enduring multiple rehearsals of the titles and names of the various town fathers with Kurzman, Thomas had Finan and Volker accompany them over the Riss and toward the entry known as the Ulmer gate. As they approached, the long shadow-finger of the portal-straddling tower held them in its narrow gloom, pointing the way home for a trickle of workers and older farm-children.

Volker grunted as a small group of more somber, muttering youngsters pushed a produce-vendor's handcart toward the purpling blue of the eastern horizon.

"What is it, Volker?" asked Thomas, wondering when the guard at the tower was going to get around to challenging them.

"Those kids. They're Swiss."

"Swiss? All of them."

"*Ja*. Spring workers, down from the Alps. Usually about ten to fourteen years old. Folks send them down here along the Jakobsweg to make money. Not enough work up-country at this time of the spring, but plenty down here."

Quinn stared, shook his head.

Thomas noticed. "Not common in your time, I take it?"

"Kids that young sent a hundred miles from home to work for someone else? That would probably have been breaking about a hundred up-time labor laws."

Thomas shrugged. "You would perhaps have preferred

them a bit older, so that the girls might be pressured to provide more than field work?"

Quinn's voice was low and hard. "As if 'employers' like that are picky about age, anyway."

Volker spoke up. "Sirs, it is not as you are thinking. The children travel in groups, and go to families they have worked with before. Mostly." He fell silent as the officers stared at his ominous addition of "mostly."

Quinn asked, "But you're not from around here, are you, Volker?"

"No, sir, but a cousin from Nuremburg traded down here, knew people who had traveled the pilgrim's route—the Jakobsweg—all the way down to Santiago de Campostela in Spain. The custom of child-workers from the Alps is traditional. It is no more subject to abuse than similar traditions."

Thomas nodded back toward the gate; they were so close that they could make out the facial features of the single guard. "The town militia certainly doesn't seem to be worried about trouble, does it?"

"No, indeed," agreed Quinn quietly.

That was about the same moment that the armed worthy at the gate noticed the four armed men approaching. He flinched, pulled himself upright, and, almost as an afterthought, reached behind him and produced a weapon that made Thomas stare, and then grin. "Oh my," he muttered out of the side of his mouth toward Larry, "they are clearly ready for all threats from any quarter."

Quinn was silent as he kept moving towards the man who was brandishing a tarnished arquebus in a poor parody of stalwart readiness. Rather than asking who the newcomers were, or their business, he nervously proclaimed, "Biberach is under the protection of King Gustavus Adolphus of Sweden and the United States of Europe, and is garrisoned by the men of General Horn."

Thomas shrugged. "We certainly do not dispute those facts."

This left the gate guard—such as he was—speechless.

As Larry produced their respective papers and explained the reason for their visit to the town, Thomas continued sizing up the guard. Who, he confirmed quickly, was not really a guard at all. An ill-fitting cuirass and helmet from the prior century were the only clear military gear upon him. Although uniforms had been little known before the up-timers began to spearhead their adoption, the garb of soldiers was nonetheless distinct from that of townsmen and workers: it was generally more rugged and furnished with belts and straps from which to hang items needed in the press of combat. Gloves were not uncommon, nor was a variety of camping tools that could double as secondary weapons in a pinch.

None were in evidence on the man at the Ulmer gate. Dressed as a tradesman—possibly a weaver, from the look of him—he lacked the lean look of a soldier, and was utterly without the wary businesslike posture and tendency towards taciturnity. He was all too glad to discover that the four oddly armed men before his town's gate were in fact legitimate emissaries of the greater powers to the north; his sudden and relieved volubility were arguably the clearest of the many signs that he was merely a townsman impressed to temporary duty as a gate guard.

Thomas nodded at the now-forgotten arquebus leaning against the gatehouse wall. "You know," he observed sagely, "I am told those work best when there's a lit match somewhere nearby. Preferably in the weapon itself."

The civilian stopped, stared, and then blushed. "I am as much a guard as you men are weavers."

Thomas frowned. "Then why are *you* on guard duty? Where is the town watch? Better yet, where is the garrison that General Horn left here?"

"Well," said the fellow, leaning on the gun-rest as he spoke, "the garrison was actually put in place by General-Major von Vitinghof three years ago, although he was only in town for one day. Most of the work was done by an assistant of his, Hauptmann Besserer, who left twenty Swedes in charge. There were also thirty German soldiers: Lutherans, mostly from Ravensburg."

"And where are they?"

"Gone." He waved west. "Back with Horn, fighting Bernhard, I suppose."

Larry frowned. "And no replacements were sent?"

"Yes, but they came late. And not many of them. They contracted plague on the way to us"—he crossed himself ardently—"and almost half were dying as they got here. The rest were very weak."

"And so there are too few left to man the gates?"

The guard looked east. "Well, I do not know. They are not stationed in the town, you see."

"Not in town? Where are they?"

"The abbey at Heggbach, about six miles east."

"There is a hospital there?"

The fellow looked uncomfortable. "No."

"Then what?" snapped Thomas. "Why send them to the abbey?"

"To keep them away from us," the man mumbled. "The abbess and many of the nuns—they had already

died of the plague, there. The survivors had gone elsewhere: there weren't enough of them left to maintain the
abbey. Besides, they were too weak to live on their own."

"And none of you helped them," finished Larry in
a flat tone.

The guard stared back in faint defiance. "There was
nothing we could do. By the time we learned, a third
of the nuns were dead or nearly so. And besides, they
are not our responsibility. At times, they had been most
troublesome. The abbess of Heggbach was frequently
in dispute with the abbey's tenant farmers, many of
whom live much closer to our walls, and who sought our
intervention. Which made for trouble with the abbey."

Larry stared at the man. "So when the sick replacement garrison showed up, you sent it into quarantine
at Heggbach Abbey. Where I presume you expected
them to die."

"I expected nothing!" shouted the weaver-watchman.
"I am a simple man given an old gun to guard a gate. I
am not consulted on such things. I just hear news like
everyone else. If you wish to complain to the *Burgermeisters*, they should still be in the *Rathaus*—although
not for much longer." He sent an appraising squint
toward the end of the tower's lengthening shadow.

"Fine," said Larry with a sharp nod, "we'll do that."

Following the guard's directions, they moved toward
St. Martin's cathedral, angling south through the reasonably wide streets once they came upon it. Thomas
chose his calmest tone, and began. "I say, Larry—"

"I know," the American shot back, "I was pretty
tough on that poor guy at the gate."

"Rather. Why?"

"I guess because what he said pushed my buttons. Yeah, I understand why they did what they did: they had the plague at their gates, and a reasonable chance of keeping it out if they were careful about how much external contact they had. But damn, so many towns around here made such an easy accommodation with turning away people in need, with turning a blind eye upon human suffering. Just like they did during World War II, up in my time."

Thomas considered. "Larry, I claim no expertise in what your histories call the Holocaust. I will simply observe that villainy, bigotry, and genocide have a long history of traveling together. The same up-time processes that enabled mass production were no less an enabling factor for mass destruction.

"However, in this time, what you see as an easy accommodation with cruelty may simply be the exhaustion of hoping for fairy tale endings. I notice in your American history that things almost always came out right in the end, as though there was some guardian angel watching over the fate of your nation. As best as I can tell, some of your more gullible leaders actually believed there was. But here, you are dealing with persons brought up on unremitting rounds of war and plague, of whole generations sucked into the maw of death." North looked up as they fell into, and then out of, the shadow of the cathedral. "You Americans never had a reason to lose hope. These poor sods were born into a world where there wasn't any hope left."

Quinn nodded slowly, pointed. "There's the new *Rathaus*, at the head of the market place. Ready for a frontal assault on close-minded and quarrelsome bureaucrats?"

Thomas sighed. "Oh, yes; I live for the thrill of that particular battle."

After navigating the closing bakers' stalls crowded along the arcades of the *Rathaus*, they made their way inside. It was the same scene of impermanence and frenzy that Thomas had seen in small city *Rathauses* throughout Germany. Often used for general meetings and other large gatherings, the ground floor of such buildings were rarely furnished with fixed partitions. Field chairs, stools, and folding tables abounded, as did arguments, exhortations, and idle chatter. Quinn waded manfully into the chaos, fixed upon a young fellow who was just preparing to run a message, flashed a *Kreutzer* at him.

The fellow's stride broke, swerved in the direction of the American. His eyes roved over the group's gear. "Yes, *Herr Hauptman*?"

"I wish to speak with either the *Burgermeister* or the *Stadtamtmann*. Where will I find them?"

The reply—"upstairs"—earned the fellow the *Kreutzer*; his reaction was a quick smile and a quicker departure.

Progress through the diminishing crowd in the *Rathaus* was still slow, due to the frenzy of the remaining workers as they redoubled their efforts to wrap up and head home. An outbound scribe descending the northern staircase attempted to dissuade them from ascending, saw that his entreaties were pointless, gesticulated toward their destination, and left them to their own devices.

Thomas was content to let Quinn continue to walk point; that way, the American would hit the first political tripwire, and they were deep in what was, for all soldiers, enemy country: the tortuous warrens of bureaucrats.

Quinn knocked on the jamb of an already-open office door. "Herr *Burgermeister* von Pflummern?"

A youngish, fit man looked up from his pile of books and papers. "Yes?" In the next second he was on his feet, his eyes slightly wider and much more cautious. "And who, may I ask, are you?"

While Quinn presented their bona fides, their papers, and their business, Thomas scanned the room and the hallway surreptitiously. Another man, older and thickly built, emerged from a larger office halfway down the hall, two other men in tow. Brows lowering, they glanced hastily at the strange group around the entrance to von Pflummern's office, and hurried toward the southern staircase.

Von Pflummern's office was half chaos, half order, leaving Thomas with the impression that it was being used by two different men. Judging from the way that pristine orderliness seemed to be encroaching on dust-covered layers of entropy, the neatness was logically a characteristic of the newcomer. A glance at von Pflummern himself, and Thomas knew him to be the recent arrival.

It was not just his comparative youth: it was his immaculate dress, hair, and hygiene. The pen he was using was neatly and newly cut, and the ink, quill knives, and blotting paper were arrayed evenly along the margins of his workspace.

Just as *Burgermeister* von Pflummern was about to correct Larry's (and therefore, Ed Piazza's) ostensible misunderstanding of what had, and had not, been offered and promised by the inner council of Biberach's

Rat, Thomas intruded a quick question: "Excuse me, Herr *Burgermeister* von Pflummern, but how recently did you replace the former Catholic *Burgermeister*?"

Von Pflummern's jaw froze, then thawed into a surprised stutter: "How, how do you—? Two months. And a few weeks."

"So you were not a *Burgermeister* at the time the aerodrome agreement was made, is that correct?"

"It is, but as the senior Catholic member of the inner council, I was fully aware of all the particulars."

"I did not mean to imply otherwise. I just noted that your office has—well, has the look of transition."

Von Pflummern flushed slightly, nodded, looked around; had there been enough space and chairs, Thomas intuited that the man's innate congeniality would have had him inviting them all to take seats. But then he stood straighter and extended a hand toward the door, back in the direction of the stairs.

"You are correct. We have had many losses, this past winter. My predecessor died of a fever, and the former Protestant *Burgermeister*, Johann Schoenfeld the Elder, died of the plague late last year. He was one of the few to contract it and he refused to come back within the walls. Now I will thank you gentlemen to see yourselves out; I must close my office and return home."

North was going to press for one more tidbit of information about the prior Roman Catholic *Burgermeister* when Quinn stuck out a hand with a slight bow. After a moment's hesitation, von Pflummern took it. Quinn bowed slightly. "I am sorry we have intruded so late in the day. As you see from my orders, I will need to speak to you at greater length, as well as the town's other *Burgermeister* and its *Stadtamtmann*."

"The Protestant *Burgermeister* is Hanss Lay. My brother Christoph is the *Stadtamtmann*. We will make what time we can for you tomorrow. Good evening, gentlemen."

Before heading back to their beddings of hay and the smell of ordure, Quinn suggested they visit a tavern a few blocks south of the market place that was known as far as Ulm for its beer. Thomas offered no resistance and made a silent footnote to inquire upon returning to Grantville if the up-timer's modest means had improved in recent days, or if he was on a rather generous operating account. If the latter, that suggested he had garnered an unusual measure of trust from the notoriously frugal (not to say miserly) Ed Piazza.

The inside of the Grüner Baum was tidy and nicely appointed: the ravages of the Thirty Years' War had indeed visited this town lightly, if even its taverns were no worse for wear. Thomas downed his first pint before the barmaid could escape the table: *"noch ein"* he ordered with a wide smile and turned to Larry. "Very nice of you, standing us a drink."

"I find your use of the singular—'a drink'—particularly ironic."

"As was intended. Now, what do you think that was all about, back there?"

"Don't know," answered Quinn, staring at a spare, morose-looking fellow across the room. "Hopefully, we'll get a better idea tomorrow."

"I doubt it," said Thomas, craning his neck to catch a glimpse of the barmaid and thereby gauge when the next frothy stein might arrive. "I get the distinct impression that the town fathers are concealing something.

Possibly even in cahoots across denominational lines, if I read that little closing scene correctly upstairs at the *Rathaus*."

"You might be right," Larry agreed. His tone suggested his attention was elsewhere.

Thomas followed his gaze, which was still fixed—and with greater intensity—upon the morose fellow sitting alone across the rapidly filling room. Who, Thomas noticed, was wearing well-worn clothes, but not of the typical, almost stolid, local cut. His garments and gear emphasized line and flow: Thomas discerned that they were not only easier to look at, but also, probably easier to move in.

In short, they were almost certainly Italian. The look of the leather, the faint hints of color and the detail of worksmanship all suggested those origins, now that he studied the man more closely.

He also noted that the fellow kept his head turned slightly, eyeing the world from one side more than the other, rather like parakeets did.

Thomas was about to remark on this odd feature when Quinn rose with a muttered, "I'll be damned," and began moving across the room. Thomas, flustered, rose, and—after a moment of desperate and disappointed scanning for his inbound pint—followed.

He arrived at the table in time to see Larry offer a quick half-bow and inquire, "I am sorry to intrude, but may I inquire: are you an artist?"

The fellow—younger than Larry—started, and in that moment, Thomas saw why he held his head peculiarly: his left eye had the subtle, milky discoloration that often followed and marked a blinding injury.

More surprising still was the fellow's response.

"Why, yes: I am. Or so I style myself. Who, may I ask, is inquiring?" The smile was congenial but also far too old and world-weary for the young face. "A factor for a patron, perhaps?"

"Perhaps," Larry answered with a grave nod. If he noticed Thomas start in surprise along with the half-sighted fellow, he gave no indication. "There are several people where I'm from who are very interested in your work."

"'My work?' At present, what few canvases I painted I was compelled to leave behind in Rome. How could anyone here know of my work?"

"Not here, Herr Schoenfeld. I am referring to up-timers in Grantville—and some of their Dutch acquaintances."

Now the younger man sat up very straight. "If this is a jest, it is in very poor taste, and I will ask you to leave. If not, I will thank you to indicate who you are, who you represent, and how you know me."

Larry answered Schoenfeld's first two queries and concluded with, "As for knowing you: in my time, Johann Schoenfeld was known as the father of Baroque art in Germany. You, sir, are famous."

Schoenfeld stared, then laughed, his tilted head back. "Famous?" he barked so loudly that several other heads in the Grüner Baum looked up from their steins. "If I'm famous, it's for failing my family and my craft. Famous for fleeing before the black tides of war."

"I assure you, Herr Schoenfeld, in my time, sketches from your early career were sought-after treasures of art history."

Schoenfeld studied Larry with his good eye; Thomas

knew he was being thoroughly scanned as well, albeit peripherally. "And so this is how you knew me?"

Larry nodded. "Before coming down here, I was briefed on everything we knew about Biberach from this time period. Other than a few brief mentions about events in the Thirty Years' War, it was best known for being your birthplace and family residence until you left for Italy."

Johann Schoenfeld leaned back, his long nose seeming to accuse them. "I am sorry to tell you that your histories are incomplete. I apprenticed in Ulm and then Basel before returning here—just before stories began circulating about the wonders of Grantville. And just when it also seemed possible that Wallenstein or the Bavarians would finally pillage Biberach. And so I fled to Italy. To escape. And yes, to work, also, but mostly to escape."

Larry shrugged. "Why should one remain in the path of war when it approaches?"

Schoenfeld's one good eye stabbed at him. "To support one's family. Which I did not. And thanks to that, my father is dead of plague."

Thomas blinked: *so, the late* Burgermeister *Schoenfeld and the artist's father are one and the same.* It was not beyond possibility that there could be two such men of the same name, and same generation, who would have died of the plague in Biberach. But it was pretty unlikely, and besides, a *Burgermeister* would have the wealth and authority to send a talented son—particularly a son who was blind in one eye— off to a safer place, a place to which a journeyman artist would logically go. Similarly, a *Burgermeister* who thought that way was also likely to be the kind of selfless man who, once infected, would quarantine himself outside the town rather than risk bringing the plague into the streets where all his loved ones and friends lived their crowded, wall-bound lives.

Thomas' hypotheses received an additional boost when the young artist took up his own drink and continued gesticulating with the other hand—which was clearly withered. "If I had not been so—so weak, so useless, this would never have happened."

Thomas, who had resolved to let Larry handle this on his own, found himself objecting: "Herr Schoenfeld, I have known many cowards. You are not among their number."

Schoenfeld looked at Thomas. "And how would you know this?"

"Because I have been in more battles than you have lived years and I can tell you this about cowards: they spend most of their time making excuses for themselves. The last thing they do is take blame upon their own back for fear that others will see them for what they really are." He considered his next words carefully. "What I see right now is a man whom God, fate, or chance—your choice—intended for a different greatness. Perhaps to inspire men through your visions of the world, rather than to cause men to expire out of it."

"As has been your lot in life," Schoenfeld added the unspoken footnote.

"Unfortunately, yes. And I will tell you that nine out of every ten so-called 'deeds of valor' were merely acts of desperation that came out well. And that there is very little glory picking your way among the dead and dying after a battle."

Schoenfeld's answer was a strange, small, poignant smile. "As you say these things, my mind's eye shows me what I have always wished to paint."

"Come to Grantville," put in Larry, "and I will show you that you did. I saw some pictures of your paintings before I came here: they are heroic, but always haunted by the horrors of war. Some critics said they could sense Breughel and Bosch lurking just beyond the margins of your canvases."

Schoenfeld's eyes—including the sightless one—were suddenly bright. "I would like to see these canvases—if for no other reason to know what now I will never paint." Then the vitality seemed to ebb out of him. "But there is too much to settle here. Too many troubles."

"Something that we can help with, perhaps?" Larry offered carefully.

"Maybe. I don't know enough, yet. I just arrived yesterday and learned—well, about my father. And the other problems. It is difficult, adapting to so much, so quickly. Perhaps, if we were to meet here again tomorrow, at about this time—"

"We shall." Quinn's voice was firm and friendly. "And now, tell us about Italy. We have heard that there is trouble there."

Schoenfeld rolled his eyes. "That is like saying that water is wet. I had been thinking of pursuing an invitation to go to the court of Count Orsini of Naples, but—"

Thomas managed to catch the eye of the barmaid and guide the lost beer to his waiting hand; listening to traveler's tales was thirsty work, after all.

✧   ✧   ✧

It was also thirsty work listening to German *Burgers* say "no" in half a dozen different ways, as Thomas discovered the next morning. It certainly made him want to have a drink. Or three.

The return to von Pflummern's office was cordial but brief. The brother Christoph—the *Stadtamtmann* and the decidedly less-congenial sibling—did not even sit, but stood behind his brother, arms crossed, his frown as firmly fixed upon his face as his sharp-bridged nose. When asked if he had been part of the negotiations, he shook his head once and spat out a crisp, "*Nein.*" And that was all.

Unfortunately, the meeting with the Protestant *Burgermeister* wasn't going much better. Another town functionary, Hans Kaspar Funk, was sitting stolidly in a chair beside the *Burgermeister*'s vast desk. As the town's *Pfarrpfleger*, Funk ensured the timely and adequate external maintenance of Biberach's churches, and he was also a member of the *Innere Rat*, or inner council. Not surprisingly, he had been named in the documents in Quinn's possession: his involvement in the aerodrome negotiations was a matter of record. Indeed, he had been Kurzman's primary point of contact for sorting out the details, once the general agreement had been reached.

Except now it sounded as though the agreement— which was written in clear black and white on the sheets that Quinn had politely advanced across the table toward *Burgermeister* Hanss Lay—had never been an agreement at all. Thomas felt the need for a drink redouble as Lay spread his hands expressively and continued his enumeration of unresolved contractual impediments. "Then there is the matter of gold."

"Gold?" echoed Quinn. "Did you expect additional compensation?"

"*Nein, nein, nein*: not gold coins. Gold that one works. Gold for goldsmiths." Lay threw up his heavy hands. "Biberach's weavers are its most famous craftsmen, yes, but what is our second most famous product?"

Aggravation, Thomas answered silently.

Lay provided the response to his own question. "Fine work in gold. We have a considerable goldsmith's guild here, and my predecessor was its senior member. His nephew, Hans Jakob Schoenfeld the Younger, is a member of the *Rat* and has made his guild's special problem very clear, we feel."

"Special problem?" Quinn repeated quietly. And somewhat helplessly, Thomas thought.

"Yes, of course. The problem with Venice."

The sudden, powerful increase in Thomas' already strong desire for a drink triggered a fleeting concern that perhaps he was becoming an alcoholic, after all.

Quinn's voice was admirably level. "Tell me about the Venice problem."

"Is it not obvious? Your airship will create easier access to Venice. This will increase the flow of raw gold stocks to this area. That increased supply will depress prices on all gold objects. It would be disastrous."

Quinn held up a pausing hand. "But as I understand it—and as Herr Kurzman explored with you—cheaper raw stocks of gold are actually good. If the finished items sell for a little less here in Biberach itself, that is only a small percentage of your final market, the rest of which lies well beyond the effects of the greater influx of raw gold. Besides, the airship means your finished gold products have much wider markets—including those in Italy. According to Herr Kurzman, you saw that advantage before he pointed it out to you."

"Yes, well, we all said a great many things. I believe Herr Kurzman is quite mistaken in this recollection of them."

Funk spoke sepulchrally from his wide-armed chair. "Besides, there is also the originally undisclosed nature of our primary business partner. We had been under the impression that the airships were being created and run by the up-timers of Grantville. But we have since learned that the true owner of these balloons is this fellow Estuban Miro."

"That is true. This was made clear during the negotiations."

"Not the fact that he is a Jew," Funk sniffed haughtily. "We are not . . . comfortable dealing with one of his kind."

Thomas forgot all about the drink he wanted. "Certainly you are not serious. This town deals with 'his kind' all the time. Jewish communities are the largest suppliers and conveyors of both raw and finished gold in this entire area. How could you be—?"

But Quinn was rising. He interrupted Thomas with a bow and a "*Guten Tag*," and was then towing the Englishman toward the door.

"But this is sheer rubbish, Larry. This is—"

Low and hasty, Quinn whispered. "Thomas. Let it be. The problems here are not about Venice, not about Miro, and not about his religion. There's something else going on here." Larry continued after they had closed the door behind them and were walking toward the stairs. "They're nervous now because their objections are all bullshit. And they know that *we* know they're bullshit."

"And do they know that *we* know that *they* know that *we*—?"

"Okay, Thomas: that's not funny."

"Really? I found it exquisitely amusing."

By the time Thomas had a stein in front of him at the Grüner Baum, he was ready for a drink again. "I think this constitutes a dead end, Major Quinn. What is our next option? Removal of the civilian government?"

"Don't tempt me. But what's standing in our way is simple ignorance."

"They are a blinkered bunch, I'll give you that."

"No, Thomas: not their ignorance. Our ignorance. Since the reasons we got were pure bullshit, that means we haven't seen the real reason for their change of mind. I just wish we had access to someone who knew what was going on in their minds between the time they agreed to the deal and then went back on it."

"You mean, someone like him?" Thomas pointed toward the bar, where a young man in military gear had just placed an order. The exchange with the owner was cordial, but not familiar.

Larry looked at Thomas. "An officer from the garrison?"

North sipped, shrugged. "You know any other soldiers in town? But why wonder when we can just ask?"

The young officer was glad for the invitation to join them and introduced himself as Georg Prum, commander of the Protestant Garrison of Biberach.

Quinn raised an eyebrow. "Commander, you say?"

Prum smiled; he was a good-looking fellow, the kind that was always presumed to have "aristocratic blood" even if he was the lowest-born pauper's bastard in a town. "The plague has a way of promoting us before our time, Major. Consider the youth of the town's *Rat*."

"I thought they were spared the plague."

"Yes—thanks largely to your up-time methods of quarantine, as I understand it. But diphtheria struck, too, and is a much subtler infiltrator of towns. As is often the case, the old and the young had a particularly hard time of it. As did we."

"And so you are the ranking officer remaining?"

"I am. And we lost our senior sergeant, as well. Not that there were many of us to begin with. From what our late commander, Captain Grieg, told me, General Horn deemed this area largely secure by the onset of winter last year and wanted all his Swedish troops back west where the primary action was. So although a garrison of fifty was withdrawn from Biberach, he only sent twenty-five of us as replacements for it. The plague and diphtheria cut us down to almost half that."

Quinn shook his head sympathetically. Thomas took a meditative sip before commenting, "You know, we were contemplating coming out to visit the abbey."

Prum pushed back one dark black wing of a trim moustache. "You'd be the first. And most welcome. Although if you do so, I doubt you'll be very welcome back here, anymore."

"Why?"

"Because you might pick up whatever stench was apparently thick upon us when we arrived."

"I take it you were not met with open arms?"

"We were turned away at the gate. Seems our predecessors had not made themselves very welcome in the town: they were such ardent Lutherans that they made the joint government difficult to maintain in any practical sense of the word. And of course, we showed up sick and too weak to really debate the matter: the half of us who were healthy enough to move under our own power had our hands full supporting those who were not. So they sent us off to the abbey—probably to die. The abbess there had died not too long before; plague also. It cleared the abbey."

"Well," Larry offered, "at least you have plenty of room."

"Not as much as you think. Toward the end, the nuns obviously had no way to bury their own dead. Half of the rooms still have one or more corpses in them. And I am not about to order my plague-panicked men to do anything other than close the doors, seal those buildings off, and let the rats have their way."

"Sounds charming," Thomas said with a barely suppressed shudder. "We'll be sure to visit your pestilential abode."

"I'm sure you will," Prum responded with admirable good humor.

Larry leaned forward. "Why haven't you sent word back to Horn's staff? Being forced to live in a plague-hole is simply unacceptable. Besides, you can't carry out your orders from there. How would you even know if Biberach was being endangered?"

"We wouldn't. And you are absolutely right: there's little enough we could do from out there. We maintain a patrol between the abbey and Ringschnaitt, but even that earns us wary looks. The town—well, particularly the *Rat*—wants us to keep to ourselves, so we do."

"What brings you to town, then?"

"Man may not live by bread alone, but one has to have it, nonetheless."

"Ah. Provisioning."

"Just so. My men will fetch it tomorrow, but I must arrange for it today. Which requires a drink—often stiffer than this one—first: the local merchants are none too happy providing us with our daily needs in exchange for the promise of General Horn's coin. Coin they've never seen."

"Which is a violation of the revised conduct code of the USE," murmured Larry.

"Yes. Well. I am not sure how much General Horn believes in the authority of the USE. He certainly does believe in the authority of King Gustav, however. Perhaps if you were to bring up the matter with His Majesty..." Prum trailed off with a rueful grin.

"Yes," Quinn answered with a matching smile. "I'll make it the first agenda item for our meeting next week. In the meantime, I don't suppose you could shed any light on why the local *Rat* changed its mind on a business arrangement it made with Grantville about three months ago?"

Prum frowned, then his eyebrows lifted in understanding. "Ah. This is the airship I've heard mentioned once or twice?"

"It is."

Prum shook his head. "I am sorry. I would not be aware of it at all except for some overheard conversations amongst common workers. And the arrangement has come undone? A pity; I should have liked to have seen such a miracle."

Thomas nodded understanding. "Any advice on what to do?"

Prum seemed surprised. "Me? About getting them to reaccept a balloon? Here?" He shook his head sadly. "If you have a long time to wait, I suppose you could try to use the power of sweet reason. But if you're in a hurry, I think you'll be disappointed. The town fathers are most intractable." Seeing the looks on their faces, Prum hastened to add, "I'm sorry to be discouraging. But now I must see to securing food for my men." He rose. "If there's any assistance I can offer, do not hesitate to ask."

"We won't," grumbled Thomas.

Larry stood, put out his hand. "It was a pleasure meeting you, *Herr Kapitan* Prum."

"Likewise, Major Quinn, Colonel Thomas."

Thomas muttered a pleasantry that even he couldn't hear as the trim young officer exited the taproom. Once he was gone, the Englishman stared up at the American. "Well, your impressions, Major?"

"Only nice guy we've met so far."

"Which is precisely why I'm suspicious of him," North grumbled.

"There is that," Quinn conceded with a small smile.

One meal, two hours, and three drinks later, Johann Schoenfeld entered with a relative whose family resemblance was unmistakable. However, the newcomer—the artist's younger brother Ferdinand—spent a great deal of time in a dark distraction, missing bits of the initial conversation in his somber preoccupation.

Granted, Thomas reflected, the evening's small talk about weather, trade, politics, trade, and oh yes, more trade, hardly made for riveting conversation. But Ferdinand seemed not merely bored or disinterested: he was fretful and barely touched his beer. Even Johann's good-natured ribbing about his sibling's second bout with impending fatherhood elicited only wan smiles.

However, Ferdinand became suddenly alert when, with the dinner hour, their server changed and the new one—a slightly older woman who was more concerned with the patrons as customers than potential husbands—clapped a friendly hand down on his shoulder and asked, "So, how is your little Gisela enjoying the new school in Nuremburg? I'll bet she misses her *Vati*!"

Ferdinand muttered congenial pleasantries that sounded both pained and evasive. The server smiled and frowned simultaneously and then swept on to the next table.

Thomas watched the brother as Quinn asked. "So, how is your daughter doing in school?"

"Well," was the brittle answer, "quite well."

"What made you decide that she start studying so young, and away from home? Are the schools in Nuremburg so much better?"

Ferdinand drew himself up. "Our schools are every bit as good as those in Nuremburg..." Then he faltered, became furtive again. "But it's a bigger town. It's a city. It's safer."

"Safer?" his brother Johann wondered. "Safer than here?"

Ferdinand was openly nervous now. "*Ja,* safer. At

least in the ways that matter most." He rose quickly and bowed. "You gentlemen will excuse me. I have a pregnant wife and it is getting late."

Thomas and Quinn rose, returned his bow, saw Johann's face folded in creases of concern as Ferdinand made for the door. "I think I should see him home. Something has been bothering him."

Ya think? Thomas wondered silently, cherishing the sassy up-time idiom.

Quinn frowned after the departing brothers. "You know, Thomas, given Ferdinand's strange answers and jittery nerves, it might be helpful to have a chat with his wife tomorrow."

And now, with a smile, Thomas got to say it aloud: "Ya think?"

The next morning, their ruse to speak with Ferdinand's wife at home was a dismal failure. Their claim that they were trying to return what might be Herr Schoenfeld's lost pipe (it actually belonged to Thomas's batman, Finan) was rebuffed by the a cronelike servant who answered the door and avoided sharing her name. She indicated that her young mistress was indisposed and added the unsolicited observation that men should not come calling to see pregnant women unannounced, and particularly when the husband or another male family member was not present. It did not perturb her sense of indignation in the least that they had started by asking to speak to the husband (whom they knew to be at work), not the wife, and that it was difficult to send word ahead when one was trying to return a lost object as promptly as possible.

Still, Larry proved a source of unflappable, under-played charm: well, then might they make an appointment for later?

The crone shook her head once and responded in her limited English: "Not possible."

Well then, would the servant herself consent to allow them in to show her the pipe, so that she might describe it to Master Ferdinand for his subsequent consideration?

Again, this was "Not possible." But then came one tantalizingly unusual piece of information. "I am house servant. I do not meet with outsiders. And I do not leave."

Really? wondered Larry. Never?

"No more. Not now. You are going now."

Larry's tone was the epitome of reasonableness; his foot was also in the gapped door. Well, what about one of the other servants? The ones who brought in the food, the water?

"*Kein*. None. The only other servant *ist* gone. It is well; she vass lazy."

Oh? And who might that have been?

A wicked glint illuminated the crone's one visible eye: she would not share much, but would be happy to advertise the failings of the younger, discharged servant. "Ursula Bodenmüller. The granddaughter, I mean. A weaver's daughter who cannot weave. *Dummkopf*. Now you go."

Larry got his foot out of the way just in time to avoid losing it.

"So," said Thomas with a smile. "Ursula Bodenmül-ler, *Dummkopf*. She shouldn't be too hard to find."

❖   ❖   ❖

And indeed, she was not.

But extracting information from her was difficult and exceedingly dull. After countless digressions into the difficulties of being a weaver's daughter, of the intellectual challenges of weaving, of the comparable intellectual challenges of shop-cleaning for a butcher, and of the intricacies of being a twenty-seven-year-old woman whose virtue was daily threatened by various suitors (of whom there was no material evidence), Larry and Thomas finally found a way to keep her talking about the household of Ferdinand and Anna Schoenfeld. Luckily, the key to their continued conversation was the daughter, little Gisela, the darling of her eye who had gone off to school in Nuremburg just before turning three. Which was rather odd timing, Ursula reflected: why send such a small child off to school in the last month of winter?

"Why indeed?" prompted Thomas, who knew not to speak further. One more phrase from him and Ursula was sure to be off on some other tangent.

But Ursula's focus remained on Gisela. "Do you know, this is what I wondered, too. There had been no talk of school for her; her mama Anna was looking forward to having her around when the new baby comes." Ursula looked crestfallen. "And to send her off in the middle of the night that way. So strange."

Thomas looked at Larry; Larry looked back at Thomas. Who urged, "They sent Gisela off to school in the middle of the night?"

"Yes, and it was as though they had forgotten they were going to do so."

"Why do you say that?"

"Well, you see, Herr Schoenfeld spoilt his little girl

rotten." Ursula smiled happily at the recollection of this dubious parenting. "But even so, Gisela was always so sweet. And she always liked sweet things. So he made sure she had a fresh sweet roll every morning. Which means I always had to buy them late the day before. Which is just what I did the day before Gisela left." Ursula sighed and stopped.

Thomas thought he was going to swallow his own teeth in frustration. "And then, the next day? The sweet roll?"

Ursula's eyes got watery. "Gisela was gone, and that old witch Mathilde had given the sweet roll to the chickens. And she wouldn't tell me why she hadn't packed it for Gisela's trip, or who had taken her to Nuremburg. And Herr Schoenfeld fired me. And Mistress Anna was sick in bed. And they took Mathilde in to live with them. The witch." Ursula's full, quivering lip threatened the onset of full-blown weeping.

Larry's voice was patient. "And you haven't heard from Gisela? You seem to have been very close."

"Oh, we were. We were. She liked me much more than that—"

"But you haven't heard from her?"

"No. How could I? She's only three, and if they have news of her, they don't tell me. Which is very hurtful. I loved her like she was my own—"

Thomas saw the lower lip become unsteady again, jumped in. "And you say Frau Schoenfeld was suddenly ill?"

"Yes." Ursula paused, frowned. "Although—" And then she thought.

Unwilling to disrupt this rare event, North and Quinn waited.

"Although," repeated Ursula with a great frown after what seemed like the world's longest ten-count, "Frau Schoenfeld took no medicines that I saw, and Mathilde was the only one allowed in her rooms, other than Herr Schoenfeld. Who was there all day. But he never sent for the doctor. But I was scared that Mistress Anna was very sick indeed. That maybe her new pregnancy was putting her in danger."

"Why did you think that?"

"Well, because her family came to the house for a long time, that day. And it was such a busy day, too. All the Swiss children had arrived, and some were already being sent out into the fields and others were being sent further north, all the way to Ulm. And even so, Mistress Anna's brothers came, even the oldest one—despite all the work he had to do with the children."

"He works in the fields with the children?"

Ursula scowled at Thomas' unthinkable stupidity. "No: he is in charge of recording their contracts at the *Rathaus*. Anna is the sister of Hans Kaspar Funk. Didn't you know?"

Larry and Thomas looked at each other a long time before Thomas said. "No, we didn't. And did anything else unusual happen that day?"

"No. But the next day, the other girls went to school also. No one saw them leave, either. And their families fired most of their servants too."

Thomas managed not to look over at Larry again. "And what two girls were those?"

"Liesel Lay and Agatha von Pflummern. But with all those Swiss children running around, settling into their jobs in town, or traveling further north or east, it's no surprise no one remembers seeing them leave. They are pretty much the same age as the ones who were arriving. It was all very confusing, that day." Ursula paused, looked puzzled. "What was I saying? Was there something else you need me to tell you about Gisela?"

Larry rose, extended his hand. "No, Fräulein Bodenmüller. You have told us everything we need to know."

Thomas and Larry walked in silence. They hadn't discussed a destination upon leaving the bloodstained backroom of the butcher's, but of one mind, they seemed to be heading for the Grüner Baum. At least that's where Thomas hoped they were heading.

Larry spoke up as they turned into the narrow street which led to the tavern. "We've been looking at this all wrong. We've been looking for a business angle, for some in-town cartel that had something to gain by undermining the aerodrome deal."

Thomas nodded. "But this doesn't smell like that. It smells more like—"

"Extortion."

"Yes," Thomas agreed, suddenly completely uninterested in a drink. "Extortion."

Sitting by the window looking out on the small lane that led around behind the Grüner Baum to various victualers, Thomas and Quinn nursed almost untouched beers. "What now?" the Englishman wondered aloud. "Try to get in to see the mothers of the other two children?"

Thomas himself knew it was a futile ploy, but nodded in agreement with Quinn's response. "We won't get access there, either. According to Ursula, it sounds as if they've also gone to a 'closed house' servant model."

Thomas pushed his beer back and forth. "Reducing all routine contacts with the outside world. All in order to conceal whatever happened to their children."

"Which, judging from Mathilde's extreme protectiveness, still has Anna Funk in a state of depression."

"Probably all of them. I hadn't thought anything of it before now, but I've overheard mention that this was an 'off' social season among the high and mighty." Thomas took a sip; the beer he had been enjoying so much during the past two days had a suddenly sour taste to it. "Apparently, the top levels of government aren't in the mood for celebration. Both *Burgermeisters* and one of the inner council are too busy trying to act like nothing is wrong."

Quinn looked around at the patrons of the Grüner Baum. "You think anyone else knows something's wrong?"

Thomas considered. "Probably not yet, because it hasn't been going on long enough. Whatever happened occurred within the last two months, if Gisela's sudden departure for 'school in Nuremburg' marks the beginning of the change. But if it goes on much longer—well, a big secret is hard to keep in a small town."

Quinn nodded out the window. "I wonder if any of them could shed some new light on it." Thomas turned, saw Schoenfeld approaching, slightly faster than a donkey cart being led by—if he wasn't mistaken—a pair of genuine soldiers. One of the them was wearing a Swedish-style helmet.

Schoenfeld's one good eye must have been quite

good indeed: he spotted Larry and Thomas staring at him, waved a brief hello, and accelerated his approach to the Grüner Baum.

"Walking like a man with a mission," commented Quinn.

Thomas nodded as the artist entered and came directly toward their table. "*Meine Herren*, may I join you?"

"We were hoping you would, Herr Schoenfeld," replied Thomas, who was happiest being generous with other peoples' money. "A drink?"

"No, thank you. No time for that." He sat and leaned forward briskly; all business, he seemed to forget that one of his hands was withered. "I have been encountering some puzzling circumstances, which may or may not bear upon the frustrations you have been experiencing as well."

"Oh?" asked Larry mildly.

"Yes. My sister-in-law Anna, usually so cheery, has been quite depressed. According to those who know her, it has been going on for some time now. They fear for her coming child. But at my other brother's house—Hans Jakob, who is also a member of the *Rat*—I am now expressly forbidden to speak of it. And I had only asked if it might help to bring little Gisela back for a visit with her mother: by all accounts, they were inseparable, a smile from one being sure of receiving a like return from the other."

Larry nodded. "And that was when you were told not to speak of Gisela any more."

"Exactly. Or of Anna's depression." Schoenfeld looked from one to the other. "And neither of you are surprised at this. In the least."

Thomas was wondering how best to respond to that frank observation without giving too much away when the door banged open and the two garrison soldiers entered. Their swagger and bold sweeping glance about the room stopped when it fell upon Thomas and Quinn. Suddenly circumspect, they made their way to the bar and ordered.

Schoenfeld kept to the topic. "You have encountered something similar. You have suspicions."

Thomas kept his eyes on the soldiers, watched the exchange at the bar. "Suspicions, yes. But no answers."

"What else have you learned?"

Larry seemed to gauge Schoenfeld carefully. "That Gisela isn't the only little girl who was sent to school suddenly, just before the *Rat* decided to cancel the aerodrome deal. It seems that the daughters of Hanss Lay and Ignaz von Pflummern also departed for Nuremburg without anyone noticing."

Schoenfeld banged his good hand on the table. "I knew it!" he announced.

"Knew what?"

"That there was something odd about this early schooling nonsense. Gisela is a little strip of a girl, barely three. So how would she get to Nuremburg without special arrangements being made long beforehand? It is not as if Biberach has one of your marvelous trains running to and from Nuremburg, after all. Even so, someone from the family would travel with her. And when I offered to bring a letter to her, my younger brother seemed ready to throttle me."

Quinn leaned forward. "You are traveling to Nuremburg? Why?"

Schoenfeld actually blushed. "Since I was not to

become an artist in Italy, then perhaps in Germany, in Grantville, maybe in the Netherlands..."

Quinn smiled. "Perhaps so. But at least travel with me, when you go: I would not like to see you hazard the Jakobsweg on your own. And travel is always more pleasant with company, no?"

It was Thomas who answered. "And it is always far more pleasant to travel with well-funded friends."

Quinn quirked a sour smile. "You mean, like me?"

"Actually, right now, I meant like them." Thomas pointed surreptitiously at the backs of the two soldiers at the bar.

Larry frowned. "What do you mean?"

"While you've been discussing disappearing daughters with Herr Schoenfeld, I've been watching those two. Who have already knocked back two of the house's finest. And are now chasing it down with a double helping of schnapps, each. And they paid full price. For all of it."

Quinn's frown went away, replaced by a carefully neutral expression. "Hmm. Not such a poor, threadbare garrison after all."

"No, indeed. And look at their gear."

Quinn did. "All new. Local manufacture, if I'm not mistaken."

"You're not," put in Schoenfeld. "I know the work of our weavers and tanners, their marks, their cuts and patterns. That's their work all right. Of course, they'd have had plenty of time to purchase some, by now. From what my brothers tell me, they're in town twice a week to pick up provisions."

Quinn turned, saw where the soldiers had left the wagon, which was now being loaded—none too eagerly—by a handful of the nearby victualers. "But why get their goods here? Why not in the market?"

Schoenfeld shrugged. "My brothers tell me that the *Rat* is worried that there could be a riot. Biberach has not had it so bad as other towns, but food is still dear. If the townspeople had to routinely watch soldiers who do nothing but sit on their hands six miles away, getting food for free—"

"I see their point," allowed Quinn, "but still, it's peculiar."

Schoenfeld shrugged. "Perhaps not, particularly given how much the people fear any contact with the abbey. So, what they don't see doesn't stir up their anger or fear. That's not even one of our town's wagons out there: that came from the abbey. And the soldiers come with it, to drive it back and forth."

Quinn rubbed his chin meditatively; he glanced at Thomas. "Because no one from town wants to get anywhere near the abbey, of course."

"Of course," agreed Thomas. *Yes, it's odd how distant and socially isolated the garrison is and yet how well-heeled its individual soldiers seem to be.*

"And look who's here to lend a hand."

Thomas looked up, followed Quinn's eyes out the window: Hanss Lay had arrived, conferring with the victualers who were loading the wagon. North smiled. "I wasn't aware *Burgermeisters* made a special point of counting out the beans and bacon for their garrisons. Perhaps a few questions are in order—"

But Schoenfeld was shaking his head. "*Nein, alles ist Ordnung*—it is correct that he does this. He is also the *Stadtrechner*."

"The what?"

"You would say . . . cashier? No, more like your word 'purser.'"

"So," said Larry with a mirthless smile. "Hanss Lay handles Biberach's accounts payable."

"Well, of course he does," agreed Thomas with a similar smile.

Schoenfeld looked from one to the other again. "What are you saying? What do you suspect?"

Larry leaned his chin in his hand and looked out the window. "Why speculate when we might see for ourselves?"

The soldiers at the bar tossed back the last of their schnapps and, leaving more coin than was strictly necessary, strode outside. Thomas suddenly rediscovered his taste for the Grüner Baum's fine beer as he turned to watch the end of the loading.

As the last space in the wagon's bed was filled—with improbably choice foods, drink, and some outright frippery—an assistant appeared beside *Burgermeister* Lay bearing a weighty box from which the ends of loaves and corked bottles protruded.

Quinn grinned. "That's a mighty heavy meal, he's carrying there."

Thomas nodded. "Evidently Prum's men are used to a very, very rich diet."

The soldiers appeared, exchanging curt nods with Lay, but no words. Thomas cheated the shutters open a little wider and strained to catch any conversation that might arise.

None did. The soldiers walked around the wagon slowly, inspecting its contents. When they were done, they stood at the front, expectantly.

Lay and his assistant approached. The *Burgermeister*

nodded crisply at the box the smaller man was carrying. "*Speiserest*," Lay almost spat at the soldiers.

One of whom nodded, and jerked his head at the wagon's seat.

"'Leftovers?'" translated Schoenfeld quizzically.

As the box hit the seat, Thomas clearly heard the faint jingle of coins. Many, many coins.

"Leftovers," confirmed Thomas. "Or, to be more precise, it is what is left over from Captain Prum's steady depletion of your treasury."

It took a few moments of whispered explanations to make matters clear to the initially bewildered, and then outraged, Schoenfeld. "So you believe that Prum and his men kidnapped all three girls?"

Quinn nodded. "Let's add it up. Lay just sent a secret payment to a handful of men who are holed up in a fortlike building that no one goes near. His daughter is one of the three missing. The other two are also children of the highest ranking men in your *Rat*. And with Lay as the *Stadtrechner*, they could manage this all from the top without anyone under them being any wiser."

"But eventually it would come out. And why would Prum not simply extort the families themselves?"

Thomas shrugged. "Probably because Prum's a right greedy bastard. He knows the real money in this town is not in the hands of any one of its citizens: it's in the hands of the *Rat*. The taxes and tariffs. Besides, this way, he can shift from extorting cash to goods however and whenever he likes. He's a clever parasite: he can feed from a number of sources, for as long as this lasts."

"But then why would he pressure the *Rat* to reverse its decision about the aerodrome? It means less income for the town, and Prum must have anticipated that it would bring an inquiry from Grantville."

Quinn frowned. "Well, to start with, an inquiry is a whole lot less troublesome than having us set up business on your doorstep. As long as traffic through Biberach is moderate and overwhelmingly local, Prum can probably control the situation. But if Biberach became a more dynamic hub of commerce, that would change: more people would be trying to make deals, ask questions.

"As far as income increase from the aerodrome goes, I don't think Prum plans to be around long enough to really see that. How long can he realistically hold on to those girls? How long before people start becoming less fearful of the abbey and traveling out there again, or the nuns come back to take possession? My guess is that he's not planning on being here come Christmas, or even first harvest. So if he can delay us from setting up the aerodrome for just half a year, he'll have achieved everything he intended to."

"Which is?"

"What else?" said Thomas, draining the last of his beer. "To bleed your treasury and merchants dry, while also keeping his wealth as portable as possible."

"And the girls?"

Thomas glanced at Quinn, who had a hard look on his face. "I doubt that Prum has a strong taste for needless killing. On the other hand, I also doubt that he would hesitate to do so if it suited his ends—or was simply more convenient." *Which it almost certainly would be, given the situation.*

Schoenfeld was pale. "I hadn't meant that," he said. Thomas thought the smaller man might be on the verge of vomiting. "I meant, how did Prum get them in the first place?"

Quinn started thumbing a stream of coins onto the table. "I imagine they used the chaos of the arrival of the Swiss child laborers to cover their actions. Lots of people running around with kids, not all of whom were happy, I'm sure. They probably got Gisela first, because the house was the smallest and had only two servants. A night time grab, probably. It wouldn't have been hard to plan it out. Prum and his men had plenty of lead time to know who held what positions in the *Rat*, where everyone lived, how many kids they had, what age, and all the rest. And once they had one child, they probably went to Lay's house under the guise of reporting on their progress in 'locating' Gisela. And when they left his house, they had his daughter. And probably had him in tow as well, to get access to von Pflummern's house: a frantic knock on the door in the middle of the night, a familiar face—and they went in right behind. And then they had the daughters of both the Catholic and Lutheran *Burgermeisters*." Quinn stood. "Let's go."

"What? Go where?"

Thomas was making sure that the straps and flaps that secured and hid his various weapons were untangled and ready for fast access. "Wherever Prum's wagon goes. But much further behind."

"But won't we lose them, then?"

"No," smiled Quinn, "we won't. Thomas, how many binoculars in your unit?"

"Two, counting my own. But why ask me? You have

one of your own. And unless I'm much mistaken, that Ruger bolt-action you've tried to conceal from me looks to have a scope."

Quinn smiled. "No fooling you, is there Thomas?"

"No, there isn't. As I've told you before. Now let's be after them."

Templeton leaned away from the Ruger's telescopic sight. "They just turned into the abbey, sir."

"Patrols?"

"One man in a blind outside the complex. About fifty yards up the road from the main entrance."

Schoenfeld stared wide-eyed at the scope, at Templeton, and back at the scope. "He can see all that? From a mile and a half away?"

"He most certainly can," Thomas assured him, before turning to Quinn. "So. Prum is not sending his ill-got gains anywhere else, at least not directly."

"Nope. And any of his men can be deemed complicit, given the size of their unit and the fact that they all seem to rotate through the privilege of coming to down to pick up the payola."

Schoenfeld frowned. "I admit their guilt looks certain. But, as a man who makes a living tricking human eyes into believing they have seen something they have not actually seen, I must point out: looks can be deceiving. It is not proven that the daughters are at the abbey, just that there is some kind of underhanded business going on between Prum's men and Lay."

Thomas was about to rebut that sometimes things are exactly as they seem, but Quinn nodded. "You have a point, Johann. And there's one last bit of evidence which will tell us whether or not the girls are in Nuremburg, instead."

Thomas kept from rolling his eyes. Six months studying under a lawyer and the once-daring and decisive Lawrence Quinn had almost been unmade as an officer and a man.

"What is this evidence? How do we get it?" asked Schoenfeld eagerly.

"Well, actually, Johann, it was you who gave us the answer to that question."

"I did?"

"Yes. So here's what we'll do tomorrow morning..."

By the time Thomas and Quinn had emerged from the *Rathaus*, Johann was already waiting for them at the head of the market place. His stance and flushed cheeks suggested barely contained agitation.

"I hope you fared better than I," he snapped when they drew near. "The moment I asked the servants if the mothers had any letters for me to carry to their daughters, it was as if I had become a plague carrier. All three doors were shut in my face. And you?"

"The same with the fathers," answered Quinn with a nod. "But with the added deceitful details you'd expect from nervous politicians."

Thomas smiled. "It was strange. When we indicated that we would have to return north to report the failure of our mission here, they were relieved. That changed around entirely when we indicated that we were returning via Nuremburg and thus would be happy to accept responsibility for delivering letters to their daughters at their respective schools. All of a sudden, all three corrected us: their daughters were not at schools, but under the guidance of private tutors."

"Did they give you names?" pressed Schoenfeld ingenuously.

"They couldn't," Quinn answered gently, "since it's pretty clear there are no names to give."

Schoenfeld nodded. "So they are concealing something."

Quinn nodded. "And now, we'll double-check it from the other end."

"How?"

"We have a radio with us. We'll use it to contact the personnel at the new aerodrome in Nuremburg. Some of the local staff there are well-connected with a number of the more affluent groups in the city, who *do* have enough personnel to make a quick round of the gates and travel-houses. Places which would not fail to notice and remember three girls of such young ages, arriving in the dead of winter in a big city, waiting for a tutor to meet each of them and take them in hand."

Schoenfeld nodded. "Absolutely. One, they might miss. But all three? It would probably be a safe assumption that if they were not seen, it is because they were never there."

Larry nodded and turned to North. "Let's get back to the men at Ringschnaitt. Are they ready to move?"

Thomas shrugged. "They were ready before we left this morning."

As Metzger, the radio operator, looked up, Thomas knew the answer before the squat man even shook his head. "So," the Englishman said turning to Quinn and Schoenfeld, "Not a whisper of them." He turned to Volker and Wright, whom he'd sent out early that morning to keep the abbey under closer observation. "Report on reconnaissance?"

Wright—who was even taller than North—spoke with smooth precision. "The garrison, such as it is, is still maintaining reasonable watchfulness, Colonel. Although from the attitude of the men we've observed, they don't seem too accustomed to guard duty, and don't much like it."

Probably on alert only because we're still in the area, Thomas conjectured.

Wright hadn't finished. "They've taken some minor steps to increase the defensibility of the abbey. As seen yesterday, they keep one man in a hidden outpost on the roadway in. They send out irregular walking patrols into each quadrant of their perimeter; never more than two men, often only one. Judging from the morning cooking fires, I suspect the small patrol complement is due to their small numbers. We also caught a brief glimpse of one man just a mile from Biberach, we think with a mount, in a concealed position, watching the roads into town."

"Keeping a close eye out for any movements by our unit, I'll wager. And the discipline at the abbey?"

Wright's smile was pinched. "Not such as I'd call it, sir. They seem to be following their orders, but in a casual fashion."

"And the girls?"

"Sorry, sir. Not a sign of them. But the abbey itself is large, even though they've closed up all the outbuildings except the stables. They could be anywhere, sir."

If they're still alive, he could hear Wright thinking

in unison with him. "Well done, Mr. Wright. You and Volker should get yourself some breakfast." *Which, for all we know might be your last with me, since Quinn already has his acquisitive hooks into the two of you.*

Schoenfeld had crossed his arms, looking from North to Quinn. "So. Prum and his men have apparently become common bandits. What do we do? Scout the abbey more closely, try to find the girls?"

Quinn shook his head. "We can't go any closer. They know we're in Biberach, and until we leave, that one nearby lookout will be watching us. Which means that the moment we move directly toward the abbey, we are putting the girls at risk. We need the element of surprise, if we are to save them."

"So then we approach under the cover of night, and charge them head on?"

Quinn shook his head. "We might manage to approach undetected, and we could probably overcome them, but not before they killed the girls. Or put guns to their heads and compelled us to withdraw."

Schoenfeld's composure disintegrated: his shout turned heads among North's men. "Then what do you plan to do?"

"Us?" Thomas said mildly. "Why, we plan to leave."

"To get reinforcements?"

"To get a fresh perspective," said Quinn.

Schoenfeld stared, livid, from one to the other. "So this is how the great and powerful United States of Europe defends the interests of one of its newest affiliates?" His withered hand trembled as he pointed it at them. "Then I will attempt what you soldiers will not. I will secure the release of those girls myself!"

North allowed one eyebrow to rise skeptically. "Indeed?"

"Yes," the rather wiry artist retorted hotly. "Judging from the artful planning that went into carrying off this scheme, Prum is a clever man—clever enough to realize that once his crime is known, his only logical alternative is to turn the girls over to me and flee the area at once."

North struggled to keep a grin off his face—but Quinn leaned forward with an earnest frown. "Johann, don't do that. It won't work. If we thought talking to Prum would work, that would be our first approach—"

"Your first approach is to flee." Johann almost sneered. "I concede your point that an outright attack would endanger the girls. But instead of considering any other solution—and particularly a solution that relies upon brains instead of brawn—you decide to give up. But I will not. I will do what must be done. Alone, if need be."

Quinn leaned forward even more urgently, evidently ready to make further entreaties that Johann not pursue such a course of action—but North took a step toward Johann with a smile and an extended hand. "And we wish you luck, Herr Schoenfeld. You are indeed a brave man, and we hope that your mission succeeds."

Johann blinked, stunned by such a rapid approval of his plan—and the de facto confirmation that his friends were not, in fact, going to provide any material assistance in the attempt to free the girls. Then, with a grimace and narrowed eyes, he turned on his heel and stalked away.

North appreciated Quinn's modicum of composure:

the American did not round on him until Schoenfeld had turned a corner, leaving them quite alone in one of Ringschnaitt's narrow lanes. "Thomas, you just sent that poor unsuspecting artist to his death. Once he's revealed that he knows about the girls and has seen the inside of the abbey's defenses, Prum will never let him go."

North shrugged. "Of course he won't; Prum may be an amoral monster, but he's no idiot. He'll figure right enough—and right away—that poor Johann is not particularly gifted at playing high-stakes poker with extortionists. In fact, what Herr Schoenfeld believes to be his ace in the hole—the threat of external intervention—is worthless, as Prum will quickly teach him."

"North, if I didn't know you any better, I'd swear you are as heartless a bastard as Prum himself."

"Nonsense; I was the legitimate product of a church-consecrated marriage, so I am not a bastard. Technically. However, you may be right about the rest. But mark me, Larry: Prum has no reason to kill Johann immediately—and, more importantly, Johann's abortive visit will actually allow us to prepare the surprise attack we need to use against Prum."

Quinn crossed his arms. "Enlighten me."

"Shh. No talking during Professor North's lecture. Let us begin by admitting that Prum will be aware that, if Biberach's town fathers were sending Schoenfeld as some kind of envoy, he would not be traveling to the abbey alone. There'd at least be a small escort, hanging back a few hundred yards. So the absence of that escort will tell Prum that Johann is acting on his own, naively convinced that the bastard will not harm him for fear of bringing searchers out to the abbey. Which Prum knows will not happen, since we can be sure the town fathers have been told—in grisly detail—what will happen to their daughters if they reveal or confirm Prum's extortion to anyone else.

"So as long as Prum refuses to allow poor Johann to return to Biberach, there's still no danger of the truth getting out. And even if Schoenfeld had gone to the town fathers first—which he is likely to claim— Prum will interpret the lack of an escort as a sign that those same civic worthies have sent the artist out to the abbey as they would send a lamb to the slaughter: to be silenced before he tells anyone else what he knows. Which you may be sure Prum will do—eventually."

"Which means we've just signed Johann Schoenfeld's death warrant."

"An overly-hasty conclusion, Mr. Quinn. Attend and learn the delicate art of dealing with inhuman monsters. Prudent creatures like Prum are also cautious creatures. So he will want to speak with Johann. Furthermore, Prum is also a proud creature—and so he will also want to gloat: it is an almost invariable characteristic of such blackguards that they must preen a bit when they feel themselves completely safe."

"And why will Prum suddenly feel himself completely safe?"

"Well, Mr. Quinn, by the time Herr Schoenfeld arrives at the abbey, the fellow Prum has watching our movements from a mile outside of town will have seen us depart northward and will have ridden back to inform his despicable master that we have all left the area. Which means that the only plausible threat to Prum is gone. And we will have departed in such a blasé fashion that he will be forced to conclude that we not only failed to resecure a site for the aerodrome, but that we remain unaware and unsuspecting of Prum's extortion. Logically, awareness of such a crime would compel us to take action rather than slouch back the way we came. All reasonable, so far?"

Quinn was still frowning, but he nodded. Grudgingly.

"So when Johann arrives with his naive threats of disclosure, Prum will no doubt press him—perhaps unpleasantly, I grant you—to confirm that we actually have left the area. Which our now-resentful friend will either emphatically confirm or unconvincingly deny—because he now believes it to be true also. That is why I couldn't let you share our plans with him."

Larry nodded. "Because now, having two separate but identical reports of our departure, Prum will be doubly assured that he is safe."

Thomas nodded. "Just so. And the moment that Prum begins basking in that mistaken sense of security, that is when we must strike. After we see how he handles Johann, that is."

"What?" Quinn's eyes had opened wide.

"Larry, the lecture is over: now we must confront brute reality. Prum will have to pull some of his already meager sentries off the line to escort and guard Johann when he approaches the abbey. And because Prum will feel himself safe, he should be pretty relaxed about doing so. And when he does, those movements will show us precisely where most of his men are positioned, how they react when the abbey is approached, and will possibly help us determine the best sightlines for a sniper."

"So that we can take out Prum immediately, when we attack."

"Exactly. If our first blow takes off the head of the serpent, the body is likely to thrash around purposelessly for a while. So before it can grow a new head, some of us will rush in and secure the girls—and Johann—while the rest of us chop its writhing coils into tiny pieces."

Quinn nodded, but he was still frowning. "Well, that all sounds fine. Except for one thing."

"Which is?"

"Which is: what if you are wrong about Prum letting Johann live for a while? What if Prum decides to simplify his hostage-holding tasks: one less person to guard, one less mouth to feed?"

North shrugged. "It's not a logical course of action, Larry. They have plenty of food and they can just let Johann sit in a cell while they wait to see if they have further need of him: as a hostage, a liaison, or an information source for subsequent dealings with the town."

"Granted—but those are all conjectures. We're talking about putting a man's life in certain danger."

"We're also talking about the lives of three young girls—and all the men in our platoon who would unnecessarily die in any frontal assault. Which would almost certainly result in the deaths of those young ladies, as well. So this way, we risk one to save all."

Quinn's eyes were unblinking and, North had to admit, rather unsettling. "And you wouldn't even let me warn him what he was walking into."

"Larry, Prum will believe Johann because, as things stand now, *Johann himself* is not only convinced that we are gone, but that we do not care about local problems. His genuine bitterness toward us is what will lead Prum to believe him, to believe that we are truly out of the picture. And once he believes that, we have the best chance of making a surprise attack that should save the hostages' lives. Now, let's get the platoon ready to pull out north toward Ulm."

Four hours later, sitting in a copse a quarter mile due north of the abbey, Quinn handed the binoculars to Thomas. "There he goes."

Johann Schoenfeld, having approached the abbey along the east-west road, did not see the man at the observation post wave to the sentries at the main building.

"Have you marked their picket?" Thomas growled behind him.

"Marked, sir," answered Lieutenant Hastings, who passed a second set of binoculars along the line to the unit's best marksmen: Volker and Templeton.

Schoenfeld was met and brought into the abbey by two armed men. Thomas relayed the key information as he saw it: "One wheel lock, one flintlock. Or possibly a snaphaunce. Can't tell at this range." Assessing the firearms they were up against was crucial tactical intelligence, gathered more easily when the members of the garrison came out from the walls and shadows of the abbey. Or leaned out the window in amused curiosity, as several others did now. "A pretty even mix of wheel locks and flintlocks throughout," Thomas added, based on the new appearances. "Are you marking their positions, Hastings?"

"They are marked, sir."

Quinn produced his own binoculars. "I want to get my own close look at how this next part goes down," he explained. Thomas lay elbow to elbow with the up-timer and watched.

After some delay, Schoenfeld appeared in a high-ceilinged upper-story room, made commandingly expansive by its several wide windows. They had heard about this room from locals. It had evidently been, at different phases in the abbey's history, a chapel, a library, and a convalescent sunroom. It was hard to tell what it had been most recently, given the chaos of pompery that had been pushed into it. An ornate chair was on a makeshift dais. An altar had been pushed off to one side, serving as a combination sideboard and weapons-rack. Prum appeared from the dark at the back of the room, wearing a red cape—a cardinal's?—and began walking in a circle about Schoenfeld, asking short questions. The answers he received seemed to instigate long responses, replete with grandiose gestures.

"Damn: poor Johann," muttered Quinn. "Trapped in the court of the Crimson King."

"Eh? What?"

"An up-time reference, Thomas. Just a way of saying that Prum is completely out to lunch."

"Don't use up-time idioms to explain up-time idioms, damn you. But if you mean that Prum is mad, well—no, I don't think so. I've seen a lot of this kind of behavior, particularly once the wars became perpetual and the armies started to become desperate and disorganized. Little men, having lived a life beneath the boots of their 'betters,' suddenly come into a moment of power. It's an intoxicating opportunity to play the part of those whom they have hated—and envied—for so long, and to exact vengeance from all who are too weak to resist, as they themselves had long been. But Prum does not stand to gain anything by killing Schoenfeld—not right away, at any rate."

"So you say. But after he's questioned him thoroughly, which might eventually include torture—"

"—Prum might indeed kill Schoenfeld and drop the body down some convenient well, where it won't be found for several months." Thomas shrugged. "Frankly, if you're trying to find a lunatic in this whole dance macabre, I nominate Schoenfeld. Granted, civilians often completely misread situations like this one, but Johann seemed sensible enough up until he did this."

Quinn sighed. "Thomas, you heard Schoenfeld the first night we met him. He's wracked by guilt, by not being here when the shit hit the fan. This isn't just about having a plan to save the girls; it's about the expiation of what Johann considers his sins, of not being in Biberach when his family and town needed him. Johann stated quite clearly that he holds himself responsible for his father's death. Feels guilty to have fled before the approach of war. And now, he's probably convinced himself that if he'd been here, he'd have been able to do something to stop this."

"So he goes to present himself for evisceration by renegades while also inadvertently providing Prum with a tactical update on our departure."

Quinn shrugged. "Yes, but if pressed, he'll probably also point out that we'll be back."

"Yes, which will only lead Prum to wrap up his extortion racket in a month or two, while the coast is still clear. Which means that the usefulness of the hostages will end sooner, rather than later."

"Listen: Johann doesn't understand our line of work, but he has a good heart—" Larry stopped and stared intently through the binoculars. "Damn, is Prum making Johann get down on his knees?"

North looked, nodded. "Yes. I think he's making him swear to something. Probably giving him his parole."

"Hmm," mused Quinn. "That's interesting. A military habit Prum's retained. Probably to give his captives—which is to say, his eventual victims—a false sense of security while he decides what to do with them."

"You sound like you're scheming, Larry."

"Me? I'm a guileless American, remember? Anyhow, I've seen enough. As you've said, now we need to mount an attack as soon as possible."

North nodded and looked over his shoulder. Dispersed back along one-hundred and fifty yards of open woods, the platoon was hiding as best it could. "Moving them all up to attack positions is not going to be a short job, unfortunately."

Hastings, hanging a few feet back, shrugged. "We could advance at night, attack under cover of darkness."

North shook his head. "A night attack is no good, particularly since we don't have detailed information about the interior of the abbey. Major Quinn and I asked Herr Schoenfeld about the layout; he'd never been inside. Not surprising for a Protestant. Not surprising for a Catholic, either: the sisters and townsfolk were not mutually welcoming. Besides, any earlier layout could have been changed dramatically by now."

"Then sir, should we move at night and attack at dawn?"

"Hastings, what part of the phrase 'quick attack' is

confusing you? With every passing minute, there is an accumulating chance that one of the enemy—either a walking patrol, or another mounted lookout—will alert Prum to the fact that we never really left the region and are now poised, weapons drawn, on his doorstep. Being discovered that way—or by some other bit of bad luck—would constitute a situation that we can safely characterize as Very Bad Indeed. Besides, moving at dark could give us away just as surely as moving in daylight: we don't know this ground, Hastings. And we've not been close enough to the abbey itself to know the best positions to assault from, or the most concealed avenues of moving into them."

Quinn thought for a moment. "I think I can help with that."

"What? How?"

"Well, you've groused about my taking four of your very best soldiers, so I guess I'll see if they live up to the hype. I'll take the four of them forward as a pathfinder force. We'll blaze a trail along the best-concealed pathways to assault positions. Give us about an hour. Once we give you the signal to get the rest of the platoon moving up in drips and drabs, we'll start looking for ways to get a sniper into an optimal position and, if possible, wriggle into some far forward positions for directing the start of the attack."

North frowned. "So you're going to go bounding off into the bush—the rather sparse bush—with Volker, Templeton, Winkelmann, and Wright—on your own?"

Quinn shrugged. "Yeah. You said they're the best. And you need to manage traffic back here. Got a better plan?"

North looked at Quinn, found the subtly diffident cheeriness of the American unnerving, and, studying his eyes for a second, resolved never to play poker with him again: he had learned how to become well-nigh unreadable.

Quinn crossed his arms. "I'll ask again; do you have a better plan?"

North sighed. "Damn it, no, I do not. So get moving—and no foolish risks, Larry."

Larry beamed. "Only sensible risks; I promise." And then he was gone into the thickets that led away from the copse and down the slight incline toward the abbey.

As North waited for Quinn to meet him and point out where he'd positioned their sniper, as well as any new details about the abbey, the Englishman scanned the skirmish line of his troops. They were fanned out along the edge of the smaller but thicker copse to which Larry's pathfinders had brought them. Wright, clearly the shrewdest of the four troopers that the American had selected, had waved them into the positions of the broad outlines of the attack his commander was recommending.

Peering over the one hundred twenty-five yards separating them from the abbey's walls, North had to admit that the American's attack concept was a good one, and he had selected good positions from which to spring it. Likewise, the concealment on the approaches had been more than adequate, and, best of all, Quinn had them positioned due east of the abbey. This put them well away from the primary source of traffic—the west-leading road to Biberach—and therefore, to the notional "rear" of the hidden sentry who kept watch over it.

The ground between the copse and the main building was mostly clear, but a smattering of low bushes had grown wild in the year of its abandonment, providing a few points of cover for a conventional approach. But at this range, and with the element of surprise against troops armed with single-barreled, muzzle-loading weapons, North and his lead squad would make a straight rush over the ground. His two supporting squads would provide covering fire until the lead squad was ready to enter the main building, at which point they would deploy to the cover of the bushes. Eventually, a few men would head down the road to set up a flanking position to the south and—

—and why the hell was Larry Quinn emerging from those overgrown bushes and walking toward the abbey, a white handkerchief held high?

"Damn it all, what is that lunatic doing?"

Thomas had expected the question to be rhetorical and inspire fearful silence among his men, but from just behind him, a voice answered his query: "He's getting inside, sir."

North turned, dumbfounded, and discovered that Wright had caught up to him again and was regarding him with patient blue eyes. "And what in the name of all that is both holy and unholy does that damned Yank think he's going to achieve if he *does* get inside?"

"The element of surprise, sir."

"Surprise? Well, yes, I'm sure Prum *will* be surprised: the person who could do him the most harm is now simply walking in his front door, unarmed. I know *I'm* surprised."

Wright's smile was small. "I think Major Quinn has something else in mind, sir."

"I doubt Major Quinn has enough of a mind to have something else in, Corporal Wright. Now, you'd better tell me—"

"No time, sir. Looks like the party is starting. Watch carefully, now; you'll need to act quickly."

"I'll need to—? Oh, bloody hell. Hastings, Finan: word down the line. We go with the plans we discussed upon arriving here, but they could be changing as we move. Everyone's eyes on me. Assign the covering squads their marks. Designate reloaders."

"Done, sir," answered Hastings.

Oh. Well. Why the hell am I here at all, then? "Very well. Be ready."

"For what?"

"As if I bloody know? Just be ready to follow my orders and my lead."

"Yes, sir."

Quinn was disappearing through the front door after a hasty body search by the guards. Only one of the two sentries went in with him. An audible commotion rose up a moment later: several of the other sentries at the windows disappeared inside, their duty overridden by their curiosity. *Well, that* does *help us by clearing the field a bit,* admitted Thomas. *But still—*"Finan: report. The enemy's patrol status?"

"None out right now, sir. And while one or two of the sentries might look a bit more alert, most of them are trying to see who the visitor is. They probably don't get a lot of excitement out here."

"Well, they're about to get more than they bargained for. Hastings, I want this to be absolutely clear: you do *not* charge with the last two squads right behind me. You keep your men back here until the lead squad is safe under the walls."

"Yes, sir."

"Finan?"

"Sir?"

"Pass the word to the lead squad: rifles back-slung, revolvers out. Except for Arnfauss and Schiltung: if we need close supporting fire on the way in, they'll provide it with their Winchesters. The rest of us will charge headlong to get to the walls before—"

"Sir," interrupted Wright, who, it turned out, had Quinn's binoculars. "The major is inside."

Thomas swiveled to look through his own glasses. Sure enough, the hare-brained American was in Prum's own Grand Receiving Room of Tawdry Squalor. Prum was already pulling out all the theatrical stops, lording it over his new, hapless captive.

Which is when Thomas noticed how calm and utterly collected Quinn was. And how calm Wright was. As if none of this were a surprise to either of them. But what purpose, what scheme, could possibly—?

"Sir, get ready," hissed Wright.

The largely one-sided conversation in Prum's audience chamber was becoming less cordial: Prum gestured at the floor imperiously. Quinn looked away, said something brief. Two of Prum's men came forward. *Larry, do as the homicidal popinjay says; don't get him angry. He might—*

The prior exchange was reprised: Prum pointed at the floor, Larry seemed to resist again. One of the two men who had stepped closer lifted a sword— whereupon, reluctantly, Larry sank to his knees—

Wright's breath stopped in mid-draw.

Thomas understood what was happening just before a sharp, distinctively up-time report sounded from the upper third of one of the higher trees in the copse. Almost instantly, Prum spun around, evidently hit in the shoulder. Thomas heard Templeton's voice utter a ferocious curse—"Bollocks!"—from that same location, accompanied by the faint clatter of the Ruger's bolt action being worked.

Thomas was raising up as the second shot barked out over their heads and Prum went down, a puff of dusky red marking the impact point just to the right of his sternum.

"Charge!" yelled North, and, nine-millimeter up-time automatic in hand, he began a long-legged sprint toward the abbey. First squad, emerging from the trees, was right behind him, cap and ball revolvers at the ready.

Prum's men appeared at the windows of the abbey; each one was greeted by the slow but steady roars of two, sometimes three, pre-sighted Winchesters. Half of the renegades sprawled back. The door guard returned fire from deeper in the archway, but did not even have an angle on—or probably know about—most of the squad that was charging in his direction. Winchesters snapped rounds at his muzzle flash. It was impossible to tell if he was dead, wounded, running, or reloading.

Wright was pacing Thomas on the charge, Quinn's own nine-millimeter in his long-fingered grip. Volker and Winkelmann rose up out of the bushes in front of them, leading the way to the gate by about ten yards. *Damn it, how did Quinn manage to get those two positioned before I had even—?*

But there was no time to wonder at the obvious—that

Larry Quinn had indeed grown proficient as a soldier—
because they were coming upon the archway. The fellow
in its shadows—the one who had returned fire at the
other squads—cast away the musket he was reloading
and drew his small sword. He went down under a flurry
of bullets from the four lead attackers. To the south, a
single musket spoke; Winchesters answered, probably
announcing the end of the soldier manning the road
outpost.

Thomas, panting, threw himself against the interior
wall of the arched entrance to the abbey. "Wright,
Volker, Winkelmann: according to what little we learned
of the interior from the farmers in Ringschnaitt, we'll
go up the stairs to the—"

"We know, sir; Major Quinn told us. Leapfrog
advance?"

Damn smart alecks. "Stop asking the obvious, Winkelmann. Start us off."

The rest of the first squad arrived as the four of
them rounded the doorway and started up the staircase.

They encountered only three men on the way to
Prum's audience chamber—all trying to run away.
One made the mistake of bringing up his weapon;
the other two sensibly surrendered. However, Thomas
reflected, perhaps the first one was the most sensible
of the three: the quick bullets he got were infinitely
preferable to what the townspeople of Biberach were
likely to visit upon any survivors.

As Thomas' men dodged into Prum's audience
chamber, a familiar voice spoke from the darkness
along the rear wall: "*Donner.*"

"*Blitzen,*" replied Volker and Wright in unison.

Quinn leaned out of those shadows. "Quickly, back here. I've been covering the approach to the girls, but I can't get them out."

The dark at the rear of the room concealed a passageway to a row of hermitage cells. All locked. All with sounds of whimpering coming from behind the thick, dark timbers. Thomas started snapping orders. "Volker, get some men up here and take these locks off. Presuming that the mutinous Major Quinn will allow you to take orders from me any more."

Volker slunk away like a child detecting the first impatient tones of what might turn into a full-blown parental argument.

But Quinn just smiled. "I wasn't in the least mutinous, Thomas: I did exactly what I said I'd do. Just not the way you envisioned it. And actually, let's be clear about one other thing: for this operation, you were *my* employee."

"Don't distract me with the facts, you impertinent Yank. Why they hell didn't you tell me what you had in mi—?"

"Because, Thomas, would you have agreed to this plan quickly?"

"What, are you mad? Agree to this—?" Thomas had planned to indicate Prum's awkwardly fallen corpse along with the others of his makeshift court who had not known to keep their heads down and out of Templeton's scope-aided field of fire. But then the three girls emerged from their prisons with grateful sobs, and Schoenfeld was heard raging in a further cell, obviously none the worse for wear. "Well, um, I suppose I wouldn't have."

Quinn smiled. "Right. And there wasn't time to

argue. You agreed that there was no way to be sure how long Prum would let Johann live. And the only reason Johann had his head in Prum's noose was because we didn't explain things to our artist friend before he went off on his quest. So every minute mattered, and I didn't have the right to ask anyone else to go in and get our sniper a shot at Prum. I was the one who put Johann in there: it was on me to start the wheels moving that would get him out."

North looked away, wondered if he'd have had the nerve—or more to the point, the fine sense of ethics—to have done what Larry had done. "Well, you may be a lunatic, but at least you're an admirable one."

Larry shrugged. "Not so much of a lunatic to miss that we really did need a pathfinder group to find a concealed route to some reasonable assault positions. And as soon as I realized that, I saw how I could put the rest of my plan in place while you were bringing up the platoon. So either way, the best thing was for me to go on ahead with my four men."

"Your men?"

"Sorry, but they are for now. And you might not see them again for quite a while."

"Well, I suppose you're not taking them to invade some other world, are you?" And then, judging from Larry's patient gaze, North understood. Yes, they were going to another world. The New World, to be precise. "The Americas, then?"

Quinn shook his head. "Thomas, you know I can't say."

"No—but you just did. Well, none of my business and not for me to repeat." With which Thomas set about putting things in proper military order: "Finan, bring Hastings in. I want a head-count of the defenders, dead and alive. If it doesn't match or exceed our preattack estimate, he's to organize pursuit teams. As soon as you've got that squared away, send a mounted courier back to Biberach. Message follows . . ."

By the time the rider to the town was dispatched, the survivors had filled in the blanks of how the garrison had evolved into a pack of blackmailing thieves.

Their group had not started out as part of a regular formation, but as members of a mercenary regiment that had been broken, reconstituted, and broken again in the years leading up to the creeping peace that had begun to break out a year after Grantville appeared. Mostly Swabians, those that had joined from some sense of religious loyalty had, by the end of 1634, found billets with more legitimate units, or directly in Swedish regiments. And those that remained—

Well, the dregs always went somewhere, and in this case, they remained with the regiment that Horn allowed to be battered down to company size, and then a single platoon after sharp exchanges with Bernhard over various contested tracts farther to the west.

With the unit exhausted and threadbare, Horn directed his staff officers to move it off the line: it was too weak, too unreliable, and too ill-equipped to be an effective fighting force. Rear-area security or garrison duty: that was its only role, now.

The unit's senior officer, a well-respected fifteen-year veteran by the name of Grieg, was all that was keeping them together. But on the journey to replace the garrison at Biberach, he showed signs of coming down with some kind of fever. By the time they reached Biberach, he was barely able to sit his horse long enough to formally relieve the garrison's commander. Already weak, he was one of the first victims of the plague that had been festering unknown in the unit, and which broke out even as the *burgermeisters* were trying to decide where to house their new garrison. Indeed, it was in dealing with them directly that Johann's father had evidently contracted the disease himself.

In the wake of the death and misery of the plague, the only officer left was the young, charismatic, ambitious, and utterly ruthless Georg Prum. The unit's senior remaining NCO tried to restrain his new commander, but he too was weak with fever. Although not afflicted by the plague itself, the fellow nonetheless died, possibly aided by some poison from Prum, it was hinted.

And so, without a moral compass, resentful of the town that had left them to die in a plague-house, and with no prospects of coming out of long years of warfare with any better prize than their own vermin-ridden hides, Prum's soldiers willingly became blackmailers. And once little Gisela was in hand, it was easy to leverage each town leader to compromise the next. And so they had become wealthy at last.

Schoenfeld had, in his few short hours among them, heard enough of the story to be able to make a full report back in Biberach, but when offered the opportunity to travel there along with the courier, he shook his head. "No," he said, "I don't think I'll be going back there—not if the offer to travel with you to Grantville still stands, Major Quinn."

Larry looked a bit sheepish. "I'm surprised you'd travel anywhere with me at all, Herr Schoenfeld."

"Johann, please. I cannot say I like the gambit you used here, but I see the wisdom of it—and I did not miss the worry in your eyes when I set out on my own." Schoenfeld pointedly did not look at North during this exchange. "So, I take it I am welcome to accompany you, then?"

Larry smiled. "You most certainly are. We'll start on our way at once."

Thomas frowned. "What? No victory parade through Biberach? No basking in the ardent hero worship of a grateful town?"

Quinn's smile broadened. "I'll let you be the recipient of that well-deserved adulation, Thomas. I've got to get back to Grantville. And you've got an aerodrome to set up."

"Well, yes, so I do. And the last thing I need under foot is a meddling Yank who shows up to change my mission, steal my men, and then ruin my battle plans. You made all of this most difficult, you know. Things will be much simpler now."

"I'm sure," said Quinn with a farewell wave, "that from here on, accomplishing the rest of your mission will seem like child's play."

Thomas scowled. "And I won't miss your so-called jokes either, Larry. Get on with you and your foolishness, now: I have an aerodrome to set up."

Add, Subtract, Multiply, Divide

Bjorn Hasseler

Kat Meisnerin
September 1635

"Just remember how you break down a verb," Friedrich concluded. "If you know the base and its meaning, the personal endings, and the rules for each tense, you can build verbs as you go instead of memorizing long lists of forms."

Katharina Meisnerin took another bite of sauerkraut to hide her grin. She remembered telling Friedrich the same thing during their first year of Greek.

"*Danke*." The sophomore went back to his own cafeteria table.

Friedrich looked over at her with a grin. "See, I listen." But then it vanished, and he stated, "Memorizing conjugation charts is confusing the Greek II class."

Katharina frowned. "*Herr* Ashmead does not teach Greek the same way that Dr. Green does. He would prefer to have us all memorizing the charts."

"I wish Dr. Green were still teaching us. It will be good to know Attic Greek, too, but it is just not the same this year."

"I know. But Dr. Green needed to stop teaching in order to try to make the deacons happy, and *Herr* Ashmead showed up at just the right moment."

"So you think it was the right thing to do?"

No, Katharina thought. "I do not think he had much of a choice. Not really." *But I wish he were still our teacher. I do not always agree with his views, but I did always like his class.*

"If you will excuse me, I need to talk to a couple people before class."

"Me, too." Katharina finished eating, returned her tray, and headed for the table where the theology debate appeared to be winding down.

"Hi, Katharina," Joseph Engelsberg greeted her. "I noticed you found a table on the far side of the cafeteria."

Katharina smiled. "How was the predestination discussion?"

"*Venimus, vidimus, versavimus.* We came, we saw, we debated." They had Latin next. "You know. Predestination, election . . ."

"I foreknew what would be said. But I left so I could not have caused it," Katharina quipped.

The bell sounded.

"May I walk you to class?" Joseph asked.

Katharina froze for just a second. This was new. "*J—Ja,*" she stammered.

"Something else came up I thought you should hear about," Joseph continued. "I heard a street preacher a couple days ago. Non-Trinitarian, works salvation. Others have heard people like him around Grantville, too."

Katharina frowned. "Preaching on the street is bold. They will be safe in Grantville, but I do not want them to lead people astray."

"Me, either. That is why I objected to what he was saying. The next thing I knew, a couple of toughs were trying to shove me around."

"Joseph! Are you okay? We need to call..."

Joseph held up a hand in a stop gesture. "I was showing a few men from Comenius' *Unitas Fratrum* around Grantville—real busters on their way back from a special mission in Saxony. They pushed back." He paused. "Have you ever had a bad feeling about something but could not explain why?"

"*Ja.*"

"I have that same bad feeling about this street preacher," Joseph said. "So that is why I chose to preach on the deity of Christ when the elders approached me."

"Joseph!" Katharina exclaimed. "They asked you to preach a sermon? *Wunderbar!* So things are going well in Rudolstadt?"

Joseph smiled briefly. "They are. The rednecks do not really even need to guard us anymore, but some of them still come." He paused. "Would you be willing to look over my notes? And perhaps suggest passages that I missed?"

"Of course." Katharina was thrilled he had asked. "I am glad they asked Young Joe to preach."

"I am not sure I am ready to be Young Joe," Joseph told her. "When your friends call you Kat, and you are not sure that is who you are? It is like that. I respect Old Joe a great deal, but sometimes I just disagree."

Katharina nodded slowly. He had put his finger on something that had been bothering her, too. "I feel like that about Dr. Green. Sometimes, from everything I can find, he is just...wrong."

Joseph nodded. "How is the church?"

Katharina shook her head. "It is not good. I am afraid the deacons are going to ask Dr. Green to step down. Everyone seems to think there will be another vote soon. I do not want to lose Dr. Green, even though I do not agree with him all the time. I have learned so much from him that I otherwise would not have. Grown. Changed. Maybe it is time for me to realize that I am Kat."

They arrived at the Latin classroom.

"How soon do you need those verses?"

Carole Ann Hardy
Wednesday, October 17, 1635

"It's not good. The church is in a real mess. Everything changed after the Ring of Fire but we still had our church. Brother Green is changing it into something we can't even recognize anymore. It's all I can do to try to hold the youth group together."

The person on the other end of the phone call spoke for a while.

"I know, Mildred. Believe me, I know. Al Green was new to Grantville before the Ring of Fire. It's not surprising that he's siding with the Germans to change the way we've always done things."

She listened some more. Finally she cut in with, "Listen, Mildred, I really need to get going. The youth group is meeting tonight.... Yes, at the church ... I'll talk to you tomorrow.... Good-bye."

Carole hung up the phone and took inventory of everything she had piled on the kitchen counter: supplies for tonight's activity, devotions book, her list of people she needed to talk to about one thing or another, snacks. She threw it all in a tote bag.

"Anna Maria!"

The twelve-year-old was doing homework in the dining room.

"I'm going to pick up Johann Diedrich and Nona and take them to youth group. Dinner is already cooking. Make sure Helena and Hans Philipp eat their vegetables."

"I will."

Anna Maria is a good kid, Carole reflected as she started the car and drove off to the high school. Johann had JROTC, and Nona had some religious activity—the BSG or whatever it was.

Carole Ann sighed. Nona was her sister Mary Jean's daughter. Roger Dobbs had gotten deployed to Augsburg, and Mary Jean had transferred from the state library to advising the Swabian administration on which books to acquire. It let her be close to Roger, and Carole Ann didn't begrudge her sister that. But Roger and Mary Jean had left their kids in Grantville. Back in '31, the four Marbacher children had shown up in Grantville. Carole Ann and Donald Hardy had adopted Johann Diedrich and Anna Maria, while Mary Jean and Roger adopted Helena, now seven, and Hans Philipp, now five. It only made sense for all four siblings to stay with the Hardys while Roger and Mary Jean were out of town. Roger and Mary

Jean's natural children, Nona and Blaine, were staying with Carole Ann and Mary Jean's brother John Grover and his wife Leota. But since Carole Ann was the youth group leader, she was still responsible for getting Nona to youth group activities.

She pulled into the high school parking lot. Johann Diedrich was waiting. He was a good kid, too. He was bound and determined to graduate at age eighteen and join the army. *That's too soon. We had Donella and Deirdre start late. It didn't do them any harm to graduate at nineteen. Too bad I couldn't convince Mary Jane to have Nona start a year late, too. It'd settle her down. Nona . . .*

"Johann, have you seen Nona?"

"*Nein.*"

Carole Ann reluctantly shut off the engine and unbuckled her seat belt. "Wait here. I'll go find her."

The first place Carole Ann checked was the classroom where Al Green had taught Greek. That's where the BSG meetings were. *I don't see why Nona can't study the Bible with some other group. Why does it have to be Al Green's group?*

Nona wasn't there. But she recognized a couple of the students.

"Hi, Missus Hardy." They'd quickly learned not to greet her with "*Guten Tag, Frau Groverin.*"

"Have you seen Nona?"

"I think she said she was meeting someone in the music wing," one of the girls offered.

"Thank you."

Carole Ann stalked down the hall toward the music rooms. *Meeting someone! Probably a boy.*

The first two music rooms were empty. Then Carole

Ann heard rock music. She'd banned that from youth group. Nona was probably in there listening to rock and roll with a boy. *I'll give her a piece of my mind!* She brushed past a German loitering in the hall.

The music died away. A man's voice drifted out. "A creedal statement set to music. For all that you insist that yours is not a liturgical tradition . . . Next time you come to a prayer service, please bring this so Brother Aidan may hear it."

Carole burst in. She was right. Nona was just pressing stop. *Caught in the act!* With a boy. Actually he was a well-muscled man, bald except for an odd topknot of hair. He looked dangerous.

"Nona Dobbs, what do you think you are doing?"

Nona looked up, startled. "I'm playing a song for Brother Oran."

"Brother Oran?"

The man held out his hand. "I am Brother Oran of the Celtic mission. Nona was kind enough to share a hymn with me." He looked back to Nona.

"What sort of weird religious group is that?" Carole Ann demanded.

"The Celtic mission. Columba brought Christianity to Scotland in the sixth century . . ."

"You're *Roman Catholic*!" Carole Ann exclaimed.

"No, not Roman . . ."

Carole Ann whirled on Nona. "What are you doing with *Catholics*? And listening to that rock music?" She ejected the tape. "I forbade you from listening to rock and roll and you defied me!" She snapped the cassette in half.

"No!"

Carole Ann was startled. The exclamation had

come from the man who claimed to be a monk, not from Nona.

"That is irreplaceable." Oran sighed. "I would have liked Bishop Aidan to have heard it."

"It is the devil's music!" Something the man had said clicked into place. "What was that about a prayer service?"

"Nona has been kind enough to join us for prayer," the monk said.

"*What?* Nona, how could you?" Carole Ann demanded. "Come with me, at once! We're late for youth group!"

Johannes Huber
Wednesday, October 17, 1635

The up-time woman sniffed as she hurried past him, towing her daughter along. Johannes Huber waited until they were gone and very tentatively entered the music room.

The man with the topknot of hair looked up at him.

"The music?" Johannes asked.

The man held up two halves of a plastic rectangle with nothing but a thin strand of something connecting them.

"It is my fault," the man said. He looked genuinely distressed.

Johannes took a deep breath and confessed, "I was listening. It was a confessional statement. I know the Schleitheim Confession and the new Dordrecht Confession but I have never heard of this one. And then I heard... some of the rest."

"Then you know I am Brother Oran of the Celtic mission."

Johannes nodded. "I have not heard of your church before. I am Johannes Huber, one of the Brethren."

"What Brethren are these?"

The two men spent a few minutes explaining their respective churches to each other.

"I fear I have caused Nona's aunt to be angry with her," Oran said. "And the song has been lost. As you say, it was an up-time creed set to music."

"Many of us Brethren are attending the Baptist church," Johannes said. "I have seen her there."

"Perhaps I could approach the priest..."

"*Nein.* Oh, it is a good idea, but the up-timers are divided. *Frau* Hardy opposes Brother Green. But there is someone else in the congregation that we can talk to—a man who can sometimes fix musical devices."

Oran's eyes widened.

An hour later they were talking to Larry Dotson at the hardware store.

Larry examined the tape carefully, poking a pencil into the spindle on one side and carefully retracting the tape.

"Yes, I can fix this," he told them. "I'll have to charge you for the repairs. It needs up-time glue, and there's not much of that left."

"I will pay what you ask," Brother Oran stated.

Larry got around to reading the label. "Huh. How'd this happen, anyway? Cassettes don't just break like this."

Brother Oran hung his head and explained.

"I don't care for rock and roll. But chanting isn't my thing, either. No offense. It'd be nice if someone would set Gospel lyrics to some of that stuff Heather Mason listens to. But there was no call for this." Larry's voice was soft as he worked on the cassette. "We Christians ought to do better." He sighed. "All right. This glue is going to have to set, and then I'll try to glue the other pieces in. Better give it until tomorrow afternoon."

"We will come back after work tomorrow," Oran agreed. "I fear I have missed the evening service and dinner already."

"Please, join my family and me for dinner," Johannes requested. "I would like to hear more about your church."

"I think those two get it," Larry Dotson murmured as he set the cassette in a safe place and went back to stocking shelves. "I wonder who else gets it."

Nona Dobbs
Thursday, October 18, 1635

The alarm went off. Nona Dobbs hit the snooze button a couple times. After crying herself to sleep last night she had no desire to face the day. But the third time it went off, she reluctantly rolled out of bed, shut it off, and started rummaging through her closet for clothes.

Aunt Carole Ann had absolutely forbidden her from going to the Celtic services. Uncle John hadn't been quite so stern, but he obviously wasn't going to contradict Carole Ann.

Nona sighed and began flipping through the hangers a second time. What was she going to do? First Baptist was becoming a never-ending source of tension.

She wasn't allowed to listen to most of her worship
tapes. It was the Celtic services that were giving her
a chance to relax and enjoy worshipping God. But if
she wasn't allowed to—

Oh! Her hand closed on the tartan skirt. This
wouldn't be backtalk. Not precisely. She started flipping hangers again, looking for a blouse that matched.

Nona paid close attention in class. As long as she
had something to concentrate on, she wasn't thinking
about being in trouble with Aunt Carole Ann.

Alicia Rice caught up to her at lunch. "What's with
the Catholic schoolgirl look, Nona?"

"Well, yes, I suppose so." Then she teared up.

Alicia had pulled the whole story out of her when
Kat, Marta, and Barbara showed up.

"What's wrong, Nona?" Barbara asked.

Nona struggled to compose herself. Alicia gave
them the abbreviated version.

"So because she thinks you were being heretical,
your aunt broke a Trinitarian tape?" Kat asked.

"Next time Mrs. Waters wants an example of irony
in English class, I know what to say," Alicia agreed.

"She saw it only as a rock and roll tape," Nona told
them. "I'm not allowed to go to the Celtic services
any more, either."

"I doubt our parents would let us go to them,
either," Marta said.

"Could you go somewhere else?" Barbara asked.
"What about Alicia's church?"

Alicia laughed. "Nona is trying to concentrate on
worship, not on having everyone talk."

Nona shot her best friend a grateful look.

"What about the other up-time churches? Church of Christ?"

"I've had enough legalistic nonsense," Nona stated.

"Ouch."

"Well, I have. Look, they don't have instrumental music in church because they can't find where it is explicitly commanded in the New Testament. That puts them in the same camp as the Calvinists—everything not specifically allowed is forbidden. If I were going to pick one of the other churches, it would be Lutheran, where anything not specifically forbidden is allowed."

"*Adiaphora*," Kat supplied.

"I like the theory," Nona said. "But the Lutherans don't really follow it. They have their own list of doctrines which must be correctly believed in order to be saved. Kat, you've called Johannes Musaeus out on that often enough."

Kat nodded vigorously. "I will say one thing for Johannes. He has a shorter list than most Lutherans."

Marta Engelsberg spoke up. "One of Dr. Green's up-time church histories says that sometimes this time period was called the Age of Protestant Scholasticism. Lots of emphasis on believing things just exactly correctly."

"Thank you, teacher." Marta was definitely the historian of the group.

"Up-time there was a reaction."

"I should hope so," Alicia muttered.

"Three reactions, really," Marta continued. "Pietism emphasized a personal relationship with Jesus and living a godly life. Rationalism looked for scientific explanations for everything. Mysticism was exactly what it sounds like."

"We want pietism, right?" Alicia asked.

"You Methodists ought to," Marta agreed.

"But pietism with sound doctrine," Kat warned. "Otherwise it will all fall apart in two generations like in the up-time."

"What do you mean 'we Methodists'?" Alicia asked.

"According to the up-time church history book, you are basically English pietists," Marta answered, "with influences from Calvinism, Arminianism, and the Radical Reformation. But also from the Moravians."

"Moravians? Wallenstein's people? I thought he was Catholic."

"Wallenstein converted to Roman Catholicism. His father was Lutheran, and his mother was an Utraquist. That's one kind of Hussite. Comenius's *Unitas Fratrum*. See, it started with Wycliffe in England. He wasn't allowed to preach like he wanted, but Jan Huss heard him and began preaching many of the same things in Bohemia. He was burned at the stake by the Council of Constance. In the up-time, about a hundred years from now, a Saxon count named Zinzendorf invited the Hussites to his estate. They became the Moravian church. One of their missionaries was preaching when John Wesley was saved. That is how Wycliffe's message got back to England."

"Missionaries?" Nona asked.

Marta told them about the Moravian missionaries and the hundred-year prayer watch.

"Orphanages," Alicia mused. "I always thought of being a missionary as going somewhere else."

"Me, too," Nona confessed. "That's why we wanted to go back to America."

"You're both some*when* else," Kat pointed out.

"We sure are," Nona agreed. "Marta, you said this Zinzendorf worked with people from different denominations? Well, I'm grounded. I can't even go to the Celtic service."

"What if we brought them to you?"

"How?"

The girls had fun brainstorming increasingly impractical ways to make that happen.

Finally Barbara asked, "Was this tape like the ones at First Baptist that are used to record the sermon?"

"Yes."

"Could the Celtic monks not record their service?"

"I think we have a tape recorder that still works," Alicia offered.

Friday, October 19, 1635

"Ugh! I am glad that is over!" Barbara declared as they entered the locker room.

"Soccer's not so bad," Alicia stated. "You should try it wearing something other than ankle-length skorts."

It sparked one more round of an oft-repeated discussion between down-time and up-time girls.

After they had showered and dressed, Nona asked mischievously, "What was that about short skirts?" She pirouetted in her skirt.

"Ah, nothing."

"You sound like you're doing better today."

"I am."

"Good, because I've got a surprise for you," Alicia told her. "Come to the music rooms."

"Why?"

"You'll see."

"I don't have long, but I can stay 'til the late bus," Nona told her. "My aunt is making me go to a youth group activity."

"Oh?" Alicia asked as they hurried down the hall.

"Michelle Carson, Melisa Higgenbottom, Aaron Craig, Jack Sims..."

"Ah, another of those up-timer youth group activities," Alicia observed. "Allen Green?"

"Strangely, his name didn't come up. And Jason Cheng had a family thing. Again."

"Again. Nona, you might want to talk to Jason and see if he's having his family plan events on Fridays on purpose. Besides, he's kinda cute."

"Alicia!"

They reached the music rooms. Alicia led Nona into one of the rooms.

"Brother Oran!"

"Miss Nona," he returned as gravely as he always did. "This is Johannes Huber."

"I have seen you at church, Herr Huber." Nona shook hands with him.

"And I, you."

"Herr Huber heard the tape," Oran explained. "He knew of someone who could fix it."

"Really?"

Huber produced the tape. Oran slid it in and pushed play. The four of them listened to the up-time song, Oran and Huber drinking it in.

"Thank you so much," Nona told them.

"I must seek your forgiveness for your aunt's displeasure," Oran said.

"It wasn't your fault," Nona said. "Really, it wasn't."

Brother Oran inclined his head. "It is kind of you to say so. I understand that you are not allowed to come to our services anymore."

Nona nodded. "I'm grounded."

"Miss Alicia brought one of these tape recorders yesterday." Brother Oran produced a second cassette tape. "Bishop Aidan agreed that she could record the prayer service."

Nona squealed in surprise. "Thank you! Thank you!" She hugged each of them. Then she switched the cassettes, and the Celtic service filled the room.

Eventually Alicia hit stop and eject. "Nona, you have a bus to catch."

Al Green
Thursday, November 8, 1635

"Chief Richards can see you now. This way, please."

Al Green followed the receptionist to the chief's office.

"Brother Green." Press Richards came around his desk and shook hands. "Please, have a seat."

"Thanks, Press."

"You asked to see me? Is this in an official capacity?"

"I don't know." Al Green sat down and sighed. "Press, I'm about to lose my job."

"Sorry, Brother Green. Wish there were something I could do about it."

"Pray, of course. But Claudette and I have been doing that, and it's looking like Albert Underwood will get his way sooner or later."

"I thought we voted to keep you on."

"That was in August. After Underwood engineered a deacons' vote of three to one with one abstaining. That part didn't set well with a lot of folks—calling a no-confidence vote on the basis of three out of eight deacons. The others didn't miss another deacon's meeting, not until October when Hale Myers couldn't get leave to come down from Magdeburg for a couple days. That vote was three to three with one abstaining. It's likely that, sooner or later, Underwood will find a way to make it four to three. And y'know, it might be that the good Lord has other plans for me. You know Joe Jenkins left us his farm, on the condition we turn it into a Bible institute."

"I heard. Do you know where Old Joe went?"

"He left town. Headed north on a steam wagon he cobbled together."

"He hasn't been in touch with you, then?"

"Nope."

"Well, Brother Green, I hear from Dan Frost that there've been Old Joe sightings across the USE. Generally trending north to Magdeburg, and then maybe toward one of the ports."

Al Green chuckled.

"So you're going to start this Bible institute. Do you plan on having a church up there?"

"I reckon we probably will, for the students and their families. Some of the Anabaptists still attending First Baptist will probably come. They won't be very welcome after Underwood gets rid of me."

"So the church is going to split."

"I'm not asking it to," Green stated. "I just think that if you tell down-time Germans they can't drink

138

Bjorn Hasseler

beer and have to worship in English, some of 'em are going find another place to go."

"And the up-timers?"

"Some of the nondenominational evangelicals who started coming after the Ring of Fire have already left. The Chengs started their own house church. They're worshipping in a mixture of Chinese, German, and English."

Press chuckled. "I bet that frosts Albert Underwood but good."

"I expect so. Claudette was talking to Kathy Sue Burroughs the other day. Her husband Reed has been preaching every Sunday. Some men from his unit, a few from other units, sometimes a handful of people from the town they're in at the time. They're in Bohemia now, and he's made contact with the Hussites. Kathy Sue's parents are up in Erfurt. Garland and Mary Sue Alcom are holding services for whomever shows up. So you might say this whole situation is multiplying churches."

Press Richards leaned back in his office chair. "So you are multiplying churches rather than dividing the congregation. But really *you* are going to add one church and subtract some members from the other."

Al Green winced. "I wish you wouldn't put it that way, Press. It's accurate enough. I just don't like the terminology. You see, add, subtract, multiply, divide is one of the ways of diagnosing a cult."

Chief Richards' expression darkened. "Funny you should mention that. Please, explain."

"Add to the word of God, subtract from the person of Christ, multiply what you have to do to be saved, divide loyalty.

"It's easy enough to tell when someone's adding to the Bible, but sometimes it's subtler, acting like the leader's books or sermons are almost Scripture. Subtracting from the person of Christ—well, He's fully God and fully man. When you leave out one or the other, you got a problem 'cause if He's not both, He can't save. As far as multiplying requirements for salvation, some groups come right out and say, 'You have to do this, this, and this.' Others at least give lip service to saved by grace through faith. But then they turn right around and say 'if you aren't doing this, this, and this, then you aren't in the will of God.' I don't mean living in sin. I'm talking about the leader's pet hobbyhorses. And dividing loyalties is dividing a person's loyalty between God and the group's leader—usually to the exclusion of their family and friends, too."

Press jotted that down on a pad and stared at it. "That's pretty catchy," he allowed. "Does it always work?"

Green ran through a few examples he knew Chief Richards would remember from up-time.

"All right, so it's a good diagnostic tool for preachers."

"Well, it's also what I came in here about, Press."

"Oh?"

"There are new groups coming into Grantville all the time now. Some of them could be trouble."

"Yeah, I know." Richards' voice was harsh. "We lost Fred Jordan trying to protect a group that probably trips at least some of what you just said. But they're harmless and being persecuted by the big churches—who've been on their best behavior since Krystalnacht, of course."

Al Green nodded. "I'm with you on that. A lot of Protestants who ought to know better slip into the more subtle form of multiplying requirements for salvation. For that matter, doesn't Underwood's position boil down to 'if you're in the will of God you'll follow these rules'?"

Chief Richards sighed. "Al, I know you must be sore about this, but not everybody's a potential cultist. I can't arrest anybody for fitting your four math points here."

"'Course not. Trying to compel people to believe the right thing is wrong—and ineffective. No, I'm hearing things about a new group. They sound like Socinians, but—"

"Bro—"

Green held up a hand. "Hear me out, Press. I'm not suggesting you investigate Socinians. If you were going to do that, you'd pretty much have to open a file on Mary Simpson."

Chief Richards winced.

"Yeah, Unitarianism is a development of Socinianism which in turn diverged from the Anabaptist movement. But this group . . . Kat Meisnerin put me on to them. She said Young Joe—Joe Engelsberg, that is—ran into a street preacher. That was in September. I've been keeping my ear to the ground, and here's what I know. I've heard of three different street preachers in Grantville and others elsewhere. I actually listened to one of them for a while. They use some Anabaptist language but they're not really part of it. They're sent out by a Brother Caspar. They describe him as a skilled speaker and a strong leader. I'd use the word charismatic except that that would confuse people, make them think he's part of Chalker and Fischer's bunch. He's not. Brother Chalker I disagree with, but he's a good man trying to point people to God. See, this Brother Caspar is having his preachers tell people God's made a new revelation to him, about how the Ring of Fire figures into the end times. His preachers are pointing people to him, telling them to follow Caspar no matter what."

Press Richards nodded. "Yeah, I know who you mean. There's been some pushing and shoving. Just another group of crazies, though, right? I mean, it's not like we've got a shortage. Uh, you didn't hear me say that."

Al Green leaned forward. "I think this group bears watching, Press. See, they quote this Brother Caspar's revelations on par with Scripture. That's the adding. They don't think Jesus was God. That's the subtracting. They had a whole laundry list of what you had to do to survive the end times. That's the multiplying. And following Brother Caspar is the dividing of loyalties."

"So you think they're a cult?"

"Oh, I *know* they're a cult. Unlike the Stiefelites or the Socinians, I think these guys have the potential to be dangerous." He let that sink in a minute. "Like I said, Press, I think I'm about to lose my job. If so, I'll be up on the mountain getting the Bible institute going. I won't hear as much of what's going on in town. So I'm saying something to you now. This could be more important than what's going on at First Baptist."

"Appreciate it, Brother Green," Richards said. "I'll pass that along to my officers. We're not going to violate anyone's rights, but after the Dreeson Incident, I don't want to get caught by surprise, either. And I'll pass it along to Dan Frost next time we talk."

"Thank you." Green leaned back.

"How long do you figure?" Press asked.

"'Til they vote me out?" Green asked. "Until Underwood finds an issue that changes one more deacon's mind, I suppose. Unless the good Lord has plans to the contrary."

Anna Mae Foster
Monday, November 19, 1635

"Well if you ask me, Brother Al Green is the number one religious problem in this town! Why let me tell you . . ." Anna Mae Foster proceeded to recite her pastor's failings into the phone at great length.

Finally the person on the other end of the line interrupted.

"That's right, Lois. Roger Dobbs ran off somewhere. Mary Jean went after him, and left their kids here in Grantville. Her daughter's been getting into all sorts of trouble. Carole Ann caught her sneaking out with Catholics, if you can believe that."

She paused while Lois replied.

"Yep, just like your Emily . . ."

Anna Mae actually edged the phone away from her ear a bit. Willard and Lois Carson hadn't spoken to their daughter Emily since she married Joe Ugolini.

"No, I have no idea if she actually intends to marry him," she finally got in.

A few minutes later, she added, "No, they were listening to rock and roll. . . ."

There was another pause.

"Yes, Lois, all of us up here at the Manning Center agree with you about that. I know everybody at Bowers does, too."

Lois spoke again at some length.

"Huh. Well, if you think we can do it. I sure want to add no rock and roll music to our list of expectations, but do you think we convince five deacons?"

This pause was shorter.

"Albert Underwood and Willard, of course. And Chauncey Monroe and Bert Dotson... Hmfph. Well, Lois, you simply must talk to Okey.... Yes, I know he's married to your niece.... No, I don't think any of the other three will change their minds although one would expect that Lincoln Reynolds would see things the same way as Bert. Desiree Reynolds was a Dotson, you know.... No, come to think of it I don't know what Larry Ray Reynolds thinks of the whole thing. Keeps to himself, don't he?"

Lois spoke for a while.

"Lois, you simply must talk to Okey. If we can't get rid of Al Green soon, the Germans are going to take the church right over!" She paused briefly. "You do that!"

Okey Rush
Sunday, November 25, 1635

Okey and Vanna were driving back to Jena after a typical Sunday of church, lunch, and seeing family. It was a bit earlier than normal, but since Thursday had been Thanksgiving, they'd seen quite a bit of family. Okey was ready for some peace and quiet, and he had this week's lesson plans to fine-tune. He still wasn't sure that having a master's degree in Public Administration qualified him to teach that subject at the University of Jena. On the other hand, he did enjoy the interchange with the down-timer students. They'd grown up with different approaches to public administration than he was used to. He tried not to fix the parts that weren't broken.

Vanna was a licensed practical nurse at the CoC clinic. She could really use a restful evening before starting another week of shifts. But evidently his wife wanted to talk.

"Okey."

"Yeah?"

"I don't like how things have gotten at church."

"I don't think anybody likes it, dear."

"Well it has to end. It's tearing the church apart."

"I reckon it could. Albert Underwood doesn't need to bring it up every deacon's meeting, though."

"If he doesn't keep him honest, Al Green will get everything his way. German services on Sunday morning, people drinking alcohol..."

"Brother said he was okay with keeping the German service in the afternoon."

"Well that's not what Aunt Lois told me."

Okey glanced in the rear-view mirror while he framed his next question. Their daughter Lissa was engrossed in a book. "Did Lois ask Brother Green about it? Because the deacons did at the October meeting, and he said the services were fine the way they are now."

"That's not what Aunt Lois said."

"Vanna," he stated in exasperation, "I was *there*."

"Okey, you know how the church has always been. Families have attended for generations. It's where everyone goes when something happens. It's one of our last pieces of up-time."

Okey thought about how everyone had gathered at First Baptist after the mine accident earlier that year. Vanna was right about that.

"If Green gets his way..."

"Al and Claudette Green were right in the thick of it, helping out after the mine disaster," he interrupted.

"But if he turns First Baptist into a church for down-timers, where are the miners going to go?"

"The UMWA gets along real well with down-timers. I don't see why that wouldn't work out at church."

"That's not what I mean. We could lose everything that makes First Baptist special."

Okey sighed. After a couple minutes, he tried again. "Vanna, Green isn't trying to implement anything different. It's Underwood who's trying to add things. There are down-timers coming to all the churches. We're not even going looking for them, really. Seems to me we ought to be hospitable."

"I don't mind taking them in. I mind them trying to change the place."

Okey figured that was probably a good place to let the conversation peter out.

Sunday, December 2, 1635

Okey suddenly had a lot of time to think. A few days ago Leahy Memorial Hospital had started treating measles cases, and as of this past Thursday, November 29, the Sanitary Commission had restricted travel. Jena now had cases, too. Since he taught public administration at the university, he'd gotten called in to advise the city council yesterday. But today he couldn't go to church and didn't have to be anywhere else, so he was staying home. Well, if you called their rented house in Jena home, that is. Vanna was on duty at the clinic, of course. He was worried about her.

. Okey prayed for the folks who had measles. Most of them were kids, and Vanna said some of them were in bad shape. Then he prayed for Vanna and the other doctors and nurses. And for the captain-general and everybody else who'd been wounded in the war. Then he decided he ought to read something in the Bible. Okey flipped some pages. He liked Acts. So did Brother Green—he preached from it a fair bit. Under the circumstances, Okey figured a rerun was permissible.

> "And on that day a great persecution began against the church in Jerusalem, and they were all scattered throughout the regions of Judea and Samaria, except the apostles." (Acts 8:1, King James Version)

He read about Philip, Saul, and Peter—all doing big, important things.

> "And some of them were men of Cyprus and Cyrene, which, when they were come to Antioch, spake unto the Grecians, preaching the Lord Jesus." (Acts 11:20, King James Version)

These were just regular guys, and they'd started the church in Antioch, the one that sent Paul and Barnabas on their missionary journeys. Now that was interesting. He had written something in the margin here. *Green: God had told them to go into all the world—Matt 28:18. They couldn't do what God wanted while they were all in Jerusalem. Antioch—fresh start, but still took care of the believers in Jerusalem.*

Huh. Grantville wasn't Jerusalem, and he and the other deacons certainly weren't apostles, but maybe there was something here that could help First Baptist right now. Okey didn't see anything in the notes he'd written in the margins. Oh, here was the date—Brother Green had preached this back before the Ring of Fire. Interesting.

So almost everybody had to get scattered before they could accomplish their mission. First Baptist had had some scattering, too—the Chengs had their own house church, the Burroughs/Alcom family was trying to do the same, and several people were either deployed out of town or had taken jobs away from Grantville. He remembered a newspaper article that called it "the American Diaspora." He thought that word was from the Bible but he wasn't sure where to look for it.

Hm, then should we send out more people? Or could we try following directions by reaching people right in Grantville? Okey thought about that for a long while. *Lord, which one is it? I don't know, and I think I might need to.*

He kept thinking about it, on and off, over the next two weeks. Vanna kept him updated on what her aunt, Lois Carson, thought, too.

Sunday, December 16, 1635

First Baptist had a weird feel today. Attendance was low for December. There were a fair number of adults, but hardly any kids around. Because of the measles outbreak, the Sanitary Commission had closed the schools until after New Year's and advised children to stay home. They'd made arrangements with Voice of America to broadcast church services on Sunday mornings, and even read a statement from Larry Mazarre over the air, making it okay for Catholics.

After the singing and the prayers, Brother Green went up to the podium to give the sermon.

"I know that between the measles outbreak and the political situation, we're all under a lot of stress. Let's take a few minutes and remember that it's almost Christmas. Think back to that first Christmas. Caesar decided to have a census. They all had to go back to their families' hometowns. Many Jews were living outside of Israel. The Diaspora, they called it."

Okey sat up very straight.

"Many years later, Peter wrote his first letter to them. They were having a hard time of it, and after the last few years, I guess maybe we can feel a little of what it was like for them. . . ."

Yeah, I guess we can, Okey agreed. He came back to what had been on his mind for the last couple weeks. *So are we dispersed to down-time and supposed to reach out to people? Or are we dispersing out of* Grantville *and supposed to get to it now?* He got a little distracted from the sermon and flipped back to Acts. *First everybody else got dispersed while the leaders stayed. But then the leaders were going out and doing stuff. And Antioch developed its own leaders and sent out Saul . . .*

Okey suddenly realized Vanna was talking to him. He shook his head. The service was over, and people were filing out of the church, shaking Brother Green's hand at the door.

"Are you going to sit there all day, Okey?"

"Oh, no. Just thinking."

When they got to the door, Vanna said, "You seemed to have really given Okey something to think about this morning." She shook hands and moved into the entryway.

Okey smiled weakly as Al Green scrutinized him.

"Actually, Brother Green, I've been thinking about that series you preached from Acts back in '98."

Al grinned. "I'm flattered, I think. You look like you have a question or three."

"I need to talk to you." Okey spoke quietly but urgently. "But they need Vanna back at the clinic this afternoon. Lots of folks coming in—a few sick and the rest worried they might be."

The grin was replaced by a speculative look. "I need to return some reading material to Johann Gerhard. Perhaps we could meet at the university, and I could answer your questions then."

"Thank you, Brother Green." They shook hands.

"What was that all about?" Vanna asked in the entryway.

"There you are!" Albert Underwood clapped Okey on the shoulder. "Deacons meeting, tomorrow night. Carsons' place at seven." He said it so that those around could hear it.

Okey nodded. "I'll see you there, Brother Albert. Is there anything I can bring?"

"Just bring yourself, young man. We've got a lot to discuss."

❖   ❖   ❖

Vanna went in to work right after lunch. Lissa, Cordula, and Agatha were giggling upstairs.

"Girls, I'm meeting someone at the university!" he called up the stairs. "I'll be back before dinner."

"Brother Okey."

"Hello, Brother Green."

"I take it you have a very serious question?"

"Well, Brother Green, it's like this..."

Al Green listened as he explained it. By the end he was wearing a bemused expression.

"So let me see if I have this straight. You think the church ought to let me go, because you think I—and some others—will follow the Great Commission. But if the church keeps me on, none of us will, at least not deliberately."

Okey flushed. "Well, yeah, that is pretty much how it seems to me. Brother Green, I'd rather you stayed..."

"...but it might not be the right thing to do," Green finished for him.

Okey nodded unhappily.

Al Green leaned back. "I think I want to stay," he said at length. "But back in August, I *knew* I wanted to stay. And, well, obviously I've taken steps to make sure I have something of an alternative." He thought a minute. "There's a deacon's meeting tomorrow night."

"Underwood should have waited until after Christmas and New Year's," Okey stated.

"You'll have to do what you think is right."

"That's not a lot of help, Brother Green."

"Claudette and I figure I'll lose at some point. Y'know, I could have resigned any day of the last five months. But I think that would be seen as an acknowledgment that Underwood's way is the right way." He trailed off into thought again. "Tell you what. Let Claudette and me pray about it tonight. Can I call the university in the morning?"

"They'll send a kid over with a message. I can come over here and call you back. I'm sorry to put you in this fix, Brother Green."

"Done in by my own sermons from '98." Green laughed.

Harley Thomas, Jr.
Monday, December 17, 1635

The Marshals' Service had moved to the new capital of Bamberg with the Supreme Court, but still had an office in Grantville. More often than not, Harley Thomas was the marshal using that office. Leta Huffman tended to hand out assignments by area. Her husband Max was the senior marshal covering Bamberg, Würzburg, Ansbach, and Rothenburg. Archie Mitchell and his team handled northern Franconia, Suhl, and the other cities in the Thuringerwald. Harley and his guys had West Virginia County, the cities in the Thuringian Backbone, and, increasingly, Saxe-Altenburg and Reuss counties. People displaced by the situation around Dresden were doing desperate and sometimes stupid things, and Saxe-Altenburg and Reuss were catching the spillover.

Harley and Vina Thomas had done the same thing as the Marshals' Service. They'd moved to Bamberg and rented out their house in Grantville to a couple of real nice families—a brother and sister who were each married with kids. They couldn't quite afford the place, but Harley and Vina had given them a break on the rent in return for retaining one of the smaller bedrooms for themselves, whenever they were in town. Harley got to stay in his own house every couple weeks or so.

For the last couple weeks, he'd been enforcing what amounted to a youth curfew, put in place to limit the measles outbreak. Nobody liked it, but after the plague outbreak along the Rhine last summer, most people's attitude was better safe than sorry. And if he spent time arguing with too-smart teenagers, it was a nice break from extraditing criminals.

The office phone rang at 8:30 AM.

"SoTF Marshals' Service, Harley Thomas speaking."

"Harley, glad I caught you in the office."

"Brother Green?"

"Have you got time for a cup of coffee at The Flying Pig?"

"Yeah, sure. Why there?"

"Because the name's amusing right now, and we don't really need to be noticed or overheard."

"Oh. Now I'm curious. I'll meet you there."

That evening

The monthly deacons meeting dragged on. Harley couldn't remember how it had ended up on the third Monday of the month. He'd heard the story from his father once.

Giving was down the past couple weeks. No surprise there; so was attendance. As soon as the Sanitary Commission gave the all-clear, both would recover. But

Albert Underwood and Willard Carson needed to talk it to death anyway. Then there was some discussion about who was cleaning what and how well.

Then Underwood put the big one on the table. "I would like to propose a vote of no confidence in the pastor."

"Second," Willard Carson said.

"Discussion?"

By now, Harley had spent a lot of time as a marshal watching how people reacted when they were on the spot. Underwood sounded confident. Hale Myers wasn't here—with the current political situation, the USE Army was being stingy about granting leaves. That should mean another three-to-three vote with Bert Dotson abstaining. But it was possible enough pressure had been brought to bear on Bert. He worked at the steam sawmill, and some of the up-timers there had an attitude toward down-timers.

"I think it's past time for the pastor to go," said Chauncey Monroe. He was Underwood's reliable third vote. He was about as open-minded as Willard, but while Willard's favorite conspiracy theory was Communists, Chauncey seemed to think that down-timers were just waiting to turn into Nazis. Harley still almost chuckled when he remember how old Fred Miller had reduced Chauncey to sputtering outrage by asking what he thought about Krystalnacht.

"... and so if he won't keep these influences out of the church, he ought to go," Chauncey concluded.

"Anyone else?" Underwood asked.

Lincoln Reynolds stirred. "I think maybe we're debating the wrong question." He sounded for all the world like he'd just stumbled onto something.

"Suppose you explain that." Underwood made it more of an order than a request.

"Every point you raise about Brother Green really has to do with the down-timers and how you don't want *them* taking over the church. The question is really, what does a down-timer have to do to be a Baptist?" Lincoln opened his Bible. "'For it seemed good to the Holy Ghost, and to us, to lay upon you no greater burden than these necessary things; That ye abstain from meats offered to idols, and from blood, and from things strangled, and from fornication: from which if ye keep yourselves, ye shall do well. Fare ye well.' That's Acts 15:28-29. King James, of course. But that's what the Jerusalem Council decided about what Gentiles had to do to become Christians. Now the down-timer Anabaptists are already Christians. So I can't see putting any more restrictions on them than this."

Albert Underwood flushed. "'Bring forth therefore fruits meet for repentance,'" he retorted. "Matthew 3:8."

"So are you saying the Council of Jerusalem was wrong?" Lincoln asked.

Harley tuned out the resultant explosion. He'd forgotten that Lincoln could adopt that innocent tone to go with his poker face. He wasn't noticeably cowed by Underwood's tantrum, either.

"Brother Albert's right," Chauncey Monroe said into the silence once the man ran out of words. "We can't have just anybody joining the church without understanding what we're like. I call for the vote."

Willard Carson seconded that.

"A motion of no confidence in the pastor is on the floor. A yes vote is a vote of no confidence. A no vote means you have confidence in the pastor," Underwood stated. "I vote yes."

"Yes," Willard said.

"No," Lincoln countered.

"Yes," Chauncey Monroe stated.

After Harley said, "No," there was a pause.

"Well?" Underwood prompted.

Bert Dotson fiddled with his watch. "Yes."

Underwood grinned. That was four.

"Yes," Okey Rush stated.

"The motion is passed, five to two. The deacon board will request the pastor's resignation. If it is not provided, a congregational meeting will be called as soon as possible."

Harley nodded to himself. Congregational meetings had to be announced for two consecutive Sundays before they could be held.

The meeting ended a few minutes later. Underwood and Carson went to request Al Green's resignation. Bert Dotson left right away. Chauncey Monroe took a couple minutes, looking very smug.

Harley kicked back in his chair. "Okey, you should know that Brother Green met with me this morning, so I knew what was up."

"Me, too," Lincoln admitted. He grinned. "It's a good thing Hale Myers couldn't make it. He's not very good at keeping a straight face."

"I'm sorry, guys," Okey said. "I didn't want to vote Brother Green out. But I think it's the right thing to do for the Baptist church. Just maybe not for us at First Baptist."

"Brother Green explained what you were thinking," Harley said. "I don't know whether I agree with you—but I'll grant that you've been doing some serious thinking about it. More'n I have."

"But now things are going to be a mess."

Harley looked at Reynolds. "Lincoln, we both knew this was coming."

"Yeah, we did," Lincoln agreed. "Didn't want to admit it."

"Okey, it was just a matter of time before Underwood caught both Hale and I out of town at the same time. Brother Green was going to lose three to two at some point. And they seem to have leaned on Bert Dotson. So don't go blaming yourself."

"Everyone will hear, probably by the end of tomorrow."

"What about the down-timers?" Lincoln sounded urgent.

"Brother Green called on some of them this afternoon," Harley told him. "He wanted them to hear it from him, especially the ones in the *Bibelgesellschaft*."

Sunday, December 23, 1635

Albert Underwood got up on Sunday morning and announced that the deacons had voted to request the pastor's resignation, but he had refused. So he was announcing a congregational meeting to take place on January 6, 1636. Meanwhile the pastor was suspended from preaching.

"Tomorrow is Christmas Eve, and Tuesday is Christmas." Dr. Sims' voice carried very well. "Who is going to preach those services?"

Attendance remained down over the holidays.

Sunday, January 6, 1636

But on the date of the congregational meeting, the church was packed. Underwood preached from the book of James. After the service was over, Al and Claudette Green went downstairs to the fellowship hall along with those who weren't members—including the Anabaptists arriving early for the afternoon service.

Harley saw an usher trying to shoo Nona Dobbs out of the sanctuary.

"I'm not going to vote," she said. "I'm not even going to talk. I wrote Mom and Dad that I'd tell them what happened."

"Let her stay," Harley told the usher. "I told my mother the exact same thing."

Nona gave him a grateful smile.

It was a long and heated meeting. A number of people spoke from both sides. The vote was called, and paper ballots were distributed, marked, collected, and counted.

"Brother Carson, Brother Thomas, would you please go get Brother Green and his wife?"

Willard and Harley came back with Al and Claudette and their kids along with a couple down-timers.

"I brought a couple Anabaptists who can report back to the others," Harley stated. "There are more people downstairs than up here. Thought at least a couple of 'em should be present."

Underwood obviously didn't like it, but nodded curtly.

After everyone was seated, he said, "We have the results of the vote. The congregation of First Baptist Church has voted to dismiss Brother Green as pastor by a vote of sixty-two to forty-nine."

Harley was watching the Greens. Al shrugged, stood up, and helped Claudette with her coat. They filed out of the pew—and were quickly mobbed by slightly less than half of the voting congregation. Harley caught Press Richards' eye, and the two lawmen subtly but efficiently opened a path through the crowd.

"What are you going to do now, Brother Green?"

"Well, you know Joe Jenkins turned his farm over to me to get a Bible school up and running. So I'll be setting up Mountain Top Baptist Bible Institute."

A different voice asked, "So who's going to preach Sundays?"

"That's up to y'all."

Underwood spoke into the microphone. "The deacons will take turns. We'll preach every eight weeks."

Harley Thomas worked his way back to the front of the sanctuary. Quietly he said, "Seven, Albert. I'm an officer of the court. It's important that everyone see that we treat everyone equally. So I'm not going to stay."

Underwood bristled. "We're not treating anyone differently."

"I know you believe that, Albert. But it looks different from Bamberg."

"Brother Thomas!"

"You got what you wanted, Albert." Harley turned around and followed the Greens out the door.

Press Richards waved him over. "I thought we lost you in the crowd."

"Nah, when Underwood said the eight deacons would rotate the preaching, I had to inform him his numbers were off."

Al Green blinked and said, "I'm not asking anybody to leave."

"Like I told him, it's a perception thing. See, people here in Grantville know Press is a good cop. But lots of people in Bamberg and Reuss and Altenburg don't know me, and I can't afford to show up as 'that guy who attends the church where everyone has to be like the up-timers.'"

"Nona Dobbs! You get back here!"

Nona darted through the crowd and hurried over to the Greens. "Dr. Green, when is church next Sunday? For that matter, *where* is church next Sunday?"

"I, uh, I, uh, wasn't planning to preach."

Carole Ann Hardy stalked up. "Nona Frances Dobbs, you come over here at once!"

"I think," Harley Thomas told Al Green, "that if Okey's plan is going to work, you should probably start thinking about your first sermon to this diaspora."

Larry Ray Dotson
Sunday, February 3, 1636

Larry Ray Dotson spent as much time as he could with his wife. Betty had been in the Pritchard Extended Care Center since 1632. Type II diabetes was a life-threatening condition here and now.

"I'm sorry I couldn't make it today."

"Shh. There's no use pushing it when you're not feeling up to it."

"How was church?"

"Kinda sparse," Bert admitted. "Okey Rush preached. He said he wasn't sure how many sermons he has in him, but he had at least one."

"What was it on?"

"Missions, but he never actually said it that way. He talked about how since we're here in the seventeenth century, some of us don't actually need to go anywhere. Others have gone all over. It was pretty good, actually. Here's the tape."

"Well, if it was 'pretty good,' I'll have to listen to it. Brother Willard and Brother Chauncey's sermons weren't 'pretty good.'"

Larry shrugged. "They'll get better with practice."

Betty laughed. "They're about to get a lot of it. Bert's next, isn't he?"

"Sure is. Harley Thomas left right away. Lincoln came to church the next week, but the other deacons voted to request his resignation and Hale Myers'. So now the Reynolds and the Myers families have left, including Desiree."

Betty patted his arm. "Your sister will be okay. She's standing up for her husband, and that's just the right thing to do."

"Bert's pretty upset with her."

"Have they talked about it?"

"I don't think so," Larry answered. "I suppose I should make sure that happens, shouldn't I?"

"You said attendance was sparse," Betty prompted.

"Well, there's no more afternoon service. The deacons voted for English services only. There are a few down-timers coming to the morning service now, but most of 'em left—some of 'em to the two Anabaptist congregations who already left, some to the Mennonites who took over for the Nazarenes, but most of 'em with Brother Green. The Stevensons and the Eckerlins left."

"They're in-laws with the Reynoldses."

"I haven't seen the Bledsoes or the Dorrmans or the Simses. I haven't heard what any of them have decided. I feel bad for the kids. Spring Reynolds liked First Baptist, and she's just not able to understand why her family isn't going back. Plus she's living at Bowers and some of the folks up there are being catty about it. And then there's Nona Dobbs, who'd like to leave, but Carole Ann Hardy won't let her."

"She's the one who had the tape," Betty remembered.

"That's got to be tough on her," Larry mused. "I'd hate to have bad feelings in our family. What do you think about inviting all of them over to the house next Sunday for dinner? We could hire a couple ladies to do the cooking. I'll grill."

"In February?"

"I'll put the grill just inside the garage with the door up and set the fans pointing outside."

"Larry, it could be zero degrees next Sunday."

"Won't matter. Bert and Lincoln will both come out and stand around the grill. For long enough, anyway."

"If you say so."

Sunday, February 10, 1636

The mid-winter cookout had cut into their monthly budget but Larry figured he could live on leftovers for a few days. Plus Desiree Reynolds and Winona Dotson both insisted on bringing a side dish. So that helped.

"Gotta hand it to you, Larry," Lincoln said. "I wouldn't have thought a February cook-out could work."

It wasn't zero, but it was definitely cold out. The grill was just inside the garage door. If you stepped past it, you were outside in a biting wind. But inside it was tolerable for long enough to cook burgers and sausages.

"It's a shame there aren't more winter sports yet," Bert said. "I did go see the high school basketball game."

"Oh? How'd that go?" Larry asked.

"Calvert High versus the Jesuit collegium. Calvert High crushed them pretty badly, of course, but they're coming along. I heard they're trying to talk the Tech College into having a team."

Once the weather and sports were exhausted, there were a few minutes of silence as they huddled around the grill.

Now or never, Larry thought. "I've been thinking about the situation at church. I got something to say."

"Figured you might," his brother Bert said.

"I don't doubt you'll both be trying to persuade me to see things your way. But think about this first. I work retail. Sure, it's just stocking shelves, but I've gotten a feel for when the store's doing well and when it ain't. Now I've never seen the church books but I do know that First Baptist's finances vary from 'we're gettin' by but not by much' to 'giving's gettin' behind.'"

"Can't disagree with that," Lincoln stated.

"Most of the down-timers and a lot of professionals have left. Some of 'em went with Brother Green, and others are working out of town. But I think it's safe to say giving is down."

"Oh, it's safe to say that, all right," Bert confirmed.

"It seems to me that if you split a church that's barely getting by, then neither half will be getting by anymore. One half needs to find a building, and good luck doing that in Grantville right now. The other half has a building that's gonna be hard to pay the upkeep on."

"Keep going, Larry. You're making sense," Lincoln encouraged.

"I don't think either group can survive on its own forever. Maybe for a few years. But five, ten years down the road? What are both sides going to do?" He waited a minute then added, "Somebody's gonna have to put it back together or else there aren't gonna be any Baptists left in Grantville."

"I don't know how we'd do that, Larry," Bert said. "Both sides are pretty riled up."

Lincoln shook his head. "Me, either."

"It's okay to disagree," Larry stated. "But we do have a testimony to the rest of Grantville. We ought to at least keep the lines of communications open so that if there's an opportunity to get back together, we still can. Or maybe we never will, but we'll find ways to work together on stuff."

"That's reasonable," Lincoln agreed.

"All right," Bert said.

"So I'm expecting both of you and your families back here for a cookout every couple months. We can make sure we're still willing to talk about it."

"'Preciate it, Larry," Lincoln said. "But how 'bout we rotate whose house it's at? It'd be tough for you and Betty to host every time."

"Thanks."

"You or me next, Bert?"

Bert grinned. "Rock, paper, scissors?"

Joe Engelsberg
Sunday, February 17, 1636

"In Titus 2:13 we have two personal, singular nouns connected by *und* and only the first is preceded by *des*. According to Sharp's Rule, they refer to the same person. Thus, our great God is our Savior. 'Savior' is further clarified as 'Jesus Christ,' so the grammar explicitly identifies Jesus as God. You can check the Greek and the English. They have the same pattern.

"Therefore we say with Paul in 1 Timothy 3:16 that 'God was manifested in the flesh.' Let us pray."

Joe Engelsberg made it a short prayer. His throat was really, really dry. He hoped he hadn't rushed his delivery too much there at the end.

Brother Green dismissed the congregation.

"Come on, Joe. You preached—they're going to want to shake your hand and tell you how you did."

Joe groaned. "I have no idea how I did."

"Oh, I do. You nailed it. A little lecture-y, but not bad considering you crammed what are normally two seminary classes into one sermon."

"*Dank.*"

They reached the door, and Joe blushed his way through a bunch of compliments. As the last people in line reached him, someone pressed a cup of water into his hand.

"You did great," Kat Meisnerin told him. "I liked your sermon."

Joe grinned. "You should. You wrote a lot of it."

"Did not. I did research. You wrote it and delivered it."

"Editor."

"You guys are cute."

Joe looked over, startled. Nona Dobbs was standing there next to Johannes Huber. She had a mischievous grin on her face.

"Now don't start," Kat told her.

"I'll leave that to Alicia," Nona agreed. She held up a tape recorder. "We both taped it."

Joe frowned. "Why both?"

Johannes answered. "Miss Nona lent me her tape recorder to record your sermon for our friend Brother Oran. I don't think he will disagree with any of it."

"And I borrowed Alicia's tape recorder because there are some kids at school who want to hear your sermon, Joe, but their parents wouldn't let them come. I know what that's like," Nona explained.

"After Brother Oran has listened to your sermon, I will try to get Zecharias Spangler to listen to it. He has been listening to some street preachers and is all mixed up."

"Street preachers?" Al Green asked sharply. "The ones who follow a guy named Caspar?"

"*Ja*," Huber confirmed.

"Tell me about him, if you would." Green pulled Huber aside.

"Nona," Joe said, "I did not hear the whole story. How is it that you are allowed to come to church here now?"

She grinned. "I wrote to my parents. They sent three copies of the same letter to Aunt Carole Ann and Uncle Donald, to Uncle John and Aunt Leota, and to Brandon and me. Brandon and I are allowed to pick between First Baptist and ... Mountain Top ... Second Baptist ... whatever this is. I'm still not allowed to go to the Celtic services, but Alicia said she'll go tape one for me every month or so."

"Are you practicing your smuggling for when you become missionaries?" Kat asked.

"Gotta start somewhere, right? And Alicia is going to get an after-school job at one of the day cares. She remembered what Marta said about the orphanages in Halle and Savannah."

"And you?"

"I'll probably go to State Tech and learn a skill that'll be useful to have as a missionary." Nona turned the question around. "What are you guys going to do?"

"According to the elders just now, work on my next sermon." Joe shook his head. "I have no idea how Brother Green did this every week."

"What's it going to be about?"

"The Trinity," Kat said. "This is going to be fun."

Fallen Apple

Robert E. Waters

September 1636
Grantville High School

Arnulf Langenberg waited impatiently outside Rachel Hill's classroom. The science teacher was grading papers, and somewhere in that pile was Arnie's extra credit. He was proud of it and had done a lot of work and research to make it the best one yet. Projects that required study of important up-time persons were his favorite. It was almost like reading fiction, for the history hadn't happened yet in his world, but it *had* happened . . . or, it would happen eventually. Or, maybe not. It was a marvelous conundrum, almost as intriguing as the dog-eared Chandler novel peeking out of his back pocket. Phillip Marlowe was in a real pickle in *The Long Goodbye*, and so too was Arnie, sitting there sweating nervously and waiting for Frau Hill to call him in. *I should just leave*, he thought, clutching the copied project papers in his hand. *I should just—*

"Herr Langenberg." The teacher's voice echoed into the hallway. "Come in. Come in."

He rose slowly, put on his best face, nodded politely. "Frau Hill. Thank you for seeing me."

"Please sit," she said, pointing to a tiny wooden chair in front of her desk. "I'm just grading papers here. Yours is somewhere in the pile." She chuckled. "And I'm sure it's just fine. Your projects usually are."

"Thank you, Frau Hill."

"So, what can I do for you today, young man?"

Her smile was genuine, as it usually was. Arnie squirmed in his seat, trying to find the comfort spot, hoping that her pleasantness would persist once he told her what he needed to say. He sighed deeply, nodded, and held up the papers in his hand so that the teacher could see the black-and-white portrait on the first page.

"Frau Hill, as you know, my project was about this man. One of the greatest scientists OTL, and certainly fascinating to me." Arnulf used the term "OTL" without thinking about the conundrum involved. The initials stood for *Our Time Line*—and referred not to his own, but to that of the American up-timers. But with the passage of time the phrase had simply become part of the lexicon of the seventeenth century.

He laid the papers in his lap. "As you instructed, I researched his life and then did my assignment. But I did not stop there. I ... dug deeper and found out more about him and his family. And, well ... I ..."

He paused, and Frau Hill said, "Yes? What is it, Arnie?"

He sighed again, wishing there was a shot of whiskey in front of him so he could down it like Marlowe, and find his courage at the bottom of the glass. "I think I made a terrible mistake, Frau Hill."

"How so?"

Arnie straightened in his chair. He cleared his throat and said with a half-smile, "I sent a letter to his mother."

September 1636
Market Overton, Rutland

Hannah Ayscough could hear her mother, father, and brother William arguing over a parcel that had arrived earlier that day. Now it was dark, time for bed, and there was a lot of agitated hand waving and muffled frustration as they sat around the kitchen table in the shadow light of the candle, arguing over...what? Hannah peeked through the crack in her bedroom wall, trying to figure it out.

In the middle of the table sat a large envelope that William had torn open. Beside it lay a ruffled stack of papers unlike any that she had ever seen, thick white and perfectly rectangular. Occasionally, her brother would pick them up, wave them in the air, then let them fall back to the table. He seemed genuinely delighted by what the papers contained, unlike her mother and father, whose faces, in the faint candle glow, seemed perplexed, confused, and sometimes horrified. Mother especially, who was close to tears on a few occasions. Father's expression was harder to divine, as his back was turned to Hannah's door, but he would occasionally look over his shoulder, as if to ensure that his daughter was not eavesdropping.

Hannah would pull her eye away from the crack lest he see it, wait for him to turn away, then eavesdrop again. This went on for a long while.

They concluded their discussion. Father rubbed out the candle, and he and her mother bid William goodbye. Her brother left, and Father folded the papers up and placed them back in the envelope. Then he and Mother went to their room, letting the waning embers from the fireplace cast dark shadows across the floor.

Hannah loved her father, but he could be careless. There it lay, the parcel still on the table, beside the cold candle. Hannah waited until the house grew still, then she carefully opened her door a margin and slipped into the firelight.

Quietly, she drew the papers out of the envelope, unfolded them, and tiptoed over to the fireplace. *Father must have forgotten that I can read*, she thought as she bent the papers toward the light to get a better look. Well, she wasn't as good as her brother, true, but she could read most anything given time. She took pride in the fact that she was one of the only girls her age in Market Overton who could read better than most boys. So she read, though the words on the paper had been copied so small that it was difficult for her to parse out their meaning. She'd never seen such small and precise script in all her life. More perfect than any print type that she had ever read before. Where had this come from?

She flipped over the envelope. On the front was scribbled her name and the address of her home. That was all.

"Who sent me a letter?" she wondered, not realizing that she had said the words out loud.

"Grantville," William said. "Well, not the town, but a boy there named Arnulf Langenberg."

Hannah jumped. She had been so focused on the papers that she had failed to notice her brother slipping back into the house. For a moment, she was scared, like a cat caught with a mouse, uncertain what to do next, but William put a finger to his lips to shush her. "Shh. Quiet, now. Let's not wake them up."

"William, I'm sorry," she pleaded. "I didn't mean to—"

He waved her off. "Don't worry about it, little sweet. It is my fault. I should have taken the papers with me."

Like he used to do when they were younger, William sat cross-legged on the floor and motioned for her to sit in his lap. She did so, snuggling into his chest and letting his hand rest on her shoulder. Hannah smiled like old times and laid her head back. William rocked a little.

"Why is someone sending me a letter from Grant-ville?" she asked.

She had heard of the place, this town that had come through time to plant itself right in the middle of Germany. The people—the so-called "up-timers"— who had come through the ring looked just like them, or so she had been told by folk in town who had visited London and had seen them first-hand. William claimed to have seen one, in fact. But he had kept quiet about it for the most part, declining to provide any real details about what they looked like, how they spoke, how they sounded, who they were. What did it matter here anyway, he had argued, outside the craziness of London's dangerous politics? Out here, what mattered was rain water, crops, soil, bread. What mattered here was day-to-day survival.

"Read it," William said. "Take your time."

She did so, squinting at the bigger words, those that she had not seen before, odd ones like *Principia Mathematica* and "calculus" and phrases such as "corpuscular theory of light" and "motion and universal gravitation." Clearly, the papers were describing the life and times of an important person, of his accomplishments and deeds. The man it spoke of was a Christian, it seemed, but he had not always been loyal to the notion of a Holy Trinity.

"Well, what do you think?" William asked.

Hannah flipped over the last piece of paper and let it all fall into her lap. "I don't understand most of it. Who is this person it talks about?"

William stroked her hair and laid a gentle kiss on her forehead. "He is the greatest scientist the world will ever know. And he is your son."

Hannah shook her head. "I don't have a son."

"I know, Hannah. But you will . . . you will."

September 1636
Grantville High School

"What in the world possessed you to write her a letter?"

Arnie wouldn't say that Frau Hill was mad exactly, but she wasn't happy either. "Well, at first, my thoughts were to just say 'Hello,' you know? I thought it might be nice for her to know that she will be the mother of Isaac Newton. I just think it's neat that we know who she is—even before she realizes who she is—and what her future will hold. I thought it might be nice for her to know.

"But then I spoke to a friend in the Committees of Correspondence, and he—"

"You have friends in the CoCs?"

Arnie nodded. "Just one. He wants me to join after graduation. Anyway, he was telling me what was going on in London, how the king was rounding people up whom he had learned would be part of the civil war there. He told me how they were being imprisoned, executed, drawn and quartered. He told me about a Frau named Jenny Geddes and how the CoCs got her out of danger. Then I got to thinking about Galileo and all of his troubles. I got scared, you know, for her life, and for his father's life. I thought, if they can go after someone simply because she would—or just *might*—toss a chair at a minister's head, what would they do to the mother of a man who, by the accounts I've read, was devout, but not always loyal to all the precepts of the church? Would these people be afraid of what Newton would stand for and for the accomplishments in his life? I mean, certainly a man of his power and influence matters more than a person tossing chairs. They might go after his mother just to make sure she never meets her future husband. They might even kill her. So . . . I warned her in the letter."

"What do you mean?"

Arnie sighed. "I told her to be careful. I told her who she is, who her husband will be, and sent her copies of these papers so that she would know who her son would become."

"Jesus!"

It was not uncommon for up-timers to blaspheme,

but they rarely did it in front of children, and in a school, no less. But Arnie could see that Frau Hill had moved from mild agitation to outright anger. If she could get away with it, she'd probably slap him.

She rose and walked to the window. She folded her arms. "When did you send this letter?"

"Three weeks ago," he said. "Through my CoC friend."

Frau Hill shook her head. "Arnie, do you understand what is called 'The Butterfly Effect'?"

Arnie nodded. "Some of it, yes. But I was trying to keep that from happening. I want them to meet, I want them to—"

"This is an entirely new timeline," Frau Hill interrupted, turning away from the window. "The Ring of Fire created a whole new world, Arnie. And we don't know what all that means yet, but what we do know is that things have changed...a lot! People are alive today that died OTL. Important people whose deaths up-time affected the way in which history unfolded there. Gustavus Adolphus is a good example of that. He died up-time in 1632. What will his continued existence mean for us all in years to come? We simply don't know yet.

"But for Newton... he won't be born for another six, seven years, Arnie. His mother and father weren't supposed to meet for another four, five years I'd imagine. It's possible that in this new timeline, they aren't supposed to meet at all."

"I don't understand that," Arnie said. "Why not? If they meet and we ensure that they survive and get married, why wouldn't Sir Isaac Newton be born?"

Frau Hill shook her head. "Some people think that

an entirely new timeline means changes in our DNA as well. They say that even within a short time after the Ring of Fire the environmental impact would—" She waved her hand. "Never mind. It involves genetics and it's complicated. But it could be that it is impossible, no matter what happens, for the man 'Isaac Newton' to be born."

"I don't believe that."

Frau Hill shrugged. "I don't know if I do either, but what we do know is that, no matter how well-meaning your intentions were, your letter will have an effect on the lives of those you sent it to, and probably a major one."

Arnie felt low. He slunk down in his chair, wishing he could become invisible, wishing he could take back writing the letter. *If I hadn't sent it at all, perhaps things would have played out in the right way*. But was that so? If what Frau Hill was saying were true, then Newton wouldn't be born anyway, and thus, the letter would have no effect at all, other than to just needlessly worry those who had received it. But no, he couldn't think that way. The stakes were too high. Something had to be said. Newton had to be born.

"Let me ask you something, Arnie," Frau Hill said, moving to stand next to his chair. "Why does it matter to you that Newton is born? I mean, our library here already has a fair amount of the knowledge that he gave the world. We don't have it all, of course, but we know the most important things. We know of his laws of motion; we know of his work with gravity, his work with telescopes. We have calculus. The world already has the gifts that he gave us, and others in time can expand upon it. Why does *he* need to exist?"

"Because he does."

"Why?"

Arnie looked into Frau Hill's eyes and saw that she was in full teacher mode. She was challenging him, pushing him to finally pause a moment and think critically about what he had done, and about what it meant to him.

"Because... his birth added to the substance of the universe."

That paused her. Her expression changed. Arnie couldn't fully read it, but she stepped back, went to her chair, and took a seat. "You're a smart boy, Arnie. You'll do well in life. But, a person lives and dies by the choices he makes. You're old enough to understand that. The way I see it, there are only three conclusions that can be derived from this situation. One, the letter never reaches her; it's lost, damaged, whatever. Or two, she gets the letter but can't read it or understand what she is reading, and throws it away, and it has little or no effect. Or three, she gets the letter, reads it and understands it, and well...," she smiled, though Arnie could tell that it was not from joy, "...in that case, we'll have to see how the butterfly flaps its wings."

October 1636
Woolsthorpe-by-Colsterworth, Lincolnshire

William Ayscough stepped aside a pace, lest his shoes and the hem of his coat get spattered by the phlegm spewing from Isaac Newton's mouth and nose. On his knees, the man seemed ill; there was no "seem" about it. He was ill, and William had a notion to turn right around and walk away. *Not worthy of my sister*, he thought as he checked his clothing and wriggled his nose against the stench of manure and tilled field grass. *Not worthy at all.*

"My apologies," Isaac said, wiping his face with a dirty cloth. He sniffled, coughed. "Can't seem to shake this malady."

"No apologies necessary, sir," William said, offering a nicer cloth. Isaac refused it. "I hope you don't mind me arriving unannounced, but I trust that you received my letter?"

Isaac stood, turned away from his work, and gave a look of embarrassment. He nodded. "I got it."

William was cautious. "But you didn't read it."

Isaac kicked up a clump of dirt, knelt and took it in his hand. He broke it into tiny pieces and let them fall to the ground. "I'm a farmer, priest. Not a scholar."

No doubt about that. "To be clear, sir, I'm an Anglican Rector. Had you read the letter, you would have known the reason for my visit. Allow me to explain."

William laid everything out. He described the letter and associated papers that the Ayscough family had received from Grantville. When he was done, he said, "So, what do you say to all that?"

Isaac shrugged, but William could see the man's eyes widen, his skin turn a damp white. "What am I supposed to say? I don't believe a word of it."

"Oh, it's true. The history has already been written. You will marry my sister, Hannah, and you will father a child with your name. And that child will become the great scientist, Sir Isaac Newton."

The farmer bent over and sneezed again into his

cloth. He wiped his nose, shook his head. "Whatever children I have will be farmers. I can promise you that."

"Not this one. This one will go on to do great things in science and mathematics, make great discoveries, all in the eyes of God. And I will help him achieve those things."

Isaac gave a wry smile. "I see what this is." He stepped closer to William, eyed him carefully. "This isn't about me or your sister. It's about you, isn't it? You have some part to play in this that you aren't telling me. What is it, sir? Did God tell you to find me? Or was it the king? What is he paying you to bother me in my own home?"

Almighty, give me strength. "I can assure you, sir, I am not here at the behest of the Crown nor—pray, forgive me—God our Father. I am here to protect my sister. And to protect you."

Isaac raised an eyebrow. "What do you mean?"

William looked left, right, to ensure that no one was near. He leaned in closer. "Our king has been busy with the incarceration and execution of those he considers a danger to his rule. He is doing this because of the histories that he has read from the up-timers in Germany, histories that tell him who will turn against him, and when. I do not know if he or anyone else would consider the birth of your son, my nephew, a danger to the state. His birth may very well be a danger to the religious community due to his disbelief in the Holy Trinity; his voice will carry weight because he will be such a prominent scientist and a great thinker. It is hard to say for sure; things are chaotic right now. But the devil is on the move, and you and my sister may very well be in his way."

Isaac considered this for a moment, turned away from William and blew his nose. He coughed, tucked away his cloth, then said, "Then she and I will never meet. That settles your problem. If she and I never meet, we'll never have children. We'll be a threat to no one."

William shook his head. "It doesn't work that way. A son will be born to you and Hannah."

Isaac huffed: "You're Anglican. You don't believe in predestination."

"What I am, sir, is a brother who fears for the safety of his sister. The information that I have just told you will, in time, get out, and when it does, I cannot control who will receive it, or how they will react to it. My sister's life matters."

"Then go and protect her," Isaac said, flinging an arm in the air as if he were shooing away flies. "Leave me out of it."

"That isn't possible either. Not anymore. We're *all* part of this matter now, and we must ensure that your son is born. He matters most of all."

"Why? Why does he matter so much?"

William smiled. "Because he will add to the substance of the universe."

On that, he agreed with Arnulf Langenberg, the young German boy who had sent the materials from Grantville. There was no disputing that claim in William's mind. A boy like his nephew is born to humanity only once in a lifetime.

Isaac stood there and thought about that last statement for a long while. William could see the man trying to work it all out in his mind, a mind confined more to matters of soil, of subsistence. Such worldly, heady concepts were obviously difficult for the farmer to understand. He cared more about getting his fields ready for the long winter. It was a lot for any man to take in on such short notice, William could not deny that, and he regretted having to come here and disturb his comfortable routine. But this was in God's hands now. Whether as an Anglican rector William believed in predestination or not, the truth of what will happen to them all in the future had been relayed to William's family, and thus, it was now part of a greater plan. *And I will see it through for myself and for God.*

"No," Isaac finally said with a flurry of hand waving. "I don't care what you or anyone else says. I'm a farmer, and that is the truth. I don't know your sister. I don't want to know your sister. Good day, sir."

He started walking away, and William said with force, "You die, Mr. Newton. You die in the other timeline, from where the Americans came. Up-time, my sister and you marry, conceive a child, and three months before he is born, you die. The history does not say how it happens—perhaps from an infection, perhaps from small pox, perhaps from ague—I don't know. But you will die, whether you marry my sister or not, for you are a sickly man, Isaac, it seems clear to me. In six years you will be dead, and you will have nothing to leave behind as a legacy, no one to care for your fields, your home. You will die alone, here, in your manor house, and no one will remember you, save the Almighty, and *that* will happen whether you marry my sister or not.

"But perhaps I can help save your life. Perhaps I can help you escape that fate at least, and perhaps you can then be a real father to your son, a real husband to Hannah. You can help me, help God, add to the substance of the universe."

Isaac stopped, turned, and fought the urge to cough again. "How can you do that?"

William offered his hand. "Come with me, my friend. Meet my sister, and I will tell you both."

Hannah sat quietly at her father's table, beside a man she did not know. She did not want to know him, in fact. He was old, not very good-looking, and sickly. He kept sniffling, his nose was red, and he smelled of manure. But then he was a farmer, and a pretty good one, by William's account. He owned a decent manor home in Lincolnshire and had sizable property. He was not rich, but he was better off than her parents. A lot of her friends would never marry such a prominent farmer or man. Her brother said that she should be honored and delighted to be betrothed to Isaac Newton. She didn't want to be. *But I can't refuse, can I? I'm not allowed.*

"Do you like cats?"

He sniffled, cleared his throat. "They're useful on the farm."

Hannah nodded, took a deep breath, pressed on. "We have three, although one is not ours. Just a stray. She kills mice."

"Yes, I guess they do that."

Another long, uncomfortable pause. Hannah could hear birds chirping outside the window of the kitchen, but it was a cold, rainy day, and thus streaks of rainwater across the glass kept her from seeing them. She pulled her shawl tighter around her shoulders. The wood in the fireplace had just been kindled.

"What kind of crops do you plant?" She asked.

"Some wheat, some barley. Beets. I also have a spot reserved for turnips. I have some goats and a few head of sheep. I'm getting fields ready for winter."

She used that last statement to say what lay heavy on her heart. "How can we go, then, if you are getting your fields ready? We must stay here."

"It's been arranged. My brothers will take care of the farm while we're away."

"And how long will that be?"

Isaac shook his head. "I don't know. Until any threat subsides. That's what your brother says, anyway."

"He says someone might try to hurt us, or kill us. Is someone going to do that?"

He shrugged. "I don't know."

William would be going with them, as a chaperone; it was the only way Mummy and Daddy would allow the trip. They were not supposed to get married yet; she was too young, only thirteen, and anyway, she hadn't flowered. The thought of it all made her sick. "I don't want to go," she said, fighting back tears. "I don't want to have children."

Isaac looked toward the door as if he were expecting someone to walk in; then he turned back and said in a whisper, "I don't want to either, Miss Hannah. But I don't think we have a choice anymore."

"Why not?"

"William says it's God's will."

"I don't care. I—"

She got up and went to the fire. She could not stop her tears. "I don't want to leave Mummy and Daddy. I don't want to leave my friends. I don't want to leave my cats. I don't care what they say. I'm tired of doing what everyone tells me to do."

Her back was turned to him. She could not see his expression. But the room fell silent, with just the crackle of the fire. Then he was moving towards her. She could hear his heavy boots along the floor, shuffling as he blew his nose again into his handkerchief and cleared his throat. He was near her then, far enough away as to keep her from catching his cold, but close enough to cast his shadow across her back. She could smell him.

"Did your brother tell you what happens to me after we marry?"

She nodded. "I read it."

He fell silent again. *Can he read?* She wondered, suddenly regretful of her impertinent response. She did not want him to feel embarrassed in the presence of a simple girl. Then he said, "All right, then you know that I die. I abandon you and our child. I'm not a smart man, Hannah, and I never will be. I'm just a farmer, but I don't want to go out like that. I like to think that I have some honor, some integrity. I'm not a healthy man either. I get sick easily...as you can see. I haven't always made the right decisions in my life. But maybe marrying you was the right decision. According to those papers, it was. So I will make you a promise."

He moved so that she could see his face. Hannah wiped tears from her cheeks, tried to look brave. "You help me now to become a better, healthier man, and I swear to you that, in the end, neither your brother nor God will dictate our future. We will be the masters of our own fate. Besides," he said, screwing up his face in a comical, clownlike manner, "according to those papers, if I die, you go on to marry an old, disgusting ogre of a preacher named Barnabas. Grr!!"

Hannah smiled and couldn't help but laugh at his ghastly expression. It was true. She would have three children by this "ogreish" man, and he would reject the son she would have with this farmer standing before her. So maybe Isaac was right: It was, in the end, better for her to marry a man sixteen years her senior, than a man nearly forty years her senior.

"Very well," she said, standing and fixing her brown dress. "We will do what my brother says. We will go to Grantville with him, and we will learn more about our son. But first," she said, reaching over to a chair, grabbing a coat, and pulling it on. "Can I say goodbye to my cats?"

November 1636
Grantville

It was cold on the walk home, but it wasn't the chill in the air that made Arnie shiver. . . . *We will be arriving on the twentieth of November, and we would like to meet you* . . . He read the line again from William Ayscough, then crumpled up the letter and stuffed it into his coat pocket.

All he wanted was to just say hello and to give them a little "heads up" as the up-timers might say. He never meant it to become a national crisis.

But perhaps it wasn't and wouldn't be. They were just coming to Grantville to pay a visit. That was all. At least, that's what the letter said. They were coming to see Grantville for themselves and to meet the young German boy who had expressed so much concern for their family's welfare. They also wanted to know more about a man who wasn't born yet, to know him as a person, as a great intellect. On that score, Arnie had little else to give them. He had sent them everything he had found on their son. There was no more to tell. But perhaps up-time teachers could give them more insight. Frau Hill, for instance. Perhaps she could tell them more, or direct them to the Imperial College of Science in Magdeburg. Surely the scholars there would know far more about Sir Isaac Newton than anyone else.

Arnie paused at the bottom of the wooden steps leading to the back door of his mother's apartment. Another shiver ran down his spine as he thought again about the Butterfly Effect. If it was to be believed, then the simple act of Newton's parents meeting before they were supposed to had changed the percentage chance of their son being born. The act of leaving England, of coming to Grantville, of the father seeking expert medical advice on what chronically ailed him . . . all of these things would change the calculus. Was it now even possible for Sir Isaac Newton to be who he becomes if his father does not die before he is born? Was his resentment of his mother's abandonment of him at age three a critical factor in his intellectual and independent-minded development? Arnie did not know, and more importantly, he was not sure if he could tell them all these things when they arrived. It could break their hearts.

He shook his head. *No, I cannot think like this. Sir Isaac Newton will be born. He must.* God would not be so cruel as to deprive the world of such a great man because of a little tear in the time continuum. *Would he?*

He entered the kitchen. His mother was there, back turned to him, working batter in a wooden bowl. "Hello, Arnulf. How was your day at school?"

He saw the apple sitting on the kitchen table. A small, red-green, knotty one. One of the last of the season. He picked it up and squeezed it. Very firm. He tossed it in the air, watched it tumble over and over. It hovered there a split second, then fell back into his hand. He smiled and took a bite.

Yeah . . . God would not be so cruel.

"Fine, mama." He paused to chew, then said, "But guess who's coming to dinner?"

Rats of War

OR

PTSD Is No Invention of the Twentieth Century

Rainer Prem

⏤ Prelude ⏤

Ulm, Swabia
April 3, 1627

"Name?"

"Peter Hagendorf."

"Where from?"

"Zerbst."

"Where's that?"

"In Anhalt, near Magdeburg."

"Can you read? Write?"

"German, Latin and Italian."

The recruiter looked up with a puzzled gaze. "*Ach, Herr Professor!*"

Peter Hagendorf could nearly see what that man was thinking. He was a middle-sized, muscular man wearing torn clothes, and didn't look in the least as if he knew Latin. Why was he even here, prepared to join a mercenary troop?

He frowned. "Not really, only six years at the *Lateinschule*. Been in Venice and Italy just the last two years."

The recruiter looked down. Peter's eyes followed him, seeing his shoes held together scantily by some withies. "Just crossed the Alps by foot."

The recruiter shrugged. "Sign here. You now belong to the company of Hans Heinrich Küllmann in the Regiment of Gottfried Heinrich zu Pappenheim. Take the *Laufgeld*, buy you some good shoes and go to Müllheim with the others."

> *"...von da aus sind wir auf den Muster-platz gezogen, in die obere Markgrafschaft Baden. Dort im Quartier gelegen, gefressen und gesoffen, dass es gut heißt."*
>
> *"...from there we went to the induction place in the upper Margraviate of Baden. There we stayed in quarters, devouring and boozing as much as we could."*
>
> —*Peter Hagendorf's Diary*

— I —

Magdeburg
May 20, 1631

The sky changed color from black to gray. Now the day had finally come. Magdeburg would be down today. Peter was waiting with his company for Pappenheim's order, looking right and left for the sign of a fellow mercenary attempting to run before him.

He took a firm grip for his saber and his pistol. No pikes and muskets today. They weren't exactly reasonable in house-to-house fighting, and Peter was sure that such a fight would happen. It was too late for Magdeburg's lardasses to surrender.

For first time since he had enlisted with Pappenheim four years ago, he would get a real piece of the cake. The pay he and his comrades got—or didn't get, at least not in time—wasn't enough to pay the beer and bread for them; less for their families following behind.

Peter's family. It consisted of Anna Stadlerin, whom he met shortly after his enrollment and quickly married. A strong woman. Four years she had accompanied him, had borne him four children and buried three of them. Only Elisabeth was still alive, and only God knew for how long. For several weeks now she was sick, nearly the whole time the regiment was besieging Magdeburg.

Anna had been seriously ill once during that time, the whole eighteen weeks during the siege of Wolfen-büttel, while the water was slowly rising behind the makeshift dam they had built. Then, when the town was finally drowned on Christmas 1627, the citizens quickly surrendered to avoid being looted. So he had no chance to look for a little extra income.

The next three years had been filled with marching and waiting. Waiting and marching. From Baden to Hamburg, from Stralsund to Wiesbaden, to Paderborn and finally to Magdeburg.

Peter wiped the thoughts away. If he could capture enough booty today, they could bring Elisabeth to a good doctor, could pay for the medicine, save her. Peter spoke a short prayer.

The possibility of capturing booty had never been as close as today. Magdeburg's city council had refrained from a timely surrender, trying to buy time for the Swedes to relieve the city. A big miscalculation. Tilly had outlawed all of the town and its inhabitants, and Pappenheim's regiment would be the first to enter the town.

Those Magdeburgers would now suffer for their stubbornness. The fact that Peter had been born only a two days' walk from this city more than twenty years ago didn't matter.

It was over time. The company was waiting behind the most forward fieldworks, weapons in their hands, with stomachs empty of food, but full of the anger of the last weeks. Peter's company had lost two captains to the fire of the defenders; the third had deserted, so they had no captain at the moment. Well, nobody to tell them what to do and what to refrain from. The lieutenant could be safely ignored.

Drumbeat! That was the sign! This was the big day. This was the hour. The regiment started its march. Slowly first, but when they noticed that nobody tried to stop them, the first line increased their pace.

When they reached the broken gate, they were nearly running. Peter lost his place in the first line when they poured through the opening in the wall. But the fellow soldiers before him soon entered the houses to the left and the right, hacking and slashing along their way, while Corporal Hagendorf concentrated on his target, followed by his privates.

The houses of the rich patricians in the New Town. Next alley left, then right. Yes, Peter could see the clean whitewashed houses behind the gaping *Neustädter Tor*.

A flash. He looked up, saw a puff of smoke, tried to evade. But it was too late. A kick in his stomach like from a horse made him stagger. A second kick hit him in the armpit.

Then the world went dark.

> *"Nachher bin ich in das Lager geführt worden, verbunden, denn einmal bin ich durch den Bauch vorne durchgeschossen worden, zum andern durch beide Achseln, so dass die Kugel ist in dem Hemd gelegen."*
>
> *"Afterwards I was brought to the camp and bandaged, because I was shot, first through the belly up front, and second through both armpits, so the bullet lay in the shirt."*
>
> —Peter Hagendorf's Diary

The next thing Peter sensed was being thrown on a cart. Somebody was pressing a hand onto his stomach.

"He's alive," he heard. "Take him to the surgeon." Darkness again.

Sometime later he awoke from somebody pulling his arms to his back.

Hot pain stabbed him. "What?" he cried.

"Be quiet," somebody told him. "I must get the bullet out of your belly."

His hands were tied on his back. Something like a fireball hit his stomach and the world went dark again.

When he awoke the next time he was lying on his back. He could see a familiar silhouette moving in front of the tent flap.

"Anna," he groaned and tried to rise.

His wife turned and came closer. "Stay down for Heaven's sake!" she commanded, pushing down his shoulders. "You're half dead. Don't move, or you'll bleed to death."

"I'm dying anyway," he gasped.

"Not if you'll follow my orders. I'll leave Elisabeth with you and go fetch more bandages. Stay put!"

She put their sick daughter next to him and left the tent.

He couldn't remember how long it had been before the flap opened again, waking him from his dozing.

Anna was back, hauling a huge tankard and wearing a bundle on her back. An old woman followed her wearing a bundle of cloth.

"This is Margarethe," Anna said. "She helped me get the bandages." Her voice was shaking.

"What's the matter?" he asked.

When Anna turned to him he could see how worried her face was. "Magdeburg is burning," she said flatly. "They set the houses on fire, from where the snipers shot you, and now the whole city is ablaze."

Suddenly she started to weep. "They are killing everybody," she cried. "Men, women and children. The streets are covered with corpses."

Peter tried to rise; he wanted to comfort her, but as soon as he lifted his head, the world turned dark again.

It was the same evening when his company mates came to visit him. The rest of the company had been luckier than him. Only a few other men had lost their lives or had been wounded.

And they *had* experienced the big day, so they could give alms to the one person who hadn't. Compared to the wealth they were able to loot from the town, it was definitely alms. But together with the wine, clothes and other things Anna had found in the town, it was at least worth the effort.

> *"Ist mir doch von Herzen leid gewesen,*
> *dass die Stadt so schrecklich gebrannt hat,*
> *wegen der schönen Stadt und weil es mein*
> *Vaterland ist."*
>
> *"I was sincerely sorry that the city burned*
> *so terribly, because the city was beautiful and*
> *because it's my home country."*
>
> —Peter Hagendorf's Diary

Breitenfeld, near Leipzig
September 17, 1631

> *"Da sind wir am Lager wohlauf gewesen*
> *die ganze Zeit über, bis der Schwede ist*

angekommen... Da sind wir ihm entgegenge-
gangen, über zwei Stunden."

"It was a good time in the camp [in Leipzig]
the whole time, until the Swede arrived....
Then we went to meet him, over two hours."
—Peter Hagendorf's Diary

From his place in the first line, Peter could look over
the whole area. A feeling of pride rose in his chest
when he saw the enormous army he was part of.

Seventeen battles formed the heart of the Bavarian
army, arranged in the Spanish Ordnance, the square
formations the Spaniards called *tercio*, framed to the
left and right by thousands of cavalrymen.

They were waiting on the only rise over the flat
grassland, the sun at their backs. The enemy had to
look up and face the rising sun. Oh, yes, old Tilly
knew well how to prepare a battle in order to win.

Far to the left Peter could see the banners of the
Black Cuirassiers. Colonel Pappenheim was leading his
famous heavy cavalry in person, and so his infantry—
far away on the right wing—was put under the order
of the young Bavarian Joachim Graf von Wahl today.

To the right of Peter's companies, he could see the
regiments of Wallies and Wangler and the light cavalry
at the rightmost position. The view to the left showed
the other battles, the big cannons in the middle.

Straight ahead on the enemy's left flank Peter could
see the Saxons. Von Wahl had already given Tilly's
order down to the companies that those were their first
target. Peter smiled. He had heard how inexperienced
they were. And their appearance proved that rumor
right. Their weapons shone in the sun, their clothes

were colorful like peacocks. Experienced mercenaries wore unremarkable clothes, didn't waste their time washing them, had muskets, dark from the heat of the rounds, pikes and swords stained by oil.

He could count only fifteen or so companies, with very few cavalry. No match for the thirty veteran companies under von Wahl's command.

This had to be the next big day after Magdeburg. And this time Peter was determined not to fall down again and miss the whole fun.

The artillery on both sides had already started their probing two hours ago. Peter could hear the steady deep pounding of the big pieces. They would certainly shatter the Swedish cannons; not much to answer came back; those were only small field pieces.

A murmur went through the battles, when the heavy cavalry far away at the left flank started an attack. *Pappenheim! Yes!* Peter fastened his grip at the musket. Dispatch riders came from the center. And now the drums were rolling.

The battles started their march. A picture Peter had dreamt of since he became a soldier. And with seventeen earth-shattering unstoppable battles advancing, the cavalry on the right started their attack.

Yes, scare the gutless Saxons away. Make them run like rabbits. This day will be our victory!

"Jesus Maria!" the men shouted while they made their way crossing the gap to the enemy. "Father Tilly!" Yes, that was better. Peter had always had problems yelling along with the Catholics around him. More perhaps than the other Lutherans and Calvinists in the regiment.

The fact that he had signed in for fighting against his fellow Protestants had taken a long time to register in his mind. Then in Ulm, it seemed to be the easiest way to get a regular income in war-torn Germany.

This time his emotions were not as churning as after Magdeburg. Here they were at least fighting against the foreign Swedes and the Saxon assholes led by the drunkard elector his own people called "Beer George."

And exactly these Saxons were now straight before them, waiting to be stomped into the ground by Tilly's glorious warriors. *Well, they'd certainly get what they wanted.*

The light cavalry had already attacked and found very few problems. The lines of the Saxons showed gaps, began to waver, seemed to break.

Don't hurry! Leave some of the glory to us!

But the cavalry didn't hear Peter's thoughts. They started to circle the Saxon regiments, and separate them from their Swedish support.

Running horses and marching men blew up more and more dust, and in the meantime Pappenheim's regiment had reached the foot of the little hill they had started from. So Peter lost his overview.

New orders were coming. *Ah, the old fox!* Tilly obviously wanted to take advantage of the Saxon's weakness. The three regiments of the right flank were slowly turning to the right, to make room for the other fourteen to their left.

Peter coughed. He wasn't the only one. The dust in the air became thicker, mingled with the smell of sulfur and ash. He had, like most of his comrades, drawn his scarf up to cover his mouth, but the hot weather of the last weeks, together with the boots of thirty thousand men, had made a desert out of the grass plains. Only from the sun's position at his back could Peter tell that they were still advancing on the Saxons.

Or at least to the place where they had been. They should have met them in the meantime. So the cowards had already panicked and left the battlefield. Peter tried to imagine the layout. With the Saxons gone, Pappenheim's regiment and the two others to their right no longer had an enemy to face. Infantry was not fit to pursue fleeing enemies. That was the task of the cavalry.

So the regiments would have to turn left and attack the Swedes from behind. *No problem.* That was even better. Somewhere their camp followers should hang around. They were easy prey for the victorious army and a good booty, too. Peter was satisfied with his tactical sense, when he noticed the drums changing their rhythm to indicate the left turn.

But soon their advance slowed down. Over the shuffling of thousands of feet Peter could hear shooting. Muskets and the high tone of the small Swedish cannons, the pounding of their rounds somewhere before him. Apparently this was not behind the Swedish lines; this wasn't an open flank. The Swedish must have managed to open a new front.

But what had happened to the imperial cannons? The regular deep pounding had turned irregular. And worse. One of their rounds even crashed into the lines of the Pappenheim regiment. A loud moaning rose, the lines wavering. *Idiots! Why don't they shoot the Swedes?* And then another round, again from the left. More men went down. Suddenly a rumor was spreading. "The Swedes have captured our cannons." That was bad. Very bad.

The regiment was still not in a place to fight. In the

meantime their advance had completely stopped, and the dust was still too thick to see anything. The men looked in the direction from where the horrendous cannon balls from their own cannons were arriving.

Again a new command from the drums. "Spread! Spread!" Somebody had reacted. But the men had no room to spread. Before him were the hindmost lines of another regiment; behind him all the lines of his own. To the right and left men from his regiment and two more to the right. So he could only stand and wait, wait and stand. And hope that none of the big balls landed on his head.

Ahead him the cries of men became louder. Each time one of the Swedish cannon balls struck it didn't only take a few men. The balls were arriving grazing, smashing through the lines like murderous skittles balls. Again and again he could see through the dust a whole row of men in front of him being hit and torn by a single ball.

Peter cursed, when his tactical sense set in again, painting a clear picture of the situation. This must have been a trap. The Saxons had been the bait, flamboyantly colorful, guaranteeing not to be ignored. They must have had an order to retreat immediately and lure the cavalry away.

Oh shit! And all the regiments on the right side were neutralized. Standing behind the other ones in the middle with no chance to fight. This was more than frustrating.

You are lucky, his mind told him. *The battles at the front are torn apart by the Swedish muskets and cannons. You can only be hit by one of our captured cannons.* In the half clear sky he could see most of the big balls traveling far over the regiment. *If none of these kills you by chance, you will stay on your feet.*

A small comfort. He *wanted* to fight, but he couldn't. He stood locked between five thousand men with no chance to advance, retreat or dodge to the sides.

Oh what a grandiose shit! Another not-so-big day in my life.

> "*An diesem Tag sind wir geschlagen worden, die ganze bayrische Armee, ausgenommen diese vier Regimenter nicht … aber was wir in der Altmark gefressen haben, haben wir redlich kotzen müssen vor Leipzig.*"
>
> "*On that day, we were beaten, the whole Bavarian army, all but these four regiments, namely Pappenheim, Wallies, Wangler and Young Tilly … But what we devoured in the Altmark we had to vomit near Leipzig.*"
>
> —Peter Hagendorf's Diary

Ducal-Bavarian Wheat Beer Brewery, Kelheim
March 1632

> "*Unser Regiment ist zu Kelheim an der Altmühl gelegen. Hier haben wir wieder gutes Quartier gehabt. Da wird ein trefflich gutes Weißbier gebraut.*"
>
> "*Our regiment took quarters in Kelheim along the Altmühl. Here we had again a good accommodation. A very good wheat beer is brewed there.*"
>
> —Peter Hagendorf's Diary

"That's impossible!" Peter shook his head and took another big pull from his stein of *Weißbier*. Being in quarters in a town famous for its beer had its advantages.

"I'm telling you the way it is. I've been there. They call their town 'Grantville,' but they're no Frenchies. They swear it had been in Northern America until last year. In the year Twenty-Zero-Zero." Thomas von Scharffenberg was another mercenary. In Magdeburg he had been the *Fähnrich* of Peter's company; and while Peter was recovering from his wounds he went to Thuringia foraging with a handful of companies. And there they had encountered a new kind of enemy.

Peter shook his head, half from disbelief, half to get his beer-drowned head free to understand.

"They've got more guns than a regiment," Franz Moser chimed in. Originally he had come from Austria, learned the craft of gunsmith in Suhl, but couldn't become a master there. "A town of three thousand inhabitants including women and children armed to the teeth like ten Spanish tercios. I honestly believe they are born with a gun in their hand."

Laughter arose around them. Gallows humor. Franz always made jokes, when the situation got nasty.

"Well," Peter said. "Three thousand armed people are not negligible. Militia are always difficult to crack, when they are fortified behind city walls."

"Grantville doesn't have walls," Thomas said smiling. "No palisades, not even a trench. It's down in a valley. Their creek goes straight through the town instead of around."

Peter tried to imagine such a town. He failed.

"And there weren't three thousand on the field.

They attacked us with not more but a company of infantrymen. Our colonel wanted to simply stomp their company but they shredded us like a piece of paper.

"They didn't even need the cavalry they had."

"Cavalry?" Peter asked. "So they *have* regular troops where they come from?"

Common shaking of heads.

"They were Scots, a company, no idea where they got them from." Thomas shrugged. "But they used them only for cleaning up. These Americans, you know, they've got weapons shooting clack, clack, clack, clack. Without pause for reloading. Burning bullets. Without heating them first. I've got a burned wound." He showed Peter the small black scar at his upper arm. "And after they had killed most of the regiment, instead of hanging the rest at trees, they took the survivors to their doctors. They cleaned my wound and stitched the edges together."

"And then let you leave, for no reason?"

"They imprisoned us," Franz said, grimacing as if from pain. "Full three days. And do you know what the worst torture was?"

Peter shook his head. First treating their wounds, and then torturing them?

Franz rolled his eyes. "They *washed* us." Everyone broke out in laughter. "They said we're full of vermin. They poured *water* over us, gave us stinking soap to rub in. What a shame!"

Peter laughed. "Do you want to tell me they were wrong? About the vermin I mean."

Franz only grinned.

Peter sobered. "And what are these people? Wizards? Witches?" he asked.

Franz shook his head. "Nah. I don't think so. These *shotguns* they have, you know, I could build them easily if I had the right tools."

"I don't think so either," Thomas said. "There weren't sudden thunderstorms, poison in the air, or evil demons killing our people. Only weapons. But what kind of weapons . . . think how not long ago there weren't any muskets. And now add three hundred and seventy years of development. I'm not surprised about *that*."

Franz suddenly grinned. "And beautiful girls they have. And their teeth . . . as if made from white marble and polished."

Peter laughed, uncertainly, trying to hide the ruins in his mouth. It was simply unbelievable. Then he got serious again. "What do you think will happen?"

Thomas shrugged. "Perhaps the Swedes will attack them. Rumor said the Thuringian princes supporting the Swede are far from happy about these Americans. It seems they try to get political influence at the expense of the Wettins, Schwarzburgs and Reußens. I heard they are threatening the town councils around them to join their so-called United States."

Peter frowned. "That would be too good to be true. Two threats eliminating each other. And if not? If they join the Swedes? Can you imagine what they could do to us?" He tried to keep his good mood, but the picture of Swedish cannons ripping the soldiers around him was still visible in his mind. And he tried to imagine musketeers firing without reloading and firing and firing.

"How many rounds do you say they have in their muskets?"

"'*Shotguns*' is what they call them," Franz repeated. "Some have magazines with several rounds, others are simply opened up like a book, throwing out the used cartridge, and then they insert the new one, close it and fire again. Ten heartbeats they need." He showed with his hands. Shoot, open, insert, close, aim, shoot, open and so on. No fiddling with fuses, no black powder to prime the pan, simply shooting.

"And then," Franz made a pause. "There is the *machine*, a gun that shoots and shoots and shoots without end. Rattattat-rattattat-rattattat. It's simply terrible if you stand on the wrong side of their barrels." His face was mirroring the horror. No sign of the jokester any longer.

Peter frowned again. "What can we do? Our regiment I mean."

Thomas took a deep breath. "Pikemen? Nothing. They're about to become extinct. Musketeers? They must learn to get cover, take aim and fire volleys. Like the guys who shot you in Magdeburg. What you can't see you can't shoot.

"So what will you do, Corporal Hagendorf?"

Peter didn't answer. His eyes traveled into the distance. Then suddenly he came to a decision.

"Yes, I will accept your proposal. I'll join your skirmishers, Lieutenant von Scharffenberg. I don't want to be locked again in the middle of a battle."

"A wise decision. And I'll tell you another thing: Wear something without colors. The Americans have suits that look like they're painted with leaves. If they stand between two trees you can't even see them."

"Hmmm. Fortunately these Americans are in Thuringia and not here in Bavaria."

Scharffenberg laughed. He rose and extended a hand. "Welcome to our little company, Sergeant Hagendorf."

Near Rain am Lech
April 14, 1632

"...*wieder fortgezogen nach Regensburg*....
nach Donauwörth an der Donau. Bald ist die
schwedische Armee auch da gewesen und hat
uns von Donauwörth weggejagt. Nach Rain
am Lech, eine Festung."

"... *moved again to Regensburg*.... *to*
Donauwörth on the Donau. Soon the Swedish
Army also got there and chased us away from
Donauwörth. To Rain on Lech, a fortress."
                                —*Peter Hagendorf's Diary*

Once again Peter noticed the mortal sound of the
Swedish artillery. And fortunately he once again was
not the target of their furor. Scharffenberg had taken
his group of skirmishers to the right flank of Tilly's
defense station. Here they were hiding behind some
trees and bushes waiting for enemies who approached
their ambush unsuspectingly.

It was a kind of warfare old Tilly detested. Peter
could understand him. It was...dishonorable, perhaps
cowardly. But according to Thomas this was the future.
This was the way the Americans had shattered their
regiment. Win dishonorably or die with honor? For
Peter this question answered itself.

He was squatting behind a bush, wearing the clothes
Anna had helped him to color with dots and smears in
black, gray, green and brown. Most of the skirmishers
had laughed when he appeared this morning wearing
the "camouflage," as Thomas had called it. But Thomas
didn't laugh. He only nodded approvingly.

Thomas had told them that the old field marshal didn't believe that the Swedes would try to force the river crossing. But you never knew. And perhaps some scattered Swedes would run before the long and rifled barrels of the Bavarian skirmishers' new guns.

Peter caressed the oily barrel. He had called the gun *Elisabeth* after his youngest daughter, who had died last year. Peter somehow had the impression that Anna hadn't taken the repeated death of their children as easy as she said. Her eyes, however, lit up when Peter had shown her the letters he had burned into the rifle's butt.

A soft whistle roused him from his thoughts. Something was happening below them. Under the covering fire of these terrible cannons men came forth and started to build a wooden bridge. They jumped into the shallow water and drove pegs into the riverbed.

"Open fire when they are in the middle of the river," Franz said at his left. "And then we blow their asses away," the jester added. Peter passed the order to his right, grinning.

From time to time a cannon ball from the Bavarian side landed between the men in the river, but the rareness of these events told Peter that the Swedish cannons had already taken their death toll. In the meantime they aimed their shots onto the wooden fortification and into the forest, which made them deafening loud.

One man to his right fired and one man in the water fell down. Then Peter fired also. Another Swede went down. While Peter rose behind a tree to reload his gun, more men in the river were cut down by the well-aimed shots.

But then suddenly he heard a strange sound from Franz's position. Like a cleaver hitting a pig's ham. Directly followed by a crack, and the sound of a falling body.

Peter slumped to the earth. "Franz! Are you all right?" No answer. Then he crawled to the left. Franz was lying there on his back.

"Franz, what's the matter?" Peter hissed. No answer. He crawled closer. First he could see nothing that could have brought the man down. Then he noticed a small hole in Franz's chest. Much too small to be a problem. Peter had survived a much bigger hole in Magdeburg.

Only a small amount of blood had emerged, but Franz was not moving and his eyes stared broken into the cloud-covered sky. Peter reached to Franz's mouth, and there was no breath. The man was apparently dead. *Witchcraft?* Then Peter saw a dark fluid emerging from *under* Franz. *Blood! Did that little ball go all the way through?* Still crouching he managed to turn the corpse over.

"*Herrgott!*" Franz's back showed a huge wound; more than a handful of flesh had been torn out. What kind of weapon had caused this?

While he was still doing this, the strange sound repeated again and again. Plop, crack, cry, and slump. Soft and clear he could hear the sound of a strange gun through the continuous roar of the Swedish cannons. Plop, crack, another falling body. But that was impossible. A gun that hit before it could be heard? Like lightning and thunder.

"*Gott im Himmel!*" Peter whispered and made the sign of the cross. Four years in a mostly Catholic troop had consequences to behavior. What else should he do?

Then he heard von Scharffenberg's voice from the other end of their line. "Down, down! Don't dare to move. That's an American 'tchoolee.'"

"*O Scheiße*," Peter shouted but stayed down. A survivor of the so-called Battle at Jena had told them about the marksmen the Americans had deployed to kill all the officers and other leaders of the scattered remnant of the Bavarian army. And he had told what the Americans' German allies called them.

But judging from the number of corpses he had heard falling down, Thomas' orders seemed a little too late.

Oh what a grandiose piece of shit! Another not-so-big day in my life.

"*Da haben wir uns gesetzt. Da ist viel Landvolk zu uns gestoßen, aber alles umsonst. Als der König mit Macht ist auf uns gegangen, mit Kanonen geschossen, dass etliche gefallen sind. Auch ein amerikanischer Tschuli ist dagewesen, hat zehn von uns niedergemacht.*"

"*There we settled. Many local troops have joined us, but all was futile. When the King attacked us with force, shot with cannons, so many died. Also an American tchoolee was there, killed ten of us.*"

—Peter Hagendorf's Diary

~ II ~

South of Ingolstadt
Early May 1632

The Swedes had finally lifted the siege of Ingolstadt. The fact that King Gustav had lost his white horse by a shot literally below his butt might have convinced him to seek greener pastures for his army and squeeze some gold out of the coffers of the rich Bavarian towns.

The Bavarian army had left Ingolstadt, too, to secure the Danube in Regensburg.

The few survivors of the skirmisher company had been kept back to support the garrison and seek for replacements in the town and around.

Peter had jumped at the opportunity to leave the stinking town and going to loot—uh—survey the situation in the small villages south of the Danube, which had been more or less devastated by the Swedish troops.

Three surviving skirmishers and a handful of slightly wounded musketeers—now also armed with the Suhl rifles formerly belonging to Peter's unfortunate comrades—were the escort for three horse wagons.

Even some of the soldiers' wives were traveling on the wagons—officially to provide first aid to possible survivors among the civilian population. But unofficially they were always the ones with the better eyes for hidden treasures, while the men could stand guard.

The first couple of villages hadn't posed any surprises. The Swedes had killed or stolen all animals for food and also looted the farmers' granaries. The people were slowly returning from the woods where they had spent the last weeks. The Ingolstadt scribe accompanying Peter's group took the names of the villagers, and then they continued.

But when they approached another village—its name was Weyering according to the scribe—Peter could see something happening when they reached the forest edge.

"Stop!" he ordered. "Musketeers take cover behind the trees and ready your rifles!"

From the distance he couldn't exactly see what was happening. Men were moving, and houses were burning.

Later he would learn that a small Swedish detachment was about to do the same thing as Peter's troop had planned. But the Swedes were not simply taking the names of the survivors but were looking for another kind of fun.

Suddenly two horses emerged from the village in full rout; the riders whipped them frantically. Two skinny villagers as far as Peter could see. Soon other riders chased them, the latter wearing cuirasses and yellow brassards. *Swedes!*

Peter thought quickly. "Group one: Shoot the pursuers as soon as they are in range. Reload as quickly as possible." He scrutinized his troop. Twelve men with rifles against nearly the same number of enemies on horses. "Group two: wait ten heartbeats, then you start shooting. And for the sake of god, try to leave the fugitives alive."

"Aiming" was a new concept for the recruits in his group, but they had practiced on the Swedish besiegers during the last weeks.

Two hundred paces. That was doable. Peter aimed at the second man in the group of pursuers. And fired. *"Scheiße!"* He had missed the man, but his bullet took the horse down. While he used one of his self-made paper cartridges to reload his rifle, he could notice that two of the Swedes were down on the first volley. And two horses. The second group scored only one man and one horse.

But that was enough. The Swedes had not expected to be interrupted on their joyride chasing for the villagers, who were riding bareback on the two plowhorses. The cuirassiers turned around and flew, the horseless men running behind them.

"Cease fire!" Peter commanded. "Unless they come back. Johann, Heinrich, try to fetch the horses! The others keep an eye on the village!"

When the fugitives reached the shelter of the forest they literally fell from their horses. Both were covered in blood.

Anna had become an experienced surgeon since Magdeburg. Peter could no longer remember how many wounds she had tended since then. She tried to help the boy—apparently a young man—first, but soon looked up to Peter and shook her head.

Then she tried to help the girl. Peter could see that the blood stains on the girl's clothes concentrated around her waist and had an idea what she had experienced before. *Oh my god, she's twelve, fourteen at most!* When he approached the girl—one eye still on his men and the village in the distance—he could see her wince and sobbingly cling to Anna.

Anna shooed him away.

Grumbling he turned to his men. "We'll stay until dark," he said. "Then I'll scout the village."

"Auf einem Sonntagsausflug mit den Jungs haben wir ein paar Schweden getroffen. Konnten sie überzeugen zu verschwinden. Und jetzt haben wir doch wieder ein Mädchen in der Familie."

"On a Sunday trip we met/hit some Swedes. Could convince them to disappear. Now we finally have a little girl in the family again."
                              —Peter Hagendorf's Diary

The boy had been shot by one of the Swedish mercenaries. The girl—Marie was her name, the only information Anna could extract out of her after long hours of trying—had obviously been raped by not only one man, all her limbs showing black bruises. Her father had been decapitated; her mother been raped like herself and stabbed afterwards.

The farm was a complete write-off. The mercenaries had bound burning torches at the tails of the farms' cattle, and when the animals flew into the supposed safety of their stable, they lit all the buildings.

The bags of the three killed soldiers and the saddle-bags of the horses were the only solace Peter's group could find on that day. At least not a bad one. They contained more than a hundred gold pieces—much more than normal soldiers carried along.

Near Zirndorf, Franconia
Early September 1632

> "Unser Regiment ist nach Regensburg in die
> Stadt verlegt worden. Mein Quartier ist gew-
> esen bei dem Marktturm, bei Johannes Strobel,
> Krämer, gutes Quartier. Dann zurück nach
> Ingolstadt, dann die Altmühl hinauf bis Zirn-
> dorf. Da war das große Lager von Wallenstein."

> "Our regiment was transferred to Regens-
> burg into the town. My quarters were near the
> market tower at Johannes Strobel, shopkeeper,
> good quarters. Then back to Ingolstadt, then
> up the Altmühl to Zirndorf. There was Wal-
> lenstein's big camp."

—*Peter Hagendorf's Diary*

The camp was a monster. The village of Zirndorf was
contained *within* the camp, and the tents and pad-
docks extended thousands of paces in every direction.

"Have you heard about Gallas' cavalry? A complete
company is missing. They only wanted to water their
horses and never returned."

This was one of the recurring jokes at the campfires
and in the makeshift taverns. Jokes about the stupidity of
Swabians had massively decreased after their regiment
had left for Suhl two weeks ago and only a handful of
them had returned to tell of the outcome.

Other stories were growing instead. "How many Spaniards do you need to burn down a castle?—None.—The
Americans will do it for them. They call it Spanish Roast."

Or: "How many Croats do you need to kill an unarmed
old woman?—Five hundred.—One to kill the crone and

four hundred and ninety-nine to get killed by school-kids in the meantime."

Exaggerating had always been a way to overcome fear. And fear was creeping through the alleys of the camp. Would fifty thousand soldiers be enough to bounce the Swedes back at last, when they would attack supported by the American wizards?

Wallenstein was certain. His generals, too. The lower ranks not as much.

Peter shook his head. He was sitting on a wooden bench in front of his tent, slowly slurping his beer. The last mug for now. Supply was slow for a "camp" which in fact was one of the largest cities of the world at the moment.

"I don't know," he told Thomas von Scharffenberg. The captain of his company was a common visitor at Peter's private tavern.

"I don't know," he repeated, "how long it will take until the next supply convoy will arrive. Perhaps the Swedes have intercepted them. And perhaps the Swedes will have killed us all before then. Do you have an idea, how many American tchoolees are with them?"

Now Thomas shook his head. "I don't know how many of these killers exist in Grantville. Our bastion is eight hundred paces away from the Swedish positions. That's certainly enough. But their cannons are bad enough."

Peter flinched. Only a little. He'd become good at hiding his fear.

Thomas took a gulp from his beer. "Do you still have these nightmares?"

Not good enough. Peter blushed. "They're getting better." His voice faded. That was a lie, and Thomas most likely knew that. It wasn't easy for Peter to admit the problems he had.

The first weeks after the battle at the Lech he awoke each night with the image of Franz's death. Sometimes he even saw Anna dying instead, broken eyes looking into a cloud-covered sky raining big cannon balls.

After the incident at Weyering the picture of Marie's parents often blended in. Her father with his head dangling only from a thread of meat; her mother with the knife still protruding from her chest. And both showed Anna's face sometimes.

Fortunately the meantime had been quiet. Only marching and waiting, waiting and marching, no violent events.

Thomas scrutinized him from the side. "You know what? You should go away. Take Anna and Marie and look for a quiet job somewhere in the north."

Peter flared. "I'm no defector. I'll keep my promises."

"You kept them longer than necessary. How long have you been a soldier?"

"Over five years. I don't know if I'm fit for civilian life."

"Then look for a post in the life guards of a prince there. Or join a town watch."

A long gaze from the side, then a deep breath. "Peter," he continued solemnly. "You're a danger to yourself and to the men around you. When the fighting starts and you begin to see dead people again...

"Come to the office tent tomorrow morning. I'll have your discharge papers ready an hour after sunrise."

After Thomas had left, Peter stayed seated. Should he accept the offer? Should he risk searching for a job? Outside the mercenary troop that had been his home for more than five years?

Anna came out of the tent. "Is he gone? What did he want?" Her belly was blown up from her fourth pregnancy.

He took a deep breath. "He wants me to leave. I'm a danger for my comrades, he said."

"Nonsense!" Anna stood very close to him. Then she poked in his chest. "He wants to save your life. You've earned it after five years. This here—" she waved her hand around "—isn't a life. Not with the Swedes' new weapons."

He lifted an eyebrow. Anna and tactical assessments did not exactly go together well.

Anna's expression changed. Now fear showed in her eyes. "If they come here with their hellfire, like the Americans did in Eisenach, we're dead. Dead! Do you hear me? You and me and..." Her voice broke. She put her hand to her belly. "I don't want to lose this child again," she whispered.

For a last time, he tried to find reasons to stay with the army. A single reason he could tell Anna. The fear of a changed world outside didn't count.

He failed.

"All right. Let's leave for Zerbst. Perhaps we'll find somebody of my family there."

"Wir sind nach Norden gezogen, nach Bamberg, dann Kronach und Lauenstein zur thüringischen Grenze. Da ist uns eine ganze Kolonne riesiger Eisenkästen auf Rädern begegnet. Und da habe ich meine ersten Amerikaner gesehen."

"We trekked north, to Bamberg, and then

> *Kronach and Lauenstein to the Thuringian*
> *border. There we met a column of gigantic*
> *iron boxes on wheels. And I saw the Americans*
> *for the first time."*
>
> —*Peter Hagendorf's Diary*

Near Lauenstein, at the Franconian-Thuringian Border
Five days later

They heard the strange sound long before they could see anything. A deep roar constantly getting louder. Some higher noises mingled in between, rising and falling.

"What's that?" Anna asked and stopped the ox cart. Marie clung to Anna's body, eyes wide open. Anna caressed her head. "Shhh. Nobody will harm you."

"I have no idea." He looked to the sky. It had stopped raining the day before, and nothing indicated a thunderstorm. The sound was anyway far too constant for that.

Suddenly some strange vehicle came around the next curve. Apparently made from iron, moving without any draft animals, but uttering the strange sound and blowing smoke. It was nearly as wide as the dirt road they were traveling on.

Before Peter could decide what to do, the vehicle stopped only ten paces away. Men jumped from its rear, clothed in brown suits with black and green spots. They wielded guns, shorter than the rifle Peter had hidden under some bags in the cart.

"*Machen Weg frei,*" one of the men said in a heavily

accented voice and waved his hand. Peter looked around, but couldn't see a possibility to put the cart aside. Both sides of the sunken road rose steeply.

He shrugged. "*Wie denn?*"

The man—Peter strongly assumed he was meeting the famous Americans for the first time—looked around, too, and then spoke quickly to his comrades pointing up the slope. Peter could understand very little of their variation of English.

Then he turned back to Peter. "*Wir helfen. Da hoch.*" He pointed again and shuffled with his hands. Then he waved at the women and pointed down. "*Kommen runter,*" he said smiling.

Peter had conflicting thoughts. These men were heavily armed, so he had no chance to oppose them. On the other hand—apart from their horrible German—they were rather friendly. He turned to Anna. "Come down, they want to pull up our wagon to clear the road."

Two men were already unhitching the oxen, while another one was pulling a rope from a pulley at the vehicle's front up the slope, around a tree and down to the wagon. Peter could see that the rope was no hemp, but apparently made of iron, too.

The confident and quick motions of the men told Peter that they weren't doing this for the first time.

The man who had spoken to Peter—obviously the leader of the group—was standing next to him supervising the actions.

"Are you—um—Americans?" Peter asked, pulling a little English, he had learned from some mercenaries, out of his memory.

The man looked at him, hesitated, but then laughed.

"Damn obvious, huh?" Then he extended a hand. "Sergeant Don Clements. Nice to meet you."

Peter took the hand. "Peter Hagendorf," he said, hesitated, and then added. "Sergeant been." He pointed to Anna and Marie. "With family."

Suddenly the sound of the vehicle got louder, and Peter saw Marie flinch.

Don's eyes followed his. "*Kein Angst!*" he shouted.

Without any of the men pulling the wagon began to move. The other Americans were at its tongue and guided it. Slowly the wagon moved up the slope. The wood creaked protesting, but then it had completely cleared the road.

The men tied the tongue to some trees, this time using a normal hemp rope.

"Wait for the whole column to pass," Don told Peter, in a mixture of German, English and gestures. "Calm the oxen during the time, the APCs are rather loud. There's another truck at the end, they will get your wagon down again. Understand?"

"Understand," Peter said.

"Been a sergeant?" Don asked. "What made you quit?"

Peter hesitated, but this man had an aura of friendliness around him.

"*Nachtmahre*," he said. Seeing Don's puzzled face he dug again in his memory. "Nightmares."

Suddenly the American's face showed sympathy and understanding. "I understand," he said. "Are you going to visit Grantville?"

Peter shrugged.

"If you'll get there," Don said. "Ask for Denyse Clements, my wife. She's a teacher at Blackshere Elementary School. She'll show you around if you like."

"Thank you," Peter said. "That's very nice."

"You're welcome. Take care of yourself," Don Clements said. Then he looked at Anna and Marie and waved to them. "And your family. Godspeed!"

They entered their vehicle again, and with a howling sound they disappeared.

Peter turned to the women. "More vehicles will come. Louder ones. Help me calm the oxen."

Not only louder, but also bigger. Much bigger than the first one. They looked dangerous, like moving castles. Through slits in their iron walls, Peter could see men inside, and guns. *Thomas, I hope you'll survive this.*

— III —

Grantville
Spring 1633

Don Clements was sitting on his front porch, enjoying the warm afternoon on his short leave from the troops.

Peter Hagendorf left the house, two mugs of beer in his hand. He handed one to Don, and then sat next to him on the bench, overlooking Dawn Drive and Sunshine Road.

"A nice corner of Grantville," Peter said.

"You say it," Don answered. "We bought that home after we married in 1993, because it's only a puddle jump from Blackshere Elementary. By now Downs is one of the quietest places in town. Most people want to live closer to downtown."

"I like it. It reminds me of my home village. Only the smell here is much better." He grinned.

Don laughed. "How's your job?"

"*Ich liebe ihn*," Peter said fervently. "Being a mounted constable is not only a job, but a real *Beruf*. Riding along the town's perimeter, protecting the people, even scaring off the occasional vagabonds. After five thousand miles on foot . . ." He stretched his legs. "Ahhh."

Don laughed again. "Tell me, how did you end here in Grantville after we met at the Franconian border?"

Peter frowned. "I have to blame it on my women. They pressed me into this 'day trip' from our inn in Saalfeld." He laughed. "And I'm happy they did. Even the lice comb and the bath Anna applied on me. And I think the new clothes Anna had hidden in her trunk contributed their part.

"I could see how Denyse sniffed the air and then laughed when she smelled the soap, before she greeted us. It seems, she and Anna are—what do you call it?— 'on the same wavelength.' Soap vibrations, perhaps." Both men laughed.

"Anyway, she invited us to stay in Grantville and to move into your house." He shrugged. "With you away in the field, and after the Croat raid, having a man in the house seemed to calm her down. Marie loves your kids and vice versa."

Then they saw a group of girls coming along the street, chatting and giggling. One of them separated and waved the others good bye, making the international sign for "we phone later."

"Hi, Dad," Marie said smiling, and kissed Peter on the cheek. "Hi, Mr. Clements." Then she disappeared into the house.

"*Dad?*" Don asked.

Peter grinned. "She said, using the American terms

for Anna and me, and reserving *Mama* and *Papa* for her dead parents seemed a good compromise for her. I'm happy that she started speaking at last. Even if she doesn't speak about her past."

He straightened. "It seems she had a good education. She's attending the middle school and her teachers are pleased.

"I only hope the nightmares go away." He shook his head.

"Hers or yours?" Don asked.

Peter hesitated. Then softly: "Both."

He sighed. "I'm seeing a *psy-cho-the-ra-pist*," he pronounced carefully, "once a week. She told me to write down my experiences in detail. You know, I took notes all the years I was walking through Europe, and she said I should try to remember and visualize each day. The good ones and . . ." he shuddered ". . . the bad ones, too."

After a pause he sighed again. "But Marie is not—not yet I think—willing or capable to do the same. Dr. DeVries says that she'd need more time. At the moment Marie is *re-pres-sing*, she says."

Don lifted an eyebrow. "*Doctor* DeVries?"

Peter laughed uncertainly. "I know, she's no official *Doktor*, but I call her that. If she can heal my soul, she deserves that title."

Their heads darted around when they heard clopping. A handful of horsemen were approaching from the direction of downtown Grantville, cavalrymen by all appearances. Don rose and opened the holster at his belt.

"That's the Swedes." Peter also rose. "No danger."

Don frowned and looked quizzical.

"Half of Colonel Mackay's men are on leave at the moment, and some Swedish companies have taken over their duties. They've just arrived yesterday."

The leading horseman obviously scanned the letterboxes of the houses they passed. Peter scrutinized him from the distance. The man's motions seemed somehow familiar.

"Thomas!" Peter shouted and waved. "*Bist du das?*"

The man looked up, smiled, spurred his horse and jumped off in front of the Clements' front yard. Peter jumped over the stairs leading down and ran to the fence gate.

"Peter!" Thomas von Scharffenberg flinched when Peter hugged him.

"What's the matter?" Peter asked.

"It's a memory of Nuremberg." Thomas smiled painfully, opened his coat and showed Peter a large scar on his left shoulder. "High speed bullet. Took me out two minutes after the start of the American attack."

He looked to Don Clements who was slowly approaching. "But I don't blame them. Perhaps I would have been dead otherwise. My company had only a handful of survivors.

"And now I'm on the other side anyway. Major Thomas von Scharffenberg, Swedish Yellow Regiment. Nice to meet you."

"Master Sergeant Don Clements, NUS Army. Good afternoon, Major."

"And while we're at it," Peter added smiling. "Sergeant Peter Hagendorf, NUS Mounted Police. That means: I'm the one who gets the beer for you two."

"Not now," Thomas said grinning. "Unfortunately

I have to organize our camp. I just wanted to check where you live now. But we can meet tomorrow at our regiment's Lutheran field service. We don't have to pretend to be Catholics any longer." He grinned again. "You're also invited for lunch with both your families. Is that—hmmm—*okay* for you?"

"Of course, thank you," Don said.

"*Natürlich, danke*," Peter said.

"Sergeant Hanebuth!" Thomas then called one of his men.

"*Ja, Herr Major?*" a handsome blond German in his thirties answered with a clear voice.

Peter looked up and thought he had seen this long blond mane and heard this clear voice once before, but he couldn't nail it down.

"Send someone here tomorrow morning at nine. With a coach for...how many people, Master Sergeant?"

"Seven, all in all. Two kids," Don answered. "Denyse will be very pleased to finally attend a Lutheran service again."

"A coach for eight," Thomas concluded.

"*Jawohl, Herr Major, verstanden*," Hanebuth confirmed.

"We must hurry," Thomas said and shook hands. "Say hello to Anna from me. We'll see you tomorrow."

North of the Ring of Fire
The next day

"*Ein feste Burg ist unser Gott*," Peter sang along with some hundred cavalrymen and half as many civilians from Grantville. He looked to the sky, half to check that the weather would stay dry, half to internalize the first Lutheran service after—*oh my*—ten or more years.

Anna had been eager to attend the service, even with her belly heavily rounded in the last month of her pregnancy.

Suddenly he noticed Marie, who was standing between him and Anna, cling to Anna and start sobbing, flinching from time to time. He caught Anna's gaze, saw her shrug and realized that she also had no idea what concerned Marie.

Peter looked around, but saw nothing what could have been the reason of Marie's being upset. He listened, again noticed the clear trained voice of Sergeant Hanebuth leading the chanting, but heard nothing that could have concerned Marie.

Until the service ended, Marie had more or less settled down but was not willing to tell what had hurt her.

"Can we help?" Denyse asked.

"I don't think so," Peter answered. "At the moment she's like she was in the first weeks after we found her. She let nobody but Anna touch her, no man even near her. I hope it will pass."

"Let's get some stew, perhaps its smell and taste will calm her down."

Half an hour later Thomas had joined the group. Peter and he were indulging in reminiscences, telling Don how the morale had been in Wallenstein's camp after the Croat raid had so epically failed, while Don entertained them with a recap of the shootout in downtown Grantville.

"Oh, by the way," Peter said to Thomas. "Have

you already met Julie Sims-Mackay? A nice young lady, I must say."

Denyse was chatting with Anna when suddenly a shriek tore through the murmuring of a thousand voices. "*Where's Marie?*" Anna shouted in panic.

"She's gone to the horses," Hailey, Don's seven-year-old daughter said and pointed.

Peter and Don looked at each other, and then started to run.

When Marie returned her family's mess kits to the field kitchen, she could hear neighing from the stables behind it. Without consciously thinking about it, she directed her step to the wooden sheds that the Scot cavalrymen had erected during the last two years to give shelter to their steeds.

When she saw a newborn foal in a separate box with its dam, she kneeled down to absentmindedly caress and hug the tiny animal.

"Still fond of horses," she suddenly heard the sneering clear voice from her nightmares behind her.

Marie's head jerked around and she opened her mouth.

But before she could even take a breath to cry, Jasper Hanebuth's large hand was gagging her mouth. "*Kein Mucks*," he said. "Not even a loud breath or you'll be dead."

Marie's eyes were wide open. Horror had caught her. A horror which brought her instantly back to that day one year ago. To the moment when one mercenary after the other forced his way into her body. When she had squinted her eyes and hoped it would only be a bad dream.

When suddenly the same sneering clear voice said: "Leave her alive for me; I'll take her later, and care for the old ones first."

When afterwards the clear, trained voice started to sing "*Greif an das Werk mit Freuden,*" and she heard the same sound she knew from her father slaughtering a pig, but the death rattle afterwards hadn't been from a pig.

And then solacing darkness had fallen around her, but this time it didn't. And this time she kept her eyes open to never forget the face of the man who had slaughtered *Papa* and *Mama*.

While Jasper dragged her into an empty box and pushed her deep into the straw covering the floor and stinging into her back through her Sunday's blouse, she kept her eyes open and drunk in the long and dirty blond hair, the beautiful blue eyes with their lustful expression, the strong nose, obviously broken on several occasions, the wide grinning mouth with the yellow and black teeth and the stinking breath, the beautiful strong chin covered in a blond short shingled beard.

Jasper wondered that she didn't show a single move of resistance, even lifted her butt to let him tear her skirt down, didn't hinder him to rip up her blouse, but at the same time crossed her arms over her breasts. *I love shy women.*

He laughed sneeringly. "I haven't any interest in your baby-breasts, but..." and as it happened often in this situation a song came into his mind, one he had heard in Grantville. *Yeah, that suits here.* He started to sing. *"Kiss me baby one more time."*

He bent over her to do exactly this. She was still lying motionless below him and fascinated him with her nice brown eyes. He removed his hand from her mouth to get his tribute and approach her lips with his.

"*Nein*," Marie said loudly, and forcefully cut his throat with the knife she had hidden in her bodice.

Her father had already taught her to slaughter, before this man had killed him. And her father would have been proud for the exactness of this cut.

She laughed, when she saw the astonishment in his beautiful blue eyes, while the blood from his veins flooded her face and her chest. *Arteria carotis* and *vena jugularis externa*, she memorized the names from her biology class.

Now her laugh got more and more hysterical, when the situation registered in her mind. Louder and louder she laughed and cried and finally shrieked.

When Peter and Don ran into the stable, their hand guns ready, Marie was still lying under Hanebuth's corpse. She hadn't even tried to get free. She was crying and laughing.

"*Mama*, I've done it. *Papa*, I've taken revenge for you." Peter could understand, but then the cries started again.

Her eyes were wandering up and down and right and left, obviously not seeing what happened.

Peter and Don heaved the corpse from her body. No chance to take the knife out of Marie's hand.

Only seconds later Anna and Denyse arrived.

Anna analyzed the situation with one look. "*Raus mit euch*," she shouted. "Out, out. Let nobody come in."

Peter nodded.

"Yes, ma'am," Don said.

"And take this piece of shit with you," Anna added.

Peter and Don each took an arm and dragged the corpse out of the box.

Then Don closed the gate from the outside.

Peter looked down at his bloody hands. Then he looked down at the bloody corpse. He saw the deep cut which extended literally from one ear to the other. His own blood started to rush along his ears.

Another image blended over the dead body. The nearly identical memory of Marie's father, his throat gaping wide open. Then the image of Franz blended in, the tiny hole in his chest, the astonished expression on his dead face.

Peter didn't notice that in the meantime he was kneeling next to the corpse. He didn't notice that Thomas had arrived in the meantime, speaking with Don.

For the first time another image blended in, the image of faceless people Peter had killed during the ambush at the Lech. The image of the dying soldiers on the dusty plain near Leipzig. The image of men, women and children he had seen die before he was shot down in Magdeburg.

Peter didn't notice the tears running from his face and dripping onto the dead man's chest below him. Suddenly a hand touched his shoulder. He looked up with blurred sight, could just barely recognize Thomas standing next to him, looking down from his height.

"That could be me," he whispered hoarsely.

"Everyone can die in this merciless war," Thomas said flatly.

"No, you don't understand me." Peter shook his head. "That could be me having killed Marie's father and mother. That could be me having raped Marie. It's more for the lack of opportunity than for the lack of willingness.

"If I hadn't found Anna, if she hadn't stayed with me along this way..." He sighed deeply.

❧ Finale ❧

A stable north of Grantville
The same day

Suddenly the sobbing and murmur from the box changed its color. A groaning sound came through, but before the men at the outside could decide what to do, the gate opened and Denyse stuck her head out.

Peter rose and wiped the tears from his face.

"We need hot water, soap, and clean cloths, *subito*," Denyse said.

Peter's jaw dropped. "What's wrong?"

"Nothing," Denyse said. "But your loving wife has kept the fact from you that her waters broke just during the service."

Peter froze. *Broken waters?* "What does that mean?"

Denyse frowned. "Men! They always start the process without knowing how to bring it to an end. Your child is about to come." She turned and closed the gate.

Peter turned to Don. "What was that about water? Is that something bad?"

Don grinned. "Tell me, you have no idea about childbirth. Is that your first one?"

Peter shook his head. "We've lost three already. God may give them a happy resurrection. But I never attended a birth. I always came home from the daily chores and another one was there."

"Since Thomas has obviously sent a soldier off to get the things the women need," Don said smiling. "Let me introduce you to the wonderful world of childbirth."

Then the soldiers came running and delivered the ordered goods.

Half an hour later the gate opened again.

"Wanna see her?" Denyse asked.

Peter stormed into the box.

Anna was sitting on a saddle blanket with a big grin on her face, Marie was huddled to her, smiling and caressing a small bundle in her arms. When she saw Peter she rose and approached him.

"What's her name, Dad?" she asked when she handed him the bundle.

Peter looked into the tiny red face of his daughter.

Before he could speak he had to clear his throat. And again.

"We wanted to call her Barbara. But I think I've got a better name for her." He paused and looked into his wife's eyes.

"I think we should call her *Hoffnung*."

Author's Notes:

When the law enforcement authorities in Hannover arrested Jasper (or Jaspar, the north German spelling of Caspar) Hanebuth—born in 1608 in Groß-Buchholz near Hannover, son of a rich farmer, Swedish mercenary, and a horse trader by profession—and questioned him on November 30, 1652, to be charged for stealing horses in Medefeld, they got no testimony from him. As it was custom they contacted the law faculty at the university and the professionals there agreed that a "peinliche Befragung" was appropriate, since several witnesses swore they recognized him.

On December 16 they started. First they showed him the tools of torture and questioned him again, but he still swore he had bought the concerned animals from some unknown men.

The torturer then dressed him in "Spanish boots" and he soon started to whine and cry for mercy. The judges who took his confession were rather astonished when he not only admitted having stolen the horses in question, but also started to confess one murder after the other. Finally they had a list of nineteen murders and ten horse thefts, which most likely was only the tip of the iceberg.

One of his victims was his long-standing *"Räuberbraut"* (robber's bride) Marie whom he had captured in 1632 near Ingolstadt and who afterwards fell in love with him and took part in several of his crimes.

He shot her because he suspected her to be pregnant from one of his buddies.

His passion of singing hymns while killing is also documented in the court papers. *"Greif an das Werk mit Freuden, wozu mich Gott bescheiden in meinem Amt und Stand"* seemed to be his favorite.

Since he had committed these murders during the Thirty Years' War, the judges in Hannover were not able to verify his confessions. But nevertheless after long hither and tither when he revoked his confession and then confessed again he was executed by the wheel on February 4, 1653.

It was a very common mode of execution at that time. The delinquent was first hit with heavy clubs or even with a wagon wheel. After his bones were broken they either delivered a coup de grace by gently removing his head with a sword or (for bad crimes) bound his now flexible body to a wheel and let him simply die.

The last execution in that style occurred in Prussia in 1841.

The court papers of Jasper Hanebuth's trial still exist in Hannover; the town has even named a street after him—no comment.

Mass murderers appeared after the Thirty Years' War, hence my notice of PTSD. Melchior Hedloff, called Schütze-Melcher from Breslau, was also questioned in the year 1653, and confessed *two hundred and fifty-one* murders—what a memory.

All events in this story up to the battle at Rain am Lech are historical. As well as shooting Gustav

Adolph's white horse near Ingolstadt, which is still on display there.

Peter Hagendorf's diary was found by chance in the manuscript storage of the Prussian State Library in Berlin in the year 1993.

He had taken notes during the nineteen years of his mercenary life, which took him over fifteen thousand miles through Germany on foot, then bought a stack of paper in 1649 and wrote down all his memories.

The author was unknown at first, but Professor Jan Peters from Potsdam University could find the birth certificate of his later daughter Margaretha in the archive of the town Pappenheim, where his name was given.

A document from Mühlhausen, where Peter managed the supply of wounded soldiers in December, 1641, gave another proof.

Jan Peters' book containing the complete transcript of the diary together with a "translation" into proofread German has the title *"Ein Söldnerleben im Dreißigjährigen Krieg."* (A Mercenary's Life in the Thirty Years' War). It was republished in 2012. The citations up to the Battle of the Alte Veste (excluding Julie Sims' role in the Battle at the Lech) are taken from this book.

The diary is the source for several master theses in Germany; the one which thoroughly explains the text is available as a download in German.

The diary is also the source for one episode of the TV-mini-series "Der Dreißigjährige Krieg" by Bavarian Television and a third of an episode (14:00-30:00) of "Wir Europäer."

OTL Peter Hagendorf was not ordered to Nuremberg. He stayed within Bavaria, marching from town to town, and waiting for something to happen.

Anna Stadlerin from Traunstein, Upper Bavaria, bore four children, and died in 1633 together with the last of them in Munich.

In 1635, Peter married Anna Buchlerin: they had six children; only two of them lived until their adulthood.

After the end of the Thirty Years' War Peter settled in Memmingen, and could apparently not manage to get back into his prior civilian life (he perhaps had been a miller before) but stayed mercenary, soldier and watchman. And it seems he had developed alcoholism, since he wrote down several bad accidents at that time wounding him.

As for the naming of the units: The Germans called a unit from several combined companies a "Gewalthaufen" (force heap). Then the French term "bataille" (battle) came into use, later changed to "bataillon" (battalion) and in the late seventeenth century institutionalized as a defined part of a regiment.

But in the Thirty Years' War the companies were combined by temporary orders, the French term being "ordonnance" (German Ordonnanz, English ordinance). Several different ordinances were used, the best-known being the Spanish Ordinance, also called Catholic or Burgundy Ordinance on the HRE side and the Dutch or Swedish Ordinance on the other.

Within the Spanish Ordinance the troops were grouped as "Gevierthaufen" (pike square, also see illustration of the battle at Breitenfeld), these had the Spanish name "tercio," which is used within the 1632 series.

Gold Fever

Herbert Sakalaucks

Outside Odense, Denmark, March 1636

Gold! Gold! Gold
Gold Fields Discovered in Newfoundland!
Free land for prospectors.
Guaranteed by the Crown.
Limitless wealth for simple work.
Ships sail monthly from Copenhagen
Special rates for families.

Hudson Bay Company

"See here Marta! It says that there are fields of gold for the taking. We won't have to spend our lives working day and night to put food on the table. A new land, free land, and no landlords." Lars was beaming, a faraway look in his eyes.

Marta gently took the flyer from her husband's grasp. She'd seen this look before; when they'd left

Stockholm to work the fishing boat, right after they were married. Later in Gdansk, when the bill collectors were hounding them and Lars had chosen to flee rather than face prison. Again and again, the dream of fast wealth or an easy job had driven Lars to look to the next town. She studied the flyer. It was printed on fine paper and the print was much sharper than normally appeared on flyers. It did say that the king was guaranteeing it, so it must be true. Better to bow to the inevitable now than delay and put up with Lars' whining and still have to give in later. Lars had no experience as a miner, but he learned new jobs quickly. She gave a silent snort. He'd had a lot of experience in that area. There was nothing holding them here. They'd rented the farm when the previous tenant died. Now it was nearly as dead as he'd been. They were always a little behind on their rent. Money was tight but they could sell the three cows. The fine print listed the cost for passage and the sale should bring enough to pay the passage for a family of five, if the flyer was true. The ship pictured looked sturdy enough and should provide a safe passage. "If you think we should, I'll go. I'm sure the children can adjust to the new land. There's not much here for them."

Lars swept her off her feet. "No man was ever as blessed with as good a wife as you! I'll start packing in the morning."

Marta started to ask why wait until the morning when she noticed the gleam in Lars' eyes. *Ah well, he always seems to be inspired by change. A wife could do much worse, and when he's good, he's really good.* She fought back a giggle as he led her by her hand to the bedroom.

South of Baie Verte, Newfoundland
Late September 1636

Marta added a dash of salt and flour to the deer steaks cooking over the open hearth fire. The fieldstone and cast-iron grill made for a tasty flavor for the meat, as long as the weather was dry. Dinners were cold when it rained. The rhythmic sounds of chopping near the stream just served to emphasize the worries that had been building over the past weeks. They had arrived at the *gold field* in June and had staked out a claim along a stream some miles south of the Company's land. Calling it a *gold field* had taken some imagination on the part of someone. When they'd landed in Thomasville, they'd bought supplies at a store that proclaimed that it could give them the secrets to finding gold, along with the tools. When they were done paying for the tools, the owner gave Lars a two minute lesson on how to work streams for gold. That was it. Fields of gold were never mentioned. Still, Lars had been certain this would be a perfect site for them to work. He set up operations, along with their two boys, and had built a rough sluice box the second day there. He'd found some color almost immediately. Housing had followed slowly, as discovering gold had driven out all other concerns. Two canvas tents had served until the trees started to change color. The color had also started to decrease in the sluice at about the same time, but Lars was certain that they were close to a big strike. That was when Marta insisted that Lars finish building a cabin before the cold weather set in. The sound of a tree falling pulled Marta back to her cooking. The steaks were in need of turning so she speared them with a knife and flipped them. Anna was playing with some pine cones by the tent flap, so Marta yelled, "Dinner will be ready soon. Go tell Papa and the boys to come and clean up. The steaks should be ready by the time they get here." Anna set two more pine cones on her pile and then skipped off to pass on her mother's message.

Marta studied the meat, trying to gauge just the right time to remove them from the flames. Lars liked his meat well done, but not burnt. The open flames were notoriously fickle, the fat helping to speed up the cooking. Sounds of Anna's return helped settle the decision. Marta skewered the steaks and piled them on the waiting platter. As Anna approached, Marta shooed her ahead to hold back the door flap. The rough-built table and benches were centered in the large room. Overhead, the canvas roof hung limp against the rafters. "I do hope they can get the cross pieces cut and raised tomorrow. I'm tired of living under a leaky roof. The weather's held too good for too long. One of these days our luck is going to run out. Snow is not too far off."

Just then, the door flap flew back and Michel and Augustus raced in. "I won!" Michel crowed. "You get to clean up tonight."

Augustus gave him a shove. "Not fair! You pushed me." He turned to his mother, "Tell him it's not fair."

Marta surveyed the two, panting boys. "I seem to recall neither one of you cleaned up last night. So tonight you both wash up and scrub the grill too."

Off to the side, Lars gave a shrug before either boy could appeal. "You heard your mother. Now sit down and behave."

After the grace was said, Marta asked between bites, "How did it go today?"

Lars paused a moment to swallow first. "We've got all but two of the trees cut down along the stream edge. We'll cut those in the morning and then start splitting them for roof poles. Once we get the roof finished, the boys and I will head for the trading post to get our winter supplies."

Marta gave him a jaundiced stare. "I hope the gold you've found is enough. It could be a very lean winter if you don't get the price you're counting on. We definitely haven't struck it rich like you said we would."

"I'm sure we're close to the big one. Once we get these trees cleared, we should be able to sluice out the old stream bed. I've got a good feeling about it." He reached across and jabbed the last steak and started to lift it. Michel stared at it. Auggie was a little more circumspect in his appeal, but both boys were definitely still hungry. Feeling guilty, Lars plopped it back on the platter, cut it in two, and gave each boy a piece. "Growing boys need their food. Make sure you wipe up the juices with your mother's bread."

Later, after the children were asleep, and as they were lying there, sweat stained from their exertions, Marta asked softly, "Do you really think you're close to a strike? If we can't get at least the minimum supplies we've discussed, I'm scared that we could starve if the winter lasts too long." She'd finally managed to voice the fears that had been haunting her dreams.

Lars turned to face her, "I promise, if we can't get enough supplies for the gold we have, I know we have enough gold to buy passage back to Thomasville. I can always get a job there in the foundry to keep us fed. Now go to sleep and quit worrying." He gave her the grin that always managed to bring a smile to her face, even when she was mad at him. She sighed and pulled her nightcap down firmly. He gave her a quick peck on the check and rolled over on his side. In moments he was snoring, the long day's work exacting its toll. Marta stared up at the canvas roof, praying he was right.

The next morning dawned cloudy and windy. After rekindling the cook fire, Marta checked the hens for eggs and then started making breakfast. As Lars and the boys wolfed down the meal, she pointed toward the sky, "I think the weather is finally changing. Getting those roof poles done can't come any too soon." Lars nodded and then wiped his plate clean. All three males hurried out, to avoid listening to Marta going on about the roof.

As soon as breakfast was over and the dishes cleaned, Marta went to the small stores shed to bring back a canister of flour. A gust of wind nearly bowled her over as she approached the shed. A quick glance back showed that the cabin's roof canvas was still in place. *That would be all we need with weather coming.* She needed to concentrate on baking today. The men had finished the last of the bread for breakfast. If the weather was going to turn, she needed to get some loaves made before the rains came. Anna helped her get the bowls and utensils out and add the ingredients as she'd been taught. As Marta was kneading the dough, the steady sounds of chopping axes ceased, but instead of the expected loud tree crash, she heard a shrill scream. She tossed the dough into a bowl. Even an emergency could wait for a second to save the precious food. As she threw the door flap back, she could see Augustus running as hard as he could back from the stream.

As he spotted her, he screamed, "It's Papa! The tree split and landed on him. Michel and I tried, but we couldn't get it off him. Please hurry, it looks bad!" He grabbed his mother's arm and tried to pull her faster. He had blood on his hands.

She shook him off. "Let me get cloths for a dressing. If it's as bad as you say, we'll need them." Sprinting back inside, she grabbed a nightshirt off the bed. When she got back outside, Augustus was frantically bouncing up and down, his fists clenched.

"Hurry, hurry, Michel said he might die!" The tears were rolling down his checks as he ran back.

When they reached the clearing, Marta stopped dead in her tracks. If anything, it was worse than Augustus had described. The tree limb had indeed split, but it appeared that Lars had tried to push off with his axe as it fell toward him and the axe had struck him as well. The front of his shirt was drenched in blood and the limb had him pinned to the ground. Michel was trying to roll the limb off, but the branches were keeping it in place. Marta looked around, frantic for inspiration. She spotted the previous day's work pile, with the cleared branches. "Auggie, bring me two large branches. We'll use them as levers."

She knelt next to Lars. His eyes were open and he tried to speak. "Just plain stupid luck," he managed to whisper. "Wind gust struck as the tree started to fall and split it. The boys were right in its path, so I tried to push it aside. The other tree twisted it and it came back on me instead. Looks like the roof might have to wait a day or two." He coughed from the exertion and blood came to his lips.

Marta fought back the tears. "You hush now! The roof can wait. I love you. Don't you dare leave me!" She was terrified. He spasmed in her arms and went limp. She realized their dream was gone. "Lars, why did we have to come here? No gold is worth your life." She broke down and wept uncontrollably.

The boys came up, branches in hand. Michel realized what had happened and dropped his branch to hug his mother. Augustus stared down, trying to wish his father awake. When it finally struck him that his father was dead, Auggie slumped to his knees, crying softly. After what seemed an eternity, Marta gave a shuddering sob and braced herself, "We have to get the tree off him. Help me with these branches, boys." They needed to do something and this was the best she could come up with. Rolling some stones near the limb, the boys stuck their branches under the limb and pushed down. The limb rose slightly, and Marta was able to drag Lars' body out from under. Straightening the body, she took Michel and Auggie by their shoulders, "Go see to your sister. Don't tell her what happened. I'll be there in a minute." She used the nightshirt to wipe the blood from Lars' mouth. Shock was setting in and she needed to be strong for the children. Looking at the body of her husband she asked, "What do I do now? You always were the one with a plan. Now you've gone and left us in the wilderness with no house and winter coming." Even in death, he had a slight smile.

They had to pack up and hope they were in time to catch the last trading ship of the season. She rose, turned away and trudged slowly back to the cabin, dreading the thought of having to dig a grave with the children nearby.

The next ten days were a living hell for the survivors. Marta managed to get the grave dug, but broke down when she finally realized that there was no minister to say a blessing on the grave. The best she could do was a simple stick and twine cross that would not even last the winter. The boys helped, but Anna could not understand why papa was not coming with them. Marta finished packing up the last of their food supplies and looked around the clearing. Another storm seemed imminent, so she hurried the children on their way north, toward the trading post on the bay. Three cold, wet days later, they finally broke through the brush and reached the shoreline. Marta scanned the shore trying to spot the trading post.

Suddenly Michel let out a whoop and pointed toward the west. "There's smoke. I think we should head toward it."

"You've got sharp eyes. Help your sister over these rocks. We should reach there before sundown." All during the struggle north, one worry had weighed her soul down. *Would they get there before the ship? If they were stranded at the trading post, there might not be room for them. Their food was not enough to survive the winter.*

As they rounded the last point, Marta could see a group of people camped along the shore by the post. *More returnees. It seems we're not the only ones returning to Thomasville. At least the ship hasn't been here yet.* They were almost to the walls of the post before a small boy spotted them and started pointing.

They were met by two older women and three men, who asked their names and why they were there. The trading post's owner, who was known simply as Hunter, stuck his head out a window to see what the commotion was about. "Another arrival, I see. What brings you here?"

Marta had dreaded this moment, but had vowed to keep the tale simple and concise. "My husband was killed in an accident. We have to return to Thomasville. We were just finishing our cabin when he died. Without a roof over our heads and winter coming on, I had no choice."

"I hope you don't expect charity. I only have enough room for me here. That's why everyone is camped out. You're lucky. The last ship of the season is two days overdue. That last storm must have delayed her." Nods from the others confirmed his statements.

Marta shucked off her pack. "We have canvas for a tent, so we won't have to impose on you. Can we set up here on the south side of the post? Hopefully, we'll get some shelter from the winds off the bay." The trader waved her on, not bothering to lend a hand, but also not denying her permission. The youngest of the three men walked over and offered to help. In talking to him, Marta learned that he was just waiting for supplies he'd ordered. He'd be making a couple of trips back to his camp, trying to beat the weather. When Marta described where they'd lived, it turned out he had been their neighbor, just three miles from where they had settled. They continued to chat as he helped her set up the tent. Within an hour, the family was bedded down for the night.

Two days later, a sail was sighted at daybreak,

coming up over the northern horizon. The overdue coastal trader dropped anchor later that afternoon. Her captain came ashore with two boats. Both were weighed down with supplies. Hunter met them at the water's edge. "What do we have here Captain? It looks like more supplies than I ordered. What do I do with them?"

Captain Nordqvist was brusque and ignored the question, "I need to sail with the tide. Please see to the unloading." He nodded toward the prospector who had been waiting on his supplies. "That gentleman ordered and paid for the extra canned food when we landed this past spring. It's his worry how he plans to get them all to his diggings." He gave the expectant passengers a quick glance. "I suppose these are this year's fools who want to return to civilization. I should have space for them, if they aren't picky. Do they have the fare?"

"As long as it hasn't changed, they do." Hunter hoisted the pouch he'd brought along. "Gold dust for all."

Nordqvist looked at the pouch with a thoughtful expression. "So many dreams in such a small pouch." He walked over to the waiting group. "Get onboard now! Don't bother with any fancy luggage, just the essentials. We don't have a lot of room and you'll all have to share a hold for this last stretch. The cabins are already filled. We should be in Thomasville by Sunday."

One man asked timidly, "How many days is that? I've lost track of what today is."

Nordqvist shook his head in disgust. "Six days, you poor excuse for a prospector. Now quit jabbering and get moving!"

Within the hour, everyone was loaded and the two boats shoved off. Marta stared at the receding shoreline, sorrow etched on her face. One of the women leaned over. "I hope that young man survives. I think snow is on the way soon. My knee says so." Marta began to answer, but the boat gave a lurch as a wave struck and her stomach reminded her about her penchant for seasickness.

Captain Nordqvist missed his estimate for making port by five days. The weather steadily worsened as he beat to the east. In the hold, it was a nightmare for the passengers come to life. The smell, as seasickness struck, was overpowering. No one was allowed on deck, for fear of being washed overboard. Slop buckets remained below and were tossed overboard when the crew could find the time and a break in the weather. Marta had made some hardtack before leaving the cabin, and the family subsisted on that for the entire voyage. Two days before docking, the storm abated and the passengers staggered on deck for relief. Marta was uncertain what she faced when they landed and finally worked up the courage to question the captain.

Surprisingly, he was much more civil than when they had boarded. "I apologize for my temper when we met. I feared a storm was brewing and I was right. If we hadn't sailed when we did, we might not have made it here. I have some time to talk now. To answer your questions, the town has grown over the past year like a weed. The foundry is working full blast and housing is tight. Do you have a trade that you can work at? Skilled workers are in demand."

Marta blinked at the question. She'd been married to Lars for fifteen years and kept his house and raised a family. She'd never been apprenticed and the only work she could remember was on her father's dairy farm. "I was a milk maid when I was a young girl. Since then, I've been a wife and mother."

"Well, there is shortage of women. Maybe you'll find something you can do." He raised a knuckle to his cap and turned away, a smirk on his face. The meaning of his comment was unmistakable.

Fuming silently, Marta vowed she'd die before she turned to that trade. Spotting the boys skylarking on deck, fully recovered from their ordeal in the hold, gave her pause. It was fine to vow death before dishonor, but what about the children? Her dreams were troubled that night with thoughts of leering, drunken men.

The harbor was crowded with ships. Workmen could be seen setting stonework for the fortresses at the harbor entrance. As they approached the only open pier, Marta could see the smoke rising from the nearby steel furnaces. Along the harbor front colliers were unloading coal for the coking ovens. Streams of dust-covered laborers hauled coal sacks on their backs from smaller ships to waiting wagons, while larger loads were swung over to be emptied by cranes in large bins. Everywhere, there was a sense of prosperity. The ship glided up to the dock and lines were tossed to waiting dockworkers to hold the ship fast. Marta gathered the children and adjusted her pack. She wanted to be among the first off. If there was housing available, she wanted to beat her fellow passengers to it. As soon as the crew finished securing the boarding plank, she led the children off.

The storm had cleared the air and the sun shone warm through the crisp air. Marta walked down the street, studying the shops and houses as they went.

Some of the taverns and eating houses looked promising for work, but housing was the first concern. The captain's comment on tight quarters meant there might not be rooms available. As the family worked its way out of the business area, rough-built houses started to appear. All looked to be inhabited and nowhere was there a sign saying rooms for rent. She stopped a number of passersby and inquired if they knew of any housing available. The answers were about evenly divided between rude comments and laughs. Two older women did say that they knew of nothing available. As they neared the edge of town, Marta was getting desperate. They had to have shelter! It was beginning to look as if they might have been better off staying at the cabin. At least there they would have had walls and a floor. Damn Lars for running out on life again and leaving her holding the bag! She'd always loved him, but it was starting to sink in that the life he provided for her and the children had left a lot to be desired.

As she looked up from her bitter ruminations, Marta realized she'd paused in front of a small church. In desperation she climbed the stairs and tried the door. It swung open, revealing a single, open room with rough benches. Near the front, a man dressed in a priest's robe was tending the candles by the altar. Realizing it was a Catholic church, Marta turned to leave, but was stopped by a question from the priest.

"Do you need help, my child? You appear troubled."

"I'm not Catholic, Father. We'll just be on our way."

"This is the Lord's house, daughter. All who need help are welcome here. Tell me what's troubling you." The kindly look in his eyes gave Marta pause. She definitely needed help for her family. Making up her mind, she herded the children inside.

"We just returned from the north and need shelter. My husband was killed in an accident and we wouldn't have survived the winter there. Do you know of any housing and jobs that I might find here in town?"

The priest frowned. "There are rooms available for single adults, but places large enough for four people... I don't know of any. You will probably have to farm out the children to a number of families." He paused. "Ah—wait. Speaking of farms, a thought comes to me. One of my parishioners has a new dairy farm a short way out of town. He recently lost his wife in childbirth and is trying to care for his new daughter and the farm. He has living quarters over the barn. It's not fancy but it's warm in winter. I'm sure he could find some space for you and your children, if you can do farm chores."

Marta's jaw dropped. "Father, I was raised on a dairy farm. I was milking cows when I was six years old. Of course I'm interested." As soon as she agreed Marta realized that she hadn't even thought about Lars before answering. Their dreams had always been his, maybe now she needed to work on some for herself.

"Come along then. We might as well make the introductions all at once." The small procession trooped out of the church and started along the path leading to the nearby headland.

Thomasville, Newfoundland, May 1637

Marta stepped out of the butcher shop, the soup bones wrapped in paper and clutched tightly under

her arm. Her gaze swept the hills that led down to
the harbor. The warm, spring weather was bringing a
carpet of flowers to the fields outside of Thomasville.
It had also brought the coastal traders into port with
the first wave of prospectors and trappers returning
from successful winters up north. She spotted a small
crowd around the Company's assay office, gathered
around a bearded prospector. She wandered over to
find out what the commotion was about.

"Look here, friends! See what the fields up north
are growing!" The prospector held up a huge gold nugget. "I found this just as the snows hit. I was caught
by a storm while trying to bring in my last cache of
supplies and had to seek shelter. I stumbled across
an empty, half built cabin close to my claim and I
waited the storm out there. By the second day, I had
to go to the nearby stream for water. I found a tree
toppled over, its roots exposed and rain washed by the
weather. At first I thought I was dreaming, but there
it was, just shining in the roots. I just had to reach
over and pluck it out. The hardest part was waiting
until the snows cleared so I could return." He held
onto the nugget firmly while he showed it off. Total
strangers shoved through the crowd to catch a glimpse
and pound him on the back in congratulations. The
prospector finally had enough of the attention and
called out, "I've been waiting for a drink all winter.
Come on over to the tavern, the drinks are on me!"
The crowd surged across the street and stacked up
by the door.

Marta suddenly realized who the prospector was
and where he had found the nugget. He was the
young man who had helped her set up the tent at the

trading post. The tree where he'd found the nugget must have been the tree next to where Lars had died. Lars had been right. He had been close to striking it rich. Her thoughts were interrupted as a tall, blond man tried to force his way upstream through the crowd heading for free drinks. She recognized the golden hair instantly. Her new husband must have finished up his negotiations with the Company's meat buyer early and was coming to meet her for the rest of the buying trip in town. She may not have struck it rich in the gold fields, but she had found a golden treasure in town that was her dream.

Hide Trouble from Mine Eyes

David Carrico

Magdeburg
July 1635

Gotthilf Hoch, sergeant in the Magdeburg *Polizei*, jumped to one side as the patrolman he was standing beside turned and puked, splashing the contents of his stomach right where Gotthilf's feet had been not a second before.

"Don't get that on the corpse," the newly appointed coroner, Dr. Paul Schlegel, growled from where he was crouched beside the victim.

The patrolman choked and hurriedly backed away to fall to his hands and knees and helplessly hurl another wave of vomit onto the ground. It sounded as if he was heaving up everything he'd eaten in the last two weeks.

It had been the doctor's previous comments as he examined the body of the young woman that had occasioned the patrolman's spasms. "Hmm," he'd said matter-of-factly, "someone has cut both her *trentono-mous sicogliceneral* from her head."

"Her what?" Byron Chieske, up-timer lieutenant for the Magdeburg *Polizei* and Gotthilf's partner on the detective squad, asked from where he stood on the other side of the victim.

"Her eyeballs," Dr. Schlegel had responded, peeling back one of her eyelids and pointing his lantern's light to reveal a congealing pool of blood in a raw red eye socket. That was when the patrolman who had discovered the body and had been hovering at Gotthilf's elbow since the detective team had arrived lost it.

Gotthilf had seen a fair number of dead bodies during his days first on the city watch and later on the Magdeburg police force that Mayor Gericke had formed to provide up-time style policing in the capital city of the USE. Nonetheless, he felt his own stomach lurching in sympathy with the patrolman. For some reason, though, when he looked across at his partner and saw that Byron's face was just as pale as the cold sweat on his forehead told him his was, that helped him settle down a bit.

"So, uh, how long has she been dead, Doc?" Byron asked after a big swallow.

The coroner placed one gloved hand on the victim's head and attempted to move it. "Hmm. She's well-progressed toward full *rigor mortis*. Given the temperature last night, that means she's probably been dead for at least six hours, maybe longer. I'll be able to get a better estimate after I get her back to the morgue and check my reference books. And I'll confirm the cause of death as well, but from reading the studies that Dr. Nichols gave me when he heard

I had become the coroner, I'll hazard a guess at the moment that it was strangulation." He reached down and pulled her collar aside. "These ligature marks are strong and deep."

Dr. Schlegel stood. He was of middling height and build, with short hair, a close-trimmed beard, and sharp eyes that peered out from under bristly eyebrows. He walked over to talk to his attendants for a moment. Gotthilf and his partner both looked to the police photographer, who nodded back in confirmation that he had taken all the necessary photographs.

Gotthilf knelt where the coroner had been, joined a moment later by Byron. They took a good close look at the poor woman who had died by violence during the night.

Wisps of light brown hair escaped from under her cap and floated in the breath of the early morning breeze. She lay seemingly calmly, body straight, hands crossed on her chest. Gotthilf looked down. Her clothing was straight and neatly arranged. He looked across at Byron, and when he caught his eye, pointed to her skirt. Byron nodded. He'd obviously had the same thought—at the moment, at least, this didn't appear to be a sexual assault.

Gotthilf reached out his gloved hand and turned one of her hands, looking closely at the fingers. "Doesn't look like she fought much. Her nails aren't torn."

"Yep," Byron replied. "We'll have to wait for the doc's autopsy report to see if there's anything under them, though."

"Yah."

Gotthilf laid the hand down, and reluctantly raised his eyes to her face. The sight of the concave eyelids sinking into the violated eye sockets caused his stomach to knot up again, but he forced himself to look beyond that. Not a girl; her skin had some pock marks and was somewhat blotchy and rough. Of course, some of the unevenness may have been due to the paleness of death. Her features were regular. There were the beginnings of lines at the outer corners of her eyes. So, early to mid-twenties, maybe. Not beautiful; not even pretty.

"What do you think?" Byron asked.

Gotthilf stood and looked up at his partner across the corpse. "A working woman," he said. "Plain clothing, somewhat worn but still pretty neat, well mended in a couple of places. Sound shoes. No jewelry. Obvious callouses on her hands. Someone's housekeeper or maid, maybe."

"Was she killed here?"

He looked around the alley where the body had been found. Pointing at the ground, Gotthilf said, "No real signs of a struggle here. No drag marks, either. It looks like she was either carried here or walked here under her own power before she was killed."

"And either way," Byron concluded, "her killer rather neatly arranged her body." The up-timer shook his head. "That's not good."

"Yah. If she walked here, she must have known her attacker or she would have struggled."

Byron waved at the coroner's attendants. They pulled their rolling body cart over, bent and hoisted the body in one smooth motion and placed it on the cart.

As they wheeled it away, Byron squatted after a moment, pointed to spots on the ground, and called out "Hey, Doc." When the coroner stepped over, he continued, "Is that about the right amount of blood to have leaked out if the eyes were cut out here after she died?"

Dr. Schlegel fingered his short beard as he considered the bloodstains. "Perhaps. There certainly wouldn't be much more than that." He frowned. "There wasn't any blood on her face, though."

"Maybe the killer wiped it off," Byron said. The doctor raised his eyebrows. "This guy went to some pains to neatly arrange her body. If he was that obsessive and tidy, he might well have cleaned her face as well."

"I'll test for that," the coroner said. He started to turn, then faced back to them and said, "Guy? You assume the killer is a man?"

"Oh, yeah," Byron said with a twist to his mouth. "We've had almost four hundred years more than you have to study murderers and their patterns. Not one chance in a thousand—maybe not in ten thousand—this was done by a woman."

"Indeed," the coroner murmured, and an expression of loathing crossed his face. "Then I hope you find him soon, so he can be executed and buried in a potter's field. This was heinous."

"We're on it, Doc," Byron assured him.

The coroner followed his attendants out to their wagon and clambered up to the seat to head for the morgue. "You're that sure it was a man?" Gotthilf asked his partner as the others drove off.

"Oh, yeah," Byron breathed. "A man with a very sick and twisted mind. I can feel it, Gotthilf. This is one very sick bastard, and we'd better catch him soon, or he may kill again."

"Agreed."

The two of them looked around the alley for additional information: anything that could be evidence. The problem with the hard-packed dirt streets and alleys in the Greater Magdeburg area, Gotthilf thought, was that in the absence of a recent rain they allowed no impressions. A nice patch of soft dirt or mud, there would have been shoe prints. Even if it had been paved with flagstones, concrete, or the up-timers' oiled and packed pea gravel, it could have shown something. But the hard-packed dirt gave nothing to the detectives.

After a few minutes, Gotthilf moved back to the rope that had been strung up between movable posts to block access to the alley. He carefully looked over the crowd gathered around the mouth of the alley. It opened out onto Kristinstrasse, one of the busiest of the major streets in the new city. Mostly women, he noticed, with a few apprentices and a passing pastor who slowed down to look as he was walking by. Nothing caught his eye; no one caught his attention.

After a careful study, he beckoned to the patrolman. Pale in the face after emptying his gut, the young man still had wit and energy enough to move smartly to where he waited.

Gotthilf took a good look at the patrolman in the early morning light. He was the scrawniest and possibly the ugliest man Gotthilf could remember ever seeing, with a beak of a nose, a somewhat receding clean-shaven chin, and a prominent Adam's apple. Almost that was enough to hide the intelligence that shone from his eyes. Gotthilf reminded himself, though, that Captain Reilly would not hire stupid men, and that he, of all men, should not judge a man by his stature or appearance.

But Gotthilf couldn't help making the silent observation that if there was ever a face that deserved to be hidden by a beard, it was this one. He wondered why it was bare.

He pulled out the latest of his many notebooks, flipped it open, and poised his pencil. "You are..." he began. The police force had grown enough that it was hard for him to keep track of all the men who weren't in the detective squad.

"Daniel Kierstede," the patrolman furnished his last name.

Ah. A bit of an eastern accent. Kierstede may have come from near Silesia. No surprise, that. Most of the patrolmen were not native Magdeburgers. Of course, something like two-thirds or more of the city residents hadn't survived the Sack of Magdeburg in 1631, so the repopulation and massive expansion of the city had drawn heavily on people from all over central and eastern Europe. German speakers from every direction of the compass, plus the odd Pole, Hungarian, and Rumanian walked the streets of the city. That was reflected in the makeup of the *Polizei* as well.

"Night shift?"

"Yes, Sergeant."

"How long have you been patrolling this stretch?"

Kierstede thought for a moment. "Since a week ago last Tuesday."

"Have you seen anything like this before, Kierstede?"

"My God, no, Sergeant!" If anything, the patrolman's pallor deepened and tinged with green in the growing early morning light. "Not even in The Chain have I seen something like this."

Gotthilf pursed his lips as he jotted a note. If Kierstede had been part of the patrols that watched over the most notorious tavern in the city, then despite his seeming youth and his size he was no rookie, as Byron would put it. Only the toughest, most alert, and sharpest of the patrolmen walked that part of Old Magdeburg, the city inside the walls, especially at night.

"But you've dealt with dead people before, right?" Gotthilf asked.

"Yes, Sergeant. I was part of the crew that had to break up that big fight at The Chain a couple of months back; the one that left three of the crowd dead and two more crippled, and cost old Johann Schwenkel his left eye and invalided him out of the *Polizei*."

Gotthilf nodded. That had been a bad night. Kierstede moved up in his estimation.

"It's one thing to deal with men beating each other to death, or cutting other men's throats," the patrolman continued. "But I was standing by Schwenkel when the knife cut his eye. I made sure the bastard that did it went down, then I turned to help him. The blood and the eye humor on his face, on my hands..." Kierstede swallowed convulsively. "And then to find a woman done to death like this, with her... eyes..." He swallowed again.

"As you say," Gotthilf murmured. "But what I meant was, have you found bodies laid out like this in this patrol area before today."

"No, Sergeant."

Gotthilf continued interviewing the patrolman,

teasing out the information he wanted. Unfortunately, there wasn't that much more information that Kierstede could provide. The body hadn't been there when he made his previous pass down the street; it was there in the pre-dawn hour. No, he hadn't seen anything else unusual. No, he hadn't seen anyone else in the area. That hour of the morning, he very seldom saw anyone except other patrolmen. No, he hadn't done more than touch her neck to see if she was alive. No, he hadn't moved the body or anything else in the immediate area. Yes, he had whistled for his patrol sergeant as soon as he had realized what he had found.

After going through everything with Kierstede twice, Gotthilf closed the notebook and slipped it and his pencil back into the inside pocket of his jacket. "Good work, Kierstede. Keep a very sharp eye out now, and if you see anything unusual on your patrols, anything that seems odd or out of place, bring it to either me or Lieutenant Chieske immediately. Also if you think of anything else. And don't be surprised if we come back to you later with more questions."

"You think whoever did this is still around, then?"

Kierstede *was* sharp, Gotthilf noted. "Yes."

A determined look settled onto the patrolman's face. "Count on me, Sergeant."

"We will."

The next day the file and mail clerk dropped a folder in the In-box on Gotthilf's desk. He ignored it until he completed reading and correcting the typed version of his last report, which he put back in the typist's work folder and put in his Out-box. Hopefully Manfred the typist would get it right this time.

That done, he reached out and picked up the folder. Flipping it open, he was faced with photographs of the dead woman. He flipped through them and sorted the close-up of her face to the top. No one looked good in the monochrome pictures the police photographer took, but she definitely looked bad.

Gotthilf looked over at Byron's desk and held up the photo. "Pictures of the dead woman from the photographer."

"Good," Byron grunted, looking up from reports he was reviewing and signing. "Any word yet on who she is?"

Before Gotthilf could respond, one of the patrolmen assigned to watch the front desk entered, followed by a young woman. He led her over to stand in front of Gotthilf's desk. Gotthilf looked at him with raised eyebrows.

"Sergeant Hoch, this is Fräulein Esther Frey. She has filed a missing person report." He handed the report to Gotthilf.

"Thank you, Schmidt." Gotthilf turned his attention to the young woman. "Please be seated, Fräulein Frey." He scanned over the report. Missing person was her older sister, one Margrethe Döhren. Different fathers, obviously; not that that was unusual with the turmoil of a decade and a half of war, especially around Magdeburg. There were lots of fractured and blended families now.

The description given would probably match half the women in Magdeburg. Not much help there.

Last seen: a day and a half ago. Gotthilf looked up at that. "Are you sure she's missing? This isn't a very long time."

The young woman nodded rapidly. "Margrethe's never been gone this long. She always comes straight home after her work. She never stays out all night. She's afraid of the dark, you see."

"Ah."

Gotthilf returned to the report. Okay, the missing woman worked for the Startzig family as a maid and child tender. He looked back to Fräulein Frey. "Have you checked with the Startzigs?"

"That was the first place I went. They didn't see her at all yesterday. Frau Startzig was quite angry." Fräulein Frey's fingers were twining about each other, for all that she was sitting still and her voice was mostly steady.

Back to the report. Clothing she was last wearing... that list rang an alarm in Gotthilf's mind. He put his pen down, and picked up a folder from his desk. He paged through it, then looked back to Fräulein Frey.

"Tell me, Fräulein Frey, does your sister have any distinctive marks on her face?"

This question obviously confused the young woman, but she raised a hand to a point right below her right eye. "She has three pox scars in a triangle right below her eye."

Bingo, as Byron would put it. He pulled the close-up photo of the eyeless dead woman from the folder and handed it to Fräulein Frey. "Is that your sister, Fräulein Frey?"

"No...no...no!"

For all the negatives of her response, it was obvious that the dead woman was indeed the missing sister. As Fräulein Frey began shaking and weeping, Gotthilf looked over to see Byron looking at him. "Ask and you shall receive," ran through his mind.

At least they had a name for the body now.

Several days later, Gotthilf was beginning to get very unhappy about the Margrethe Döhren case. He hadn't been happy about it to begin with, needless to say. But no leads were turning up. Not one. Thus his current frame of mind, standing in an alley not far from the police station.

He and Byron had interviewed Frau Startzig, the dead woman's employer, who was shocked and horrified about the murder—and obviously feeling a bit put out by it, as well, as she mentioned more than once the disruption it was causing her family to have to seek out a new and reliable assistant maid and child watcher. But the good Frau had been unable to do more than identify the last time she had seen the victim, which was when she left work at her regular time on the evening before she was murdered. She had seen no evidence of anything unusual in her servant's behavior; no indication that there might be any kind of problem either personal or otherwise.

They had walked with Esther Frey as she had retraced her sister's usual routes between their rooms in a very modest rooming house in the west of Greater Magdeburg to the Startzigs' new house, which had been built in the Neustadt district of Old Magdeburg, in an area inside the walls that had been mostly destroyed by fire back in the 1620s and hadn't been rebuilt until recently. Nothing unusual had been noted, although there was one route that came a little closer to The Chain than he would have liked if it had been his sister walking it.

As the days passed, no residents or citizens had come forward to offer any information. Nor had any been gathered when they started doing interviews of those residents and businesses whose buildings were near the travel routes. Rumors, yes; plenty of those. Facts? Not a one. Nothing.

Finally, after all that labor had developed exactly nothing, they were down to trying to tap the informers that Byron had been cultivating among those who were on the streets every day. And that brought his mind back to the present.

"Talk to me, Hans," Byron said, tapping his finger in the thin chest of the scruffy little man that they had just pulled into a nearby alley.

"What do you want, Lieutenant?" Hans Schmidt— and wasn't that a remarkable name, Gotthilf thought to himself—sounded very resigned. And he probably was, since he wasn't much more than a failed thief who was just trying to keep body and soul together with whatever day work he could find.

"I want the killer of Margrethe Döhren, is what I want." Byron poked him in the chest again.

"Who?" Schmidt sounded perplexed. "Oh, wait a minute . . . is that the one where her eyes were . . ." The little man's face took on an expression of incipient nausea; which was appropriate, Gotthilf had to admit. The whole case was one to make a man sick.

"Yah," Gotthilf responded. "That's the one. So give."

Schmidt shrugged, and held his hands out, palms up, looking back and forth between the two detectives. "Sorry, Lieutenant, Sergeant, I have nothing. Everyone is talking about it, but nobody says anything, if you know what I mean."

David Carrico

"Is that because they don't know anything, or because they're afraid to talk?" Gotthilf asked.

"Everyone's afraid, but not that kind of afraid. They would talk if they knew anything." Schmidt ducked his head. "Nobody wants someone around who could do that to a woman. But no one knows anything—not that I have heard."

Byron muttered something, then said, "If anyone knew anything, if anyone had heard anything, who would it be? Who would be the best person to talk to us about this?"

Schmidt fingered his straggling whiskers, combing a few crumbs out of them as he did so. "I don't know...maybe Demetrious."

"Demetrious," Byron said. "I don't know that name."

"Old guy," Schmidt said, "tall, sort of skinny, white hair. Not from around here." By which he meant Thuringia or Magdeburg provinces in general and Magdeburg the city in particular.

"Yeah, I gathered that," Byron said. "That's not exactly a German name."

Schmidt shrugged again, and continued, "He might be from Rumania, or someplace like that."

"So what does this Demetrious do, and where can we find him?"

"He runs a cup game..."

"A cup game?" Gotthilf interrupted.

"Yah, the magic cups," Schmidt replied, holding his hands palm down in front of him and moving them in circles.

"Oh, God," Byron muttered. "Don't tell me we've got a thimblerig operator in town."

Gotthilf made a note to himself to ask Byron

what a thimblerig was later on. "But where do we find him?"

"Last time I saw him, he was hanging around where Canal Road meets the main road out of the shipyards. Can I go now?"

Byron jerked a thumb over his shoulder. "Get."

Schmidt got.

Gotthilf looked up at the darkening sky. "Tomorrow?"

"Yep," Byron replied. "He's someplace warm and dry by now. We'll look for him tomorrow."

As it turned out, they didn't go looking for Demetrious the next day. When Gotthilf arrived at his desk that morning, there was an envelope lying in the center of the desktop between the In-box and Out-box. He picked it up, curious about what it was. Middling quality paper; a manufactured envelope of the type sold in one of the new stationery stores that sold supplies to small businesses; and sealed, not just with adhesive on the flaps, but also with an irregular blob of wax.

He looked over at Byron, who was seated at his own desk reading one of the ubiquitous reports that always seemed to appear in his In-box like mold suddenly appearing on bread overnight. "Do you know what this is?"

"Nope," Byron muttered, not looking up. "Saw it when I came in, but it's got your name on it and says 'Confidential.' Figure you'll let me know if it's something I need to see."

Gotthilf looked at the handwriting; solid, even, with a bit of a slanted line. Educated person; probably male from the firmness of the strokes. He opened the envelope by breaking the seal and sticking a finger under the top flap to separate it from the other flaps.

The envelope only contained two scraps of paper. One looked to be from a newspaper; the other appeared to be a fragment of a book page. It only took a moment to read them.

"*Scheisse!*"

Gotthilf heard Byron's chair scrape across the floor and crash against a wall at the same moment that his partner appeared at his side.

"Show me."

Gotthilf handed the scraps to Byron and waited for him to read them. This took a moment longer than it had taken Gotthilf, because the up-timer was not skilled yet in reading the fraktur script with which the book scrap was printed. Gotthilf was glad of that, because it gave him that much longer to slow his breathing and try to counteract the adrenaline surge that had spiked through him when he realized what he was holding.

Byron looked up. Gotthilf could see anger blazing in his eyes like a beacon. "C'mon," was all he said. "This has to go to the captain."

An hour later Gotthilf was standing in the office of Mayor Otto Gericke. He stood to the left of Captain Reilly, with Byron standing on the other side. Reilly had just handed the scraps to the mayor.

Gotthilf had no problem recalling the contents of the scraps. He suspected that they were burned into his memory so strongly that he would be able to recall them the moment before he drew his last breath.

First, the raggedy-edged newspaper scrap. It was a short article that looked to be from the *Magdeburg Times-Journal*.

> A woman was found most vilely murdered two days ago in an alleyway off of Kristin-strasse in Greater Magdeburg. Her name was Margrethe Döhren, a woman of good repute who resided in Greater Magdeburg. She is survived by her sister, Esther Frey.

The word "good" had been crossed out.

The second scrap was actually about a half-page from a pocket Bible. It had been very neatly trimmed out of the Bible, apparently with a very sharp knife. A block of text from the book of Job had been outlined in black.

> *Let them curse it that curse the day, who are ready to raise up their mourning. Let the stars of the twilight thereof be dark; let it look for light, but have none; neither let it see the dawning of the day: Because it shut not up the doors of my womb, nor hid trouble from mine eyes.*

The mayor laid the scraps down on his desk, and folded his hands together before him, interlacing his fingers. "So why have you brought this to me?"

Gotthilf watched out of the corner of his eye as Captain Reilly turned his head and said, "Lieutenant Chieske, would you address that, please?"

"Mayor, it is better than nine chances out of ten

that those..." he pointed at the scraps, "...were sent to us by the killer."

The mayor's brows drew down, and his face took on a look of distaste. "Why? And again, why are you bringing this to me?"

Byron sighed. "Because, Mayor, the killer is seriously sick in the mind. The mutilation of Fräulein Döhren's corpse alone proves that. This is just another symptom. It's a message at three levels."

The mayor spread the two fragments out before him. "How so?"

Byron lifted a hand with all fingers but the index folded down. "One: crossing out the word 'good' in the newspaper article is telling us that the killer thinks there is some question as to the character and morals of the victim."

The second finger raised to stand along the index. "Two: the inclusion of the Bible page with that passage circled is a taunt to the *Polizei* and yet could be evidence of a sort if we can combine it with other facts."

The ring finger now stood along the first two. "Three: although the killer may not recognize it, the sending of these scraps is a call for help. At some point, somewhere in his mind, he wants to be caught."

Mayor Gericke nodded, then pursed his lips for a moment. "All right. I understand what you are saying. But for the third time, why are you bringing this to me? Just do what you have to do to catch this..." his mouth twisted in disgust "...this murderer."

"The problem, Mayor," Captain Reilly picked up, "is that we don't have enough information to identify and capture the killer yet. And our experience from the uptime tells us that this is likely just going to be the first of several murders. This has all the earmarks of being what was called up-time a 'serial killer' on the loose. So first of all, this is a heads-up warning for you, so that you won't be surprised if other similar murders occur."

The up-timers used a term—*blind-sided*—that Gotthilf thought was appropriate to the situation. No leader, and especially no politician, liked to be caught unaware of anything happening in their realm of responsibility.

"Second, the use of the Bible page does open up another possible line of investigation. We may need one of the pastors in Magdeburg to talk to us about this."

That, Gotthilf thought to himself, opened a political door that the detectives didn't want to barge through without some help from the mayor in first figuring out who to talk to. Lutheran pastors in Lutheran provinces were usually influential people in their own right. Lutheran pastors in the very capitol of the USE really needed to be approached carefully, and Gericke's assistance or direction would help.

"Third, this not being a 'normal' murder, but a mutilation of a woman, it could attract attention from the Committees of Correspondence."

No one wanted the CoC to get stirred up about this, Gotthilf thought. No one.

It was another two days before Gotthilf and his partner finally caught up with Demetrious. They found him where Schmidt had said he would be, near the junction of the Navy Yard road and the Canal Road. A tall thin man in worn clothing, slightly stoop-shouldered, that Gotthilf took to be the man they were looking for had a table set up and was moving his upside-down cups around on the surface of it, watched closely by a group of the ship-workers on the way home for the evening. There was a lot of yelling, a lot of shoving back and forth among the workers, and more than a little laughter.

Just as they arrived at the edge of the crowd, a burly worker who was standing across the table from the thimblerigger reached out and tapped one of the cups with a finger.

"Are you sure?" Gotthilf heard Demetrious ask in a melodious accent.

"Yah. Show me," the man said.

Demetrious shrugged and lifted the cup from the table, exposing . . . nothing.

The crowd exploded in shouts and laughter. The loser just shook his head, smiling. "Come on, boys," he said in a loud voice. "Time for a beer."

They marched off together, chattering among themselves and vowing that next time one of them was going to find the ball under the cups.

Demetrious carefully lined his three cups up on the table. From what Gotthilf could tell, they were carved from wood, with a small hollow made in the bottom of each. The old man reached out and placed a small ball in the hollow base of the center cup with care. Then he straightened and put his hands behind his back. His head turned and tilted to look at them, much like a bird's would, and the gleam in his eye was also birdlike. Gotthilf suddenly had a feeling much like he thought a bug would have when caught in the gimlet gaze of a raven. Then Demetrious smiled, and the feeling passed.

"Good evening, my friends," the old man said. "Would you care to partake in a game of chance?"

Byron snorted. "Not hardly. Gotthilf, here you see one of the oldest scams in the book. There are pictures from five hundred years before now that show men fleecing the unwary with this very setup." He waved a hand at the cups on the table.

The old man's smile grew wider. "Oh, the history of the game goes back much farther than that, friend," he said. "Me, I have no doubt that when Christ entered to cleanse the temple, he probably ran into someone playing the game at the very gates."

Byron laughed, and replied, "You're probably right, Herr Demetrious."

Demetrious tipped his head in acknowledgment. "Ah, it is good to know that one's reputation abounds. But please, will you not try a game with me? Perhaps you, *meine Herr*?" He looked at Gotthilf.

Byron looked over and said, for all the world as if the old man was not right there, "Gotthilf, there is no such thing as a random game of chance with this man. He is in total control of the game at all times. If you win, it's because he gives it to you. If you lose, it's because it's all in his hands. It's all illusion. It's sleight of hand."

Demetrious' grin grew wide enough to almost split his face. "It is true; I have some small skill at the game."

Byron snorted again. "You're old enough you probably invented the game. It wouldn't surprise me if it wasn't your big feet that Jesus tripped on as he entered the temple that day."

Gotthilf looked at Byron in surprise. For some reason, the normally laconic up-timer was bantering with Demetrious. He'd have to dig an explanation for that out of Byron later.

Demetrious laughed. "You flatter me, my friend. I am neither so old nor so renowned."

"Maybe so," Byron said. He pulled out his badge wallet, and flipped it open to show the snarling lion mask. "But that's not why I'm here tonight. Lieutenant Byron Chieske of the Magdeburg *Polizei*. My partner, Sergeant Gotthilf Hoch."

Gotthilf had his badge out a moment later.

Demetrious looked at the wallets carefully, smile gone. He raised his eyes to their faces, hands behind his back again. "I have done nothing wrong," he said calmly.

Byron looked over at Gotthilf. "We didn't say you had," Gotthilf said as he put his badge away. "But the word from the streets is that from time to time you may hear things that no one else in Magdeburg hears."

"Ah," Demetrious said. He looked away from them for a moment, then returned his gaze. "And what if I do?"

Gotthilf placed his hands on the gaming table. "Any word, any breath, any hint of a thought that has anything to do with the death and mutilation of Margrethe Döhren, you bring or send to us." He leaned forward. "Anything. At. All."

The old man looked at them both, first at Gotthilf, then at Byron, then back to Gotthilf. At length he gave a small sigh. "A very nasty business, that."

Gotthilf straightened but said nothing. Byron stood as if he were a statue. Tension built.

"All right," the old man said at last. "I will do so if you will keep my name out of the stories. I would not have the other fishes in the channels I swim in turning on me."

"Agreed." Gotthilf nodded.

Demetrious picked up his cups and stowed them in jacket pockets, then picked up his table and made it collapse into an easily carried form. When he was done, he looked at them one last time. "I cannot guarantee word. I cannot hear what is not said. And even if there is word, it may take a while to find."

"Understood."

The old man turned and carried his table away from them.

Byron blew breath from his lips.

"Think he can help us?" Gotthilf asked.

Byron shrugged. "Maybe, maybe not. We'll keep looking on our own."

"Yah."

The two started back to the station. Gotthilf looked up at Byron as they strode along. "So what's a thimblerig?"

"Well, they used to call it the shell game . . ."

August 1635

Gotthilf was approaching the police station building when he heard his name.

"Yo, Gotthilf!"

He looked up to see Byron standing by a horse and wagon waiting in front of the building. Byron was beckoning, so he broke into a trot for the last few yards. Byron was already climbing up in the wagon when he arrived. The up-timer reached a hand down, which Gotthilf grasped and allowed his partner to give him a pull up to the seats on the wagon bed.

"Hope you didn't eat much breakfast this morning," Byron said with a twist to his mouth. "We've got another body."

Gotthilf's stomach suddenly got a hollow feeling.

"Another woman?"

"Yep."

The red-haired driver clucked to his horse and got her moving. The wagon rumbled down Kristinstrasse away from the police station, gravel crunching under the wheels. Gotthilf turned to his partner.

"So, what do we know?"

Byron shrugged. "Only that there's a dead female victim. Word got to the station about five minutes ago. Doc Schlegel will meet us there."

Gotthilf turned forward again, watching the people moving down the broad street. Kristinstrasse was one of the major boulevards in the new city. It started in Old Magdeburg at the west end of Hans Richter Square, pierced the city wall through a new gate that Otto Gericke had forced the Old Magdeburg city council to agree to, crossed the canal that surrounded three sides of the old city, and headed due west through the mixed residential and light industrial area that had built up away from the river. There was usually a lot of traffic on the street during the day, and today was no exception. Pedestrians, light wagons hauling parts or supplies to the factories along the river, newsies—mostly women—hawking newspapers, even Committees of Correspondence members—again often or mostly women—handing out broadsides with savage political cartoons or bad poetry; it was a regular stew of people before him.

The wagon turned into a side street and traveled past two more cross-streets before it pulled up at the mouth of an alley. Byron looked at a wagon nearby, and said, "Doc beat us here. C'mon."

The two detectives hopped down from their wagon. Gotthilf nodded to the patrol sergeant and foot patroller who stood at the mouth of the alley as he moved past them. They were keeping the growing crowd of curious or concerned or downright nosy onlookers from tromping all over the crime scene, although that was starting to be more of a challenge as the number of bodies standing and craning their heads increased.

Byron didn't say anything, just went and stood well to one side where Dr. Schlegel could see him. The coroner stood beside the corpse, bent over to look at it closely. As with the first scene, the hard-packed dirt in the alley prevented the creation of much in the way of footprints, so he wasn't contaminating evidence just by standing there. He took a metal probe from a pocket and gently moved the victim's collar a bit. Gotthilf could see dark stripes on the neck.

The police photographer, Nathaniel Crüger, showed up with his assistant just as the coroner stood and joined the detectives. They all retreated a few more steps to get out of the photographer's way.

"Talk to me, Doc," Byron muttered, eyes on the corpse.

"Another unfortunate like the Döhren woman. I'm getting too much practice in studying ligature marks, I'm afraid. It's almost identical in occurrence: killed sometime after dark; appears to have been strangled, probably from behind from the looks of the ligature marks on the throat; body and clothing carefully arranged; and her eyes were removed, probably after she was placed here."

"*Scheisse!*" Gotthilf said in disgust at the thought of another wanton mutilation.

"Agreed," the coroner said.

Byron didn't say anything, but Gotthilf heard him inhale slowly, then expel all the air in a forceful sigh.

This was not a good thing, Gotthilf thought. Murders happened when a city was as large as Greater Magdeburg was; even murders of women. But this kind of violence—this kind of systematic and senseless mutilation—this was unheard of. And there was a thought that now filled his heart with dread.

He looked over at Byron. "So, do we have a serial killer?"

Byron was silent for a long moment, jaw muscles twitching as he clenched his teeth. Finally, he said, "Looks like. We'll have to wait for Dr. Schlegel's autopsy and coroner's report to be sure." He nodded to the coroner, "but I'd put ten bucks on it right now."

"No bet."

The three of them stood in silence and watched as the photographer took his pictures of the crime scene.

Afterwards, after the preliminary examinations were complete and the coroner's attendants were taking the body to their wagon, Byron talked to the coroner and Gotthilf stood at the mouth of the alley and looked at the people. Mostly women, he noticed, but that didn't surprise him. The word would have spread very quickly, he was sure. "I just wish things would spread back to us that quickly," he muttered.

He noticed that Daniel Kierstede was one of the patrolmen that had been called in to help block off the alley and keep the crowd out of the investigators' way. When Kierstede looked his way, he jerked his head at him. Kierstede stepped over to where Gotthilf was standing, all the while keeping his eyes on the crowd.

"Did you find her?" Gotthilf asked.

"Not this time." Kierstede sounded thankful, for which Gotthilf couldn't blame him.

"Any clue as to who she is?"

Kierstede shook his head. "Not from any of us."

Gotthilf looked up as the messenger approached his desk. He had headed for Byron's desk first, but had veered for Gotthilf as soon as he saw that Byron's chair was empty. He handed an envelope to Gotthilf and headed for his next stop, riffling through the other envelopes he was carrying.

After reading the short note inside the envelope, Gotthilf grabbed his jacket and headed for the captain's office.

Bill Reilly, captain of the Magdeburg *Polizei*, was an up-timer, just like Byron Chieske, one of the three and a half thousand or so residents of Grantville, West Virginia, who had suddenly found themselves transported from the year 2000 to 1631 into the region of Germany known as Thuringia. The effects of that event—miraculous or otherwise—had been almost immediately felt, and were continuing to spread.

One of those effects had been the rebirth of Magdeburg after the Sack of 1631. And one of the effects of that effect had been the creation of the Magdeburg *Polizei* in early 1635, with the two up-timers seconded from the Grantville army troops by General Frank Jackson to be the *Polizei's* first leaders. And just as the population of Magdeburg itself was something of a mongrel, so was its police force. The captain, even more so than Byron, was responsible for finding and hiring men to be patrolmen in the melting pot of societies and cultures that was Magdeburg. Gotthilf had seen him dealing with those issues, and competing for good men with the industries and the army. He had a great deal of respect for Captain Reilly.

The captain looked up from his conversation with Byron when Gotthilf appeared in the doorway to his office. He said nothing, but his raised eyebrows did ask a question.

"Sorry, Captain," Gotthilf said. He turned to Byron. "The coroner wants to see us 'as soon as it's convenient.'"

Byron looked to Reilly. "This will keep. Just get back with me later," said the captain.

As Byron started to stand up, Reilly spoke again. "Oh, yeah—the mayor did go with me to a meeting of the senior pastors in town. They're all in agreement that any of them will be willing to help you with background for these murders. Just remember who they are, and deal gently with them. We've got enough heat coming our way right now." He waved his hand in dismissal. "Go, go."

Moments later the two detectives hustled out the front door of the station and headed for the nearest cart, since their regular driver appeared to be elsewhere. "City morgue," Byron snapped as they jumped in. The lurch as the driver urged his pony into motion dropped Gotthilf into his seat with a thump.

The morgue was some distance from the station, in a street that was mostly warehouses. No one wanted to live near the morgue, it seemed.

When the cart pulled to a stop, the two of them jumped down. Byron headed for the door. Gotthilf took two steps, then turned back to the driver. "Wait for us."

The driver touched a finger to the brim of his hat and reached down and set the wheel brake before he settled back in his seat.

For all that Byron's legs were longer than his, Gotthilf had caught up with his partner by the time he'd taken two steps inside the morgue. His nose twitched. There was a faint smell of decay. Given the purpose of the place, and the fact it was August, he supposed that shouldn't have surprised him. Still, the building was almost brand new, and it had only been in use by the newly appointed coroner for a few weeks. He'd hoped it would be longer before it took on the air of its purpose, so to speak.

One of the assistants opened the door into the morgue itself and the two detectives entered to find Dr. Schlegel waiting on them.

"Tell me you found something we can use, Doc," Byron said.

"I just find the facts," the coroner said, wiping his hands on a towel. "It is your job to find their application."

"Right. So what have you got?"

"First of all, a name. According to Frau Maria Züchner, who claims to be her mother and came here yesterday afternoon after the rumors made their rounds, yesterday's victim was one Anna Seyfart. Age, twenty-three. Occupation, assistant to Frau Anna Schneider, who is—"

"Probably the most in-demand seamstress in Magdeburg for the leading families," Gotthilf interjected. He shrugged when the two men looked at him. "My mother patronizes her almost exclusively. You learn these things around my mother and sister. Anything else?"

"Ah, right," Dr. Schlegel said. "Unmarried, but not a virgin. As to the autopsy..." Gotthilf watched as the doctor laid two folders side by side on top of a freshly scrubbed exam table.

"I cannot absolutely verify that the two women were killed by the same person," Dr. Schlegel began, "even after discussing the cases with Dr. Nichols and reading the up-time reference books. They were both killed by strangulation, yah, but look here." He pointed at one picture, then another. "It was not manual strangulation. Some type of cord or ligature was used on each of them."

"Damn," Byron muttered. "No chance of matching hands to the marks, then."

Gotthilf nodded, remembering an earlier case they had solved, where the murderer of a wealthy factor named Paulus Bünemann was eventually identified because of a distinctive lack of a fingermark.

"I'd say not," the coroner replied. "The ligature that killed Margrethe Döhren was thin, and was placed near the base of the neck, below the larynx. But the ligature that killed Fräulein Seyfart was thicker, and was placed across the larynx. It may have been the same murderer, using different tools, but the second attack was made with more force. The ligature marks cut deeper, and the larynx itself was partially crushed."

Gotthilf felt of his own throat.

The doctor noticed that movement, and smiled. "Indeed, Sergeant Hoch, from what I have learned it would take a significant amount of force to do that."

"So we may have two killers, then?" Gotthilf asked. "The second stronger than the first?"

"Possibly," Dr. Schlegel responded. "But look at this." More pictures were pulled out of the folders.

"The two women were posed in exactly the same manner. No differences at all."

Still more pictures were pulled out to display.

"And the eyes were removed from both of them in exactly the same manner, with the same cuts, and I would swear with the same tool. Look at these," the coroner pulled yet more photographs out, displaying the naked eye-sockets. "See here and here," he pointed from one photo to the other, "see how the tissues are cut in exactly the same manner?"

Gotthilf bent over the pictures. The photographs were grisly, yes, but lacked the immediacy of having the tissue in front of him, so he was able to view them with perhaps a bit more objectivity than he otherwise would have.

"See, this line here? This slice across this muscle?" The doctor's probe traced the line on one picture, then moved to the other. "Compare it to this one."

Gotthilf was no doctor, but he could see a definite similarity between the two mutilations. After a long moment of study, he straightened. "Anything else?" he asked.

"I don't know what tool was used, but it was very sharp. And the use of it was very precise."

"How so?" Byron asked.

"Precise enough to be a skilled surgeon, even by up-time standards," Dr. Schlegel said. "Precise enough that the eyeballs were removed without cutting or puncturing them. There was no trace of vitreous humor in the orbits of either woman, which would have been impossible to totally clean out if an eye had been penetrated. I am impressed by the skill, and appalled by the use to which it is being put."

"Great, we've got a Ripper on our hands," Byron muttered. Gotthilf barely heard him, so he didn't think Dr. Schlegel had. He stored that statement for later discussion.

"So, we may or may not have multiple killers, but after the murders have been done, it's one person," Gotthilf said.

Byron nodded. "I'd bet that way. And I still think it's only one killer."

"But the differences?" Gotthilf objected. "Why weren't the methods exactly the same?"

"Because it's not the actual death that he's obsessive about," Byron said. "It's what happens afterwards." Gotthilf watched his partner tap his finger against his lips, then cross his arms. "Was Fräulein Döhren raped or otherwise sexually assaulted?"

The coroner shook his head. "No. She was not a virgin, but there was no evidence of recent sexual activity of any kind."

"So they had that in common, as well," the up-timer mused.

"You think that's a factor in this?" Gotthilf asked.

"I don't know," Byron replied. "But obsessions that lead to murder almost always involve sex one way or another."

It was late in the day when they returned to the police station. They had gone over every bit of the forensics data with the coroner and viewed the body of Anna Seyfart themselves. Again, nothing presented itself that hadn't already been seen; no new revelation or interpretation of the evidence jumped out at them. Gotthilf was grinding his teeth when they climbed down from the wagon and stepped into the station house.

"Captain wants to see you both, soonest," the desk sergeant said as they entered. They turned as one and headed up the stairs to Captain Reilly's office.

"Not good," Byron muttered.

"What's it about?" Gotthilf asked.

"Dunno," Byron shrugged. "Probably got something to do with these murders."

Which was the only thing Gotthilf could think of, as well. But why?

That question was answered as soon as they entered the captain's office.

"Where do we stand on the murder/mutilations case?" Reilly asked as soon as they stepped into his office. He did not invite them to sit down.

"Same place we did this morning," Byron replied. "According to the autopsies, we may be looking at two killers or one, but the post-murder obsessiveness is definitely one person. I'm betting we've got one killer who obsesses over the after-death stuff but not the exact manner of death."

"So, what, we've got our own Jack the Ripper here?"

Byron flashed Gotthilf one of those *I'll explain it all later* looks, then said, "Maybe, maybe not. There are some parallels, but so far he's not a copycat killer."

"That's not good enough," the captain said. "I've had a steady stream of visitors in my office today, beginning with one Frau Schneider, apparently *the*

dressmaker in town, then followed by what seemed
like most of her clientele, all of whom demanded that
the murderer be caught now, or else. The afternoon
was capped off by a visit from Mayor Gericke, who
indicated his concern about this case, and wondered
why we hadn't caught the murderer yet. After all, it's
been over a week since the first woman was found
dead, strangled and eyeless."

Gotthilf clenched his teeth. There wasn't anything
to say to that diatribe that wouldn't sound like self-
justification. He stole a glance at Byron, who was
playing statue again.

Reilly's stiffness relaxed all of a sudden. He waved
a hand. "Sit down, guys, sit down."

After they did so, the captain continued, "I'm sorry,
you probably don't deserve that, but we are starting to catch heat over this, and if we don't find the
killer soon, we're going to be neck-deep in political
mud. Brief me, so if the mayor comes back I can say
something besides 'We're trying.'"

Byron pointed a finger at Gotthilf, who pulled out
his notebook.

"Two women: one twenty-two, the other twenty-four;
both unmarried; both living in the western section of
Greater Magdeburg; both working in Old Magdeburg
or at least having frequent business there. Neither was
well off, although Fräulein Seyfart had a better job and
obviously better connections than Fräulein Döhren.
According to their families, neither woman had suitors,
or even male friends. Both often walked to and from
Old Magdeburg via the bridge and gate in the northwest corner of the Altstadt. We have no witnesses that
placed them anywhere on the evenings of the nights in

question. We know when they left their places of business or service, and we know when they were found the next morning. Other than that, nothing."

"You're certain they were mutilated in the same manner?"

"Dead certain," Byron said, "no pun intended. The photos from the autopsies are clear."

"And you think they were killed by the same man." That was not a question.

"I'd bet every dollar I have on it," Byron replied.

"Then you're missing something. If we have a serial killer, one twisted and obsessed enough to mutilate his victims in exactly the same manner, then the victims have something in common. Find it, and it will lead you to him."

"Here," Byron shoved a large up-time book at Gotthilf, who barely caught it. The up-timer's finger pointed to a column of text with a heading of "Jack the Ripper." Gotthilf sat down at his desk and started puzzling through the up-time English and printing. When he was done he looked up at his partner.

"This is what you think we are dealing with? This insanity?"

"Insanity, yes," Byron said. "Not exactly like the Ripper, though. Like I told the captain, there are some real differences between what we've seen and what happened in London in 1888. But similar, oh yeah."

"It says they never captured or tried this Jack the Ripper."

"Yeah," Byron muttered. "Lots of crazy theories as to who he was, but no one had ever absolutely proved any of them before the Ring fell."

Gotthilf closed the book and handed it back to Byron, who stuck it in his desk drawer. "We will do better than that, Byron. We have to."

"So what do we have?" Byron looked at the two case folders that lay on the table.

Gotthilf flipped them open and pulled out the autopsy stats on both women. "Physically, Fräulein Döhren was five feet three inches tall and one hundred forty-five pounds, Fräulein Seyfart was five feet two inches and," he flipped a page, "one hundred thirty-eight pounds."

"So, both women were short and stocky in build." Gotthilf, no towering giant himself, directed a stern look at his partner. "Well," Byron amended his statement, "stocky, anyway."

"Right. Hair," Gotthilf looked back and forth, "Seyfart was 'dark blonde,' Döhren was 'light brown.'"

"Pull the close-up photos out again," Byron said. Gotthilf laid them out on the table. "Hmmf. Round-faced, both of them."

"Yah," Gotthilf replied. "So they wouldn't be mistaken for sisters, but similar size, shape, and appearance."

"Yep." Byron stared at the two pictures. "I could see one of them being mistaken for the other, especially if the light was not good, but..."

"Why kill them both?"

Byron tapped a finger on Seyfart's autopsy stat sheet. "Why does Döhren's sheet show her eye color but this one doesn't show Seyfart's eye color?" A moment later, he snorted. "Stupid! No eyes to see."

"We got Döhren's from the missing person report her sister turned in," Gotthilf replied. "It looks like

Dr. Schlegel didn't think to ask Seyfart's mother about her eye color when the body was identified."

"We need to pin that down tomorrow."

"Yah."

"Hmm. Döhren was blue-eyed."

Gotthilf looked at his partner. "Is that significant?"

"Dunno. If Seyfart's eyes weren't blue, then probably no significance. If they were blue," he shrugged, "then maybe. Hard to tell without more evidence."

Gotthilf laid out two additional lists and started comparing them. "Personal belongings: clothing, shoes, a few dollars apiece, a stub of a pencil in Döhren's pocket, a bit of ribbon in Seyfart's. Nothing remarkable there, or unique. Hmm..."

After a moment, Byron said, "What?"

"Sorry," Gotthilf looked up. "I was just trying to think if this was important...both of them had a rosary in a pocket."

"Rosary?" Byron looked surprised. "I thought that was just a Catholic thing."

"No," Gotthilf replied. "Many Lutherans still use them. My mother and sister both carry them."

"So what do you think?"

Gotthilf shrugged. "To quote my partner, dunno."

"So," Byron said the next morning, "have you been able to catch up with the sister and mother yet?"

In between other tasks on other cases, Gotthilf had managed to do additional interviews with Esther Frey and Maria Züchner about their sister and daughter, respectively.

"Yah," he replied. "Fräulein Seyfart's eyes were indeed blue."

Byron grunted. "Okay, so that makes them just that much more similar in physical description. Anything else?"

Gotthilf paused as he stepped over a steaming pile of horse manure in Canal Street. "Where's the CoC when you need them?" he muttered, which evoked a laugh from his partner. The Committees of Correspondence were fanatical about cleanliness and civic hygiene, and the sight of a small hill of fresh manure this close to the canal waterway would ordinarily be guaranteed to send local CoC members into a frenzy. However, it appeared that none were in the immediate vicinity, which meant that the equine perpetrator of the crime was able to escape, along with his driver accomplice.

"A few things," Gotthilf said, pulling out his notebook. "Both of them described the victims' eyes as a dark blue. Döhren's sister said her eyes were 'piercing,' and Seyfart's mother used the words 'sharp' and 'penetrating.'"

Byron grunted again. "Okay. Flag that as distinctive."

"Does it mean anything?"

"Not yet. But it's the first really strong element we've found. What else?"

Gotthilf looked down his notes. "They were both friendly and outgoing women."

"Any boyfriends?"

"No. Both Frey and Züchner were adamant about that. And I'd say a bit disappointed, too, especially the mother."

"Understandable. Next?"

"Both women were strong church-goers, more than Sunday, anyway."

"Ah. Make a note of that, too."

Gotthilf nodded, then asked, "Why?"

"Because this kind of murder, there has to be some kind of passion behind it," Byron said. "It may be sexual—probably is—but this wouldn't be the first time in history that an atrocity has been committed for a religious reason."

Gotthilf didn't like that thought at all, but he tucked the thought away for later mulling over. "So what do we do now?"

"Do you know what churches they attended?"

Back to the notes. "Ah, Döhren attended St. Ulrich's, and Seyfart..." his finger ran down the page, "also attended St. Ulrich's."

Byron stopped in his tracks. "They both attended the same church?"

"Yah."

"Damn." Byron slammed a fist into his other hand. "Captain knew what he was talking about. We should have already found this."

Gotthilf started putting facts together. "Oh, you mean it's a connection."

"Yep. Similar appearance with distinctive eyes, similar temperaments, and now attending the same church? Oh, yeah, have we got connection."

Just as Gotthilf was about to ask what they would do now, the office messenger walked by and dropped an envelope on Gotthilf's desk. He took one look at it and yelled, "Martin!"

The messenger reversed his path and came back to where Gotthilf stood. "Yes, Sergeant?"

Gotthilf pointed at the very familiar looking envelope. "Do you know where that came from?"

Martin shrugged. "Morning mail drop, I think."

Gotthilf waved him on and looked at Byron, who

echoed Martin's shrug. "Take it down to the fingerprint guys, and see if they can develop any. Envelope paper is pretty coarse, and all they've got is the powder, so I'm not expecting much there. Depending on what's on the inside, maybe, maybe not."

The fingerprint department was a couple of older men who had recently been sent to Grantville for training. Mostly they took fingerprints with ink of convicted criminals or people arrested for various issues. This was only the second or third time they would be asked to try to develop prints from an object.

Gotthilf pulled out a handkerchief and swaddled his hand before gingerly picking the envelope up at a corner. He didn't expect much either, but it was worth trying.

He was back in less than an hour, carrying two familiar looking scraps of paper now somewhat smudged with fingerprint powder. "No visible prints on the envelope, and nothing clear on these," he reported.

"So what did we get this time?" Byron asked. "As if I can't guess."

One was another newspaper article from the *Magdeburg Times-Journal*.

> Another mysterious murder of a woman has occurred in Magdeburg. The body of Anna Seyfart was discovered yesterday in an alleyway off of Canal Road in Greater Magdeburg. She is survived by her mother, Maria Züchner. Frau Züchner and Fräulein Seyfart's friends ask for prayers for the soul of Fräulein Seyfart. "She was a good girl," her mother said.

The word "good" had been crossed out.

As with the previous mailing, the second scrap of paper was a portion of a page from the Bible, again neatly cut out with a knife. And again, a block of text was outlined.

> *And when ye spread forth your hands, I will hide mine eyes from you: yea, when ye make many prayers, I will not hear: your hands are full of blood.*

"So what do we do next?" Gotthilf asked when Byron looked up, jaw muscles clenched and anger obvious on his face. The confirmation that they had been right to fear the presence of a serial killer in their city was not a good thing.

"Wasn't the pastor at St. Ulrich's one of the pastors on the list Mayor Gericke said we should contact?" the up-timer asked through barely parted lips.

"Yah."

Byron pivoted and grabbed his jacket. "Get the pictures and the other messages from the files, and then we go interview the pastor at St. Ulrich's, is what we do."

"Right."

"So talk to me about this Dr. de Spaignart," Byron murmured as they waited in the narthex of St. Ulrich's church.

"Dr. de Spaignart is a very learned man, quite the writer," Gotthilf replied. "Strong preacher, really well connected through both his family in Saxony and his connections with the congregation here. St. Ulrich's parish is for the most part the eighth quarter of Old Magdeburg, and most of the wealthy and influential people live here."

"First Baptist Church," Byron muttered. Gotthilf looked confused. "Never mind. How old is he?"

Gotthilf shrugged. "I don't know. He looks to be early forties."

"What kind of man is he supposed to be?"

"According to my father, he's a smooth talker, and really is smart about politics and economics in addition to theology. And he's been known to argue with Matthias Decennius, the *Caplan im Dom*—the head pastor at the cathedral—at length over doctrinal issues."

"Not afraid of confrontation, then," Byron said.

"Definitely not," Gotthilf replied.

"You know him?"

"A little. My father knows him better. This is our church."

"Shoulda guessed." Two men, one older than the other, entered the narthex from an interior door. "You take the lead."

Dr. Christian Gilbert de Spaignart was an impressive man. Physically he was broad across the shoulders, with iron gray hair and a matching short-trimmed beard. He was shorter than Byron, but taller than Gotthilf, which was a description that covered most of the men in Magdeburg.

He also dressed well; very well. By Gotthilf's estimation—informed by more instruction from his mother than he cared to remember—the suit the good doctor was wearing was made of the finest wool he had ever seen, and probably cost more than all of Gotthilf's clothing put together. Put that together with the way de Spaignart carried himself, and it was easy to be impressed.

"*Guten Tag, meine Herren.*" Dr. de Spaignart spoke very precise German, if with a Saxon flavor. He was definitely not going to be conversing in Amideutsch, Gotthilf decided. "Mayor Gericke gave me to understand that you might be arriving for a conversation. With what may I be of assistance?"

"I am Gotthilf Hoch," Gotthilf responded, pulling out his badge wallet and flipping it open for display, "Detective sergeant in the Magdeburg *Polizei*. This is my partner Lieutenant Byron Chieske." Byron had his badge out by then.

De Spaignart glanced at both badges, then returned his gaze to Gotthilf. "Are you related to Johann Hoch?"

"My father," Gotthilf replied as he put the badge away.

"Ah. I thought I recognized you. I have seen you in our congregation, have I not?"

"Yah," Gotthilf confessed, steeling himself for the next comment from the pastor.

"Although not as often as I should." De Spaignart's eyes seemed to twinkle, and there was a hint of a smile flirting with the moustache and beard that framed his mouth.

"*Mea culpa*," Gotthilf said. "I plead that my work as a policeman has kept me extremely busy."

"It is a worthy work," the pastor said, his smile broadening a bit, "but if you are so busy you cannot come to at least at least one service a week, you are perhaps busier than the Lord ever intended for you to be."

Gotthilf felt himself smiling back. "I will keep that

in mind, Pastor." He turned his gaze to the other man. "And this is?"

"Ah, please excuse my oversight," de Spaignart said. "This is my archidiakon, Laurentius Demcker."

Byron looked a bit confused until Gotthilf said, "That would be the assistant pastor, Byron."

Demcker, who looked to be a few years older than Gotthilf, said nothing but simply nodded.

"I do not wish to appear impolite," de Spaignart said, "but I am supposed to be in another meeting soon. What is it you wished to speak about?"

Gotthilf pulled the two close-up photographs from his folder, tucked it under an arm, and held the pictures up before the two pastors. "Do either of you recognize these two women?"

"Is there a reason why I should?" de Spaignart asked.

"Because both of them were members of St. Ulrich's congregation," Byron spoke up in a matter-of-fact tone.

"Were?" de Spaignart was quick to notice. "Has something happened to them?" His eyes switched back and forth between the two detectives.

"Do you recall reading the news stories of the two women recently murdered and found in alleyways in the exurb?" Gotthilf responded.

"Yes. What—" de Spaignart stopped in mid-phrase as the connection occurred to him. "Are these the ones . . ." his voice trailed off.

"Whose eyes were gouged out of their heads? Yes, sir," Byron continued in the matter-of-fact tone.

Demcker looked nauseated. De Spaignart controlled his face better than his assistant, but even his eyes widened.

Gotthilf continued to hold the photographs up, and

after a moment the senior pastor leaned forward a little and peered at them closely. "No," he said after long scrutiny, "I do not recognize them. Laurentius, do you know them?"

The younger man swallowed hard, then leaned forward and gave the photographs a long study of his own. At length he reached out and touched one of them. "Her," he murmured. "I recognize her. She would come early to the mass and stay afterward, praying. She knew all of the songs, and sang loudly. Although not well."

Gotthilf turned the picture around. "Margrethe Döhren. Are you sure?"

Demcker nodded. "Every Sunday, and sometimes during the week as well."

"Ah," de Spaignart. "She is the one who would stand as close to the pulpit as she could get. Now I remember her."

"Can you tell us anything about her? Or about her friends?" Gotthilf asked.

"I'm not sure I ever spoke with her outside of a service," de Spaignart said. He looked to his assistant. "Have you, Laurentius?"

The younger man thought for a moment, then shook his head. "No. I cannot think of anything at the moment."

Gotthilf pushed the other photograph forward a bit. "This is Anna Seyfart. Can either of you tell us anything about her?"

Both men shook their heads.

Gotthilf returned the photographs to the folder. "Thank you for your time, Dr. de Spaignart, Archidiakon Demcker, and please, if you can think of anything about these two victims, anything at all, please send a message to the police station. It might prevent another tragedy."

"Another?" the senior pastor pounced. "Is there a risk of another such murder?"

Byron nodded. "Until we catch the murderer, there is a very real chance he will do it again."

"Shocking!" de Spaignart declared. "What is our world becoming, that such things will happen in the streets of a civilized city?"

To which neither Gotthilf nor Byron responded. What could they say? The ability of man to kill or torture mankind should not be a surprise to someone who was well-read in the Bible, after all.

"I really must be off to my meeting," the senior pastor declared. "Good day, Lieutenant Chieske, Sergeant Hoch." He nodded, then swept through the outer door.

Demcker lingered for a moment. "Did these two . . . unfortunates . . . leave any family behind that we should be tending to?"

Gotthilf nodded. "A sister for one, and a mother for the other."

"I will examine our rolls," the archidiakon said. "We should look after them. Good day." He turned and reentered the church proper, leaving the two detectives looking at each other.

September 1635

Gotthilf stared at the two files on his desk. Almost two months since the first murder and mutilation; over a month since the second one. No solutions yet. No one arrested. And despite the cooling of the Magdeburg weather as the seasons turned toward autumn, he and Byron were feeling the heat. The mayor's office had asked for weekly updates; Frau Schneider and her customers—including his own mother—were keeping public interest stirred up; and there was a rumor that the Committees of Correspondence were taking note of the lack of closure of these two cases.

The CoC. That was all they needed.

Captain Reilly stepped into the room, looked at Byron and Gotthilf, and jerked his head toward the hallway. "My office. Now."

This time the two detectives were left standing after Reilly settled behind his desk.

"Where do we stand on the murders?" the captain growled.

"Döhren and Seyfart?" Byron asked.

"No, Julius Caesar and Marc Antony," Reilly snarled. "Of course Döhren and Seyfart. Do we have anything on them? Any leads? Any prospects of leads? Any hint of a suspect?"

"No," Byron shook his head.

Gotthilf just looked at the In-box on the captain's desk. There wasn't much he could add to this conversation.

"Why not?" The captain's voice had an edge to it that would cut glass. It was doing a pretty good job of flaying them, Gotthilf thought.

"Because we don't have the forensics capabilities we need for a case like this," Byron replied.

Gotthilf decided to interject a comment. He couldn't let Byron take all the heat. "And because the murderer is stone cold silent."

Reilly's eyes swiveled to him. "What do you mean?"

"He has said nothing to anyone," Gotthilf said. "After this long a time, almost always we get some kind of feed, some kind of hint from the rumor mongers on the street. With this one, everyone is afraid, everyone is talking, but there is nothing that could be from the murderer. The only voice he's given us are the two Bible verse excerpts he cut out and mailed to us."

"This guy is unnatural," Byron picked up. "He's not talking to anybody. And he's sharp enough to not leave evidence behind. Nothing that we've been able to find. Photographs, magnifying glasses, primitive fingerprint kits and autopsies can only give you so much. Even if we had access to those DNA tests they were starting to roll out back in 2000 before the Ring fell, I doubt we'd have found anything that we could test.

"Captain, we've done everything right," Byron continued. "We've interviewed the family and friends, even casual acquaintances. We've canvased the neighborhoods along their usual paths. We've grilled the employers. We've been reduced to asking for rumors from the street people. I'm about to start taking out ads in the newspaper."

Byron ran his hand through his close cropped hair. "I'm absolutely certain that the same person committed both murders. I think the autopsy evidence proves that. I'd swear that there's a sexual angle to this, but there is no evidence of rape: no semen, no signs of sexual activity at all, much less any bruising or abrasions or other signs of being forced. No indication even of penetration with foreign objects. Dr. Schlegel had to study up on it, but he was consequently very thorough in the autopsies. Nothing. Zip. Nada."

He sighed. "There's a sexual agenda in play here. I can feel it. But I can't figure out what it is."

Gotthilf watched Captain Reilly absorb all of that. Muscles played along the captain's jawbone.

"Do I need to assign someone else to this case?" the captain finally asked.

Byron shook his head slowly. "No. We've kept the other detectives informed, in case they ran across anything that might apply. But they haven't been able to think of anything else to add."

A long moment of silence passed. Gotthilf was starting to get very uncomfortable when Reilly finally said something.

"You two are the best detectives we have. You have got to crack this case, and soon. The political pressure I'm getting on this is getting worse by the day. And the mayor let something slip this afternoon: if there's another murder, if this isn't solved soon, he may bring troops into the city to patrol the streets."

"God, no, Captain," Byron blurted out an instant before Gotthilf did. "That will kill the *Polizei* if he does that. Nobody will believe us or trust us after that!"

"Exactly," Reilly ground out. "So I don't care what you have to do, I don't care whose coattails or skirts you have to lift, I don't care whose tender feet you step on. Find. Me. This. Killer." He stared at them for a moment. "Now."

Another long moment passed. "Is that clear?" the captain's tone was level, but Gotthilf really didn't want to be around if the captain ever spoke like that again.

"Yes, sir," the two detectives responded in unison.

"Get it done. Now get out."

❖   ❖   ❖

Next morning, Gotthilf found his steps slowing as he drew near the police station in the early morning light and saw Byron waiting for him by the wagon and driver they usually used. This time Nathaniel the photographer was waiting along with Byron, his kit already in the wagon.

"Don't tell me," he said when he stopped next to his partner.

"Okay," Byron responded. "But get in."

They climbed into the wagon. Byron must have already instructed the driver where to go, because he shook his reins and clucked his horse into motion without a word from them. The horse was wheeled around and headed back east on Kristinstrasse, until the next corner, then turned north. They traveled six blocks, then stopped at the mouth of an alley.

"Come on," Byron growled as he jumped down and headed into the alley.

Gotthilf and Nathaniel followed. "Where's your assistant?" Gotthilf asked the photographer.

"Flat on his back," Nathaniel responded. "Fell off a step and broke a bone in his leg."

Gotthilf winced.

"I think the lazy lout just got tired of carrying all this rig," Nathaniel continued with a grin as he set his case down well away from the body.

Gotthilf stood well back from the body as Nathaniel unpacked his camera and set to work. Another young woman, laid out carefully with clothing neatly arranged. Looked like another working-class girl. Clothing was drab; from what he could see her shoes were worn. Ice gathered in his stomach as he saw that her face was round, and what he could see of her hair was either dark blonde or very light brown. He couldn't see her face clearly yet, but at this point he was willing to bet she was missing her eyeballs.

He and Byron were silent. There was nothing to be said at this point. Gotthilf took one look at his partner, but the narrowed eyes and the bunched muscles at the back of the jaw told him all he needed to know about the up-timer's frame of mind.

Of course, he realized as he felt his own teeth clenching that his mind was in the same state. He clasped his hands tightly behind his back to keep his fingers from unconsciously flexing, seeking to find the neck of the killer in their grasp.

Gotthilf came out of his rage enough to realize that Byron had drifted over to stand beside him. He looked at his partner.

"Was the captain really that angry yesterday?"

Byron nodded, but said nothing for some time, watching Nathaniel work. He finally said, "Yeah, he was pretty pissed. Not so much at us, although he's not happy that we're taking so long. But the political heat he's taking must be getting really bad, or he wouldn't have let so much of it drop on us. And the bit about the army..."

"That's not good," Gotthilf responded.

"Nope."

"We've got to solve this case, and soon."

"Yep."

"Maybe we'll find something with this one."

Byron just nodded. They turned and watched the photographer.

Nathaniel seemed to take forever with his photographing, although Gotthilf figured it probably wasn't any longer than any other crime scene "shoot," as Byron called it. Finally he stepped back and started putting the camera equipment away.

"Did you get some good face shots?" Byron asked.

"Three of them," Nathaniel answered. His grin was long gone.

"Need copies as soon as possible."

"They'll be on your desks by lunch time."

Nathaniel swung his pack up off the ground and headed for the street, exchanging words with the coroner as they passed each other.

"Another one?"

Dr. Schlegel set his case down beside the body and opened it up.

"Looks that way," Byron said. He stepped closer, hands still in his jacket pockets.

The coroner shook his head. "Same as the other two." The probe in his hand pointed to the eyes. "Eyeballs removed. I'll have to examine the tissue in autopsy, but..."

"Yeah."

The probe moved down to push the collar in different directions. "Ligature marks. Placed more like the Döhren woman than Seyfart, but very similar otherwise."

The coroner made a few simple tests, then sat back and looked the corpse over. "I'll confirm it with the autopsy, but I'd say the pattern will almost exactly match the other two murders. This is victim number three."

Dr. Schlegel stood and motioned to his attendants to come remove the corpse.

Gotthilf stared at the dead young woman. It took

him a while to realize that he didn't really feel much nausea, even though she had also been murdered and mutilated in the same manner as the two previous victims. He was already angry because of the senseless violence; now his anger increased because he realized that he had started to become inured to even this level of atrocity.

"Last one," he whispered to himself. "This is the last one."

Two days later the case file on Gotthilf's desk was fatter by another set of crime scene photographs and another autopsy. Said photos documented the condition of the body very well. Unfortunately, they provided no more illumination as to who the killer was than the previous victims' photos had. Dr. Schlegel had confirmed that the removal of the eyes of the third victim from their eye sockets had been done in the same manner and with the same technique as the previous victims. He even ventured an assertion that the same tool had been used in all three mutilations.

And they knew who the third victim was. One Justina Hösch, wife of Lorenz Mühlhäuser. They had not been married long, and Herr Mühlhäuser had been down at the police station the morning after the murder but before it had been publicized. He had been out looking for his wife much of the previous night, and was not in a good mood when he arrived at the station. His reaction on being taken to the morgue and asked to view the latest victim was not a positive one. It had turned out to be advantageous that the coroner's assistants were sturdy men—and that there were several of them.

Gotthilf opened the file and looked at the autopsy. Amongst all the other details, which simply confirmed that Frau Hösch looked much like Fräulein Döhren and Fräulein Seyfart, was the one hard-fought fact that had been extracted from Herr Mühlhäuser before the shock finally caught up with him: his wife's eyes were blue, of a particularly dark and piercing shade.

He looked over at Byron's desk, where his partner was reading another report.

"Hey, Byron."

"Hmm?" The up-timer didn't look up.

"What's that saying . . . the one about how many times something happens?"

Byron took his eyes off the page in his hand. "Huh? Oh, you mean the one that goes something like 'Once is happenstance, twice is coincidence, but three times is enemy action?'"

"Yah."

Byron set the paper down. "Why?"

"Because all three of the victims had dark blue eyes." Gotthilf didn't have to specify who the victims were. There was only one set of three victims on the minds of the entire police force at the moment.

"Hmm, yeah. Maybe so. But we don't have a connection yet."

Before Gotthilf could respond, Martin the messenger walked through the door from the hallway, carrying an envelope with care, his fingers only touching the very edges of it. He walked to Gotthilf's desk and displayed it.

"This came for you, Sergeant."

Gotthilf looked at it. Same style envelope; same styling of his name and "Confidential"; same handwriting.

He pulled a pair of gloves out of his jacket pocket and put them on, then took the envelope from Martin. From his other pocket he pulled a switch-blade knife and flicked it open, using the blade to open the envelope. Holding the envelope over his desk, he turned it open side down and shook it.

Unlike the previous communications, there was no newspaper story clipping. What fell out of the envelope was a third clipping from the Bible.

> *And if the people of the land do any ways hide their eyes from the man, when he giveth of his seed unto Molech, and kill him not: Then I will set my face against that man, and against his family, and will cut him off, and all that go a whoring after him, to commit whoredom with Molech, from among their people.*

"Sonofa..." Byron breathed from where he was reading over Gotthilf's shoulder. "I was right. There is some kind of sexual angle in play here."

Gotthilf nodded, but his mind was racing. Something was trying to jump out at him...something... something...then it connected. He flung open the case file and pulled out the previous two Bible excerpts and lined them up.

"And here's your connection," he said, using the tip of the blade to point to the same word in each excerpt.

Byron's eyes narrowed and his jaw muscles bunched, then he nodded slowly. "You're right. The eyes are connected to this guy's sexual obsession, somehow, someway."

Gotthilf inhaled sharply. Whether he meant to or

not, the murderer had finally told them something real, something about himself. Two somethings. Now the hunt could begin in earnest.

When the latest missive from the murderer arrived back at Gotthilf's desk from the fingerprint department, smudged with powder from another fruitless attempt to find a fingerprint, Gotthilf put it in an envelope along with the other two fragments cut from the Bible and one of the smaller envelopes in which the fragments had arrived, and stuck the envelope in the same inside jacket pocket where he carried his notebook and pencil. He looked over at Byron's desk. His partner was in a long meeting with the captain, with no expectation of seeing him anytime soon.

Not wanting to lose the rest of the afternoon to mundane tasks in the office, Gotthilf scribbled on the back of a piece of used note paper. The note he dropped on Byron's desk read, "Gone to talk to the preachers again. G."

Gotthilf grabbed his hat from the peg on the wall it was hanging from and clattered down the stairs. Stepping out the front door of the police station, he gave a shrill whistle. A moment later, a police vehicle pulled up before him. He looked up to see the red-haired driver that he and Byron usually used. They grinned at each other, and he clambered up into the light wagon.

"St. Ulrich's church," he said, pointing toward the Old City.

They arrived at the church a few minutes later. Like most of the churches in Magdeburg, St. Ulrich's had been damaged during the Sack of Magdeburg, although unlike some it hadn't been totally destroyed.

Nonetheless, it had taken some time to repair the building, and the final touches had only been applied that summer. There were a few places in the exterior walls where the fresh mortar in some of the stonework was a pretty obvious clue as to where some of the repairs had been made.

"Wait for me, please," Gotthilf said as his feet touched ground again. He looked around to see a group of clergy standing by one of the side doors to the church, so he headed that direction.

"Good afternoon, Archidiakon Demcker."

"And a good afternoon to you, as well, Sergeant Hoch," Demcker replied. Gotthilf looked as his two companions and raised his eyebrows. "Ah, excuse me. Sergeant, this is Archidiakon Simon Schönfeldt, from Heilige Geist Church, and Pastor Timotheus Agricola."

"Currently serving at St. Jacob's Church until Pastor Doctor Paulus Gronovius recovers from his illness," the second man said, completing his own introduction.

Schönfeldt was an average looking individual. There was nothing physically remarkable about him. In fact, he and Demcker bore a certain resemblance to each other, as if they were patterned after a model "Young Lutheran Pastor." Agricola, on the other hand was the shortest pastor Gotthilf had ever seen; slight of build and not much taller than he himself was.

The other thing Gotthilf noticed during the introductions was their dress. They were all dressed in dark sober clothing, as befit pastors. None of them was clothed at the level of sumptuousness that Dr. de Spaignart had worn the other day. Surprisingly, though, it was Agricola who was most well-dressed of the three.

"Is Dr. de Spaignart in the church at the moment?" Gotthilf asked when the introductions were concluded.

"Alas, no," Demcker replied. "Can I be of assistance in his place?"

"Perhaps," Gotthilf replied. "I need to consult with you about some scripture references that may apply to a case we are working. But since I have three of you here, I would also like to ask if any of you have heard any rumors or whispers about the recent spate of murders?"

"You mean the slain women? That's right; there was another one recently, wasn't there?"

That was Agricola. The man's voice was rather high in pitch, and a bit nasal. Not an especially pleasant sound, especially when combined with a heavy Saxon accent.

"Yes."

The three pastors looked at each other, and one by one they shook their heads.

"If you hear of anything," Gotthilf said, "send word to the police station and we will come talk to you."

"I have heard nothing about them other than what I read in the papers," Agricola said.

"Nor have I," Schönfeldt added. "Other than a few of the older women gossiping that the unfortunates may have been selling their bodies."

"I would not be surprised if that were the case," Agricola replied. "For all that we preach against it, more of these lower class women do that than we might imagine." He shrugged. "And if that is the case, then it is perhaps understandable that they came to such an end."

For a moment, Gotthilf had to bite his tongue to

hold back an outburst. "No one deserves to die alone in the dark, murdered and mutilated," he finally said.

"I agree," Schönfeldt interjected, "but it is also true those who commit sins must bear the consequences of those sins. Jeremiah says, 'Behold, I will visit upon you the evil of your doings, saith the Lord.' Even if one of them was from my own parish."

Ah, Gotthilf thought to himself. Frau Hösch was a parishioner of Heilige Geist Church, so of course Schönfeldt should know of her. Interesting way he presented it, though.

Agricola nodded in agreement with his fellow.

There was silence after that.

Gotthilf finally looked to Demcker. "About those scripture references . . ."

The pastor looked to his friends. "If you will excuse me . . ."

"Certainly," Agricola said. "I will speak to you in a day or two." He nodded his head, turned, and left.

"Actually, I'd like to stay, if I might," Schönfeldt said.

Demcker looked to Gotthilf. Gotthilf shrugged, then nodded. It was no concern to him if the other pastor wanted to see what was going on.

"Then let us go inside," Demcker said.

He led the way through the doors and to a small room that Gotthilf decided must be the vestry from the robes that were hanging on the walls. There was a small table shoved into one corner with a rickety looking chair beside it. There was a large Bible lying open in the middle of the table, surrounded by books. Daylight shone through a small window high in one wall, and there was an oil lamp in a bracket mounted to a wall over the table.

"Erm," Demcker said, looking a bit abashed. "I use this for my study. It is much quieter than my rooming house. But I have no other chairs."

"That is not a problem," Gotthilf said with a smile. "I am very used to standing."

Demcker clasped his hands in front of him. "So, Sergeant Hoch, what assistance can I," he looked at Schönfeldt, "or rather we, provide?"

Gotthilf pulled the envelope from his jacket pocket, took the three sliced pages from it, and laid them on the table. "What can you tell me about these?"

Demcker and Schönfeldt both bent over the table to scrutinize the page fragments. After a minute or so, Demcker put a finger on the first piece that Gotthilf had received. "This one," he said, "this is from the book of Job." He sat down and began turning pages in the Bible.

"Chapter 3, I believe," Schönfeldt said.

The pages stopped turning, and Decker ran his finger down a column of print. It stopped, and he compared the fragment to the verses his finger had found. "Correct," he said. "Verses 8 and 9."

Schönfeldt touched another piece. It was the second one he had received, Gotthilf noted. "Isaiah Chapter 1," Schönfeldt said. "Verse 15, if I'm not mistaken."

"Of course," Demcker said. Again the turning of pages; again the finger running down a page and stopping; again the comparison. "Exactly so."

They both looked at the third fragment. "I am not so certain about this one," Schönfeldt said. "Deuteronomy, perhaps?"

Gotthilf got the feeling that they had forgotten him. "No," Demcker said. "I believe Leviticus." Pages were turned slowly as they were scanned by both men. "Ah. Here." He pointed to a column.

"Chapter 20, verses 4 and 5," Schönfeldt said. He clapped a hand on his fellow pastor's shoulder. "I bow to your knowledge, my friend."

Gotthilf cleared his throat. Both pastors jumped a little. Gotthilf suppressed a smile as it became clear that they had indeed forgotten he was there.

"Was that what you needed, Sergeant Hoch?" Demcker asked.

"It is a beginning," Gotthilf said as he pulled his notepad and pencil out of his pocket. "What I would like your opinion on now, if you will, is taking those three passages together, what does that say to you about the man who sent those to me?"

"Would that be the murderer?" Demcker asked with a frown.

"We believe so," Gotthilf responded.

Demcker picked up the page fragments and stared at them one at a time for long moments, then handed them to Schönfeldt.

"If the murderer did indeed send them, then he is a most disturbed individual."

Gotthilf snorted. "We have three murdered and mutilated women. I believe that he is somewhat more than 'disturbed.'"

Demcker grimaced, but nodded. "Can you disclose if the women were raped?"

Gotthilf thought for a moment, then said, "Under seal, I can say that they were not."

Demcker folded his hands, interlacing the fingers, and raised them to cover his mouth, as if in prayer. He sat that way for long moments. Gotthilf noted that his fingers were turning red as his intense grasp cut off circulation.

The young pastor looked up, pain in his eyes.

"I would say," he began, "that this man has been wounded by a woman in the past, probably in a sexual manner. But this is not revenge, no. This is not hot-blooded anger wreaking death and destruction." He swallowed. "This is judgment, cold-blooded and hard. This is a man who has forgotten the mercy of the Lord. He has forgotten the *lex talionis.*"

"The what?" Gotthilf asked.

"An eye for an eye," Schönfeldt said from where he stood by the window, carefully examining the page fragments. "The punishment must be fitting for the crime. Exodus Chapter 22."

"Ah," Gotthilf made notes. He looked up. "Please continue."

"The fact that he made no sexual assault upon them proves this. He is not visiting vengeance. Rather, he has set himself up as judge rather than wronged lover, passed sentence, and is now serving as executioner." Demcker closed his eyes, and his shoulders twitched. "But he is not an impartial judge. This man is so filled with rage he should by rights be a conflagration in the midst of the city."

"No," Schönfeldt looked up. "Not fire. Ice. Rage, yes; but a cold rage. A deep-seated, icy burning rage that has been rising for long and long, until it over-flowed its well."

Demcker opened his eyes. "Simon has the right of it, I think. But multiple slayings would indicate that the woman who injured him is gone. He has no recourse against her, or there would have been only one murder. He found someone who he thought was like her, and executed judgment. But it did not satisfy. And so he has struck again. And yet again."

"And will continue to kill until he is stopped," Schönfeldt said in a heavy voice, "because there is no peace for a person such as him. Not now; not now that he has usurped the Lord's throne of judgment."

Gotthilf scribbled notes furiously. So far nothing they had said contradicted his own observations about this case. In fact, they reinforced his own thinking that Magdeburg was going to be in trouble until they caught this man.

Pencil still, he looked at the two pastors. "Is there anything else you can tell me?"

"About the man, no," Schönfeldt said. "At least, not directly. But about his surroundings, perhaps."

Gotthilf raised his eyebrows.

Schönfeldt's mouth quirked. "Sergeant Hoch, have you attempted to identify the Bible that these pages were cut from?"

"We contacted Zopff and Sons and a couple of other printers," Gotthilf said. "They all said that the paper was of middling quality, the type-face was probably from Leipzig or somewhere to the south, but they couldn't put a printer's name to it."

Schönfeldt nodded. "You should know, Sergeant, that most pastors are bibliophiles. And when it comes to Bibles, those of us here in Magdeburg can discourse on their makeup and construction with the best of the printers. Show us a page, and we can tell you which edition it is from, and probably the name of the printer and the year in which it was printed. These mutilated leaves of the holy book," he presented the fragments in a fan shape, "these speak to me."

He reached into his own jacket and pulled a small Bible from an inside pocket. He handed it and the fragments to Demcker and said, "Laurentius, compare these, if you would."

Gotthilf moved over by the table and watched as Demcker leafed through the Bible and found the matching passages, then compared them to the fragments. One by one, they matched as to page and format. He raised his gaze to look at Schönfeldt, but said nothing.

"Dr. de Spaignart was born in Torgau, in Saxony, and still has family in that region. He often travels to the Leipzig book fair, and he did so last year," Schönfeldt said. "He returned with many books, including several copies of that small Bible. He gifted one to me, and to Laurentius, I know. I don't know where the others went."

Schönfeldt leaned forward slightly. "I will say that the paper of the fragments matches the paper of my copy. The type-face matches my copy. From what I can tell, the ink matches my copy. So there is perhaps a way to cast a net and ensnare this man, by finding those who received other copies."

Gotthilf flipped to the front of the small Bible, and noted the details about the printer and the edition.

"That will not be so much of a help as you might think," Demcker said. "I had just started as Dr. de Spaignart's assistant when he made that trip. Not only did he bring copies back, he also arranged for a local printer to order a shipment of them and sell them here in Magdeburg." No doubt receiving an honorarium from each copy sold, Gotthilf observed to himself. "So there are more copies than you know of, Simon. And," Demcker hesitated, "there is some small issue here as well. I, uh, lost my copy."

"What?" from Gotthilf.

"Oh, Laurentius," from Schönfeldt.

Demcker shrugged. "I had it here in the church, and misplaced it not too long after Dr. de Spaignart gave it to me. I was quite upset about it for a while." He shrugged again. "I finally concluded that someone else needed a Bible more than I did."

Gotthilf looked at Demcker, who returned his look with a clear gaze of his own. If the man was lying, Gotthilf thought, he was remarkably good at it. Not that Gotthilf thought that a pastor was above lying if the cause was strong enough, but Demcker had not impressed him, in their short acquaintance, as being someone who would have any facility at prevarication.

"Well," Gotthilf said, "I suggest you try to find it. Being able to prove your copy is at hand and intact may be something you want to do in the future."

Both pastors looked scandalized at the thought. Gotthilf gave them his best sardonic stare. "If Judas, called by Jesus himself to be one of the Twelve, could turn his back on our Lord and betray him, none of us, including you, are above suspicion."

That brought a blush of anger to meld with their scandal, but both finally ebbed away. Schönfeldt sighed. "Truth, Sergeant Hoch, no matter how little we would like to hear it." He nodded to Gotthilf. "I assume you will wish this conversation to remain under seal?"

"You may tell anyone who asks that I asked for your help about identifying certain scripture passages.

Do not disclose your observations about the killer, or the information about the fragments to anyone, not even your superiors, unless and until I or my superiors approve it."

"I will not lie for you," Demcker said with a stern look.

Gotthilf smiled. "I'm not asking you to lie. Simply don't say anything about this to anyone. Let them draw their own conclusions."

Schönfeldt nodded, and said, "Agreed."

"One last thing," Gotthilf said, pulling the smaller envelope one of the fragments had come in from the larger envelope in his pocket and handing it to Archidiakon Demcker. "Do you recognize this handwriting?"

Demcker studied the envelope with care, Schönfeldt looking over his shoulder. They both looked up. "If this is from someone I know, he is disguising his hand well. I cannot say that I know it at all."

Gotthilf received the envelope back with a bit of disappointment; but not much, because he hadn't expected anything.

As Gotthilf retrieved the Bible fragments and restored them to his envelope as well, Schönfeldt said, "And now I really must be off. Sergeant Hoch, I wish I could say I enjoyed our conversation, but I do hope and pray you catch this fiend soon. Laurentius, I will see you next week, if not before then. Goodbye to you both."

Gotthilf watched him leave. "A good man, that," he said quietly.

"Indeed," Demcker said, rising from his chair. "One of the best. And I need to be about my duties as well, Sergeant. Is there anything else?"

"I think not," Gotthilf said, as he started to turn away. A thought occurred to him, and he turned back. "Except...who is the biggest gossip in your congregation, Archidiakon Demcker?"

Byron showed up at work the next morning with dark circles around his eyes. He headed for the department coffee pot as soon as he walked in the door and poured a cup of what he usually sneered at with comments like "liquid sludge." He took a long drink of it before he headed up the stairs to the detectives' office. No word had yet been spoken, and even for the normally terse up-timer that was unusual.

Gotthilf followed him up the stairs and through the doorway.

"Rough night last night?"

Byron growled. There was no other word that could describe the sound. Then he said, "Yeah. I made the mistake of going by my sister-in-law's place to give her and her husband a warning."

"Warning?" Gotthilf was a bit confused.

"Yeah. Marla has blue eyes."

"Oh." The import behind that crashed into Gotthilf like a brick dropped from the roof of a church. "You told her she needed to stay home and be safe."

"Yeah."

Gotthilf had met Marla. He suppressed a guffaw with difficulty. "And how did she take that?"

A sheepish smile played around the corners of Byron's mouth. "Not very well. She wouldn't have taken it well at any time, but at seven months pregnant..." He winced. "She let me know in no uncertain terms what I could do with my suggestion." The smile faded.

"But I told her to watch out anyway. Franz was there, and he heard. I can trust him to keep her safe."

Marla Linder was the most well-known musician in Magdeburg, and one of the most well-known uptimers as well. Byron's wife Jonni was her older sister. Gotthilf hadn't met Jonni yet. She hadn't yet made the move from Grantville to Magdeburg. Something about children in school, Byron had said. But she and the children would be coming soon.

"Girl's even stubborner than her sister," Byron concluded.

"That couldn't have taken the entire evening," Gotthilf noted.

"Nope," Byron conceded. "But running down Gunther Achterhof did."

Gotthilf looked at him in surprise.

"It took me most of the evening to find him, and I had to drink more bad ale than I can remember seeing before in order to get my message to him without blabbing it before the entire town."

"Message." Gotthilf kept his tone level, although he wanted to grab his partner by his shoulders and shake him.

"I gave him a hint that any woman he knows who has blue eyes should be escorted until this case is closed."

Gotthilf sat back in surprise. "You did what?"

Byron shrugged. "I talked to Captain Reilly about it yesterday in our meeting. It's a risk, but we both thought that giving the CoC an unofficial heads-up could work to our advantage. And if it keeps even one woman from this guy's hands..." His own hands clenched and unclenched.

"Point," Gotthilf said. He mulled on the idea of the CoC being even indirectly allied with the *Polizei*. That would take some getting used to.

Byron slugged back the last of his coffee, and shuddered. "Crankcase drippings would taste better than that."

Gotthilf chuckled. "What was it you used to say about the lowest bidder?"

"I know." Byron scrubbed his hands over his face, then looked up. "So, what did you find out yesterday?"

It took Gotthilf about ten minutes to fill his partner in on everything he had picked up from the pastors. Byron was wide awake by the time he was done with the recital. "That's kind of scary," he said.

"Yah," Gotthilf replied. "But I think Archidiakon Demcker is probably right."

"Yep," Byron said. "And that's part of what scares me. A righteous fanatic can be a lot more dangerous than just a general nut case."

Gotthilf considered that thought, and considered some of the men who had passed through Magdeburg in the last five years.

"Point."

"So where does this lead you next?" Byron asked.

Gotthilf grinned. "We have a date."

"You sure about this?" Byron asked as they walked up to the door.

"Yah," Gotthilf replied. "What have we got to lose? At best, we might learn something. At worst, we waste a little time listening to an old woman ramble."

"Okay. Let's do it, then."

Gotthilf raised his hand and rapped the bronze

door knocker against the door twice. They stood for a long moment, but just as he was about ready to knock again Gotthilf heard a latch being drawn and the door opened. A slightly stooped frail-looking woman with gray wisps of hair slipping out from under her cap looked at them; first at Gotthilf, then up at Byron. She smiled.

"My, you are a big one, aren't you?"

"Good morning. I am Lieutenant Byron Chieske of the Magdeburg *Polizei*, and this is my partner Sergeant Gotthilf Hoch."

They both presented their badges. The woman looked at them, and her smile widened.

"Sorry lads, I couldn't read those if I wanted to. Don't see as clearly as I used to. With the *Polizei*, you said?"

"Yes," Gotthilf replied. "Are you Frau Maria Backfennin verheiratet Weygoldin?" Since he had never met Frau Backfennin before, Gotthilf was being very formal, addressing her as "Frau Maria Backfennin married to Weygold."

"That I am," she said. "Come in, lads, come in. I don't want to let the warm air out."

They stepped across the threshold, and followed the woman into a small room with several chairs in it. She settled in one, propped her feet up on a stool, and picked up some knitting, folding short wrinkled fingers around the needles and the yarn.

"Sit down, lads, sit down," she said, needles beginning to move. "And tell old Frau Maria why you've come calling? Who sent you my way? Was it Pastor de Spaignart?"

"No," Gotthilf said. "It was Archidiakon Demcker."

The old woman giggled, and for a moment he could see the ghost of her face as a girl, with a wide smile and bright eyes. "And I'll wager he told you I was a horrible old gossip."

"Well . . ."

She giggled again. "And so I am, lads, and so I am. But with Michael dead all these years, and my eyesight fading, what else do I have to keep myself busy? You can only knit so many scarves and socks, after all." She lifted her hands with their work for a moment, then dropped them back into her lap. "So what is it you want to know?"

"Tell us everything you know about Fräulein Margrethe Döhren, Fräulein Anna Seyfart, and Frau Justina Hösch."

The knitting needles slowed, then stopped. "Those are the women . . ."

"Who were murdered and mutilated," Gotthilf completed the sentence. "Yes, that's correct. What can you tell us about them?"

After a moment, the needles started working again. There was a long moment of silence, then Frau Backfennin said, "I don't know that last one. She must not attend St. Ulrich's."

"She doesn't," Gotthilf said. "She attends—attended—Heilige Geist Church."

"Ah." The needles continued moving, small clicks of sound happening as they did so. "The other two, them I knew. Fräulein Döhren, she should have been a nun. She would sing all the songs, as loud as she could. And she would stand as close to the pulpit as she could, staring at the pastor as if he was Jesus himself."

"Did she have any friends?"

"Not many." The old woman's mouth twisted in distaste for a moment. "I never knew her from before the sack. She started coming to St. Ulrich's a couple of years ago. She never really seemed to make friends with any of the other women. Not that very many of them would have wanted to be her friend anyway."

"She was unpleasant?"

"She was poor," Frau Backfennin said sharply. "The kind of woman the others would accept at church so they could feel pious about having the poor in their midst, but not the kind of woman they would invite to share a meal or ask her opinion of things. Sanctimonious old harpies, most of them," she muttered.

Gotthilf bit the inside of his cheek for a moment to keep from laughing. He could tell from Byron's face that he was struggling, too. When he felt in control again, he asked, "Did she have any men friends?"

"Was anyone courting her?" The old woman snorted. "No."

Byron spoke up. "Were there any men who..."

Frau Backfennin snorted again. "Did she whore herself out, either on her own or by some pimp? Not that I saw or heard. Unlike that Seyfart woman."

"Ah," Gotthilf said. He got his notepad and pencil out. "Tell us about Fräulein Seyfart, then."

"She was a nasty piece of work. She had no friends at St. Ulrich's either, but not because she was poor. No, she was everyone's friend to their face and their worst enemy behind their backs. Most women learned that about her the hard way, and usually quickly. But she was so adept at flattering those who could help her that she managed to stay close to several important and influential women in the church." The old woman worked her mouth as if she was tasting something unpleasant.

"Frau Schneider," Gotthilf prompted.

"Her and others," Frau Backfennin shot back. "All of whom should have known better but were taken in by sweet words and a devil's smile."

Gotthilf bit his cheek again as he made notes.

"And the men?" Byron prompted.

"The men were even bigger fools than the women," she said tartly. "She would play with all of them; flatter the old men, tease the young ones."

"Did she..."

Frau Backfennin frowned and ran her fingers along the knitting. "Tch. I got so worked up about Fräulein Seyfart I dropped a stitch." She grasped the yarn and pulled on it to carefully unravel half a line of the knitting. "If you go by the standards of Matthew chapter 5, she committed adultery or fornication in her heart with every man of the church. But actually making the beast with two backs? Not that I would swear to," Frau Backfennin answered with a sour expression. "She was that careful, especially since many of the men were the husbands and sons of the women she was also flattering."

She started the needles moving again. "Both of them, though—Döhren and Seyfart both—I think would have gladly spread their legs for the same man."

Gotthilf's eyebrows went up. "And who would that be?"

"The archidiakon, of course."

"I like her." Byron chuckled as they started walking back to the station. "She reminds me of Grandma

Pearl, my Grandpa Buck's wife. Sharp as a razor but heavy as a hammer."

"Yah," Gotthilf said. His mind was still whirling with the last revelation the old woman gave them. "And now we have a suspect. But not one I would have expected."

Byron sobered. "Yeah. I can tell you stories about erring preachers from our time. But I don't think they're exactly unknown here and now, either, are they?"

"No," Gotthilf replied. "But it is still not something you want to believe."

"Check it out," Byron said. "You can't accuse him or exonerate him without checking it out."

"Point," Gotthilf sighed.

Gotthilf beat Byron to the police station the next morning, but not by much. He had poured himself a cup of the execrable stationhouse coffee and was taking his first sip when Byron walked through the door. Byron had taken two steps toward the coffee maker when his name was called.

"Chieske! You down there?"

They both looked up to see Captain Reilly standing at the head of the stairs to the second floor.

"Right here, Captain."

"My office! Now!"

Gotthilf offered his cup to Byron, who gulped down the remainder of the contents and grimaced.

"Come on," the up-timer said, "let's go face the music."

Gotthilf followed Byron up the stairs and down the hall to the captain's office.

"Shut the door," Captain Reilly growled from where

he stood with his hands behind his back looking out the window.

Gotthilf did so, and took his place beside his partner. Reilly didn't say anything for a long moment, but from the set of his shoulders Gotthilf could tell that he was not happy. The captain finally turned around and faced them, back to the window, hands still clasped behind his back.

"Mayor Gericke is being pressured to bring in army troops," he announced. "He really doesn't want to do that, and God knows I've been arguing with him about it, because it will be seen as his failure as well as ours. But if we don't catch this killer soon, he won't have much choice. Some of the notables are already talking about appealing to the emperor."

"That would include most of the city council of Old Magdeburg, I would guess," Gotthilf ventured.

"He didn't name any names," Reilly responded, "but given how those guys just about have a collective stroke every time Gericke tells them they can't do something, I'd say you're right on the money. They haven't been happy since Gustav appointed Gericke to be the mayor of Greater Magdeburg and restricted their authority to the area inside the walls. If they can take him down and maybe replace him with one of their own, they'll go for it like a starving fox after a chicken."

Gotthilf nodded. That's how he saw it, as well.

"But that doesn't matter at the moment," Reilly continued. "We've got to get this guy, now, or we're all going to be deep in the kimchi."

"We got a suspect yesterday evening," Byron said.

"Who is it?"

Gotthilf looked to Byron, who gave him a small head motion toward the captain.

"It's one of the pastors," Gotthilf said.

"Who?" Reilly repeated.

"Laurentius Demcker, the archidiakon to Dr. de Spaignart at St. Ulrich's church in Old Magdeburg."

"The assistant of the most learned and most political of the pastors? Are you nuts?"

Captain Reilly didn't sound pleased, Gotthilf noted. But then, he might be excused at having another political implication loaded onto his plate.

"Aw, come on, Cap. You saw enough of the televangelist scandals up-time to know that just because a man is a pastor that doesn't make him a saint." Byron had a disgusted tone to his voice.

"Is he the man?" Reilly asked after a moment.

"Not sure, Cap," Byron interjected. "But he could be. And if he isn't, he may be able to give us leads to the real perp."

"Chieske, if you finger this guy and he's not the killer, you're going to drop us all in the chamber pot. The church will hang us from their crucifixes."

"Get us two days, Bill. If we can't get the guy by then, we'll deserve to have the troops in the streets."

Reilly stared at them both. Gotthilf returned a level gaze to the captain. "All right," Reilly said. "I'll talk the mayor into two days, somehow. But if you don't have me somebody in handcuffs by then, it's going to hit the fan, and there won't be any going back after that."

"Two days," Byron repeated. "We'll get him, Cap. Promise."

"Get after it, then," Reilly said, waving at the door.

Gotthilf almost trotted to keep up with Byron's long-legged strides down the hall. They rumbled down the stairs side by side. No one said anything, but the way between them and the outside door cleared almost like Moses parting the Red Sea. They burst outside and down the front steps and came to a stop by the first police vehicle.

"We've got to split up," Byron said. "I'm going to go hammer this Demcker guy, since I've met him. You go talk to the other one that was there, whatsisname."

"Schönfeldt," Gotthilf said.

"Yeah, him. I'll meet you in the square by the *Rathaus* in the old city in three hours and we'll compare notes. Got it?"

"Yah," Gotthilf said as Byron swung up into the first vehicle. The up-timer gave directions and the driver urged his horse into a trot.

As his wagon rumbled down the gravel of Kristinstrasse, Byron tried to remember everything said by the instructor of the class on interrogation he had attended a year before the Ring fell. He'd been an older guy named McPherson, probably in his later fifties, thinning gray hair and a brusque manner; but he'd known his stuff. He should have, having been a criminal investigator first for the Army's Judge Advocate General Corps, and then the West Virginia State Police, ending as a captain.

McPherson had walked in front of the instructor's desk at the front of the room and hopped up to sit on it. He'd held up the textbook and growled, "Read this on your own time. There's good information in it, and it's not bad for teaching about interviewing witnesses.

But it's a total failure as far as teaching anything about interviewing suspected perpetrators, and that's what we're going to spend most of our time this semester looking at. Here's the short version, people."

Byron remembered students, himself included, scrambling to get pens and notebooks ready to capture what was coming.

"Your goal is to get the perp talking, and keep him talking by any means you can. The more he talks, the longer he spins out his story, the more he'll let slip and the more you can get a read on his personality, emotions, and responses.

"There are two rules, people," McPherson had said. He'd held up a finger. "First, you've got to convince him you're sympathetic to him, on his side. You'll have to play on his likes and fears to do that." McPherson had held up a second finger. "Second, never ask a yes or no question. Never let a perp have a chance to say 'No' to anything. That will break the flow, and there's a really good chance he'll clam up at that point."

McPherson had slid off the desk onto his feet. "If you don't learn anything else this semester, learn those two things. Clear?"

Byron came back to his present as the wagon pulled to a halt in front of St. Ulrich's Church. "Clear, Captain," he whispered.

The second vehicle pulled up, and Gotthilf climbed aboard the light cart.

"Where to?" asked the driver.

"Heilige Geist Church," Gotthilf said. "As quick as you can."

The cart rumbled into motion. As the driver guided

his horse down Kristinstrasse toward the bridge into the old city, Gotthilf looked through his notes from yesterday's interview with the pastors and racked his memory for all the things that hadn't made it into the notes. They were drawing up in front of the church as he came to the end of that exercise. He still wasn't sure how he would approach Archidiakon Schönfeldt as he clambered down from the wagon.

"Wait for me," he told the driver. "I don't know how long I'll be, but if your boss gives you any trouble about it later, tell him to come talk to me."

"We will be here," the driver said as he set the brake and climbed down from the wagon seat.

Archidiakon Demcker rose from his chair by the table in the vestry room as the church sexton ushered Byron into the room. "What can I do for you, Lieutenant Chieske?" he asked.

Byron waited for the sexton to leave the room, then closed the door behind him. "I need to ask you some more questions about the same matters you discussed with Sergeant Hoch yesterday."

"Of course," the young pastor said. "Please, take the chair," he added as he stepped over and seated himself on a low stool.

"Gotthilf said there was only one chair in this room," Byron said as he settled into it.

Demcker gave a faint smile. "I had a feeling that there might be other conversations following upon yesterday's, so I asked Sexton Held to find another seat."

Byron grinned back at the pastor. "Good thinking." He sobered after a moment, and said, "The murders of these women are about to stir a passel of trouble in Magdeburg. We have got to find the murderer, and soon."

"Murderer? You are so certain that these acts were done by one man?"

Byron nodded. "Yeah, we are. I can't reveal evidence to you, but we have evidence collected in analyzing the crime scenes and the autopsies that make it clear to us that a single man committed the murders and mutilated these women."

Archidiakon Demcker shuddered. "It is hard enough to consider someone killing young women like that. It is almost unthinkable to think that they would mutilate the bodies in so grotesque a manner."

"Except that someone did think of it," Byron retorted. "Not only thought of it, but did it. Three times."

"Which only proves the theological thesis that man is a depraved creature," Demcker responded sadly.

"That's as it may be," Byron said. "I'm not here to debate general theology. I've got to catch a specific killer, soon, before he kills again."

Demcker nodded. "I understand. I will help in any way I can. Ask your questions."

Byron sat back in his chair and crossed his legs, presenting an air of comfort.

"Would you say that the men and women of your church get along, Archidiakon?"

"As much so as any group of people," Demcker responded.

"They're nice people, then?"

"For the most part, yes."

"Do you like the women of your church, Archidiakon?" Byron asked.

✧   ✧   ✧

Gotthilf encountered Archidiakon Simon Schönfeldt as soon as he entered the side door at Heilige Geist Church.

"Oh, hello, Sergeant Hoch," the pastor said in surprise, stopping short as Gotthilf appeared in the doorway.

"Archidiakon Schönfeldt," Gotthilf responded. "Is there someplace we can talk?"

"About?"

"The things we discussed yesterday."

Schönfeldt's mouth tightened a bit, then he said, "Come this way." He led the way to a small room much like the one Archidiakon Demcker had used at St. Ulrich's Church.

"Another vestry?" Gotthilf asked with a smile.

Schönfeldt responded with a smile of his own. "I learned this from Archidiakon Demcker. Our sexton hasn't learned yet to look for me in here. I can actually have an hour or so for my own study if I step in here when no one is looking."

"Ah," Gotthilf said. "That I can understand."

There were two low stools along one of the walls. Schönfeldt pulled them out, sat on one and waved Gotthilf to the other. "What can I do for you today?" he asked.

"What can you tell me about Archidiakon Demcker?"

A look of astonishment crossed the pastor's face. "Laurentius? Why? You don't think that because he lost his copy of that Bible he..."

"No," Gotthilf responded, "this is not about that. Or at least, not only about that. We have testimony that there may have been a connection between him and at least two of the women who were murdered."

"Ridiculous!"

Schönfeldt's eyes flashed and his face flushed.

"Laurentius is one of the gentlest souls I know. He would no more be able to murder someone than I could walk on the clouds."

"You know him well, then?"

"Well enough," Schönfeldt said.

"How long have you known him?" Gotthilf pulled his notebook out again.

"A little over two years, since right after I arrived here in Magdeburg."

"Ah," Gotthilf said. "Where did you come from?"

"Jena," Schönfeldt said. "I was invited to come by Pastor Jonas Nicolai to serve as his assistant here at Heilige Geist church."

Gotthilf jotted notes while Schönfeldt was talking. He looked up and said, "So are you the newest pastor in town?"

Schönfeldt thought for a moment. "I believe I am. Laurentius came from Hamburg a few months before I did. And I believe the next newest is Pastor Agricola, who is serving St. Jacob's while Dr. Gronovius is ill."

"I see." Gotthilf added more notes. "So you came from Jena, Archidiakon Demcker from Hamburg, and Pastor Agricola from Saxony, by his voice."

"Leipzig, I believe." Schönfeldt's voice was flat.

Gotthilf looked up. "Is there something wrong with Pastor Agricola?"

Schönfeldt made a face. "Not necessarily something wrong. He is like many young pastors, and not a few older ones, who seem to think that their chamber pots do not stink."

❖   ❖   ❖

"What?"

Demcker looked confused. Byron stared at him, eye to eye, and said, "Do you like women, Archidiakon Demcker?"

"Inasmuch as they are God's children and members of the parish, yes." There was still a trace of bewilderment in the pastor's eyes.

"Oh, come now, Archidiakon. You mean you've never admired a shapely woman, or admired a well-turned leg in your time here?"

Now the pastor looked away. *"Retro me, Sathanas,"* he muttered.

Oh, touched a nerve here, Byron said to himself. *Of course, he knew if he said "No" I wouldn't have believed him.*

"Do you like to touch women, Archidiakon?"

Demcker turned white.

"I mean," Byron pressed on, "sometimes you have to offer a hand of guidance or correction, don't you?"

Demcker started to flush.

"Soft, aren't they?"

"Lieutenant, I . . ."

"Really soft," Byron interjected. He uncrossed his legs and leaned forward, elbows on his knees. "Especially if you have to correct them, put them in their place. They ask for it sometimes, you know. I've seen it."

Demcker opened his mouth, eyes narrowed, then froze. After a moment, his mouth closed, and he turned away.

Gotthilf looked back to his notebook. "A common failing in humanity, I believe."

Schönfeldt sighed, and said, "You are right, Sergeant. I wrestle that demon myself."

There was a moment of silence while Gotthilf thought, then he asked his next question. "Is Archidiakon Demcker the type of man who could or would encourage a woman to desire him?"

Schönfeldt snorted. "Absolutely not!" He leaned forward a bit and spread his hands wide. "Sergeant Hoch, Laurentius Demcker has only one heartbeat, and that is to be a pastor to his people. I've never known anyone who has the passion to be a shepherd that he has. His first thought when he wakes up each morning is to pray for someone in his congregation. His second is to think of someone who needs comfort or help, and see to it that they receive it. His last prayer at night is that God will prepare him to minister the next day to those who are weak, wounded, or failing. Of all men I know, pastors or not, he is the least likely to prove to be a wolf who preys on the flock rather than the shepherd who prays for them."

"A paragon of pastors, then," Gotthilf murmured as he made notes.

"Aye," Schönfeldt agreed, "far better than I. And perhaps the sad thing is that he will likely remain a simple pastor his entire life, while others will use him as a stepping stool in their climb to rank and renown."

"Someone like Pastor Agricola?"

"Or even myself," Schönfeldt replied. Gotthilf noted that he didn't deny the comment about the other pastor.

"Do you think that rankles him? Archidiakon Demcker, I mean?" Gotthilf asked with interest.

"No," Schönfeldt said with a sad smile. "It would

me; it does rankle me on his behalf. But Laurentius would probably prefer serving as he does now, for it would mean he would see the people more and see their needs better than he would if his rank were higher." He shrugged. "I will not claim sainthood for him, but he is a better candidate than most."

"Come on, Archidiakon," Byron insisted. "What's the harm in admitting the truth, here?"

Demcker turned back to stare at him, head slightly tilted. "Why are you doing this, Lieutenant?"

"Just looking for the truth, sir." Byron was a bit nonplussed. Everything he knew, everything he'd seen in other interrogations and in the roleplaying coached by Captain McPherson said Demcker should have been furious by now. Instead, all he was getting was a quizzical look from the pastor, and what looked to be a bit of a sad expression.

"Well?" Byron prodded.

Demcker sat up straight, and sighed. "I am only human, Lieutenant. If it gratifies you to hear me admit it, then yes, I have been tempted; am often tempted. But I am called to be a pastor; to be a shepherd. It is my responsibility to watch over the flock, to shield it; not to be a ravening lion that feeds on it. I will not so dishonor my people; I will not so dishonor myself; I will not so dishonor my God."

Byron leaned back for a moment and looked at the young pastor. His eyes were clear and steady, his facial expression was not angry, his body language was no tenser than one would expect after being indirectly accused of murder. If this guy was lying, he was the best that Byron had ever seen.

He leaned forward, good humor gone and deadly serious. "We have a witness who states that the two women from your congregation who were murdered both had the hots for you."

"Hots?" Poor Demcker looked very confused.

"Lust. They wanted to have your babies."

Byron almost laughed again as the pastor went absolutely white with a most aghast expression on his face. It was obvious that he had been struck speechless. It was a very long moment before Demcker could muster words.

"I understand what you are saying," Demcker said the words one at a time, slowly. "I cannot speak to the state of mind of those unfortunates. I will say that if they harbored such delusions, it was not from any enticement or encouragement from me."

There was a moment of silence after that declaration, then the young pastor continued in a quiet voice, "On the hope of my salvation and eternal life, as God the Father, God the Son, and God the Holy Spirit bear witness, I swear to you, Lieutenant Byron Chieske, that I did not commit these awful murders; that I had and have no relationship with any woman in our congregation other than that of pastor and parishioner; and that I have in no way attempted to entice or seduce any woman. So help me God."

Byron sat back in the chair, holding Archidiakon Demcker's gaze with his own. The pastor did not flinch, fidget, glance away, or otherwise in any way betray nervousness. Every instinct that Byron had, every signal that he received, every measurement he could make told him that the young pastor was not lying.

❖   ❖   ❖

"So you believe that Archidiakon Demcker had no untoward relationship with either Frau Margrethe Döhren or Frau Anna Seyfart?" Gotthilf returned to his main topic.

Schönfeldt shook his head, and said in a tired voice, "He could not have; not and be the man and pastor I know him to be."

"And therefore Archidiakon Demcker did not murder either woman?"

Schönfeldt simply shook his head again, wordless.

"Then who did?" Gotthilf muttered in frustration.

"Let's say for the moment that I believe you," Byron said after a moment. "In that case, let me ask you if you can think of anyone else that we should consider a suspect? Anyone at all?"

Demcker shook his head slowly. "If I suspected one of my brother pastors of something so heinous, I would have already taken it to my superiors. As for one of my parishioners, no, I know of no one who could have done this, and I have no one to suggest."

Byron stared at him in frustration. "Right."

When Gotthilf jumped down out of his wagon in the square surrounding the *Rathaus*, he found himself facing Byron. They spoke at the same time.

"He didn't do it."

"Demcker didn't do it."

Byron snorted. "Okay, so we're in agreement on that. Truth to tell, the man impresses me. I may visit his church sometime to hear him preach. But that means we've missed something, and we're running out of time. Any other ideas come to you?"

Gotthilf had been bothered by something ever since he left Heilige Geist church. Something was stirring around in the back of his mind, something that was important, but he couldn't draw it into the light of day. The entire ride to the square he had been trying to tease it out, trying to grasp it firmly, but it kept eluding him.

"Not yet, but there's something..."

Someone stepped between them at that moment, muttering, "Follow..."

Byron gave him two steps, then followed in his wake. "Wait," Gotthilf told their drivers, then he in turn followed his partner.

Within twenty steps they all drifted into a nook between two buildings, and Demetrious turned to face them.

"I had about given up on you," Byron said bluntly.

Demetrious shrugged. "I am not a miracle worker."

"Do you have something that will help?"

Demetrious shrugged again. "I have something. You will have to decide whether or not it will help you."

"Give." Byron's voice was very hard at that point. Gotthilf was in a similar frame of mind.

"You know a boy with no eyes?"

Byron flushed and he started to raise a fist. Gotthilf grabbed his arm. "Byron, he means Willi."

Both of their minds flashed on the blind boy they had rescued from virtual slavery in their first case as partners.

"What about Willi?" Gotthilf asked Demetrious.

"The breeze whispers that the boy may know something that will help."

"What is it?" Byron demanded.

"Best you get that from him," Demetrious murmured. "There are those near him who do not let his voice be heard." With that, he pushed past them. A moment later he was lost in the crowd.

Without a word, the two detectives returned to their vehicles. Byron sent his back to the police station, and climbed up in Gotthilf's wagon behind his partner.

"*Das Haus Des Brotes* in the exurb," Gotthilf ordered, "and fast!"

What could Willi know? That refrain was running through Gotthilf's mind in the trip from the square to the bakery run by the family that had fostered Willi after his rescue from the man who had abused him. What could a blind boy know that no one else in the city knew?

The detectives jumped from the wagon before it even came to a complete stop in front of the bakery on the corner of Kristinstrasse and Canal Road. Frau Zenzi—Frau Kreszentia Traugottin verh. Ostermannin, known as Zenzi to one and all—was brushing a bit of mud from the steps up to the door. Her husband, Anselm, was the baker for *Das Haus Des Brotes*, but she was the one the buyers dealt with.

"Good day to you, Frau Zenzi," Gotthilf called out.

"Lieutenant Byron, Sergeant Gotthilf," she responded with a big smile. Nothing about Frau Zenzi was small, but her smile was especially large and warming to anyone who received it. "My two favorite *Polizei* men. What can I do for you this fine afternoon?"

"We came by to talk to Willi. It's been a while since we've seen him," Byron said.

"He's around on the back steps, taking a break," the shopkeeper pointed around the side of the building.

"Thanks," Byron said. The two detectives headed that direction.

Gotthilf could hear whistling as they drew near the back corner. They rounded it to see the boy, flour-smudged cloth tied around his head, whistling one of the Irish songs that Marla Linder had made popular in Magdeburg. He was sitting on the top step next to an older man.

Willi broke off the whistling, cocking his head to one side as he turned blind eyes toward the detectives. "Lieutenant Byron and...that must be Sergeant Gotthilf with him."

"Right," the older man said. He shook his head. "I still do not understand how you can tell that."

Willi giggled. "Everyone walks differently, Papa. I can hear it."

"Willi, Herr Anselm," Gotthilf said. Byron nodded.

Willi had really blossomed in the months since Byron and Gotthilf had rescued him from the man who had been running a faginy racket in part of Magdeburg. He had settled in with Anselm and Zenzi with the church's blessing, and had quickly become a part of their lives. He'd filled out physically as well, becoming a solid chunk of a boy instead of the waif that they had found begging on the street.

"So, Willi," Byron began, "I hear you may know something we need to hear about as policemen."

"Wait a minute," Anselm began, bristling a little. "Willi's only a child. You have no right to involve him in your work."

"Seems like he's been involved in our work before," Byron said. "He's with you now because of the work we do."

"Papa," Willi said, smile gone, "he's right. If I can help them, I must, because they helped me. And besides, it's the right thing to do."

"But..." Anselm began. Willi's head turned to face him, blind eyes behind the masking cloth still pointed in his direction. "All right," Anselm sighed. "For all that you're not her blood and bone, you have your mother's strength of will."

"And don't you forget it," Frau Zenzi's voice was heard as she stepped into the door behind her two men. "Willi, you tell them what you think you heard. But you two," she leveled a very direct gaze at the detectives, her former smile absolutely vanished from her face, "you'd best be sure that nothing comes back to touch my boy."

Byron nodded.

"As if he were our own kin," Gotthilf said.

She nodded in return. "Go ahead, Willi."

Willi stood and stepped back up the steps to the doorframe. "Excuse me, Mama." Frau Zenzi stepped back inside the shop and the boy stopped inside the door. "It was the evening of the night when the last woman was killed."

"Are you sure?" Gotthilf asked.

"Yes. I remember Mama talking about it two days later, and I knew that it was the same night."

Gotthilf motioned for him to continue, then grimaced as he remembered the boy couldn't see him. "Sorry, Willi. Go on."

"I was standing just here in the doorway, with the door only part way open, getting ready to come out and sit down to enjoy the evening air, when I heard them."

"Heard who?" Byron asked.

"A man and a woman, walking down the alley. And either they were hurrying or they weren't very tall, because their steps came close together."

"As close as mine?" Gotthilf asked. For once his lack of stature might be of use.

Willi tilted his head, considering. "Almost that close, yes."

"Okay, so you could tell there were two of them by the different steps, and you could guess at height by the speed of their steps," Byron said. "But how did you know they were a man and woman? Were they talking?"

Willi nodded his head. "I only heard a little bit. She said, 'Why are we going this way?' and he said 'I can't let some people know about us yet.'"

Gotthilf stiffened, and said, "Is that exactly how he said it?"

Willi's face showed a frown, partially masked by the cloth around his eyes. "What do you mean?"

"Can you describe his voice? Can you make your voice sound like his?"

"A screechy kind of voice," Willi said, changing the pitch and accent of his voice, "that sounded something like this."

Byron looked at Gotthilf and raised his eyebrows. Gotthilf's thoughts were chasing in circles. Almost he could place that sound. He shook his head and pulled out his notepad.

"Do you remember anything else?" Byron asked.

"No," Willis said. "They turned the corner right after that and I couldn't hear them anymore."

"And what time of day was that? You said it was evening, but can you be more precise than that?"

"It was almost full dark," the boy replied. "I can feel it when it turns dark. The air gets colder, even in summer."

"I can vouch for that," Frau Zenzi said, putting her hands on Willi's shoulders. "I made him close the door right after that, and it was as he says."

"All right," Byron said as Gotthilf scribbled notes hastily. "If a couple of days later you thought maybe this might be involved with the murders, why didn't you say something then?"

"That was my fault," Anselm said from where he still sat on the steps. "I didn't think this was anything very important, and I didn't want to see Willi mixed up in something ugly, so I told him to say nothing." He sighed and spread his hands. "You have to admit, it doesn't sound like much."

"Except that when we put that little bit together with the other bits we have, it sounds like Willi may have been the last person to see—or hear, rather—Justina Hösch alive."

Willi swallowed audibly.

Anselm ducked his head. "I am sorry," he muttered.

They spent a few minutes going over Willi's account again, Gotthilf adding a few more notes to his page. But it was obvious that Willi was remembering only a few brief seconds of an encounter, and without sight there really was very little more he could tell them.

"Okay," Byron said, bringing the discussion to a close. "Thanks for your help, folks. And if you think of anything else, or if you see or hear anything else that seems at all odd, make sure you let us know. Notify a patrolman right away. He'll get word to the station house, and we'll be here as soon as we can after that."

"Good job, Willi," Gotthilf said as he shook the boy's hand.

"Yeah, great job, Willi," Byron repeated.

Anselm and Zenzi drew the boy back inside the bakery, and the two detectives turned to walk back out to Kristinstrasse.

"Well," Byron murmured, "have you thought of whatever it was the boy pointed you toward?"

"Hmm?" Gotthilf replied.

"Oh, come on," the up-timer said. "I could see the wheels start turning in your head the moment the kid tried to mimic the voice he heard. Kid better stay with baking. He's not much of an impressionist."

"No, he almost had it, I think. It just won't come to me."

"So you think there's something to what he said? Or how he said it?"

The very moment that Byron asked his question, all the different thoughts that had been hanging just outside Gotthilf's grasp all day came together for him.

"I," Gotthilf pronounced with seeming calm, "am an idiot."

Byron looked taken aback. "How so?"

"I didn't ask the right question. Come on."

They hustled back to the wagon and jumped in as Gotthilf gave the address information to the driver. "So what did you miss?" Byron asked. Gotthilf just shook his head and made a sideways motion with his hand, not wanting to derail his thought processes.

Their wagon pulled up in front of a familiar house. The two detectives were standing before the door a moment later, and Gotthilf rapped the door knocker with some force.

This time the door opened quickly, with Frau Backfennin standing there, wisps of gray hair again straggling from beneath her cap, eyes blinking in the light.

"Yes?"

"Frau Backfennin," Gotthilf said hurriedly, "it's Sergeant Hoch again, with my partner Lieutenant Chieske. We have two more questions for you if we can have just a moment more of your time."

"Come in, boys, come in," the old woman said with a smile. "I have little on my hands but time these days. Come give me some company and liven up my day, please."

Frau Backfennin led them to the room they had used in their previous conversations, despite their protestations that this "would only take a moment." She settled into her chair, then looked at them with lowered eyebrows. "Sit down, boys, sit down. I'm not talking until you do."

The two detectives looked at each other. Gotthilf shrugged; they sat down.

"Now, you said you had some more questions?"

There was a hint of a giggle in the old woman's voice. Gotthilf had no trouble believing that she must have been quite the lively maiden, back in her youth.

"Frau Backfennin," he said, "when you and I talked the other day, toward the end of our conversation you said that you believed that the two victims who attended St. Ulrich's Church both, ah . . ."

"Would have spread their legs for the archidia-kon," the old woman completed the thought. "Yes, I remember saying that. And I meant it. I've been on this earth longer than most people, and I've seen more fools and foolishness in my life than you youngsters would perhaps credit, including fools in the church."

"All right, Frau Backfennin," Gotthilf said. "We believe you. But here's the first question I need to ask: when you said the archidiakon, did you mean Archidiakon Laurentius Demcker, the man who is the archidiakon today?"

Frau Backfennin got a guilty look on her face. "No."

"Then why didn't you say so then?" Byron interrupted.

She flushed a little, ducked her head, and muttered, "I wanted you to come back."

The two detectives looked at each other, then back at her.

"Why?" Gotthilf asked.

The old woman looked up at them with a defiant air. "I can't see to get out much anymore, and hardly anyone will come by except my daughter. You brought a moment of excitement to an old woman's life. Is it so wrong to wish for a bit more of it?"

Gotthilf felt compassion for Frau Backfennin. For someone so lively to be so restricted . . . he felt pity for her. Nevertheless . . .

"Your lack of forthrightness could have put Archidiakon Demcker in danger of being executed for murder," he said quietly.

Frau Backfennin paled, and her hand went to her throat. Then she squared her shoulders and sat up straight. "You shouldn't be misled by the foolishness of an old woman," she pronounced crisply. "That young man is a credit to the parish and the quarter. Oh, he's sometimes too credulous, too willing to believe the best of people, and he's not the sermonizer that Dr.

de Spaignart is—at least, not yet—but the church and the parish do better with him than they have in years."

Gotthilf felt an inner tension release, at the same time that he simultaneously mentally kicked himself for overlooking that question the first time he had interviewed the old woman and felt his gut tighten as he began to look in a new direction.

"Thank you, Frau Backfennin, that clarifies things very well, and it's a great help to us. Now, I have one more question, please: if you weren't referring to Archidiakon Demcker, who were you referring to?"

"Why, the one who was there before him, that Saxon lickspittle Bauer, him who changed his name to Latin to be more impressive."

Name change . . . Bauer . . . farmer . . .

"You mean . . ."

"Yah, him; the one who was Dr. de Spaignart's shadow and would have been his child if he could have but entered the old man's loins to claim to be his seed."

Gotthilf blinked at that, and looked at Byron. The up-timer's eyes were almost as wide as his felt. Even for the old woman, that was a rather strong statement.

"Ah, thank you, Frau Backfennin," Gotthilf said. "That answer also helps us, but it means we have a lot to do in a very short time. We must go."

The two detectives stood. The old woman remained seated and picked up her knitting from beside her chair.

"You boys can find your own way out, I'm sure. But I have one request."

"Yes?" Gotthilf was a little wary of what the old woman might desire.

"When this is all over, you come and sit here and

tell me the whole story, all right? From beginning to end, with all the details."

Gotthilf looked at Frau Backfennin, and for a moment he saw not just a hunger for knowledge, but a pining for involvement, a longing for connection. The lively, beautiful, vivacious young woman was trapped now in an old woman's body, having outlived almost all of her contemporaries. She was truly lonely, he saw.

"I will," he said. "Or at least as much of the truth as I can tell anyone."

"Good," the old woman sniffed. "You see to it that you remember that."

A moment later the two detectives were out the door standing by the wagon staring at each other.

"I was right," Byron said. "She's the spitting image of my Grandma Pearl."

"What do we do now?" Gotthilf said.

Byron narrowed his eyes in his "thoughtful" look. "Let's go talk to Archidiakon Demcker."

They weren't far from St. Ulrich's church, so in a short time they were dismounting from their wagon and heading toward the side door. Just as Gotthilf was reaching for the handle of the door, it opened before them to reveal Archidiakon Demcker and his friend Archidiakon Schönfeldt. Everyone stopped short, surprise on every face.

Byron recovered first. "We've got to quit meeting this way," he quipped. That evoked chuckles from the others.

"If you need to see Dr. de Spaignart," Demcker said, "he left for Rudolstadt this morning to visit with Pastor Johann Rothmaler. I expect him to return in perhaps three days."

"Actually," Byron replied, "we'd like to speak with you in your pastoral capacity."

"You as well, Archidiakon Schönfeldt," Gotthilf added.

The two pastors looked surprised, then looked at each other. After a moment, Demcker said, "Certainly. Come this way, please."

They ended up in a side chapel. "We should be undisturbed here," Demcker said. "The sexton is home sick today, and it's a couple of hours yet before the evening mass." He looked at the detectives. "So am I cleared of suspicion, since you are coming to me in this manner?"

"We think so," Byron said.

Gotthilf nodded to reinforce that statement. "However, the fact that *you* are does not mean that there is not a pastor under suspicion. We do not at this moment have sufficient evidence to request either a search warrant or an arrest warrant. We have a need, however, to examine his church."

The two pastors looked at each other. "We could do that, I suppose," Schönfeldt said. "In the absence of the district superintendent, I would think two of us would be an adequate substitution for this purpose."

Gotthilf relaxed a little. "That would be good."

Byron stirred. "It's that simple?"

"The churches do not belong to us," Demcker said, "although some pastors have been known to forget that. They belong to the district, so none of us can claim ownership or priority from that standpoint. As long as we are not destroying anything that belongs to him or removing anything that belongs to him without good cause, I doubt the superintendent will say much."

"Now?" Byron asked.

Demcker looked at Schönfeldt, who nodded and said, "The sooner we do it, the sooner we either clear our man or we know the truth."

"Right," Demcker said. He turned to the detectives. "Let's be on our way, then."

Gotthilf led the way out of the church, followed by the pastors with Byron bringing up the rear. He climbed up in the wagon first, then offered a hand to the others. "By the way," Demcker muttered, "just who *are* we looking at?"

Gotthilf turned to the driver. "St. Jacob's Church," he ordered.

"Oh." Demcker and Schönfeldt stared at each other for a moment, then they both looked at the detectives. "Are you sure?" Demcker asked.

"No," Gotthilf answered. "But that's why we have to look, and that's why you're coming along with us."

It didn't take long to drive the few blocks to St. Jacob's Church. It was located in the northeast corner of the Altstadt, the old part of Old Magdeburg, which prior to the Sack of Magdeburg in 1631 had been the poorest quarter of the city. Because of the prevailing winds, that quarter had mostly escaped burning. It had an even more old and run down look now, Gotthilf admitted to himself, than it had before the Sack.

"God must indeed have a sense of irony," Demcker said quietly.

"How so?" Schönfeldt replied.

"Because humble St. Jacob's, least of all the churches of Magdeburg, was the only one to survive the Sack and occupation almost unscathed."

Schönfeldt snorted. "Indeed, and that would be because there was little or nothing in the church to steal." A reluctant smile crossed his face. "Which proves your point, I fear. As well as reinforcing the many scriptural lessons about not desiring or trusting wealth."

"Indeed," Demcker echoed his friend in word and smile.

A moment later the wagon came to a halt before the church in question and detectives and pastors all descended from the wagon, all at that point equally grim-visaged.

They entered through the main door into the rear of the nave. The two pastors looked around, examining every angle, wall and recess, then led the way across the empty floor toward the pulpit and choir.

"He may not be here at the moment," Demcker said. "It is an hour or so until the evening service, after all."

Gotthilf finished his own looking around. "I see nothing to remark on here. Is there somewhere else in the church we should look?"

Demcker nodded, and led the way to a small door set to one side. That led to a small room. "Vestry," the pastor said, looking around. They all spent several minutes looking closely at everything in the room, taking the robes off their hooks, feeling the pockets.

At the end of the exercise, Gotthilf summed it up, "Nothing here."

"Where does that door go?" Byron asked, nodding toward the corner farthest from the door they had entered through.

Schönfeldt walked over and opened it, and they filed through after him. The room was even smaller than the vestry, dimly lit with a small window high in one wall, with a rickety table and lopsided stool in one corner and another door on the opposite wall.

There was even less in this room than in the vestry. And from the looks of it, it had not been usefully occupied in ages.

Byron opened the other door.

"Outside," he announced, a fact the rest of them had already gathered from the flood of light that had entered the room.

"Wait," Gotthilf called out as Byron moved to close the door. Something had caught his attention. "Move the table away from the corner."

Byron and Schönfeldt picked the table up and moved it as Demcker set the stool to one side. "Ah," Gotthilf muttered, putting on his gloves, "there *is* something there."

He went to one knee by the corner and picked up a small wooden box with a lid. Carrying it to the pool of light entering through the open door, he cradled it in one arm and opened the lid. "Aha," he said softly.

"What?" Byron asked.

Gotthilf tilted the box so that the others could see.

"It's a book," Byron said. "Is that good?"

"It's not just a book," Demcker said faintly. "It's a Bible, and I believe it's mine. I recognize that scrape on the cover." He reached for it, but Gotthilf moved the box away from his hands.

"Byron," Gotthilf said, "gloves."

Within a moment Byron had his gloves on and Gotthilf tilted the Bible into his waiting grasp.

"Open it up," Gotthilf said, "and turn to Job. Chapter 3, wasn't it?" he asked the pastors. They both nodded, eyes lighting in understanding but faces grim with the expectation of what might be found.

Byron opened the Bible in the middle. It fell open to Psalms, so he leafed pages backwards. "Job," he muttered as he turned the pages, "Chapter 15, chapter 12, chapter 9..." He slowed down, turning the pages with care. "Chapter 7, Chapter 6, Chapter 5, Chapter..."

He stopped, then slowly lifted a half page. Gotthilf hissed. Archidiakon Demcker closed his eyes. Archidiakon Schönfeldt looked furious.

Byron carefully closed the Bible, then placed it back in the box. Gotthilf closed the lid with equal care.

"You two," Byron said to the pastors, "are our witnesses that we found this here. You are the official ecclesiastical representatives that allowed us access to this church in the momentary absence of the serving pastor. You will be asked to sign affidavits to that effect, and very likely testify in court."

Archidiakon Demcker's eyes were now open, and the hard light in them was rather at odds with his usual temperament. Gotthilf was rather glad that the he was not the soon-to-be recipient of the wrath that had been brewed up in the young pastor's heart and soul.

"I think I saw a sack in the vestry," Archidiakon Schönfeldt volunteered.

"Would you get it for me, please?" Gotthilf asked, and a moment later he carefully placed the first major piece of evidence they had collected in this case other than bodies in the sack, then took custody of that from the pastor.

"Now," Byron announced, "we will head for the police station, then find the nearest magistrate after that and get a search warrant for the person and residence of Pastor Timotheus Agricola."

Byron had an edge of implacability to his voice. Gotthilf was fine with that. He was feeling just a bit implacable himself.

When their wagon pulled up in front of the police station, Archidiakon Demcker said, "How long will this take? I must do the evening service, since Dr. de Spaignart is in Rudolstadt."

Gotthilf looked to his partner. Byron nodded and headed for the door.

"Do you need to leave as well?" Gotthilf asked Schönfeldt.

"Well, I should be at the church to support Dr. Nicolai for the evening mass, but I think I can explain that I had been called upon by you officers of the law to assist with an issue that touched on clergy." Schönfeldt gave a half smile.

"And we will indeed back you on that," Gotthilf grinned back. "Do you know where Agricola lives?" Schönfeldt nodded. Gotthilf turned to the driver. "Take Archidiakon Demcker back to St. Ulrich's church, then return here. If we're not ready when you get here, wait for us. You are our driver for the rest of the day. Got it? No one else's."

The driver nodded as Demcker climbed back into the wagon. "Yes, Sergeant," he said, then shook his reins and clucked to the horse. Gotthilf headed into the station followed by Archidiakon Schönfeldt as the wagon headed back to Old Magdeburg at the trot.

Byron was standing in front of the station sergeant's desk talking to Captain Reilly. He broke off and turned to Gotthilf. "Send that to the evidence guys now, so they can try to get fingerprints off of it." He turned back to the captain. "We've got this case, Captain. We got three solid pieces of evidence this afternoon that come close to nailing our suspect to the wall. We need search warrants for his residence, and we need, what, three..." he looked back to Gotthilf, who nodded. "...three patrolmen to go with us."

Gotthilf grabbed Martin the mail clerk and handed him the bag. "Get this to the evidence room *now*, and tell them I want fingerprints from the contents by the time we get back. Don't drop it, don't break it, and by all that's holy, don't touch it! Got that?" He must have had a snarl in his voice, because Martin gave him a wide-eyed look and a short jerk of a nod before he took off almost at a run.

After Byron and Captain Reilly finished their conversation, the captain looked around at the handful of patrolmen who were hovering nearby trying to hear what had Lieutenant Chieske so worked up. "You, you, and you," he pointed to the three toughest looking of the eavesdroppers, "you're with Chieske and Hoch. Georg," he said to the desk sergeant, "adjust the schedule and rota until they get back, and get word out to the patrol sergeants." He looked back at the detectives as the delegated watchmen gathered behind them. "Are you guys still here? Go catch this guy before he kills someone else!"

The crowd of them blew out the door of the station and coalesced at the just-returned wagon. "Load 'em up," Byron ordered with a sweep of his arm. Everyone scrambled into the wagon and found a seat on the benches that faced each other. Gotthilf found himself sitting between Daniel Kierstede and Archidiakon Schönfeldt, with Byron sitting across from him.

"Head for the mayor's hall," Byron shouted, "and make it fast."

Everyone grabbed for a handhold as the wagon jerked into motion. Gotthilf leaned over to Kierstede, and said, "Glad you're with us."

"Are we after the guy who killed those women, Sergeant?"

"That we are, Daniel, that we are."

The patrolman got a very hard, very focused look on his face. "Good. I want to see that man hanged."

"Well, I think the list of people who would volunteer to pull the lever to release the gallows trapdoor is pretty long by this point," Gotthilf said, "but you might be able to bump most of the line since you found the first body."

"Who do I see?" was the patrolman's response.

Byron gave a short hard bark of a laugh. "I like your attitude, Patrolman Kierstede."

"Why is the pastor with us?" Kierstede asked. The other patrolmen perked up at that question.

"He knows the man we're going to be dealing with," Gotthilf said. It was the truth, he thought to himself as the patrolmen made their own assumptions about that statement. It just wasn't the whole truth. That would come out soon enough, but it would be distracting for it to be public at the moment.

It didn't take long for the police wagon to arrive at the mayor's hall. The building was large enough to accommodate all the functions that Otto Gericke had to oversee, between the reconstruction of the old city, the planning and construction of the new city, and all the affairs of government for the province of the Imperial City of Magdeburg. It wasn't very ornate—yet—but Gotthilf assumed that would come with time and money.

The wagon pulled to a stop. Byron and Gotthilf jumped out. "Archidiakon, you're with us," Byron said. "The rest of you wait here."

Byron led the way as Gotthilf and Archidiakon Schönfeldt followed. "What are we doing here?" Schönfeldt whispered.

"We need a magistrate to sign a search warrant anyway," Gotthilf muttered back, "and this case has so much notoriety that we need to give Mayor Gericke a quick report that we've found a suspect, so he'll know to hold everyone at bay for a little while longer. Since the mayor is also a magistrate, this allows us to kill two birds with one stone, as the Grantvillers would put it."

They marched down the hall and into the mayor's offices like a storm front, people scattering out of their way. "Albrecht," Byron said to the mayor's secretary, "we need to see Mayor Gericke now."

"The mayor is occupied..." Albrecht began.

The door behind him to the mayor's personal office opened. "Send them in, Albrecht," Mayor Gericke's voice came through the open door.

The three of them filed past Albrecht's desk and into the mayor's office. Gotthilf closed the door behind them.

"Lieutenant Chieske, Sergeant Hoch, and..." the mayor's eyebrows rose, "Archidiakon Schönfeldt, is it not? Why are you here?"

"We have a suspect for the murders and mutilations

of the three women," Byron reported. "We need search warrants signed for the residence of the suspect." He offered two folded papers to the mayor.

Gericke took the papers, opened them, and began to read. Gotthilf could tell when he got to the name of the suspect, as his eyes widened and he glanced at them sharply before returning to the documents. He read through them all with obvious care. At the end, he looked back up to the men standing before his desk.

"I suspect I know now why Archidiakon Schönfeldt is with you. Are you certain about this, Lieutenant?"

"Very certain," Byron replied. "I believe we have enough information now to arrest him on suspicion of murder, and certainly enough to support the search warrant. And if we find anything at all in his rooms, we will have enough to charge him with premeditated murder."

"But a pastor," Gericke said. "I have seen them heated enough to have an apoplexy, and God knows that Martin Luther is probably not the only pastor who has thrown an inkwell or a book or something similar at an opponent. But this just simply isn't the kind of thing I can see a pastor doing."

Schönfeldt stirred. "With respect, Mayor, I have heard much of the evidence they have gathered, and I and Archidiakon Demcker were present when the most damning piece they have yet was found. No matter how my heart wants to agree with you, in this I must stand with these men."

"But why would a pastor do something like this?" Gericke almost sounded plaintive. "Feuds with kings, feuds with other pastors, feuds with professors and guild masters and even mayors I could understand. But this...this..."

"Cold-blooded murder," Gotthilf interjected. The mayor nodded sharply. Gotthilf continued, "We may never understand, Mayor Gericke. These are the acts of a deranged mind. We can eventually prove the circumstantial case: the who, the what, the when, the where, the how. Grasping and proving the motivation— the why of it all—is often the hardest thing to do, and sometimes we never accomplish that."

The mayor stared at them for a moment longer, then sighed, picked up a pen, and signed the warrants. He pushed them back across the desk to Byron when he was done, and said, "It is a matter of great grief when a man of God goes so far astray. Do it quietly and with as much respect as possible."

Byron picked up the warrants and passed them to Gotthilf, who tucked them into his jacket. "To the extent that he allows it," the up-timer said. "But all bets are off if he threatens someone else."

After a moment, the mayor nodded. He waved toward the door. "Go do what you must."

They filed out of the office in silence. Gotthilf could feel the brooding gaze of the mayor on his back even as he closed the door behind them.

The detectives, the pastor, and the attending patrol-men finally arrived at a rather new rooming house in the northern part of Old Magdeburg called the Neustadt. Much of that part of the old town had been destroyed in a fire in the 1620s, and had not been rebuilt before the Sack. Since then, however, building had practically filled the space between the walls, and it had become one of the more prestigious areas for newly affluent members of the capitol's society to dwell in.

Byron's eyebrows raised slightly. "Kind of up-town place for an assistant pastor," he said.

Archidiakon Schönfeldt shrugged. "His family is well off," was all he said.

Byron looked back at the patrolmen. "Any of you know who's in charge here?"

"Old pensioner named Röloffse," one of them responded. "Last door on the left."

"Ready?" Byron looked to Gotthilf, who gave a firm nod in reply. "Everyone with us, then."

The up-timer led the way through the front door, followed by a host of clomping feet. He arrived at the identified door, and rapped on it sharply as Gotthilf arrayed himself at his partner's side. It was opened in a moment by an old man of middling height, iron gray hair, and deep furrows on his face. "Who are you, and what do you want?" he barked.

"Lieutenant Chieske of the Magdeburg *Polizei*, Herr Röloffse," Byron responded curtly, holding out his badge, "and my partner Sergeant Hoch." Gotthilf flashed his own badge. "We have a warrant to search the residence of one Timotheus Agricola."

Gotthilf took one of the search warrants from his pocket and handed it to the old man. Röloffse took the paper in his right hand and shook it open with a sharp motion. It was only then that Gotthilf noticed that he was missing his left arm from above the elbow. The sleeve for that arm was pinned up so it wouldn't flop around.

Herr Röloffse peered at the warrant closely, spending

some time in reading it through. When he was through, he handed it to Gotthilf, who returned it to his pocket.

"The man's a pastor," the old man said. "What right have you to be pawing through his things?"

Gotthilf stepped to one side and motioned Schönfeldt forward.

"I am Archidiakon Simon Schönfeldt of Heilige Geist Church, Herr Röloffse," he said. "They are here with the knowledge of the church."

"Hmmph." The old man still looked skeptical. "I guess you'd be wanting me to show you which room is his, then."

"If you would," Gotthilf said.

"Clear the way, then."

Everyone in the hall stepped to one side or the other and opened a path for Röloffse. He strode through and led them back down the hall to where a flight of stairs led upward.

They mounted to the third floor, then followed the old man back down the hall toward the rear of the building. Gotthilf was glad that no one was opening doors and sticking heads out. Their little processional would have occasioned comments and discussions that he would just as soon not have to deal with at that moment.

Röloffse stopped at a door. "Here," he said.

Byron first knocked at the door. No response. Knocked again. Still no response. He tried the door. It was locked. He looked at the old man.

"Got a key?"

A hint of a smirk crossed Röloffse's face. "Yah. We own the locks on the doors."

Byron stepped back and motioned to the door. The old man detached a large ring of keys from his belt and held it up before his face in the light from the window at the end of the hall. Gotthilf was surprised at the nimbleness of the fingers in Röloffse's one hand as he rolled keys around the ring, counting, "... fifteen, sixteen, seventeen, and eighteen. Here we are."

Röloffse applied the key to the lock in the door and turned it. The click of the lock mechanism turning was loud in the hallway. He removed the key and tripped the latch so that the door stood slightly ajar. Stepping back with a broader smirk, he waved at the open door.

"Thanks," Byron said brusquely. "We'll take it from here." He waited for the old man to head for the stairs, then turned to the patrolmen. "Any of you have gloves?"

Kierstede pulled a pair out of his jacket. The other two just shook their heads.

"Right. You two stand out here and guard the room," Byron directed. He motioned with his head, and Gotthilf and the rest followed him into the room.

"Gloves," Byron said.

Gotthilf looked at Schönfeldt as he pulled his own gloves on. "Pastor, you stand there by the door and watch. Do not touch anything unless we tell you to."

Schönfeldt nodded.

Gotthilf and Byron looked at Kierstede. Byron motioned to Gotthilf, then started looking around on his own.

"Touch things only if you have to," Gotthilf instructed the patrolman. "Be careful about how you move things. Look everywhere you can, every place there is to look." With that they joined the lieutenant in the search.

Agricola's residence was a suite of two rooms. One

was a sitting room with a sofa and chairs clustered around a small table and a desk and chair shoved up against a wall on the far side of the room. The other was a small bedroom, from what Gotthilf could tell looking through the door.

There was a mound of books piled on the desk. Gotthilf began there, picking them up one at a time and leafing through the pages with care. Somewhere around the third book he saw out of the corner of his eye that Kierstede headed into the bedroom. An aimless whistling began sounding from in there as Gotthilf continued to page through the books.

He was in the middle of the eighth book when Kierstede called out, "I think I've found some-*urk*!"

There was a clatter from the bedroom and the patrolman rushed through the sitting room with his hand clamped over his mouth. As the sounds of explosive vomiting echoed in the hall, Gotthilf dropped the book and beat Byron through the door to the bedroom by a split-second.

There they found a small wooden box lying on the bed with its lid beside it. In the box were several small jars. Gotthilf picked one up.

"*Scheisse!*" He recoiled in horror, his own gorge rising.

In his shaking hand was a small clear glass jar filled with a clear liquid. Floating in the liquid, almost as if they were peering at him, were a pair of blue eyes. He managed to set the jar down without dropping it, then backed up a step, hands fisted at his sides.

Byron didn't say anything, but Gotthilf could see his jaw muscles bunched up; always a sign of anger in his partner. The up-timer picked up the other jars in the box. Two of them were also filled with the same clear liquid as the first, and pairs of blue eyes floated in them as well. The third was empty.

Each of the three jars Byron held was set down by the up-timer with care beside the one that Gotthilf had pulled out of the box. Then Byron took a deep breath, held it for a long moment, and released it in a controlled manner.

"Archidiakon Schönfeldt," the up-timer called out, "would you come here, please?" Gotthilf remarked at how calm his voice seemed.

Schönfeldt appeared in the doorway. Byron beckoned him forward. "I think we have found our evidence, sir, to arrest Pastor Agricola for premeditated murder. What do you think?"

Gotthilf saw an expression of pure horror come across the pastor's face. "O merciful God in heaven," the man whispered, hand flying to his mouth. After a long moment, his face set in a rigid expression. He lowered his hand and looked at the detectives. "Arrest him," the pastor said, "and make your case in court. If he is convicted, there will be no outcry from the church."

"Byron," Gotthilf said.

"What?"

"Agricola's killed three times," Gotthilf pointed out, "but there's a fourth jar there. We need to find him now."

Byron's head swiveled to focus on Schönfeldt's face. "Where is he going to be at this moment?"

Schönfeldt pulled out a pocket watch. "He should be at St. Jacob's church, close to finishing the evening service."

Byron grabbed the pastor by the arm. "Come on! Gotthilf, seal the room!" he threw over his shoulder as he pulled Schönfeldt through the bedroom doorway and toward the hall.

Gotthilf followed them, stopping long enough to close the door to Agricola's rooms. He looked at the two guards. "You two will stand guard over this room until the coroner arrives. No one enters until then. No one. I don't care if Emperor Gustav Adolf shows up, he doesn't get in. Got it?"

"Got it, Sergeant," one of them answered. "But do we have to stand here smelling his puke?"

"Until someone comes to clean it up, yes," Gotthilf responded as he grabbed a white-faced Kierstede by the arm and pulled him along toward the stairs.

"You owe us, Kierstede!" sounded from behind them. The patrolman waved a shaky hand in acknowledgment as he started down the stairs.

Gotthilf clattered down the stairs as quickly as he could, towing Kierstede in his wake. He arrived at the ground floor almost under the nose of Röloffse, who stepped back in surprise.

"There's been an accident in the hallway up there," Gotthilf said as he trotted by the old man. "You might send someone up to clean it up."

They burst out the front door and hurried to where Byron and the pastor were already in the wagon. Gotthilf boosted Kierstede into the wagon, then grabbed Byron's outstretched hand and was yanked up by main force.

"Go!" Byron ordered, and the driver popped his horse into a reckless trot.

The day was becoming twilight, and curses followed them as people had to dodge the wagon. Gotthilf heard something over the rumble of the wheels. Archidiakon Schönfeldt was talking aloud. For a moment, Gotthilf couldn't understand it, then it registered with him that the pastor was speaking in Latin.

> *Requiem Aeternam dona eis,*
> *Domine,*
> *Et lux perpetuae luceat eis.*
> *Requiescant in pace.*
> *Amen.*

It was the prayer for the dead from the Requiem Mass. As Schönfeldt finished with the *Amen*, he would start over again at *Requiem*. Gotthilf looked away from him. The man had just received a serious shock, and if this helped him cope with it, that was okay with Gotthilf. And in the back of his mind he figured that any prayers to God were a good thing, particularly at this point in time.

The wagon rumbled over the bridge into the old city, pedestrians scattering like birds. Gotthilf reached across and grabbed Kierstede. "When we stop rolling," he shouted, "you get two blocks away from the church and blow your whistle for a patrol sergeant. When he shows up, you tell him I said we need the coroner at the rooming house we just left, on the third floor. If he thinks you need to go along with the message, you do that, otherwise you run back to the church and find us. Got that?"

Kierstede gave a firm nod. His color was back to normal, so Gotthilf thought he could handle that assignment. He looked to Byron, who nodded but said nothing.

Despite the horse's quick trot, it was still another minute or so before they arrived at the church. As soon as the driver pulled the horse up short and the wheels stilled, Kierstede was off the back of the wagon and hurtling away from the church in pursuit of his orders.

Gotthilf and Byron jumped down from the wagon; Archidiakon Schönfeldt followed at a bit more deliberate pace, but still wasted no time. They faced a very small group of parishioners exiting the church in the deepening twilight.

"Small crowd," Byron remarked.

"It is a sad but unremarkable fact that a weekday evening service never attracts many attenders even in the larger churches," Schönfeldt replied in a quiet voice, searching the crowd as much as the detectives were. "Most attend only on Sunday." He stiffened. "There he is."

Gotthilf followed the pastor's gaze and saw Agricola emerging from the church talking to a youngish woman.

"All right," Byron murmured, "let's approach him quietly and ask him to come with us to answer some questions. Archidiakon, you stand here."

Byron stepped out and Gotthilf followed his lead. They approached the man that Gotthilf could only think of as "the perp" with ease. Although Gotthilf's hand itched to be holding the .32 caliber revolver that was sitting in his shoulder holster under his jacket, he made it swing freely at his side, and concentrated on keeping a pleasant expression on his face rather than the anger and loathing he felt inside.

"Pastor Agricola?" Byron called out as they neared the man.

"Yes?" Agricola was more nasal than Gotthilf recalled it. The pastor turned slightly so he could see them without losing sight of the woman he was speaking with.

"Lieutenant Chieske of the Magdeburg *Polizei*," Byron replied. "I believe you've already met my partner, Sergeant Hoch."

Gotthilf kept the pleasant expression on his face by slipping by main force of will.

"Do you need something, Lieutenant?" Agricola made it clear by tone and expression that he felt he had better things to do than speak with the police at that moment.

"We would appreciate it if you would come down to the station and talk to us," Gotthilf said. "We have some questions about a case we're investigating that we think you could help us with." Gotthilf was proud of how casual he sounded.

"I think not," Agricola responded tartly as he turned back to the young woman.

"I'm afraid we must insist," Byron said in a cooler tone as he took a step closer. Gotthilf sidled to the right to put a slight separation between himself and his partner. It was taking more self-control to keep his hand off of his pistol.

The young woman standing by Agricola said, "No need to see me home, Pastor. I can make my way alone."

She started to step away. Agricola's left hand snaked out to grasp her arm. "No! Don't leave."

At that, Gotthilf's right hand moved inside his jacket to rest on the butt of his revolver. He could see from the corner of his eye that Byron's right hand was behind his back and under his jacket, obviously grasping the up-time Colt automatic he carried there. Neither one of them moved.

"Go away! Leave!" Agricola shouted at them. "I have nothing to do with you. I know who you are, men whose hands are bloody with the lives of those you have brought down."

Byron snorted. "Bit of the pot and the kettle there, I think." Agricola's brows lowered in confusion. The up-timer straightened, although his hand remained behind his back. "Timotheus Agricola, I arrest you on the charge of premeditated murder. Let her go and come with us."

Agricola shook his head sharply. "No!" he said, "No! You cannot do this to me. I am a pastor, a man of God, doing God's work and God's will. You have no cause and no right to do this. Go away!"

Byron took a step closer, angled away from Gotthilf. Gotthilf stepped once in a similar manner as he said, "Herr Agricola, you are under arrest for the murders of Margrethe Döhren, Anna Seyfart, and Justina Hösch."

The young woman's eyes had opened wide in panic, and she was trying to get free from Agricola's grasp. Although he looked to be scrawny, he must have had a fierce grip, as her struggles were in vain.

"You don't understand," Agricola's nasal tone intensified. His eyes flicked back and forth between the two detectives. "I have done nothing wrong."

"You shall not murder," Byron said. "Exodus chapter 20."

Agricola's face twisted. There was a flurry of movement as his right hand reached over and pulled the woman in front of him. His left arm looped around her neck almost in a choke hold, and his right hand dropped into a side coat pocket and pulled out something metallic which he raised against her neck.

"Knife!" Gotthilf called out as he took two steps to his right. His pistol was out but hung at his side. He couldn't take a shot. Not yet. Too much risk of hitting the woman.

"Get back!" Agricola ordered in a strained voice. "Don't move!"

Byron raised his left hand and made a calming gesture. "Herr Agricola, just calm down. We don't want anyone to get hurt here."

"You will address me as Pastor!" Agricola shouted. "I am a man of God!"

"Fine, Pastor Agricola, fine," Byron said. "We'll call you that. But calm down, and let's not hurt anyone."

Gotthilf saw Agricola's gaze shift past him, then he felt more than saw Archidiakon Schönfeldt step up beside him. "Timotheus," the pastor said in a calm voice.

Agricola seemed to settle a bit. "Simon," he responded.

"I have seen the Bible with the cut pages," Schönfeldt continued in that calm voice. "I have seen the eyes in your rooms." There was a long silence during which Agricola seemed to shrink a bit. "Timotheus... why?"

For a moment, it seemed as if Agricola's arms were going to drop. Gotthilf tensed to spring forward, but then Agricola tightened and his eyes seem to light up.

"Are you against me, too, Simon?"

Schönfeldt spread his hands, and repeated, "Why, Timotheus?"

Agricola hesitated for a breath, two, then said in a very low voice, "I have the French disease."

Gotthilf saw Byron mouth "Syphilis," and nod.

It was called variously the French disease, the English disease, or the Spanish or Spaniard's disease depending on where you might be in Europe. But regardless of the name, syphilis was still as nasty a venereal disease in the 1630s as it was in the future that Grantville came from.

"Oh, Timotheus," Schönfeldt muttered.

"I was young," Agricola said, "barely nineteen when I met her. I was studying medicine at the university in Leipzig. I'd never lain with a woman before, but when I met Annalise in a tavern that night, I was captivated by her. She had the bluest eyes, and they ensorcelled me. I spent my money on her, and she took me to her bed. Twice only, I swear it. But when I ran out of money and was reduced to stealing bread from my friends to survive, she moved on.

"When it became clear that Annalise had left me a gift to remember her by, I went looking for her. I don't know what I would have done if I'd found her then, but she was gone. No one in Leipzig knew where she went. And when I let slip to one tavern maid why I was looking for her, she laughed a cruel laugh and said that she had done likewise to half the men in town."

Schönfeldt shook his head in sorrow.

"I began to study religion in penance for my sins," Agricola continued, a distant expression on his face, "and I distanced myself from women. For years I found comfort in serving God. But then, one day I saw her eyes, staring at me. Those blue eyes, laughing at me, teasing me, taunting me, telling me my faith was weak and worthless."

There was a moment of silence.

"What did you do?" Schönfeldt finally asked.

"It was obvious to me that Annalise had been a succubus," Agricola responded in a voice of reason. "And now she was inhabiting a new vessel. But she didn't recognize me, so I was able to get her alone. When I commanded her in the name of Christ to come out, she did not do so. So I silenced her. And then I removed her from her vessel."

Gotthilf felt nausea listening to this account from what was becoming more apparent by the moment to be a very deranged man.

"And then?" Schönfeldt prompted.

"Then I saw her again. And again I removed her from her vessel."

"How many times now?" Schönfeldt asked.

"Three," Agricola responded.

"And have you seen her since then?"

"Yes."

Gotthilf shivered. No telling how many times this lunatic would have killed if they hadn't found him today.

"Timotheus," Schönfeldt said, "is Annalise in the woman you are holding?"

"No," came the drawn-out reply.

"You need to release her."

"No. I need her."

"Why?" Schönfeldt replied.

Gotthilf's attention was attracted by movement behind Agricola. Someone had appeared in the doorway behind the pastor and his hostage, someone who was moving very carefully and very quietly up behind them, taking care to remain in Agricola's blind spot. Gotthilf kept his eyes focused on Agricola's face, letting his peripheral vision see the moving figure. He tensed, and rocked forward onto his toes.

"Because..."

At that moment, the figure behind Agricola resolved into Patrolman Kierstede as he sprang forward and wrapped his arms around the pastor, getting both his hands on Agricola's knife hand and pulling it away from the woman.

Byron and Gotthilf joined the struggle an instant later. Byron broke Agricola's grip on the girl by main force; from the sound of it, he may have broken some of Agricola's fingers as well. Gotthilf caught the girl as she was spun away from the knot of struggling men. He steadied her on her feet, then passed her to Archidiakon Schönfeldt as he moved forward.

"Watch over her, please. I've got to help Byron."

It took all three of them, detectives and patrolman, to wrestle Agricola to the ground and get him restrained. Gotthilf secured his wrists with his handcuffs.

"Cuff his ankles," Byron directed Kierstede. "He's so skinny, your cuffs should go around them. At this point, I don't care if he gets a little bruised. I don't want him capable of running."

Gotthilf ended up sitting on the backs of Agricola's thighs and pressing down on the backs of his calves with all his weight in order for the patrolman to secure cuffs around the pastor's ankles. Once that was done, he jumped up and away from the bound form.

Agricola writhed on the ground for a few moments, grunting and whining. Then he collapsed on his face and began weeping.

Schönfeldt drew close. "Is it over?"

"No," Byron said in a hoarse voice. "We've caught him. That just ends the pursuit. The hard part starts now."

Kierstede had sounded on his patrolman's whistle, calling in the local patrol sergeant and nearby patrolmen to secure the area. Their wagon had been sent off to collect the police photographer and bring him back. Gotthilf turned to the young woman, who was still standing, wide-eyed and shaking, beside Archidiakon Schönfeldt. "Excuse me, Fräulein," he said as he pulled his notebook out to make notes, "what is your name?"

"El . . . Elsbeth Vollenweilder," she stammered, clutching her hands together.

"Fräulein Vollenweilder," Gotthilf noted, "did you know Pastor Agricola well?"

"No," she said, staring at the man on the ground. "No, I just met him. Would he really have hurt me?"

Gotthilf looked at her; her eyes were dark brown. "Probably not, but we've made sure of it now."

He asked her more questions, calming her down in the process. She really had nothing to tell. She was new to the Magdeburg area, and tonight had been her first encounter with Agricola. Brown eyes or not, Gotthilf mused as he put the notebook away, she was fortunate that it wasn't her last encounter.

The photographer had arrived and begun his work while Gotthilf was interviewing the young woman. Head down, Gotthilf followed behind him, quartering the area, examining the ground with care.

"What are you doing?" Byron called at him from where he stood by Agricola.

"Looking for the knife, or whatever it was he was threatening Fräulein Vollenweilder with."

"I think it went that direction," Kierstede said, waving toward the near side of the church.

Gotthilf headed that direction, and before long found something glinting in the last of the light of day that really rocked him back on his heels. It wasn't a knife—it was a spoon. "Nathan," he called out, "come shoot this." The photographer obliged, taking two pictures of the spoon where it lay. Then Gotthilf put his gloves back on, bent over and picked it up, after which Nathan took three more photographs.

A spoon; but not just any spoon. This was an up-time spoon, made of thin stamped metal of the kind called stainless steel. Gotthilf had seen its like before in the case involving Harold Baxter. But was this really what Agricola had been holding at Fräulein Vollenweilder's neck? And if so, why?

He carried it back over to where his partner was standing. "Byron, do you have your flashlight with you?"

"Yep." The up-timer pulled the small flashlight out of his pocket and flicked it on. The bright white light illuminated the bowl of the spoon.

"The edge of the spoon bowl is sharpened," Gotthilf said in surprise. "Why would anyone sharpen a . . . Oh."

Gotthilf and Byron adopted identical expressions of disgust. Byron flicked the light off and put it away. Gotthilf pulled a waxed paper envelope out of a jacket pocket, enfolded the spoon in it, and tucked it back into a pocket. An outside pocket, this time.

Kierstede looked at them both, perplexed.

Gotthilf lifted a fist to eye-height, then made a digging and rotating motion with it. It took a moment to sink in that the spoon had been what Agricola had used to cut the victims' eyeballs from their heads. Kierstede paled in the light of the lamps held by a couple of the patrolmen.

Another wagon pulled up behind theirs, and Captain Reilly descended from it and headed their way. Byron and Gotthilf pulled their tired bodies up straight, echoed by the patrolmen standing around the area.

"Who is that?" the captain asked, pointing at the manacled body on the ground.

"That," Byron said with a sigh, "is our serial killer."

"Doesn't look like much," Reilly replied. "Who is he?"

"Pastor Timotheus Agricola," Gotthilf said. He jerked a thumb behind them. "He was serving here at St. Jacob's Church."

Reilly frowned. "You guys sure about this?"

"Oh, yeah," Byron said.

"We found the missing eyes in his residence," Gotthilf added, "apparently preserved in gin or something as some kind of trophy."

Reilly looked like he wanted to curse, but restrained himself after he looked at Archidiakon Schönfeldt out of the corner of his eye. "You have anything more on him than that?"

"Oh, yeah," Byron repeated. "He confessed."

"He what?" Reilly was flabbergasted.

"He confessed in public to our Archidiakon Schönfeldt there—who, by the way, could be the hostage negotiator on my team any time. The short version is he thought he was fighting cases of demon possession."

"Uh-huh. And the real case?"

Byron looked sad and sour at the same time. "We probably won't be able to prove it until we have an autopsy done at some point, but from his own admission he has syphilis. I think we've got a bad case of tertiary stage syphilis shredding his mind."

"Al Capone crazy, huh?" Reilly said.

"Worse, I think," Byron said.

Something else to talk to Byron about, Gotthilf made a mental note.

"Gotthilf's got lots of notes," Byron said. Gotthilf patted his jacket pocket. "We'll write up our reports tomorrow."

"Good." Reilly looked around. "I'll take him back to the station and we'll lock him in a holding cell for tonight. He'll be Mayor Gericke's problem tomorrow."

It took a few minutes to get Agricola loaded onto one of the wagons. Reilly rode with him, along with a couple of patrolmen. The rest of the patrolmen returned to their patrols. The patrol sergeant put Fräulein Vollenweilder up on his horse and took her home. That left the two detectives, Kierstede and Archidiakon Schönfeldt staring at each other. They were joined by Archidiakon Demcker, who stepped out of the shadows to join them.

"How long have you been there?" Gotthilf asked.

"Long enough to figure out what happened. So Timotheus really did it?"

Byron sighed. "I need a beer if we're going to go over this. C'mon."

They all trooped to The Green Horse, where they collected mugs of beer and settled around a table. They let Archidiakon Schönfeldt explain the evening's happenings to Archidiakon Demcker. That worthy had nothing to say when the accounting was concluded. All he could do was shake his head and mutter a prayer.

"The really interesting thing, in a ghoulish sort of way," Byron concluded, "is how this is going to play out in the courts. In the up-time, the American legal system held that someone who is insane could not be severely punished or executed for acts committed while insane. I don't know what the Magdeburg law will hold."

"If the judge is merciful," Demcker said softly, "he'll get the ax. Otherwise he'll be broken on the wheel. The law about murder is severe."

There was a moment of silence, then Byron said, "Some Jena law student may get a thesis out of this case."

Gotthilf snorted. "More than one student, and more than one thesis, I suspect."

Byron gave a tired chuckle. "You're probably right." His gaze swiveled to Kierstede. "Daniel, my man, if you can't hold your stomach any better than you have in this case, being a cop just may not be the job for you."

"It's the eyes," Kierstede said hollowly. "I can handle anything else, but this stuff with scooping out women's eyes just got to me. I'll deal with it."

"You'd better," Gotthilf said. "You'll see worse than this if you stay with this job."

Kierstede said nothing; just gave a determined nod.

Byron's eyes came back to Gotthilf. "And you, partner, have a tough job tomorrow."

"What? Writing the reports?"

"Nope."

Gotthilf racked his brain, came up with nothing. "What?"

A sinister smile slowly appeared on Byron's face. "You have a date."

Now Gotthilf was really confused.

Byron's smile grew larger. "With an old widow-woman."

Gotthilf's confusion compounded.

"To tell Frau Maria Backfennin what happened."

Gotthilf put a hand to his eyes and groaned as everyone at the table laughed.

"You promised."

The Blauwe Duif

Kerryn Offord

July 1634, the Øresund, near Helsingør,
30 miles north of Copenhagen

Pieter Kervel stood at the tiller of the *Blauwe Duif*
as she sailed down the narrow strait between Seeland
and Skåne that was the main sailing route connecting the North Sea to the Baltic. They had loaded a
cargo of salt at Setubal, in the Low Countries, and
were heading for Danzig, the largest port on the
Polish coast. This was their first passage through the
Øresund since the New Year. In a normal year they
would have made their first passage of the year at
the end of winter, but the last few months had been
anything but normal. First there had been the invasion
of the United Provinces, which had closed Setubal
and Amsterdam to normal trade, and then there had
been the conflict in the Baltic, which had forced up
insurance premiums, making the route less profitable
than the alternatives. The recent Peace of Copenhagen

had changed all that, and he'd finally considered it time to make the passage. Today the sea was calm, the wind was steady, and the sun was shining. Pieter wasn't expecting any problems as he headed for the toll station at Helsingør.

KAABOOOM!

The *Blauwe Duif* heeled violently as the blast sent water into the air. Pieter barely kept his hold on the tiller as it was nearly whipped out of his hands. Then the ship righted herself. Pieter realized there had been an explosion, and his immediate thought was some of his cargo had exploded. But, that wasn't possible. They were only carrying salt on this trip and salt didn't explode. He turned then to his next concern, the safety of his ship and crew. A quick visual inspection revealed all the sails still set, and all the lines still in place. Whatever the damage, and he could feel through his feet that there had been some damage, it wasn't topside. He spotted a couple of crewmen getting back to their feet. "Man the pumps!" he called.

The first mate appeared from below decks and signaled that all was not well as he hurried up to Pieter. "We've been holed," Dirck Arentsz said. "The hull's staved in forward of the main mast. We're taking in water fast, and some of the cargo has broken free."

That was what Pieter had feared. He glanced landward. Beaching the *Blauwe Duif* was his only hope of saving her. He swung to starboard. "See what you can do about slowing the inrush of water and securing the cargo. I intend trying to beach her."

"I'll do what I can, Pieter." Dirck took one step away before stopping and looking back over his shoulder. "Lucas was in the hold."

Pieter winced. With loose cargo that couldn't be good. "Is he hurt?"

"We haven't found him yet."

Pieter couldn't help but picture Lucas trapped under a couple of casks of salt while the water rushed in. But now wasn't the time to worry about a single seaman. He had a ship to save. "Keep an eye out for him, but stemming the inflow of water is more important."

The battle to save the *Blauwe Duif* had been lost from the moment the explosion breached the hull. The crew wasn't big enough, nor was it well trained enough in damage control to stem the flow. All they managed to do was slow it enough for them to get everyone above deck and an injured Lucas safely into the ship's boat. He was the worst of the injuries, with a broken arm and a leg that had been crushed when a cask of salt had rolled over it. The rest of the crew sported a selection of cuts and bruises with a sprinkling of sprains, broken noses, and lost teeth.

As the *Blauwe Duif* sank beneath the waves Pieter was left wondering what had sunk his ship.

Copenhagen, a couple of days later

Morgens Kaas af Sparre held a very important, and lucrative, position in King Christian's Øresund Tolls Commission, but right now he would have given anything not to be Superintendent of Tolls for the Øresund. He sighed and concentrated on what Pieter Kervel's lawyer was saying. Also listening attentively were the representatives for the insurers of the *Blauwe Duif* and her cargo.

Jan Dircksen paused his oration while he carefully polished his spectacles. Putting them back on, he continued. "Therefore, the loss of the *Blauwe Duif* is clearly the result of the Kingdom of Denmark's failure in its duty to ensure that the passage for which it charges a toll was safe from abnormal hazards to navigation."

Morgens winced at the choice of words. You couldn't get a more abnormal hazard than a minefield. He had foreseen that the minefield would interfere with trade when it was first proposed as a way of protecting Copenhagen from the USE Navy, and had pleaded the case that a safe channel be left mine free when it was initially laid. Either his pleading had been listened to, or more likely, the relatively small numbers of mines available had dictated that there had to be some areas with few if any mines. Either way, there had been a narrow channel, right under the guns of Kronborg Castle near the port of Helsingør, where there were no mines. Obviously, they hadn't advertised the existence of the safe channel during the war, but upon the cessation of hostilities the channel should have been marked, and there should have been commission vessels in the Øresund to warn incoming vessels to use the safe channel. Unfortunately, one of his subordinates had failed to carry out his instructions. The *Blauwe Duif* had not been warned about the presence of the minefield and had sailed right into it. Not only did she hit a mine, but she also managed to sink in the middle of the safe channel.

His brother-in-law, Christian Friis af Haraldskær, counsel for the Øresund Tolls Commission, leaned over and whispered into his ear. "They have a strong case. We may have to settle."

Morgens flicked Christian a scathing look. Four years studying the arts and five years of civil law and that was the best he could do? Morgens had already realized that they were going to have to settle. It was now a matter of how much it was going to cost.

"... It is my considered opinion that the Kingdom of Denmark owes my client compensation for the loss of a contract worth seven hundred and thirty-six rigsdaler to deliver a cargo of salt to Danzig." Jan lowered his papers and dropped his head in a minimal bow before sitting down.

Morgens mentally compared that with the usual freight rate for salt from Setubal to Danzig. It was significantly higher than normal, but for one of the first ships to pass through what had until recently been a warzone, it was within acceptable limits. He turned to the lawyer for the underwriters of the voyage. "Do you have anything you wish to say?"

"Yes." Melchior Borchgreving grabbed a handful of papers and stood. "My clients, the underwriters of the last voyage of the *Blauwe Duif*, intend claiming for the total loss of the ship and her cargo." He started to read from the papers in his hand. "Item, one ship: a fluyt of one hundred and sixty *scheepslast* burden, valued at nine thousand two hundred and ninety-five rigsdaler..."

"Hold it!" Christian held up his hand to silence the lawyer. "That's the price of a new fluyt of a hundred and sixty scheepslast. You aren't going to tell me your clients underwrote a vessel of the *Blauwe Duif*'s age for her full replacement value, are you?"

Morgens was in full agreement with his brother-in-law. No underwriter in their right mind would insure a vessel of the *Blauwe Duif*'s age for her full replacement value. Such an action would only encourage ship-owners to insure their old and worn out vessels and then wreck them for the insurance. He started checking his book of tables, found the entry he was looking for, did some quick calculations on his abacus, and announced the pertinent numbers. "The Diminished Value of the *Blauwe Duif*, a fluyt of one hundred and sixty scheepslast on the Baltic Trade for seventeen years, is one thousand, five hundred and fifty rigsdaler. We may be willing to compensate your client up to that amount."

Melchior continued as if Christian and Morgens hadn't spoken. "Next, there is the matter of the cargo the *Blauwe Duif* was carrying when she sank—a hundred and sixty scheepslast of salt destined for Danzig."

Morgens checked his paperwork to find the current price the Sounds Toll Commission was prepared to pay for salt, and winced. Total compensation for the loss of the *Blauwe Duif* could cost as much as thirty-eight thousand rigsdaler, or nearly a sixth of the total value of tolls collected in the last full year of collection—1632. However, there was a light at the end of the tunnel. "Surely the salt is being transported in casks, if so, it could be salvaged."

"It was my understanding that the commission did not intend salvaging the *Blauwe Duif* or her cargo," Melchior said.

Morgens hadn't intended salvaging the *Blauwe Duif*. The *Blauwe Duif* had sunk in over sixty feet of water and the local salvage operators couldn't work at those depths. Normally they would just mark the wreck and leave her there. Unfortunately, the insurers had good grounds to claim compensation not only for the loss of the *Blauwe Duif*, but also for her cargo. An attempt to salvage the *Blauwe Duif*, or at the very least, her cargo, would have to be made. Morgens hoped that Admiral Simpson's divers, with their up-time dive equipment, could do the job. "That was the original intention. However, since our last meeting, I have spoken with Admiral Simpson of the USE Navy and he has offered the use of his up-time divers."

Morgens wasn't being totally untruthful. He had talked to Admiral Simpson as soon as he heard of the sinking of the *Blauwe Duif*, but it hadn't been about borrowing Al and Sam Morton to salvage the ship and cargo. No, he'd approached the Admiral about getting rid of the mines before they caused him any more problems. With the war over, Morgens expected traffic through the Øresund to return to normal, which was an average of more than ten ships a day over the summer and autumn. Unfortunately, the wreck of the *Blauwe Duif* was blocking the only channel through the minefield, and every day it remained blocked was costing the tolls commission a small fortune.

Admiral Simpson had responded to his request for help with the less than satisfactory news that the USE Navy didn't have any mine clearing capability. Morgens had pressed him, but the best he'd been able to get out of the admiral was a promise to get his engineers onto the problem right away. In the meantime he had offered Morgens the Morton brothers—the heroes of the defense of Lübeck. Even as Morgens spoke Al and Sam Morton were in the Copenhagen armory examining several uncompleted mines. Their inspection was interrupted by a messenger. They were to report to Johannes Verlacht's office immediately.

Johannes Verlacht was the former senior engineer aboard the SSIM *Monitor*, which had been lost to a spar torpedo during the attack on Copenhagen. He could easily have obtained a new assignment on one of the remaining ironclads, but he'd been seduced by the contents of the Copenhagen armory.

He was drooling over the plans for King Christian's wooden submarine when Sam and Al knocked on his door. "Come in!" he called. When he saw who had knocked he gestured towards the chairs arranged around the office. "There's been a change of plans. Grab a chair and sit down."

Sam fell into a chair. "What do you mean there has been a change of plan? Don't they want us to clear the mines from the Øresund?"

Johannes waved for Al, who was still standing, to sit down. "The powers that be have decided that it is more important that you salvage the *Blauwe Duif*'s cargo."

"But what about the mines," Al protested. "We just spent the whole morning learning everything we could about the things."

"That's good to hear," Johannes said, "but you will have to pass that information on to whoever gets assigned the task in your place. Right now it is more important that the *Blauwe Duif*'s cargo be recovered."

"Why?" Sam protested. "What's so special about the ship's cargo?"

"Its value," Johannes said. "The Øresund Tolls Commission has decided that they want to recover the more than three million dollars worth of salt the *Blauwe Duif* was carrying.

"The Danes have hard hat rigs," Al said. "Why can't they use those?"

Johannes shook his head in gentle negation. "The Danes have exactly one hard hat rig, and with the publicity surrounding the king's adoption of it as a method of execution, you are unlikely to find anyone willing to use it."

Al winced. One of King Christian's wartime creations had been a hard hat diving system. From what he'd heard, it had been as faithful a reconstruction of an up-time hard hat system as local materials allowed, except for one little detail. The air supply had lacked a non-return valve. When, during the first demonstration dive, the air hose had broken lose, the pressure of the surrounding water had attempted to squeeze the contents of the dive suit—in other words, the diver—through the only opening in the suit, which had been the coupling in the helmet where the air had entered.

"So we get nominated for the job?" Sam asked.

"I'm afraid so."

"Can we use the Danish hard hat rig?" Al asked.

Sam turned to his brother. "What? Are you serious?"

"Do you want to move a whole ship's cargo using SCUBA?"

Sam paused for a few seconds before shaking his head. "At sixty feet it'd be a real pain."

"That's what I was thinking," Al said. "It won't be ideal, but we could work split-shifts: one working in the hard hat rig in the morning while the other does the afternoon shift." He turned to Johannes. "Would we be allowed to use the king's rig?"

"After we add a non-return valve," Sam added.

"We can only ask," Johannes said, "But how is your non-return valve attached?"

"Usually they are screwed in between the helmet and the whip hose," Sam answered.

Johannes shook his head slowly. "I think you'd better check out the king's hard hat rig before you make any more plans."

Al had difficulty holding onto the contents of his stomach. Their guide had taken them to where King Christian's latest execution device was displayed. The human remains had been removed from the dive helmet and were now sitting beside the helmet in a large glass jar of alcohol, still in the shape they'd assumed when they attempted to fill the helmet. It was probably one of the most gruesome sights he'd ever seen.

He turned from the gruesome sight and concentrated on the much safer sight of the dive equipment. He immediately identified a problem with the whip hose. "I think I know why Herr Verlacht suggested we look at the dive rig. They clamped the hose to the helmet."

"We can probably work around that, but I've spotted a major problem." Sam pointed to a mark in the helmet. "Have a look at this. It looks like they cut it open to get the body out."

"I did wonder how they did that." Al bent down to examine the helmet a bit more closely. The copper had been carefully cut, and then just as carefully repaired. He straightened up and turned to his brother. "I don't know about you, but I don't think I'd trust this helmet."

"I don't want to use it either, but what do we do?" Sam asked. "The admiral ordered us to give the Danes 'all assistance.'"

Al shrugged in resignation. "I guess we ask them to make us a couple of new rigs, with non-return valves."

"It'll take ages for them to make two new rigs," Sam protested.

"Yeah," Al agreed. "I doubt the artificers in Copenhagen are going to be any quicker than Asmus Brockmann was back in Lübeck."

"We could ask for the rigs he made to be sent to Copenhagen."

Al liked the thought of using their old hard hat rigs, but he knew it wasn't possible. "Matt and Miquel need them to clean up the little mess we left blocking the River Trave. The Lübeck city fathers would raise merry hell if we tried to shut down that operation to help the Danes."

Sam's shoulders slumped. "Yeah, well, you do realize that leaves us salvaging the *Blauwe Duif's* cargo using SCUBA?"

Al had realized that, and he wasn't any happier than his brother. "It's all we've got until they can make some new hard hat rigs."

Grantville, the office of Kitt and Cheng Engineering

Louie Tillman didn't like public speaking, even if it was only to an audience of two, but with a career in the U.S. Navy that lasted thirty-two years and included two tours on minesweepers he was the best qualified person to lead the minesweeper project. Fortunately, Jason Cheng and John Kitt were good listeners, and being engineers, easily absorbed the technical details. "And that is an 'O' sweep—so called because it uses something called an Oropesa float." He illustrated the end of his prepared presentation by drawing a circle around the float in the diagram of the "O" sweep he'd drawn on the meeting room's blackboard. "Can you build one?"

Jason nodded. "It all looks pretty straight forward enough, except for the explosive cable-cutter, but I've got a few ideas for that I'd like to try. However, I do think it'd be a waste of resources to build all of the sweep gear here in Grantville. We'll probably need the services of one of the Grantville machine shops to make the explosive cable-cutter, but we can design everything else so that it is well within the capabilities of the naval yard in Lübeck."

"Will they be able to follow your engineering drawings though?" Louie asked. "We don't want to get everything built and find you can't connect the explosive cutter to the rest of the sweep."

"We haven't had any trouble with the local crafts-men, so I don't envisage any problems in Lübeck. Not with Derek Modi there to supervise," John said.

"I'd forgotten about Derek being in Lübeck," Louie said. "He had something to do with the rolling mill there, didn't he?"

Jason nodded. "He got it built on schedule, and on budget."

Louie whistled in admiration. During his career in the Navy he'd seen many a project manage to be completed either on schedule or on budget, but very few of them, and certainly nothing as complex as a rolling mill, had been both.

The Øresund, off Helsingør, a couple of days later

SCUBA was not the best way to salvage a cargo of over four thousand casks of salt from a ship sixty feet underwater. If they'd been using hard hat equipment they could have stayed underwater long enough to recover all of the casks in a few days, albeit a few very long days. But working at sixty feet they were draining their SCUBA tanks down to the reserve in only twenty minutes. That meant they had less than twenty minutes of working time per dive, and with mandated surface intervals between their dives of up to three hours to keep their accumulated nitrogen levels manageable, they were going to be lucky to accumulate seventy-five minutes of actual working time per day.

Sound travels easily underwater, so Al and Sam had no difficulty hearing the warning bell that signaled the minesweepers were about to detonate a mine. They carried the one hundred and forty-four pound casks they were holding—which under water felt as if they only weighed twenty-four pounds—to the cargo net and dropped them into it before heading for the fifteen foot decompression stop, where they would stay for three minutes. According to their dive tables they didn't need to make this decompression stop, but their dive tables hadn't been created with their workload in mind. With no decompression chamber available, they were erring on the side of caution.

Back on the surface Al passed his fins to the crewman who'd appeared at the ladder the moment they surfaced. "This is getting old fast," he said to his brother.

"It's the third time today we've had to cut a dive short," Sam agreed as he passed up his fins to the waiting Jörgen Ibsen. "Still, I'd rather not be in the water when they detonate a mine."

"True." Al had no idea what the lethal radius of the shockwave from a mine might be, and they might be taking safety to the extreme by leaving the water while a mine was detonated, but it was better than finding out the hard way that they were too close. He climbed the ladder onto the sailing barge that they'd been allocated as their diving tender and reached down to give his brother a hand up. "You want to catch the action?"

"Why not? It'll help pass whatever surface interval Henrik insists we take before we can go down again," Sam said as he started to remove his dive gear.

There were three whaling boats on the water, with the closest no more than fifty yards away. Two of them were lying parallel some fifty feet apart, their full complements of rowers doing just enough to hold their position against the current. A hundred yards or so behind them, the third whaler, with only two pairs of rowers, was also maintaining its position while two rifle-armed crewmen watched on. The front whaleboats each had an end of a weighted rope, which was supposed to find mines by snagging the mooring lines. The ringing of the bell that had brought Sam and Al out of the water was a warning that they'd found a mine.

The mines they were finding were sixty gallon Bordeaux wine barrels that had been suitably modified. Each barrel had been about two-thirds filled with gunpowder before a wooden plug was put in place. This created a cavity that served as a buoyancy chamber as well as somewhere to put the fusing mechanism.

Outside the mine there were five horns, which were the contact fuses. Anything striking those horns with enough force would activate the fuse, causing the mine to explode. Or at least, that was the theory.

Henrik Mortensen rang the dive tender's bell and lowered the flag that announced they had divers in the water. This was the signal the whaleboats had been waiting for. Almost immediately a man waiting at the stern of one of them slid into the water, and, with what looked like a simple carpenter's saw in hand, dived under the surface. He popped up some ten yards from the whalers to take on air before diving down to continue sawing through the mooring line. A couple of additional trips to the surface for air later a mine popped up, to be followed by the swimmer, who'd wisely swum away from the mine before surfacing. While he was being picked up the current carried the mine away from the whaleboats.

It only took a couple of minutes for the mine to drift a hundred yards, and as soon as it was a safe distance away from the sweeping whaleboats the marksmen on the third whaler opened fire. It took five shots before it exploded in a cloud of white smoke and water.

With the excitement over, Sam and Al wandered back to where they'd stowed their equipment. Henrik had been totaling up their bottom time, and the dive tender's skipper had good news for them. "I'm calling an early end to the day. All this coming and going has stuffed up the schedule so badly that you can't start the next dive before it's time to knock off for the day."

Al was happy to call it a day. They might have spent less than fifty minutes actually moving the heavy salt casks from the hold to the cargo nets, but he was still exhausted. "How many did we do today?" he asked Henrik.

Henrik called out to one of the men operating the boom crane that was transferring the results of the latest dive onto a waiting lighter. "How many did they do this time?"

"Thirty-three."

"And ninety makes a hundred and twenty-three," Henrik said. "At your current rate of progress, and taking into account things will take longer the deeper you go into the holds, I can see it taking over a month to salvage all of the casks."

"Shit!" Sam muttered. "What's the bet they have the new hard hat rigs finished just as we remove the last cask from the wreck?"

Next day

Someone had been busy overnight. Instead of the disorganized arrangement of the first day of combined operations, today they were organized. Al and Sam were scheduled to make five dives lasting no more than twenty minutes, with the first surface interval of the day being two hours forty minutes and the others lasting three hours. It made for a long day, but with the sun shining for over seventeen hours a day, it was silly to waste any sunlight. Some smart fellow, and Henrik made sure Al and Sam knew who that fellow might be, had suggested to the crews of the whaleboats that they synchronize schedules. The rowers could rest when Al and Sam were diving, and sweep for mines when the divers were on the surface. It meant they didn't have to wait for the divers to surface before detonating a mine, and Al and Sam could keep to their dive plan, maximizing their bottom time. It was a mutually satisfactory arrangement.

Al and Sam were in the middle of their second surface interval when the warning bell sounded. They glanced at each other, and then at Henrik, who was already making his way to the dive tender's bell. They might have agreed to dive to a schedule, but they were still acknowledging that there were no divers in the water, just in case something went wrong. It was all being done in accordance with the latest Occupational Health and Safety regulations, but with it being their lives on the line, neither Al nor Sam were complaining.

Everything seemed to be going well. The diver had entered the water and started cutting the cable. They watched him dive another three times before the mine popped up. They covered their ears when it came time for the marksmen to detonate the mine. Nothing much happened with the first shot. Al wasn't even sure where it hit, but there was no such problem with the next shot.

KAABOOM!

Al uncovered his ears and smiled at his brother. "Now that never gets old."

After lunch they spent another sixteen minutes moving salt casks, before enduring another boring three hour surface interval. During this time the whaleboat crews found another two mines, bringing the total found over two days to seven. It didn't sound like many, but they were sweeping the edges of what should have been the safe navigation channel.

That day ended with a total of seventy-three minutes of bottom time, in which they managed to offload another one hundred and eighty-six casks.

Al looked at the tally Henrik was keeping and wanted to weep. There were something like forty-three hundred casks of salt aboard the *Blauwe Duif*, and in two days of diving, they'd barely scratched the surface of the task at hand.

The days fell into a pattern. Al and Sam were fitting in five dives a day, and moving up to two hundred casks a day. Meanwhile the whaleboats were slowly expanding the cleared channel, finding and destroying at least three mines a day.

There was no real excitement on the twelfth day when, during Al and Sam's second surface interval of the day, the whaleboats found yet another mine. Everything was running according to the established procedure as the swimmer went in and cut it free, and once it drifted a safe distance away, the marksmen on the following whaleboat fired at it.

They were used to mines not exploding with the first couple of shots, but a fourth shot rang out, and then a fifth. Sam turned to his brother. "Maybe they missed the horns."

"They hit all five horns," Henrik said. "What happens now?"

Al glanced round to see Henrik had joined them. He had a telescope in his hands, which explained how he knew the horns had been hit. "If the marksmen can't set it off by shooting at the horns, then they have to set a charge on it and blow it up that way."

"Is that dangerous?" Henrik asked.

"The actual setting of the charge isn't that dangerous. What's dangerous is whatever is happening inside the mine. It could go off at any moment," Sam said.

"Which is why they're going to wait a good ten minutes before approaching it," Al said.

Ten minutes later one of the whaleboats rowed within fifty yards of the mine before stopping to let a swimmer slide over the side with a length of slow match tucked behind his ear and a fused stick of dynamite between his teeth. The swimmer used a combination of dogpaddle and sidestroke to swim up to the mine. Once there he carefully placed the stick of dynamite on top of the mine and after blowing on his slow match, lit the fuse and swam away.

He hadn't swum more than ten feet before a seagull landed on the mine, and moments later started to peck at something sticking out of one of the damaged horns.

KAABOOOM! BOOOM!

"Holy shit!" Al shouted. Not that he could hear anything. He hadn't been expecting the double blast of the gunpowder and dynamite, and had been caught with his ears uncovered. He looked around to check that Sam and Henrik were okay. They were, but both were staring white-faced at the slowly dissipating cloud of white smoke.

They watched on in silence as a whaleboat approached a body floating in the water and gently hauled it aboard. Nobody could have survived that blast, Al thought. Not being so close to it.

The diving team hadn't previously had any social interaction with the whaleboat crews, but you had to do something to show your respects when a man died.

So Al, Sam, Henrik Mortensen, and Jörgen Ibsen set out that evening for the tavern where the boatmen usually hung out. They heard them long before they saw the light spilling out of the tavern.

"Do Danes mourn someone's death by having a party?" Al asked.

Henrik shook his head. "Not that I'm aware of."

"I'll go ahead and see what's going on," Jörgen said.

He was waiting for them when they got to the door. "They're celebrating good news. Soren Hemmingsen survived the explosion."

"What?" Al demanded. Soren Hemmingsen was obviously the name of the swimmer, but Al had seen how close he had been to the explosion. It just wasn't possible that he could have survived.

"It's true," Jörgen said. "He's a bit of a mess, but they say there's nothing that won't heal."

Al was still trying to wrap his mind around what he'd heard as he trailed his companions into the tavern. It went against everything he'd ever learned about diving—a diver that close to such a big explosion should have been killed. It was in this confused state he was introduced to the leader of the whaleboat crews.

"It shouldn't have taken young Soren nearly getting himself killed before you joined us," Oluf Andersen said as he shook Al's hand.

Al rescued his hand from Oluf's strong grip. "We can't drink when we're diving." It wasn't much of an excuse, but it did contain an element of truth. Alcohol and SCUBA diving didn't mix. Al couldn't remember the details of what the complications were, but he did remember that alcohol in the system could increase the risk of decompression sickness.

Oluf snorted. "Erik doesn't seem to have any trouble drinking."

The name didn't mean anything to Al. "Who?" he asked.

"Erik Andersen. Soren's replacement." Oluf smiled. "You didn't think we'd stop sweeping just because one man has been injured?"

Al had thought that. "I would have thought you'd have difficulty finding a replacement so quickly."

Oluf shook his head. "The money's too good. They upped the diver's bonus for destroying a mine by setting a charge on it to a whole rigsdaler. There were a number of volunteers. Erik was the lucky one."

That was about one hundred dollars, and Al knew it wouldn't have been enough to get him to go that close to a live mine with damaged fuses. "If all it takes is money, maybe we can hire a couple of locals to use the new hard hat rigs when they arrive."

Oluf snorted. "No way. No amount of money will get a sane man into one of those killing machines." He reached a hand out to each brother. "Come, have a drink with me."

Al didn't want to seem stand-offish, but there were some things a sensible person didn't do. "I'm serious. We'd love to have a drink with you, but it's a really bad idea to mix diving with alcohol."

Oluf gestured in Erik's direction. "He's drinking, so you can drink. Come, I'm buying."

"But he's free diving, while we're using SCUBA. With repeated dives you build up nitrogen in your system, and . . ."

"Nitrogen?"

It was obvious that Oluf had never heard of nitrogen.

Al took a deep breath before attempting to explain what nitrogen was. The explanation created more questions, and soon Al and Sam were the center of interest as the boatmen asked about the science of diving. The evening ended with Al and Sam carrying the drunk Henrik and Jörgen back to the dive tender.

The next evening the diving team once more joined the boatmen at the tavern, but having had nothing better to drink than boiled water that first evening, this time Al and Sam came prepared, with coffee and a coffee pot.

A barmaid brought out a couple of mugs and the steaming coffee pot that had been simmering on the stove out the back. She poured coffee into Al and Sam's mugs and stood waiting expectantly. Oluf noticed the smell and asked what they were drinking.

"Coffee," Al replied as he took the first sip. It was just how he liked it, and he told the barmaid so. She smiled and placed the coffeepot on the table before walking away.

"She likes you," Oluf said.

Al blushed. He'd noticed the looks she'd been giving him. She was a very attractive woman, as barmaids tended to be. But he had heard stories about how they earned their living and wasn't interested in that kind of encounter. To distract him, Al offered Oluf a sip of his coffee. Oluf's reaction didn't bode well for the future popularity of coffee locally.

"It's an acquired taste," Al said as he had another sip. "Me and Sam were talking today..."

"During your copious free time," Oluf said after rinsing his mouth out with beer.

"Hey, those breaks are compulsory," Al said. He was all ready to further justify their long intervals between dives when he saw the smile Oluf was trying to hide. "Ha ha, you got me. Yes, during our copious free time, Sam I and I got to thinking. What do you think about using a sort of spar torpedo to plant the explosive charge on a mine that's refused to explode?"

Sam butted in. "Yeah. If you put a stick of dynamite on a long pole, you wouldn't have to get as close as Soren did."

"But when the mine explodes, the boat will be too close," Oluf protested.

"The mine will only explode if something upsets the fuses. So you have your marksmen pick off any birds that try to land on it," Sam said.

"But when the dynamite explodes, surely the mine will also explode?" Oluf asked.

Al shook his head. "The dynamite won't set off the gunpowder. It needs a source of ignition."

"But surely dynamite going off is a source of ignition," Oluf said.

"Sure," Al agreed, "but by the time it ignites the gunpowder, the mine will be broken open. All you'll get is an enormous powder flash."

Oluf's raised brows said more than words.

"Gunpowder needs to be confined to explode," Al said. Oluf still looked dubious. "Hey, I can prove it."

"Please do."

Al looked around for the source of the interruption. What he found were a lot of interested faces. Just like the previous evening, they'd attracted an audience. "I'll have to hunt around for what I need."

"What do you need?" one of the boatmen asked.

"A couple of anvils would be nice, and of course, some gunpowder."

The man nodded. "I can get some gunpowder, but what do you need the anvils for?"

"I want to recreate a demonstration I saw years ago. A guy placed an anvil on its working face and filled a cavity in its base with gunpowder and lit it. It just flared off, but when he repeated the experiment by putting the second anvil on top of the gunpowder, it exploded, sending the second anvil high into the air."

"I'd like to see that," the man said. Others agreed, and one suggested he knew where they might be able to find a couple of anvils.

"If you can get them for me, I'll get everything set up for a demonstration tomorrow before we start work."

"Tomorrow?" Oluf asked. "What is wrong with now? There is still at least an hour of daylight." He turned to the tavern. "Who wants to see Al's demonstration?"

There was a roar of agreement, and Al found himself dragged around to a local blacksmith's shop where Oluf and his friends persuaded the blacksmith to lend them his anvils. These were carried to the seashore where the larger one was set into the sand. Al took the offered barrel of gunpowder and filled the cavity. He then lit a fuse and hurried away. Twenty feet from the anvil he joined the others watching the fuse burn. When it hit the gunpowder there was a massive flash and a cloud of white smoke.

"That was pretty," Oluf said. "Now make it explode."

Al checked his audience. "This is going to be dangerous," he warned. That got nods of understanding, but not a lot else. Al remembered he was dealing with people who were clearing mines for a living and tried a different tack. "If this goes as I expect, that anvil"—he pointed to the second anvil—"is going to shoot over a hundred feet into the air, and I have absolutely no idea where it's going to land. So, I'd like everyone to back off at least a hundred yards."

There were snorts of disbelief, but Al was having none of it. "Either you fall back a safe distance, or I won't do this."

That threat finally got some movement. When the audience was far enough away Al loaded the cavity with gunpowder, set the fuse, and with his brother helping, lifted the second anvil to cover the gunpowder. He waited until Sam was at a safe distance before he lit the fuse and walked very quickly to where Sam and the others were waiting. He glanced over his shoulder a couple of times just in case the fuse burned faster than usual, but there was still fuse left when he reached the others.

KAABOOM!

The explosion sent the top anvil shooting high into the sky. It was a very long four seconds before it landed fifteen feet from the other anvil.

"Can you do that again?" someone in the crowd called out. His request was soon met by a roar demanding that Al repeat the experiment. He glanced at Sam, who shrugged his shoulders and walked over to get the gunpowder barrel.

Naturally someone complained about the noise and the watch was called out to deal with the unruly rabble that had congregated on the beach in order to make loud noises that disturbed honest citizens' sleep, or at least that was what the members of the watch said when they arrested everyone.

The next day started very much like any of the preceding dozen or so days, except that Al and Sam were sleep deprived and Henrik more sarcastic than usual.

"Did the sleeping beauties have a nice sleep?" Henrik asked when Al and Sam stumbled aboard the diving tender.

Al glared at the dive master. "You could have come and bailed us out." They'd spent an uncomfortable night in the town lockup with the boatmen, who'd all been a little the worse for drink.

Henrik's brows slowly rose. "Now why would I want to do a thing like that?"

Al wasn't taken in. He could guess why Henrik might have a grudge against him and Sam. "We woke you up?"

"Of course you woke me up. You woke the whole town up."

"If you were awake, why didn't you come and bail us out when we sent a messenger around to get you?" Sam demanded.

Al slapped a hand over Sam's mouth before he could stuff his size nines in any deeper. "We'll be ready to dive by six," he said as he said as he hustled Sam past Henrik.

It was deep into their first surface interval and Al and Sam were napping in deck chairs under the warmth of the morning sun when they were woken by Jörgen calling out.

"Fire! There's a ship on fire."

Al rubbed the sleep from his eyes and stared out across the water in the direction Jörgen was pointing. There was no land due south of their position for over thirty miles, so he was probably right to say it was a ship. Al struggled to his feet and walked over to Henrik, who was studying the smoke through his telescope. "What is it?" he asked.

"So, the sleeping beauties have finally surfaced. Here, have a look. Maybe you will recognize her."

Al accepted the telescope and set it to his eye. "It's a ship all right, but she's not burning. It's a steamship."

"What?" Jörgen protested. "What's a timberclad doing way out here?"

"It's not a timberclad," Al said. He could understand why Jörgen might have jumped to that conclusion. The timberclads were probably the only steam ships he'd ever seen, but Al had a little more experience with them. "I think she's the *Puffing Willie*."

"The tugboat from Lübeck?" Sam had arrived and was staring in the direction of the smoke.

Al nodded. "It has to be her. There aren't any other single stackers in the Baltic."

"As far as we know," Sam said.

Al shrugged. "As far as we know then, but I'm willing to bet it's the *Puffing Willie*."

"She's over six miles away," Henrik said. "That means you have plenty of time to complete your next dive before she gets here."

Al gave the smudge of smoke on the horizon a last glance before heading below to get ready for the next dive.

❖   ❖   ❖

The *Puffing Willie* didn't steam past the dive tender. Instead, well before she came near, she turned to steam into Helsingør.

"Can we go back to the harbor and find out what she's doing here?" Sam asked.

"You can borrow the dinghy," Henrik said, "but you better be back before noon."

Their next dive was scheduled to start at twenty past twelve. Al glanced at his diver's watch. It was just after ten thirty, and it would take maybe fifteen minutes each way to get there and back, leaving an hour at most. "Let's go next surface interval."

Sam nodded. "Yeah, give them time to get settled."

It was just after one o'clock when Al and Sam arrived in Helsingør. After securing the dingy they wandered over to where the *Puffing Willie* was tied up. Except that she wasn't the *Puffing Willie*. The name *"Osprey"* was written across her stern, and a naval ensign fluttered above it.

"And you were so sure she was the *Puffing Willie*," Sam said.

"That's the USE Navy's ensign," Al said. "Maybe they changed her name when they commissioned her."

"So what's she doing way out here?" Sam asked.

That was a good question. The *Puffing Willie*, or *Osprey* as she was now called, was a small river tugboat, and she didn't have the bunkerage to make the trip from Lübeck, where she'd been based, to Helsingør without making multiple stops on the way. "I think she might be a minesweeper now." Al gestured towards the equipment on the after deck of the *Osprey*. "All that stuff looks new, and those blimp things look like something I've seen in pictures of minesweepers in action."

"Al, Sam, just the people I need to see. Come on aboard," a voice called out from the deck of the *Osprey*.

Sam recognized the man who'd called out. "That's Mr. Tillman. I wonder what he wants?"

"There's an easy way to find out." Al walked over to the gangway connecting the *Osprey* to the wharf. "Permission to come aboard, Mr. Tillman."

"Permission granted," Louie Tillman said.

"You're cutting it a bit fine," Henrik said when they arrived back at the dive tender over an hour later.

"We've got new orders," Al said as he passed a folded document to Henrik. "How long will it take you to get ready for sea?"

Henrik glanced at the orders. "Destination—Wismar." He stared into the distance for a few seconds before speaking. "I can be ready inside an hour. How long will it take you two to get ready?" he asked. "The current will be turning in our favor in about twenty minutes."

The tidal range at Helsingør was negligible, but it did signal the change in flow of water into or out of the Baltic, and the current in either direction could be as much as three knots. For a sailing ship capable of only six or seven knots that could be either a great boon, or a great hindrance.

"I want to say goodbye to Oluf, but other than that, there's nothing stopping me being ready to sail in an hour," Al said.

"Same here," Sam added.

Henrik nodded. "Right. We'll dock to off load the salt and take on provisions. While we're doing that you can hunt up Oluf and his colleagues to say your goodbyes. I'll ring the bell when I'm ready." he looked pointedly at the brothers. "Just make sure you're back before I stop ringing the bell."

"But Oluf and his colleagues are out sweeping," Sam protested.

"No, they aren't." Henrik gestured out to sea. "They were called in shortly after the *Osprey* docked."

"I wonder why," Sam said.

"It's awfully quiet," Sam observed as they approached the tavern Oluf and the other boatmen frequented.

"That's a bad sign," Al agreed as they approached the door. The last couple of times they'd been here the tavern had been bustling with activity, but right now it was almost silent.

Heads looked up when they entered the tavern and Oluf waved them over.

"What's happened?" Al asked.

Oluf sighed. "A man from the tolls commission arrived with the steam boat. Apparently it's a mine-sweeper, and we are now 'surplus to requirements.'"

"Sorry," Al muttered.

Oluf clapped a hand on his shoulder. "It's not your fault. Besides, we knew it was only a short-term job." He sighed. "But the money was good while it lasted."

"What will you do now?" Al asked.

Oluf shrugged. "Some of us will move on. Me? I'll return to ferrying cargoes between Helsingør and Helsingborg."

"The *Osprey* brought a couple of the new hard hat rigs. There's sure to be demand for trained dive crews," Al suggested.

Oluf shook his head. "Those things are dangerous."

"We looked them over and they look as good as the ones we had back in Lübeck," Sam said.

"Looked? Is that all? If you could say you had used them you might find someone willing to risk a painful death." Oluf shook his head in negation. "But as you only looked, no one with any sense will risk them."

Al realized he'd never convince Oluf and his colleagues. Maybe if their first experience of hard hat diving hadn't been King Christian's failed experiment, they might have been more willing to try it. There wasn't anything they could do, so Al and Sam left.

Rasmus Brahe was a lesser twig in the great Brahe family, but he had high hopes of soon securing a much more important position within the tolls commission. He'd already saved the commission eight rigsdaler by dismissing the boatmen who'd been sweeping for mines the moment he arrived in Helsingør rather than let them finish the day.

He left the inn where he'd enjoyed a very good lunch and ambled to a lookout point so he could watch the activity on the Øresund. He easily located the *Osprey* puffing smoke from her single funnel as she chugged up the Øresund, but he couldn't see the dive tender. She should be out there. Rasmus didn't understand what was going on. The up-timers should have been out on the water using the new hard hat rigs he'd brought up from Copenhagen.

He ran to the dock, but all anyone could tell him was the dive tender had taken on provisions, paid their bills, and left. He was forced to cool his heels until the *Osprey* came in to find out what had happened.

✧   ✧   ✧

"What do you mean they've gone?" Rasmus demanded when the *Osprey* finally docked and he was able to talk to Louie Tillman. "They're supposed to be salvaging the *Blauwe Duif*."

Louie needed all of his thirty-two years in the navy to keep a straight face as he commiserated with the bureaucrat. "Unfortunately, the Navy requires them elsewhere, Herr Brahe." He smiled. "Still, they did find time to check out the new hard hat rigs you brought with you and they said they were completely happy with them."

Rasmus cursed under his breath. This was bad news. He had the hard hat rigs but with the Morton brothers gone he had no one to use them. He was going to have to find some new divers and handlers.

Rasmus looked around Helsingør first, but not even the boatmen who'd been clearing mines were interested. He'd ended up heading back to Copenhagen, but even there he'd been forced to troll through the prisons. Niels and Poul Madsen had been on death row awaiting execution when Rasmus offered them the job and, after hearing that the glitch that had killed Laurs Jeppsen had been fixed by the up-timers, the brothers had leapt at the opportunity to cheat the executioner. He'd arranged their conditional release and seen to their training before shipping them, still in chains, to Helsingør. The training had been the best he could devise, based on descriptions he'd culled from newspaper articles describing the diving operations on the River Trave.

The heavy helmet was slipped over Niels' head and locked into place. He didn't like the feeling of confinement, but he'd learned to live with it during his training. It was a small price to pay for continued life.

He heard the pump start and the hiss-click of the non-return valve—that most important of additions to the diving suit. He held up a hand to indicate everything was working and he was ready to go down.

The face plate was closed and locked in place. He was now totally dependent on the air-hose for air. Two men helped him stand up in the heavy suit and walked him to the landing stage—a light platform on a swing arm that would take him from the deck to the water in one easy movement. Once there he took his position and waited for his brother to join him. Moments later they were swung over the water and lowered into it.

Niels checked that his brother was okay before manipulating his air-regulator and the exhaust-valve to reduce his buoyancy. Slowly he sank down to the *Blauwe Duif*.

Four hours later Niels was dying to go to the toilet. He was also feeling cold, and fatigued, so he was pleased to hear the clang of metal on metal that indicated topside thought it was time they came up. He passed one last cask to his brother before climbing out of the *Blauwe Duif's* hold and waited for Poul to join him. Only then did he close the exhaust valve a quarter turn. This slowed the rate air escaped from his dive suit and caused it to balloon out a little, giving him positive buoyancy. He started to float gently upwards. This was in accordance with what they'd been taught back in Copenhagen. Unfortunately for them, Rasmus had failed to realize that Matt Tisdel and Miquel d'Alcaufar were able to surface without making decompression stops because they were working in less than thirty feet of water and their no-decompression time limit was effectively infinite.

Poul surfaced soon after Niels and they were soon being swung aboard the dive tender. Moments later they were being helped to unsuit. Free of his heavy dive suit and nearly two hundred pounds lighter, Niels dashed for the heads. He returned to find his brother talking to the bureaucrat who'd arranged their pardons. They were conditional on them completing the salvage of the *Blauwe Duif*, but as they came with payment for their work, Niels wasn't complaining. Money was always useful.

"You are making very good progress," Rasmus told Niels when he joined his brother.

Never one to speak when he didn't have anything to say, Niels grunted.

That didn't seem to deter the bureaucrat, who then asked if they were having any problems.

"It's very cold down there," Poul said.

Niels nodded. "Tomorrow we want more clothes to wear under our suits."

"I will see that you get some more clothes. But other than that, did you have any problems?" Rasmus asked.

Niels shook his head. He had to give the bureaucrat credit. He had listened to all of their complaints and requests while they were being trained, and even done something about some of them. The four hour limit had been established because that was the longest either he and his brother were comfortable holding their water, so he was sure that tomorrow there would be more woolen socks, pants and tops. "Thank you," he muttered.

"Good, good. Well, you two have your lunch and rest a little," Rasmus said before walking off to have his lunch.

They'd been back in the water a little over two hours when Niels started to feel tired, stiff, and worst of all, itchy. He put it down to the long confinement in the dive suit and the hard work he was doing, and tried to ignore it.

Three and a half hours into the dive the itching was starting to become unbearable. It was as if he had ants crawling all over his body. He shuddered at the thought and tried to relieve the itching by rubbing against the *Blauwe Duif's* timbers, but any relief was momentary. Still, he told himself, it couldn't be long to go now.

He heard the ring of metal on metal that was the recall. "At last," he muttered to himself. He turned to climb out of the hold, and noticed Poul was trying to rub his back against the hull. So it wasn't just him. He smiled at the thought, but then the itching reminded him that it was time to get back to the surface where he could get out of his suit. He got clear of the hold and tightened the exhaust value. The dive suit started to inflate, and he put a hand on the air-regulator control valve.

He shouldn't have ascended at more than twenty-five feet per minute, but the sensation of insects crawling all over his body was driving him mad. Instead of opening the control valve only a little, he opened it as wide open as he could. The suit started to balloon almost immediately and he shot to the surface. On the way up his joints started to hurt. The closer to the surface the worse it got. Near the surface he started to scream.

Rasmus stared down at the two bodies laid out on the dive tender's deck. He didn't know why they had died. All he knew was that the two divers had seemed perfectly fine when they started their second dive, and there hadn't been a problem until they returned to the surface.

"The suits are cursed," one of the topside crew muttered. The rest of the crew crossed themselves and stepped a little farther away from the suits that were still in the disrobing area where Niels and Poul had been pulled from them.

Those few words rang like a death knell over Rasmus' hopes. He'd had enough trouble finding Niels and Poul, but once this story got out—and there was no way he could stop that from happening—even condemned men wouldn't be interested. A pardon was no good to a dead man, and with the sound of Niels' and Poul's screaming themselves to death still echoing in his skull, Rasmus wouldn't blame them for preferring an easier death at the hands of the executioner.

He couldn't understand what had gone wrong. The dive gear had been redesigned after consultation with the Morton brothers, and they'd appeared quite happy to use them if they were made to their specifications. Niels and Poul hadn't had any trouble during their training dives, and the divers working in the Trave River were using similar equipment with no problems.

Rasmus could be sure of only one thing. The tolls commission was not going to be happy with his failure to salvage the cargo of the *Blauwe Duif*.

❖   ❖   ❖

Oluf and his fellow boatmen heard about the accident, and how the divers had come to the surface, screaming in pain. It only went to reinforce their belief that the dive suits were killers. If anybody had bothered to ask them though, they might have been able to supply a clue to what happened to Niels and Poul. They didn't know much about diving, but if they'd been prompted, some of them might have mentioned that first discussion with Al and Sam Morton about nitrogen and nitrogen buildup. Instead, the new dive suits were locked away in a storeroom deep in the bowls of Kronborg Castle and the whole messy episode was quietly consigned to history.

Prison Break

Walter Hunt

— 1 —

Miolans, Savoy

Phillippe de la Mothe-Haudencourt often found himself
reflecting on his own life and upon the twists and turns
he had experienced. It would have been different if
the Ring of Fire had not interfered with what—once
upon a time—had been a promising courtier's career.
But that was a matter of history now: at least five
years' remove, and given the rate of change that the
Ring and the up-timers had brought, five years was
an eternity.

He had made his choice, attaching himself to the
army of Henri Tour d'Auvergne, now Marshal Turenne,
and he had accepted the responsibility for staying
behind in Lyon so that when Prince Gaston and his
entourage arrived, he was there to offer apologies
and excuses.

Now he was in Miolans, the Savoyard prison in the mountains, by order of King Gaston. He had been given a choice: either voluntarily permit himself to be seconded to the insipid Jean-Baptiste LeBarre, the warden of Miolans—or plan to become a resident of one of the several aptly named groups of cells that comprised it.

It wasn't much of a choice, but Gaston wasn't one to offer much of a choice about much of anything.

That being said, it was still a long way from Paris or Lyon—or Marseilles, for that matter. He could attribute the loss of his career as a courtier to the elevation of the youthful Turenne to command of an army: it was, as the up-timers said, an *offer he couldn't refuse*. It had certainly dulled his courtier's instincts, preventing him from very pragmatically jumping when it was in his best interests to do so. Instead, he patriotically took the fall for Turenne.

And here he was. *But at least*, he thought, *I am not an inmate*. The food wasn't terrible; LeBarre had at least a few books, and the views were magnificent.

They were especially handsome when viewed from the lookout tower on the north side of the prison-fortress. It was one of his favorite places: far from the prison cells, far from LeBarre, and—in his poetic ex-courtier's imagination—a place that gave at least the illusion of freedom.

As he looked out across the vista, he heard a heavy tread on the stone steps. He turned, straightening his sleeves and giving the slightest adjustment to his belt, and presently a rumpled figure appeared at the top of the stairs. The other man looked exhausted, as if the climb had been far too much for him. He did not speak, but rather gave a weak sort of wave and stumbled to a stone bench. He leaned back, his arms splayed out.

De la Mothe tried, and probably failed, to suppress a smile as he said, "you must be *Dottore* Baldaccio."

After a moment, the other man seemed to gather himself. He leaned forward, hands on knees, panting, then looked up.

"You are Monsieur de la Mothe, I take it."

"At your service."

"What in the name of the Lord God, the Blessed Virgin, and all of the saints of Heaven convinced you to arrange our conversation up here? I nearly suffered a fit of apoplexy with those thrice-damned stairs."

"Perhaps your humors are out of balance, monsieur *Dottore*."

Baldaccio scowled at him owlishly. "My humors are just fine, monsieur, and they are not in any case subject for discussion."

"As you wish. To answer your question: this is a beautiful setting; it is far from the prison and prying eyes and ears. Your letter indicated that circumspection was the order of the day, and I was uncertain whether that extended to the warden. So—" He extended his hands, mock-theatrically, as if to indicate that there was no need to finish the sentence.

"The warden? You mean that *capatosta* LeBarre."

"Yes." The Italian word sounded like an insult; if so, it was undoubtedly apt.

"You are quite correct, Monsieur de la Mothe," Baldaccio said. He seemed to have recovered at least some of his breath, and his aplomb. "As my letter said, this is a matter most secret."

"Since it is the first I have heard from anyone of authority in some time, I am eager to hear what you would have of me."

"In a few days a prisoner will be transferred to Miolans. This is a very special, and very secret, prisoner. He will require special handling."

"Torture is not my province, Doctor."

"*Torture?* Oh, no, monsieur, you misconstrue my meaning entirely. If it was simply a matter of putting this prisoner to the question—whatever question—there are plenty of people down below who are more than adequate to the task."

"I completely agree."

"Yes. Well then. Let me be more clear. The prisoner is not to be harmed: indeed, he is to be most attentively cared for. It was thought that you were ideal for the task."

"I am to be . . . some sort of *servant*?"

"Not precisely. It was intended that you be the principal . . . gaoler, I suppose one might say. The person charged with this prisoner's care: his interlocutor with the outside. Because no one . . ." Baldaccio's voice lowered and he waggled his finger at de la Mothe in a most ungentlemanly way. "*No one* is to know that he is here. Indeed, no one is to even learn his identity."

"I don't understand."

"It will all be made clear to you. What you must understand *now* is that this is a duty of supreme importance." Baldaccio sat up straight, giving the impression that *he* was of supreme importance—the dispenser of weighty tasks. "I shall be here to examine the prisoner and certify that he is in good health—and thereafter he shall be in your care."

"I see." De la Mothe did *not* see, but could also discern that no more was to be gotten from this buffoon. "How long am I to . . . *take care* . . . of this prisoner?"

"I suppose," Baldaccio answered, "it depends on how long he lives."

Baldaccio made himself at home in Miolans for the next two days, engaging in regular banter with the warden. The two of them made quite a pair; de la Mothe, who was also present at the dinner-table, watched them as they each so obviously tried to have mirth at the other's expense, missing that it was being done in return. It was very much like a low-quality, low-priced play that could not last a night in Paris . . . but it was all the entertainment that was to be had.

On the afternoon of the third day a carriage arrived, coming eastward from the direction of Lyon. It was escorted by four hard-faced men on horseback, who cleared everyone out of the courtyard before permitting the carriage door to be opened. De la Mothe viewed the scene from an upper story; one of the guards noticed him and began to raise his musket, but the leader waved him off, pointing to de la Mothe and then to his own nose, an obvious reference to de la Mothe's most obvious facial feature. In another circumstance it was the sort of thing that gentlemen fought duels over—but not now or here. De la Mothe congratulated himself for not having flinched when the musket was first raised, nor turning his head away from the scene.

Finally the guards were satisfied that there were no other observers. The leader opened the carriage door and assisted someone to descend. The prisoner—for such he was: de la Mothe could hear the clink of chains as he stepped down onto the dirt—was heavily cloaked, so that no indication of his identity was visible. In quick order he was taken by two guards and hustled into one of the side-buildings, rather than the main entrance.

Clearly this had all been planned in advance by someone who knew the prison well.

Shortly, Baldaccio—who had largely ignored him since their conversation—presented himself at de la Mothe's rooms. He was furious: not at de la Mothe, apparently, but at LeBarre. He came into the sitting room and reclined against the couch without so much as a courtesy.

"What's wrong, *Dottore*?"

"What's wrong? What's *wrong*? *This*," he said, reaching inside his doublet and drawing out a key at the end of a fine silver chain. "I was given this by my patron to pass on to the warden for his keeping."

"A key."

"A very *special* key," Baldaccio said importantly. "It has to do with the prisoner. I offered it to the warden and he laughed at me. Directly in my face, if you can imagine it! 'No,' LeBarre said to me. 'You keep it, you'll have more need of it than shall I.'"

"And?"

"And then, when I informed him that I had no use of it at all because I planned to take my leave and return to my laboratory in Turin, he laughed again. 'No, no,' he said: 'you won't be going anywhere. Your place is here, and here you will stay.'"

De la Mothe smiled, and considered the possibility of laughing in Baldaccio's face. "So you have somehow become a prisoner here as well? Why?"

"To attend to whatever *medical* needs that the prisoner might require. You shall be his cupbearer, and I his leech, I suppose. We will become fast friends."

I doubt it, de la Mothe thought to himself, but he said, "Do you think it is time that we meet this prisoner?"

"I am not to be permitted," Baldaccio answered. "But you should go. Yes, indeed, monsieur: I think it is time that you learn just why it is you—both of us—are to be confined here."

"Where is he?"

"In the Sighing Tower. He has been given a very nice accommodation." Baldaccio looked around de la Mothe's rooms. "Nicer than *this*, in any case."

After shooing the *Dottore* out of his rooms and locking the door, de la Mothe made his way down to the courtyard and across to the tower in question. It was an older part of Miolans; two of the escorts he had seen earlier were guarding the entrance, but on his approach they stood aside, allowing him to pass through the arch and onto a circular stairway.

He was a dozen steps up when he first heard the noises: the mountain breeze passed through slits in the walls, making a sound that was soft at first, but grew louder as he ascended—and, indeed, it sounded very much like the discontented sighing of some unquiet soul. It was eerie, but he supposed that he might become used to it after a while.

At last he reached the uppermost floor of the Sighing Tower, and there he found a barred door. He opened it and found himself in what was, indeed, a comfortable room: there were plain, but well-made tapestries hung on the walls, a thick carpet on the floor, a table with two chairs, and an ornately-carved *prie-dieu* in the corner. The robed figure he had seen in the courtyard stood near a small, high window, facing away from him, the hood of the robe pulled over his head.

"Monsieur?" he said. "Allow me to present myself—I am—"

"I know who you are, Monsieur de la Mothe," the man said. The voice sounded vaguely familiar, but it echoed strangely.

"But I do not know who you are."

"Nor, I expect, is this intended." The man turned to face him, and slowly lowered the hood of his robe.

For a moment de la Mothe was struck dumb, unable to find words—an inexcusable situation for a proper courtier. Before him stood a man in what might be the garb of a monk, unremarkable except that from the neck up his face was invisible: upon his head was a metal shell, like a helmet with a full face mask, secured just below the chin by a heavy lock. Only his eyes, and the smallest part of his mouth, were visible.

Suddenly he knew what the key was for.

"Your patron, Monsieur de la Mothe, and my captor, has no intention of having you or anyone else know who I am. I expect that we are being spied upon at this very moment." The masked man laughed for a moment and looked away, then focused again on him. "I have been instructed that upon my life I am not to reveal my identity to you or to any other person, and that you are to be the only person I shall see or communicate with. We will become well acquainted with each other, monsieur, though we shall only talk of trivialities."

"Why...this is heinous, monsieur! This punishment is cruel and—"

"By comparison to those things that happen some levels below us, monsieur, I expect that this is scarcely a jest." He reached his hands—old and weathered, but hands clearly not accustomed to labor—from the sleeves of his robe, and placed them on the iron that encircled his head. "My captor—of whom I am also enjoined not to speak—caused this to be locked upon my head based on an inspiration from some up-timer book. It was decided that merely killing me was sinful, but keeping me prisoner where no one could look upon my face was more *humane*. Up-timers," he added, snorting, and lowering his hands to his sides. "I commend them for their *civilized* ways."

"I find this a terrible punishment," de la Mothe said. "No man should suffer such a fate. I shall complain to the warden."

"He has no control over this, Monsieur de la Mothe. Nor do I. Nor, I fear, do you. We are all prisoners here...for better or worse." He folded his hands in front of him. "I think we should all become accustomed to it."

— 2 —

Le Massif Central
Southeastern France

There were times that Terrye Jo Tillman felt pangs of regret over the change in her fortunes. A few months ago she had been settled as the head telegrapher for the king of France—well, the man who claimed to be, and had been crowned king of France, Gaston d'Orleans; she had been well-fed, well-clothed and had a nice apartment and workspace on the Rue San Antoine in Paris, good contacts and good prospects.

Now she was sleeping rough, eating in an army mess—a well-equipped one, she had to admit, but still—and working with inferior equipment.

And, to be perfectly frank, on the run from that crowned king. And under the command of a woman who had once been her nemesis: Sherrilyn Maddox, former P.E. instructor at Grantville High. But that, she thought to herself, was a few hundred years in the future—one that never would come to pass in this timeline.

Terrye Jo had seen what dwelling on the past, and becoming swamped with regret over what might have been, could do; it still hung over her dad—though at least they were talking, since the not-so-chance meeting in Reims during the coronation. She wasn't going to let that happen to her: being out with Maddox's Rangers beat spending any time in His Majesty's prisons in Paris—which would have happened, but for Colonel Erik Haakonsen Hand. The future was whatever came, and whatever she made of it. Whatever had happened was in the past and there was nothing she could do to change it. Maddox's Rangers had escorted the up-timers employed by the USE embassy to the French border, in accordance with the royal decree banishing all up-timers from the kingdom; then they'd found their way back, equipped with a small portable radio set. At night she set it up and listened, hoping to hear Georges—GJBF—but she never picked up his "fist" or heard his call sign; she wondered if he was in some prison, or worse, for associating with up-timers... or if he had his old job back, and good riddance to the up-timer.

They'd been making good time through fairly wild country, stopping at night after long days' rides. After eating, most of the troop settled down to sleep, but she'd usually set up the radio and listen to what she could find.

It was on the fourth night that she heard a familiar "fist"—someone she knew: Henri Durant, one of her protégés from the Castello del Valentino. There wasn't much to it: a brief chat with Sylvie, his sister, who—she gathered from the conversation—was still in Turin, while he was elsewhere. It took her a few nights more to find out where, and when she did, it was troubling.

Henri was at Miolans, the prison in the mountains between Turin and Lyon—the place with dungeons named Hell and Purgatory and some other things. He wasn't a prisoner, as far as she could tell—but he complained about some important figure who was. There was no name for this big shot, but there was another name that she heard that finally made her mention it the following morning to Sherrilyn.

It was already chilly even in late August, and she could see her breath as she sat on a fallen log and pulled on her boots. They didn't look as handsome as when she'd had them made in Paris, but at least the *cordonnier* had made them well.

"Daydreaming again?"

She looked up and saw Sherrilyn Maddox standing in front of her, arms crossed, a faint smile on her face. At Grantville High, that would usually mean laps on the track. But there was no track here in the mountains, and she was skilled help—and a fellow up-timer.

She didn't answer, but finished pulling on her boot and adjusting the fit. She stood up, picking up her hat and putting it on; the jaunty feather had been lost somewhere.

"You're up early," Sherrilyn said. "I usually have to kick you out of your bedroll."

"I wanted to tell you about something I heard last night late." Terrye Jo smiled. "Didn't want to mess up your beauty sleep, and I know you're up early."

"Something you heard?"

"A name."

"Huh. Well, breakfast is cooking, but let's take a little walk."

"Sure."

They followed a path that led toward a clearing in the trees, a small promontory that overlooked a beautiful valley, where the first leaves were just beginning to change.

There were some flat rocks; Sherrilyn dropped onto one and Terrye Jo sat on the other. "All right, what did you hear?"

"I told you that my old friend Henri Durant was at Miolans. He was on the air last night and he mentioned that there was an important prisoner there, and there was also another VIP; last night he used a name."

"Someone important?"

"Someone named de la Mothe."

"*Phillippe?* Phillippe de la Mothe-Haudencourt? Skinny guy, big nose?"

"There wasn't a description, or a first name, but Henri seemed to think he was someone important."

"He *is*. The marshal had to leave him behind at Lyon and has regretted it ever since. A very sentimental man, our Marshal Turenne." Sherrilyn stood up and walked around, stamping the cold ground. "I thought I might run into him while we were in Paris, but it's a big city. And now he's in prison..."

"Miolans isn't just a prison, Sherrilyn. It's..."

She had been with Gaston when she last saw Miolans. She remembered it clearly, especially the sounds from below when the door was unlocked. The sections had names like "Hell" and "Purgatory"...When the warden had been hesitant to permit her to tour, Gaston assured him that up-time had things far worse—and at that, the French king-designate, as he then was, was probably right. De la Mothe had been waiting at Lyon when the royal party reached it; Terrye Jo hadn't seen him, but word had come how angry Gaston had been that only de la Mothe, and not Turenne's army, had been there to receive him.

Sherrilyn was waiting for her to finish the sentence, but it must have been clear from Terrye Jo's expression that she'd already said plenty.

"We have to do something," Sherrilyn said. Her face was set in a grim expression. "We need to get him out of there."

"That's not what our orders are," Terrye Jo answered. "The marshal is expecting us to be in Marseilles in a few weeks."

"This is a side trip. All we have to do is ride up there, grab him, and boogie. We should be able to manage it, right? This prison is in the middle of nowhere."

"It's a fortress. It's not very heavily guarded, if I remember, but it's still got defenses—"

"And we're as well armed and as well trained as anyone in Europe. All we need is a plan, and I'm reasonably sure we can come up with one."

"I thought we didn't go cowboy anymore."

"Funny, you know, that's a word in French now? When someone goes off on their own they call it *le cowboi*. I *love* how we're messing with down-time languages. We don't exactly go cowboy anymore, but this is a special circumstance."

"Sherrilyn, in the space of a few months I've come to really respect you. The PE teacher thing—that's pretty far away now, and I'm glad to have a chance to do something rather than get sent home. But Miolans isn't in France, it's in another country—it's in Savoy. Don't you think this might cause, I don't know, an international incident?"

"Isn't the duchess of Savoy Gaston's sister? It's all in the family, isn't it?"

"Another. Country."

"You worry too much, Terrye Jo."

"Are you planning to let the marshal know about this little side trip? Or doesn't he worry about this either?"

"Not exactly. But if we do this right, we get in, grab Philippe—"

"Philippe?"

"The Sieur de la Mothe. Phillippe blah blah Haudon-something de la Mothe."

"I didn't know you were on a first name basis."

For a moment, the PE teacher scowl flashed across Sherrilyn's face, then she smiled. "Okay. He's a good guy, Terrye Jo. I don't want to see him in this prison, and if we do this right, all we have to do is get in, grab him, and get out before it becomes an international incident."

"What about Marshal Turenne?"

"It's easier to get forgiveness than permission. Philippe's a valuable guy, and is in tight with the authorities in Marseilles. The marshal is going to need help from the locals, especially if the Spanish actually *are* thinking about invading from there. I don't think he's going to turn him away, or tell me I shouldn't have done it."

"I still think it's a bad idea. This sounds a lot like a Wrecking Crew operation."

"I guess it does...look, sometimes it's necessary to draw outside the lines a little bit. Turenne can't order me to do this for the exact reason that it *could* be an international incident." She took off her hat and ran a hand through her hair. "You're right, I'm not *completely* sure about it, but I'm *mostly* sure.

"Did I ever tell you that I almost had to do a little *le cowboi* in Paris? I heard that you might have been arrested, and I was ready to go bust you out of prison. They talked me out of it."

"No," Terrye Jo said. "You never told me that."

"Well, it's true. An up-timer held against her will—in a down-timer prison—is never good. In a country where up-timers are marked as the enemy it would be even worse. Especially for a woman. But it's the same with Philippe de la Mothe. He's friends with folks that are opposed to King Gaston, so he's probably being treated like crap.

"That's getting me worked up."

"Copy that," Terrye Jo said. "And I'll go along with whatever you decide—I'm guessing that the Rangers will go wherever you lead. I just...have my reservations, that's all."

"Until our dustup in Rome last year, I'd say, 'what could possibly go wrong?' But I know that a lot of things could go wrong. If we're going to accomplish this, I'm going to need to know everything you remember about Miolans...."

— 3 —

Miolans, Savoy

Henri Durant pulled off the headphones and carefully set them on the worktable beside the radio apparatus. He tried to rub the sleep from his eyes; the pendulum clock on the shelf above, kept carefully wound, showed 5:25—he would be on duty for nearly a half hour more, until his replacement, a young Savoyard mechanic named Gilles, arrived for duty.

Having a novice in the radio tower during the early part of the day was for the best. The most clear reception was at night; it was when the radio waves were full of telegraphers and the occasional voice, heard crackling and far away, speaking Italian or French or English or Amideutsch, talking about the most interesting things or, more often, nothing at all. The world of the airwaves had become like a vast town square, squawking and complaining and shouting... and listening.

It seemed like a hundred years ago that Mademoiselle Tillman had come to Turin with the other uptimers, to set up and operate Duke Victor's fine new radio. He and his sister Sylvie had been just servants then, working in Castel Valentino's spacious stables... a worthy employment, but no more than that. She had taken them both on as apprentices, first to work when their usual day's work was done, and then as part of her permanent staff on the condition that they learn the arts and skills of the mysterious, magical device that talked and listened to the world. Then the prince, Monsieur, had come and taken Mademoiselle Tillman away, to be on his royal staff in Paris—but instead of simply returning to the stables, Sylvie had been promoted to the head position, and Henri had been sent to Miolans, where His Grace had ordered a new radio to be built.

Henri talked to Sylvie every night: a few minutes of talk about the most interesting things . . . or, more often, nothing at all.

Sighing, he donned the earphones once again and settled himself in his chair. He turned the great circular disk to its lowest position, and began to slowly move it up through its range, pausing at carefully marked frequencies with known broadcasters.

There was quite a bit of regular traffic even this close to the end of the night, though many had signed off. They were mostly French and Amideutsch speakers, though he did listen in on an interesting exchange between two Spanish telegraphers—he could follow it mostly because they were halting and inaccurate with a lot of *QSMs*—unusual, since Spain was well-known for its aversion to up-time technology. It was something to do with what was going on in Rome.

It was engrossing enough that he did not hear footsteps behind him and jumped when he felt a hand on his shoulder. He practically tore the headphones from his head and whirled around, only to see Gilles—the lumbering, unsubtle man in the flesh—start back.

"I didn't mean to startle you," Gilles said. He gestured toward the high window, where early morning light was already filtering in. "The lauds bell has rung."

"So you've made your morning oblation?" Gilles was very devout, but not of the school that thought the Ring of Fire—and up-time technology—was the work of the Devil. *Thank God*, Henri thought to himself.

"*Oui*, of course. The curé asks after you."

A likely story, Henri thought. "He knows that I keep faith in my own way."

Gilles sniffed and dropped into the other seat beside the work table. The chair legs seemed to cry out in protest. "Really quite singular," he continued. "One of the *prisoners* was at the mass, if you can imagine."

"Well, the curé doesn't like Hell or Purgatory, *certainement*."

"*Non*. It was the *special* prisoner, Henri. He was all the way in the back of the chapel away from everyone, except his *valet de chambre*, that la Mothe fellow. He was wearing gloves over his hands—I saw them when he crossed himself—and a heavy cloak and hood that completely concealed his face. The *Dottore* told me that it's a wonder he could see where he was going."

"*Dottore* Baldaccio attends Mass? I thought he was a man of science."

"Even men of science bow before the glory of God," Gilles said, his face assuming a beatific smile. "And I will have you know that *Dottore* Baldaccio is a particular friend of mine, and takes a great interest in the work I do here."

"Does he indeed."

Gilles gave Henri a curious look, as if trying to determine some hidden meaning; then, finding none, returned to his subject. "The prisoner has not been there before," Gilles said. "I wonder why he was permitted to attend. Perhaps he is a monk or priest. Still, he made no confession."

"How could he? No one is permitted to speak to him."

"Well, that's true enough. But if he is a monk—imagine, a monk sent here to Miolans!—shouldn't he have a confessor?"

"Maybe he confesses himself to Sieur de la Mothe."

Gilles frowned. Humor was something of a foreign language for the big Savoyard, especially where it intersected with matters of the Church. "Well," he said at last, spreading his hands. "Who knows with these things." He rubbed them together as if he was about to make fire. "Are you ready to be relieved?"

"Well past," Henri said. "Have a good shift." He stood, patted Gilles on his broad back and walked through the narrow door and down the steps, on his way into the cool morning air.

A few hours later, Gilles laboriously took down a message from a source he'd never heard of: it was something routine, a visit by a troop of soldiers heading along the road to Turin. He finished making a fair copy and carefully filed it away. By mid-morning there were a half-dozen messages piled on top.

In the highlands near Chambery

"I still don't like this plan," Terrye Jo said, squinting up at the sky, which was filled with low clouds. "I feel like we're riding into Mordor."

"That's more than a bit melodramatic."

"Sherrilyn," she said, "it's a freakin' *prison*. If anything goes wrong all they have to do is throw us down the stairs."

"Nothing will go wrong."

"What makes you so sure? Do you feel it in your knee like a change in the weather?"

Sherrilyn glared at the younger woman, tightening her grip on her horse's reins. Terrye Jo would have bet on white knuckles inside her riding gloves.

"Are you *asking* me to kick your ass? Look," she said, frowning like she used to do when the PE class wasn't behaving, "no plan is perfect, but this one is very, very simple. We are a troop of soldiers—"

"I know. I sent the message. It wasn't Henri who took it: I didn't recognize the fist. It was someone new, someone not very good. They may not have even gotten it right."

"So much the better. So, as I was saying: we're a troop of soldiers headed for Turin. We just want to stop to water and fodder our horses. Once we get inside—"

"We all pull out our weapons and say, 'nobody move or the nose gets it.'"

"Come again?"

"*Sleeper*. Woody Allen. Forget it. What possibly makes you think that even if we are able to get your friend out, they won't come after us? They have soldiers—guards—"

"You told me that the warden was a boob, and that they didn't have many guards because they relied on being remote to keep prisoners from escaping."

"Well, yes, but—"

"Nowhere. Wildernessville."

"They have a radio."

"We take the crystal."

Terrye Jo thought about that for a moment, then said, "this is really one of those things where no one does anything until we're well away, and then all they can do is complain."

"Right. And who are we going to get in trouble— King Gaston? We don't *like* King Gaston. Marshal Turenne? The duke of Savoy already doesn't like Turenne. Believe me," Sherrilyn said, "once we get Henri away and back to the marshal, he'll thank us for it."

— 4 —

Miolans, Savoy

Warden LeBarre poured another glass of what he supposed was excellent wine into Phillippe de la Mothe's glass. He smiled his insincere smile, and de la Mothe returned it in equal measure.

"So tell me, monsieur," LeBarre said, sipping from his own glass. "How are you getting on with your charge?"

"With the mystery man? I attend to his needs, which are few; we talk—"

"I know."

"I know you know." There was a hollow space beneath the floorboards of the tower room where the masked prisoner was kept; LeBarre's inept spies had a great deal of trouble keeping quiet. "We talk about inconsequential things—the weather, the lives of the saints, that sort of business. All rather boring, really."

"It is for the best that way. But...surely you have your suspicions as to his identity."

"I am firmly committed to keeping my head attached to my shoulders, Monsieur le Warden. Whatever I privately think, I do not intend to discuss it with you or anyone else."

"Yes, yes, of course...still, who could be counted so great an enemy to have this punishment?"

"I would say that the punishment is mild when compared to some of the pleasures your torturers inflict. He is well-fed; he sees the sunlight, and is permitted a few books and the freedom to move about. You even very graciously permitted him to hear mass a few days ago."

"But the mask—"

"Compared to fetters and hot iron pokers, it seems a mere inconvenience."

"Perhaps we should have one fitted up for you." He laughed with equal insincerity.

"You have consistently told me that I am a guest here, rather than a prisoner. It might have been that the king wished to condemn me to this or that, but his royal mother decided that she had a better use for me. I would not want to impair my usefulness even to satisfy you."

"I...only meant—"

Invoking Marie de Medici, even if not by name, was enough to make LeBarre shudder in fear; if the matter were not so serious, and if—and it pained de la Mothe to even think thus—the goodwill of the prison's warden were not crucial to his good health, he might have laughed in his face.

"Her Highness the dowager queen does what she

wishes, but does it largely out of the sight of the king. If it is far from the center of real power, so be it—but you doubt her influence, and her capability to do mischief, at your own peril, monsieur."

"I do not...I do not doubt it in the least, Monsieur de la Mothe. I would not dream of doubting her in this matter. And if you ever have the honor of an interview with her, I hope you will convey my fondest respects."

Of course, you insipid little worm, de la Mothe thought. *As if I'd ever get a chance for an audience with Marie de Medici...though she seemed to be on the outs with Gaston.*

She couldn't be scheming against him, could she?

"Should that ever happen," de la Mothe said, "I will not hesitate to do so."

De la Mothe took the prisoner his meals three times a day: a small *pétit dejeuner* early in the morning—a small sweet roll from the warden's own kitchen and a dish of weak coffee; a bowl of some sort of stew in the afternoon, usually with an apple that de la Mothe cut into sections so that the masked man could manage to eat it; and a light repast after vespers, usually again whatever the warden had on his table—mutton most often, as LeBarre seemed to favor it.

His charge was always gracious and polite. Inside his apartments he didn't bother with the hood: de la Mothe always got a good view of the locked, masked helmet, reflecting the light through the windows or the flicker of candles, which he was permitted, and which he carefully husbanded between uses. The latter were only to be used when de la Mothe himself was present, and it was he who was to take a spill from the fire and light it.

On the evening after his *tête-a-tête* with LeBarre, de la Mothe had brought the dinner up as usual and had lit the candles. The masked man was reading slowly from his breviary, his soft whisper echoing weirdly from within his metal prison. He did not acknowledge his keeper, which was a little surprising; after a few minutes, de la Mothe rose and walked over to the table where the prisoner was intently reading. He wasn't sure what he might do—rap on the helmet? Tap him on the shoulder? When suddenly the man reached out and with a surprisingly strong grip pulled de la Mothe's hand down to the table, palm splayed flat.

The masked man lifted his head, and de la Mothe could see the eyes through the shadowed holes. They were fierce, feverish, reflecting the flickering candle light. He did not speak; but de la Mothe felt something under his palm.

The prisoner nodded once, very slightly, and let go of de la Mothe's hand. He lifted it and came away with a small scrap of cloth: a scapular, bearing a worn image of a radiant heart—the Sacred Heart of the Saviour.

"It opens doors," he said in an almost inaudible whisper.

Anyone listening to the exchange, and it was almost certain that someone was, would likely be unable to make any sense of it.

De la Mothe took the scapular and began to tuck it into his wallet, but the masked man softly clapped his chest with his open palm. De la Mothe stopped;

he nodded, briefly kissed the image, and pulled it over his neck and settled it over his breast under his blouse.

He walked over to the corner where the fire threw light and shadow into the room. "You know, my friend," he said, "I begin to doubt whether either of us will ever leave this place alive."

"We have an audience for our conversations, I do not need to remind you."

"I don't care," de la Mothe said, turning to face the room. "The warden tried to play at questions with me this afternoon—he wanted to know if I had any suspicions as to your identity. I assured him that who you are, what you are, is nothing I care to discuss in public. But it troubles me to think about it, about who and what would anger the dowager queen of France so much that she would do—"

"She is a very dangerous woman," the prisoner interrupted, holding up a hand. "She is not the king, and she is not the Lord God." He genuflected, and de la Mothe followed suit. "But . . ." he raised his hand to the metal mask that covered his face. "She appears to be well-read in up-time literature, and she does have a macabre sense of humor. I have learned to be patient, Monsieur de la Mothe. You, too, must be patient." He clapped his hand to his chest once more, as if to remind him of the small gift that had passed between them. "And trust in Divine Providence."

"Until—"

"As long as necessary, my friend. As long as necessary."

— 5 —

Miolans, Savoy

Henri had become fairly comfortable at the fortress—he was liked and respected, holding the responsible position of head telegrapher. It was not often that he felt a cold chill.

A few mornings after the conversation with Gilles about the special prisoner, he was taking his early constitutional along the main parapet. He looked out at the road leading west toward Lyon, and saw a troop of soldiers approaching. They bore no banner and, while obviously well-equipped, wore no livery or uniform.

He asked the use of a spyglass from his friend Guillaume, an older pensioner among the guards, and gazed through it. To his surprise, it seemed that the column was being led by a woman—possibly an up-timer—and that riding beside her was another woman. With a start he recognized her.

What in the name of all the saints is Mademoiselle Tillman doing here? He thought. *And what is she doing riding with a group of soldiers?*

It was then that the cold chill struck with full force.

This couldn't happen in a void—someone must know about it. There must have been a message, but he didn't remember recording one.

He took the stairs two at a time down from the wall, crossed the courtyard and to the tower where the telegraph was located. The wide wire array caught the morning sun as he ran inside, bounding up the stairs as quickly as he could.

Gilles was sitting at the apparatus, painfully tapping out some message with one beefy finger. When Henri came in, he sent the last few characters and then turned to face him.

"Is there something wrong?"

"Did you record a message regarding the arrival of some soldiers?"

At first the big Savoyard looked at Henri as if he was speaking a foreign language, but then the question seemed to register. He nodded and gestured toward the "in" tray.

Henri reached up and pulled down a small stack of pencilled messages, all carefully numbered and dated, in various hands including Gilles' blocky script and his own more careful lettering. There was nothing regarding soldiers—

Then, suddenly, he saw that a slip of paper had fallen down behind the shelf. It was from three days earlier, and noted that a troop would be coming from the west, stopping to water and fodder their mounts.

"Did you find something?"

"Yes. Yes . . . nothing critical. Go back to work."

"You're sure? I remember getting that one, Henri. I didn't recognize the call sign."

Henri took the message and tucked it into his vest. "Don't worry about it. I'll take care of it."

"If I—"

Henri jerked a thumb at the apparatus. "Aren't you supposed to be listening?"

Gilles took the hint, put the earphones back on, and hunched his shoulders—a sign that he was concentrating.

❖   ❖   ❖

Henri was torn: clearly there was something about to happen—and the fortress was unready. If he hadn't picked out Terrye Jo Tillman, who he considered a friend but who he hadn't heard from in ages, his duty would be clear: go directly to the warden and inform him exactly what was coming. But he had, and things were more muddled because of it.

Up-timers had been proscribed in France by order of King Gaston. If she was here—if the two *Grantvilleuse* women were here—they might be escaping that proscription. He had nothing against Terrye Jo: in fact, as far as he knew, neither did His Grace. These soldiers might be friendly. But the warden might misinterpret things, for whatever reason . . .

He hesitated long enough that the troop reached the bridge over the foss that surrounded the fortress, and was slowly crossing it, by the time he resolved to go down to the warden's reception room.

"Let me handle this," Terrye Jo said to Sherrilyn as they dismounted in the courtyard. She could already see Warden LeBarre walking quickly to meet them.

"Mademoiselle—Mademoiselle—" he began, clearly unused to such exertions—and also clearly not in possession of her name.

"Tillman," she said. "Monsieur LeBarre. I was here last spring with His Highness King Gaston." She smiled her best disarming smile. "You made some insightful remarks about the cruel world of up-time."

"Mademoiselle Tillman," he said, panting just a bit. "Insightful? Ah, yes. The tortures." He smiled in a slightly disturbing way. "Have you come back to observe?"

"No, monsieur. Nothing like that. I am traveling with this troop, and they have need of water for their mounts, and to rest and fodder them before we travel on. I told the colonel—" she gestured to Sherrilyn, who was standing next to her horse, innocuously adjusting the strap on a saddlebag—"that you had been most hospitable, and that it would be an ideal place to stop. I hope this is not too great an imposition."

"Imposition?" He blinked, looking at two dozen well-armed soldiers in his courtyard. He glanced nervously at the walls; there were eight or nine guards, two with flintlock muskets in none-too-good repair, the rest with halberds that had seen very little use. "No, not at all. In fact, I—I was just taking my breakfast. Perhaps you would care to join me, mademoiselle."

"We'd love to."

"We," he repeated, glancing again at the soldiers. "Mademoiselle . . . my table is very modest, very small—"

Terrye Jo smiled again. "I meant only myself and the colonel. The rest of these fine lads will remain in the courtyard." She beckoned to Sherrilyn. "Breakfast?"

"Breakfast," she repeated, nodding. "Sounds like a plan."

"After you, monsieur," she said, gesturing toward the main hall.

LeBarre turned and led them across the yard and under an archway. Terrye Jo and Sherrilyn followed close behind. As they passed from the bright sunlight into the dim coolness of the building, Sherrilyn caught Terrye Jo's eye and nodded.

LeBarre's small dining room was just off the main hall, and the table was set with bread—still warm, from the smell—a wedge of cheese and three apples.

There was a pitcher and a ceramic mug on the table as well. LeBarre turned to his pantry cabinet and pulled down two additional mugs . . . and when he turned around he found himself face to face with the business end of a handsome reproduction of an 1861 Colt pistol.

"This can be very easy," Sherrilyn said softly but menacingly, "or very, very hard."

"Madame," he said. He looked at Terrye Jo. "Mademoiselle. There is nothing here to rob—this is a prison, not a treasure house."

He seemed unusually calm, even with a dangerous weapon wielded by a dangerous person pointed directly at him.

"We only want one thing," Sherrilyn said, "and we'll be on our way."

"And that thing is?"

"One of your prisoners."

LeBarre looked suddenly very alarmed. This was a sore point of some sort; Terrye Jo wasn't sure just why.

While she tried to figure it out, someone came through the door. "Warden," he said, "I—"

Terrye Jo Tillman didn't have the dramatic flair that Sherrilyn Maddox had acquired as part of the Wrecking Crew, but her reflexes were still fairly good. She whirled, drawing her own pistol, and suddenly found herself face to face with Henri Durant. Her former apprentice stopped speaking and slowly raised his hands in front of him.

She gestured with her weapon, directing him into the room to stand next to the warden, who stood with a mug in each hand, unmoving.

"This is very dangerous ground, *mesdames*," the

warden said. "The prisoner you seek—it would be worth my life to give him up."

"Because he ticked off a high and mighty?" Sherrilyn said. "Believe me when I tell you that anyone who's capable of angering someone important has a friend in a high place who'll protect him. And you."

"This is an...unusual case. The important person is very important indeed."

"He's right," Terrye Jo said. "The king of France is pretty important."

"The king? *Non*," LeBarre said. "His *mother*."

"Phillippe de la Mothe pissed off Queen Marie?" Sherrilyn said, sounding incredulous. "I mean, I know it's supposed to be easy, but—"

"De la Mothe?" LeBarre's face brightened. "You're here for de la Mothe?"

"...Yeah," Sherrilyn said. "Who did you think we wanted? The Count of Monte Crisco?"

"Monte *Cristo*," Terrye Jo said.

"I know. Joke. Forget it." She waved her pistol at the two men. "Just who do you have that's that important?"

LeBarre got the alarmed look on his face again. Sherrilyn moved her thumb to cock the hammer of the pistol, but it was more for effect: it was obvious that the warden was scared of something—or someone—more than he was scared of having Sherrilyn Maddox blow his head off.

"We want Phillippe de la Mothe-Haudencourt," Sherrilyn said. "Terrye Jo, why don't you get this other guy to take you to him."

"Mademoiselle Terrye Jo," Henri said, his voice quavering a bit, "I don't know what—"

"Wait. You know her?"

"I trained Henri as a telegrapher," Terrye Jo said. "So yes."

"Then maybe he'll do a friend a favor," Sherrilyn said. "Assuming you're still friends."

"I'll . . . take you to him," Henri said. "He is . . . not a prisoner, though. He is responsible for a prisoner."

"Durant—" LeBarre began.

"You shut up." Sherrilyn waved LeBarre to a seat at the table; he took two steps and sat, still holding the two mugs and looking bewildered, looking as if he wondered how he could suddenly be at his own dining-table at gunpoint. Still, there was less fear in his eyes than Sherrilyn expected.

"Lead the way," Terrye Jo said. She smiled—but didn't lower her pistol.

Henri Durant did not speak as he ascended the tower stairs ahead of Terrye Jo. She didn't holster her weapon, but let the edge of her riding-cloak wrap around it so it wasn't so obvious. Her old friend looked scared and wary; she wanted to reassure him, but she also wanted to carry through the mission—to get the man they came for and get out before anyone needed to blow *anyone's* head off.

Finally they reached the top of the tower. There was a barred door, secured from the outside. A guard lounged in a chair nearby, but jumped to attention as they approached. He reached for his halberd, but froze when he saw Terrye Jo, who made her pistol once again visible.

"Henri," she said, waving him over to the guard, "get the keys and open this door."

"Mademoiselle Tillman," Henri said. "Mademoiselle Terrye Jo. It is very dangerous, this thing you are doing. It would be far better if your troop left at once."

"We're here for a reason, Henri. I'm not in command, but the person who is will absolutely kick my ass if I don't do my part. Now get the door open before I have to do something we'll both regret."

Henri Durant hesitated only a moment more, then walked to where the guard stood. He extended his hand and received a ring of keys, then stepped to the door and inserted the correct one in the lock. He swung the door outward to reveal a reasonably spacious cell; a well-dressed man stood facing the door, with another man sitting at a small table, his head turned away: he seemed to be wearing some sort of metal helm. When he turned, Terrye Jo saw...

"Damn," she said. "Not the Count of Monte Cristo—it's the Man in the Iron Mask."

Sherrilyn knew that it would be easy to let her attention drift, so she made a point of studying the warden of Miolans while she waited for Terrye Jo to return with Phillippe de la Mothe-Haudencourt. LeBarre had reacted with surprise and annoyance when she'd stuck her pistol in his face, but he didn't seem to be angry now—he was almost smug.

"I must commend you for your nerve, 'Colonel'—assuming that to be a title you deserve," he said. "That you believe that you can come right in here and get what you want so easily."

"'Nobody move or the nose gets it,'" she answered. "Eh?"

"Never mind. Yes, it's a legitimate title—I was

commissioned by a marshal of France. Thanks for the compliment: yes, I see no reason why we can't get what we want and get out, no one gets hurt."

"Perhaps in that up-time world of yours," LeBarre said. "But we are not so gullible. As soon as I was informed of a troop of soldiers coming to Miolans, I was suspicious. What's more, I am completely unconvinced that you are here to 'rescue' that popinjay de la Mothe. You want our special prisoner."

"Special prisoner?"

"Please do not dissemble with me, *Colonel*." He might have accepted that she was deserving of the title, but it was a sneering tone nonetheless. "You think that you can meddle in the affairs of your betters, but you cannot hope to succeed."

"So? What are you going to do about it?"

"More to the point, Mademoiselle," LeBarre said, "it is what I have already *done* about it. You may have found it easy to get into Miolans . . . but you may find getting out much more difficult."

"I don't think there's much time," Terrye Jo said to de la Mothe. *Yep*, she thought to herself: *that's some nose*. "You'd better come with me, monsieur."

De la Mothe turned to face the masked prisoner. "*He's* coming with me."

"Who is he, anyway?"

"I am not sure," de la Mothe said. "But I would not condemn him to remain in this state."

"Let's get the mask off," Terrye Jo said. "Do you have the key?"

"The warden has it. And I don't know where he keeps it."

She reached into her belt for a second pistol and handed it to de la Mothe, then walked over to the masked prisoner.

"If you will permit, Monsieur," she said, and took hold of the lock just below the chin. She gave it a slight tug; it seemed very solid. "With the right tools I could probably pick the lock, but it would be easier if I just used the key."

"You are an up-timer," the prisoner said. "Is that not so?"

"Yes. I assumed that was obvious."

"You go at this problem the way all up-timers do," he said. "Straight ahead, with no regard for consequences."

"Right now, I'm mostly concerned with getting this mission done and getting out of here. Monsieur de la Mothe is right, though: no one should be given this treatment. Frankly, I think we should let *everybody* out—except that this is the middle of nowhere."

"I think it's a splendid idea," de la Mothe said, without looking away from Henri and the guard. "Though I confess that I don't know why you're here."

"Because when Sherrilyn Maddox gets an idea into her head," Terrye Jo said, "she doesn't let go of it."

"Colonel *Maddox* is here? To rescue me? *Très gallant*," said de la Mothe. "*L'homme masqué* is right: I should have seen her hand in this from the very beginning. She is the most up-timerish of all of the up-timers I have ever met.

"But it cannot be possible that we will simply ride out of here unopposed."

"We'll see about that. In the meanwhile, we should get downstairs and see what's happening. Henri,"

Terrye Jo said to her former apprentice, "I'm sorry, but I have to do this. Go sit over there." She pointed at the little table. "And you, Giuseppe, or whatever your name might be—go sit next to him."

With weapons still drawn and aimed at Henri and the guard, they backed out of the room, then securely locked the door before making their way down the stairs—de la Mothe helping the masked man to keep him from a misstep.

Sherrilyn's knee had begun to throb, but she wasn't about to sit down while she was keeping an eye trained on—and a gun aimed at—LeBarre. She'd relieved him of the cheese knife, so he was contenting himself with bread torn from the loaf. The smell of it was making her hungry, but she wasn't about to let herself be distracted by that either.

Through the thick glass windows of LeBarre's pantry she could see that the rest of the Rangers had organized themselves as she'd ordered. One of the senior men had put his head in and had received orders, and a warning that there might well be visitors, and to find the radio shack and disable it.

She was just beginning to think that Terrye Jo had been gone too long—*what's the freakin' delay, child?* Ran through her head—when she heard footsteps: two or three sets, coming at speed. She placed herself against a sideboard, where she could keep her eyes on the doorway and on LeBarre, and raised her pistol.

The first person through the door was Phillippe de la Mothe-Haudencourt, and for a moment her stomach gave a most unprofessional jump. Even in whatever situation he was in here in Miolans, even in the middle of nowhere, it was clear that he hadn't stopped paying attention to his appearance: the moustaches were carefully trimmed and arranged, his clothes were properly arrayed, and he removed his hat and gave Sherrilyn a most gentlemanly bow.

"No time for that," she snapped, but she was far less annoyed than she tried to sound. He seemed to see right through it. But the *noblesse* only lasted a moment before he stepped aside to reveal a man dressed in rough-spun clothing with some sort of helmet on his head. Terrye Jo was just behind, sharing her attention between the doorway and Sherrilyn.

"The Man in the Iron Mask?" She looked from the door to LeBarre. "Are you serious? Who the hell has been reading Dumas?"

"You need to ask," LeBarre said. "But in all earnest, madame. *Everyone* reads Dumas. There is someone who has paid particular attention."

"Enough of that. We're going to get that thing off, Monsieur, whoever you are."

"There will be consequences," he said, the headgear making his voice sound strange and hollow.

"Don't care," Sherrilyn said. "Terrye Jo, do you think you can get that off, or will I have to shoot the lock?"

"I think I have the tools," she answered, and disappeared, presumably headed for the courtyard.

"It sounds like our friend the warden has called up reinforcements," Sherrilyn said to de la Mothe. "He assumes that we're here for the masked man. Whatever got you put here in this spot, monsieur?"

"Friends in high places."

"Such as who?"

"Madame," the man said, "if you unlock this prison

and learn my identity, you put yourself and everyone here, even Monsieur le Warden, in extremely great danger. Those who did this will spare no efforts to pursue you."

"Let 'em try."

"Your up-timer bravado is impressive."

"Your up-timer bravado is foolhardy," LeBarre said. "Like that prancing fool—what's his name? Leffer?"

Sherrilyn turned to face LeBarre, pointing her pistol directly at him and cocking the hammer. "Lefferts. Harry Lefferts. Say one more word about him, monsieur, and I will most assuredly blow your head all over this room. Are we clear?"

"Abundantly," LeBarre answered. His voice was more level than Sherrilyn would have expected.

"She means it," de la Mothe said. LeBarre shot him a nasty look.

Terrye Jo reappeared in the doorway, rucksack in hand. "If you'd sit down, monsieur," she said to the masked man, "it'll be easier."

He took up a position on a small settle and placed his hands on his knees. Terrye Jo knelt down and opened the rucksack, pulling out a rolled-up piece of leather; she spread it out, and reached for a pair of small picks. In short order she was working on the heavy lock.

"I don't need to wonder how you learned to do that," Sherrilyn said admiringly. "Army, I'm guessing?"

"Grantville High," Terrye Jo said without turning around.

"Really."

"Good thing that's a long time ago and a long time from now," she said. "Now let me work."

De la Mothe and Sherrilyn exchanged a glance but kept quiet. After a few minutes there was a satisfying click as tumblers fell into place, and Terrye Jo gave the lock a jerk; it opened and came easily off in her hands. She carefully separated the front of the helmet from the shell and drew it up over the prisoner's head.

He was a bearded man past middle age, with what remained of a clerical tonsure. His piercing eyes were his most compelling feature, and they looked from LeBarre to Sherrilyn and finally to de la Mothe, who looked extremely surprised.

"Père," he said, kneeling and placing his hands on those of the other man. "If I'd known . . ."

"It's all right," he answered. "It was not intended for you to know. Whatever problems this solves, it creates a host of new ones. Still," he added running one of his hands through thinning hair that glistened with sweat, "it's good to get that cursed thing off and take a deep breath."

"Care to introduce us?" Sherrilyn said.

"You don't know who this is?"

"We don't exactly live in a world with cable TV, Phillippe. He's obviously a priest, but I have no idea which one."

De la Mothe scrambled to his feet. "Sherrilyn— Colonel Maddox. I have the honor to present Joseph Tremblay, Cardinal *in pectore* of the Holy Mother Church. A . . . confidante and particular friend to the late Cardinal-Duke de Richelieu."

As they stood in the courtyard, Sherrilyn heard a low, sharp whistle from the wall: the signal for *incoming*.

"We need to get all of us out of here," she said.

"But I really am not sure how. We're not leaving you behind, Eminence," she added to Tremblay, "but I think you're the one they want the most."

"That is without doubt," he said. "Though they may not know they are after me."

"What do you mean?"

"I would assume that Queen Marie kept my identity a close secret." He gestured toward the mask, which Terrye Jo had hung from her saddle. "They may only know that they are to protect a masked prisoner."

"If we bug out and there's no masked prisoner with us," she said, "they may not bother with us."

"If there's no masked prisoner, Colonel," Tremblay replied, "they'll assume that you removed the mask."

"We weren't going to leave it in place."

"For which I thank you, mademoiselle. But it causes this predicament."

Sherrilyn looked at the ground, and kicked the dirt with one boot. *This was supposed to be simple. Harry always said that simple plans were the best—in and out, clear objectives, quick solutions.*

Terrye Jo is going to give me such a raft of abuse— she told me so. She said this wasn't going to be easy, and the girl was right, and there'll be no way to deny it. They'll assume we took the mask off.

Unless they see someone wearing it.

"Phillippe," she said, "are you up for a fast ride?"

"Meaning what?"

She went to Terrye Jo's horse and picked up the mask. "His Eminence pointed out the obvious a minute ago—that anyone coming to reinforce Heritage USA here is going to be looking for a prisoner wearing this thing." She held it up. "We didn't come to break him out—we came to break *you* out—but they'll assume otherwise. So we need to give them what they want: a man in an iron mask, escaping."

"And how do I come into this?"

She didn't answer, but looked from him to the mask and back again.

"You're not serious."

"My boys can all ride reasonably well," she said. "But you're the best horseman I know. Put this on, and the two of us haul it as fast as we can—they'll go after us."

"And the rest can leave without being pursued. Unless, of course, they split up."

Sherrilyn whistled loudly, with a slightly different pitch than the warning. One of the men turned and put up a hand with one finger down.

"There are about forty men," she said. "If they stay together we can outrun them. If they split up, we outgun them. Bastien," she said to an older Ranger standing a few feet away. "You're in command—you know how this plays."

The man smiled in a way that would be disturbing if he were on the opposite side of the fight; to Sherrilyn it was vaguely reassuring.

"So what do you think, Phillippe? Are you up for this?"

He gave a dubious look at the mask, shuddering very slightly. "This is a stupid plan."

"You're damn right. But it's what I've got."

"Very well, Madame. My fate—and apparently my head—is in your hands." He reached out his hand and took the heavy metal mask, taking a moment to gaze into its depths.

❖   ❖   ❖

Sherrilyn only heard about it later, when Bastien and Terrye Jo related the story; her part was exciting enough. When the troop of soldiers approaching Miolans from the direction of Savoy came into sight— but not weapon range—of the fortress, she and de la Mothe—wearing the iron mask—burst across the bridge and rode as hard as they could in the opposite direction. It took the troop commander a few moments and a couple of harsh commands to get his men moving, but they responded to the sight, at least half of them taking off after their quarry.

In the meanwhile the remaining force approached Miolans, only to be suddenly greeted by the sight of two dozen Maddox's Rangers, all armed with fine, well-made rifles that caught the pale afternoon sun, and all aimed at them. Their muskets were well made, but they'd have to advance close enough to fire.

That would be at least two rounds for each man on the wall, more than enough to thin the ranks.

"No one knows what happened to you, Your Eminence," de la Mothe said a few nights later. "His Highness the Prince of Condé offered sanctuary to the young former Cardinal's Guardsman, D'Aubisson, who managed to get out of the Châtelet. He made a public complaint at court, but it seems that His Royal Highness had no idea you'd been imprisoned."

De la Mothe placed a wooden bowl and spoon in Tremblay's hands and sat down next to him.

"There's no need for you to serve any longer as my *valet de chambre*, Monsieur de la Mothe."

"It is my pleasure, Eminence. Frankly, being an enemy of Queen Marie does not trouble me in the least."

"It should. My former master—" Tremblay crossed himself—"God rest his soul—never stopped being wary of her, even after the Day of Dupes, even after she went into exile in the Low Countries. I don't think even King Gaston should take her lightly."

"I didn't say I took her lightly, Eminence. I just said that I don't care if she considers me an enemy."

Tremblay smiled; his expression indicated that it was not something he had much practice in doing. "Very well. I see the distinction." He took his spoon and buried it in the stew in his bowl and drew it to his lips. "Ahhh. I cannot say that I ever became accustomed to that mask."

"I only wore it for a few hours, Eminence," de la Mothe said. "I can't say it was a pleasure."

"That Dumas fellow had a vivid imagination."

Sherrilyn came up to stand next to the two men. "He sure did. Apparently he's a real favorite with down-timers."

"We all like to be amused at how we are portrayed," Tremblay said. "I shall have to become more sinister, apparently."

"I don't think I appear at all," de la Mothe said. He ran a finger along his moustaches. "Though I confess that I have not read the entire *oeuvre*."

"We cannot all be celebrities," Tremblay said. "But it really does not matter—the world he described, at a distance, is one that does not exist: it never did, and never will. We have the Ring of Fire to thank for that."

"Or curse for it," Sherrilyn said. "In the meanwhile we'll just have to do the best we can."

Love Has a Wet Nose

Walt Boyes and Joy Ward

Jena, Germany 1634

Henry leaned against the tavern window, staring blankly through the tiny panes of watery looking glass at the quick rain shower coming down outside, and trying to avoid looking at the couple in the seats across from him. Too many memories, too much pain.

The couple, in their late thirties, held hands and talked softly as they seemed to fit together like a puzzle. They were dressed well, if plainly, and both completely naturally wore something like up-timer dress. He was slightly balding, and was sharing small talk with the slightly dumpy blonde woman nestled next to him as they looked out at the midsummer shower and the scenery.

Henry averted his eyes and made a point of not engaging the sweet couple. They reminded him too much of his loss, his François. He and François had been just as in love but all that was gone. He could tell no one and yet he had to watch others in their love.

Henry wiped at his eyes, hoping the couple wouldn't see him and feel moved to talk to him. He couldn't bear that. Their love was so evident, so palpable, to talk with them would tear him apart.

Henry's thoughts went back a couple of years when François was still alive. He and François had traveled together under the cover of swords for hire, serving in mercenary companies for the Protestant side. It was not unusual for young men to band together to hire out as a team. The two of them had gained a slight fame among their colleagues. Both were known to have competent sword arms and were expert shots with both wheel-lock pistol and musket. François and he had become underofficers in a regiment mostly made up of French Huguenots and some English and Scots. They had fought well at Breitenfeld and other major battles and had been looking forward to a little bit of peace, now that the USE had made a de-facto truce between the Catholic and Protestant sides.

But their relationship had been much deeper than simple sell swords. Henry and François had been lovers. Occasionally they would step out with a pair of young women to maintain their cover as eligible rakes. After all, their love was outlawed by state and church. Of course, everyone knew there were powerful men who preferred men to women but those whispers were often silenced by money and power. Henry and François had little enough of either.

So they moved around, took commissions from those who could afford them and kept their love silent.

Until this past Spring when François started to complain of pain in his belly. Henry's mind slid back to that evil day. The tavern seemed to wash away in the rain.

"Oh, *le bonne Dieu!*" François gasped as he doubled over on his horse. He swayed in the saddle, and then fell to the ground. Henry reined in, turned his horse around and rode to him, slid from his horse, and knelt in the stinking muck by François' side.

"Aieee!" François gasped, clutching his belly.

"What is it, my friend?"

"It feels like a cramp, but not one. Ahhh! It is easing now." François started to get up, and Henry helped him to stand. One of the men held François' and Henry's horses, and François mounted again.

"I seem to be fine, now, *mon ami*," François said, waving Henry off.

It was not too bad at first, at least that's what François tried to say. That night in their tent, François repeatedly woke up in pain, sweat pouring across his lithe body and soaking his shoulder-length chestnut curls. Nothing helped.

Henry tried to find an up-time-trained doctor but there were none in the backwater town in which they were stationed. There were only barber surgeons, and the occasional hedge woman but none could help his love, his François. They were terrified of surgery on the abdomen.

That night François died, taking Henry's life with him.

Henry came to as he sat in the window, staring, but his eyes saw a different scene; the day he met the man who would change his life.

"You there!" The accented voice cracked like a whip. Henry spun around as a horse sidled to a stop next to him. He was working on his horse's tack, a job he never let one of his troopers do.

He looked up, into the eyes of a tall, slender man with longish chestnut hair, worn in a pony tail.

"Yes?" Henry said, continuing to massage linseed oil into the leather.

"I am looking for Monsieur Henry Cooper," the tall man said in fractured-sounding English.

"That would be me."

"Ah, *c'est bon*! Monsieur Cooper, I am François de la Roche, and I have orders."

Henry reached for the proffered leather message pouch. His hand touched François' and a spark flew between them.

Henry, born in England to a cooper father, and François, born two years earlier in France to a stonemason, never thought they would be parted. Having found each other in a war, they thanked God for bringing them together. They would laugh about their cross Channel union during their late mornings lying together in their bed. Each would tell the other what their families would say when they returned with their sacks of hard-earned gold and their cocky partner in tow. Henry would toss his dark brown hair back from his high cheekbones and affect his father's long stride pacing across the room. The two lovers would laugh and the laughing would turn to something more physical, though just as pleasant.

But then that day, that evil day, that Henry woke to find his François really and truly dead. He had been torn away by Death. His dashing Frenchman had died in his sleep from something within his belly. The pain had been getting worse and worse until the night François grabbed his abdomen and screamed. François said that he felt he had been run through with a blade but there was nothing on his skin. He had not been stabbed but by dawn he was dead.

Henry hated remembering that night but he kept wondering was there something he could have done? All he could do was remember the smell of the stale sweat as it poured off François' pain-wracked body. In the days that followed, Henry made his own vow. He would make Death pay by stealing as many of the living from his grasp as he could.

Henry was brought back to the present in Jena where he sat in the café. The man was calling to him, asking Henry something.

The woman across from him giggled at something her husband had said. Henry looked up, momentarily pulled into the present. He looked up. Into the woman's brown eyes. He had to return her warm smile.

"Are you new to Jena, young man?" She straightened her blue wool skirt as if she needed to remove unseen wrinkles or crumbs from a tasty pastry. She wrapped her left hand, with a simple wedding band, around a cup of some steaming liquid and nodded toward the balding man.

"Do you mind if my husband and I share the time with you? You seem to be alone and, well, we see each other quite a bit." She laughed and squeezed her husband's arm as he threw a mock frown her way. "My husband is Helmut Woltman and I am Eugenia Beckerin," she said. "We are going to work in Grantville at Leahy Medical Center. We have been taking some courses at the medical school here. Are you here to study at the university?"

Henry smiled. "I'm heading to the medical school, in fact." Henry blushed and looked out the window. "I had a few years of medical training before becoming a soldier. I plan on joining the next class. Are you both doctors?"

"I am a nurse-midwife," Eugenia said, "and Helmut is a physician's assistant. That's a new term for what used to be called 'barber surgeon' but with much more up-time training." She looked as if she would swell with pride and gave her husband a private smile.

Eugenia continued, looking at Henry, "How did you decide to be a doctor? Please don't mind me saying so but you look to me more like a soldier than a doctor."

"I spent some few years at University in England, where I am from," Henry said. "School did not agree with me, so I left to become a soldier. I am Henry Cooper, at your service." He doffed his soft, dark green hat to her as he bowed from his seat.

Henry was a well-built, broad shouldered man well past six feet tall. The years in the wars had added a scar over his left eye. With chocolate brown eyes that had turned many ladies' attention, Henry had made his living by his good right arm for well over a decade.

"So you have left the regiments?"

"Yes, Frau Beckerin. I have spent a few years in the military but I prefer to fight for lives rather than death. I look forward to being a reminder and carrier of health rather than of Death. I have been told that having already received two years of medical training in England I will have a shorter training period here."

"We wish you well, my friend. My husband and I are on our way to see Grantville. We can't wait to see all the marvels of the up-timers." The sweet-faced matron reached over and squeezed her husband's substantial arm again, giving him a smile.

He smiled back at her. "My wife has been a fan of the Barbie dolls and hopes to come across a spare from one of the up-timers. I told her that is highly unlikely but I am looking forward to studying in the famed library." The man smiled as he reached up to remove his brown cloth cap to wipe his balding pate.

"Barbie dolls?" Henry asked. "What are they? I have not heard of them."

"The up-timers have many arts that we do not, including the making of toys," Helmut said. "One of their toys is a doll that is about so high, perhaps a foot, and is a poppet based on a woman. She has enormous bosoms and a thin waist, and is used for dressing up with expensive clothing made especially for the doll. They are disgustingly expensive, but Eugenia wants one."

"And perhaps I'll be able to get one," she said, smiling.

Henry let the couple talk on as he pushed the memories back and focused on the on busy, sun-washed street outside the cozy café as the drizzle gave way to afternoon sun.

A few minutes later Henry found himself walking out of the tavern and into the Jena streets on his way to the university's medical school and a new life. As Henry moved through the bustling city he kept wishing he could share it with his best friend, his love, his François. But François lay back in the churchyard in France. Tears rose unbidden again. Henry pulled back towards a building, away from the milling crowds of what seemed to be university students and shoppers.

Before long, Henry's long strides brought him to the medical school. His new life began when he walked through the high, stone archway.

True to his unspoken vow, Henry dedicated himself to medicine. He never missed a class, never missed a chance to learn something new. He became the perfect scholar. At night when other students were sharing ales at one of the taverns ringing the schools of Jena, Henry cloistered himself in this small, seedy room.

Even his classmates noted his studiousness. Most among them spent their time between their books and the taverns. While they thought Henry to be nice enough, both male and female students noticed his lack of frivolity. The males had heard of his soldierly past and Henry wore his blade regularly, so they dared say nothing to him. The few female students noticed his strong physique, fine brown hair and eyes and wondered what it would take to catch his eye.

Henry was the first to volunteer to see patients with the visiting doctors. He was first to volunteer to help carry supplies or bandage the poor needing help. Henry did not care if the patients were rich or poor; he was there to help when he could. He became known among Jena's poor as a visiting angel.

He would see the farmers with broken arms and legs as well as the children with scrapes and burns. Some, like the cooper with no way to pay Henry for his help with his wife's early pregnancy, gave him what they could and blessed his way. As he finished his schooling he reached out and helped even more people, with more dangerous illnesses. He did not limit himself to the wealthy burghers and generals as so many of his classmates did.

Only one among the students became friends with the taciturn young doctor in training who haunted the medical library. She was also a loner, intent on her studies. Frieda was from Austria and as dedicated to becoming a healer as Henry. Occasionally, after class the two would sit in a nearby tavern, drinking tea and discussing the lectures. Other students would watch them, thinking they were more than friends but nothing was further from the truth.

Frieda was young, just twenty when she began her medical studies, but she was very observant. She realized that Henry never eyed the other women, never laughed at the usual crude jokes made by his male fellows. Of course, she said nothing to anyone else.

Henry threw himself into his studies, and later his practice, because it gave him a way to avoid the memories a few minutes longer. When approached by a young woman seeking his attentions, he would politely tell her he did not have the time to become involved and did not want to play her affections for a few nights' frolic. In this way, Henry remained true to his François and avoided uncomfortable questions. After all, he could not announce his preferences since they might have caused him to be dismissed from the medical school or if he was very unlucky, be sentenced to death.

Jena, Germany, Late in 1635

Then the time came for Henry and Frieda to graduate, at the top of the class, of course. They had, as the up-timers said, "aced" the medical curriculum. Both had done four years' work in less than two. Henry had studied medicine in England, before turning to a military career, and he'd kept up his studies as a soldier, always talking to the doctors that served with the regiment. He remembered one in particular, a flamboyant doctor named Gribbleflotz. He'd learned a lot from him.

Henry was going on to study in Grantville, while Frieda was returning to Vienna to teach. Frieda decided she had known Henry several years now and he should trust her. She decided they should talk.

Frieda asked Henry to go with her to a new teashop that had recently opened across town. This way, she felt, they could have a little privacy away from the usual tavern crowd.

How should she start? Why not just jump in? So they sat and sipped their strong tea in silence.

"This is a sad time for me too, Frieda, with leaving and all. You have been my best friend here." Henry lifted hid cup in salute to his fellow graduate.

"Um, yes, I'll miss you too but that wasn't really why I asked you here." Frieda took a long gulp of the tea.

"Frieda, there you are." A tall, red-haired woman swept over to the pair and hugged the blond Frieda. Frieda, a bit flustered, hugged her back.

"Henry, this is my friend Magda. Magda is in Jena studying up-timer engineering. We grew up together in a small town near the Turkish border in Austria."

Magda laughed. "*Ja*, Frieda was always doctoring small animals like birds and rabbits. Anything hurt in the village ended up in her rudimentary clinic."

"Not to mention all the times I had to repair you and your brothers after one of your inventions or experiments." Frieda giggled at the memories and took a bite of the strawberry tart in front of her.

Magda put her black bag filled with papers down

in a wooden chair at the table and sat down. It was only a few moments before an even younger woman in an apron and a yellow cotton dress made her way to the threesome. Magda ordered a tea and a piece of cake.

When the tea arrived, Magda raised it in a toast. "To the new doctors!"

Frieda looked from Magda to Henry. "Henry, please come over tonight for a celebration with a few folks."

Henry stared into his mug of tea for a minute, searching for some way to gracefully beg off. Henry had never been invited to her home, and he did enjoy her company. He could think of no reason to refuse her invitation. "*Ja*. I would like that."

He stayed for a few more minutes, long enough to be sure of Frieda's address.

Bottle of Riesling in hand, Henry found himself in front of Frieda's rooms shortly after dusk a few hours later. He knocked tentatively on the dark wooden door.

While Henry stood in the faint light from the street, he wondered if this was a bad idea. He and François went to social events together where François would shine. Henry never thought of himself as a glittering conversationalist and he was always afraid of giving the two of them away to prying eyes and wagging tongues.

Of course, François was gone . . .

In what seemed to be only a minute, Frieda was standing in the open door, pulling Henry in to the warm room.

No one else was there other than Frieda and Magda. "Am I early? Did I get the time wrong?"

The two women exchanged a smile. Frieda put her hand on his arm. "No, no. We are all here. Come; let's open the lovely wine you brought. Is that my favorite Riesling?" The shorter blond woman swept the wine away into the kitchen where she pried off the cork and poured the clear liquid into three glasses.

She shared them out to Magda and Henry, who had moved to a table draped with a paisley cloth. They pulled out chairs and began to sit down when Frieda stood still and looked appraising lay at Henry.

"Henry, do you trust me?"

Magda swirled the light wine around in her glass as she exchanged a meaningful look with Frieda.

"What is the matter, Frieda? Have we not shared these last few years together in medical school? And why only us here? Did the others cancel?"

Frieda smiled and took a step towards the taller auburn-haired woman. "My question to you is can I trust you with my life and freedom?"

"Are you in trouble? Do you need help?" Henry's pulse quickened.

"No, but I could be if I trust the wrong person."

Henry glanced around the small but comfortable apartment. "Of course you can trust me but what..."

Frieda took that moment to place a distinctly non-sisterly kiss on Magda. Henry watched in silence.

The two women pulled apart slightly and looked at Henry.

"So?" Frieda grinned at him. "Did I guess wrongly?"

"What do you mean?"

"Are you shocked or scandalized? Have I trusted wrongly?"

"No, of course not."

"I have been watching you since we met, Henry, and I figured you would understand. Magda is my very special friend. I wanted you to know her and know you are not alone."

Henry's thoughts flashed back to his François for a moment and the tears seeped out. He still missed François so much! He welcomed Frieda's admission but he very much wished François was with him.

The two women exchanged looks and each reached out to lay a caring hand on Henry's shoulders.

Frieda's otherwise jovial features took on a worried look. "We did not mean to alarm or cause you pain. I just wanted to encourage you the way I've been encouraged by some of the up-timers and their writing."

He wiped at his eyes with one blue cotton sleeve. "What do you mean? Encouraged? Who could you possibly tell without fear?"

"Let us sit down, share this good wine and talk." Magda settled herself at the table. Frieda and Henry followed her lead.

"What do you mean about encouragement?" Henry asked as Frieda uncovered some hard cheese and bread on the table. "I will not share your secret. Your secret is mine, as you have deduced, but our loves are forbidden and illegal. How could you be so rash as to talk to others about it?" He looked around nervously as if expecting church or civil representatives to slide out from under a chair or crash through a window.

"According to some of the up-timers, in the future people like us will not be hunted and despised." Magda took a sip of her wine.

"I overheard one of the up-timer women in the cafe talking about her relative who was like us. The up-timer seemed to genuinely miss her cousin, I think it was, and her cousin's partner she called him. She and her friend did not seem to be in a hurry so I struck up a conversation with them and worked my way back to the subject. According to the up-timer woman, in *her* time, most people did not seem to care too much if one was like us. She has problems understanding why it is a problem for people of our time. She even said that she expects things to change, just like the up-timers have affected other issues in our world."

"I pray you and she are correct." Henry dearly wished that François could hear all this. "Here's a toast to good friends, love, and the up-timers!" He lifted his glass and met the glasses of the two women. *"Prosit!"*

They talked through the Riesling and into a red wine from Burgundy. They talked about the up-timers, their new ideas and what they brought with them to medicine and engineering and other facets of life. They promised to write, often. Afterwards, Henry headed home with the new ideas and hopes for the future seeding his mind with ideas.

That night, Henry cried himself to sleep, again. He was glad for Frieda and Magda but François was still dead.

A few days later, Henry moved to Grantville to start his internship, as was the custom. He had practiced as a doctor's assistant in Jena but now he would be able to practice on his own. He could not wait to see this epitome of new thought and the best medicine. Now he could truly begin his war against Death!

He rode the train from Jena to Grantville, luxuriating in the speed and comfort of the newly built transportation. It was now springtime so he watched the fresh countryside glide by. How unlike his first trip into Jena by cart! How exciting! He only wished he had someone to share it with. Once again, François rose to mind. Could Magda and Frieda be right? Could the up-timers actually change ideas and even laws so he too could love?

That was too much to hope for. He just hoped Frieda and Magda would not be stupid and let the wrong person know their secret. It could cost them both more than their careers; it could cost their lives. He shivered at the thought of how others like them had died.

No, Henry would concentrate on his first quest— stealing some of Death's quarry from the bony one. His life was dedicated to healing. He pushed thoughts of the up-timers from his mind and watched the train pull into his destination, Grantville.

Grantville, Early Spring 1636

Henry got settled in a small set of rooms near the hospital in Grantville, which overlooked the street and a few stores. These rooms were slightly smaller than the ones he had in Jena but with only one flight of stairs to climb. Those in Jena had been on the third floor. Henry felt absolutely rich since he was getting paid a decent salary as an intern, even though things in Grantville were ridiculously expensive. But there was an inexpensive café called Cora's in the street below where he could eat and watch the throngs of people from all over the world flow by. Jena had been big but Grantville was much more interesting. In such a short time, it had become the intellectual capital of Europe.

Henry would sit by the window and watch as the wide array of people of all ages and types moved past. It was his favorite entertainment after hours of making rounds with the Grantville doctors or visiting patients in their homes. He would order a bowl of the café's delectable soup and wash it down with some juice or ale and watch people. The café smelled of soup and coffee and spices.

Grantville offered a smorgasbord of people to watch. Up-timers and down-timers in up-timer-inspired clothing drifted by in the new denim material. The new entrepreneurs and captains of industry strode past on their way to building their fortunes. But Henry's favorites were the people with their pets, usually dogs because they could be walked on leashes without fear of harm. Henry loved to watch the dogs and their humans. He loved dogs but his time in medical school had made it hard to have a pet. Before then, he and François had moved so often having a dog would have been difficult.

Grantville, Fall 1636

One evening in the late fall when evenings were turning cold, Henry was sitting in his favorite seat by the window when he noticed a small, furry creature huddled outside the door. It had no leash and seemed to be alone. It was a dog, but one that was so dirty and matted it could have been a castoff fur blanket waiting to get swept away by the street cleaners.

He watched the dog through the window. No one came to collect the poor soul and few paid it much attention beyond avoiding it. Henry's heart hurt for the poor thing that would from time to time look up and around as if looking for someone. Then it would lay its head back on the cold street as if giving up the search.

Henry could not stand to watch without doing something.

"Cora, do you know who that dog belongs to?" Henry pointed to the heap of fur on the sidewalk in front of the window.

"Nope. Never seen it before," Cora said. "You taking it home?"

Henry nodded, and paid his bill. He grabbed a leftover piece of bread from his plate and went outside to where the dog lay. He held the bread out to the dog as he spoke quietly. "Come here, little one, I won't hurt you. Here's some bread. I have more at home."

At first, the small ragamuffin only looked at the bread as if it was another empty promise in a life already filled with too many. But before long the smell of the bread enticed the dog to Henry, who petted him as the dog wolfed it down. "Would you like to come home with me, little one? I'm alone too. We could keep each other company. I've been told I do not snore too badly so I shan't keep you awake at night." Henry laughed at his joke but realized the idea was already warming him against the chilly air.

Henry gathered the small canine bundle in his arms. "Our first job after more food and water will be a bath, I think. You are a smelly mess, you are! And what is your name? You do not look like you will be very big so you do not need a huge name but you must have one with dignity. I must think on this very important matter. Names should not be given lightly. Maybe after a night of food and rest your name will be more apparent." Henry realized that he was babbling, but he didn't care. He'd had no one to talk to in so long.

When Henry took the dog, young but a bit beyond puppyhood, home and bathed him he discovered the dog was off white with soft hair that when brushed made the ten-pound or so dog look twice as big. His big dark eyes were matched with a wet, pink nose.

"What a serious face you have, my young prince. That is your name, is it not, Prince? Surely you have the look and breeding of a prince so Prince it will be."

Henry smiled and felt better than he had in a while. He had not realized how much he missed having someone to care for. Prince was not another human but Henry saw plenty of those as a doctor.

No, Prince was exactly what he needed to fill his heart and home.

Henry had to leave Prince at home when he went to the hospital but Prince went everywhere with Henry otherwise, including to visit patients in their homes. Prince was so well behaved he actually became part of the therapy for some patients, especially children and the aged. Prince would stand next to the patient, waiting to be noticed. Some would stroke his fine coat and others would ask if he could sit in their laps where they could cuddle him. Prince seemed to take it all in as his job and due, sitting quietly sporting a bright blue or purple satin collar.

Henry still thought about François from time to time but now there was less pain and more good memories. Prince was helping Henry heal just like he helped Henry's patients.

While Henry was still in Grantville a round of the flu hit and he found himself working even longer hours to keep up. Instead of only caring for his own patients Henry was called upon to take the patient load of at least one other intern who had fallen ill.

Henry usually spent a great deal of time in the less expensive parts of Grantville. As an intern he was given the poorer or less affluent patients. He was fine with all the patients, seeing each healing as a victory in his personal struggle with that old enemy, Death.

But when the doctor, a down-timer named Rathkin, who was overseeing Henry's internship, became ill, Henry inherited his patients as well. Among these were some in the emerging middle class, such as traders bringing all manner of items into and out of Grantville.

Henry took Prince with him to visit these new patients. Most were suffering with a strain of the flu. According to the up-timers, influenza should have been fairly easy to treat but the strain that was hitting Grantville this time was not so benign. Henry spent much of his time explaining how to keep a sufferer hydrated, warm, and well-fed, and dealing with cranky and out of sorts patients on their way back to health. This would be the perfect time to bring his sweet canine assistant.

The visits went as planned until Henry got to the last house of the day. It was a large home in the area favored by Grantville's merchants and traders. Henry presented himself at the ornate carved door and was promptly admitted by a distinguished, fifty-something butler who could have taught lessons on the craft. "Signor Cantalupo is in his rooms. Please come with me, Herr Doktor."

Without waiting for Henry's reply the butler turned on his heels and proceeded up a large winding stairway. As he followed the butler, Henry noticed numerous apparently expensive paintings hung over the stairs and all along the otherwise richly appointed walls.

The butler stopped at a door on the second floor, waiting for Henry to catch up. Prince seemed to know they were close to a patient because he started moving around in his perch in Henry's backpack. Prince rode there so Henry could keep his arms free when traveling around the city.

Henry followed the butler into a bedroom as finely decorated as the parts of the home he had already seen. Rich red bedding filled out a huge four-poster bed. In the bed was one of the most enchanting men he had ever seen. François had been a blond and gorgeous but this man was night to his day. He had long lustrous raven black hair spilling across his olive skin. When he opened his eyes, Henry almost had to take a step back from what the haunting gray revealed.

Henry had not had this kind of reaction to anyone since François. He knew he could not, would not let the patient know. He would be tightly controlled. To do otherwise could be dangerous.

Henry took a moment, pretending to look in his medicine case, then approached the patient's bed. "Good greetings, sir. I am here because your doctor is sick. Nothing dangerous but I am his intern and will be seeing you for the time. I hope you will not mind."

The man smiled up at him. "Of course I do not mind, but I hope Doktor Rathkin will be well soon. He is a good man. What is your name?" He spoke with a touch of an Italian accent.

The smile was blinding. Henry had to compose himself once again. "Thank you for bearing with me. I am Doktor Cooper, Henry Cooper."

"As you probably know, I am Antonio Cantalupo. I welcome you and hope you can help me with this illness. I really must make a trip to Venice soon to pick up a shipment. How soon can I travel?"

"Herr Cantalupo, we cannot rush your healing too quickly. The influenza cannot be hurried. Many people start to feel better and overdo activities, and then they relapse, and sometimes die."

"May I ask for as quickly as possible? Winter will soon be on us and then I will not be able to move goods for some months. Sooner is better."

"I will do what I can and the rest will be up to your body to reach health quickly."

Prince decided it was time for him to be introduced because he started to move around more in the backpack, even giving a short, discreet bark or two.

"Your backpack seems to have developed a mind of its own, Doktor Cooper." Cantalupo laughed, followed by a rough cough.

"Careful now, Herr Cantalupo. You will cough soon enough but sit back and rest. I'll introduce you to my assistant." With that, he pulled the backpack off and laid it on the bed, letting Prince nose his way out.

The butler, who was still standing near the bed, moved towards Prince as if to take him away. Before he could, Cantalupo waved him away. Prince walked across the red velvet to the patient's open arms. Cantalupo stroked the soft off-white coat on Prince's back and Prince gently licked his face.

"What a dignified, lovely dog! What is his name?

Adler, you can leave us now." The butler gave a stiff bow, left the room and closed the door behind him.

"He is Prince."

"He definitely behaves like a Prince. Where did you get him? I would love one just like him."

"First we treat you, then we may chat." Henry was determined to maintain his calm, no matter how handsome the patient. He listened to Cantalupo's heart, took his temperature and quickly ascertained that in fact he had a case of the flu. Cantalupo was fairly young and healthy.

"Have you had the influenza before?"

"In Italy, two years ago. It was terrible. I recovered but was coughing for a month."

"You will survive this one, too, if you take care of yourself."

The whole time Henry worked, the patient had petted Prince, cradling him like a baby.

"Now Doktor Cooper. Tell me about Prince here."

This was Henry's last patient for the day so he let himself relax a little. "I found him on the street in front of Cora's. He had no home. I had no one at home so we fit each other well." Why did he tell this patient so much?

"I too am alone but it sounds as if there are no others like him. That is too bad." Cantalupo looked out from under long, black lashes at Henry. "Maybe I can ask that you share him with me another day. I would welcome his company." Unspoken was that he would welcome Henry's company as well.

At that moment, Henry reached across to pet Prince. Cantalupo reached across at exactly the same moment. Their fingers touched. It felt like Henry had touched an up-timer's electrical outlet. The two men looked at each other as if seeing the other for the first time. Cantalupo smiled shyly, like a young girl at her first dance. "We both love dogs, do we not?"

Henry gulped. He had not felt like this since he first met François. He felt his heart beat just a little faster as he returned the Italian's smile.

The two men, both alone and lonely, sat for a few minutes petting Prince.

"Maybe there are other things we both like, Doktor Cooper? Please call me Antonio. May I call you Henry?"

"Yes, Antonio, please do. I cannot stay too long today but I will be back. I will bring Prince with me."

"That would be marvelous, Henry. I will look forward to seeing both of you."

Henry had to once again catch his breath. Maybe there was hope for him. Maybe the up-timers were changing things so he could hope to live a life in love like other people. Maybe there was love for him after François. Maybe, just maybe, he could be truly happy again, openly happy. Time would tell.

On his way back home, Henry held Prince and even kissed him on his pink, slightly moist nose. "Well Prince, you seem to be my Cupid, so I guess Love has a wet nose."

The Red-Headed League

Virginia DeMarce

~ Section I ~

Besançon, September 1635

"I can read an encyclopedia as well as anyone else."
Henri, duc de Rohan, continued to pace around the
room. "In less than three years, I will be dead."

"Not necessarily," Grand Duke Bernhard countered.
"You were killed in a battle we fought at Rheinfelden,
which is an encounter I see no need to fight in this
world. How old are you? Fifty-five or so? You could
live another thirty years."

"Or I could be dead next month. So, yes, I have
read the encyclopedias and I am utterly determined
to see my daughter married to a Protestant while I
am still alive."

"To just about any Protestant in your more frantic
moments. To a suitable French noble Protestant in
your more rational ones. If not to a foreign Protestant

prince, preferably Calvinist. Or . . ." Bernhard rotated his shoulders restlessly. "Are there Protestant space aliens in this up-time 'science fiction' you have been reading these past few months? One of them might be the best choice."

"I am *not* in a mood for raillery," Rohan grumped. "Even if my friend Ron Stone claims that I am 'fixated.' I *died* and the French crown controlled her. For years, they did not let her marry at all. Then they gave her a list of Catholic nonentities acceptable to them and she picked one because 'at least he's handsome and a good dancer.' Frivolous women! That is not a potential son-in-law acceptable to *me*. Neither are grandchildren who will be reared Catholic as a condition of the king's permitting my daughter to marry at all. So . . ."

"So what do you plan to do about it?"

"With *your* permission, O sovereign lord of the County of Burgundy, I will bring my wife and daughter to join me here in Besançon. Or, if you prefer, I can return to Berne and have them join me there."

"You're not going anywhere," the grand duke answered, clasping his hands behind his back as he paced. "Berne does not need you. You have accepted duties to Burgundy. Think of the piles of paper on your desk. Think of the hordes of petitioners who will be devastated if you do not hold personal meetings with them." His smile turned feral. "Think of the committee meetings that you are scheduled to chair, which will spare me from doing it. In any case, it will take a while to get your ladies here. This kind of thing isn't urgent enough to justify the cost of one of those aircraft." His shudder was not staged. His wife's all-too-frequent jaunts on the Monster unsettled his stomach. "You can borrow a couple of my better officers for such a mission and they can ride horses like normal people."

Rohan stopped pacing and steepled his fingers. "Ruvigny, then."

"What?" Bernhard raised his eyebrows at this apparent *non sequitur*.

"Ruvigny. He's an officer in your service and we know him well."

"The redhead? The one with the truly remarkable nose?"

Rohan nodded. "And freckles. Don't forget the freckles. Yes, that's Henri de Massué de Ruvigny."

"Why him?"

"His family are clients of my father-in-law. They have been since long before Sully even became my father-in-law. Thus, they are in a way clients of my wife, so it's mostly a matter of *entré*. She will receive him at least, possibly as a welcome rather than unwelcome guest, and perhaps if I am fortunate, even pay some attention to the message he presents on my behalf. Maybe."

Bernhard unclasped his hands and fingered the little goatee he was currently wearing. "Not a bad choice. He's a good officer, but he'll make a better diplomat someday, if he ever has the money to support an ambassadorial career. Someone ought to find him a wife with a dowry. Who else do you want?"

"Ask him. He knows the younger officers better than either of us do. He'll make a good choice."

Bernhard's private secretary stuck his head around the doorpost as a signal for the meeting to break up.

✧   ✧   ✧

Ruvigny chose August von Bismarck. Bismarck, he told the duke, was reliable and solid. Unflappable. The kind of officer a commander could depend on.

They also happened to be good friends, on first name terms, and so far said friend hadn't had any luck at all when it came to promotions. This kind of expedition could give August a chance to bring himself to the favorable attention of more powerful people. But there was no point in mentioning that to the duke and grand duke just yet.

Whereupon Rohan wrote letters and they begged the best horses that the regiment would let them take.

Bismarck's horse turned out to be reliable and solid. The kind of horse a man could depend on. Ruvigny's horse went lame four days out, so he had to hire a far less satisfactory one.

"So," August said the next afternoon. "Did you find out anything about yourself from the famous up-time encyclopedias?"

Henri dropped his reins onto the gelding's neck and stared out toward the peasants who were still harvesting in the fields, weeks after the end of this very unsatisfactory summer. "Britannica 1911. On what I'm paid, I just asked the researcher I hired in Grantville to look up the main article for my family name, if there was one. It's not as if I can afford to hire someone for a thorough search. There was an article about my oldest son. King Louis XIV revoked the Edict of Nantes in 1685, crushing everything I did after I retired from the army. I served as deputy general of the Huguenot Synods to the royal court from 1653 onwards, trying to maintain our rights. Ultimately I failed, so I went into exile and died in

England. My oldest son received an Irish title, earl of Galway. He never married. Neither did my other two sons. No descendants, male or female. The French crown confiscated our estates. The teacher had it right, I guess. 'Useless, useless; everything is useless.' Or, maybe, 'Futile, futile, everything is futile.'" He picked up the reins again. "But for some reason, I keep working." He raised his eyebrows. "You?"

August grinned. "Same encyclopedia; same procedure; same reason, since I'm always broke. I got less detail but more optimism. About two hundred fifty years from now, *somebody* named von Bismarck, Otto to be specific, had worked his way up in rank from country gentleman to *Fürst, Herzog, und Graf*. He guided the multitude of small German states into becoming a united country. He wasn't very nice about the nation building, either. Gustav Adolf and Stearns have proceeded with considerably more tact. Whether or not he was related to me directly, I have no idea, but since we were both born at Schönhausen in Brandenburg's Altmark, there's likely to be some connection. I'm going to assume that one of my brothers or cousins managed to hang onto the land, such as it is, paid off the mortgages our father loaded on it in pursuit of such luxuries as family portraits and comfortable beds, and kept begetting heirs." August sighed. "My lord father wasn't very frugal. He kept trying to press additional new fees out of the peasants, the peasants kept suing him, and the courts kept deciding in their favor. He left a huge mess for my mother to deal with after he died."

Henri shifted restlessly in the hired saddle. It didn't fit him right. "There are millions of people, I suppose, who wouldn't find anything at all in those books. My son received an article because he became a general."

The sun was shifting steadily into the west. August pulled his hat down to protect the pale forehead that his persistently receding auburn hair seemed to be enlarging with every day that passed. "Rise high in the army and qualify for the small immortality of an encyclopedia entry. At the rate I'm receiving promotions, which is not at all, it's no wonder the up-timers never heard of me. I'll die still a captain, whether it's next summer or twenty summers from now."

They plodded onwards toward Paris.

Brussels, October 1635

From: Susanna Allegretti, Brussels
To: M. Leopold Cavriani, Geneva

Most honored patron and friend,

I regret that I must request a favor from you. Because of certain difficulties that have arisen here in the household of the king and queen in the Netherlands, I feel that it will not be wise for me to remain in my current situation any longer than absolutely necessary. If it would be possible for you to arrange for me to transfer to the household of the *Stadthouder* in the northern provinces, I would be sincerely grateful.

Your devoted friend and servant,
Susanna Allegretti

From: Susanna, in Brussels
To: Marc, wherever you may be
(c/o M. Leopold Cavriani, Geneva)

My dearest heart,

I'm getting so mad about all of this that if I weren't a seamstress who can't afford snags in the lace and satin that earn me my daily bread, I'd be biting my fingernails right to the quick. Or, more usefully, kicking the non-gentleman colonel from Lorraine where it would hurt him the most. Which I can't, because he has "important connections." Of course, with all the excitement about the expected baby, nobody could expect the queen to have time to worry about the trials and tribulations of one of her dressmakers. Not even if she is an outstanding dressmaker, which I have become if I may be so bold as to say so.

No matter how impeccable the personal conduct of the king and queen in the Netherlands is, its impact on the court as a whole is not strong. Of course, one could say the same about decades of impeccable conduct on the part of the marvelous archduchess, who is, alas, still old and still ill.

So. This obnoxious *exile*, even after the truly entertaining demise of his duke last spring, simply will not take no for an answer, and what's worse, most of my colleagues in *haute couture* don't see why I'm not willing to say yes to his demands (which truly are more demands in the English usage than requests in the French usage). He's offered generous terms, they say, and it's not as if I'm some *petite bourgeoise* subject to the rules of German guilds. When he ended an arrangement with a generous settlement (they say, they say, they all say, or at least most of them say), not that I think that he has enough money to do that, apart from any considerations of morality, then I would have a bigger dowry than I do now and could make an even better match than expected with some other upper servant in the court than I can now aspire to.

But I don't want to do this, so I have written your father asking him to get me sent to the court of Fredrik Hendrik and his wife in the Hague.

> I miss you so much.
> Where are you?
> Susanna

Paris, October 1635

Bismarck didn't have any idea how they would be received at the ducal residence and he hadn't wanted to ask. He certainly hadn't expected that within minutes after they presented their credentials, the duc de Rohan's daughter would dash into the entryway and throw herself into Ruvigny's arms with a squeal of "Henri! I haven't seen you for ages!"

"Well, if it isn't the itsy-bitsy, teeny-tiny, seed pearl, all grown up." Ruvigny responded to her enthusiasm with a brotherly hug, looking her over. "Our daisy has grown petals."

In spite of the double entendre, it was definitely a brotherly hug. Bismarck knew a brotherly hug when he saw one. After all, he had four sisters to go along with his three brothers. Before he decided that he would rather embrace a military career than continue dragging around in the genteel poverty that had been their mother's lot since the wars devastated the Altmark shortly after his father's death, he had lived in an affectionate household. Even though she, all of her offspring in tow, had made nightmarish treks that took them to Magdeburg, Hamburg, Salzwedel, and Braunschweig in search of semi-permanent refuge from the marauding armies, in sorrow and in joy the eight of them had hugged each other all the time. Their mother, even though she prided herself on exercising *firm and serious discipline* in their upbringing, had hugged them. For that matter, they had hugged their father, before he died. He shook his head, throwing off the memories as unsuited to his present duties.

As for itsy-bitsy, Ruvigny was not teasing. The young duchess was really very short. Pretty enough, he supposed, in the way that it's hard for a girl to be ugly when she's seventeen and healthy, with a clear complexion, but certainly short.

Introductions followed, with the accompanying protocol, etiquette, and general necessary *politesse*, with the the little duchess excusing her mother's nonappearance as hostess on the vague grounds of "she's busy."

As they migrated from the entryway toward a side salon, Bismarck whispered, "Is there something you haven't been telling me?"

Ruvigny shrugged. "Oh. Well. About five years ago, during the Savoy campaign, La Valette sent me to Venice to recruit a regiment of light cavalry. The duke was there, then. I stayed with the Rohans."

"And he paid attention to me," the little duchess said. "I was twelve. He talked to me and teased me and told me stories about the campaigns and...and nobody else there ever paid any attention to me at all. Henri is my best friend ever."

Bismarck added "has very sharp ears" to his mental list of what he knew about the duc de Rohan's daughter.

They woke up the next morning to still no senior hostess to welcome them and what seemed like a mass invasion of the Rohan *palais* by the staff of every theater in Paris.

An expected invasion, apparently.

"Oh, Henri, you have to stay in Paris just a little bit longer," Marguerite proclaimed. "I won't let you go. What need does that upstart Bernhard have for you right at the moment? Winter's coming on. Nobody's going to fight anybody, probably. We're putting on a ballet for the court. I'm dancing the lead role and everyone will be there—utterly everyone. You have to dance, too, Henri. Remember how we used to dance on the balcony of the house in Venice?"

"What I am is utterly out of practice, little daisy," Ruvigny protested. "I've been doing other things these last few years, remember?"

"Oh, poof. You can do it. Mama got Isaac de Bense-rade to script it. He's the very newest literary sensation this year." She grabbed his arm and towed him in the direction of the ballroom, Bismarck trailing along behind.

The little duchess turned around. "You dance, of course . . . don't you?"

"I would say that I'm modestly competent in a ballroom. I've never even seen a ballet."

"Well, that's disappointing. *Autres temps, autres mœurs*. I suppose that applies to other places as well as other eras. You can watch."

Three hours of strenuous rehearsal later, the little duchess, not even mildly winded, plopped herself down next to Bismarck while Benserade and the choreographer put the male chorus, once more, through the final routine.

"Benserade is a slave driver. Even before the cast rehearsals started, he had me in here for five straight days, just learning my own part."

"If you are as careful of your reputation and virtue as all say that you are, mademoiselle, I am surprised that you spend all these hours in the company of a young man in his twenties, quite unaccompanied." He looked around. "Well, unaccompanied except for a company of costumers, not to say several set designers, a half dozen carpenters, and ten or so miscellaneous servants."

Marguerite sniffed. "Benserade is no threat to my reputation. I could take him to bed and he wouldn't be a threat to my virtue. Everyone knows he's tilted. Everyone who matters, at least."

Bismarck blinked.

"A bit out of plumb, like the king. But Louis only tilts this far"—she placed her elbow on the chair arm and moved it about ten degrees to the left—"and he, Louis, tilts both ways." She moved it an equal number of degrees to the right. "Isaac's all the way to the left..." Her arm went down to a right angle, parallel to the floor. "...but that doesn't keep him from being very entertaining."

"Out of plumb?"

The little duchess viewed Henri's German friend with exasperation. "Are you so naïve? I am telling you that he is out of kilter. As our Provençals would say, *gai*. Slanted. The man is not straight. He might be a threat to the reputation of my cousins, Maximilien or François, but not to mine. Don't you have a word for it in German?"

Bismarck almost strangled, but swallowed very hard. "None that we use in the presence of respectable young ladies of seventeen years, Your Grace."

"How odd. In any case, very shortly absolutely everyone will know that he's the very best at planning galas and spectacular entertainments and we will have sponsored him first. Someday, he'll be in their new *Académie française*. There's hardly any doubt about that, and he's one of ours—a Huguenot, I mean—so there is also no way that Maman will let Richelieu and Mazarin seize the glory of having discovered him for the Catholic party. This ballet will be a real coup for the Protestant cause."

Bismarck had difficulty envisioning a ballet directed by a sodomite as a coup for the Protestant cause, but was tactful enough not to say so.

Some hours later, the young duchess disappeared to be dressed, so that she might join her still-invisible mother for a yet-unspecified mandatory social occasion.

Ruvigny and Bismarck headed off for a tavern, to meet some of Ruvigny's old friends from his first years in the Royal Guards in Paris. Who were late, of course. They ordered ales while they waited.

"I had no idea you were on such close terms with the Rohans," August said, shoving his mug around the table and leaving a wet streak.

"It's not the Rohans, really," Henri answered. "I don't know the duke very well and I've never presumed on any acquaintance with him for advancement in the service of Grand Duke Bernhard. It's the family of the senior duchess—that is, it's the Béthunes who are our patrons. Our families have known each other just about forever. It was through her father, the duke of Sully, that my father got his sinecure as lieutenant-governor of the Bastille. I was only three when Papa died, but Maman has repeated constantly to all of us, ever since, just how much gratitude we owe to the Béthunes. Sully himself was godfather for my oldest brother, who died in the Royal Guards. Sully's wife and one of his sons were godparents for my sister Rachel. For my little brother Cirné, too, but he died when he was hardly more than an infant."

He shifted uneasily on the bench. "I'm not comfortable with Rohan's politics. At the siege of La Rochelle, I was with the royal forces. If the Huguenots have any hope of surviving in France, they'll be better off practicing a policy of 'respect the crown and placate the king' rather than rebelling."

"Doesn't Peter, in the Epistle, say 'honor the king' rather than 'placate the king'?"

"At the French court, it's 'placate the king.' Not that such an approach succeeded either, according to the up-time books. Nobody loved Sully when he was chief minister, even though he perhaps did more for France than anyone else under Henri IV. The Catholics hated him because he was Protestant and the Protestants hated him because he was loyal to the crown. It's hard to deal rationally with fanatics."

The elder duchess appeared at breakfast the next morning, not apologizing for anything but making a fuss over Ruvigny. She wasn't bad looking, Bismarck thought, for a forty-year-old woman who had borne ten children. But nowhere nearly as good as his own mother, who had borne eight. Mutti must be a dozen or so years older than the duchess. The last time he had seen her, which was nearly ten years ago now, she would have been about the same age as the woman to whom he was making a bow in this year of 1636. She had looked a lot younger and healthier, in spite of all the troubles of the war.

Making a fuss over Ruvigny stopped the instant he carried out their mission and handed over the letter. The duchess did not respond to the duke's letter with appropriate wifely compliance, much less biblical submissiveness. Her reaction was more along the lines of indignation amounting to anger. Fury, perhaps. Even the ire of the classical Furies themselves.

"No way!" she screamed at Ruvigny. "So 'chaos is coming.' I am quite prepared to manipulate, to the benefit of Rohan, any political advantage that is to be attained from looming chaos, but I can only do that in Paris. So 'danger lurks.' I am not prepared to abandon the court. Nor will I agree to send away my daughter, who is at long last getting old enough to play her own part and therefore belongs at the center of the world, in Paris, and not in the boondocks of the

County of Burgundy. Doesn't he think I am capable of protecting her from some forced Catholic marriage?"

No one of any importance, she finished, ever went to Besançon. Or ever would, in all probability. Certainly not within her lifetime.

After which she flounced out.

"That went a lot better than I expected," Ruvigny said.

Bismark thought that the French ate breakfast too late. He had practically starved before food appeared on the table.

The breakfast, as late as it was, didn't last long because there was another rehearsal, to which he was again relegated to being a spectator and involuntary recipient of the female lead's constant chatter at those times she was not onstage. Today, she was trying to explain her mother, "because I do not want you to think poorly of her, M. von Bismarck. Henri, of course, already knows it all. He lived through a lot of it. Not when she got married, of course, because he wasn't even born yet.

"She was ten years old when the late king—Henri IV, that is—commanded that she should marry my father. Not just be betrothed to him, at that age, which would not have been so unusual, but marry him. The ceremony was in the temple at Ablon. She wore a white dress, and some joker asked, loud enough for the other guests to hear, 'And who is it that presents this child for baptism?' Papa was twenty-five. He went back to the army and Maman got to live with her mother-in-law."

She stopped. "How old were you when you got married, M. von Bismarck?"

"I'm not married. I'm twenty-five and I can't afford to get married, any more than Henri over there in the chorus line can. Maybe not ever."

"Do you have a mistress?"

"If I could afford a mistress, I could afford a wife, and I would much rather have a wife, I assure you."

"Does Henri have a mistress?"

"No, mademoiselle."

"Oh, good. But then Maman grew up. By then, though, Henri IV was dead and the Rohans were in revolt again. Politically, at least, Maman has always been fiercely loyal to Papa. She has defended the Rohan cause tirelessly to the court; she has raised immense amounts of money for his ventures, even when she and my grandfather thought they were too risky.

"And, of course, she had to bear him children after she grew old enough. I am certainly legitimate," the little duchess said proudly. "That is why Papa is so concerned about my marriage and sent the letter that has irritated Maman so much, you understand. Uncle Soubise has no children at all, so I am the only hope for continuing Rohan. Papa can be sure that I am the legitimate heiress of all that Rohan represents, because Maman was quite conscientious about her behavior until Papa gave up begetting after none of my eight brothers and sisters survived early childhood. She didn't take lovers until after that."

Bismarck could not think of a tactful reply. At least, not one that was relevant.

At which point, Benserade and the choreographer beckoned her back onstage.

Bismarck hoped that they would have lunch, or maybe dinner, or just a snack, pretty soon, but was afraid that they wouldn't. It was a mystery why the dancers, whether ladies-in-waiting and courtiers or actors and ballerinas, had not been reduced to skeletons.

The next day was more of the same. A ballet in Paris appeared to involve as much in the way of logistics as a minor military campaign. The little duchess and the ladies in waiting, and the men of course, danced in the traditional style, but the ballerinas hired from the theater were doing two pieces in the modern *en pointe* style that the up-timers had introduced. Since their presentations meant that the other female dancers were offstage quite a bit, though both the courtiers and actors partnered the professionals in their display, Bismarck was subjected to more chatter.

"The night of the ballet, you will be presented to M. de Gondi. Be very, very, careful. He is Maman's current lover, and extremely prone to take offense at the slightest thing he can interpret to be a discourtesy. Also, he has a retinue of favorites who follow him around and take offense on his behalf. Henri fought some duels when he was younger, before I ever met him, but I do believe that he has outgrown it. It would not be good if either you or he got trapped into one while you are here and it would not be beyond some of the courtiers to entrap you into having to fight one, just to embarrass Papa. Don't trust anyone. That's the best. Anyone, even one you think is now your closest friend or most committed ally, may well betray you tomorrow if some advantage is to be obtained from it."

"Lover?" Bismarck had learned most of his French in a classroom and was not certain of his comprehension at times, particularly when a conversational partner spoke with excessive rapidity. Which all the French seemed to do most of the time. He wanted to be sure that he had heard clearly.

"Yes, her current lover. But truly, everyone says that Maman is quite fastidious. It's not as if she's one of those women who claim to be ladies but fuck the footmen for fun. She only takes one lover at a time and all of them have been politically influential and members of the highest nobility."

Marguerite sighed. "Even though in the case of the Nogarets, she chose two full brothers at different times, Cardinal de La Valette and the comte de Candale." She wrinkled her nose. "Which is just... not fastidious."

Bismarck's eyebrows were practically up in his receding three-point hairline.

"So, what was I saying? It's not as if Maman has a reputation like *la Chalais*, for whom a man published a poem in praise of her slit."

She punctuated that by nodding her head firmly.

"Her husband, the comte de Chalais, killed the comte de Pontguibault in a duel because of that poem. It was a big scandal at the time—that must have been about a dozen years ago. But Chalais was beheaded later on, because *la Chevreuse* seduced him into one of her conspiracies against Richelieu. She's a *very* distant cousin of Papa's, from the Rohan-Montbezon line." She paused. "You *will* remember what I told you about duels, won't you? It just will cause too many complications if you or Henri cause a duel while you are staying with us."

Bismarck blinked in the face of this apparently never-ending gossip. It might be true that nobody ever paid attention to her, because when she did have a captive listener, her mouth overflowed with everything she was thinking. Much of which was astonishingly world-weary and far more cynical that a girl her age should be, he thought.

If anybody asked him, which nobody was likely to.

At least, when the day of the performance finally arrived, he would be in the audience rather than backstage. He hoped.

He hoped, but he knew that sometimes hope was in vain. He had seen the modern English translation of the Bible in the school library when he was studying at Helmstedt. Well, not the modern of the up-timers but the modern of his own day, the one sponsored by King James. The passage Henri had quoted on their ride to Paris had not employed "useless" or "futile." "Vanity," the Teacher had written, speaking the Word of God. "Vanity, vanity, all is vanity."

Solomon must have visited Paris at some stage of his career. But, then, he had been presiding over a royal court of his own. With wives in the plural, concubines by the hundred, and troubles of his own.

Monogamy had a lot to be said in its favor.

Marguerite propped her chin on the heel of her hand. "And then there's Tancrède."

"Another . . . ah . . . lover?"

The little duchess managed to convey jaded disgust with one short glance. "My half-brother."

"The duke also has affairs? An affair? His junior officers, at least during my term of service, have not been aware of any."

"My *maternal* half-brother. He's six. Trust me, M. von Bismarck. One has not truly lived until one has

ridden, most of the time in a closed carriage, from
Venice to Paris, with a pregnant, motion sick, middle-
aged woman who is expecting an illegitimate child and
knows that it will have to be fostered out because her
husband draws the line at accepting a possible male
heir whom he has not fathered. After such a wonderful journey, it's hard for a girl to retain any illusions
about the joyous and sacred nature of motherhood,
no matter what the preachers say in their sermons."
She paused. "Candale begat the boy. He and Maman
slept together in my own father's house. That's really
bad taste, don't you think?"

Bismarck nodded. Bad taste was the least of it,
from the perspective of a devout Lutheran.

Even ballet rehearsals finally come to an end.

"It's actually true, what she said when we arrived,
isn't it?" Bismarck asked that evening as he finished
taking off his boots and leaned back, wiggling his toes.

"Huh?" Ruvigny was half-asleep already.

"That nobody other than you paid any attention
to her when she was in Venice and twelve years old.
Nobody pays any attention to her now that she's in
Paris and is seventeen years old, as far as I can see,
other than dressing her, rehearsing her for that ballet,
and parading her around to salons and court appearances. She's the greatest heiress in all of France and
she's completely neglected. Nobody listens to her at
all. Nobody even tries to provide her with some kind
of...moral compass. Not as far as I have seen."

"Not since her grandmother Rohan died," Ruvigny
answered. "That must be five years ago, now. The
duchess' parents, Sully and his wife, are still alive,
but Marguerite doesn't see much of them. He's in

retirement in the country, which amounts to a nice way to say house arrest, writing his memoirs and dreaming of his 'great design' for a federation of all Christian nations."

A month later, Bismarck and Ruvigny reluctantly set out from Paris. Reluctantly only because they were returning to Rohan with the his wife's final refusal to either join him or send his daughter to him. The duke would not be happy.

"Why did the duchess have to delay so long? Basically, she gave us the same answer a month ago, the instant she read the duke's letter. She just postponed, then delayed, then procrastinated, and finally dragged her feet about giving us her written answer. Now we're headed back to Burgundy in the middle of what looks like it could be the most miserable winter I've ever seen. Even worse than last year." August looked up at the lowering gray sky, which was drizzling tiny pebbles of sleet onto the half-frozen mud of the ungraded track that was pretending to be a road in eastern France.

"She's not the one who has to ride in this," Henri pointed out. "She may have put things off so long so she could add that she didn't want to risk the seed pearl's health by traveling in midwinter to the rest of her excuses."

"He isn't going to like it."

"*Entendu*. Maybe all the church bells ringing to celebrate the child of the royal couple in the Netherlands will distract him. Too bad it was a girl."

"But healthy, which isn't something the Habsburgs can always count on. That augurs well for the future." August hunched his shoulders against the sleet.

"Sometimes it's better for the heir to come second, with a girl first to undergo the process of having her head stretch out the mother's hips for childbearing."

The duke wasn't happy. He was far from happy. As soon as they reported to him, he started to compile a yet another list of acceptable—acceptable to him—matches for Marguerite. "It's more urgent with every day that passes," he insisted. "As Grand Duke Bernhard said, when he declined the honor of fulfilling the role of her husband himself, she needs someone who can be Rohan for her."

⌐ Section II ⌐

Brussels, December 1635

From: Susanna Allegretti, Brussels
To: M. Leopold Cavriani, Geneva

Most honored patron and friend,

Not having received word from you, I conclude that your other obligations have taken you to places that the postal service does not reach. Because of the difficulties I mentioned in November, I am taking prudent measures to avert what otherwise might become a series of unfortunate events.

I will remain here in Brussels for the time being, awaiting your further advice.

Your devoted friend and servant,
Susanna Allegretti

The old cobbler looked up from his workbench. "Are you sure that you want these shoes altered the way you described? They will be very unstable to walk in, and the points are likely to damage the floors."

"Yes, Joseph. Exactly as I described." Susanna hopped down from the wide window sill on which she had been perching and took one of them in her hands again. "The wooden heels themselves—whittle them down from about here..." She pointed. "...just start a quarter-inch below where they attach to the sole and keep whittling until they are very narrow when they meet the floor. They're only about an inch and a half high altogether—that's what is fashionable now—so the wood shouldn't break when I put weight on them. Then stiffen the matching fabric, mold it to look like it is covering a normal shoe heel, and glue it to the unwhittled quarter-inch of the wooden heel at the top." She pointed again. "Right here. The false fabric heel should be just a little off the floor—an eighth of an inch, maybe. Not enough that a casual observer will notice but enough that it won't snag."

"Every pair? This will ruin them and shoes do not grow on trees, *petite Suzette*. You have to pay for them."

"Yes, Joseph. All five pairs. I have my reasons."

From: Susanna in Brussels
To: Marc, wherever you are
(c/o M. Leopold Cavriani, Geneva)

My dearest heart,
　　　Should you hear stories that a certain overly-persistent Lorrainer colonel of my lamented

acquaintance has a broken instep, do not be concerned for me. I will be perfectly fine, I promise.

> Wishing you were here.
> With all my love,
> Susanna

Besançon, January 1636

Leopold Cavriani came into town with his son Marc late in the month, dusted the snow off his nose and kicked the slush off his boots, did not curse the slippery cobblestones, inquired where the duc de Rohan might be found, and expressed cheerful relief when informed that his quarry was not at the top of the citadel.

"It's just a little garrison up there right now, Sir," the hostler said. "I'm plenty sorry for them, too, because their teeth must be frozen, not to mention their balls, the way the wind whips across that hilltop."

Cavriani sent Marc off to look for their mail, conferred with Rohan, and then with the assent of Grand Duke Bernhard annexed Colonel Raudegen temporarily. The contents of the mail packet proved to be very unsatisfactory—either a great deal of correspondence had gone astray or some malefactor had been purloining bags from the postal system. He borrowed the use of Bernhard's radio to check with Potentiana in Geneva, by way of multiple short resendings, only to get the dismaying news that none of the missing mail had arrived there, either.

So on the basis of the most recent information he had, which was far from recent enough, he sent Raudegen, with Marc as assistant, off to stage some interventions in England and the Netherlands.

"England first," he counseled, when it became clear that whatever Marc's mind might be advising him, his heart was of the opinion that Susanna Allegretti had priority over anyone or anything else. "You should find her at the Hague, or wherever Fredrik Hendrik's court is right now. Keep an eye on the newspapers to see where he is and if his wife is with him or spending the winter more comfortably in a town house in Amsterdam. I sent the request for Susanna's transfer to the head dressmaker in Brussels back in November."

London, February 1636

Travel conditions being what they always were in the middle of winter, especially when it came to crossing the English Channel . . .

"I hope I never see this place again," Marc said as they disembarked in London. "We've been here five minutes and that's five minutes too long. How Huygens endures it more or less permanently, I simply can't imagine. It may be preferable to being burned at the stake by the duke of Alba during the Eighty Years War . . ." He paused and took a second look at the London docks. "But not by much."

"Early March is said not to be the most salubrious season in England," Raudegen remarked mildly.

"What is?"

"Someone told me once that it was August 23, if I recall correctly. But it may have been July 26."

"I wouldn't precisely call it internment," Soubise said. "I've not been in the Tower the way the king kept the envoys from the USE. Then, of course, he's on considerably firmer ground in having precedent on handling an errant French nobleman who is temporarily unwelcome in his homeland rather than when handling unnerving strangers from the future. It's a perfectly nice house here on the Strand, if somewhat small for my needs, and luckily I brought my valet and cook with me. Thanks be to God the Almighty, for otherwise I'd have been wearing English tailoring and eating English food for more than half a year."

"Your brother thinks that you have accomplished all that you can in the matter of Ducos and his fanatics."

"Not as much as I hoped I would. I wanted to chase them all the way to Scotland. But..."

His secretary spoke up.

"Since my master was not, in fact, under house arrest, as the English authorities kept assuring us, though they also would not let him leave London, he has proven to be an excellent envoy. He has hosted at least three formal dinners each week, this house being inadequate for dancing parties. He has established a salon which the most elite *literati* of London..." He cleared his throat. "...the most elite *literati* of London, such as they are, have attended. Thus, everyone of importance in London is aware that the House of Rohan does not in any way condone these regrettable assassinations."

"The Dreeson Incident was very regrettable," Soubise interjected, "but I would not have been heartbroken if he had succeeded with the pope."

The secretary cleared his throat. "My lord de Soubise has not only regularly attended divine services at the French Protestant Church on Threadneedle Street, founded by the good offices of and under the charter issued by the late King Edward VI, but has also heard sermons here in his own house from the pastors of the other Huguenot churches in and near London. Additionally..."

"You would not believe how many sermons I have heard in these past months," Soubise exclaimed. "Certainly enough to be a lifetime supply for any normal man. Biblically sound and well delivered, but sermons nevertheless. Forgive an old sailor for saying it if either of you are of a pious bent, but there ought to be some kind of limit, some entire *statute* of limitations, on theological pontificating."

"What my master is attempting to convey," the secretary said, "is that by dint of his efforts, every French pastor in the British Isles is now aware of Ducos' perfidy. Engravings of him and of his men, made from the best descriptions that M. le duc de Rohan could obtain in Grantville, with their names printed beneath so far as the Grantville authorities identified them, are now in wide circulation. Every pastor who came here received several copies, and each week at the church in Threadneedle Street, all visitors from other parts of England and Scotland are invited to take copies. Additionally, the pastor in the City has been so cooperative as to arrange a series of mid-week guest sermons, which have been delivered by the pastors from other cities, such as Bristol and..."

"What he means," Soubise said, "is that we've papered the whole country with wanted posters and that's all I've managed to do, because aside from the three men I brought with me and a few Huguenots I've managed to hire, the rest of my staff, I'm sure, are English spies. And I'm still stuck in London, because I can't get leave to return to the Continent. Richelieu apparently takes a certain glee in having me 'stranded' here and the English are more than happy to oblige him."

After considering the situation, Raudegen concluded that since Soubise did have a limited ability to move about in the streets, at least on Sundays, removing him to France would not be a major challenge. Removing him along with the valet, secretary, and cook would complicate the process to the point that in his opinion, since their specific charge was only to retrieve the duke, the three should be left behind to fend for themselves, which meant enduring whatever punitive consequences the English government might choose to visit upon them as retribution for their employer's transgressions.

Marc objected for humanitarian reasons.

Raudegen discussed the traditional relationship between omelettes and eggs.

"If you won't extricate them, then I'll do it myself. That's what I'll call it. An extrication, and as such, it should be made with all due delicacy. The only servants we should leave behind are the ones the English themselves planted in his household. There's no reason for us to pay to import more English spies onto the Continent. There are enough there already."

On Thursday, Milord's cook complained about the quality of the vegetables delivered. The footman who had done the ordering countered that vegetables were always shriveled at this time of year. The cook sent him back to the market and complained again about the produce to any staff member who would listen. The footman came back, bringing no satisfaction.

Cooks did not usually lower themselves to go to

the market in person, but with a dramatic screech, the temperamental Frenchman left the house this day, taking the unsatisfactory footman with him. He did not return when expected, but then neither did the footman, so no one raised an alarm, given that he had prepared in advance sufficient cold meats and aspics for the household's supper.

On Friday morning, the housekeeper (English) told the butler (also English) that the cook and footman had not returned the night before. As both were missing, the butler saw no reason to inform the intelligence service in any panicked manner, since they had probably just fallen victim to ordinary thieves or cutthroats. The housekeeper instructed the under-cook to proceed as well as might be, while the butler sent another footman to try to pick up their trail from the market.

On Friday afternoon, the valet told the butler that there were problems with milord's tailor. Since this was a frequent occurrence, given the pickiness of the irritating little Frenchman, the butler just nodded as the valet left by the back door. Since the valet did not ordinarily join the other servants for meals, the under-cook just sent up trays to his room as usual for Friday supper and Saturday breakfast. The maid who carried and retrieved the trays happened to be a Huguenot. For two mealtimes, she got to eat a lot more than she was usually allotted and was happy to do it.

On Saturday, the secretary gave instructions to the housekeeper that all the servants were to attend the earliest service the following day, because milord expected a dozen guests for Sunday dinner. The under-cook had hysterics, but the housekeeper managed to calm him down.

Hearing of the instructions, the butler knocked on the door of the room where milord's secretary worked and asked rather stiffly, "Surely not the coachman, sir? For early services?"

"No, of course not," the secretary answered. "Use your common sense, man. He will be needed to drive milord to church and will attend services at the same hour we do, as usual."

The Huguenot staff members attended the church on Threadneedle Street, of course, just like their heathen Calvinist master. The English servants, in a procession headed by the butler and rearguarded by the housekeeper, attended a proper divine service at the nearest Church of England parish.

It was unusual for all the servants to be gone from the house at once, leaving only milord and his secretary there. It was not, however, unprecedented. It had occurred on a few other occasions when milord hosted Sunday guests.

There was no precise precedent for Marc's arrival in the house and Raudegen's arrival in the rear garden.

The English servants returned before the Huguenots did. They had a much shorter walk, after all. They entered through the back door. They did not leave through the back door, or any other door, at least not for quite a while. They found all the interior exits from the back hallway, a dingy and windowless narrow passageway, barricaded, and the rear door mysteriously barred behind them.

The Huguenot servants did not return at all, having taken the words of God to heart and, per instructions, departed hence unto another place as soon as the preacher delivered the charge and the Aaronic blessing.

Milord and his secretary left the house on the Strand by the front door, of course. The coachman arrived from the stables with punctilious promptness. Milord kept a generously-sized four-person carriage, which was just as well, since it already contained four people before milord and his secretary entered it this lovely Sabbath morning.

The coachman drove decorously toward the church on Threadneedle street.

Then he passed it.

The coach was later found on the docks, with the missing footman who had accompanied the cook to market gagged and bound up in it. He had some explaining to do.

The next morning, a party of Dutch and Flemish businessmen took ship for the Hague with their various servants and attendants. Two had letters of passage from Constantijn Huygens who was, of course, well known, at least by name, to all English customs officials. The other four were identified by their passports as middle-level employees of the Courteen and Crommelin mercantile firms.

The papers were all perfectly authentic. They simply didn't happen to belong to the men who were using them at the moment.

The Hague, March 1636

The newspapers were still celebrating the February birth of Ernst Wilhelm, infant grand duke of the County of Burgundy, first child of Bernhard and Claudia. While it might seem premature to a rational man that the columnists were discussing the possibility that someday this babe might marry the Netherlands' own Baby Archduchess (a cutie if ever there was one!), that didn't stop the reporters.

Soubise heaved a sigh of relief at being on solid ground again after the unpleasant Channel crossing. Marc gathered up the various passports and letters of passage. He would find someone his father knew in the Dutch diplomatic service to have them returned to Huygens in England by way of a diplomatic pouch.

Soubise inquired where the *Stadthouder* was to be found, made a courtesy call, and grumbled, though he admitted that there had been no point in his staying longer when he'd done all that he could.

Fredrik Hendrik, who of course knew the elder Cavriani, fingered the wispy blond moustache that matched his wispy blond hair and wispy blond goatee and asked Marc about his *Wanderjahr*.

Marc answered that he really did not have many entertaining tales to tell of his travels, because, "I am a prudent man. It's difficult to make much of the thugs who did not beat me up in Marseilles because I didn't stay around long enough for them to locate me. I did mention to that bargemaster on the Rhône that there was a place in the hull that looked perilously thin, but when he ignored me, I left the boat at the last stopping point before they would have needed to pull it out to do the portage over the rapids. That particular pool was very deep and tended to swirl, I had heard. It was too bad they lost the wine, though, for it was a good vintage and would have made a nice profit for the seller. I only hope the shipment was insured. In the matter of those people in Lyon who might or might not have been Spanish spies...all I can say is that the aggressive pseudo-barmaid did not seduce me, because I went up to bed early and put a bar across my door." He pushed back the curl that constantly fell down into the middle of his forehead and shrugged, both palms pointing upwards. "Some of us were born to have exciting adventures and some were not. Odysseus will never need to envy me."

He paused. "If I may inquire..."

"Permission granted."

"I need to contact *Froken* Susanna Allegretti. Per my father's arrangement, she was to be transferred from Brussels to your wife's staff some months ago. She is a highly skilled dressmaker. She would be with your lady wife."

But she wasn't. Not to the best of the *Stadthouder*'s knowledge. Nor, for that matter to that of his wife Amelia, her ladies-in-waiting, the steward, or anyone else. Nobody had even heard of her, much less of any proposed assumption of her into the household. There were no letters in the files. There was no notation in regard to compensation in the ledgers. The Hague had no knowledge of her existence.

"Which means," Marc said firmly, "that I am going to Brussels. Raudegen, you can escort Soubise directly to Paris if you wish, but I'm going to Brussels. Anything could have happened to Susanna since the last time Papa heard from her. Anything!"

Raudegen was more inclined to the view that one should never attribute to malice those things that could be adequately explained by stupidity and suggested that M. Cavriani's request for her transfer had most likely just been lost in the mail or misplaced on someone's desk, so the girl was still snug and comfortable where she had been the preceding autumn. Nevertheless, having developed a sneaking fondness for the little dressmaker when he escorted her from Basel to the Netherlands eighteen months or so earlier, he agreed to the Brussels option, which meant that Soubise had to endure it with what little good grace he could manage.

Soubise's valet, secretary, coachman, and cook took the news about the proposed detour with even less grace.

⟶ Section III ⟵

Paris, June 1636

"I'm glad Uncle Soubise is here," the little duchess said over a folder of fabric samples. "I hadn't seen him for ages, but I like him even though he blusters most of the time and mutters the rest of it. He doesn't really mean any of his complaints. He's nice."

Susanna looked up. "Should I be sitting in your presence, Your Grace? I have been concerned about this. After all, your status and mine..."

"You're not here as a dressmaker for me. You are here as the fiancée of M. Cavriani, whose father, if not noble, is most certainly very rich and knows everyone. Consequently, you are here as Maman's guest. You will stand in my presence in the public rooms, of course, should you be called to be present. In the private rooms, you are my own guest because I invited you in. Here, I say that you may sit. Maybe you are even someone who might become my friend, if we know one another long enough. Friends can sit to look over a book of fabric swatches, can't they?"

"I guess so."

"Then that's settled. Now, about Uncle Soubise, what I wanted to say is..."

Susanna meditated for a moment on whether or not she was now on such terms with Marc that she ought to start practicing how to acquire intelligence data.

Yes, she was.

"Marc says that your uncle is much shrewder than he pretends to be."

"Papa thinks so, too, that Uncle Soubise is undervalued." Marguerite hesitated, as if she were about to reveal a secret sin. "I have read some of the drafts of Papa's *mémoires*. Grand-père Sully's also. I started just because I miss them, but parts are terribly interesting. Don't tell mama. She loathes the *femmes savantes*, so I wouldn't want her to think that I am in danger of becoming intellectual. I don't think it's likely that I will become a *savante*, do you, even though Grand-mère Rohan was almost one? I don't think they had a word for it, way back then. But Papa thinks that if the English commanders and the authorities in La Rochelle had listened to Uncle's advice during the last revolt, then things might not have gone so badly for us. I don't remember much about that time, though."

"How old were you?"

Marguerite calculated. "Ten, when it started. Eleven when it finished. I don't remember the revolt before that at all, because I was only six. I only know what people tell me." She closed the sample book. "They don't usually tell me very much. Where has Colonel Raudegen gone?"

"To start making overtures, more or less. Put out feelers at the court by way of military men who know Grand Duke Bernhard, get some sense of the mood from former associates of your Grand-père Sully, that sort of thing. Marc is speaking to various associates of his father—bankers, financiers, people that Gaston will need if the government is to have funds. This all has to be done before your mother starts hinting at *salons* and *soirées* that the allegiances of the Rohans would be more likely to move in the king's favor if he revoked the exile decree. The king has a lot of popular support right now, but it's still far from universal support. If quite a few people start murmuring about how it would be desirable for your uncle to come back to France, he and his advisers may, ideally, conclude that it is their own idea. It's not as if she's requesting permission for your father to return. That would be a lot harder."

"Yes, because they know that Papa is very calculating and ambitious. He shows it. I suspect that Uncle is also. He just isn't obvious. But Uncle is *already* here."

"You know that. I know that. Colonel Raudegen knows that and your mother knows that. It is entirely likely that several dozen royal spies know that. The new king does not, officially, know that. Right now, it will be a lot better if he and his advisers don't officially know that. If he reverses the edict as a 'gesture of magnanimity,' Colonel Raudegen says, then they will wait a couple of weeks of discreet 'travel time' before your uncle 'arrives.' Otherwise, if the king won't reverse his exile, they'll have to take him on to Burgundy. But if the hints to the court receive favorable hints from the court, then your Maman can make a formal request."

"Will the king let Uncle Soubise stay?"

"Marc thinks . . ."

Marguerite's mind suddenly flitted away. "I saw Marc kiss you at breakfast this morning."

"I kissed him back," Susanna said. "It wasn't the first time and it won't be the last time. I'll probably marry him some day, when we are old enough, if I can learn to live among Calvinists."

"I thought that you are his fiancée."

"Our families haven't signed any contracts. His father forwards our letters to one another, though. My mother and stepfather are aware that his father, though a Calvinist, is likely to provide for his future very well indeed. So. Well. Anyway, M. Cavriani was there the first time we kissed each other."

"So. Well. Anyway," Marguerite mocked her. "It sounds to me as if you are indeed his fiancée, whether you know it or not. I have never kissed anyone. I never will, unless I get married. Perhaps then I will have to. Would I have to kiss a man if we were only betrothed but not married yet? I hope my husband will be very businesslike about begetting and not"—Marguerite made a little gesture that somehow reminded Susanna of worms, spiders, slugs, snails, and swarms of things that crept and crawled—"not put his hands all over me or slobber all over my face. How can you stand it? How can Maman stand it? Also," she assumed a facial expression that would have suited a seventy-year-old Puritan, "it's bad for your reputation."

Susanna raised her eyebrows. "Don't you have something more important to worry about than my reputation? You're in the middle of a country that's cheering for a usurper and from all I hear, the usurper is on the other end of the spectrum from trustworthy. For what it's worth, Your Grace, I assure you that my *virtue* is quite intact. As for *reputation*, girls like me don't have one. Or need one, for that matter."

"Girls like you? It's women like Maman and the other court ladies who don't have reputations. Not, at least, good reputations. Don't you *want* a good reputation?"

Susanna's forbearance snapped. "Where would I get one? You've lived in courts all your life. You know what the morals are, and they aren't what your Calvinist preachers would like them to be. They're not even like the way your ordinary provincial official or school teacher or shopkeeper or artisan manages his household. Even in the Netherlands, where both couples—the king and queen and the *Stadthouder* and his wife—are personally so well behaved, it doesn't mean that the people who revolve around them follow their example. No one raises an eyebrow when a servant becomes a nobleman's mistress. And if, when he ends it, she comes away with a generous settlement, she has a *better* prospect for marrying some other upper servant rather than a worse one. If I had given into that Lorrainer colonel, my dowry would have been a *lot* bigger than it is."

Marguerite bowed her head. "It's just really hard to think of virtue separate from reputation. Isn't reputation a mirror of a person's character?"

Then she popped her head up again, her eyes bright. "What colonel?"

Susanna tsked. "Not one you know. Just remember. Reputation is nothing but what 'they say.' A lot of what 'they say' can be really malicious—rumor, insinuations, allegations. But I don't have to care. I am who I am and Marc believes me and not anyone else's gossip.

And if he damages my 'reputation' by kissing me, he'll take the greatest of care for me, for myself and not for what anybody says about me."

"It's almost worse," the little duchess concluded, "when what 'they say' is true rather than false."

"Even Paris should be better than this." Ruvigny tapped his finger on his kneecap, watching Gerry Stone clear up their camp beside a road in eastern France. "He'll finish washing the dishes any minute now. When Rohan dumped him on us once the vaccination project got delayed, we should have at least given him time to unpack before we headed out again."

"It wouldn't have done any good," Bismarck pointed out dismally. "The infernal instrument is small. Portable. Pocket-sized."

Gerry sat down, pulling out the harmonica that he played often, if not particularly well. *Oh bury me not, on the lone prairieeeee . . .*

Bismarck spoke through the wailing. "Even with a recalcitrant duchess to retrieve, Paris will be better than this."

"This is the morning that Soubise is to 'arrive'?" Susanna asked.

Marc nodded. "We expect him shortly before noon. I—well, people I know—planted perfectly true reports in the Amsterdam papers that he had left England and met with the *Stadthouder* in the Hague. We discreetly avoided pinning down just when this occurred. Vague is your friend. The Paris papers picked that up, of course. Raudegen has managed to cobble together a decent-sized retinue to 'accompany' him, since he could hardly be expected to travel with just a secretary, cook, and valet. He's hired several plain but good quality carriages and a half dozen bodyguards, and rented a couple of dozen trunks. The trunks are empty, but as far as the reporters and the gawkers along the street are concerned, he'll have about as much luggage as would be expected if he were coming from the Low Countries. He'll hold a news conference, of course."

"Will the duc de Sully and his wife be coming soon?" King Gaston, not one to lose a public relations opportunity, had not only revoked Soubise's exile, but also added a *lagniappe* by ending the house arrest of his father's old first minister.

"No." It was the duchess who replied to Susanna. "My parents are old; my mother is not well. In their case, it's the appearance of the thing that matters. My father is happy and profoundly grateful, but they won't return to Paris."

Marguerite pelted into the breakfast room. "Henri is back again! With M. von Bismarck and an up-timer. A genuine up-timer. I've never met one before. I saw Madame Mailey when she came to negotiate the treaty after the League of Ostend *débâcle,* but I never got to meet her because Maman," she waved at her mother, "could not decide if it was acceptable etiquette for us to be presented to her, or that she must insist that the USE's ambassador plenipotentiary, being a commoner, must be presented to us. And I saw the famous physician, too, but only at a distance. He is very impressive, for a surgeon."

"Why," the older duchess asked, her voice like ice, "is he here?" A well-choreographed morning was suddenly descending into chaos.

"With all due respect, Your Grace," Ruvigny said as he came through the door, "you must know."

"The duke wants us to leave Paris? Still wants it? Wants it again?"

Ruvigny handed over a packet of letters.

"I would not say that he wants it, Your Grace. I would say that this time he requires it."

"There's a limit to how long the duchess will be able to drag her feet," Raudegen said. "Soubise is making public appearances now and has managed to get whispers that Rohan has requested that she join him circulating around the court. If she is seen to refuse, then rumors about an unconditional breakdown of her marriage will follow in short order. As long as Rohan appears to condone her actions, her standing remains unimpeachable. Once he withdraws that toleration . . ."

Whispers did not quite cover it.

"Hell and damnation!" Soubise yelled. "You have to go. Rohan's demands, not requests, have ratcheted up to a level that not even you can ignore or refuse. Since I'm here, I'm the one who can and will stay in Paris to advance the Rohan causes at court. Get your promiscuous little tush off to Besançon."

The relations between the duchess and her brother-in-law had never been marked by familial affection. She glared at Soubise in return. "This is absurd, you know. Within three months, you will find yourself crosswise with the king and get your head cut off."

"Perhaps so, but I am philosophical about it. Better for the family to lose a crusty old bachelor uncle than to lose its heiress."

With the senior members of the household making

life in the *palais* rather unpleasant, the younger ones
followed Marc's principle of "when in doubt, duck."

Gerry went and matriculated at the University of
Paris, just on general principles in order to have his
name on the register. "It's getting to be sort of like
that 'Kilroy was here' cartoon," he said to Bismarck.
Explanations followed. And, on the theory that he
hadn't time to unpack the smaller kit from his duffel
bag before he left Burgundy, he vaccinated the entire
Rohan household against smallpox.

"Will you stop that? Better, you *will* stop that."

Gerry took the harmonica out of his mouth and
the strains of "Your Cheatin Heart" ceased to resonate
through the Rohan stables.

"Do you want something different?"

"I don't want that instrument of torture at all. Think
of something else to do."

"Uh?" Gerry looked at Ruvigny. "Can I ask something?"

"Yes. I don't guarantee an answer."

"The duchess; the older one; her hair."

"What?"

"Is it for real? Those tight little ringlets screwed
down to her scalp? Or is it a wig? Up-time, I remember, a lot of the little old ladies used to go to the
beauty shop and get permanents. A lot of the time
they'd end up with hair that looked like that."

"It's real. A lot of the French nobility have really
curly hair like that." Ruvigny paused to think. "Soubise
does—take a close look the next time you see him.
So does the duke—it's just not so obvious because
he's bald in front and usually ties his back hair down

in a queue unless he's making a formal appearance, when he lets it loose and tries for a comb-over. Our little daisy is lucky that hers isn't so frizzy. Curly, but not frizzy."

"Oh grief," Marguerite said to Bismarck. "Candale's back in Paris. His only redeeming quality is that he's usually off serving in the army. He'll probably come slithering around again. I thought Maman had decided to stick with Gondi for a while longer."

"Which one is worse?"

"I don't know, really. I avoided Candale when he used to be around and I avoid Gondi now that he's around. 'They say' that Candale is agreeable and lively, but he's never seemed that way to me. His first marriage was annulled on the grounds of nonconsummation, you know, even though his wife brought him a ducal title and he only inherited that of comte through his mother. He tried to keep the ducal title, but her second husband—that's Schomberg—also claimed it. He was nineteen when he married her, poor, and very ambitious. She was rich; not just an heiress but of full age, already in possession of her estates and wealth, not having to answer to guardians. They don't have any children. Candale has never remarried, though it's been over fifteen years and he's Epernon's oldest son."

Marc pushed the curl back off his forehead. "What's de la Valette doing these days? Is Candale fronting for his brother?"

"Hmmn," Marguerite said. She wrinkled her forehead. "Which brother? Louis? The cardinal? He's with the army right now, I think. I haven't heard anyone say that he's up to anything in particular, though of course he'll be scrambling to ingratiate himself with the new king. Bernard was taken captive by the USE two years ago, of course, and hasn't come up with a ransom yet. Old Epernon, their father, is still alive. He's ancient, at least eighty years old. Still, he's the duke and he holds the purse strings. He won't pay, because having Bernard rotting somewhere in Brunswick means that Epernon controls his son, who's the heir after Candale. Nobody likes Bernard. His first wife was one of the legitimated bastard daughters of Henri IV. Everyone thinks that he poisoned her after the match became no longer politically advantageous. The politics of the Nogarets are just too complicated to sort out, even for them, probably."

Gerry shook his head, He found the customs of the French nobility that allowed a father and his three sons to have four different names dizzying. Not being the kind of person who worried about saving face, he said so. "I thought I understood the German system," he said. "They use places too, but it's consistent. Wilhelm, Bernhard (before he moved out of town), and Albrecht are all *Herzog* and all *von Sachsen-Weimar*."

"The French designations aren't personal names, exactly," Ruvigny explained. "They're the names of estates or lands that the family holds. Rohan is a dukedom. Soubise inherited the estates from which he takes his title from his mother. They are not a dukedom and he is not a duke."

Bismarck contributed with some disdain the opinion that the lands on which a lot of those *"de* Somewhere" and *"sieur de* This or That" titles were based often didn't amount to more than a large farm. "Not that our estates amount to much more than a large farm," he added cheerfully. "But though we may be *Nieder-adel*, we're also *Uradel*."

Gerry frowned. "I know 'lesser nobility,' which is mediatized sometimes and nontitled sometimes and... stuff. But what's *Uradel*? Original nobility? Prehistoric nobility?"

"Basically, it means that when the first ruler who wandered through Brandenburg hired the first clerk who could put quill to parchment and started keeping government records, we were already there. Those of more exalted rank did not create us; they just found us in place."

"But anyone with a '*de* Somewhere' is a noble? I can rely on that?" Gerry asked.

Soubise shook his head. "Not up north. Just like in the northwest of the USE, there are some commoner families with 'von' because they're so close to the Dutch and there 'van' doesn't signifiy nobility at all. Around Dieppe, for example, you'll find a family of artisans, maybe—ship carpenters or something. They're named X and most people will call them X. But because there are a dozen families named X in the Catholic parish and the priest has to keep track of how they are all related to prevent marriages within the forbidden decrees set up by the Council of Trent, he'll write them as *X de Y*, with Y simply being the little village they lived in before they moved to the city. Some of the other X families will be written *X de Q* or *X de R*."

Gerry groaned and thanked God for a good memory.

Acts of royal magnanimity rarely occurred without some expectation of *quid pro quo*.

As June turned toward July, King Gaston's advisers floated a suggestion to the duchesse de Rohan that it would be so delightful if her daughter Marguerite married one of the king's close supporters.

"For supporters," the duchess snorted, "think sycophants. Favorites. Not *mignons*, since he doesn't tilt that way."

"Can he make her do that?" Gerry asked Henri later. "Can't her father refuse?"

"Not really, if the king is directly involved. Kings can make marriages—just as Gaston's father did for Rohan himself. Kings can unmake marriages, for that matter, just as Louis refused for years to acknowledge Gaston's own marriage to the current queen, the Lorraine duchess. Right now he's being tactful, since he just took the throne, but if King Gaston decides to press the issue, Marguerite will marry his candidate and no one else."

The Royal Guards placed a respectful watch on the Rohan *palais*, disguised as security forces. The king made continuing demands that the two Marguerites be in near-constant attendance upon his wife or daughter. Royal Guards accompanied their carriage every time it left the mews. All this interfered with the general routine.

"I don't like this," Marguerite told Ruvigny. "Maman brought her little bastard Tancrède back from Normandy three years ago. At first, she had secluded him there with one of her old servants—after all, what can one do with an infant but send it to the country in hopes of more healthful air?—but when he got old enough not to need a wet nurse, she changed her mind. Especially, with the uncertainties that arose around the activities of the League of Ostend, she was uneasy about having him so near the coast. Since then, she goes to visit him clandestinely at the home of his foster parents. Not just now and then, but regularly, dressed as an ordinary Parisian *bourgeoise*. She doesn't take the carriage with our crest on the door, but all this surveillance may uncover this and give the king another lever to use in pressuring us."

Ruvigny knocked on the door of the small home in a Parisian suburb.

The maid-of-all-work who answered wore a cap that was askew, an apron with its strings half-untied, and one shoe. She didn't appear to be dirty or slatternly. She was just disheveled.

"*Monsieur?*"

"*Madame LeBon, s'il vous plaît.*"

It appeared that Madame, may the Lord in Highest Heaven reward her, had taken the boy to the park.

Ruvigny raised an eyebrow.

The maid pulled her cap straight and reached behind her to secure the apron strings into a bow.

"Madame's ward is a very . . . active . . . child."

"Might Monsieur Lebon be at home?"

"*Hélas, non.* Monsieur LeBon is at work. If he has finished speaking with the head of the new school, that is."

"New school."

"The boy has been deemed old enough for lessons. As I said, he is . . . active. The former school could not deal with it when he crawled under the desks, climbed up the bookshelves, or pulled the pages out of his *cahier* and folded them into air gliders."

Ruvigny nodded.

"Neither could the school before that. Or the school before that one. Madame will not permit the child to be caned, oh perish the thought, so..." She suddenly stopped talking and opened the door a little farther. "But would you like to come in? Just let me see if I can find where he hid my shoe...he thinks it is so funny to hide things."

Ruvigny followed her. In this house, no space was devoted to a vestibule. The door opened directly on the room in which the family sat, ate, prayed, and slept. Because of the compact space, it didn't take the maid long to retrieve her shoe from the storage bench that provided the main seating area.

The maid rattled on. "So there is to be a new school, if one can be found that will accept him. Teachers *talk* to one another, you know." She made this sound as if it were the deepest of conspiracies.

Whereas the maid had thanked the Lord in Highest Heaven for the park in a loud voice, Ruvigny mentally praised Him for perfect timing. Schoolmasters were inclined to ask curious questions when one of their pupils disappeared without an adequate explanation.

After some time he asked, "When is Madame likely to return from the park?"

"When she is about to collapse from exhaustion or the boy starts to scream that he is starving, whichever comes first."

"Perhaps, then, it would be more prudent for me to find them in the park. If you would be so kind as to direct me...?"

He found Madame and the boy at a duck pond. The boy was soaking wet. The ducks appeared to be panicked, but not quite panicked enough to abandon the bread crumbs that Madame was strewing at the edge of the water. The child was trying to catch the drake nearest to the shore and chanting, "Ducks with white feathers. Ducks with brown feathers. Ducks with gray feathers. Drab ducks, drab ducks. Jean who has been to *L'Amérique* says that they have ducks with blue feathers. Ducks with green feathers. Ducks with little red feathers on their heads. Feathers he says are 'iridescent.' Madame, what does 'iridescent' mean? Do you think that I can ever go to *L'Amérique*? Do you think that I can ever go to the moon? If I can make paper fly through the air, why can't these big balloons that Pierre at the tailor's shop told me about—they are made of silk, he says, and cow guts—why can't they fly to the moon?"

"*Pardon, madame*! I come on a matter of some urgency."

"In regard to the child? You must speak with my husband," she said.

"Why do you assume it concerns the child?"

"Nothing else in our lives is urgent." She turned. "Tancrède, come, we must go home."

"I'm not hungry yet."

"Now." She grabbed his hand.

"*Non*." He dug in his heels.

"Come," Ruvigny said. "I can tell you not only about silk balloons, but about machines that fly."

"Airplanes!" The child, Tancrède, pulled himself out of Madame's grasp and barreled toward Ruvigny so fast that it was impossible for him to save his trousers from the dripping water. "I saw one, I saw one, I saw one. It went over the city and I saw it. Nobody can tell me how men can make them fly. How do they fly?

How do birds fly? Do airplanes have bird guts inside them and feathers inside their wings? Where do they build them? Can I go see them build airplanes? I've been to the zoo but I've never seen anyone build an airplane." He stopped. "Who are you?"

The LeBons proved to be amenable to returning the boy to the care of his natural mother.

Somehow, Ruvigny was not surprised.

Containing him in the rear quarters of the *palais* Rohan proved to be challenging.

"What are these? Where did I find those? I found them under the bed; aren't they interesting? We didn't have a chamber pot this shape at the Lebons' house. What's it made of? I'm sorry, I didn't mean to break it. Can we go to the park? I saw horses out the window; I want to visit the horses. I don't take naps; naps are for disgusting little babies that still drool. Why can't I go see the LeBons again; they're nice to me. You're no fun! No, I won't give it back—it's interesting. I saw you kissing Marc. I drew pictures on the wall with the duchess' rouge because I couldn't find any pencil and paper and I like to draw pictures. Why? Where did M. de Ruvigny go? When's supper? Why?"

Susanna raised her eyes to the skies. *Why me, O Lord in Highest Heaven? I'm a dressmaker, not a babysitter.*

When she verbalized the question, Raudegen said, "Because Ruvigny can trust you. It's a very open question how many of the *palais* staff we can trust. Trust in the absolute sense, or trust to be discreet. They are paid very little; reporters pay for stories. Christ himself said, 'Lead us not into temptation.'"

❖   ❖   ❖

La petite Rohan would be a true prize. The royal advisers agreed on that. Her husband should be Catholic, and preferably an adherent of the *dévot* party. The royal advisers agreed on that. Then, of course, the question arose of who would be the best match, upon which there was far less unanimity. Each of them appeared to have a son, a nephew, a brother, a ward, a cousin, or a protégé who would benefit from marrying the Rohan estates. For every candidate, there was an objection. This one was in feeble health, so might die and leave her as a powerful widow; that one was already betrothed and the relatives of his fiancée, who had also thrown their allegiance to Gaston, would be profoundly offended if the match were broken off. Soissons was a prince of the blood and an ally (he had, in fact, been the first fiancé of the king's first wife who had given birth to little *Mademoiselle de France* before she died), but a Rohan marriage might bring him too much power.

"Does it have to be someone mature?" The question floated through the room.

"What do you mean? The king needs strong allies."

"Why not find someone the same age as *la Rohan*. He could be a trifle younger, even—someone malleable. Perhaps if we chose a royal ward who is not yet of age, it could be arranged for his guardian, our lord the king, to assume responsibility, temporary *of course*, for the Rohan estates. Her husband need not control her; the king would be in a position to control them both. That would prevent the problem of a constellation of too much power concentrated that led you to refuse Soissons."

Young. That brought a sizable flock of new candidates to the fore, but still no unanimous agreement.

"The king has been displaying his magnanimity. Why not prepare a list of, let us say, six candidates who would be acceptable to the crown and give her the liberty of choosing among them."

The other advisers looked upon this suggestion and found it to be good. The comte de Lafayette had two sons of acceptable age. The younger of Effiat's orphaned sons, the one who had inherited the Cinq-Mars title, was sixteen.

"Not fully orphaned," someone complained, "and his mother is a harridan."

"He's pretty, though, which might appeal to a girl. All that curly auburn hair. And he dances well."

"There's the de Bussy heir. He studied under the Jesuits."

Sheer *ennui* finally brought agreement on six names. The list didn't suit everyone, but compromises rarely do.

"They can't leave from the *palais*," Raudegen said. "I say that from a professional perspective. There are simply too many Royal Guards. They can't disappear from the court when they are attending the queen and *la Mademoiselle*. It's not just that they are closely observed there, although they are. There are too many people milling around around in random patterns. An escape party would run too much risk of encountering someone utterly unexpected."

"Maybe they could leave from the *palais* if there was a party going on," Ruvigny commented. "Something like the ballet they held last summer. There would be a couple of hundred guests coming and going and a major congestion of horses, carriages, servants, caterers, etc."

"Possible." Raudegen moved and looked down into the courtyard. "What kind of party?"

"We can check with Benserade. He'll come gladly, being reasonably thankful just now that he never succeeded in obtaining patronage from Richelieu and Mazarin."

"It would be easiest for them to leave if it's some kind of an outdoor production. Down in the courtyard there."

Benserade, when consulted, pointed out that outdoor productions were lamentably subject to the vagaries of the weather.

"Even better than a ballet," he said. "Hire the new Théâtre du Marais. It's in a remodeled tennis court on the Vielle Rue du Temple, right opposite the Capuchins. They renovated it just two years ago, so it's all modern. It wouldn't be a good idea to use the Hôtel de Bourgogne, even though they've accumulated a lot of indoor sets over the years, because that theater had too many long-standing ties to Richelieu—right now, they're probably all thinking that having it on the Rue Mauconseil was prophetic. It might offend the king for the duchesses to sponsor a production there."

At this point, they had to take the new and better escape concept to the ladies themselves.

"Not a ballet again," the duchess said. "It would be all too *déjà vu*. We must find something different. A contemporary play will be too dangerous." Her voice was firm. "There are just too many chances to offend. It will have to be a pastoral, classical theme. Comedy, not tragedy. Certainly not a satire. Pyramus and Thisbe, perhaps?"

"Oh, Maman. That's so overdone."

"I want something incorporating dance and music with the dialogue," the duchess continued. "Not an opera, because Mrs. Simpson is sponsoring operas in Magdeburg. Not a musical comedy, because the queen in the Netherlands is sponsoring musical comedies in Brussels. We need something else. Something that will *not offend the king*. Perhaps even something that will placate the king."

Gerry's thoughts turned to science fiction and fantasy. "You need the development of a scion from obscurity to glory. Scions are really good, like in Terry Pratchett's *Guards! Guards!* Well, probably not just like Pratchett, considering how Carrot turns out at the end, no matter how great an author Pratchett is—was—will be—used to be—still is? Anyhow, focus on the scion. I must have read twenty books that go something like the following, by different authors. Or not so many different authors. Eddings used to write the same story over and over again. He just changed the names. Brooks did pretty much the same with the Shannara series. So, to start, you've got this family living somewhere in Fantasia."

"Fantasia?"

"Well, that's actually an old Disney movie, but you can make it generic. There was this glorious book called *The Tough Guide to Fantasy Land* that came out just a couple of years before the Ring of Fire, I think. It was one of Diana Wynne Jones' things. We have it at home, but that's neither here nor there and you don't need it to make this play."

"Focus," Bismarck said. "Focus."

"You know what he's talking about," Ruvigny interjected. "Arcadia. Heroines named Amerinde and heroes named Cleonice. We've all read them."

"Think about it, guys," Gerry barreled on. "You won't even need enough time for someone to compose new music. Oh, your composer will have to add the high notes and low notes and chords and such, but I can give you enough pre-cooked melodies to carry it off. Especially since this thing won't exactly have a performance run."

He pulled out his harmonica.

"First scene. The Birth of the Scion. Daddy, Mommy, and attendants admire the new prince. All you'll need is a cradle and a spotlight. Someone sings, *Sleep my child and peace attend thee, all throught the night; guardian angels God will send thee, all through the night* and everybody dances around the cradle. Somebody can translate it into French.

"And then he's a toddler. Here's the tune. *Bimbo, Bimbo, when you're gonna grow? Everybody loves the little baby Bimb-bi-o.*" He bit his lip. "Don't use the word 'bimbo.' Some of the professional actors are bound to have little kids who are used to being around the theater and won't freeze on stage."

Benserade nodded. "One of Béjart's boys will do. The little one—Louis, I think his name is."

"Then the scion turns into a teenager and all his wonderful, extraordinary, excessive talents and abilities start to shine. From what I hear, it's hard to go overboard on flattery in this day and age. Fawning on monarchs is right up there with getting a Ph.D.—Piled High and Deep. *When you gotta' glow, you gotta glow. So glow little glow worm, glow.*" Gerry cocked his head. "I'd think up some slightly different lyrics for that, if I were you, and not call Gaston a worm by inference, but this would be the *tour de force* for whoever dances the part of the Scion. You know, lyrics about how, as he grew up, his qualities began to shine so much that he practically glowed when people looked at him."

Bismarck ran his hand though his receding hairline.

"Then he goes on some kind of a quest where he meets a foreign princess who is the true love of his life. Everybody will be able to tell that she's clearly a perfect match for him, because her dance sounds almost exactly the same and uses the same chords. *Three little maids who all unwary, come from a ladies' seminary.*

"Then everyone dances a few more dances, the Scion is received as king with overwhelming joy. You go back to the lullaby and as the young king and queen are crowned, with his mama dripping tears and pride in the background, you have God singing from the roof *Go, my children, with my blessing, never alone. Waking, sleeping, I am with you; you are my own.*"

Gerry leaned back, exhausted from this long excursion into the field of derivative imagination. "And they go off the stage. Outdoors, you have a crew shoot fireworks off. You can't do fireworks inside the theater—it's too dangerous, which is a pity. Up-time, there was some night club where a couple of hundred people burned alive because it caught on fire when they shot off fireworks indoors. They'll distract the audience's ears from what you're doing, though."

"Fireworks distract eyes, too," Marc pointed out. "All the outside gawkers will be looking up, or at least most of them."

"Can you write this?" the duchess asked.

"Nope," Gerry said cheerfully. "I'm a one-note wonder. One note at a time on the harmonica; one finger on the piano, for that matter. Plink, plank, plunk. I'm

no musician. I can't do chords. I'm no playwright. I
can't do dialogue. But I sure can borrow ideas from
bad books. You'll have to get your people to take it
and run with it."

The conversation degenerated into cacophony.

"Montdory can take the lead. No, he can direct.
No..."

"Whatever you do, don't touch Montfleury with a
ten-foot pole. Everyone knows how strong his ties to
Richelieu were."

"Scriptwriter? Has Gaston forgiven Voiture yet?"

"DesBarreaux could do it," Benserade said, "but
by all that's sacred, don't put his name in the pro-
gram if he agrees. Much less Sanguin. Schelandre is
Calvinist, which might be an advantage, but he's old
enough that his scripts sound fusty and in any case
he's out of town, campaigning. With all apologies to
you soldiers," he nodded at Ruvigny and Bismarck,
"wars are a nuisance as far as literature is concerned.
Not for subject matter—they provide a lot of grist for
the mill there—but for trying to find time to write
if a man is sitting in some uncomfortable tent with
people likely to shoot at him any day."

Bismarck, being wholly without literary ambitions,
guffawed.

Benserade barreled on. "Mairet's good, and he's
willing to write happy endings instead of being focused
on the prestige of writing tragedies, but he's hung up
on classical unities, plus he was born in Besançon,
which isn't politically correct right now. I say get
Rotrou, even if he has been writing for the Hôtel
de Bourgogne. It will get his name before the new
king, and right now they need all the help they can

get over there if the theater is going to survive the change in regime. He writes fast. Last year he told me he's already done more than thirty plays and he's not thirty years old yet. Some of those are translations or adaptations, though."

Then there was the matter of casting, which caused another conversational jumble.

"Marguerite will be the princess, of course."

"But who is to dance the young king?"

"Well, Cinq-Mars, since he's Gaston's current candidate for Marguerite's hand. Seeing them on stage together will appease M. Gaston's advisers."

"If Cinq-Mars dances the prince, in the coronation scene you can even throw in a reference to the heroic death of the former king in battle, and that will apply to the marquis' father and take everyone's minds off what happened to Louis."

"With you, Madame Duchesse, center stage as the proud and happy dowager in the finale."

"I can get Soûlas to come and be an acting coach," Ruvigny said.

"Who?"

"That theater-mad ensign who ran off to join a troupe of actors. They'd hoped to go to England last year, but didn't make it because of the political troubles there, so he's somewhere down in the Marais district, looking for work. Who knows? If Montdory likes him when he sees him working on this, he may get a permanent slot."

"So you've taken care of the religion and politics of the playwrights. Does it make any difference if the professional actors you bring in are Catholics or Huguenots?" Bismarck asked.

"Not really," Benserade said. "The Catholic church excommunicates actors, just for being actors, and the Calvinists aren't precisely thrilled with them either, so no one will expect them to be in good standing."

Bismarck wandered into the mews loft that Gerry had taken to calling the *chop shop*. "The moon will be full on the sixteenth."

Raudegen looked up.

"They've gotten to the point of setting a date for this extravaganza. That's what they've decided to call it. An *extravaganza*. As far as I'm concerned, they can call it anything they please, but do we want moonlight for this project, or don't we?"

"It would give decent illumination for several days before and after. Unless it's cloudy, of course. We could see better to drive by night if the moon was out. If we had bad luck and someone followed us, though, they could also see better. It's a toss-up."

"The fireworks will make a better show without moonlight," Ruvigny said.

"Understood. Let me go tell them to pick one of the dark of the moon weeks, either before or after the middle of the month."

One could not of course very well give a gala in honor of the king and queen unless they agreed to come. The duchess sent out feelers in advance. Their Majesties agreed, but Gaston's people insisted on insinuating Tristan l'Hermite, a hanger-on with literary ambitions (thus far not realized, in the sense that none of his plays had actually been performed) into the planning. His presence had a stultifying effect on conversation.

Except for Benserade and Cinq-Mars, who flirted madly backstage during the rehearsals.

"Oh," Cinq-Mars said. "I just adore skirts; they're so wonderfully swishy, don't you know, with all those petticoats. I hated it when I was taken out of my baby skirts and made to put on 'little man' breeches. They're *so* tight and uncomfortable. At home, I've always snitched my sister's clothes to lounge around in, whenever she would let me."

Tancrède adored the harmonica.

Gerry was quite willing to share. "Just don't lose it," he warned.

"I won't. Thank you so much, sir."

Tancrède's future did not involve a career as a musical prodigy.

He did lose the harmonica.

"Keep looking, kid," Gerry said, "but don't worry Susanna too much if you can't find it. I have a spare."

On his way out, he threw a different admonition at Susanna. "If you're the one who hid it, I don't blame you, but I do want it back."

"I am so incredibly thankful," Bismarck said, "for my two left feet."

"My inability to carry a tune," Gerry added.

They had found a comfortable refuge in the chop shop.

Within certain parameters of comfortable, of course. The hay was softer than any chair in the most luxurious rooms in any château in France, but it did tend to prickle.

"Would you mind if I asked something?"

"Nah."

"Why don't you object to addressing the duchesses as 'Your Grace'? I've heard that the up-timers believe that all men, well, ladies too, are created equal."

"I just make myself not think of it as giving a title to a person. I'm giving the title to an office. Say, the spring we got transferred here, if our class had taken a field trip to Washington, DC, which we didn't, and I had gotten to meet President Clinton, which I never did... but if I had, I wouldn't have called him 'Bill.' I'd have called him 'Mr. President' and I should have. That's only polite. It was a matter of the office he held. In spite of Monica Lewinsky and all."

Bismarck enjoyed what Gerry could dredge up from his recollections—"Hey, I was only eleven"—about Monica Lewinsky. A lot.

So did both of the duchesses when Bismarck had him repeat it after supper that evening as they all stood around in the back rooms, free, for once, from the busy ears of l'Hermite.

While Gerry played the *raconteur*, Susanna was walking around and around Marguerite, looking at her sharply. When he had finished, she turned toward Ruvigny. "There's no way on earth to disguise her as anything other as a noblewoman." She sighed and curtsied to the duchess. "Much less you, Your Grace!"

"Why not?" Marguerite snipped, in full objection and protest mode.

"Because . . ."

"Because," Gerry interrupted. "When people say that up-timers act like nobles, they aren't really thinking. They mean that we act different from them, and we pretty much don't kowtow to anybody just because he thinks he's better than we are. Or she. We don't really act like nobles, though. We don't have the mannerisms. We don't act subordinate, but we don't act entitled, either. Because we—make that most of us—don't think we're better than they are, either." He cocked his head. "I've got to be fair. Some up-timers do, of course—think they're better than someone else, that is. They did even back in West Virginia. There was a sizable bunch who thought they were a lot better than the hippie Stones."

"But," Marguerite persisted. "How can you tell?" She glared at Susanna, who gave an exasperated sigh.

"I've been dressing ladies of the high nobility for eight years now. Gerry's perfectly right. I can tell, and so could anyone else who took a close look."

"Disguise the duchesses as lesser noblewomen," August suggested. "Someone like my mother or sisters. The lady of a country manor, somewhere out in wherever France's equivalent of rural Brandenburg is." He grinned. "A lady like that will think of herself as just as much automatically entitled, in her own bit of the world, as a duchesse de Rohan is in France as a whole. But a country lady traveling with her daughter and a small entourage won't attract much attention."

Susanna eyed Marguerite critically. "Yes," she said slowly, nodding her head. "Yes, that might work."

"I will be her bodyguard," Raudegen said. "You"—he pointed at Marc—"are the assistant to the steward at her manor. The rest of you"—he pointed to the four redheads—"are her staff. Upper servants—household servants. There's enough difference in your ages. Three brothers and a sister. This family is not wealthy— Susanna will be doubling as maid for the ladies and nanny for the child. Susanna and Gerry won't have any problems in the role; you other two are their brothers in the local militia. I've brought you along for extra muscle because of all the unrest. You've have been in the armies long enough to know how ordinary soldiers act. Now, what is your name?"

Gerry grinned. "Lapierre," of course. "Or Stein, since three of us are more at home in German than in French. Henri's accent in German is execrable, but maybe he can keep his mouth shut."

"Why would a French country lady have servants named Stein?"

"Alsace. She's heading home."

Raudegen nodded. "That will do. She and her daughter are French-speaking upper class. The four of us are German-speaking peasants. Cavriani? Any preference?"

Marc shook his head. "Either one is fine."

"It's getting out of the theater that will be the trick. We're lucky that Cinq-Mars has that curly red hair and wears it *au naturel*. In that last scene, Gerry can substitute for him and get Marguerite away when they promenade out. We'll need to use plenty of spotlights, multi-colored and strobing around the stage, to distract people's eyes from noticing that the lead actor has changed."

"Who will distract Cinq-Mars from realizing that he's not onstage at the high point?"

"Benserade, of course."

"What if you end up needing more than fireworks?" Gerry asked Raudegen.

"I've been thinking the same thing myself."

"Well, I don't have the famous Stone Boys' Box of Tricks with me, but I might be able to cobble some primitive stuff together. Down-time kitchens don't offer the chemical options that up-time kitchens did, and we don't want to draw attention to ourselves by buying any gunpowder, or stuff like that. If you can get them to order a few extra fireworks, though, and a couple of dozen of those little earthenware storage containers."

July turned inexorably into August. The letters from Rohan turned just as inexorably from demanding and requiring to threatening the most dire of consequences if Something Wasn't Done and Soon.

"We can't hurry this," Raudegen wrote back patiently. "Trust my professional judgment, please. This is an instance in which haste would make waste."

"They're smoke bombs that put out unbelievably nauseating smells, basically, but they aren't working as well as I hoped they would." Gerry eyed the sputtering firepot with dissatisfaction.

"At least they seem to be reliable," Raudegen answered. "Finish up the rest of the supply." He walked away.

Gerry kept standing there. He wrinkled up his forehead. *They need more zip. The fuses are way too slow, for one thing,* he thought. *Before I finish them up, I'm going to talk to Susanna and see if there's something up in the dressmakers' stash that would burn faster if I unraveled the fabric and twisted it into fuses.*

On performance night, as if to spite everyone's nerves, things went well. Rotrou had indeed written the script in such a way that in the last scene, the "king and queen" did not dance, but had the remainder of the cast dance around them. Nymphs floated around in billowing, if salaciously knee-length, chiffon skirts. Muses in classical draperies struck attitudes. The Scion's crown was so immense that it shadowed his face nicely. God sang and the leads processed off the stage with great dignity.

The dignity held until they were well in the wings. Then Gerry took a firm grip on Marguerite's wrist and scampered as fast as he could move in order to get her safely outside in the course of the after-performance confusion.

Marc and Susanna were already on their way out of town with the first carriage. It also transported Tancrède and most of the supplies for the trip. They planned to wait at a predetermined location for the second carriage to catch up.

Bismarck, reins in his hands, waited at the stage door at the back of the theater until the older duchess came out.

Raudegen and Ruvigny would follow on horseback as soon as they were reasonably certain that there had been no slip 'twixt the cup and the lip.

The fireworks were a success.

The royal party exited from their boxes, there being too many to fit in a single box.

There was a lot going on outside the Théâtre de Marais. The crowd went oooh! and the crowd went ah! at every detail of the dresses and hair styles.

Cinq-Mars saw the Rohan ladies leaving, the only person to notice, but why should he care? Once the choreographer told him he wouldn't be needed in the last scene, he had made his own plans to take advantage of the after-performance confusion. He slipped into a dressing room and formally accepted an offer of employment at the Théâtre des Marais. He would act under a pseudonym like all the others of course, but he had a vision. Someday he would become a tremendous success, adored by all of the *literati* of France, a power to be reckoned with. He would become the pet of all the salons. He would make and break careers. Until then, he and Isaac were going out for a late supper.

Some days later, upon receiving notification from the authorities that they could only assume that some really unfortunate event had happened at the gala, his older brother heaved a private sigh of relief behind his public display of grief. The boy's tendencies were embarrassing and probably could not have been disguised forever. It's one thing to have your brother beheaded for conspiring against the monarch, as happened according to the up-time encyclopedias. That could be considered one of the normal hazards of belonging to the French nobility. To have him survive and perhaps eventually be burned at the stake for sodomy would have caused excessively unpleasant difficulties for his surviving relatives. There was no guarantee that even rank and wealth could have protected him if he became flamboyant enough. He did not push the authorities to pursue the matter energetically.

"We have a problem," Ruvigny said.

Raudegen grunted.

Four Royal Guards had apparently been paying attention to what they were supposed to instead of the distractions that had been laid out for them. They were trotting down the street, positioned to keep the carriage Bismarck was driving in sight.

"Good men," Raudegen said. "They have enough sense not to try to stop it until they've figured out the size of the opposition. I hope they get commendations. But for right now, let's spook their horses."

Ruvigny had been more in demand by the the Rohan ladies, which meant that Raudegen had the experience with the little smoke-and-sparks-spitting firepots. Gerry called them oversized sparklers.

"A half dozen should be enough." He hefted down one of the saddlebags and reached inside his buffcoat for a flint—the new kind with the little fuel reservoir and small roller.

Ruvigny led their own mounts around a corner, since a man's own horse was usually just as subject to spooking as someone else's.

Raudegen lit the first fuse and went to toss the ersatz Molotov cocktail down the street toward the riders.

"What? Oh the hell! Goddamn this fucking fuse!"

The first firepot went off while he still held it, throwing sparks in all directions before the clay cracked, split, and spilled the spitting gunpowder out on his hand. He had lined up the other five quite neatly on the ground next to him. The closest caught a spark from the first. That fuse also ran much too fast and hot. The pot exploded, throwing potsherds rather than just cracking, and ignited the rest. He fell to the ground, nauseated with pain.

"They didn't work as reliably as I had hoped," he groaned, once Ruvigny had pulled him up, shouldered him around the corner, and boosted him onto his horse.

Ruvigny walked around the horse's head to the other side. "How's the bleeding?"

Raudegen glanced down. "It's actually mostly cauterized, I think."

"You're just lucky you throw overhand. If that first pot had been on a level with your head, you might have lost your eyes instead of just your hair. Use this hand to hold the cloth against the cuts on your scalp above your ear unless the burns are so bad that you can't stand the touch. Otherwise, just try to balance in the stirrups. I'll put him on a lead rein."

Raudegen grimaced. "They worked, though. Those guards are riding some thoroughly spooked horses, if they've even managed to keep their seats. City slicker horses with no battle experience."

They couldn't move rapidly, but the carriage Bismarck drove was moving even more slowly through the moonless gloom. When they caught up, Ruvigny transferred Raudegen into it. Gerry winced, straightened the mangled fingers as well as he could, and improvised a splint.

"That's all I can do here. My med kit's in the duffel. Marc and Susanna have it."

It was still dark when they caught up with the other carriage. The new splint reached from beyond the tip of Raudegen's middle finger to above his wrist. Gerry sprinkled the mess with sulfa powder from his duffel bag, and wrapped it in a clean bandage. "That's the best I can manage until we get some daylight and I can actually see what I'm doing. Even these new-model lanterns with the mantles flicker."

Ruvigny looked at the splint and bandages critically. "That will never grasp a sword, or anything else, again, despite the best care that our angel of mercy can provide you."

Raudegen also looked at the splint and bandages. "There goes my career."

"Nah," Gerry said, tying the final knot. "Don't go all 'if it weren't for bad luck, I'd have no luck at all' on me. You're already too high up the totem pole. The grand duke will just kick you up higher—probably assign you to Erlach for planning and logistics, with your very own private secretary to write down what you think for you."

He lifted a beaker to Raudegen's lips. "Now drink this. It's not like you're some ordinary person, like a tailor, who actually needs to use his hands to earn a living. It's not like you're a clockmaker or a lens grinder. Or a blacksmith, for that matter. No matter how well it heals, though, that hand will ache in bad weather and be a constant nuisance. You'll remember tonight every day for the rest of your life."

— Section IV —

"I can't help it," Gerry said. He had his arms clutched across his chest, shuddering and shivering as if it were February rather than August. "Ever since Rome, when I shot Marius after he shot at the pope, I can't help it. I did fix Raudegen's hand before I lost it, but I can't help it. My gun was at his throat and it went off. The blood just sprayed out of him, all over everyone. It almost took his head off. I'm sorry guys, but it was my fault, too. I changed the fuses, after Raudegen tested them the last time, trying to get more bang for my buck. I know you're soldiers; you've probably seen worse, but

I can't help it. Marius' head just sort of exploded and now Raudegen's hand blew off and it's my fault again because I didn't tell him that I changed the fuses. Nurses and doctors probably see worse all the time, I know. I'm probably a disgrace to Lothlorien Pharmaceuticals. I'm okay with vaccinations, like I did back at the *palais*, but when I have to look at the insides of someone's body, I just can't help it and it's all my fault again. He's just lying there on the carriage bench because I gave him some opium; he's just lying there."

It was not the most opportune moment for someone else to join the party. Candale was really very fortunate that neither Ruvigny nor Bismarck shot him when they were alerted by Marc's sudden *Pssst!*

"The duchess invited me," didn't go very far as a rationale with anyone other than the duchess.

"See, I am already dressed in the guise of her husband, an Alsatian country gentleman," didn't go much farther.

"With all due respect, monsieur le comte," Ruvigny said, "You are just what we don't need."

"It's my fault," Gerry said. "If I hadn't blown Raudegen's hand up, we would be two hours ahead of him by now."

Candale looked into the carriage that was now occupied by two duchesses and one comatose colonel.

"Shouldn't you really be going back to your regiment?" Marguerite asked him. "I'm sure it misses you."

"If you people wake up this child or disturb Colonel Raudegen," Susanna hissed through the window of the first carriage, "it will not matter because all of you will find yourselves dead before morning."

❖   ❖   ❖

Bismarck took Gerry up on the driver's seat as they headed on through what was left of the night.

"What were you chanting?" Susanna asked him when they stopped for a rest. "It sounded like you were chanting while you drove."

"I was reminding Gerry. 'The just shall live by faith. Jesus Christ, our God and Lord, died for our sins and was raised again for our justification.' He needs to remember that now and always."

"Do you believe it?" Marguerite asked. "Actually believe it?"

"I do." Bismarck bowed his head. "In joy and happiness, in suffering and sadness, help me at all times, Christ the salvation of my life."

To avoid Candale, who usually paced his horse next to the duchess' carriage, Marguerite decided to ride with Susanna.

"Have you read the Bible?" she asked.

"Mostly only the parts in my missal."

"People are supposed to read it for themselves. Grand-mère Rohan read a great deal of it to me when I was a child and of course the preachers read it in the Temple. You haven't missed much. It's a very disappointing kind of book."

"What?"

"Oh, it's true. It's supposed to be the story of God's chosen people, but they were horrible, smiting one another all the time. The sons of Adam must have married their own sisters, because no one else was alive, and Abraham most certainly did, for it says so. There was the man who cut his concubine in twelve pieces and distributed them to the Twelve Tribes. They were supposed to be God's people, but they were not one bit better than we are, and some of them were worse. Even Henri IV only had a dozen or so mistresses besides his wives and less than two dozen bastards that we know of. David and Solomon had lots more wives than two, and at the same time instead of divorcing the first one, plus all those concubines. If the preachers want to denounce libertines, then they ought to denounce those. Don't you think?"

Susannah was about to reply, but Tancrède woke up.

"Are we there yet? Tell M. von Bismarck to stop the carriage, please; I gotta go. I'm hungry; when's lunch? These turnips are really nasty. I'm a *boy*. I don't care if you're older; you're nothing but a *girl*. I don't *want* to sit still. Read me a story. Can I ride in the carriage with the lady who used to visit me at the LeBons? Why can't I go visit the LeBons; they were always nice to me. Will you read me another story, please. I'm hungry; when are we going to stop for supper? I liked the first story better—read it again, pleeease! I gotta go. I don't *want* to behave myself. If you had brought books with short words, I could read my own stories. Are we there yet? I gotta go right now."

Closer acquaintance only reinforced Marguerite's already ingrained hostility toward Tancrède.

"There are four of us," Bismarck said while Susanna followed the boy to his chosen spot behind a tree. "Four boys born within a space of six years. With my sisters, eight of us born within twelve years. I believe that we may owe our lady mother an apology for existing."

"It's a farce," Marguerite proclaimed. "In a just world, Candale's old valet would not have been sur-named LeBon. LeMal would make a lot more sense for this one."

Tancrède, by fate and fostering surnamed LeBon, showed up in time to regard her with a defiant pout. "I don't like you. I want to ride with the other lady."

Marc put an end to the impasse by picking the boy up and plopping him in front of Candale, muttering, "I understand that you're responsible for his existence, so you deal with him for a while and give Susanna a break."

"*Merci,* M. de Candale, for letting me ride your horse. Am I going to get to ride a horse the rest of the way? I like Susanna better than I like Marguerite. I want my *own* pony to ride. I wanted a pony before, but the LeBons always said that there is no room for a pony in Paris. Do you live in Paris? No? You're in the army? Do you have armor? Do you have a sword? Do you have a pistol? Can I shoot it? Hey, look at those cows. I gotta go. Honest, M. de Candale, I gotta go right now. If you don't let me go right now I won't be able to hold it."

Candale did his best to ignore the child, but the boy wiggled. He squiggled, wriggled, and upon occasion lunged toward something that caught his eyes. Two hours later, he started to cry.

"His legs hurt," Bismarck said. "Marc, you can't put a child who has never ridden on a horse and expect him to stay there all day." He picked the boy off, motioned for the coachman to halt, followed him into the bushes for yet another "gotta go," and returned him to Susanna.

"Do you always pay him so little mind as on this trip?" he asked when he pulled his horse up next to Candale's again.

"There's no way under the law that I can make

him my heir and I have no intention of raising false expectations by making a fuss over him. It's not as if I'm a king who can furnish his *légitimés* with titles and estates the way Henri IV did for Vendôme and the others. I've provided him with foster parents since he was born. I've paid LeBon and his wife. If the duchess wants to send him to Saumur when he gets a few years older, I'll pay his school fees. Not," he added, "that she can't afford to pay them herself.

"If my father ever dies and I succeed to the title, maybe I can do a bit more, a commission or something, but that will depend on the fates. My father may be immortal. The odds are against it, but he will manage it if any human can, or at least achieve a personal return to the era of Methuselah."

"Well, if we aren't there yet, when will be be there?" Tancrède squirmed his way up from the floor of the carriage and stuck his head out the window.

"It's about two hundred and fifty miles," Susanna said. "We have been on the road for eleven days. I think it will take at least another week. We will be in the County of Burgundy, though before we come to Besançon. We will reach Dôle first and then follow the Doubs River, more or less, until we reach Grand Duke Bernhard's capital city. It is a very twisty river."

"Will I be able to go fishing when we come to the river? I love to fish."

"Maybe once we get to Besançon, you can go fishing. I don't think there will be time while we are traveling."

"What worries me most," Marguerite said, "is that we are just driving along—well, the men are mostly riding along—without any opposition. We haven't been pursued, as far as any of them can tell and all of them except Marc and Gerry are accustomed to military campaigning and knowing who is chasing you and finding the people you are chasing. Marc has been asking questions at every inn and stable. Even when we came through Auxerre, there was no more than the normal in the way of checkpoints."

"I noticed that we haven't even had to use the elaborate fiction about being a household from Alsace." Susanna nodded. "Why does this worry you?"

"Because it's likely, I think, that there must be problems in Paris that make even the disappearance of the Rohan heiress and her mother unworthy of the royal attention. Under the circumstances it is good to be insignificant, but I can't imagine what is causing it. The only reason I can think of that the king would not have sent people to find us is that—well, I don't know what may be causing it. How can I even guess, when I am riding and riding and riding in this carriage with no gossip at all?"

Marguerite was not alone.

"I haven't heard a single word of news from the court," the duchess told Candale. "Not a single word since we left Paris. I didn't even manage to buy a measly, out-of-date, provincial newspaper when we came through Auxerre. Raudegen, curse him, says it would not fit with my *persona*. You could get one for me. Even the most countrified of country gentlemen might occasionally buy a newspaper. It's maddening. I just know in my heart that Soubise is ruining everything. The next time I do hear something, it will probably be that Rohan has lost what minuscule remnants of royal favor that I had managed to retrieve for the family."

Candale ducked his head toward the carriage window. "Have you seen those new *kaleidoscopes* that are coming out of Augsburg?" he asked. "Fascinating. When I was in Nancy, I attended a lecture on how they are made. Mirrors, and a few little specks of colored glass. Every design is made with the same pieces, but it changes every time you turn the tube, which amounts to an object lesson on how the court functions. The pieces rarely change, but from one turn to another the picture alters a great deal. The Rohan piece will still be in the little compartment, no matter where it falls at each turn and another turn will always come." He smiled. "Also, I think you underestimate your brother-in-law. It's very possible that a lot of royal interest is currently directed toward the old Rohan holdings in Brittany."

The conditions in eastern France had not changed significantly since Ruvigny and Bismarck had observed them on their first trip to Paris the previous October. The villages were still half-depopulated from plague that passed through the region in the summer of 1635. The road was better than it had been in January, if one considered dust better than half-frozen mud, but it was not better because anyone had been doing maintenance on it. Trade, Marc reported, was down.

Innkeepers warned of wandering bands of ex-mercenaries, most of them men who left Lorraine after the grand duke and the king in the Low Countries started to make a real effort to restore order there. They weren't huge bands of bandits, the townsmen emphasized, but rather mostly small groups, six to a dozen men, enough to steal some livestock or fall upon a farm wagon, but even a small village was safe enough from them if the inhabitants were determined and well armed, which most of them were, since after this many years of war almost every peasant had managed to steal some kind of a musket or take a long-barrel from a former soldier who lay passed out drunk. Never call it theft. The French were law-abiding people. However, the Lord assured his children that He would provide, and if he chose to provide by making soldiers careless with their weapons, who were they to question His will?

"I don't recall," one innkeeper who doubled as a village *maire* commented to Marc, "that I've seen a single probate settlement in this district in the past five to ten years in which the deceased did not have a gun included in his inventory." He looked the party over. "Three women and a child, but also six men, all mounted. Don't worry about them. They won't even think of coming near you."

The ambushers, when they came, were neither ex-mercenaries nor bandits. They were just desperate. The ambush did not take place in a dramatic vale with overhanging cliffs, nor in the face of an oncoming storm. The landscape did not feature abandoned medieval ruins; neither were they lured into it by a piteous cry for help. As Marc would say later, it wasn't an ambush that would furnish anyone with a good after-dinner story. It took place in the middle of the morning, in full sunlight, on the edge of one of the half-depopulated villages. No riders on thundering mounts drove down upon them. In point of fact, they had halted, dismounted or gotten out of the carriages to stretch their legs, and were wandering around the vicinity of the well for one simple reason.

"I have to go," came the cry from the carriage.

"If you ask me," Bismarck commented to Gerry, "he's figured out that having to go is a way of getting out of the carriage and running around for a bit."

"Well, can you blame him? It's not natural for a boy to be cooped up like this. Dad let us run around and scream all we wanted to."

"Even if he is crying 'wolf,'" Marc added, "nobody else has volunteered to run the risk after that interesting episode suffered by M. de Candale the second time the boy rode with him for a while."

"Again! How many times this morning does that make?" Marguerite asked.

"The bright side," Susanna said, "is that at least he doesn't wet the bed."

"Anybody else who needs to go, go now," Raudegen ordered, an implacable tone in his mild baritone voice. He looked at Ruvigny. "I can't believe I just said that."

As a point of fact Tancrède was just behind a hedge, going.

The attackers took out Candale and Ruvigny first. They were standing next to one another, just casually chatting, and got bashed on the head by villagers wielding a couple of pieces of window frame. They didn't get bashed tremendously hard, nothing like a cavalryman with a saber could have done in battle, but it was enough to knock them down and daze them temporarily.

Raudegen turned and, in spite of the practice he had been doing at every opportunity, automatically reached for his sword with his injured hand. Another attacker swept a bladeless scythe handle at his knees.

Bismarck scrambled up, pushed the two duchesses

into one of the carriages, and stood at the door, his weapon out.

Marc, at the well where he had been lowering the bucket to get water for the horses, pulled the bucket up, pivoted, and threw the water on someone's head; then ran to grab the reins of the horses on the front carriage, thinking in a disorganized way that if the riding horses spooked, they'd be able to chase them down eventually, but stampeding draft horses could destroy the carriages before anyone managed to catch them. Susanna came around from where she was standing in the bushes to keep an eye on Tancrède and grabbed the reins of the horses harnessed to the other carriage, the one that the duchess usually rode in. It was a neat trick, since she had to keep holding onto Tancrède with her other hand.

Gerry, still in the coppice where he had retreated for his turn at taking care of private business, pulled his harmonica out of his shirt pocket and made it wail. "Ghost Riders in the Sky" produced a sound effect that bore no resemblance to the plinky little flutelike separate notes he had played to provide the melodies for the extravaganza, even when the instrument was in the hands of an utterly incompetent musician. He hoped profoundly that none of the attackers headed in his direction. He still had his pants down.

Tancrède pulled his wrist out of Susanna's grasp and ran toward Marc at the well. She was about to start after him, carriage horses or no carriage horses, when an appalling shriek arose from behind its low mortared wall, closely resembling the sound of a soul in torment, the drawing of fingernails over a slate board magnified by a thousand, or, perhaps, an untutored six-year-old blowing into a harmonica with all the power of his breath.

With two sets of shrieks coming at them from opposite directions, Ruvigny picking himself up to come into the fray, Candale immobilizing the boy that Marc had drenched with water, Marc demonstrating the usefulness of a small but practical dagger, and Raudegen's now having a businesslike sword in his functional hand, the attackers hesitated and faltered.

Three middle-aged women, a boy who might have been as old as thirteen, two old men, one of them very old indeed, and a scrawny dog.

"We need the horses," one of the women explained. "We just saw you here. It's not that we expected anyone to stop at our well this morning. It's not as if we had time to plan. We just saw you, grabbed whatever we could find, and ran out."

"What do you want horses for? Not to ride, certainly."

"To sell," one of the old men said. "To trade," the other quavered. "To eat," the strongest of the women answered.

There weren't any men. Between the war and the plague, they were gone. Because they were gone, most of the harvest had not been brought in last fall. Because they were starving, they butchered the last ox so that the rest of them might survive the winter, but that meant that this spring they had not been able to plow, but only dug the kitchen gardens with spades, so there would be no grain, not that they had any seed to plant if they had an ox to plow with, because the previous fall's harvest had rotted in the fields, as they had already told milords. The cows had been bred last year; two of the calves had survived, but the only bull calf had died, so there was no prospect of having them bred again even if they waited two or three years, which they had hoped to be able to do. They had no money to pay stud fees to the village three miles over, which still had a bull.

"Yes, we knew we might have to kill you to get the horses," the strongest woman said. "But what more right do you have to be alive than we do? How is it different for you to be dead than for the six of us and the children younger than Jean over there to be dead? If we don't do something, we will all be dead by winter. Eight of you; thirteen of us counting the other children. We could survive for a year, live well for a year, on what you are taking with you on a drive down this road from some place we have never been to some place we will never go."

"You have fine animals," the oldest man added. "Just one of your horses sold in Auxerre would bring the money for a blacksmith to put blades back on our tools, with some left over. The foragers stripped off all the metal. I know how to bargain. I don't walk well, but Jean here could put me on the most docile one and lead us to Auxerre. The price of that one horse would buy us metal for the blacksmith and a donkey to bring me home. Then we would have a donkey."

"Why don't you just leave?" Gerry asked.

"What would we do?" The second man snorted. "We are serfs, yes, and tied to the land, but that means that this land is also tied to us and we have the right to farm it. If we leave, we won't have a right to farm anywhere else. All we know how to do is farm."

❖   ❖   ❖

"We ought to have done something," Gerry insisted that evening. "There was a man who fell among thieves..."

He leaned back against the wall. This inn was surprisingly good for eastern France—clean and tidy, if not spacious. The proprietor, a German from the Palatinate, had managed to get out, with some of his money, enough to buy another inn, ahead of the Imperials back in 1622. He kept chickens and rabbits to feed his guests, a couple of goats for milk, and his wife cultivated a good-sized garden. The village was strong enough to keep random marauders away. Recent events, the death of the king and the troubles, though, had caused him to question his decision to settle in France, but in the end no man could successfully defy the will of God. If he was destined to die a pauper, then he was destined to die a pauper. At the moment, he delivered a second round of beer to the table.

"We didn't punish them. Beyond that, what can a person do?" Raudegen lifted his good hand, counting off on his fingers. "If we left a horse with these people, we would be short a horse and perhaps that would cause us to fail in our charge. If we left a horse in this village, there would still be other villages, behind these hills"—he gestured to the left side of the road they had come in on—"and behind those"—he gestured to the right—"where the people are living in equal misery. You can't help them all. You can't even find them all."

His logic was, in its own way, inexorable.

"I'm wondering about that *maire*," Gerry continued. "The one who told us that all the estate inventories that he recalled included guns. Just how many inventories do you think he's seen, this past year, with the plague and stuff? When it comes to defending their villages, dead men can't shoot guns, even if they owned one when they were alive."

"In the matter of weapons," Susanna gave Tancrède a nudge. "Now, before you have to go up to bed."

"I'm sorry, Gerry." Tancrède clasped his hands behind his back and dropped his head. "I told you a lie, I didn't really lose the harmonica you loaned me. I just didn't want to give it back." He looked up. "That's stealing isn't it? But I took very good care of it. I hid it so that nobody else could find it." He looked down again. "But I almost did lose it, because when Susanna and Marc came to take me away from Paris, I just *barely* had time to get it and stick it inside my breeches."

"You're a hero, kid," Gerry said, his voice rough. "Thank you for being polite and apologizing. That's the right thing to do when you've made a mistake. Keep the harmonica with my compliments. You may need to save the day again some other day."

It was the duchess who took the boy up to put him to bed. She often did, if an inn was decent.

Gerry watched them go. "We've turned into a team, I think," he mused. "We ought to start calling ourselves something. Teams always do in RPGs and comics, or most of the time, at least. I don't suppose that *Teenage Mutant Ninja Turtles* would do."

"What's an RPG?"

"What are those, whatever you called them?"

"One up," Bismarck said with glee. "I've seen a comic. It's like a whole bunch of broadsides bound together."

"Turtles?"

"Hey, Dad was opposed to bourgeois culture, but we went to public school. He didn't try to home-school us or anything. I know just about as much about Raphael and Donatello and Michelangelo and Leonardo as anyone else. Not to mention Splinter. I loved Splinter. He sort of reminded me of Dad."

"Those," Marguerite said, "are famous artists. Not Splinter, whoever he is, but the rest. Italian painters whose canvases cost a lot if you want to buy one from a dealer. Not turtles. I have at least that much education."

"The turtles were named for famous artists. They're still turtles. Mutant turtles."

This required about an hour of discussion. At the end, Gerry was still of the opinion that the name would not do. He looked around the table. "We could call ourselves the Carrot Tops, after Corporal Carrot, but I'm the only one who's really carrotty. The rest of you have more decent shades of red heads."

"What do carrots have to do with red hair?" Susanna asked. "Carrots are white, or sometimes purple."

"Up-time, carrots were orange. Mutations along the way, maybe."

"What's a mutation?"

"Remember what I told you about the turtles?"

Gerry scratched his head. "Now there was some Sherlock Holmes story that Dad read to us. He likes the writings of A. Conan Doyle and his philosophy of reading out loud was that it had to be something that he enjoyed reading, too. The *Red Headed League*. That's it. We can borrow that. Doyle won't mind; he was dead even up-time. Maybe we can make Corporal Carrot our mascot."

"Should we make Cinq-Mars an honorary member?" Marc asked with a grin.

"Why on earth?"

"Well, you said that he did assist us, if only by lounging around backstage and not alerting anyone that Gerry was making off with Marguerite and that the duchess was heading for the hills."

"Since this whole project is basically about who Marguerite is marrying, or not marrying," Gerry said the next evening, "we ought to take stock. What's the status of the rest of us marrying? Maybe we could do one of those mass marriages some day, all lined up one after the other, like the Moonies."

"Moonies?"

Gerry found himself with more explaining to do. "There was this preacher from Korea. I saw pictures in the papers. He'd arrange marriages between men and women who followed his cult and then marry them off to each other, hundreds at a time, all the guys in suits and the women in fluffy white dresses."

"Where was Korea; in America?"

"I thought up-timers were supposed to marry for love!"

"Mass polygamy?"

Gerry rapped on the table for attention. "No, guys. Korea's somewhere south of China. Was then; still is, I suppose. No polygamy; one husband to one wife, but he married hundreds of couples in the same ceremony. And yeah, generally speaking, at least in the US of A, people were expected to marry for love, but we weren't all clones of each other."

"What's a clone?"

"I'm pretty sure that German doesn't have a word for it. Nor French. Nor the folks over the channel in England in this day and age, for that matter. It's like this..."

By the time he finished with that, it was time for the adults go go up to bed.

The next night after supper, he persisted. "Start with Ruvigny. Henri, what are your preferences in a bride? Prerequisites?"

"A dowry—150,000 livres would be nice, but what do I have to offer in exchange?"

"There is sure to be some banker somewhere," the duchess said. "Some *noblesse de cloche*, who would regard friendly ties to the Maison de Béthune as a quite sufficient compensation for a penniless son-in-law."

"*Noblesse de cloche*?" Gerry wrinkled his forehead. "Bell nobility? I've never heard of that. In Rudolstadt, at the Latin school, they instructed us about the difference between *noblesse d'épée* and *noblesse de robe*."

"It's not a legal term like the others," Marguerite said. "It's what you call slang. Wealthy townsmen, rich urbanites, social-climbing *bourgeois*. Men who live within hearing range of the bells in the steeples of city churches."

"Do your best," Ruvigny assured the duchess. "Given the right girl with the right dowry, I'm perfectly prepared to go into matrimony with good intentions and live in amicable fidelity for the next forty-plus years."

"Er! Okay. What about you, August?"

"God-fearing. Ah, nice and plump, if I can take my choice. Ideally with a equally nice dowry."

"Define *nice* in comparison to Henri's *nice*."

"Where I come from, it's a trousseau and usually

about four thousand to five thousand *Thaler*, to be paid in installments, but you have to calculate in the reality that dowries and dowers are hardly ever paid in full. You can use the promissory notes as security for loans, though, even if they haven't been paid out. When collection time comes, the lender has to deal with your father-in-law, because a betrothal contract constitutes a legal obligation. Four to five thousand is plenty if you're farming in the *Altmark*. It wouldn't go very far to support the lifestyle of a colonel, if I ever get that rank. But I'll probably still be a captain when I die or retire, whichever comes first, so the question is moot. I can't afford a wife."

"Candale?"

"Not until old Epernon dies. I can't afford a wife on my own funds and he's too tight to fund another try after the fiasco with the duchess of Halewijn. That cost him a bundle and the family didn't get anything out of it in the end, neither a title nor heirs." He turned to Raudegen. "Anything to contribute?"

"I had one, once. She died a long time ago, in Bayreuth, before I joined the army. The baby was stillborn. My mother arranged it, but everything was all right. Our families were friends and we were friends. There wasn't any money involved because all of us were refugees from Lower Austria and there wasn't any money around. Ferdinand II confiscated everything when he drove the Protestants out." He shrugged. "I'm hardly likely to marry again."

Not even Gerry had the nerve to ask anything on the order of *what was her name?* Raudegen's expression did not invite further questions. He stood up and disappeared in the direction of the stairs.

After a short period of silence, Marc opened his mouth. "I don't suppose you have to speculate much about my marriage." He winked at Susanna. "I give it five years, more or less. But what about you, Gerry? You started it all."

Gerry winked back at him, grinning at Bismarck. "God-fearing is good, but since I'll probably marry a pastor's daughter, it's not likely to be a problem."

"Why a pastor's daughter?"

"Because most of the girls I'll meet will be the daughters of pastors. It's propinquity. It's hard to marry someone you haven't met." He looked at Marguerite and cleared his throat. "Unless you're a member of a royal family or such. Or a Moonie. Plump isn't bad, but I think 'willing to put up with me' would top anything else. I don't have to worry about it yet, because it will be at least fifteen years before I can go looking for a wife—longer, if I keep getting yanked out of school to do this, that, and the other for Dad and Ron."

"Let's set up a wager," Ruvigny said. "Each of us makes up a list of the order in which we think we'll wed, and throws some money in the pot. We'll invest it. Marc can take care of that, or get Cavriani to do it. Then when the last of us ties the knot, or dies unmarried, we'll open the envelope that we deposited with the money, compare the lists, and the winner who was closest to right will collect the pot."

"Great idea," Bismarck said. "As long as it's cash that we get from the investment. A part of the widow's dower assigned to my mother, all specified in the marriage contract, consisted of annual allotments of *Wispel* of rye—nineteen *Wispel* of rye. By the time the last of us marries, that would be a lot of rye piled up."

"What's a *Wispel*?"

"Um." Bismarck ran his hand through his hair. "About twenty-four American bushels, I think."

"What on earth did she do with it?"

"She had it ground into flour and we ate it. Brandenburg is really strong on rye bread. Rye bread, cabbage soup, and pork sausage. That's a meal that breeds up real men."

Every French person in the room shuddered.

"Henri," Marguerite asked. "Do you ever think about Jericho?"

"What?"

"Jericho. It was one the stories that Grand-mère Rohan used to read me from the Bible. When the Chosen People marched around the walls for seven days and they fell down. Then Joshua's men killed everyone in the city except the harlot who helped them and her family. You know it, don't you?"

"I know it."

"Have you ever stopped to think about·La Rochelle? And Magdeburg? The sieges and the sacks? It was the Catholics who were outside the walls. It was the Huguenots and the Lutherans who got massacred. Could God be trying to give us a hint about something? That we're on the *wrong side*, maybe? Is that why God let Louis's armies defeat Papa and Uncle Soubise and send them into exile?"

"Trust me, little seed pearl. If God talked directly to Tilly or Richelieu, nobody heard him." *This is way above my pay grade*. "Ah, who else have you talked to about this concern?"

"Nobody. Nobody ever listens to me. Hardly anybody

else ever listens to me at all, and I couldn't very well ask Susanna, because she's Catholic. And she doesn't know any more about her religion, honestly, than I do about mine. As far as I can tell from things she's said, not discussing theology but just talking about how she lives, for her it's mostly habits and actions; smells, sounds and colors. Habits of going to mass on certain days, actions like the incense censers going down the aisle and smells like the incense burning in it; sounds like the bells they ring with the incense; colors in the stained glass windows and the idolatrous statues of the saints. And, especially for her, because she loves fabrics so, the brocades and tapestries, the embroideries and laces, on the paraments and vestments. She's used to it and when she goes to church it's like she is pulling a warmed blanket around her on a cold day and cuddling in. Calvinist churches aren't cuddly."

"They aren't supposed to be cuddly, little daisy. They are designed to be spare, to focus our minds on God's Word as expounded from the pulpit."

"I'm not sure that Susanna even connects what Richelieu and Tilly did with what she feels when she goes to mass."

"It has to be tonight," the duchess said to Candale. "I've deferred to your preferences this far, but we're getting too close to Burgundy. Once we pass the border, it will be far harder for us to slip away and getting back out through the grand duke's border posts without being stopped would be a very chancy matter. In any case, the escort I arranged before we left Paris will be waiting for us on this side."

"Assuming that they have arrived in a timely fashion,

which isn't a very safe assumption given the travel conditions I've observed."

"Be reasonable, Candale. They are men traveling on horseback; they won't have had to concern themselves with carriages and the various other delays this party experienced. They've probably been waiting for several days, spending my money on wine."

"Are you still absolutely sure of this?"

"I am utterly sure of this. There will be nothing for me to accomplish in Besançon. I have no connections in the grand duke's picayune little court, the archduchess is Catholic and Italian to boot, and Rohan will keep me sidelined from his concerns. I belong in France, where I intend to see that Soubise does not garner any glory that may still be available for our cause and that we collect every ounce of advantage that we can from the new king's political uncertainties. Even though we have *still* heard no news, there are bound to be political uncertainties. Bah, I hate that German colonel. But even without fresh news, I can be certain that there are political uncertainties because the world hasn't come to an end yet." She took a deep breath. "We evaluate, and we throw Rohan's influence behind the party that appears most likely to triumph. I belong in France, and so do my children."

"On the basis of candid observation thus far," Candale said, "it is not easy to travel with children. It will particularly not be easy to travel with the boy *sans* Susanna. Having him will slow us down immensely— delay us as much going as he has delayed us coming. He can't ride—the plan was that all of us would ride once we rendezvoused. If you bring him, your escort will have to find a carriage again. Marguerite will not

come voluntarily: I'm more than sure of that. In any
case, if you take her, willing or not, Rohan will never
stop his pursuit. Do you want Raudegen, Ruvigny, and
Bismarck on our tails all the way?"

"Tancrède, then. Please Candale? Just let me bring
Tancrède."

They all woke up no more than an hour after the
last of them had gone to bed, to the banshee wail of
a six-year-old blowing on a harmonica just as loudly
as he could. Susanna jumped out of bed and dashed
toward the cot in the corner of the chamber where
he was sleeping. Or, more precisely, had been sleeping. Bleary-eyed, she tried to make out shapes in the
darkness. The harmonica howled again. She scurried
faster, grasped an arm that was much too long to
belong to a child, and bit the attached hand. Hard. A
soprano scream joined the shrillness of the harmonica
as the hand's owner tried to shake her off.

Tancrède untangled his legs from the sheet and
started kicking.

Susanna got an arm around his waist. "Don't kick
me. Kick him. Kick her. Kick the other person."

Marguerite woke up in the adjoining room she was
sharing with her mother and, still half-asleep, managed to light a lantern. The men poured out of the
rooms across the hall, at first trying to break through
the inside bar to the room where Susanna was, until
Marguerite yelled that the door to her room was
unbarred and open, so they could enter through that.
Three of them headed that way, but by the time they
arrived, the intruder was gone through the window
and Susanna remained in possession of the prize.

A few minutes later, the duchess wandered in, clutching together a long, loose cloak thrown over her nightclothes. "What's all the excitement? I had to go to the necessary."

"Are you sure," Marguerite hissed, "that you didn't just find it 'necessary' to pay a visit to M. de Candale's room?"

Susanna unbarred the second door. Candale, who had been standing outside it, came in. "No, she did not. Nor do I think she appreciates your impertinence."

"Just what happened, anyway?" Marc asked.

"I wasn't asleep," Tancrède said. "But I'm not supposed to get up and wander around at night, so I didn't. Not this time—sometimes I do, when I'm at home with the LeBons and know my way around, but I don't know my way around any of these new places. I was just lying there, playing with my harmonica. I sleep with it under my pillow. Somebody opened up the window. I thought it might be an interesting monster, so I just waited. But it was a person and the person tried to pick me up, so I blew and blew and blew and blew and . . ."

"All right," Bismarck said. "We believe you. You blew."

"I tried to make out some trail," Raudegen said, "but whoever it was headed back toward the outbuildings. It's dark and there's just too much of a mess of footprints in the loose dust behind the inn. The best thing to do is for the rest of you to go back to bed. Ruvigny, you stand guard on the ladies' doors inside. I'll take the outside."

"Let me take the outside watch," Candale said, "since I have two hands available. If Susanna's teeth did their work the way she describes, you and he would be evenly matched if he dares to come back, but I will have the advantage."

In the morning he was gone, and so was the duchess.

"I could have told you if you asked me," Tancrède said. "But you didn't. I knew it was the lady I ride with sometimes who tried to take me out of my bed. She smelled just like she always does."

Bismarck predicted the worst possible vocational outcome for all of them if they turned up in Besançon without the duchess. Raudegen, who was, after all, on this particular venture, not responsible to Rohan for getting the duchesses to the duke but rather, along with Marc, for getting Susanna to someplace she would be safe, was inclined to let them go. Bismarck reiterated that Rohan would not like it. In his opinion, it could be a career-ruining event for Ruvigny—well, for him, too—to turn up without the older duchess.

"Not," Marguerite said, "if you bring me. Maybe only career-discouraging or at worst career-transferring. Henri can always go to Grand-père Sully and find another patron. And you work for the grand duke, not for Papa. Well, so does Henri, for that matter. Papa just borrowed you. I doubt that the grand duke will place so much importance on all of this."

Raudegen pointed to Gerry. "What did you tell me the night of the extravaganza? 'If it weren't for bad luck, I'd have no luck at all?' Bismarck seems to be adopting it as his motto."

"Theme song, actually." Gerry played a few notes. "Gloom, Doom, and Agony on Me."

"Up-time must have been a very strange world," Marguerite said. "A world in which people turned deep, dark, depression and excessive misery into a joke."

"Some didn't," Gerry said. "They ended up doing stuff like committing suicide. If Magda and Pastor

Kastenmayer, he's the Lutheran pastor in Grantville, hadn't talked to me, there was a point when I might have done something stupid like that myself after we came home from Rome. A person just has to keep going. It helps to laugh about it if you can. When you can. Sometimes it just all drops down on your head at once, but the rest of the time, you might as well make jokes."

"*Melancholia*," Ruvigny said. "The ancients knew about it."

"More practically," Raudegen said, "we might as well sell one of the carriages here, and those two horses as well. We don't need two carriages without the duchess and it never hurts to have some additional resources. Especially since the duchess took most of the money, but I can't honestly complain about that, since she provided it in the first place. At least Candale was decent enough to only take his own horse."

"Rohan didn't send money to get them out?" Susanna asked.

"Not enough to last Ruvigny and Bismarck in both directions. He expected his wife to pay her own way to join him. She has more money than he does. As for Marc and me, it's been an expensive trip, especially the time in England. We cashed in the last bank draft from Cavriani in Brussels."

"Keep the little carriage," Marc advised. "As we get up closer to the Jura, the roads aren't meant for vehicles at all. We may end up selling it, too, in a couple of days, to someone who's headed out in the other direction."

The grand duke had guards on the Burgundy side of the border where the road crossed toward Dôle.

Unfortunately, the king also had guards stationed on the French side.

Raudegen dismounted, handing his reins to Gerry, and talked to them. He called up Marc, who also dismounted, handed his reins to Gerry, and talked to them. Raudegen produced paper. Marc produced more paper. The guards shuffled paper.

Susanna, looking as nursemaidly as she could, stepped down from the carriage, lifted Tancrède down, shot the guards an apologetic smile, and said, "He has to go."

Gerry trotted after the two of them, leading the horses.

"Hey you," one of the guards yelled. "Come back here." He was speaking French, but his gestures indicated what he meant in any known human language.

Gerry answered. "I'm going that way"—he pointed— "and I'm in plain sight. I'm supposed to keep an eye on the kid." His voice was sulky, his German accent was provincial, and his facial expression indicated that although his body was moving, his mind had never fully caught up with it.

Just a dumb ol' country boy, that's me. He'd seen the role played up-time. He'd seen it played down-time. One of his classmates in Rudolstadt had been a genius of a mimic. He could probably do it in his sleep. He watched Susanna take Tancrède back to the carriage and then ambled over to the guard who had yelled, still leading the horses. "What'ya want?" It was bad *Hochdeutsch* in a dialect that probably couldn't be understood ten miles from the speaker's home village, but it was definitely some variety of down-time German. It was also amiable, cheerful, and unthreatening.

"Go back, stupid." The guard shoved him back towards the carriage.

Tancrède started to screech, in French, of course, "Why are we stopped here? I want to go home. I'm tired. I want to go *hoooome!*" What he truly wanted was to go back to the LeBons in Paris, but there was no reason to mention that to the border guards. Let them assume that "home" was someplace in Burgundy.

One of the senior guards looked up in annoyance and shuffled more paper. Marc walked back to the carriage, stuck his head in, and talked to Marguerite, with much waving of hands. "Marguerite," Tancrède screeched, "I want to go home!"

None of the alerts that the guards had received from Paris said anything about a child and they were supposed to be watching for an older woman and a young one, not two young ones. The alerts mentioned two army officers, but said nothing about four red-headed siblings from Alsace. They didn't even adumbrate the *personas* of a bodyguard and assistant steward, though, naturally, no sensible man would send a young woman he cared for out traveling without such precautions. After more shuffling, the lieutenant handed the papers back to Raudegen and motioned them through.

Bismarck flicked the reins in a disinterested manner, stuck his legs out straight as far as they would go, and slouched his shoulders, about as far away from the image of a smart city coachman as a driver could be unless he was in charge of a donkey cart. Raudegen and Marc climbed back on their horses. Gerry climbed back up to ride postilion. Ruvigny prayed that the two extra horses tied to the carriage, the one that Gerry usually rode and the one Bismarck rode when someone else took a turn driving, would be taken for spares. It wasn't as if they were highly bred chargers. In accordance with the party's original fairy tale, they were just utility horses, the kind that could be used for pulling something light or a servant could ride if he needed to keep pace with his betters. Only Raudegen and Marc rode halfway decent mounts and they were no prizes.

Ruvigny rode ahead of the carriage and Marc next to it, with Raudegen bringing up the rear. Ruvigny was well into the space that separated the two sets of posts when Bismarck brought the carriage up to pass through. Suddenly, one of the indolent-looking guards gazed lazily into the window, stopped looking lazy at all, and cried out, "Stop them! I've seen that girl in Paris. She's the one we're looking for." He leaped to grab the collar of the lead horse.

Ruvigny started to turn back, but was blocked by another of the French guards. Bismarck jumped off the bench and onto the shoulders of the soldier who was gripping the collar. Marc, from the other side of the carriage, leaped off his horse and onto the bench, to take charge of the reins. Gerry, like a monkey, climbed up the back of the carriage, across the roof, and came down on another soldier who was heading toward the collar of the other horse. Raudegen yelled, "Go!" and Marc went, right toward the Burgundian border post. Not very rapidly, though, since each horse had a Frenchman on his collar, each Frenchman had a limpet on his back, trying to pull him off the collar and in the opposite direction, and the spare horses had no idea what was going on and were inclined to dig their feet in and refuse to move at all. The speed of Marc's brave steeds was more comparable to that of two snails than to that of the legendary Pegasus as they dragged their burden along toward the border of the Grand Duchy of Burgundy, inch by reluctant inch.

Two of the soldiers grabbed guns from the guard-house. Old guns. Functional, but not the modern design. Those went to Turenne's army—not to undistinguished infantry companies in regions of the country where nobody expected anything to happen right now. Of course, the officers here kept their men drilled. Something might happen here someday, just not in the immediately foreseeable future, and the French military establishment was in a constant budget crisis. Wherefore, they had to go through the whole, by current standards stupendously, excruciatingly, slow, routine of getting them ready to shoot. Which they did precisely as they had been trained to do. They might be on the far edge of what was happening, but their officers knew that could always change and some day they might be, on very short notice, *in medias res*. There was no such thing as a stable front in seventeenth-century warfare. Armies moved around.

They aimed at the carriage. One shot grazed the flank of one of the spare horses, who reared and broke his lead, but not before slowing the progress of the carriage even more. The other man might well have made his shot except that Bismark, taking advantage of the delay caused by the slow fuse, dropped off the soldier he had been pulling down and ran directly toward the muzzle of the gun.

Raudegen's horse didn't like any of this noise and confusion at all. He'd wrapped the reins around the wrist of his very incompletely healed hand, but that didn't give him much control, and he'd had very little time to practice using his sword with the "wrong" hand since they left Paris. The horse refused to come around, much less move in the direction of loud noises. Raudegen threw the sword.

It didn't hit the shooter. No reasonable man could have expected it to, under the circumstances. It did flash by the side of his head, into his peripheral vision, the light reflecting off its blade, just close enough that he closed his eyes and flinched a few seconds before he was ready to pull the trigger.

The shot would have hit the carriage, right where Marguerite was sitting. If she had still been sitting there, that was. She was on the floor with Tancrède. Susanna was on top of them. The carriage wasn't very large.

It did hit Bismarck, but, thanks to the flinch, not quite in the chest.

Marc got the carriage onto Burgundian soil. Gerry dropped off the second soldier who had been hanging onto a horse collar, landing on his rear end with a thump. The soldier dropped off in turn, landed more adeptly, and ran back toward French soil before the Burgundian border guards could catch him.

The rest of the escape party, being no fools, did not remain to conduct a brave and valiant rear guard action. They scrambled after the carriage as fast as they could, Raudegen dragging Bismarck, with his good hand, by way of a firm grasp on the other's collar. He left the sword behind. It was just an ordinary sword. He could buy another one.

"You're an idiot, you know," Ruvigny said bracingly while Gerry patched Bismarck up. "Normal people don't run directly at guns. At least not when they're on foot. We're all a little strange, I suppose, in that we've chosen a profession that causes us to run right out to get shot at, but we do it on horses, while we're wearing armor. The infantry on foot don't normally charge guns. At most, they just stand there and take it, hoping that one of the balls doesn't have their number."

Gerry, although he was stoically continuing to swab the wound out, was going from pale to greenish. Ruvigny turned to him. "How did you do it? Tricking that soldier into thinking you were a down-time peasant when you're an up-timer."

Gerry fought down his gag reflex. "Think about it. I was twelve when the Ring of Fire hit. I've lived nearly a third of my life down-time. Most of that time, I've been going to school with either a majority of down-timers in Grantville and now at the university in Jena or to a school where *everybody* else was a down-timer when I was at the Latin School in Rudolstadt."

He rearranged the tools he was using to probe at Bismarck's shoulder. "This is going to take a surgeon, you know, once we find one."

After that bit of drama, the rest of the trip to Besançon was just a slog.

— Section V —

Besançon

Rohan was not happy, but he was pragmatic. "Has she resumed her liason with Candale, then?"

"I wouldn't put it past her," Marguerite said.

"I saw no sign of it while we were still in Paris

last summer," Ruvigny shook his head. "He was rarely around. On the way here, he shared a room with the other men every night."

"It's probably political, then, but that's really neither here nor there." Rohan looked at Raudegen. "I'll have a letter ready by morning. With Bernhard's approval, if he will agree to continue to second you to me for a span of time, you will be on your way back to Soubise shortly thereafter. He needs to know that she is out there, somewhere, spinning her intrigues."

"You have probably been receiving more information here, through the radio connection to the USE, Your Grace, than we did the last two weeks we were in France. Do you have any sense where they might have gone?" Ruvigny asked. "We speculated, of course. Brittany? Back to Sully? To the USE to negotiate La Valette out of captivity?"

"Back to Paris to make Uncle Soubise's life miserable," Marguerite contributed. She paused. "Why don't you divorce her, Papa?"

"No." Rohan shook his head. "I won't say never, but not as long as your grandfather is alive. I respect and admire him more, perhaps, than you can believe. In my estimation, Sully is one of the greatest men of our age with perhaps the greatest of political visions."

"Do you believe, Henri?" Marguerite asked.

"Believe what?"

"The teachings of John Calvin. The tenets of the faith. What the theologians write and the preachers say?"

"How come you ask?"

"Because Susanna believes, I think. Bismarck believes. Gerry believes, in his way. But I'm pretty sure that Uncle

Soubise does not believe, really, nor Papa even. Nor Maman, at least only that God's favor has not fallen upon her and she is predestined to damnation, so she might as well do as she pleases on the way there. Do you believe?"

"Sometimes . . . sometimes I think that we—Rohan, Sully, Coligny, Bouillon, the great Protestant houses and their clients—have been placed in France to defend the faith of those who do believe." He paused. "I am prepared to expend my life's blood defending the right of Huguenot believers to follow their convictions, without forced conversions, without expulsions, without confiscations. Is that belief? Make of it what you will."

Ruvigny was standing, his back against the wall.

"I hadn't given it enough thought," Rohan said to Marguerite. "Here you are and your presence will completely disrupt my bachelor household. You must have a mature woman as your companion, since the duchess did not come. How many ladies-in-waiting will you need? A personal maid. A chambermaid." He ticked items off a list as he muttered. "It's already September. There's not a lot of time left to bring suitable persons here."

"If I may speak, Your Grace," Ruvigny said, "you no longer have close personal ties with the major Huguenot families, and the constellations at court are changing every day. You can't be sure that any woman you bring from France won't be acting as an agent for Gaston. Or for the now-diverging interests of her own father and brothers. Or for the duchess, as far as that goes."

"Then what do you recommend? She can't stay here without a proper establishment."

"Temporarily, borrow someone from Archduchess Claudia."

"Her attendants are Catholic. Well, mostly—she has accepted a few Protestants as a concession to the grand duke, but they are all Lutheran." Rohan chewed on his upper lip for a moment. "As for that, this girl who traveled with you . . . she's Catholic, isn't she?"

"Betrothed to Cavriani's son." He steepled his fingers, briefly considering the relationship among the downtime equivalent of lies, damn lies, and statistics. "So it is possible that her Catholicism may be interpreted as a temporary or interim condition. We should certainly behave in such a way as not to discourage her from converting if or when the possibility should arrive. In addition to that . . ." *Ah*, he thought to himself. *What would we do without the subjunctive case?*

"I know Cavriani. I enjoy conversing with him. However, I'm never entirely sure whether I'm on solid rock or shifting sand when I'm dealing with the man. Still . . . oh, well, yes. The girl can stay in Marguerite's household until Cavriani sends for her and Marc. That doesn't reduce the need for suitable Calvinist attendants."

Rohan did not fully understand why they were all in his conference room. Why were all of them taking such an interest in Marguerite's marriage? It wasn't as if, aside from Ruvigny, they were Huguenots. The up-time boy had even stuck his hand up in the air and replied, "Present," when he called the meeting to order.

"Now, as to the Catholic nonentity to whom the crown married her according to the up-time encyclopedias, impelled by Anne of Austria and Cardinal Mazarin: he was a terrible *mésalliance* to be forced on the ducal house of Rohan. They married Marguerite off to a minor Poitevan nobleman, merely a *seigneur* with not even a title, of no special fortune. Nonetheless, I am having difficulties in locating matches of suitable rank among the Calvinists. Rupert of the Palatinate is out of play. Or even among the Lutherans." He slammed his hand on the table, palm down. "By now, my minimum requirement is a *Protestant* nonentity."

"Don't pick a dumb one," Gerry advised. "It's like breeding horses, if you don't mind my saying so, Your Grace. Look at every single one of the possibilities and ask yourself, 'Would I mind having a grandson just like this guy?' If your answer to yourself is, 'I'd rather have a pig,' then he's not the right choice, no matter how many political connections his family has."

"So," Bismarck said. "One requirement on the list is, *smart*."

"Smart, kind, and reliable," Gerry qualified. "You can vary the proportions but you need all three of those. At least, if you're honestly trying to make a decent marriage for her, Your Grace, and not just using her as a pawn in your political games."

Ruvigny looked at Rohan uneasily. People, at least most people, didn't say things like that to dukes. At least not more than once.

Rohan ignored the up-timer completely, going back to his original train of commentary as if the boy hadn't said anything. "Not one of these possibilities is acceptable." He slammed his hand down flat on the table again. "I can't identify a single French nobleman of suitable rank who would place Rohan first. Not with any certainty. And she needs someone to be Rohan for her." He frowned down at the papers in front of him.

"I'm here, you know," Marguerite grouched at her father. "Sitting right here at the table."

Gerry, blithely indifferent to the peril in which he kept placing himself, ignored her and kept on talking to the duke. "Yeah, I can see that, Your Grace. Politically, I mean." He gestured toward Marguerite with this thumb. "For some important guy, she'll just be a territorial annexation, so to speak. Land and money walking on two feet, to add glory to him. The tail that some dog would be wagging. As an even better analogy, she'll be a commodity on the futures market and her husband will be speculating that she'll retain her value—survive childbirth and not have anything happen to cause the French crown to seize the Rohan estates."

"There's a story that Gerry told me and the young duchess," Bismarck whispered to Ruvigny. "About some emperor and some new clothes and a child who calls it just the way he sees it."

Gerry was still full steam ahead. "But some unimportant guy doesn't have the clout you want." He leaned back. "Maybe there really isn't anybody suitable. Like there wasn't for Queen Elizabeth of England last century."

Bismarck shook his head. "She needs a husband. On that, I agree with the duke. Otherwise, she won't have the heirs she needs. That Rohan needs. That queen of England got it wrong. She'd have been better off to find some guy, even if he wasn't ideal, and have a half-dozen kids, than let Mary of Scotland's son take the throne after her."

"I'm here, you know," Marguerite grouched at Bismarck. "Right here at the table, guys."

Gerry glanced at her. "Yeah, I know you're here, but I wouldn't count on any of them—your father and his advisers—listening to you. Face facts. It's not as if you actually have any say in the matter. Not even if you think you should or I think you should. You know all of us guys in the Red Headed League better than you'll have a chance to know the man you eventually marry before you have to stand up in the church to say 'I do.'"

He turned back toward Rohan. "But why does any guy you pick to marry her have to be Rohan for her at all?"

The duke popped his head up from studying the papers. "What do you mean?"

Before Gerry could answer, Bismarck gestured. "Why can't she be Rohan for herself? She has us, Your Grace, if Grand Duke Bernhard will accept our resignations in your favor. Just give us a few years. Ruvigny for her Secretary of State, so to speak. Raudegen, when he gets back, as Chief of Security." He nodded at Marc. "Head of the intelligence service." At Susanna. "The voice of common sense I suppose. I nominate me for her commander in chief." He started to nod at Gerry. "Uh, chaplain? You could always convert to Calvinism. I'll have to if I become her general. It won't be that complicated—the Brandenburg Electors are Calvinist already: they just didn't force their subjects to give up Lutheranism, but they'll be pleased enough if one of them does. She'll have your whole Red Headed League, with Raudegen and Marc as bonuses."

"Nope," Gerry preempted him. "I'm going to be a *Lutheran* pastor and as soon as this is over, I'm going back to Jena. *Finally!*"

Marguerite looked at him. "Are you sure?"

"I am, Your Grace. I know who I am and I know what I am. Out at Lothlorien, where I grew up, we had lots of vinyl LPs and a lot of those were Pete. He sang it, 'Keep your eyes on the prize.' You have to hold on and keep an eye on where you're going. And there was Horton."

Nobody else in the room had the vaguest idea what either vinyl or and elpee might be. This wasn't Grantville. It wasn't even Magdeburg or Bamberg. Neither did they know who Pete might have been. Nor Horton.

"Horton?" Marguerite asked.

Rohan tried, though. "Horton. Frau Dunn's late husband, the one who was involved at Suhl. You know the up-time nurse that Grand Duke Bernhard brought here, don't you? She prefers that we not speak of him."

"Not that Horton." Gerry nodded his head. "The other Horton. 'I meant what I said and I said what I meant.' *That* Horton—the elephant who was faithful, one hundred percent."

Rohan finally broke the ensuing silence. "A fable perhaps, similar to those composed by Aesop?"

"I tell you," Gerry said. "We had a lot of books out at Lothlorien, but Dad bought them at yard sales and flea markets, so they were pretty beat up. So we didn't give them to the State Library. They're still out at the dome. I'll have Ron go find Horton for you, when he hatches the egg and when he hears the who. 'A person's a person, no matter how small.'"

Murmurs of translation fluttered around the table, along with the making of lists of topics to be investigated further.

Bismarck thought that even though Gerry had so casually refused the jocularly offered ducal chaplaincy, a prize which almost any cleric of any denomination would grasp with both hands, there might yet be, in the form of this scrawny, unprepossessing, boy, someone, finally, who would give thought to providing a moral compass for a girl who certainly would need one. Still . . .

"*Are* you sure," he asked Gerry after the others left, "that your true desire is to serve God for pure love of him? Are you sure that you aren't trying to atone for what you see as your own unforgivable transgressions by following this path, relying on works rather than faith and grace? Are you sure that you aren't following the same mistaken path that Luther took when he vowed to become a monk?"

During the last course of that evening's dinner, Marguerite leaned her chin on her hand and asked dolefully, "Do any of you care what I think about it? Anybody? How can I be Rohan for myself if nobody listens to me?"

"I'm listening, little daisy. What do you think?"

She sat up straighter. "Don't indulge me in that soothing voice, Henri. Do even you *really* want to know what I think?"

"I do." That was Bismarck.

"Me too." That was Gerry.

Susanna and Marc waved from the other side of the table.

"Well then." She pushed back her chair and stood up. "If Papa won't divorce Maman and marry again to have more heirs, *I think* that he should make

Uncle Soubise get married. He can put on 'crusty old bachelor' as what Gerry calls his public face as much as he wants to, but he's several years younger than Papa—not too much past fifty. If he had children, then it wouldn't all depend on me. And it shouldn't all depend on me, because I'm a girl."

"Girls can do things for themselves," Kamala Dunn, the up-time nurse who had joined them for dinner, began with the almost automatic up-timer's reaction. She started to say more...

Marguerite pressed her hands together. "I know that I'll have to marry the man Papa chooses...and...and get pregnant...whether I want to or not, because it's my duty under God. If my husband is kind, like Gerry said, then it shouldn't be so bad. But what if I die in childbirth, the first time? What if the baby dies with me? What will become of Rohan then?"

Nobody answered.

She reached up blindly, clasping the wall tapestry behind her in her left hand and squeezing it into pleats. "What if I'm like Maman? What if I become pregnant time after time after time and I watch the babies die? And die, and die, until my husband tires of it and says no more, so that I will know that God has cursed me because I have failed in the only reason women are on earth, to give male heirs to their husbands? And then she had Tancrède, after Papa said there would be no more childbearing, and he was a boy and was healthy and he lived and she thought it was a sign that God had forgiven her for being a daughter of Eve, for as the preachers say, the pains of childbed are God's retribution on us for her sin?"

Marguerite's voice rose higher and higher in a pathetic wail. "So Maman loves him and she at least tried to take him with her when she went her own way this time, but she left me behind. She didn't even *try* to keep me. She just left me behind."

Letting loose of the tapestry, she sank back down in her chair. "But I am a daughter of Eve, too, so my babies will die and die, and the preachers will tell me that I must humbly accept God's will. And then there will still be no more Rohan!"

She looked at them, almost desperately. "Do you know what it's like, to have your brothers and sisters die, and die, and die?"

Bismarck shook his head. "Our family has lost none."

"Nor ours," Gerry said. "Presuming that Frank and Giovanna are okay, that is. Wherever they are by now."

"Yes," Susanna said. "I'm from my father's second marriage, so I mostly didn't see it. But almost all the children of my father's first marriage have died, seven out of eight. I remember two of them besides Maria, who is still alive. My full brother and sister also died. I barely remember them at all—I was just four when Ercole died and five when Lucretia's time came. It's my half-brothers Giuseppe and Gian Armando that I miss. I was eight when Seppi died and twelve when the smallpox took Mando."

Ruvigny bowed his head. "You know that only Maximilien and Cirné died. Max was already in the Royal Guards. The other four of us are fine."

Gerry thought of slipping out, but the radio room was at the top of the citadel. No reasonable person would climb up the citadel in the dark if he didn't have to. He'd try tomorrow.

Which he did, really, really, the first thing in the morning, Ron wasn't home, but he got a response from Missy.

"At *this* hour?"

"It's important. Honestly."

"Oh, all right. I'll trek over to the State Library, see what I can find, and get back to you."

He waited for an hour an a half for the response, climbed back down the path, and then wandered into the breakfast room.

"You know that Catholic nonentity your father keeps harping on, little duchess?"

Marguerite, who had been staring miserably at her griddle cakes, raised her head.

"He wasn't entirely useless. You had six kids. Four of them lived and had kids of their own. I don't know why the duke didn't think to mention it to you. He obviously has that same article about your family from the EB1911 that Missy just looked up for me, or he wouldn't have known who your husband was."

Marguerite pursed her lips. Her eyes lit up with new interest. "Who *was* he?"

"Uh. I forgot to ask her."

From: Gerry, in Besançon
To: Ron, in Grantville

Dude, just a second thought. When you go up to Lothlorien to hunt for those Dr. Seuss books I asked you to send, can you dig out *Yertle the Turtle*, too? I'm pretty sure we packed it in the same crate. I'll give it to Ruvigny and Bismarck to think about. I'm not sure the rest of these guys are anywhere near ready for Yertle yet, much less Max.

And if Pratchett's *Guards! Guards!* is in there, send it, too, please.

Say hi! to Dad and Magda for me, if they're around instead of off somewhere saving another section of the world.

Greetings and salutations and all that, Bro. See you soon, I hope.

                                        Gerry

"Don't let Maman get custody of Tancrède," Marguerite warned her father. "She's an *intrigante*. She'll try to use him, somehow. Don't let Candale have him, either—that would be tantamount to letting Maman have him." She bit her lip. "Especially if you do die in two years, my lord father, which I most sincerely hope that you do not."

"What are you thinking?" Ruvigny pushed away from the wall.

"That she might use him to become regent of Rohan for a far longer time than she will be if I inherit. I'm almost nineteen."

Bismarck looked doubtful.

"She could, you know. Now that I am out from under her control, if she has Tancrède she can invent some fairy story about how he is a legitimate heir. She could peddle it to his advisers as how she and Papa hid him, for fear of the evil machinations of Richelieu. Now, under the magnanimous generosity of a new monarch, there is no reason to fear. She can bring him out of the shadows into the protection of the royal sunlight. I could practically write it myself, and Benserade most certainly can write it. Heroic. Sentimental. Shocking. Touching. The Epic Poem of the Protective Mother and her Defenseless Son."

Marguerite flicked her finger. "With a chorus of lawyers. If nothing else, Papa, if you are so sure in your heart that you will die soon, then put a very explicit, unmistakable, unarguable statement into your will that the kid is a damned bastard and no way and under no circumstances should he be acknowledged as your heir."

"He should be safe from her right here," Rohan said. "Or safe from her ambitions, which amounts to the same thing."

"I won't have him here." There was a certain air of focused menace slithering around the room. Most of it was slithering out of Marguerite. "I won't have him in my household."

"It's my household," Rohan pointed out.

"I won't have him in any household where I am."

"We can't send him back to LeBon in Paris," Ruvigny pointed out. "If Gaston's supporters get hold of him . . . That would cause more complications than even the improbable scenario that you are predicting, my panicked little puppet. I had planned to take him up to Leiden. Board him anonymously with a university professor who would bring him up to be a specialist in ancient linguistics or something," Ruvigny said. "It was an actual plan. It was a workable plan before everything went sour in France."

Marguerite glared. "I take it that you developed this plan before you actually met the little demon."

"I do agree," Bismarck said, "that he scarcely comes across as a prime candidate for a career in Babylonian linguistics or anything of the sort. I don't think the sciences would be a prudent choice. I hate to think of what he could achieve in an alchemical laboratory."

Gerry cleared his throat. "We can take him." He waved his hand vaguely. "Marc and I. We're leaving anyway. We can take him with us."

"Why?" Rohan asked.

Gerry looked at Marc. There were limits to what you ought to say to a duke and he had reached his.

"He means," Marc said, "that we've got something that as far as we can tell is pretty much missing in the whole French upper class. We both have fathers, good ones, with experience in bringing up boys. Either one would take him—Dr. Stone or my dad."

"I think that Magda would *like* to have a kid," Gerry said. "It looks as if she's not going to have any of her own. But she's Lutheran, like me. If you want him brought up Calvinist..." His voice trailed off.

"Then I can take him to Geneva," Marc inserted. "Being a Cavriani will probably be enough to keep him busy when he grows up. Um. I agree with August that he's not likely to turn into a pedant. Being a Cavriani is enough to keep even a kid as energetic as Tancrède busy."

He thought, *enough to occupy even a boy as naturally ambitious as the child of a certain sneaky French count and that conniving French duchess is likely to grow up to be.*

He didn't say it, though. Instead, he looked at the younger Marguerite. "Busy enough that you won't always have to be thinking of him as a threat just over there on the horizon—on the margin of everything else you have to think about."

Ruvigny nodded. "Busy, and well out of the way of anyone who might be considering how to use him as a pawn in some power play." He thought of the elder Marguerite. His voice firmed up. "Anyone at all."

"I should stay here," Susanna said. She and Marc were standing in a not-very-busy hallway, his arms around her waist and hers around his, their foreheads resting lightly against each other. "Not go with you. Here as the dressmaker for the duchess. I should work for *la petite Marguerite*. Not Archduchess Claudia."

"Why?" Marc tried for a judicious, impartial, tone of voice. He wanted to take her with him. To Geneva or wherever came next.

"Because I haven't learned enough," she answered. "Brussels was a very Catholic court. It's just as Catholic as Vienna was, at least when you're down in a dressmaker's workshop. When you're there, you know that the alliance with Fredrik Hendrik exists, but it's really kind of abstract. You don't see it or experience it. I never went up to Amsterdam or Rotterdam or . . . or Leiden, or . . . the Hague. Not to any of those northern cities. So I need to be where I'm working directly with Calvinists. To find out, you know, if I can stand living among Protestants. The way you found out in Naples whether you could stand living among Catholics. See what happens with the grand duke and Archduchess Claudia, now that they have a child." She wrinkled up her forehead.

"I'm not sure how much you will learn about living among ninety-nine point nine nine percent of the world's Calvinists by working for the little duchess," Marc said. "I don't think anyone could reasonably describe the Rohan family as typical of the breed.

You could just come to Geneva with me. It's full of Calvinists."

"All of the ladies in Geneva wear black dresses with white collars."

"There is that problem."

"So the little duchess is better than nothing. Even if the Rohans are not typical, I will meet their associates."

Marc lifted his head and nodded. The nod was affirmative. Reluctant, but affirmative.

"If Rohan agrees to having you in her household longer term, then all right. I'll be back."

He was thinking, *no, no, we've agreed to take Tancrède to Geneva and we'll be doing it without Susanna.*

She was thinking, *serves them right for agreeing to take that kid to Geneva with them and expecting me to babysit him the whole way without even asking in advance whether I'd be willing.*

Since September was often the last month to offer decent weather for fairly easy travel, October if you were lucky and November only if you liked to gamble, Marc and Gerry were off to the livery stable the next morning.

The rain kept pouring. It dripped off Marc's cape, down onto the hand by which he was holding Tancrède. The boy pulled away from his increasingly slippery grasp and dashed into a passageway to which the description *alley* would have assigned undue dignity. It had been swept, but the running water was scouring residual slime from deep between the cobblestones and dropping it into the occasional puddles that formed in low spots. Tancrède splashed through them, uncaring, in pursuit of a feral cat.

Gerry dashed after him, indifferent to the muck landing on his boots and the hem of his cloak.

Marc stayed where it was cleaner. *Mama will be thrilled to have another little boy to bring up*, he thought to himself. *Of course she will.* If he thought it often enough, perhaps he would convince himself.

That Papa would be thrilled went without saying. Ruvigny's "Anyone at all" really shouldn't be interpreted as applying to Leopold Cavriani.

Scarface

Eric Flint

PART I

Magdeburg, capital of the United States of Europe

Chapter 1

December 4, 1635

"Something is happening, Eva. I'm sure of it!" Elisabeth von Schwarzenfels hurried her pace still further—and she was already walking quickly. Any moment now she'd break into a trot, her companion thought with amusement.

Eva Katherine von Anhalt-Dessau reached out a hand and seized Elisabeth by the shoulder. "Slow down, Litsa! I'm too old to keep up with you when you rush about like this."

Litsa glanced back at her and made a sarcastic

noise halfway between a whistle and a hoot. "Too old! All of twenty-two!"

Eva smiled but didn't relinquish her grip. "The difference between twenty years of age and twenty-two is quite significant," she said. "Wait and see! And what's the hurry, anyway? You said yourself we were headed for a meeting in Government House. When did those ever start on time?"

"With Rebecca Abrabanel in charge? And all those in attendance are up-timers except for her? They'll start on time, don't think they won't!"

Litsa had a point. As young as she was, the wife of Michael Stearns—once the prime minister of the United States of Europe and now a general fighting the Poles in Emperor Gustav Adolf's army—already had a reputation for being a formidable political figure in her own right. Eva's brother-in-law Wilhelm Wettin had replaced Stearns as the USE's prime minister, and Eva had heard him tell her sister Eleonore that you underestimated Rebecca Abrabanel at your peril.

As for up-timers, in the few short years since the Ring of Fire they'd developed a reputation of their own. That reputation had many facets, but prominent among them was the American penchant for being obsessively punctual. They even had an expression for it in English which had by now worked its way into the Amideutsch lexicon: "anal-retentive." Eva thought the funniest part of it was the firm belief among the Americans that it was *Germans* who were given to an absurd attachment to order and routine.

Whether she had a point or not, though, Eva wasn't going to let her younger friend force her out of her normal circumspection. She'd been born into one of the most prominent families in the Germanies, which were part of the *Hochadel*—the German upper nobility. That was true of Litsa's family as well, but where Litsa's folk were of fairly modest means Eva's were not. Anhalt-Dessau was a wealthy principality.

But wealth and prominence were no protection against smallpox, which had struck Eva when she was a child. She'd survived, but not without suffering rather bad scarring, especially on her face. Thankfully, her eyes hadn't been damaged. Everyone told her they were quite pretty, in fact. But the same could certainly not be said of her cheeks and much of the rest of her face.

It had been taken for granted by everyone in her family, as far back as she could remember, that because of the pox scars she'd never get a husband despite the dowry she'd bring. Nothing in Eva's own experience had suggested anything different to her. Boys had ignored her completely during her teenage years, and while the same was not generally true of young men now that she was in her twenties, they certainly didn't seek out her company.

So be it. The pox had not affected her mind. She loved to read, and had several close friends among women her age. The worst of her situation, as far as she was concerned, was that the older women in her extended family kept pestering her to enter a women's foundation. That was something she had no interest in doing. For all that she was usually the quiet one in any gathering of friends, she greatly enjoyed their company and their conversation and had no desire to forego them for the sake of contemplation.

Despite her best attempt to keep Litsa to a reasonable pace, the two of them were walking very quickly
when they came around a corner and almost barreled
into a small group of men. Litsa came to an abrupt halt
and Eva had all she could do not to stumble over her.

When she regained her balance she realized that her
friend had become tense. Looking over Litsa's shoulder,
Eva saw that the five men were quite young, except for
one who looked to be in early middle age. Judging from
their clothes, all of them were workmen—and judging
from their scowls, none of them were friendly.

She was suddenly apprehensive herself. As a rule,
the streets of Magdeburg were fairly safe, especially in
daylight. Add to that the weather—it was a clear day,
but a cold and windy one—and neither she nor Litsa
had been worried about being accosted by thieves.

But the main reason they hadn't been worried
about it was because the streets of Magdeburg, particularly here in the vicinity of Hans Richter Square
and Government House, were patrolled by squads
organized by the Committees of Correspondence. For
all that people of Eva's class complained about the
matter, given the political attitudes of the CoCs, the
fact remained that the patrols were quite effective in
keeping crime to a minimum, especially in the streets.

Normally, the worst that people of wealth or nobility might expect from an encounter with CoC patrols
was brusque rudeness—and that was not even a given.
Depending on their leadership, some of the patrols
were quite courteous, even pleasant.

But judging from the expression on the face of
the older man who seemed to be in charge of this
patrol, he was not given to courtesy under the best of

circumstances—which these were certainly not. Ever since the emperor's incapacitating injury at the battle of Lake Bledno, the political tensions in the USE had been escalating rapidly. The Swedish chancellor Oxenstierna was in Berlin organizing what looked more and more like a counter-revolution in the making.

And unfortunately, Eva's brother-in-law was not only the current prime minister but had been foolish enough—such was her privately held opinion, anyway—to side openly with Oxenstierna. She could only hope—

"I recognize the pox-faced bitch," said one of the younger men. "She's one of the sisters of Wettin's wife."

So much for *that* hope. The group of men started clustering around them still closer, and the sense of menace was now quite open.

Eva glanced around, hoping to spot a policeman, but there was none in sight. The capital city's new police force was surprisingly good, when it came to solving crimes and apprehending miscreants. But it was not a large force and made it a point to avoid open clashes with the city's Committee of Correspondence. So the police did very little in the way of patrolling the streets.

The only other people in sight were two men coming around a corner. Given the way their heads were lowered against the wind and their faces completely obscured by the hats they were wearing, she doubted if they'd even seen the confrontation taking place a block ahead of them.

And once they did spot it, they'd almost surely cross the street or turn back in order to avoid getting involved. They would also know that this was a CoC patrol, and very few people in Magdeburg wanted to get crossways with such.

Perhaps diplomacy—soothing words—

Not in Litsa's company, alas. "Why are you imped-ing us?" her friend demanded angrily. "I'm a journalist with *Simplicissimus* magazine here to do a story." She pointed to Government House, visible in the distance. "On . . . something happening in there," she concluded, a bit lamely.

There were times when Eva thought Litsa had the brains of a goose. *Simplicissimus* magazine was not openly hostile to the Committees of Correspondence and the Fourth of July Party, no. But they were not on especially friendly terms with them, either. "A journal of criticism of society and the arts" was the way the magazine's editors had characterized it when Stearns had been the prime minister. And while Stearns himself had maintained a civil stance toward the magazine, the same could not be said for others in his camp.

Certainly not the CoCs! Americans, from the long experience of their own history in that world of the future, tended to be fairly relaxed about political wrangles. The same was not always true of their down-time supporters and adherents.

"*Simplicissimus*, is it?" sneered the older man. "Just another pack of counter-revolutionary shitheads."

"Oh, that's nonsense!" exclaimed Litsa.

Eva decided to try a more deflective approach. "Shitheads, maybe. But counter-revolutionaries? They're much too concerned with fussing over the latest poetical styles—"

That turned out no better. "Shut up, poxface!" said the man who'd recognized her. He stepped closer and raised his hand as if to strike her. "Nobody wants to hear any crap from a Wettin."

Litsa seemed determined to plumb the depths of reckless obstinacy. "She's not a Wettin! She's—"

"Litsa, enough!" said Eva. Explaining to irate plebeian roughnecks that Eva was one of the daughters of the prince of Anhalt-Dessau and only related to Wilhelm Wettin by marriage would hardly be an improvement.

"I said, 'shut up!'" repeated the younger tough. He cuffed Eva with his hand.

She evaded the force of the blow easily enough by hunching her shoulders, lowering her head and backing away. Unfortunately, instead of being satisfied the fellow took another step toward her and raised his hand again.

But that was as far as he got. A hand seized his wrist and pulled him away.

"Easy there, fellow," said a man's voice.

Looking up, Eva was surprised to see that the voice belonged to a stranger. She recognized the broad-brimmed hat, though, because of its distinctive plume. This was one of the two men she'd spotted approaching them earlier. Glancing to the side, she saw that his companion had come to a halt not far from the small group of CoC men.

But her gaze immediately came back to her wouldbe assailant and the man who'd blocked him. Angrily, the tough jerked his hand out of the man's grasp and reached for a dirk belted to his waist.

"I really wouldn't do that," said the man wearing the fancy hat. Oddly, his tone remained cordial—and more oddly still, the expression on his face was an outright grin.

The CoC man started to draw his blade. The man

he confronted brushed aside his buff coat—which Eva
recognized as the informal armor worn by experienced
cavalrymen. Thereby revealing, nestled in an expensive-
looking holster, one of the peculiar American pistols
whose smallish size did nothing to disguise its lethality.
The pistol rested on the man's left hip, with its butt
facing forward, ready for a cross-draw.

"There's an old saying where and when I come
from," said the man in the buff coat. Alerted by the
pistol, Eva finally detected the traces of an American
accent. But it was a very faint trace. The man's German was fluent and easy.

"Don't bring a knife to a gun fight," he said. Then
he rattled off something in Italian, but he spoke too
quickly—that sounded quite fluent also—for Eva to
understand what he said. Her own Italian was passable at best.

Not that the meaning of whatever he'd said wasn't
obvious. His companion was a big man with a dark
complexion and a distinctly non-German appearance.
Although he'd been spoken to in Italian, judging from
his clothing Eva thought he was Spanish. The man
took a couple of steps to the side, opening the flank
of the CoC group. He also moved aside his coat,
exposing a short sword to view.

The Spaniard's expression was one of exasperation.
He replied in Italian also and this time Eva was able
to follow most of it. *You swore off*—something—*and
we don't need*—something something—*business to
take care of, Captain.*

Eva looked back at the "captain." He was quite a
handsome man. Not as big as his Spanish companion,
but very well put together. His shoulders were broad,

his stance was poised and relaxed. His hands were now . . . very still.

Eva had been around enough soldiers to know she was in the presence of a veteran—and it was obvious by the worried expression on the face of the older CoC man that he knew it as well. What had started as a simple exercise in harassing two young upper-class women was becoming a much more dangerous enterprise.

The captain's grin broadened. "But I'm a sporting man!" he said cheerfully, staring at his young opponent—who still had his dirk only half-drawn. "So let's have no talk of gun play. Knives you want, knives it is." And with that he brushed back the right side of his coat and drew out his own—

Knife? The thing was grotesque! It reminded Eva, more than anything else, of paintings she'd seen of old Roman gladii.

"We call this a Bowie," said the captain, as cheerfully as ever.

The young tough's face was now very pale. It had finally dawned on the fellow that the man he confronted was not only much better armed than he was but was also more experienced in real mayhem—and quite obviously willing to prove it.

Eva glanced at Litsa but saw there would be no help coming from her. Litsa had gone from excessive brashness to frightened paralysis.

"Please!" Eva exclaimed. "There's no need for this!" She stepped forward, interposing herself between the two might-be combatants.

The key to resolving the conflict without bloodshed, she decided, was to appeal to the newly arrived American officer. The CoC men were too angry and confused to be able to react intelligently.

"You have the advantage of me, Captain. I am Eva Katherine von Anhalt-Dessau. And you are . . . ?"

He shifted the grin to her and made a slight bow. Just enough to be polite, not enough to lose sight of his possible antagonist. "Captain Harry Lefferts, at your service."

Litsa lapsed into blasphemy. "Oh, dear God!" she exclaimed, her hand now going up toward her throat. "You're . . . *real*?"

Eva almost laughed. Truth be told, she'd thought herself that the "Captain Harry Lefferts" of current folklore was mostly nonsense. Seeing the man in the flesh, however . . .

Maybe not. Glancing at the group of CoC men, she saw that they didn't seem to have any doubts about the captain's *bona fides*.

Very gruesome *bona fides*, in some respects. One of the tales, as she recalled, had Captain Lefferts disemboweling a man in a duel. Judging from the easy way he held his blade, the legend might very well be true.

The man facing him obviously had no doubt at all. Hurriedly, he slid his dirk back in its scabbard and scuttled away a few steps. "I didn't recognize you, Captain!" he protested, holding up his hands.

"And so no harm is done," said Lefferts, as cheerily as ever. He slid the huge knife back into its scabbard and turned toward Eva, then extended his arm, crooked at the elbow. "May I escort you to your destination?"

A rather charming man too, Eva decided. He seemed to have no reaction at all to the scars on her face. That was normal, of course, for young men of her own class who already knew her or had been told what to expect when they encountered her for the first time. But when strangers met her, especially young men, they usually kept a certain distance. The reaction was subtle, as a rule, but Eva had come to recognize it quite well.

But with Captain Lefferts...nothing. That couldn't be from his American origin and upbringing. By all accounts, smallpox had been eradicated in the world they came from.

"We were on our way to Government House," she said, as they started walking.

"What a coincidence," said Lefferts. "So were Vincente and I."

Looking over her shoulder, Eva saw that Litsa had taken the Spaniard's arm and they were following just behind. Farther back in the distance, the knot of CoC men were still staring at them.

She continued to puzzle over the problem, as they made their way to the east. Before long, she decided the best solution was simply to ask.

"You do not seem—what word should I use? 'Dismayed' is too strong. Concerned, perhaps—no, I think the American idiom is 'put off.' By my pox scars."

He looked down at her. "Why should I be? Everyone who reaches adulthood has scars. No way to avoid it. Some are on the outside, some are on the inside."

He looked away, and for the first time since she'd met the man his good cheer seemed to...not vanish, no. But it certainly diminished.

"The ones on the inside are a lot worse than anything smallpox can do," he said. "I'd swap them in a heartbeat. And I might ask you the same question. The scars don't seem to concern you, either."

Eva shrugged. "I've lived with them as long as I can remember. I was very young when I came down with the pox. The scars are a fact of my life. There's nothing I can do about them, so I just ignore them."

That was not really true, though—as the feel of the man's arm under her hand drove home to her. He really was quite attractive, which was simply enhanced by his exotic origin and history. Eva normally ignored such feelings, because she knew they would lead to nothing but disappointment, but she was finding that hard to do with Captain Lefferts.

Don't be a silly goose, she told herself firmly. And, within a short time, long habit and well-practiced self-discipline had brought her wayward sentiments to heel.

They were silent the rest of the way to Government House. Once they reached the entrance and were allowed to pass through by the guards, Lefferts and his Spanish companion took their leave.

"Duty calls, I'm afraid," he said to her. The bow he gave her was a lot deeper than the one he'd done in the street—and perfect in every respect. He might be an up-timer, but he'd clearly learned the ways of his new century. He seemed as fluent in that regard as he was in his speech.

Eva was not surprised. That too was part of the folklore about the captain, and by now she'd come to the conclusion that, for once, folklore wasn't just prattle.

After Lefferts and the Spaniard were gone, Litsa was practically jumping with excitement. "Captain Lefferts! Himself! In the flesh! What did you think of him, Eva? Tell me!"

The young princess of Anhalt-Dessau pondered the matter, for a while.

"I think he's a nice man," she said eventually. "Who would have imagined?"

Chapter 2

Missy Stone leaned back in her chair. The expression on her face was one of calm, impassive deliberation with just a slight hint of sarcasm under the surface.

Her husband Ron wasn't fooled, though. Missy did sarcasm really well. Really, really, really well. As she immediately went on to demonstrate.

"So let me summarize the situation," she said. "Just to make sure I've got everything straight in what I might at first glance confuse with a pile of spaghetti. Or a pile of morons trying to make the Guinness Book of Records for the world's biggest clusterfuck."

She gave Rebecca Abrabanel a little smile. "Do I need to translate that last term?"

Rebecca returned the smile with a serene one of her own. Rebecca did imperturbability really well. Really, really, really well.

"No need," she said. "The meaning is clear enough from the context."

"Fine, then." Missy leaned forward a bit. "The landgrave of Hesse-Kassel, Wilhelm V, who just died fighting the Poles near Poznan, spent most of last year and a good chunk of this one trying to grab a piece of the Rhineland for himself."

She raised her hand abruptly, forestalling any would-be corrections. "Excuse me, I misspoke. Trying to grab a piece of the Rhineland for the glorious cause of Hessian posterity, I should have said. My confusion was probably due to my haphazard American education. Back in the day—high school, I'm talking about—when we referred to 'Hessians' we meant the cruddy bastards who were paid goons for the British crown during the revolution. You know, the ones George Washington—first in war, first in peace, first in the hearts of his countrymen; that guy—thumped in that battle in New Jersey. Trenton, if I remember right."

Ed Piazza winced. He'd once been the principal of the high school Missy had attended and was now the president of the State of Thuringia-Franconia. "I'm glad to see you were paying attention in class."

"Are you kidding? Ms. Mailey taught American history. You goofed off at grave risk to your self-esteem. That woman did sarcasm really well."

"Still does," Ed muttered. "Something else she passed on."

"Unfortunately for the self-esteem of Hessian posterity," Missy continued, "Wilhelm V's heroic efforts came to nothing. Leaving aside, of course, the dead people he left scattered up and down the Rhine in the course of his labors. By all accounts I've heard, his bombardment of Bonn when he had it under siege was particularly relentless and indiscriminate. Still and all—the dead and maimed were mostly peasants and townsmen anyway, with no posterity worth mentioning—the poor landgrave wound up with nothing to show for it. Thwarted at one end by the stubborn citizenry of Bonn and Cologne; thwarted at the other by the unsympathetic attitudes of the emperor and his Swedish chancellor. How am I doing so far?"

Rebecca made a little wiggling motion with her fingers. "Allowing for a heavy dash of editorial commentary, quite well. Do go on."

"So now we come to the present moment. The landgrave's widow Amalie Elizabeth is sulking in her tent—well, palace—because she feels unappreciated by the emperor, who is in no position to assuage her melancholy because he's *non compos mentis*. That means his brains are now mostly compost, thanks to getting bashed on the head by an uncouth Pole who took exception to being invaded by foreigners."

She half-turned in her chair to look at her husband, and then faced forward again to look at Rebecca and Ed Piazza. "And because the USE is on the verge of collapsing into outright civil war and some people—that would be you—want to make sure the landgravine of Hesse-Kassel stays neutral when that clusterfuck gets underway, you think it'd be a great idea if my exactly two months, two weeks and two days old husband pulled up all his stakes—that would be me, among other things—and headed to Hesse-Kassel in order to placate the sullen widow by handing her a freshly minted pharmaceutical industry along with a very hefty bequest to the local college."

"I'd hardly call it a 'local college,' Missy," protested Ed. "Marburg University is one of the top schools in the USE."

"That's like calling the short order cook at what used to be McDonald's—back when it was a hamburger joint rather than a hotbed of insurrection—one of the finest chefs in Grantville. But never mind. I'm nothing if not magnanimous and broad-minded. Which is why there's no way in hell—"

"Hold on, Missy," said Ron. "We're only talking about a year or so. And I can see some up-sides to getting out of Grantville for a while."

Missy gave him a sidelong look that was heavy on slitted eyes and light on newly-wed admiration. "Name one."

"I wouldn't have to deal with Herr Karl Jurgen Edelmann."

Missy's lips tightened. Edelmann was the father-in-law of Ron's father Tom Stone. He was also the man who managed the Stone family's immensely profitable chemical and dye works, Lothlorien Farbenwerke.

Edelmann was a very capable and competent manager. Even an honest one. He was also overbearing, condescending, rigid—and, worst of all, seem to think his authority extended to the pharmaceutical side of the business, a subject about which he knew absolutely nothing and cared even less except in terms of profit.

"Okay, I'll give you that one. Name another."

"We'd both get away from your grandmothers."

Missy now had a frown to match her tight lips. Her grandmother on one side was Eleanor Jenkins; on the other, Vera Hudson. Insofar as a small town in West Virginia had an analog to aristocracy, those two families were at the center—and neither Eleanor nor Vera was prone to forgetting it.

And... Missy had married one Ron Stone, whose actual father was uncertain and whose "family" consisted of the little all-male band of hippies who'd once been Grantville's most disreputable assemblage. The fact that since the Ring of Fire the Stones had become the richest American family in the known universe—only Morris and Judith Roth could compete with them in that regard—was neither here nor there so far as Eleanor Jenkins or Vera Hudson were concerned.

Leading up to their wedding, Missy had fully intended to keep her own last name. Like many spirited American girls born in the last two decades of the twentieth century, Missy would insist that "I'm no feminist" while simultaneously subscribing to at least ninety percent of the major tenets of feminism—a woman keeping her own name when she got married often being one of them.

Besides, it was down-time custom anyway. The Americans had been surprised after the Ring of Fire to discover that the tradition of a wife taking her husband's last name was pretty much restricted in the here-and-now to England. Nobody on the continent of Europe followed the practice.

But, in the end, she'd changed her mind. One too many snide remarks by one of her grandmothers had done for that. "Missy Stone" she'd be—Melissa Maria Stone, for legal purposes—and if the old bats didn't like it they could choke to death on their own spite.

"I'll give you that one too," Missy said. "Hell, it probably counts double."

Ron shrugged. "Look, I'll grant you the Hessians—and please name one down-time ruler who isn't—are obsessed with land-grabbing. But let's not get too high-up-on-our-horsey about it. Up-time foreign relations usually sucked too, whenever practical necessity reared its ugly head."

"Not *this* bad."

"Really?" Ron gave Missy a sidelong look that compared favorably to her own when it came to sarcastic undertones. "Remember how friendly the up-time United States was to the so-called 'moderate' regime of Saudi Arabia? Those would be the guys who had the female half of the population under permanent lockdown and executed people for witchcraft. 'Moderate,' my ass. But they were squatting on lots of oil and that was all that mattered."

He looked back at Rebecca and Piazza. "Fact is, Missy, I don't want Oxenstierna running the show. Neither do you. And say what you will about Hessians, there's a reason we learned about them in the history books back up-time. They can field one of the strongest provincial armies in the Germanies, if they choose to do so. And if a civil war's coming I'd just as soon they didn't—and you don't feel any differently about it. What the hell. We spend a year or so in Hesse-Kassel, get a pharmaceutical industry off the ground so maybe the landgravine will stop fretting over the fact her province doesn't have any traditional heavy industry, and we toss some money at a good university in order to make it a really top-notch one. The two things the Stone family has is lots of money and no big inclination to spend it on ourselves."

He raised his fist and coughed into it. "There'll be some conditions, of course. The top priority has to be creating the best science library in Europe. That goes without saying. We'll need it both for the business and the university."

Missy's expression abruptly shifted. The look on her face was now that of a raptor intently studying a rodent. The young woman had an interest in everything involving libraries. "Best library," she said, waving her hand in a gesture that encompassed...

Pretty much everything. "You can't qualify it. I mean, where do you draw the line?" she asked. "One man's science is another man's art."

Piazza raised his hands in a gesture that readily conceded the point. "Best library, period," he said. "I have no problem with that."

Given that he wasn't proposing to spend any of the SoTF's money on the library, Ed's concession was entirely pro forma. Ron Stone would spend his money however he chose, and he was clearly not a man inclined to deny his wife the occasional trinket. Pair of earrings, Europe's finest library...

"We think the most immediately critical issue," said Rebecca, "is to step up the production of chloramphenicol. The plague epidemic that ravaged Lorraine and other areas along the Rhine this past summer and autumn has largely died down. But that may simply be due to seasonal factors, in which case it is likely to flare up again in the spring."

"That wasn't helped any, of course, by the political chaos in the area," added Piazza. "For which we can mostly thank the king of France's younger brother, Monsieur Gaston."

Plague—any kind of epidemic—was always made much worse if an area was ravaged by fighting. Armies were usually the single biggest vector for disease, not only because the soldiers were carriers but because the destruction they brought with them up-ended whatever medical care might exist in the area. Even after armies left a region, the chaos they created remained.

Ron frowned. "Are you expecting us to operate in

Lorraine? If so, we'll need credentials that will be accepted by whoever's now in charge there—*and* some kind of a reliable security force. By all accounts I've heard, Lorraine's pretty wild and woolly."

"The official authorities would be Duchess Nicole and her new husband, General Aldringen," said Rebecca. "They have the imprimatur of King Fernando in the Netherlands as well as Grand Duke Bernhard of Burgundy. In essence, if not formally, Lorraine is now a semi-independent principality which operates as a joint protectorate of the Netherlands and Burgundy."

Ron grunted. "All of which is a fancy way of saying that Nicole and Aldringen don't have much in the way of an army themselves."

"And neither Fernando nor Bernhard is going to station significant forces in Lorraine because they don't want to risk ticking each other off," chimed in Missy. "And I'm willing to bet that most of what little Nicole and Aldringen have in the way of military forces are stationed where they can best forestall another French incursion. Which is a fancy way of saying that security in most of Lorraine is going to suck rocks."

She gave Rebecca another little smile. "Is that colloquial expression clear in context also?"

Rebecca chuckled. "Quite." Again, she made that little wiggling motion of her fingers. "We have already begun negotiations on the subject with the duchess of Lorraine. She is willing to have you bring your own security force into Lorraine, provided it is not too large. And, of course, provided it is reasonably well-behaved."

At this point Ed Piazza's face displayed a bright smile. "And we've found what we think are the best people to head up the force." He pressed a button on an old-fashioned intercom positioned on his desk. "Send in the two captains, please."

A few seconds later, the far door to the office opened and two men were ushered in by Piazza's secretary. The one in the lead had a large flamboyant hat and a grin that was more flamboyant still.

"You have *got* to be kidding," said Missy.

Chapter 3

Eva had only been in Government House twice. On both of those previous occasions she'd spent all of her time dealing with the officials who regulated housing development in Magdeburg, so that portion of the huge building was the only part of it she was familiar with.

Eva's older sister Eleonore was in the process of completing Wettin House in the capital, and felt that Eva would make a better intermediary with the city's authorities than she would. Eleonore was firmly convinced that all of Magdeburg's officials were hard-core members of the Fourth of July Party and would therefore be hostile to the wife of the leader of the Crown Loyalists. Whereas they might be fairly reasonable when dealing with a younger woman who was only related to the prime minister indirectly.

Eva found the logic flawed, herself. First, because whether or not they were members of the Fourth of July Party, most of the city's officials were just that, first and foremost—*officials*. As such, they had a reverence for rules, regulations, and proper procedure that Eva thought bordered on idolatry. As long as they were presented with the right documents, correctly filled out and witnessed in a clear and legible hand, they were not given to excessive disputation. Eva was well organized and efficient, and while her own hand was good but not superb, her family was more than wealthy enough to employ the finest secretaries. The handwriting of some of them took calligraphy to the level of art.

Secondly and more importantly, she thought her older sister simultaneously exaggerated the partisanship of the city's officials and underestimated their intelligence. She hadn't found the officials she dealt with to be particularly obnoxious. If they held strong political convictions, they seemed to be able to keep them under control when necessary. As for their intelligence, they would have had to be dim-witted indeed not to recognize Eva for who she was.

Faces marked by smallpox scars were hardly uncommon in the seventeenth century. But there weren't that many young women resident in Magdeburg who belonged to one of the premier Hochadel families, since most such stayed out of the capital due to its radical plebeian reputation. With all the various tasks falling to the Wettins and their in-laws, Eva had been out and about the city for months now.

So, between her facial scars and her expensive clothing and frequent appearances in public, Eva was rather well known to the city's officials. Her identity, at least. And if any of them were hostile to her because she was the new prime minister's sister-in-law, she had seen very little evidence of it.

The incident on the street with the CoC patrol had been unusual, and probably due to the recent sharp

escalation in political tensions. In any event, those
had not been officials of any formal government body.

All this she had just explained to Litsa. Who was
her usual unsympathetic self.

"In other words, you have no idea where we should
go. Lot of good you turned out to be." Litsa looked
around intently, as if she could discern which corridor
they should take by sheer force of will.

"You *asked* me to come," Eva pointed out. "I never
said I'd make a good guide for you—and you never
raised the matter."

Litsa ignored her. She pointed down one of the
corridor. "That way, I think."

"Why?" But Litsa was already ten feet away, strid-
ing rapidly.

Eva hurried to catch up. "Why don't we ask somebody in one of these offices? I'm sure they would
know where we could find Rebecca Abrabanel."

Litsa ignored that also. Reaching an intersection,
she hesitated only a split-second before charging down
the corridor to the left. "It's probably this way," she
said, apparently guided by mystical insight.

Eventually, Eva had had enough of her friend's
headstrong charging about. She more-or-less seized
Litsa by the scruff of the neck and marched her into
the nearest office in the corridor they were now found
in. The sign on the door read *Sanitation and Sewage
Department*. She figured they'd have a practical view
of the world if anyone did.

When she and Litsa entered they found themselves in a small chamber whose walls were covered
with shelves holding very official-looking cartons of

documents. There were two desks in the room, both occupied by young men.

The men stared up at them as if they were apparitions. Eva suspected the department didn't get much in the way of passers-by.

"We are looking for Representative Rebecca Abrabanel," she said. "We believe she has an office somewhere in Government House."

The two men looked at each other. Then, back at Eva.

"She *did* have an office here a while back," said the one on the left. "Well...she shared one with two other delegates. But all the members of the House of Commons have moved their offices over to the new parliament building."

The other young man added: "Only people working for the executive branches are still located here." He seemed pleased by that fact.

"The federal offices are upstairs," said Young Man Number One. He pointed with his finger above his head to confirm that "upstairs" meant what everyone thought it meant. Then, pointed to the south with the same finger. "Offices of the province of Magdeburg are that way, on this floor." The finger went to the north. "For the municipality, that way."

"It used to be quite chaotic," said Young Man Number Two. "But no longer." He seemed immensely pleased by that fact.

Eva knew where the new parliament building was located, of course. It had been under construction for quite some time. She went back out into the corridor but Litsa was ahead of her almost at once, rushing toward the entrance onto Hans Richter Square.

Once in the square they turned to the north. Litsa would have been trotting by now if Eva hadn't physically restrained her with a hand on her arm. As it was they were moving at a very fast walk.

"What's the hurry?" she complained.

"She might leave at any moment."

They went past the royal palace, shortly after which they turned into the entrance to the parliament building. There followed some frustrating minutes while Litsa tried to bully her way past the guards to no avail and Eva eventually sweet-talked them into letting them enter, playing heavily on her sister-in-law relationship to the prime minister.

Eventually, they found their way to the office assigned to Abrabanel in her capacity as a member of the House of Commons from Magdeburg Province. At which point they were informed by Abrabanel's secretary, a very formidable-looking middle-aged woman, that the delegate was actually in the very same Government House they had just come from. It seemed she was in a meeting with Ed Piazza, the president of the State of Thuringia-Franconia.

"In his capacity as the head of state of one of the USE's provinces," the woman explained, "Ed Piazza is also a member of the House of Lords. He is thus entitled to an office in Government House which is"—here she sniffed disdainfully—"considerably larger than the one assigned to Delegate Abrabanel, even though everyone with half a brain knows that it is the House of Commons which does all the real work for the nation." She sniffed again. "The House of Lords is just a preposterous holdover from the darkness of the past."

Clearly an adherent to the CoC view of things.

"I will say that at least President Piazza uses his office," the woman added. "He's here more often than not, these past months. Most of the so-called 'lords' never show their faces except on formal state occasions."

Eva thanked her politely and off they went. Right back to where they'd come from.

"Why would Piazza be here more often than he's in Bamberg?" Eva wondered along the way. "He governs a whole province—and probably the most populous and richest one in the USE, at that. You'd think that would keep him busy enough."

"I told you something was up," Litsa replied. "Lots of somethings! Clearly Piazza is here to help organize a counter-revolution against your brother-in-law."

Eva pondered the matter as they went back onto the street and hurried south. She thought Litsa was probably right in her broad assessment, but also reflected the unthinking bias of her class—well, *their* class, since Eva belonged to the German nobility also. But she tried not to let her position influence her thinking; or at least, no more than was probably inevitable.

It would be more accurate, she thought, to say that Piazza was *defending* the revolution against the counter-revolution that was obviously being organized in Berlin—and mostly by Oxenstierna, not Wilhelm Wettin. Eva was by now quite sure that her brother-in-law, once a duke of Saxe-Weimar, had let his own unthinking class prejudices lead him into a foolish alliance with the Swedish chancellor. Everyone knew—well, everyone in the Hochadel who was politically aware, at any rate—that Oxenstierna had never liked

his monarch's acquiescence to the radical attitudes of
Mike Stearns and his followers toward the privileges
of aristocracy. Now that Gustav Adolf was incapaci-
tated by the terrible injuries he'd received in the
Polish campaign, his chancellor was taking advantage
of the situation to carry through what was in fact a
counter-revolution.

Or try to. Eva was skeptical that Oxenstierna and
his followers would succeed.

She rarely expressed any opinions of her own on
political issues, but that was not because she didn't
have any. She was just reticent by nature. Unusually
among her class of people, Eva actually *was* a "crown
loyalist" in the precise sense of the term. She firmly
believed that Gustav Adolf was the best monarch in
Europe—and the best by what Americans called "a
country mile." (An expression she found both charming
and quite accurate, having grown up as a girl in the
countryside.) That being the case, why would anyone
in their right mind think that a chancellor would have
a better sense of what was good for the realm than
his king did?

If Gustav Adolf had decided an alliance with the
Americans and a willingness to accept at least many
of their principles as the basis for forging a unified
Germany were good ideas, Eva was inclined to trust
his judgment. One thing she knew for sure. Say what
you would about the former prime minister Mike
Stearns—and the people around her usually had the
harshest things possible to say about him—the chaos
that had ravaged the Germanies for a decade and a
half before his arrival had subsided a great deal once
he held the reins of power. Eva understood why most

of the members of her class detested the American. But she also understood why so many of the lower classes supported the man. Stearns had kept them *safe*.

Would Oxenstierna—and her brother-in-law Wilhelm Wettin—do the same? Possibly. But she thought it was more likely they'd plunge Germany back into chaos.

A sudden thought caused her to laugh. Litsa looked at her. "What's so funny?"

"I was just thinking..." She waved her hand. "Never mind. Too hard to explain."

It *was* hard to explain. The two of them had just been accosted in the street by a gang of ruffians who, one could argue, had been created by the Americans. And on one level, the argument was true enough. Without the Americans, the Committees of Correspondence would probably never have arisen. But it was ridiculous to think that the Americans had created the anger which produced those committees in the first place. No, for that Eva's own class had only themselves to blame.

However they came to be, the CoCs now existed and could sometimes pose a threat. Eva thought it was significant—certainly ironic!—that when she and Litsa had themselves been threatened, it had not been one of the nobility who came to their assistance but an American.

And not just any American! (That was the part that had made her laugh.) No, it was the legendary *Captain Lefferts*. The one man in the world, even more than Stearns himself, who embodied everything the Hochadel detested about the up-timers.

Disrespectful toward them, even derisive. Brash. Bold. A state-sanctioned criminal, in all that mattered!

Alas, a very successful one. A man who was reputed to have slain a nobleman in a duel and seduced his wife in the bargain! (Several other wives too, according to folklore.)

She had no trouble, now that she'd met the man, believing either side of that charge. He *was* quite charming. Good-looking, too. Eva knew plenty of noblewomen, married or not, who'd be susceptible to the captain, whatever they thought of his political beliefs.

Not *her*, of course.

She laughed again, but this time too softly for her friend to hear. By now, Litsa was half a dozen paces ahead of her.

Eva could hardly claim any great virtue in that, of course. Scarred the way she was, she'd never had much difficulty fending off the advances of would-be seducers. Not any difficulty, being honest about it, since there had never been any, and she didn't imagine there ever would be.

After they returned to Government House, Litsa charged up the nearest flight of stairs she could find. Being a provincial leader of the nation, not the province of Magdeburg, Piazza would surely have his offices on the upper floor.

But which upper floor? There were three, in all. Litsa would have ferreted out the truth by direct examination, but Eva opted for the dull-witted but energy-efficient *let's ask somebody who'd know* approach.

Third floor, as it turned out. She also got directions as to where the office was on the third floor, which turned out to be useful as well because otherwise Litsa would surely have explored every one of the wrong corridors before they found the right one. There turned out to be quite a few.

Finally, they reached their target—just in time to see the door to Piazza's office open and four people emerge.

She recognized the one in the lead immediately, of course. So *this*—whatever it might be—was the business Captain Lefferts had in Government House.

She was quite delighted to see him again. And then, in the way she had, immediately examined the cause of that delight.

Eva had learned the Americans had a term for her state of mind. Not surprising, really, since they seemed to have a term for everything.

Introspection, they called it. The term fit her perfectly.

So, she suspected, did another up-time expression: *introvert.* She wasn't sure about the terms *geek* and *nerd.* She was sufficiently thoughtful, perhaps, but she didn't think she had enough in the way of obsessive interest in any one thing to properly qualify. Eva was interested in almost everything.

She'd ask the captain, she decided. He would probably know, since he seemed to be the exact opposite of whatever a *geek* or a *nerd* was. Certainly an introspective introvert!

Not here and now, of course. She was much too shy to ask him anything personal in public.

Or in private, now that she thought about it. So why had she been so quick to ask him why he didn't seem to be bothered by her pox scars? She'd *never* asked anyone that question before.

By now, Litsa was well into introducing herself to the young couple who accompanied Captain Lefferts and the Spanish soldier, and explaining her mission. Which more-or-less came down to: *tell me everything you know that* Simplicissimus *magazine would want to publish.* She was speaking in English rather than Ami-deutsch because Litsa—as was true of Eva herself—had deduced that the young couple were also Americans from hard-to-define subtleties of posture and dress.

Fortunately, Litsa's English was quite good, if not as good as Eva's own. But as gracious approaches to an interview went, Litsa's reminded Eva of yet another American expression she'd heard: *a bull in a China shop.* She'd had to have the term "China shop" clarified, of course. In her day and age, no one thought of China as the source of fine tableware.

The young couple were frowning at Litsa. They were obviously having some trouble finding the sense in Litsa's torrent of words.

Captain Lefferts suddenly grinned and nodded toward Eva. "Have her explain it," he said. "You'll get a coherent answer. Reasonably short, too."

Litsa abruptly fell silent. She stared at Lefferts, then at Eva.

"Well, tell them, Eva!" She sounded a bit cross.

Eva was mute. Literally struck dumb.

Lefferts shook his head. "This will go much easier over lunch. There's a pretty good restaurant in the basement. Ron and Missy can use the time to continue to lecture me on the subject of prudence and common sense while we're at it."

He stepped alongside Eva and extended his arm again, crooked at the elbow.

"If I may, Your Serene Highness."

Not knowing what else to do, Eva took his arm.

Not knowing else to say, she said: "Is that actually my correct title in English?"

"Well ... More or less. I had to be a little creative because there's no direct equivalent in English for your title. Your father's rank is between that of a *graf* and a *herzog*—what in English would be called a 'count' and a 'duke.' It's usually translated into English as a 'prince'— the same term that sometimes gets applied these days to Mike Stearns—but that's not really accurate."

Lefferts' inimitable grin reappeared. "The exact translation of your title *Eure Durchlaucht* would be 'Your Transparency.' But I thought that would be improper, under the circumstances."

"Oh," she said. For once, thanking her pox scars. Without them, she was sure her face would be bright pink.

Chapter 4

"Okay, Harry," said Ron Stone, after the waiter in the rathskeller had taken their orders. "Why do you want to work as our security guy in Lorraine? That's pretty much the opposite of what you've gotten famous for—and can you do it legally in the first place? Last I heard you were still a soldier in the USE army."

Missy Stone put a hand on her husband's arm by way of a restraining gesture. "Hey, we got company." She looked at Eva and Litsa. "What's happening here is that Ron and I are going to help Hesse-Kassel set up a pharmaceutical industry and we're also going to be visiting Lorraine. For that we'll need a security team and Rebecca proposed that we hire Captain Lefferts for the purpose. Before we go any further, though, would it be easier for you if we spoke Amideutsch?"

"Somewhat," replied Eva. "But I would prefer to improve my English, so please continue."

"Let me work my way backward, on your questions," said Lefferts. "I talked to my boss—that's Mike Stearns, in the real world, screw the formalities—and he gave me the go-ahead to do whatever I wanted to do. As long as I cleared it with Becky first."

Missy frowned. "When did you talk to Mike?"

"A few weeks ago. I went up to see him in Berlin when he brought Gustav Adolf in from Lake Bledno. I then came back to Magdeburg to see what Becky might want me to do."

Eva had a brief moment of disorientation until she figured out that "Becky" was a reference to Rebecca Abrabanel. American nicknames were sometimes peculiar.

"And what did Becky want you to do?"

Harry shrugged. "She didn't really have much. She's already got a security force with those Yeoman Warders who came over from England after they helped us spring everybody from the Tower of London. Being honest about it, they're better at that kind of work than I am." He nodded toward his Spanish companion. "Probably better than Vincente, too."

The Spaniard was frowning slightly. Eva was fairly sure that was simply because he was concentrating on following a discussion in a language he was not very familiar with, not because he was offended by the captain's remark.

"She's actually the one who came up with this idea," Lefferts continued, "after I explained my situation to her."

"Which is what?" asked Ron Stone.

"I need to make as much money as I can, as fast as I can. Given my somewhat limited skill range"—his grin appeared—"superb for what it is, but it's not what you'd call a real money-maker unless I start robbing banks, which I'd just as soon avoid."

Stone was frowning, now. "And just how much do you expect me to pay you?"

Lefferts shrugged. "Whatever you can afford. It's bound to be more than I get from a USE captain's salary. Which I wouldn't have to give up anyway, because I'm still on the army's payroll. Just assigned to 'detached special duty,' like I have been for the last—what is it now?—better'n four years."

"Becky doesn't have the authority to do that," protested Missy.

"No, she doesn't—but Frank Jackson does. And he's cool with it."

Eva puzzled for a moment over the idiomatic term "cool." It meant *agreeable*, apparently.

Missy barked a little laugh. "You UMWA guys! Talk about a mafia."

Lefferts just smiled in response. Eva wasn't sure what "UMWA" or "mafia" meant either. But she'd ask someone later. The comment was obviously a side remark, not germane to the discussion itself.

"You still haven't explained why you need a lot of money," said Ron.

"It's my niece, Julie."

Missy made a little face. "I was sorry to hear about that, Harry."

Ron was looking back and forth from his wife to the captain. He was obviously puzzled. "What am I missing?"

His wife nodded toward Lefferts. "You remember I told you Julie Miller had something wrong with her but nobody knew what it was?"

"Ah . . . vaguely. She's what, now? Three years old?"

"A little over," said Lefferts. "She was born on August 23, 1632."

"Anyway," Missy Stone continued, "she was finally diagnosed a few weeks ago. The poor kid's got cerebral palsy."

Her husband winced. "Jesus," he said, in the casual way Americans blasphemed. "There's no cure for that. I mean, even up-time there wasn't."

Litsa's curiosity was, as always, easily aroused. "What is 'cerebral palsy'?"

"It's what we call a 'neurological disorder,'" Missy explained. "Basically, it's brain damage that takes place before a child is born, for reasons that are mostly unclear. The main symptoms are a cluster of movement problems. They vary from one person to another, but they usually involve poor coordination, tremors . . ." She made another face. "All kinds of nasty stuff. There can also be problems with seeing and hearing, speaking—sometimes even the ability to reason is affected. And some people with cerebral palsy get seizures too, if I remember right."

"And there is no cure?" asked Eva. "Not even in the world you came from?"

"There's no cure," Captain Lefferts said firmly. "But—" He looked at Ron Stone. "That's why I need the money. My niece is going to have cerebral palsy her whole life. But she might be able to live a normal lifespan, have kids, a career—the whole nine yards—depending on how severe her symptoms are and depending on how much care she gets, especially during her childhood. That can make one hell of a difference."

"Yes, it can," agreed Missy. "But..." She shook her head. "Harry, most of the care you're talking about doesn't even exist yet."

"You're right," said the captain. "My sister and her husband looked into it. What Julie's going to need are a pediatrician—"

"Excuse me," said Eva. "A what?"

Lefferts smiled at her. "That's a doctor who specializes in treating children. It's a medical specialty that doesn't exist yet. So are most of the others she needs." He started counting off on his fingers. "Julie will also need a physiotherapist—that's someone who knows how to help people with movement and coordination problems—a speech and language therapist, an occupational therapist, and an orthotist. I had to look that one up myself. It's someone who knows how to make devices to correct deformities and support bad joints."

He sighed and leaned back in his chair. "And depending on whether or not she's got visual or learning problems, she might also need an educational psychologist and a special ed teacher."

He looked at Eva. "'Special ed' is slang for 'special education.' It means teachers who specialize in handling kids with learning disorders."

She nodded. All the concepts were clear enough. But...

"Did you really have people who specialized in all those things?" she asked.

"Yes, we did," said the captain. "But we don't in the here and now—unless someone can generate enough money to make it worth someone's while to learn how to do them. Or at least some of them. If nothing else, I want to make sure my niece gets the best daycare available. My sister Jill's willing to quit her job—she works for Grantville's administration—but she'd rather not because they need the money."

He'd hung his hat on a peg when they came into the rathskeller. Now he ran fingers through his thick hair. "Most of all, I don't want my parents to sell their house—which is what I know they'll do if I or someone else can't come up with enough money to take care of Julie properly. It's right in town so they'd get a small fortune for it."

He smiled crookedly. "What's the world come to when real estate prices in Grantville are like they were in Manhattan or Tokyo back up-time?"

Eva wasn't familiar with Manhattan or Tokyo but she understood the point. The value of land in Grantville was higher than it was anywhere else in Europe, and had been for at least the past year. The town that had come from the future was now Europe's premier tourist attraction—and many of the visitors elected to stay there permanently, if they were rich enough to be able to buy a home or have one built, in the small amount of land that was available.

"That *would* probably raise enough," said Missy.

"Yeah, it probably would. And then what?" asked Lefferts. "My mom and dad have lived in that house since they got married back in '73. More'n thirty years ago, now. They love that house—and they have no desire at all to leave Grantville. Which is what they'd have to do, of course, if they sold it."

Eva was feeling disoriented again. The *Captain Lefferts* of folklore was a man who carried out daring escapades, fought duels, seduced noblemen's wives—half the maidens in Europe, too, if you took the tales seriously—and was either a pirate himself or the bane of pirates, depending on who was telling the story. He was not a man who worried about the well-being of his parents and fretted over providing good care for an afflicted niece.

Truth be told, it had never occurred to Eva before this very day that Captain Lefferts even *had* parents or a family. Adventurers of legend never did, really. They just came and went like disembodied phantoms.

She felt a sudden surge of warmth toward the captain. So she'd been right! He *was* a nice man. At least, once you got underneath it all.

She hesitated then. The solution to the captain's problem was obvious. But Eva was not accustomed to interjecting herself into the affairs of strangers.

Still... Something about Lefferts made it easy for her to overcome her natural reticence.

"You should write a book, Captain," she said. "That would make more money for you than even selling a home in Grantville."

Lefferts was staring at her as if she'd turned into a phantom herself.

So was everyone else, she realized, looking around the table.

"But it's so obvious!" she said. "A book titled *The Adventures of Captain Lefferts* would sell extraordinarily well. And since Captain Lefferts needs the money quickly he could sell all the rights instead of waiting for royalties to come in. Which"—she waggled her hand back and forth, indicating uncertainty—"is probably a risky venture in any event, even with the new laws."

Copyright, in the up-time sense of the term, was a new concept in Europe. At the Americans' insistence, copyright laws had been adopted by the United States of Europe. But whether they would be effective or not was still uncertain. On the other hand, if Lefferts simply sold the rights to his book, the publisher would be able to collect all the money from the sales, at least until pirated editions began to appear. But that always took some time, even without copyright protection, and Eva was sure that a book by the notorious American captain would sell like . . .

"You have an expression for it," she said. "In American idiom, I mean. Sell like some sort of cakes."

"Sell like hot cakes," supplied Missy. She gave her head a sudden quick shake. "Good Lord. Harry . . . she's *right*. If you wrote an autobiography—wouldn't have to be more than a collection of anecdotes, really; the bestselling titles nowadays have to be short—they'd sell out as fast as they could get printed. I hate to say it, but you're probably more famous than any up-timer except Mike Stearns. And while everyone knows he's way more important than you"—she gave him a stern look—"nobody's ever accused him of fighting a duel because he seduced the wife of a nobleman."

"Dammit, that's *not* what happened," Lefferts said, scowling. "The guy was a fuck—fricking wife-beating shith—asswipe before I ever came on the scene. Yeah, fine, I had what they call relations with the lady—but she was a *widow* by then because I'd already put the fuck—fricking jackass in the ground after he picked a fight with me because I beat him at billiards. Her way of showing gratitude, what it was. I didn't *seduce* anybody."

Eva clapped her hands with delight. "Oh, that story is even better than the legend! You'd make a fortune!"

Again, he ran fingers through his hair. This gesture, this time, was more one of exasperation than anxiety. "Look, maybe I would—in theory. But in the real world, I ain't—I am not—going to be writing any books. Are you kidding? The best grade I ever got on an essay I wrote in high school was a C-minus."

Again, he scowled. "And that came from Mr. Wilson in so-called 'industrial arts' which is what used to be called 'wood shop' and 'metal shop' until they started insisting you had to write essays as well as make stuff. The best grade I ever got for an essay from Ms. Mailey was a D."

He made a snorting sound. "Me? Write a book? Yeah, sure—when pigs start flying."

Litsa pointed at Eva. "Have her write it for you. What do you call it? A vampire writer?"

Missy burst into laughter. "Oh, I like that! 'Vampire writer! But, no, the actual term is 'ghost writer.'"

Missy turned to Eva: "A ghostwriter is someone who actually writes the book while someone else takes the credit for it. They're often hired by celebrities to write autobiographies for them. The more honest ones don't try to claim they actually wrote the book. The byline will be something like: 'as told to' or 'as told by.' In your case, if Harry decided to do it that way, it would be 'The Adventures of Captain Harry Lefferts, as told to Eva Katherine von Anhalt-Dessau.'"

Eva shook her head, quite vehemently. "Oh, no! I would not feel right doing that."

Lefferts was giving her an intent look. "Why not? You'd be doing all the work. All I'd have to do is brag, which some people claim I'm really good at. Maybe even somebody at this table."

"Actually, Harry, you've never been much of a braggart," said Ron.

His wife gave him a skeptical glance, but Ron shook his head. "No, I mean it. There were always stories about Harry—him and Darryl McCarthy—about as far back as I can remember, in school. That was true even when I was there, which was years after Harry and Darryl graduated. But I don't remember anyone ever saying that Harry and Darryl were the actual source of the stories."

"We weren't, usually," said Harry. "That's because we'd either have gotten into trouble or it was something that only . . . Well, my dad taught me that some things a guy does he just doesn't talk about or he's a jerk."

He'd looked away from Eva for a moment, but now he was giving her that same intent look again.

"Can you write well?" he asked.

"She is famous for it!" said Litsa. "In her whole family—mine, too, and several others. Eva is a tireless—what's the word for it in English? I know there is one because I have heard it. Correspondinger, something like that."

"Correspondent," said Missy. "It can either mean a news reporter or just someone who writes a lot of letters."

"Yes! That's Eva! She's usually quiet in conversations—not like today, and what's gotten into you, Eva?—but she's always writing to someone. And the letters are marvelous. I know, I've gotten many of them. Well-written, interesting—she's very, how do you say it? observant, I think—and there's always something funny."

"It's a deal, then," said Lefferts. "But I'm not doing anything crooked. Nobody's ever accused me of being a liar and I'm not about to start. So we'll do it like Missy says—'Adventures of me, as told to Eva.' Make clear that she wrote it, not me. And we'll split the money fifty-fifty. I wouldn't feel right taking more than that, since I'm not doing anything except shooting my mouth off."

Shooting my mouth off was another colloquialism that Eva was unsure about, but she hardly noticed because she was in the grip of vast uncertainty. She felt like she'd been tossed out to sea in a tiny lifeboat.

"But—but—but—" She took a deep breath, and calmed herself. "I'm sorry. It's a fascinating idea, but..." Firmly, she shook her head. "The captain said he needed the money quickly. But if he is to serve the Stones as a security chief in Lorraine he will need to be leaving soon. We would not have time for him to finish telling me all his tales."

"You will have plenty of time!" said Litsa. She beamed at the young Stone couple. "Since I need to accompany this expedition in order to write about it for *Simplicissimus* and you need to accompany me because I need a companion for such a journey. So you can interview the captain along the way."

Ron and Missy Stone looked at each other. Ron shrugged. "What the hell," he said. "The publicity can't hurt. And since we're a married couple Litsa and Eva can use us as chaperones so nobody'll squawk that anything's improper."

Missy looked at Litsa. Then at Eva. Then at Captain Lefferts.

Then beamed herself. "This is a trip. Okay, then, it's all settled."

Chapter 5

December 12, 1635

Gerry Stone finished reading the letter and set it down on the side table next to his chair. The letter had been written by his oldest brother Frank and handed to him by Ron, who was the middle brother of the three.

"Okay. I'd say that establishes this guy Vincente's credentials as well as you could ask for. He started off as Frank and Giovanna's captor, during which time he treated them as well as possible, and then wound up helping Harry and the others to get them out of captivity. So we owe him. Big time."

"We owe Harry, too," said Ron.

"Yeah, we do. That whole Wrecking Crew of his, even more. Half of them got killed trying to rescue Frank and Giovanna." Gerry leaned forward in his chair, resting his elbows on his knees. "You want to set up some kind of fund for them? You know—what the cops call a widows and orphans fund. At least on TV that's what they call it."

"We can't," said Missy. She was sitting next to Ron on a divan facing Gerry. The piece of furniture was down-time made but modeled on an up-time stuffed sofa. The things were still fiendishly expensive but they were staying at the fanciest hotel in Magdeburg. Had it been left up to Ron, they'd have checked into a much cheaper hostelry, but Missy had put her foot down.

We're some of the richest people in Europe, and screw it, I'm not risking bedbugs. Just suck it up, hippie husband of mine. You can be thrifty some other way.

Ron might have argued the point, but Missy was usually not given to extravagant spending. If anything, she was on the frugal side herself. There were some matters, however, on which she thought pinching pfennigs was stupid—and flirting with unnecessary insects was one of them.

"Why can't we?" asked Gerry.

"Because there aren't any widows and orphans," replied his brother. "At least not that Harry or either one of the two guys who're still with him know about. They were all loners except for the Sutherland couple, who didn't have any kids. And both of them are dead now. Juliet was killed in Rome during the first rescue attempt, and her husband George was killed later in Italy when the pope was attacked. As far as Harry and Donald and Matija know, there aren't any family members to be supported. Or at least they don't know who they are or even where to look for them."

Gerry shook his head. He was only seventeen years old, but by now, more than four years after the Ring of Fire, he was no stranger to the harshness of the seventeenth century. He suffered himself from PTSD due to the death of a man in Rome whose head he'd more-or-less blown off. In a good cause, sure—keeping the pope from getting assassinated. Gerry still had recurring flashbacks and nightmares about it and thought he probably would for the rest of his life. That killing was at least partly responsible for his decision to become a Lutheran pastor.

He wondered, for a moment, if Harry Lefferts had the same sort of traumatic reactions. He'd been through enough to get them. Lefferts being Lefferts, of course, he'd probably never admit to it. Gerry

couldn't remember a time when *macho* hadn't been
Harry Lefferts' middle name.

He didn't much like the guy, but...

"We owe him," he said firmly. "And I assume you've
got something in mind, or you wouldn't have called
me up here from Jena."

"How's university life treating you?" asked Missy.

Gerry chuckled. "The University of Jena ain't like
WVU, I can tell you that. Or any other up-time
university I ever heard about, except maybe Oxford
and Cambridge. And why do I get the feeling you're
dodging the question?"

Ron and Missy looked at each other.

"Just tell him," Missy said. "All of it at once. The
business with Harry's the least of it."

His brother tugged his earlobe. "It's like this, Gerry.
We gave you a sketch of what Rebecca and Ed want
us to do in Hesse-Kassel."

"Yeah, I got that. I think they're probably spooking
at shadows, though."

Ron shrugged. "Maybe. But even if they are"—he
looked at his wife—"me and Missy have been talking about it. The truth is, it'd be good for the whole
country to develop a real economic center outside of
Magdeburg and the SoTF. Something 'high tech'—or as
close to it as we can get in the here and now, anyway."

"Hesse-Kassel has a lot going for it," said Missy.
"For starters, it's got a ruler with a brain. Whatever
you think of her politics—which aren't actually all that
bad, relatively speaking—Amalie Elizabeth is sharp."

"That's what I hear," Gerry agreed. "What else?"

"It's already got a good university."

"Marburg. What else?"

"The population's fairly sizeable. Kassel has an observatory—the first one ever built in Germany—and a permanent theater building."

"Yeah, I've heard of it. The Ottoneum. And quit dancing around. I get it that Hesse-Kassel provides a basis—probably as good as any in the USE outside Magdeburg and parts of Thuringia—to create a combination of a college town and a high-tech center. So what's making you twitchy? Neither one of you usually has any trouble getting to the point."

Again, his brother and Missy exchanged glances. Then Ron sighed and leaned back in the divan.

"The more we thought about it, the more Missy and I realized we're not big enough and rich enough on our own to do what's needed in Hesse-Kassel."

"'Cause it's not just Hesse-Kassel," Missy chimed in. "We've got Lorraine—hell, pretty much the whole Rhineland—to deal with, too."

"And plague isn't the only problem," said Ron. "That whole area's become a witches' brew of diseases. Typhus probably kills just as many people, and there's a lot of smallpox outbreaks too."

Gerry was getting exasperated. "Bro, I get it. You get one disease—usually because an army's been tromping through the area wrecking everything—and you get all the others piling on top. Get. To. The. Point."

"We've got to build a *big* pharmaceutical industry in Hesse-Kassel. We can't do that unless we can stimulate other people besides ourselves to invest in it."

"Ah." Gerry leaned back himself. "Oh."

Now it was his turn to run fingers through his air. "You know Dad'll have a shit fit."

"Yeah, I know. But Dad's in Padua, for starters.

Secondly, he put me in charge of the business because he'd rather be teaching. Thirdly, much as I love him he's not always real practical."

Gerry chuckled. "Tell me about it."

"We've been talking to Melissa Mailey," said Missy. "Even before this Hesse-Kassel thing came up, your father's policy was becoming a headache. She says the problem is that Tom basically wants a socialist pharmaceutical industry—but without any of the other prerequisites for it."

Gerry didn't have trouble following the logic. "Yeah, I agree. He wants medicine made at cost—'the profit motive's got no business mucking around with people's health.' I've heard him say it at least a dozen times—but what that really means when the industry's this small is that it stays small."

Ron nodded. "If we had a well-developed advanced industrial society, you could probably do it the way Dad wants it done. Most of the money up-time Big Pharma spent on so-called 'research' was spent developing copycat drugs so they could slide around some other big pharmaceutical corporation's patents. The real medical advances usually came from university research funded by one or another government. But that's just not true in this the year of our apparently absentminded Lord 1635. If you want a drug developed by anybody except us, they've got to be able to make money at it. And we're just not big enough to do everything that's needed. Not by a long shot, even with all the money we make in dyes and chemicals."

It was a little amusing the way he and Missy got simultaneously disgusted looks on their faces. "And any time we want to siphon money from the dye and chemical works, we've gotta have a knock-down fight with your dad's asshole father-in-law," said Missy, almost snarling.

"All Dad's policy is really doing is stifling the development of a pharmaceutical industry. Well, slowing it down, at any rate. We *are* doing a lot on our own, even doing it at cost."

Gerry stood up and went to the window. The hotel fronted on Hans Richter Strasse and was within sight of the Dom and the southern part of Hans Richter Square. As vistas went in Magdeburg, it was pretty good. He pushed open the window to get some air. The capital of the USE was already notorious in Europe for its pollution and poor air quality, but unlike most large cities it didn't smell that bad. The pollution came from industrial smoke and soot, not open sewage. Magdeburg was one of the few places on the continent that had a functioning sewer system, and even the ever-present horse manure was cleaned up on a regular basis.

"Dad is going to have a shit fit," Gerry repeated. "I'll back you up if it comes down to a real fight with him, but I don't know if Frank will. He's usually pretty sensible but after spending all that time with the Marcolis..."

He made a little twirling motion with his finger next to his head. The Marcoli family that their oldest brother had married into wasn't exactly crazy, but when it came to their political views they could do a pretty good imitation. They might react to what Ron was proposing with a furious denunciation of bloodsucking profiteering.

"Well, if comes to that I've got a secret weapon,"

Ron said. He pointed to Missy with his thumb. "She calls it the nuclear option. I quit and tell Dad and Frank they can damn well run the business themselves instead of sticking me with it."

"'Course, it'd be kinda nuclear for us too," said Missy, "seeing as how we'd be plunging from the heights of ye upper boo-joi-zee to whatever pitiful class you belong to on a librarian's salary. Which I don't even have yet because I'll still studying."

She didn't seem the least bit fazed by that prospect, though. Gerry wasn't surprised. One of the many things he liked about his new sister-in-law was that she didn't seem to share any of the snotty attitudes of so many members of her family. Her father was okay, but her grandmothers...

It was as if Missy had been born into the Stone mindset, not just married into it. Well...within reason. She was more levelheaded than any Proper Stone, but she didn't care about money all that much.

Gerry smiled and turned away from the window. "It won't come to that. Dad and Frank would rather lose an arm than give up what they're doing and come back up here to deal with Herr Pain-in-the-Ass Karl Jurgen Edelmann. They'll throw a hissy fit—Dad will, anyway; I'm not sure about Frank—but they'll give in once you make clear you're really serious about it."

He resumed his seat. "Speaking of which—being serious about it, I mean—are you ready to do what's needed yourself, Missy? It'll mean quitting school, at least for a while."

Missy made a face. "I don't like the idea, but that's mostly due to my innate caution. You know me: measure five times before you cut, and I got the feeling

I haven't measured library work more than three and a half times yet."

"You'll do fine," Gerry reassured her.

"Yeah, I figure I will too." She gave Ron a quick but very affectionate smile. "It helps that I know I won't have to pinch any pfennigs if I don't need to."

There was a knock on the door. Ron got up. "That's probably Eva," he said, moving toward the door. "That's Eva Katherine von Anhalt-Dessau, Gerry, so try to be polite. Harry managed to talk her into being his agent as well as his not-so-ghostly writer and she's been spending the last three days going from one printer to the next trying to talk them into the deal."

He opened the door and a very well-dressed female figure came charging through,

"Swine!" she hissed. "All of them—no! I insult honest pigs, who, say what else you will about them, are not cowardly."

She snatched off the scarf which had been covering her head. The head now exposed was topped with hair so dark it was almost black, tied up in a bun at the back of her head but with curls clustered around her face.

Gerry thought the face itself would probably have been very pretty if it weren't for the smallpox scars. But as pox scars went, hers were not that bad. Some pox-scarred faces were hideously ugly, with the features distorted and in some cases effectively destroyed. This young woman's scars were all over her face and especially heavy on her cheeks, but they were simply scars. She looked like an up-timer who'd suffered from really terrible acne as a teenager.

She was of average height for a seventeenth-century

woman and had a rather buxom figure, which was well-displayed by the bodice she was wearing. Many women with pox scars didn't expose any part of their bodies but this woman's bodice was cut low enough to display most of her shoulders and the upper part of her chest. That was perhaps because she didn't appear to suffer from much in the way of scarring except on her face. Gerry could see a few pox scars on her left shoulder but none anywhere else. There were no scars at all on her forearms and hands, which were exposed by the sleeves ending just below her elbows.

"I take it you had no success," said Missy. She'd also risen to greet the newcomer and now gestured toward one of the chairs in the room. "Please, Eva, have a seat."

Nodding her thanks, the young woman sat down. She moved very gracefully, Gerry noticed. He couldn't discern any part of her figure below the waist, given the voluminous skirts she was wearing, but he was pretty sure that if she'd been wearing up-time female athletic clothing that the body thereby exposed would be quite shapely.

He wasn't surprised, though. In the time that had passed since the Ring of Fire, Gerry had observed that upper class women suffering from pox scars tended to react in diametrically opposed ways—they either withdrew into quietude, rarely venturing outside their family homes, or they became vigorously active. A fair number of them were accomplished equestrians, and some even hunted. He wouldn't be at all surprised if this woman did herself.

"What happened?" asked Ron.

Eva looked a bit weary. "The same as all the others.

They don't want to take the risk. When I pointed out that we were offering to sell all rights, they all respond with"—her voice got a little sing-songy—"'we don't know what will happen with the new copyright laws.'" She shook her head sharply, sending the curls back and forth. "We'd be better off if we still had the old laws," she said.

Gerry understood the point she was making. Traditionally, since there were no copyright laws in existence, an author sold whatever he'd written to a printer for a flat sum. Thereafter, it was up to the printer to sell the copies he produced, either directly or through intermediaries. Eventually, if a work was popular enough, pirated editions would appear—except they weren't really "pirate editions" since there were no laws regulating them—and would soon undercut the printer's sales. But if he'd carried out his business energetically, he'd have made a nice profit by then.

Under the influence of the Americans, the United States of Europe had adopted up-time copyright laws, although without the absurd timespans that had come into effect by the end of the twentieth century. The term of a USE copyright was twenty years, renewable for another twenty. But nobody yet knew if the new laws would work as intended.

"Never mind, Eva," said Ron. He nodded toward his wife, who had resumed her seat next to him. "Missy and I have been talking it over and we decided that it would make sense to add a publishing industry to the mix we're going to propose to the landgravine of Hesse-Kassel." He smiled thinly. "If nothing else, we figure we can get her to enforce the copyright laws in her own province. Between Hesse-Kassel and the

SoTF and Magdeburg, we ought to make out okay. So we'll publish Harry's book—well, your book and Harry's, I should say—and we'll do it the way it ought to be done. We'll pay you an advance against royalties which will be big enough for Harry's fifty percent to take care of his niece for at least three years. By then royalties should start coming in."

Missy sniffed. "We figure most readers willing to buy a book will live in one of those three provinces. Enough of them, anyway. We'll have to see how the Crown Loyalist provinces do. Meaning no offense."

Eva's face was split by a wide smile. She had excellent teeth, Gerry noticed. Much better than those of most down-timers, even those of the upper nobility.

"I am naturally a supporter of my brother-in-law," Eva said. "But I fear the support weighs more lightly on me than it perhaps should."

That made Gerry laugh. She turned to look at him and for the first time he got a good look at her eyes.

Which were, quite simply, extraordinary. They were a shade of bright green somewhere between shamrock and emerald which made a striking contrast with her very dark hair. Gerry realized that his initial impression had been skewed by the scars. Eva was a beautiful woman whose appearance had been distorted by smallpox, but was not defined by the disease.

The distortion was a shame, of course. But he didn't think it was really that great a one. This was a person who'd make her own way in life, he thought, no matter what the circumstances.

One of the many things Gerry Stone liked about being a pastoral student was that he wasn't as much of a smart-ass as he'd formerly been. Still not given to fawning-over-established-truth, granted; but he was a lot better at extending goodwill toward people in general than he'd been as a smart-ass.

So, silently, he extended his goodwill toward Eva Katherine von Anhalt-Dessau.

Loudly, he extended his goodwill—such as it was—to his older brother. "Just give me a little warning before you go public with your new pharmaceutical company, will you? So I can head for cover before Dad finds out. What are you going to call it, by the way? Medicines By Mordor, Incorporated? Gouge, Fleece and Plunder, LTD? Or you could go with a simple family name, embellished a little. Stoneheart would work nicely."

"Ha ha ha," said Ron.

PART II
Kassel, capital of the Province of Hesse-Kassel

Chapter 6

February 17, 1636

> On some subjects, the captain is extremely
> reticent. "Close-mouthed," in the American
> idiom. Of nothing is that more true than his
> reputed—I can even say, notorious—exploits
> in the amatory field. If the tales are to be
> believed, Captain Lefferts' only rivals in this
> area are figures of ancient myth or the legends
> of the up-time universe regarding such men
> as Casanova and Don Juan.
>
> Yet, press him as you will, the captain
> maintains his reserve. The issue is one which
> both amuses and exasperates him.
>
> There are only two such matters on which
> Captain Lefferts is willing to speak, and then
> only about the men involved. Those have to do
> with his famous duels with the Italian patrician
> Agnelli and the French comte de Champcourt.
> In both cases, the captain felt compelled to "set
> the record straight," as Americans would say.
>
> "It is not true that I disemboweled Agnelli
> to demonstrate my savage nature, which is

*just a fancy way of saying I was showing
off. I did it for the good and simple reason
that Agnelli was a noted swordsman and the
sword is not a weapon that is very familiar
to Americans—although it has become familiar
to me since that duel. So, not being stupid, I
saw no reason to try to match his skill with
a sword. Instead, I met him with my trusty
Bowie knife. The realities of sword-against-knife
being what they are, I had no choice but to
grapple with the man and the rest came as
you might expect.*

*"As for Champcourt, the duel had nothing
to do with his wife. I did not even know the
woman at the time. The duel happened because
he accused me of cheating at billiards—a
game in which it is impossible to cheat. The
man was just angry that he lost and looking
to pick a fight."*

The sounds of horsemen entering the courtyard
below distracted Eva, but just for a moment. She wasn't
sure whether she ought to include in her account the
fact that Captain Lefferts had most certainly come to
be acquainted with the comte's wife *after* the duel.

In the course of their journey to Kassel, she'd
come to know the captain quite a bit better. One
thing that was clear to her by now was that Léf-
ferts considered it exceedingly uncouth for a man
to speak at all on the subject of his sexual liaisons,
much less boast about them. *A gentleman doesn't
talk about such things* was the way he put it once,
when he was in a formal mood. *Only an asshole*

brags about getting laid was his alternative version, spoken after he'd had perhaps too many drinks in the tavern they'd been staying at.

As was true of all Americans whom Eva had encountered, to one degree or another, Captain Lefferts fit rather poorly into down-time conceptions of proper human behavior. Very gallant, in some ways; quite coarse, in others. Sophisticated one moment, the next... what the up-timers themselves called "a country rube."

Lefferts was more acclimated to the seventeenth century than most of his countrymen. But there were still ways in which his up-time origins surfaced. Sexual attitudes were perhaps the most prominent of those, and so she decided to leave off any further discussion of the comte of Champcourt's wife. The captain would only be irritated if she did otherwise. And...

As time passed, she found herself increasingly unwilling to aggravate the captain. One of the ways in which Harry Lefferts' sexual attitudes were different from those of down-timers—you might almost say, exotic or esoteric—involved Eva herself. She was unsettled by the growing realization that the captain was attracted to her. Even quite attracted, she thought.

Why? Were he a down-timer, Eva would assume the attraction was due to her probable dowry. And while an up-timer would view such an attraction as being repellent, even repulsive, Eva herself would simply view it as logical. For people of her class, marriage was usually a practical matter. Partly political, partly financial—and always with a view in mind to continuing the family lines. There being no other mechanism for that purpose than sexual intercourse, marriage became the legitimate vehicle for the activity. The whole thing was about as "romantic," to use the term Americans were so fond of, as a farmer breeding his livestock.

If she thought Captain Lefferts were eyeing her from the standpoint of advancing his interests, Eva would know how to respond. Favorably, yes—it was not as if she were likely to have any other prospects—but also with caution. Not caution about his "honorable intentions"—another peculiar American concept—but about his thrift and financial competence. Would he squander the dowry or use it to good purpose? Would he provide for their children or leave them, and her, at the mercy of the fates?

But Eva didn't think Lefferts was thinking in those terms. She didn't know *what* he was thinking about her.

Her own thoughts on the subject, though, were quite clear to her—and quite inappropriate. They mostly involved feverish fantasies which until the past few weeks she hadn't known she was even capable of having.

What to do?

She pushed the issue aside and took up her pen again. It was one of the marvelous up-time "fountain pens" which were such a pleasure to use. Missy Stone had given it to her as a gift. One of the byproducts of the long and sometimes arduous journey to Kassel in mid-winter had been that Eva and the up-time woman had become friends.

Eva decided she'd written enough about the amatory reputation of Harry Lefferts. There was already sufficient material on the subject to satisfy most readers, and she wanted to return to the subject which the captain was much more willing to discuss—the exploits that had made him famous in the first place. Those, with the notable exception of the catastrophic events in Rome, were something in which Lefferts took genuine pride, even if his accounts were laconic and understated.

She'd begin a new chapter. The book was coming along quite well, she thought.

"So that's it," Ron Stone concluded. He set the papers he'd been using as speaking notes down and looked around at the five other men sitting at the table. "Any questions? Comments?"

The men looked at each other. Then, Reichart Hümmel cleared his throat. He and the man sitting across from him, Jost Bresch, were the two most prominent apothecaries in Hesse-Kassel.

"You are not proposing a consortium, then?"

Ron shook his head. "No. As it stands, I'm twisting the Sherman Anti-Trust Act into a pretzel—never mind; it's an up-time reference—but I draw the line at forming an outright cartel. If there isn't some real competition between the different pharmaceutical companies, we won't expand the industry fast enough."

He pointed to Hümmel with his left forefinger and Bresch with his right. "The two of you will each form separate companies. Call them whatever you want. The only conditions I place are two: First, you have to found them and maintain them here in Hesse-Kassel. Two, you can't collude with each other once we get the industry up and rolling."

Watching her husband, Missy was simultaneously pleased with the way he was handling the meeting and—being honest—a bit disconcerted. Another man might have added stern warnings to the effect that he'd catch Hümmel and Bresch if they tried to collude. But Ron didn't think that way. His silent and supreme self-confidence that he could enforce his provisions was ultimately far more intimidating than any snarling would have been.

In the short time they'd been married, two things had already become clear to Missy. As young as he was—he'd just turned twenty-one in December—Ron had the makings of an extraordinarily capable chief executive officer. A very large part of that talent was due to the fact that money as such meant almost nothing to him. He looked at money the same way a potter would look on a pile of clay. Just a raw material that wasn't useful until it was molded into shape.

Thankfully, that meant Ron was also not given to letting greed determine any of his decisions. The decisions themselves could sometimes be pretty cold-blooded—as, indeed, was the purpose of this very meeting. But however rich they might eventually become, Missy was pretty sure she'd never be greeted on a Christmas morning by a waif named Tiny Tim gazing at her reproachfully.

Well... Gazing at her, maybe. This *was* the seventeenth century, after all. Waifs abounded. But reproachfully, no.

"In exchange," Ron continued, "I will provide you with the formulas and the procedures we've developed to manufacture chloramphenicol—"

There was a slight hiss in the air from the sound of indrawn breaths. *Chloramphenicol* was almost a magic word nowadays. It was the American miracle drug, which could even—not always, but very often—cure someone of the plague. It was also effective against a number of other diseases.

The formula for the drug was no longer much of a secret, and hadn't been since Mike Stearns had surreptitiously released it to the Spanish besiegers of Amsterdam two years before. But a formula was one thing, the exact procedures for turning that formula into medicine . . . something else. Those were the product of trial and error, long effort and experience.

"—and what we've so far discovered about the process of making vaccines against typhus and typhoid fever." He made a self-deprecating little shrug. "I'm afraid we're longer on theory there than we are on some of the practical issues involved. But we're still a lot closer to being able to manufacture those vaccines in quantity than we are to mass production of penicillin or streptomycin."

He leaned back in his chair, now looking at the three other men sitting farther down the table. One of them was a representative of the Berenger Bank, founded in Hamburg almost half a century earlier. The other two men were from the Fugger financial interests. The Fuggers were backing Hümmel; the Berenger Bank was financing Bresch.

"I think we should now get into some of the marketing issues," Ron said.

Oh, joy, Missy thought to herself. She spent the time that followed by reviewing in her mind the library filing system she intended to propose to the landgravine for the new science library that would be attached to the University of Marburg. It was basically the Dewey decimal system, but with modifications from the Library of Congress as well as, for some purposes, the classification system used by the up-time U.S. Superintendent of Documents.

Had the men in the room been able to follow her thoughts, they would have been even more bored than she was. *Suum cuique*, as the Romans said. To each her own.

"The Americans have an expression," said Litsa. "'The elephant in the middle of the room,' they call it. What it means is—"

Smiling a bit ruefully, the landgravine of Hesse-Kassel waved her hand. "Yes, I've heard it—and I know what it means. The great subject that a conversation avoids by focusing on smaller issues. You are referring, I imagine, to Hesse-Kassel's landlocked status."

Litsa nodded. She had her hands clasped together on her lap, in order to keep them from flying about the task she'd *like* them to be about, which was taking copious notes. But it had taken her almost a month to get this interview with Amalie Elizabeth, and she didn't want to risk irritating the landgravine. Rulers in the early seventeenth century were not accustomed, as were their late twentieth-century counterparts, to having inquisitive journalists writing down every word that came out of their mouths that might be of interest.

So, Litsa would have to rely entirely on her memory. Unhappily, it had not occurred to her on any of the several occasions when she'd visited Grantville to see if one of the fabled up-time "tape recorders" might be available for purchase. She had been told the things were not especially bulky—and the sleeves of her bodice were full and loose. She could have probably attached the device to her forearm using some of the equally fabled "duct tape" and then—a few quick motions of Litsa's nimble fingers when the landgravine wasn't looking—and she could have recorded the entire conversation.

But, at least on this occasion, it was not to be. Happily, Litsa had a very good memory and when she wanted to be was an attentive listener.

"Yes, that issue," she said. She did not, of course, add what she could have, which was: *your husband having spent many months last year trying to seize one of the cities on the Rhine by main force and failing completely . . .*

Most unwise. Especially in view of the recent demise of said husband fighting the Poles—a task at which he'd also fallen short.

"It's not as big a problem as you might think," said Amalie Elizabeth. "Hesse-Kassel still holds the town of Dorsten on the Lippe river, which gives us access to the Rhine."

Litsa was impressed by the landgravine's self-assuredness. She wondered how much of that was sheer bluster. It was true that the Hessians had kept troops stationed in Dorsten ever since they captured it in February of 1633, and she'd heard that they were even improving its fortifications. But since the formalization of the provincial structure of the USE at the Congress of Copenhagen, Dorsten was a town in the province of Westphalia, not Hesse-Kassel. At the moment, the Danish prince Fredrik who had been appointed as the province's ruler was presumably preoccupied with the chaotic political situation that had resulted from Gustav Adolf's incapacitating injury at the battle of Lake Bledno. But sooner or later he was bound to turn his attention back to his province's affairs, at which point Hesse-Kassel was likely to be unceremoniously ordered to vacate Dorsten.

But even if the Hessians held Dorsten, the river on whose bank it was situated was hardly suitable for industrial purposes. Litsa would investigate, but she was pretty sure the Lippe was only navigable with rafts and small boats.

Of course, if the pharmaceutical project now underway here in Kassel bore fruit...

She'd have to ask Ron Stone if the Lippe would be adequate as a transport route for medicines and medical supplies.

No, better to ask his wife Missy. She was less likely to be reticent and more likely to know the answer anyway. It was a bit eerie, how much information a really devoted librarian possessed. Nothing to suggest an actual pact with the Devil, of course. Still...

Chapter 7

The details of the assault on the Tower of London led by Captain Lefferts in his successful effort to free the American envoys held captive by King Charles were long obscure. The reason for that, it is now clear, was the need to keep the participation of Julie Sims and her husband Alexander MacKay hidden from the sight of the English power. But since the famous riflewoman made her own escape from Great Britain early in 1635, that issue is moot. Her husband's father had already been murdered by the British king's assassins

*before they fled Scotland, so there is no need
to fear further retaliation for the role played
by Sims and her husband in the escape from
the Tower.*

*And what a role it was! When the assault
began—*

Eva had ignored the continuing sounds of the
horsemen in the courtyard, but a new voice broke
through her concentration.

"Nous sommes ici, Capitaine?"

It was the voice of a very young girl, speaking
French. Her accent was thick with rural origin—it had
sounded more like *noos sumb izi, Capitan?* although
the meaning had been quite clear. "Are we here?"
But the title of her address had been unmistakable
and Eva knew of only one captain.

Well, actually, she knew several. But there was only
one who concerned her.

She set down the pen, rose and went to the window.
Looking out onto the courtyard, she saw Captain Lefferts lean over and hoist a girl into his arms. She looked
to be perhaps eight years old, and so skinny it was no
effort at all for a man as strong as Harry Lefferts.

"Yes, we're here," he said, smiling at the girl. The
captain's French was fluent but he normally spoke
with a Parisian accent. Eva was not surprised at all,
though, to hear that Lefferts was shading his voice
with an accent closer to that of the girl's. It was the
kind of thing his phenomenal linguistic skill would
enable him to do—and something he *would* do, from
that deep if so often hidden wellspring of kindness
that she knew abided in the man.

She felt a sudden, very powerful surge of emotion—
which she hurriedly suppressed without examination.
Eva was usually given to introspection but on this
subject...Caution was called for.

"Captain Lefferts!" she called down.

Still holding the girl, the captain looked up at her
and smiled.

"Meet Barbeline Cayel, Eva," he said, lifting her
a bit higher. "Barbeline, this is Her Serene Highness
Eva Katherine von Anhalt-Dessau."

Like the girl herself, her face was thin, coming to
a pointed chin. At the moment, the expression on
her face was a frown.

"She's a princess?" The girl sounded dubious. "I
didn't think princesses got sick." Her little hand
stroked her cheeks. "The scars—that's smallpox, for
sure, Captain. I've seen it."

Several different possible responses came to Eva
but within less than a second she chose the one that
her instincts guided her toward. Perhaps it was the
captain's influence, too.

"No, we get sick just like everyone," she said. Eva
stroked her own cheeks in a gesture mirroring the
French girl's. "I got the pox when I was very young.
Younger than you, even."

Now the girl's expression was sympathetic. "Did it
hurt a lot? I got the plague and it really *hurt*."

"That sounds awful. Come up here and tell me all
about it, Barbeline."

"Do I call you Princess or Serene Highness? I'm
not sure because I never met any royal people."

"You can call me Eva."

✧   ✧   ✧

"I found her in southern Lorraine," Lefferts explained, looking over at the bed where Barbeline was sleeping. The girl had been very tired after the long journey. As soon as she'd had something to eat after coming up to Eva's room in the inn, Barbeline had started to nod off. Eva had told the captain to place the girl on her bed.

By then, Ron and Missy Stone had come up to the chamber. They were also curious to hear how the captain—*Harry Lefferts, of all people!* was the way Missy put it—had come to informally adopt an eight-year-old girl.

"We heard about her—me and Vincente—when we were passing through the area on a scouting expedition. She'd become something of a legend in the villages in the area. She lived in a hut she'd made for herself, eating nobody could figure out what, and spending all her time tending a grave."

"Tending a *grave*?" asked Ron.

The captain's expression, heretofore full of amusement, became suddenly somber. "Yeah, a grave. Such as it was—just a pile of rocks she'd put over the place where the guy got buried after he died. In a field some twenty yards from a dirt road."

"Her father?" asked Eva.

"No. Not her father. Her father was long dead by then. Like almost all the people in her village—and she herself, damn near—he'd already died from the plague."

The captain now looked at his two fellow Americans. "She was tending Jeffie Garand's grave, guys."

"Oh, hell," said Ron.

Missy stared at the girl on the bed. "*She's* the one?"

"Yeah, she is."

Eva must have looked puzzled, because Missy looked her way and then shook her head. "You probably never heard the story, Eva, but it was all over Grantville before we left. Jeffie Garand was one of the Americans who went to the Rhineland to help fight disease. He ran across a little girl who'd come down with the plague and been abandoned by everyone. Just been left alone by the side of the road. Jeffie insisted on breaking quarantine and staying with her. Then he caught the plague and died."

She looked back at Barbeline. "Everyone just assumed the girl had died also."

"Not everyone," said Lefferts. To Eva's surprise, his voice now had an undertone of anger. "After she recovered, Barbeline tried to go to Fulda to let Jeffie's wife—he must have told her about his family—know where he was buried."

"That's—what?" Ron shook his head. "Must be a hundred and fifty miles."

"More like two hundred, the way the roads go," said Lefferts. "She didn't realize how far it was. No way she could have made it all on her own, an eight-year-old girl, especially not in winter. But she didn't get any farther than Merkwiller-Pechelbronn, about thirty-five miles up the road. The Americans who'd been staying there had already left, but everyone had heard about Jeffie dying because he tried to save a dying girl. Stupid bastards blamed Barbeline for it, I guess. They refused to talk to her, wouldn't let her stay there—some of the village kids even threw stones at her."

Eva grimaced. Village children were notorious for petty cruelty. Being fair, children who lived in palaces were no saints, either.

"Anyway," the captain continued, "eventually Barbeline gave up and went back. She's been taking care of Jeffie's grave herself since then. Don't ask me what she's been eating or how the hell she stayed alive in that little hut she built, in the middle of winter, because I have no idea. Probably by stealing."

He gave the small figure curled up on the bed an affectionate look. "That is one tough little girl, take it from me. The only way I talked her into leaving Jeffie's grave was by making a deal with her—I'd have a real headstone made up by a mason, if she'd come back here to Kassel with me. I didn't stint on the cost, either."

Still looking at Barbeline, he shook his head. "I think what clinched the deal is that I had the mason carve an inscription into the stone along with Jeffie's name."

"What'd it read?" asked Ron.

For just a brief moment, the captain—a man for whom the term "abashed" Eva would have thought completely foreign—looked uncomfortable. "It read, 'Good-night, sweet prince. And flights of angels sing thee to thy rest.' It's from Shakespeare."

Ron and Missy stared at him.

"Yeah, I know," said Missy after a moment. "It's from the end of *Hamlet*. But since when—"

Lefferts chuckled. "Since when did I ever read Shakespeare? Not in high school, for damn sure. Believe or not, it was after I burned down the Globe Theater. Ms. Mailey made such an unholy fuss about it—you want to talk about carrying on and on—that I got a little curious. Off and on since then I've been reading the guy. Whoever 'the guy' really is, and I'm not getting anywhere near that wrangle because what difference does it make anyway? But I like that part at the end of *Hamlet* so I guess it stuck with me. I had to give the mason the words just from memory but I think I got it right."

"Yeah, you did," said Missy. "I always liked it too. And let me say here and now, Harry Lefferts, that I take back any sarcastic thing I might have ever said about you—although I reserve the right to say some sarcastic stuff in the future, should you give me cause. Which, knowing you, you probably will."

He grinned at her.

"What are you going to do with the girl now?" asked Ron.

Lefferts looked back at Barbeline. "I don't really have any idea. Take care of her, I guess, until I figure something out."

Ron and Missy looked at each other. Then Ron shrugged and said, "If you want, Harry, me and Missy could probably look after her."

"Thanks, guys. But I think we'd better wait and ask Barbeline when she wakes up. Trust me—this is not a little girl who's going to agree to anything she doesn't want to agree to. Like I said, she's tough. Think 'pocket battleship.'"

When Barbeline awoke, some time later, the issue was placed before her. Her response was immediate and granite-sure.

"No," she said. "I want to stay with the captain."

"You should say 'thank you' to them," said Lefferts.

The girl seemed dubious again, but looked back at the Stone couple and added, "Thank you."

Chapter 8

That night, several hours after sundown, Eva laid down the pen and decided to quit for the night. She'd gotten most of another chapter written on the escape from the Tower of London, but there were several details she was not clear about. There was no point in continuing until she'd had a chance to talk to the captain again.

Moved by a sudden impulse, she rose from her little writing table and went to the door. Captain Lefferts might still be awake and she could ask him the questions immediately, while they were still fresh in her mind.

But at the door, she hesitated. Was that really why she wanted to see if he was still awake?

She couldn't decide, and the uncertainty made her feel half-mad. Normally, Eva found it easy to assess her own moods and sentiments. But whenever they moved in the direction of Captain Lefferts, they became chaotic, confused—

Well, not exactly. Chaotic, yes; confused, no.

"*Ah!*" With that little inarticulate cry of frustration, she opened the door and went into the corridor beyond. Litsa's room was directly across from hers, that of the Stone couple a short distance away. The captain, along with the other men in their party, slept on the floor below.

The hallway was very dark. Feeling particularly foolish, Eva went back into her room to fetch a candle. Lighting it from her reading lamp, she went back into the corridor and headed for the stairs.

She was light-footed and wearing slippers, so she made little noise going down the stairs and even less once she reached the corridor on the floor below. Captain Lefferts' room, thankfully, was not far away—the second one on the right.

As soon as she reached the landing she could see the crack of light below the door to the captain's room. He was still awake, apparently. Moving quickly so as to keep her cautious instincts at bay, she went to the door and knocked on it.

"Come in," came the captain's voice.

She opened the door and went inside. Lefferts was sitting at a small table with a book open before him. When he saw her, he smiled broadly. "What can I do for you, Your Serene Highness?"

Not sure what to say, she looked around and saw that Barbeline was curled up on the bed alongside the wall. She felt even more foolish than she had walking into a dark corridor with no candle. She'd completely forgotten about the little French girl. As attached as Barbeline had so obviously become to Captain Lefferts, she'd no doubt insisted on staying with him.

Seeing the direction of Eva's gaze, the captain glanced at the girl on the bed and his broad smile became a grin. "It seems I've acquired my own barnacle. Or maybe—me being me—I ought to call her my own pilot fish. I offered to get her a room of her own, but she insisted on staying with me. She is one stubborn little kid."

Eva had no idea what to do. The half-formed desires and intentions that had driven her to the captain's room disintegrated.

"I . . . I don't—" She threw up her hands, turned

and left the room. Behind her, she heard the captain say "Eva—wait." But she ignored that and sped back up the stairs.

Moments later she was back in her own room. She went to the table and stared down at the manuscript she'd been working on. She began turning the pages, but she was so addlepated she had trouble even making sense of the sentences she was reading.

—fortunately, Tom Simpson was a big man and a decisive one. He just picked Ms. Mailey up and started down the escape ramp. Within seconds—

—bishop Laud was still unconscious. That was Tom at work, again. The man's fists are as big as a—

—not sure how many men Julie took off the wall. At least ten, I figure, but it might have been—

"Eva," said the captain.

Startled, she turned and saw that he was standing in the open doorway. She must have forgotten to close it behind her.

Forgotten? Eva knew herself too well to believe that.

"What's wrong?" asked Lefferts.

Suddenly—finally—everything made sense to her. For a moment, all she felt was relief. Eva really, really *hated* being confused and uncertain.

No longer. She knew what she would do. And while she was uncertain as to how the captain would respond, that didn't matter. Not so much, anyway. Whatever else, she would not spend the rest of a lifetime cursing herself for being a coward.

She stepped away from the table and gestured at the chair with her hand. "Please, Captain. Sit down. I have things I wish to say."

Looking far more solemn than he normally did,

Lefferts sat down in the chair. While he did so, Eva went to the door and closed it.

Turning to face him directly, she said: "I was born in September of the year 1613. So I am not even twenty-three years old, yet. I am quite healthy. I survived smallpox and I've never had a serious illness since. Barring ill fortune, I still have two-thirds of my life ahead of me. Perhaps more, with the new medical knowledge you Americans have brought with you."

She couldn't meet his direct gaze for the next words. So she looked slightly aside. "I do not—whatever else—want to spend every day of that life ahead of me regretting that I lacked the will to do something which—"

She started to falter, then.

"Eva—"

"Please, Captain." She held up her hand. "I need to say this."

He laughed, softly. "Fine. But will you—finally—call me 'Harry' instead of that damn 'captain'?"

"All right—Harry." Still not finding the words, she decided to approach the matter indirectly. She reached up and touched her cheek. "The pox scars. They are mostly just on my face. There are not very many anywhere . . . else. In most places, none at all."

He rose from the chair. "It doesn't matter, Eva. Either way, I don't care. I never would, I never will. I don't even notice them any more, really. They're just part of you."

"Sit down," she commanded. He obeyed.

She was finally able to relax a bit. She believed him, but it was important that she remain in control.

"I will show you." She began to disrobe, starting

with the bodice. "There are some scars here, on my left shoulder." Turning around: "And some there, in the middle of my back."

Once the bodice was off, she faced him again. "None at all on my breasts, though, as you can see."

He started to rise again.

"*Sit,*" she commanded. "I am not finished."

It took longer to remove the rest of her clothing, especially since she insisted on showing him the line of scars that ran down the back of her left thigh and the little clusters on the outside of both ankles.

"None on my feet," she concluded. Taking off the slippers, she turned away from him again and lifted each foot so he could see the soles. "Not one scar there, anywhere."

She started to turn around but the captain was on his feet again—and this time it was quite obvious he would not listen to any command to sit back down. He picked her up—so easily; the man was very strong—and brought her to the bed.

He was gentle, though, laying her down. As he began removing his own clothes, Eva laughed and clapped her hands.

"You don't boast anyway, Captain—Harry—but it wouldn't matter if you did. You and I both know the truth." She was probably grinning like a maniac. "*I* seduced *you*, not the other way around. Captain Harry Lefferts! Brought to bed by *me*. Eva Katherine von Anhalt-Dessau, the ugly one."

"You are not ugly," he growled, sliding nude onto the bed. His hand began to caress her. "You are so, so beautiful."

❖   ❖   ❖

There were some surprises for Eva, in what followed, but they simply involved the sheer pleasure
of it all. She hadn't foreseen that. Some pleasure,
certainly; but nothing like the reality.

As for the intimate details, all of those were much
as she'd thought they'd be. Eva was a virgin, but she
was hardly a *naïf*. Marriage and sexual intercourse
were practical things, in families of her class. Probably in families of any class, she imagined, although
she didn't know for sure.

She been told by her mother, her older sisters,
married friends—close servants, even—of how it all
happened and what to expect, and in detail that she
knew up-timers would have considered downright
clinical. Not to mention appalling. They were peculiar,
that way, the Americans. Full of fuzzy notions they
called "romance" but they let their children stumble
into the business completely unprepared except for
what they might have learned from other children
who were just as ignorant as they were. It was a little
amazing they managed to breed at all.

The biggest surprise, though, was how long it lasted.
She'd never heard the American expression *wham-
bam-thank-you-Ma'am* but it would have captured
the sense she'd had of how rapidly sexual intercourse
took place.

Not with the captain—Harry—however. He seemed
determined to prove that he could outlast any fable
ever told.

Which was just fine with Eva. She thought she'd
probably feel some remorse for this night in the time to
come. But regrets? Never. Not one. Never-never-never.

When Harry was finally spent, he lay on his back

staring up at the ceiling with Eva's head nestled on his shoulder. "Jesus H. Christ," he said. "If I wasn't such a suave and debonair fellow, I'd say that was the best lay I ever had."

She slapped his chest. "Just remember! *I* seduced *you*. I am *not* one of your conquests, Captain Lefferts."

He grinned, his hand stroking her hip. "Can't deny it. I put up one hell of a fight, too. For all the good it did me."

Not more than a few seconds later, the door swung open again. This time, it was Barbeline standing there.

Eva and Harry froze. They were completely naked on top of the bedding—most of which was on the floor by now.

But the French girl took it quite in stride. "You didn't tell me Eva was your wife, Captain." Eva had no trouble, this time, deciphering the thick country accent.

Barbeline covered her mouth, yawning. "Sorry, I was just worried when I woke up and you were gone. Promise you'll wake me up when you come back to the room."

And with that, she turned and left, still yawning.

Eva and Harry looked at each other.

"What should we tell her?" asked Eva. "In the morning."

"I don't know," said Harry. "But I do know this much. I do not want this to be a one-night stand."

One-night stand. Eva was not familiar with the idiom, but its meaning was obvious.

That was an issue she simply hadn't considered, she now realized. Her thoughts had never been able to get past . . . *this* night.

There was a lot to think about, and she had no idea where it might eventually lead. But she didn't have to decide everything at once. All she needed to decide was whether this would be a one-night stand or...

Not.

"Okay," she said. Proving, for perhaps the millionth time since the Ring of Fire, that some American idioms were more contagious than either smallpox or the plague.

Chapter 9

Eva awoke some time after dawn, with the pale light of winter spilling into the room. She was a bit surprised, at first, because she was normally a light sleeper and woke before sunrise. But then, feeling the warm body pressed against hers and remembering the night that had just passed, the surprise vanished.

This being the first time in her life she had awakened in the same bed with a man—both of them naked and neither of them pristine in that state—she wasn't quite sure what to do. Running through in her mind the various and lengthy pieces of reminiscences and analysis she'd gotten from other women in her family, she found nothing that was particularly useful.

Apparently, she was free to explore the possibilities. What was the American term? Ah, yes. "Free style." She thought it had mostly to do with swimming but saw no reason the same principles couldn't be applied in these circumstances.

So, she began styling freely. And, within a very short time, Captain Lefferts—no, he wanted to be thought of as "Harry" now—responded in much the same manner.

So passed a very enjoyable time, of uncertain duration. When it was over and they'd both rested a bit, Harry raised himself up on an elbow and gazed down at her.

"In case I need to start thinking about it, is there much chance you're going to get pregnant? Not to be blunt or anything."

"From last night and this morning?" Eva considered the problem. "It's not impossible but it's not likely, either. It's the wrong time of the month. That was probably partly what I was thinking—insofar as I was thinking at all—when I came to your room."

She rolled toward him so she could see his face better. "As for the future, I can't say. Assuming you haven't changed your mind about the one-night—what is it? stance? status?—"

"Stand," he said.

"Yes, that. If you still feel the same way—"

"You bet your sweet ass I do."

That idiom made her laugh, with its truly grotesque affection. "Well, in that case, it's hard to say. I've been told that you up-timers have methods for preventing pregnancy. Is that true, and if it is, are you so equipped?"

"The really reliable ones are only usable by women," he said. "They're hard to come by, any longer, although there are some fairly effective down-time substitutes. As for me, well...I ran out of up-time rubbers—condoms, they're also called—some time ago. And despite what seems to be my reputation I'm not always in the mood for sex—and I haven't been for quite a while, until I ran into you." His tone darkened considerably. "Not since Rome."

He fell silent for a few seconds. Eva didn't try to prod him into talking about Rome. She knew Harry was upset over what had happened—the details of which she still didn't know because he wouldn't talk about it. Some day, she would ask. Not today.

He sighed and stroked her hair. Then, his good cheer returning, said: "They're making some rubbers down-time now. I'll look for some, but it may take a while, especially to find ones that I'd trust even a little bit. From what I've seen and heard, a lot of these so-called condoms are about as effective as spitting in the wind."

That assessment was close to the one Eva had gotten from her relatives and friends. As soon as she got a chance, she'd investigate the methods she might be able to use. But in the meantime....

"I'm afraid we'll just have to be careful and abstain at certain points in my cycle," she said.

His expression became stern, like that of a man determined to perform a duty he found unpleasant. "I really don't want to get you into trouble with your folks, Eva. We could abstain altogether."

"Put that evil thought entirely out of your mind, Captain Lefferts."

Ron Stone had never liked wristwatches and had refused to wear one back up-time. Since arriving in the seventeenth century and becoming far wealthier than he'd ever imagined he'd be in any time or place, he'd commissioned a jeweler to make him a pocket watch. The arrival of Grantville in Germany in the year 1631 had jump-stated watchmaking by at least a quarter of a century. In the old timeline the balance spring—critical to any watch that hoped to be accurate at all—hadn't been introduced until 1657.

But while the best-made down-time pocket watches could remain accurate over the course of a day within a few minutes, they were heavy and bulky. Not a problem, of course, for a man in the full splendor of his august presence to pull the great thing out of his pocket and make a public display of his affluence. But for a man who'd been sitting through a tedious and detail-consumed business meeting for hours, Ron would have appreciated just this once having a wrist watch that he could glance at surreptitiously to see just how much longer his suffering was likely to last.

It didn't help any that the meeting had started at six-thirty in the morning, before the sun had even come up. People whose only access to night light came from fires, hearths, oil lamps and candles were usually of the *early-to-bed-early-to-rise* persuasion. Another thing which the Ring of Fire had jump-started was the proverb *The early bird catcheth the worm*—not that any down-timers Ron had ever met needed old saws to leap out of bed when or, often enough, before the local roosters started crowing.

He, on the other hand, coming from a civilized time, was a night owl by nature. As far back as he could remember, his idea of a proper diurnal cycle started when the sun had been up long enough to get comfortable and warm everything up properly.

He put his hand over his mouth in what he hoped would pass as a thoughtful pose, so at least he could yawn. And entertained himself for the next ten minutes or so by visiting silent curses on every apothecary who ever lived, beginning with the unknown founders of the nefarious trade back in Babylon somewhere around 2500 BCE.

Being fair about it—not that he was inclined to be at the moment—most of the tedium and ennui of the day was not caused by the apothecary aspect of the business so much as it was by the money side. Sea gulls and pigeons did not squabble over crumbs with anything close to the relentless enthusiasm of Herren Hümmel and Bresch. Their bankers were even worse.

But, eventually, it was over. For that day, at least. Ron rose from the table and finally pulled out his pocket watch.

"Two-thirty in the afternoon," he said. "It's amazing, sometimes, how time flies."

And with that, he sped out the door.

"Hi, hon," he said, closing the door behind him. "And I used to think your library study seminars were dull. Fool that I was! When it comes to boring they don't—"

"That fucking son-of-a-bitch!"

That brought Ron up short. Gaping a little, he stared at his wife. Who, for her part, was standing by the window and bestowing a furious glare upon the world beyond.

"Uh, Missy, what's . . ."

"What's the problem? *Your fucking buddy Harry Lefferts*, that's what the problem is!"

Ron tried to figure out by what peculiar logic Harry Lefferts had become his "buddy." It was quite the enigma. Over here, Harry Lefferts, the quintessential

hillbilly roustabout who only fell short of outright
"jock" status because he was too much of a rascal to
abide by the discipline of athletic coaches. Over there,
Ron Stone—or rather, Elrond Stone, that being his
legal given name—who was raised in a commune and
until the Ring of Fire had fully enjoyed his status as
a teenage hippie.

"*Men! Why is it so hard for you not to think with
your dicks?*"

Ah. The mystery was solved. Ron and Harry were
"buddies" by the mere fact of belonging to the same
half of the human race.

The wrong half, to be precise.

It didn't take Ron more than an instant to deduce
the specific source of Missy's indignation. Unfortunately,
he didn't take an instant longer to deduce a more
salubrious way of expressing his conclusion.

"Look, hon, it's been obvious since the day they met
that the two of them had the hots for each other."

Missy's glare was transferred from the innocent
world outside the window to the guilty-as-hell miscre-
ant within the room. "*Had the hots for each other?*"
she demanded. "Oh, sure! Let's just pretend that
one of them isn't the worst rake in Europe and the
other isn't a sheltered girl barely half his age. She's
probably—no, excuse me!—she *was* probably a virgin."

Barely half his age. In point of awkward fact, Harry
was thirty and Eva was twenty-two—hardly an out-
landish age spread even in the century they'd come
from, much less this one. The count of Schwarzburg-
Rudolstadt was a man in his mid-fifties with a wife
who'd been a teenager when they got married—and
was still no older than Eva. But Ron didn't know any

American, including Missy herself, who didn't have a good opinion of the man. Grantville could have had a lot worse neighbor.

He decided a flanking approach was probably called for. "I really think you—we—shouldn't be jumping to conclusions. Has Eva herself said anything to you about it? Made any complaints or anything?"

Missy flung her hand to the side, as if batting away a noxious insect. "Eva! She only left her room once today, and that was to use the toilet. Such as it is."

She made a face. When you lived in Grantville you didn't think much about the ubiquitous availability of up-time toilets. That was the single biggest drawback to relocating anywhere else except Magdeburg—and even then, only parts of Magdeburg. Anywhere else, you'd only find American-style plumbing in the palaces and town mansions of people rich enough to afford to get it installed.

Amalie Elizabeth, the landgravine of the province, had installed exactly two up-time toilets in her palace here in Kassel. One for her and one for everybody else who came to visit. But the inn where Ron and Missy were staying, despite being the best one in the city, had nothing but what amounted to an indoor outhouse.

Missy's plumbing distraction was brief. Within seconds she was back to the subject that had aroused her fury, worrying at it like a terrier attacking a rat.

"He's a *rat,* is what he is. He's had the girl in bed all day. He's taking advantage of her innocence—"

Ron raised his hand abruptly. "Missy, cut it out! You know perfectly well that if there's one thing no down-time girl is—including and probably even especially a princess—it's 'innocent.' They do sex education in this century in a way that'd have given every fundamentalist back up-time a heart attack or a stroke."

She subsided, slightly, but she was still obviously fuming.

"Have you talked with Litsa?" Ron asked. "I know she's here because I heard her singing in her room when I passed it. And judging from the tune she was singing, she was in a fine mood. That wasn't any lament or dirge, I can tell you that."

Missy shook her head.

Ron studied her for a moment. "Just been working up a head of steam in here by yourself, huh?" He extended his hand. "C'mon, Missy. Let's do see what Litsa thinks. She's probably the best friend Eva has."

By the time Missy finished expressing her concerns, Litsa was obviously fighting to keep a grin off her face.

"Why is this funny?" demanded Missy.

Litsa shook her head. "I'm sorry, it's just . . . I don't mean to be rude, but you Americans sometimes have the most peculiar attitudes. Didn't any unmarried women in your time—girls, too—get pregnant without being married?"

"Sure," said Missy. She gave Ron a glance that had its full share of Missy's current disenchantment with all things male. "Could have happened to me, if I hadn't been able to keep ol' octopus-hands here at bay."

Ron tightened his jaws a bit. As a depiction of their courtship, that was completely unfair. Missy had been no slouch herself in the groping department. But he didn't make any protest.

"And how was it handled?" asked Litsa.

"Depended on who it was. And what the family's attitudes were. Sometimes you had what they called a 'shotgun wedding.' That means—"

Litsa laughed. "I am familiar with shotguns, and the meaning is quite clear. Much the same happens in this time, on occasion. But surely not always, not even with your people."

Missy shrugged. "No. Sometimes people got abortions, sometimes they had the child and gave it up for adoption, and sometimes they just went and raised the kid themselves." She gave Ron another of those *damn-your-gender* glances. "Herselves, I should say."

"And was it a great scandal?"

"Sometimes." Missy pursed her lips. "To be honest, in our town—not much. But we were just lowlife hillbillies, not nobility. People used to make nasty jokes, anyway, about how inbred we supposedly were."

Litsa laughed again. "Compared to down-time nobility—much less royalty? You have to be a genius to keep track of how many cousins are married to each other in the German aristocracy." She shook her head. "The custom here is that such a child is quietly birthed and then unofficially adopted by the whole family. They are called 'a child of the clouds' and no one asks any impertinent questions as to exactly who and by what process the infant came into the world. Every noble line has such a child—usually more than one—somewhere in their extended family. It is really not—what do you call it?—a big deal."

Missy frowned. "But . . . What happens to the woman? Does she get disowned?"

"Not *here*. I believe it does happen in England, but

they are barely better than barbarians. We Germans are a civilized folk." She nodded at the door, beyond which and across the corridor a certain couple was presumably still engaged in the activity whose frequent consequences were under discussion. "When her father died, Eva was left with a trust fund, as were all his children. That fund legally belongs to her; it is not under the control of her brother John Casimir, who is now the head of the family. So no matter what happens, regardless of how furious her brother or anyone in the family might be with Eva for her conduct or situation, she will be able to support herself in comfort for the rest of her life. Fairly modest comfort, to be sure. But she'd be able to afford a suitable residence and employ one or two servants—and a nursemaid, should she have a child."

Litsa made a dismissive gesture. "But that's not probable. Her brother John Casimir is quite fond of his youngest sister and he's a jolly sort of fellow who spends most of his time hunting. It's very unlikely that he would be outraged even if Eva did get pregnant. I imagine he'd be more amused than anything else and make coarse jokes about how his stubborn and determined little sister—she's well known for it in the family—managed to get herself a bastard despite her pox scars. And did so not with a sweaty young stablehand but with one of the most glamorous men in Europe, to boot!"

She bestowed a gleaming smile on Missy. "I am really quite happy for Eva. She has always been very—what's the term?—stoic, I think, about her scars. She handles the disfigurement better than most people would. But somewhere deep I am sure there has always been a great deal of sorrow. There will be much, much less after she is done with Captain Lefferts."

Again, she laughed. Litsa really was in an extraordinarily good mood. "I read that marvelous up-time story just a few months ago—the one by the Dickens fellow, called *A Tale of Two Cities*. Captain Lefferts can now take for his own the hero's slogan at the end: *It is a far, far better thing that I do, than I have ever done.* And he doesn't even have to get his head cut off!"

Missy stared at her. "That is so wrong," she said.

Ron started laughing. Missy glared him and started to say something, but then just threw up her hands and stalked out of the room.

Ron returned to their room a while later, bearing a plate of pastries he'd finagled out of the inn's cook.

"Look, hon, I brought a peace offering."

Missy was back to glaring out the window. She turned her head, looked at Ron, looked at the plate, and went back to glaring out the window. "Fat chance, buddy."

But she relented soon enough. Missy had a ferocious sweet tooth and for some reason being angry always made her hungry.

"You planned—*mumph mumph*—this," she said accusingly, starting on her second pastry.

"Well, yeah," said Ron, who'd taken her place at the window. "I know you pretty well by now."

"Scheming—*mumph mumph*—bastard."

He looked thoughtfully at the winter landscape below and then up at the sky, which was overcast. "I was a child of the clouds myself, you know. Nobody's really sure who my father actually was. Biologically speaking, I mean. But it never mattered—not to my dad, who was, is, and always will be Tom Stone. Not to my brothers Frank and Gerry. And it sure as hell never mattered to me."

He turned away from the window. "Eva'll be fine, Missy. I'd be a lot more worried about Harry. I think Grantville's goodest ole boy may have finally met his match."

Chapter 10

February 25, 1636

Harry held Eva in a close embrace, which she welcomed more for the personal comfort than the shelter it provided from the bitter February wind in the courtyard.

"I'll come as soon as I can," she said. "Damn Litsa—and Missy too!"

Harry chuckled and kissed her hair. "We're not talking more than a couple of months."

That brought precious little solace. Eva had now had the experience of spending a week or so enjoying the pleasures of connubial existence for the first time in her life. Using the term "connubial" expansively, and who cared what fussy rhetoricians might argue? The prospect of now spending two months without her lover in her bed every night—that is to say, the way she'd spent the first two hundred and fifty or so months of her life—was horrendous.

"Damn Litsa," she repeated. She left Missy out of this second curse because even in her current state of distress Eva was fair-minded enough to admit that Missy was more sinned-against than sinning. The American woman had not planned on traveling to Lorraine at all, and had only been added to the expedition when it became clear that the business negotiations her husband Ron was involved in were going to continue for quite some time. It turned out that printers were even more disputatious than apothecaries. Working out suitable arrangements for launching an up-time-style publishing industry in Hesse-Kassel was going to take at least as much time and effort as it had taken to get the pharmaceutical side of the project underway.

So, a switch had to be made. Ron would stay in Kassel while Missy would go to Lorraine. Her protests that she had nothing she could do of any use in Lorraine—as opposed to her valuable work in Kassel expanding the new library and improving the university—fell on deaf ears. Well, not deaf ears so much as the cold stony terrain of necessity.

"Somebody's got to show the flag in Lorraine, Missy," Ron had argued. "It can't just be Harry on his own. It's got to be an up-timer with real credentials when it comes to health and medicine."

"What I know about pharmaceuticals could fit on a three-by-five card," she responded through tight lips. "I fumble putting on a band-aid. I hate the sight of blood."

"You eat your steak rare, for Pete's sake."

"Doesn't count. The cow's dead. It's not really blood any more."

"Of course it is."

"See? I told you I don't know squat about health stuff."

But, in the end, she gave in. She understood the logic, no matter how much she protested against it. Even in the late twentieth century, personal connections mattered in any kind of transaction. In the seventeenth century, they were essential. A hired agent showing up in Nancy, the capital city of Lorraine, and trying to present himself as the direct representative of Lothlorien Pharmaceuticals, would be looked at cross-eyed by Duchess Nicole. The wife of Lothlorien's part-owner and chief executive officer, on the other hand, would be taken for good coin.

But that had produced a further delay, since the work Missy had been doing in Kassel was important in its own right and she couldn't just up and leave without ruffling a lot of feathers—in particular, Amalie Elizabeth's, which had been the feathers whose much-desired unruffled state had been the main purpose of the expedition in the first place.

And, on the other hand, Harry didn't think he could delay any longer getting back to Lorraine. "Vincente's been on his own for weeks now," he'd said, explaining his decision to leave.

"I understand. I'll go with you," was Eva's immediate response.

"You can't!" protested Litsa. "I need your help putting all my notes into a good article. You know I don't write very well—and I promised *Simplicissimus* I'd have the first installment ready for the May issue. It needs to be posted by the end of the month. No later than March second or third, anyway. That's just a week away! You can't go now! You can't!"

Eva barely managed to restrain herself from pointing out—oh, so very, very sarcastically—that if Litsa didn't write well perhaps she should reconsider her ambition to become a journalist. But...

That would just hurt her friend's feelings. Worse, really. Litsa's decision to pursue journalism was the first time in her life that she'd set herself any goals at all, beyond enjoying herself. In truth, Eva approved of her friend's new-found purpose and didn't want to see it undermined.

"All right," she said, sighing, then held up an admonishing finger. "But it has to be all finished by the end of the month! No later!"

Litsa looked smug. "My notes are all assembled. If it takes longer than a week to turn them into a proper article that won't be because of *me*. And what difference does it make to you? We can't travel to Lorraine until Missy is ready, and that won't be until April."

"I'm leaving Matija behind," Harry said, nodding toward one of his two companions. "He can escort you when you're all ready to head for Nancy."

Eva glanced at Matija Grabnar, who was helping Donald Ohde finish loading his saddlebags. Normally, two women on a trip from Kassel to Lorraine's capital wouldn't need an escort, beyond a servant. But the ravages visited on the Rhineland by Monsieur Gaston's army and the forces pursuing him, followed by an outbreak of plague, had unsettled the whole region. There was still nothing like organized banditry, but the area was now full of destitute and desperate people, who could sometimes pose a danger.

Having someone like Matija along would eliminate that problem. Grabnar looked exactly what he was—a very experienced, very capable mercenary soldier. Just one man like him would cow any small band of amateur brigands who might think a couple of young women were an easy enough target for them.

If such would-be brigands even had that much fortitude. Missy was not a very accomplished horse-woman and had no experience at all as a hunter. Still, she was solidly built—no one would mistake her for a fragile damsel—and she'd be carrying a shotgun in a saddle holster. For her part, Eva was a very good horsewoman and an accomplished hunter. The boar spear that would be hanging on her saddle had been used more than once, and used well.

And, finally, there were her pox scars. Normally a social handicap, in these circumstances they would perhaps be of some help. Anyone who didn't know Eva, looking at her, usually added ten years to her age and two or three trolls to her temperament. In truth, it was not likely that anyone would attack them even if they didn't have Grabnar for an escort.

"We're ready, Captain," said Ohde. He was already in the saddle.

"Coming," replied Harry. He gave Eva a last kiss—not stinting on it, either—and turned away. A moment later, he was astride the horse. If they didn't know the man and his history, no one watching the practiced ease with which Lefferts got into his saddle would imagine for an instant that he'd come from a time when men rode machines instead of animals—and that Lefferts himself had never once ridden a horse before the Ring of Fire.

There was a little joke made about him by his regular companions. Other Americans, they said, had been displaced in time. The captain had found his.

Within half a minute, they were out of sight.

"Damn Litsa," Eva said. Realizing she was just talking to herself, she added: "And Missy, too. Even if not so much."

Yes, that was unfair. She was not in a fair mood.

By suppertime, however, her mood had improved. Eva found it difficult to maintain a foul temper—even when, as today, she was actively striving to do so. She didn't exactly have a "sunny" disposition. She was much too reserved and introspective for that. But, perhaps for the same reason, she also found it hard to lose her sense of perspective.

Going for two months without copulating, in any proportionate scale of suffering, didn't really compare with breaking a leg or contracting a major disease. It was more akin to bad indigestion.

Not even that, being honest about it. She even had her appetite back.

Hearing Missy muttering something, sitting next to her at the dinner table. Eva cocked an eyebrow. "I didn't catch that."

"I was just grumbling about the injustice of life. How the hell do you eat as much as you do and keep that figure?"

Eva pondered the problem—which she'd never really thought about. That was another peculiar quirk shared by most Americans, especially American women.

For reasons that were impossible to ascertain, they had an obsession with their weight. Slenderness was considered a virtue when any rational person knew it might put you at risk of getting sick—and at terrible risk should the harvest fail.

"I don't know," she replied. "It's just the way it is."

"You made a pact with the underworld," Missy accused.

"You're being ridiculous. Pass me the turnips, please. And the butter. Some more pork and bread would be nice, too."

After they finished eating, Eva even found herself drawn into Missy's discussion with Litsa concerning the developments with the library. That was to be the subject of the next installment of her friend's articles for *Simplicissimus,* now that she was done with the pharmaceutical enterprise.

"Honestly?" said Missy. "The biggest problem—and don't you say a word to anybody or I'll have every academician within a hundred miles running to complain to the landgravine—is that we don't have any trained librarians here, except me. Not *one,* so far as I can tell, in the whole benighted province."

"But surely . . ." Eva frowned. This was another problem she'd never considered before, and probably not one that was simply due to American fetishism. On most subjects, Missy Stone was as level-headed as anyone Eva had ever met.

"Surely those same academicians know how to find a book they're seeking," interjected Litsa.

"Sure—as long as it's *theirs.*" The look on Missy's face was one of great exasperation. "Each and every one of those oh-so-august-and-if-you-don't-believe-me-just-ask-them *perfessers* has concocted his own idiosyncratic way of organizing his books. That's 'idio' as in 'idiot.' It never seems to occur to them that the whole purpose of a library is to make it possible for anyone to find a volume they're looking for, which might have been acquired years earlier by someone they've never met and never will. That's the whole point of classification."

She poured herself another glass of wine. This was her third of the evening—which was quite unusual, for Missy. "No sooner did I beat them into submission over the issue of having a classification system at all—thankfully, I've got two big clubs: Amalie Elizabeth's temper if she loses it and my husband's money if I take it away—than the wretched lot of so-called scholars started arguing with me about the basis of the system itself."

She drank half the glass in one long swallow and almost slammed it down on the side table. "Oh, but no!" Missy began mimicking a pedant's speech and doing quite a good job of it. "The system devised by this Dewey fellow, whoever he was, fails to take into proper account Aristotle's division of all knowledge into three types: *episteme, techne and phronesis.*"

Now she raised her chin and gazed at her two companions down as long a nose as Missy could manage. She wasn't quite what Americans meant by "snub-nosed" but pretty close. "Since you up-timers are *grievously* deficient in your classical education, the terms refer to—"

"Scientific knowledge, craft or skill knowledge, and practical wisdom," Eva translated.

Missy glowered at her. "*Et tu*, Eva?"

Litsa laughed. "She's just showing off. Most people don't bother to learn Greek. Most of them don't even know that much Latin. She's always been too smart for her own good."

Eva shook her head. "I'm afraid there are few people in the world who can be as pig-headed and arrogant as university scholars. Dukes and margraves are abashed in their presence—in the minds of the scholars, at any rate. Have you brought them to heel yet?"

"No, but I will. See reference above to landgravine wrath and Missy takes her ball home and won't play any more. But what a ridiculous waste of my time."

She finished the rest of the wine and then contemplated the empty glass for a moment. "Damn. That's three glasses, isn't it?"

Planting her hands on the arms of the chair, she levered herself upright. "I'm off to bed, before I turn into an outright lush. I can't wait to get to Lorraine where all we've got to deal with are plague-carrying rats."

When she entered her room, Eva discovered Barbeline sitting on the bed. The French girl looked simultaneously apprehensive and stubborn.

"I don't want to sleep alone," she announced. "It was all right before, when the captain was still here and I knew he was close by." She looked down at her feet, which were several inches shy of the floor. "Please?"

"Of course, girl. Which side of the bed do you want?"

"The side nearest the wall."

"It's yours. And you can sleep here every night if you want, until we leave."

"I'm going with you, right?" Barbeline sounded very nervous, which was not like her at all.

"We already agreed you'd come with me—all three of us."

The girl had actually wanted to accompany Harry, when he left with Ohde. But the captain had firmly refused, explaining that he'd be traveling very fast and for long hours, not just to get to Nancy but to investigate the countryside as well. It would be too strenuous for Barbeline. She could come later, with Eva and Missy, at an easier pace.

"I just wanted to make sure."

After Eva had blown out the lamp and lain down, Barbeline nestled against her. A few minutes later, very softly, she asked, "Can I call you *Maman*?"

Eva's answer didn't need any thought at all. "Yes, you can."

PART III
The Duchy of Lorraine

Chapter 11

April 2, 1636

"What a mess," said Harry Lefferts. He leaned back and straightened up from the table where he, Vincente Jose-Maria de Castro y Papas and General Johann von Aldringen had been examining a map of Lorraine. "Oh, my aching back," he complained, kneading his spine with a fist.

Aldringen gave him a glance that fell considerably short of sympathy, as you might expect from a soldier in his late forties hearing a much younger man complaining about back pain. Especially one who, like Lefferts, was obviously in superb physical condition.

"God help France—not to mention its neighbors—if that bastard Gaston ever becomes king."

Aldringen grimaced. "The Almighty will need to help us in particular."

Historians of the future world Harry Lefferts had come from would call this period of European history "the Thirty Years' War." But from the standpoint of the people alive at the time it was not so much one war as a tangled cluster of wars. Each of which, by the time it ended, had produced offspring.

In terms of sheer chaos, destruction and bloodletting, the Thirty Years' War was reckoned by many of those historians to have been the single worst period in European history since the collapse of the western Roman Empire. No one would ever know for sure, but estimates placed the number of people killed in central Europe as upwards of a quarter of the entire population—a much greater death toll than either of the world wars of the twentieth century.

That much, at least, central Europe had been spared in the universe created by the Ring of Fire. The worst of the destruction would have come in the second half of the Thirty Years' War, and the arrival of Grantville in the middle of the war followed by the alliance the Americans made with Gustavus Adolphus had brought peace and even prosperity back to the Germanies. A unified nation had been produced for the first time in German history, and the victory of the new United States of Europe in the Baltic War had rocked all of the hostile powers surrounding it.

Especially France, which had suffered a catastrophic defeat at the Battle of Ahrensbök less than two years earlier, in May of 1634. Ever since, Cardinal Richelieu's hold on power had been shaky—and the ambitions of Monsieur Gaston, the scheming and unscrupulous younger brother of Louis XIII, had become turbocharged, as the Americans would say.

From March through July of 1635, those ambitions had led Gaston to ravage Lorraine, partly with his own army, partly from the forces he set loose, and partly from the forces sent to stop him. Why had he done so? A coherent answer was hard to come by. Even by the standards of the Thirty Years' War, most of whose battles had been semi-accidental collisions of armies seeking plunder, Gaston's "strategy" was impossible to distinguish from whim and caprice. Hither and thither he'd marched, looting and pillaging along the way, for no clear reason anyone could deduce except that Gaston seemed to feel he needed to be doing *something* that advanced his ambitions. In the end, he'd gone back to France with nothing to show for his efforts. But between the chaos he'd unleashed and the plague that came with it, much of Lorraine had become a disaster area.

The few cities in the duchy and most of the big towns had been spared, for the most part. Nancy had been too strongly defended for Gaston to attack with his relatively small army, Toul had been occupied by Bernhard's Burgundians, and Metz had surrendered to King Fernando rather than undergo a siege. Thereafter it had been directly incorporated into the newly expanded Netherlands.

But the countryside had suffered badly, especially in the lowlands. The terrain of the Vosges region was difficult enough that Gaston had stayed out of it, so southern Lorraine had come through relatively unscathed. But most of the duchy's population lived north of the mountains and it was those areas between the Moselle and Rhine rivers which had suffered the worst consequences, as well as the lands bordering the Meuse.

It would be inaccurate to characterize the situation in those areas as "sheer chaos." Enough of the local authorities and village leaders had survived to maintain at least a semblance of order. But many of the peasants had been reduced to desperate conditions, and that degree and extent of destitution acted like acid poured over the social terrain. The fact that the lawlessness that resulted was on such a small if ubiquitous scale made it all the harder to control.

Especially since the most of the duchy's military forces—which were none too great to begin with— had to be kept stationed at the French border, lest Monsieur Gaston be struck by another whimsy and take it into his head to march back into Lorraine.

"What have we got now, Vincente?" Lefferts asked.

The former officer in the Spanish army wagged his head back and forth briefly. "Let us call it a company."

Lefferts' lips twisted into a crooked smile. "Lot of help that is, the way you down-timers define a 'company.' That could be anywhere from a hundred to a thousand men, depending on the dance between recruitment and whatever's stipulated in your contract."

Vincente and Aldringen both smiled as well. The charge was true enough, being honest. The so-called "Early Modern Era" along with the Renaissance that had preceded it were the great periods of mercenary armies in European history. Although he was a Spaniard himself, Vincente had been not so much an officer of Spain as he'd been an officer in command of his own company employed by the Spanish crown.

Johann von Aldringen's history was even more complicated. A Lorrainer by birth, he'd briefly attended the University of Paris before joining the military forces of Spain. Twelve years later, in 1618—just as the Thirty Years' War was getting underway—he'd left Spanish service to become a soldier for their Habsburg cousins in Austria. As an officer in the imperial army he'd played an important role in defeating the Protestant forces under Mansfeld at Dessau in 1626, and was ennobled by way of reward. He'd served in the Mantuan War from 1628 to 1631, whose plunder had made him a wealthy man.

In the old time line, he would have been dead already—killed fighting the Swedish army on the Danube in July of 1634. But in this new universe he'd instead gotten another promotion of sorts. He'd been jointly selected by King Fernando of the Netherlands and Grand Duke Bernhard of the newly formed County of Burgundy to become the husband of Duchess Nicole, thereby helping to restabilize Lorraine.

Nicole had been willing enough. True, Aldringen was almost twice her age and she'd barely known the man before they were married, but that was a common situation for Europe's royalty and high nobility. Politics was always paramount, and between having a respected and accomplished general as her spouse and the joint support of the Netherlands and Burgundy, her duchy's chances for survival had been greatly improved.

The biggest threat to her now was disease, not invading armies. The plague had died down, for the moment, but it could well return—as could typhus, dysentery, typhoid fever and smallpox. In order to keep disease under control she had to restore order to Lorraine—with most of her own army forced to stand watch at the border with France.

So, she'd employed the renowned Captain Lefferts to handle the job. And while Lefferts was far better known for producing disorder than constraining it, he'd had the good sense to offer a partnership to his new friend and companion Vincente Jose-Maria de Castro y Papas, whose experience and skills were quite different from his own in many respects. For all intents and purposes, the new mercenary force being assembled in Nancy would actually be commanded by Vincente, not Lefferts.

In part, that was to help assuage whatever anxieties Nicole and her new husband might have—as rulers always did when it came to mercenaries in their employ. Lorraine was solidly Catholic, as were the duchess herself and General Aldringen. Captain Lefferts was also Catholic, formally speaking, but he made no secret of the fact that his Catholicism rested very lightly on his shoulders. Vincente, on the other hand, was a true son of the Roman church. The Spaniard attended mass regularly. The American... was said to make an appearance from time to time. Semi-annually, at best, and always on a holiday and full of alcoholic good cheer.

"We have about one hundred and sixty men, for the moment," said Vincente. "Recruitment has been slow, but I think that is mostly because people are still unsure how long we will be here. There aren't many stray mercenaries in Nancy—and most of those, we've already hired. That means we'll be depending on local boys from here on, and few of them will risk leaving an existing job for one that might be gone in two or three months."

"We'll be around longer than that," Harry said, "but you're right—that's something we still have to prove." He glanced at his wristwatch. The device was still quite functional because Harry Lefferts was a stern traditionalist, in some ways. When he'd bought his first good wristwatch upon graduating from high

school, he'd insisted on getting the old-fashioned kind
that you wound up yourself. No newfangled, unproven,
and chancy batteries for him, thank you very much.

"I've got to leave. I told the gunsmiths I'd visit
them today and finalize some purchases."

Aldringen nodded. "I think we've gotten as far as
we can today, anyway. There's no point planning any
more patrols until we have enough men to send out
on them."

Sometime after midnight, Harry woke up abruptly.
He was sweating and from the tension in his forearm
muscles he knew he'd had his fists clenched.

"Damn," he muttered, staring up at a ceiling he
couldn't see. "I'd hoped I was done with them, at
least while I was asleep."

It was the same nightmare he'd often had—as
well as having it in the form of a flashback while he
was awake.

*A street in Rome. Juliet Sutherland, her face twisted
with terror, desperately trying to outrun a troop of
cavalrymen—something a person much slimmer than
she couldn't have done. The cavalrymen passed over,
her shattered and crushed body lying behind. A man
in a dark cloak emerged from the ranks of Spanish
infantry coming after the cavalry. He stepped forward,
aimed a pistol, and shot Juliet in the back of the head.*

Harry had seen the face of the first cavalryman
who trampled Juliet quite clearly in his rifle scope.
He'd committed that face to memory. But he'd never
been able to get a good look at the man in the cloak
who'd executed her.

You could say—Harry would say it himself—that

the cloaked man had simply been doing his duty and had even been merciful, since there was no way Juliet would have survived her terrible injuries. Instead of dying slowly and in agony, she'd died instantly and felt no pain at all.

Harry sat up, swiveled in place, and lowered his feet to the floor. The feet were bare and the floor was cold, but he didn't notice at all.

Yes, you could say all that, and Captain Lefferts would fully agree. And if the time ever came when he encountered that cavalryman, he would kill him. And if the time ever came when he figured out who the man in the cloak was, and found him, he'd kill him too.

He knew from experience that he wouldn't be able to get back to sleep for a while. Although...

He hadn't had that dream—not once—during a recent week-long stretch of his life. So, closing his eyes, he brought those memories up instead.

And fell asleep within minutes.

He arose the next morning feeling more clear-headed than he had in years—maybe ever. Immediately he rose and started getting dressed.

"For once in your life, Harry," he said to himself, "don't be a fucking idiot."

He found Vincente having breakfast at the inn's common table.

"Join me?" asked the Spaniard.

Harry shook his head. "No, I want to get an early start on my patrol."

"The squad won't be ready for at least an hour."

"I won't need them. I've decided it makes more sense for me to see what's happening near the Rhine. Tell Sergeant Fischart to lead the patrol heading out to the Meuse."

Solemnly, Vincente nodded. It was only after Harry had left the room that he allowed the smile to show.

"Now who do I know who might be heading this way across the Rhine?" he asked no one in particular.

Chapter 12

April 5, 1636

"Where are we, anyway?" asked Missy, looking around the small meadow they'd stopped in. There wasn't much to see: a meadow like many others they'd crossed since leaving Hesse-Kassel, a forest surrounding the meadow that didn't look any different from most of the terrain they'd encountered, and a small road passing through the meadow that just barely made the grade from being classified as a dirt path.

Without waiting for an answer, Missy lifted herself from the saddle and slowly lowered herself to the ground. "I'm really not sure riding is easier than walking," she complained. "Just different muscles in my legs hurting, is the only benefit I can see."

Litsa, already off her horse, smiled at her. "You will get used to it. Another few thousand hours in a saddle and it will come very easily. And I have no more idea than you do where we are. Somewhere in Lorraine, southwest of the Rhine and northeast of Nancy."

"Gee, thanks," said Missy, now standing on the

ground. "Why didn't you just say 'somewhere in Europe' and save some breath?"

Litsa's smile widened to something suspiciously close to a grin. She started to make some quip in response but a rustle in the thick brush not far away drew her attention. Barbeline had been riding in front of Matija for the last stretch. He'd lifted her down after dismounting himself and she was now heading for the brush to attend to pressing personal business.

Suddenly Matija shouted and raced toward her. "Barbeline—*no!* Stay away—"

A wild pig came charging out of the brush. "Boar!" cried Litsa.

Eva, who was still in her saddle, had far more hunting experience than her friend. The charging pig was a sow, not a boar—which was no comfort at all. The sow was almost certainly nursing piglets in that brush, and was now protecting them. Sows in that state of mind were even more ferocious than boars, and while they weren't as big and didn't have the pronounced tusks of male pigs, they were still dangerous. Sows bit with their teeth rather than gouging with their tusks the way boars did, and the bite of a sow could inflict terrible damage.

As this one now demonstrated. Matija raced forward, snatched up Barbeline and flung her aside, and then started to draw his pistol. But as quickly as he'd moved, he hadn't moved quickly enough. The sow's great canine teeth clamped onto his lower leg and, with a jerk of her powerful neck and shoulders, brought him down. He cried out in pain. The cavalryman's boots he was wearing had kept her tusks from penetrating into his flesh, but his knee had suffered some sort of injury—a fracture, dislocation, or perhaps a torn ligament.

The sow clamped her jaws onto his right thigh, gnawing and tearing. Blood spurted everywhere; not enough for a major artery to have been severed, but those were still terrible wounds. She relinquished his leg and went for his face. Matija's pistol was knocked aside by her charging shoulder and he had to let go of it in order to seize her by the throat and try to hold her off. He wouldn't be able to do that for more than a few seconds, though. He was on his back with only the strength of his arms and the sow was digging her hooves in furiously.

Eva was on the ground with the boar spear in her hand without really thinking about it. She charged forward and sank the blade into the sow's ribcage. It was not the ideal place to plant a spear but she hadn't dared aim closer to the animal's throat or shoulder for fear of striking Matija instead.

If she'd been lucky, the spearhead would have slid between two ribs and pierced the sow's heart. But, not to her surprise, it got stuck in the ribcage instead. Now the enraged sow twisted to attack her instead of Matija—and with that poor placement of the spear the beast was likely to shake herself loose.

At least Matija could now scramble away from the pig and try to retrieve his pistol.

If he could find it in time. The pistol had sailed into another patch of brush and he was forced to scrabble on his hands and what use he could get out of his uninjured leg. He was bleeding badly from his right leg.

The sow outweighed Eva by at least thirty pounds and was driving her backward. That wasn't what worried Eva, though. If she'd had a good placement of the spearhead she could find someplace to brace the butt of the spear—on the ground if nowhere else. But the sow's furious energy was already working the spear loose from her ribs. The pig would tear herself up badly in the doing, but once she got free—

Ka-boom!

The sow was hammered off her feet by a tremendous blow to the right shoulder. The impact tore the spearhead lose at the same time. As the beast scrambled back onto her feet, squealing furiously, Eva brought the spear level and braced herself for the charge.

Thankfully, she'd turned down Missy's offer of up-time women's clothing. Blue jeans were comfortable, she didn't doubt, but for the purpose of protecting her legs against a sow's sharp fangs they'd be about as useful as a nightgown. The leather trousers she was wearing, with a slit skirt on top of them, would be a lot better protection.

But there was no need. *Ka-boom!* The sow was knocked down again, blood gushing from her neck. With the tenacity for which wild pigs were notorious, the sow tried again to get back on her feet, but she was now rapidly losing her strength.

Eva strode forward and drove the spear into the sow's throat, the blade passing all the way through and pinning the pig to the soil below. The animal's legs thrashed furiously and briefly, and then she was suddenly quite still.

Looking over, Eva saw Missy with her shotgun broken open in that up-time design that looked so peculiar to down-timers not familiar with the weapons. Missy was feeding shells into the two open breaches.

Trying to, at any rate. Her hands were trembling and she dropped the first shell. Hissing curses under her breath, she managed to get the second shell loaded and then snapped the weapon shut. Hurriedly bringing it back to her shoulder—

"There's no need, Missy!" said Eva loudly. "The pig's dead."

The young up-time woman stared down the double barrels of the shotgun at the sow lying on the ground.

"Are you sure?" Missy shook her head. "Never mind. Stupid question."

She took a deep breath and slowly lowered the shotgun. Then, remembering Matija, looked toward him.

Litsa and Barbeline were already tending to him. Or at least Litsa was—the French girl's contribution was mostly to hold Matija's hand and insist he wasn't really hurt all that badly even though the eight-year-old knew perfectly well the statement was preposterous. *Any* eight-year-old would have known that, much less one as wizened by a harsh life as Barbeline.

Matija's leg was soaked in blood—so was one of his hands, although Eva thought that was probably blood from his leg—and his face was pale and drawn. His eyes seemed dull, too.

Missy turned to Eva and held out the shotgun. "I need to look after him. Do you know how to use a shotgun?"

"Only in theory." Eva held up the spear. "I'll be fine with this. I doubt if there will be any more pigs, anyway."

Missy set the shotgun down and hurried over to Matija's side. She placed a hand on his forehead and then felt for his pulse. "He's clammy and his pulse is weak and rapid. He's in shock. We need to get his legs raised."

"Just a moment," said Litsa. She'd torn off a strip of her undergarments and was binding Matija's wounds with it. A few seconds later, she finished tying the jury-rigged bandage. Meanwhile, Barbeline had found a short log about four inches in diameter and was trying to drag it over.

"It's not thick enough, Barbeline," said Missy. "We need something—" Looking around, she pointed to the pack on Matija's horse. "That'll do. Eva, can you—?" She broke off, seeing that Eva was already starting to take the pack off the horse.

"What else should we do?" asked Litsa. None of them thought it odd that two women born and raised in the seventeenth century were looking for emergency medical guidance to a woman born in a far more sheltered time and place. That wasn't because Missy had any medical training, because she didn't. What the American did have, as they'd learned by now, was a semi-encyclopedic knowledge of a multitude of things. Missy herself ascribed that to her library training and a very good memory. Whatever the source, they'd found her to be a fount of information.

"Turn his head to the side," Missy said. "In case he throws up, which he might. We don't want him choking on his own vomit. Other than that, we need to keep him warm."

Litsa grimaced. Winter was past and there were daffodils blooming in the meadow. But they were still far from summer. It was a fairly typical day in early April, as far as temperature went. A bit chilly, but nothing that a healthy person couldn't withstand with a modicum of clothing. There was no way it could be called "warm," though.

Eva dropped the pack next to them. While Missy and Litsa got Matija's legs raised and pushed the pack under them, Eva brought down her own pack and dug out the blankets she used whenever they stopped for the night. Like any experienced traveler, she was unwilling to use bedding provided by inns, since they were frequently infested with lice and bedbugs.

"We can cover him with these," she said. "But one of us needs to go look for help."

"Litsa, you go," said Missy. "You're a better rider than I am."

"Eva's better than me."

"Yes, I know. But she's also better with a spear and right now I want that spear around in case another boar shows up."

Litsa chuckled and looked over at the dead pig. "That was a sow."

"Looked like a boar to me. Actually, it looked like something risen from the Pit of Damnation. That was *scary*."

"You handled it well," Eva reassured her.

Missy held up her hand. It was visibly trembling. "Let me see your hand, Eva."

Eva held up hers. It was not trembling.

"Steady as a rock. Right. You stay. Litsa goes."

After Litsa left, Eva saw that Barbeline had been dragging up more logs—or branches, rather. These were much lighter than the log she'd tried to use to raise Matija's legs.

She started to ask what the girl was doing, but then realized the answer. Barbeline had survived on her own for weeks living in a hut she'd made out of branches and whatever else she'd been able to find.

No fool, she, eight years old or not. Eva glanced at the sky and saw that they were now in mid-afternoon. Unless Litsa had extraordinarily good fortune, she wouldn't find a village whose inhabitants were willing to help in time to be back before sunset. They were going to have to spend the night out here, and it was bound to get quite cold. Not below freezing, no, but cold enough to pose a potentially mortal threat to Matija.

So. A hut—and a fire.

She hefted her boar spear and gauged the surrounding woods. She didn't think it was likely that there was another pig out there, and even if there were, the chances were low that it would be dangerous. Feral swine normally avoided people. The risk came from sows nursing piglets and from boars trapped during a hunt and striking out at whoever came near.

Bears were always a possibility, of course. But they normally didn't attack either, unless surprised or provoked.

"Barbeline, don't go far into the woods. Not more than a few feet."

The French girl shook her head. "Won't be many good branches that close to the meadow, Maman."

"No, but there'll be plenty of small ones for a fire. I'll get the bigger branches. You find what we need to get a good fire started—and we'll need enough wood to keep it going all night."

Missy rose to her feet. "I'll help. There's really not

much I can do for Matija now. We've stopped the bleeding and he's mostly unconscious anyway. The key thing is we have to keep him warm."

By sundown, they had a jury-rigged hut—more like a lean-to shed propped up against the thickest oak they could find that was on the edge of the meadow. And they had a fire going as well. Matija was too nauseated to want to eat, but the rest of them dined on the dried meat, cheese and bread they had in their packs.

They'd be crowded, all four of them packed into the small shed made of branches. But that was all to the good. In truth, Matija would get more warmth from the bodies surrounding him than he would from the fire, since they had to keep it a certain distance away lest it burn down the shed.

"And now we wait," Eva said. "And hope Litsa's found someone."

"I love adventure stories," said Missy. "Which I define as tales told about someone else freezing their butts off in a shed made out of branches in the middle of a forest full of bloodthirsty wild pigs."

Somewhere in the distance, there was a peculiar coughing noise.

"Don't forget bears," said Eva.

"And there are trolls, too," added Barbeline. Seeing the look on the faces of the two older women, she shook her head. "Well, there *are*."

But she didn't seem especially bothered by the thought. And why should she? By the time she was eight years old, she'd survived being orphaned and struck down by bubonic plague. Trolls, pfah.

Chapter 13

When Eva woke up, she immediately sensed the absence of Barbeline's little form. For all the French girl's fortitude, at night her child's nature came forward and she pressed herself tightly against Eva, almost clinging. It could be a bit annoying, but Eva never chided her for it.

She sat up abruptly. Missy was awake, having taken the last watch for the night. She was sitting at the entrance of the shed with the shotgun propped against her shoulder. The fire was still burning but it was low.

"Where's Barbeline?"

Missy pointed to the woods to the west. "Over there. Going to the bathroom, as they say." The American frowned. "Although now that I think about it, she's been gone quite a while. I haven't heard anything, though."

The girl was probably all right, then. If she'd been attacked by an animal, there'd have been plenty of noise. Still, Eva was a bit worried, so she rose to her feet and went out into the meadow, heading in the direction Missy had pointed out.

She hadn't taken more than ten steps, though, when Barbeline's voice came from her right, more than a quarter of the way around the meadow from where she was supposed to have been. "I'm over here, Maman!"

The little girl emerged from the woods. She had a piglet in each hand. Dead piglets, from the way they were hanging limply.

"These will make a good breakfast," Barbeline announced cheerfully. "Two for each of us. There are six more still back there."

She trotted past Eva, dropped the piglets next to the fire and headed back in the direction from which she'd come.

Since there was obviously no danger, Eva let her go and returned to the shed.

Missy was staring at the piglets. "Did they starve to death already?"

The up-timer had that odd streak of naiveté. Eva shook her head. "No, Barbeline probably strangled them."

"Oh."

"They'd have died anyway, without their mother. They're too young to survive on their own."

"Yeah, I know, but . . ."

About a minute later Barbeline dropped off two more carcasses and headed back to where she'd found the piglets.

"We'd better stoke up the fire," Eva said. "And hand me the knife out of my pack, would you? I'll dress them."

Breakfast was ready before long. As they dined on very tender pork—Barbeline with gusto, Eva with appetite, Matija weakly and Missy as if she were eating dead giant spiders—Barbeline swallowed another bite and said happily: "They're much tastier than rats. And cats, when you can get them."

The American looked at the girl as if she'd suddenly become a giant spider herself. Eva had a hard time to keep from laughing.

True, Barbeline could be a little unsettling. But since Eva seemed destined to become her adoptive mother, formally or otherwise, she figured if nothing else she'd have a very resourceful daughter to look after her when she was in her dotage.

The girl was hard-working, too. No sooner had she finished her pork breakfast than she went over to the carcass of the dead sow and tried to drag it back to the shed. Given that the pig weighed at least three times as much as Barbeline did, she was making slow progress until Eva and Missy came to help her. But it was quite apparent that the French girl *would* have gotten that pig to the fire even if it had taken her all day. And Eva had no doubt at all that she would have figured out how to dress the carcass even without a knife.

Given that Eva had a knife she always kept very sharp, that task wouldn't be particularly difficult.

"Do we really need to do this?" asked Missy, looking at the dead pig distastefully. Eva suspected that she'd had little experience either hunting or butchering. Meat that had been dressed and prepared for the kitchen looked a lot different from meat still on the proverbial hoof—and still encased in hide and fur.

"Yes," said Eva. "We have no way of knowing how long it will take Litsa to find help. And even if she finds it quickly"—Eva glanced at the forest surrounding the meadow—"this is a poor rural area. Poorer still, after the armies went through it, and the plague. Having a dressed pig to offer to the local peasants will gain us a considerable amount of good will."

Missy nodded. "Makes sense. Okay, I've never done this. What do you want me to do?"

Eva wielded the knife, with Missy and Barbeline helping with the rest. She worked carefully and slowly, since she didn't want to get stains on any of their clothing. It was difficult to dress a large animal without getting bloody, but she'd had quite a bit of experience and managed the task.

"Maman's good at everything," Barbeline pronounced. That simple statement brought a flush of pride and pleasure to Eva she wouldn't have expected. But all she did in response was nod sagely. Mothers didn't boast. That was a father's prerogative.

Not that *this* girl's adoptive father ever had, in Eva's acquaintance with him. From his reputation, you would have thought Captain Lefferts to be a vainglorious sort of fellow. But he didn't seem that way at all to her.

She wondered where he was, and wished he were there with them. That thought produced another flush of pride and pleasure. Quiet Eva, with her pox-scarred face. Who would have imagined the adventures she'd get herself into?

Not she herself, for a certainty, until she'd met the captain.

"Isn't life grand?" she said.

Coincidentally, that statement came just as she finished cleaning the knife. The look Missy gave her almost made her laugh again. "I didn't mean because I get such a thrill out of gutting a pig!" she protested.

By sundown, Litsa hadn't returned. They made ready to spend another night in the woods. They'd be quite a bit more comfortable, at least. Barbeline had spent all day gathering various items to improve their shed—moss, twigs and grass, which she used to seal the interior and improve their bedding. The girl seemed indefatigable.

Matija had improved, too. He'd recovered from the shock and was no longer at risk of losing his life. The biggest problem he faced now was the pain caused by his wounds. But, as you'd expect from a man with his history, he handled it with silent impassiveness.

He spoke little. Just lay there with his eyes usually closed—but with his pistol again at his side, which obviously gave him a great deal of reassurance. Barbeline had found it lying in some brush and returned it to him.

Matija had recovered enough that he could take the first watch this night, allowing Eva and Missy to get more sleep than they had the previous one. As Eva lay on her side with Barbeline cuddled tightly against her, a sudden thought occurred to her.

"Do you know how to read and write, girl?"

"No," said Barbeline.

"I'll teach you."

"Do you really think I can learn?"

"Oh, yes."

Help finally arrived just before noon the next day, although Litsa herself wasn't with the people who came. It was a party of two men, a boy about twelve years old, and three women. Two of the women looked to be in their twenties; the other was a woman in her forties who, from appearance, seemed to be the mother of one of them.

None spoke any language other than a dialect of French that was close enough to Barbeline's for the girl to be able to translate.

"They say Litsa came to their village and told them about us. But she didn't stay. She went on to see if

she could reach a bigger town. Maybe even Nancy."
Barbeline shook her head. "None of them have ever
been to Nancy, though. They say it's far away."

That didn't mean very much. Rural folk like this
were often illiterate—semi-literate, at best—and rarely
traveled any great distance from their village. "Far
away" could mean a hundred miles—or ten.

There was another exchange between Barbeline and
the villagers. Frowning, the girl turned to Eva and
Missy. "They say Litsa told them you'd pay them if
they helped you. They want to see the money. They're
not very trusting of strangers."

That, too, was pretty much a given. Missy went
back into the shed and emerged with some silver coins
in her hand. In the meantime, Eva had offered the
carcass of the pig as a gift to the villagers.

They were appreciative of the pig, but seemed
almost dazzled by the coins. They would have handled
currency very rarely.

Within a short time, cannibalizing some of the large
branches from the shed, they had a litter jury-rigged.
Once Matija was placed on it, they set out from the
meadow, with the litter carried between two of the
horses. The villagers had no horses themselves, so
neither Missy nor Eva chose to ride. They would walk
like all the others.

The journey was not particularly arduous, but it
was very hard on Matija since there was no way to
keep the litter from jostling. They'd soon left the
road, such as it was, and were making their way across
open ground. The forest was more in the nature of
interconnected woods than the sort of forest one
would encounter in North America or Russia, and

the villagers took care to avoid the worst parts. Still, it was fairly rough terrain.

By late afternoon, they reached the village. It was very small, just half a dozen huts, three on each side of an open space that could be called a "street" only by the most charitable of souls. A few faces peered at them from open doorways, insofar as the term could be applied to cloth flaps. Only one of the huts had an actual wooden door, and it looked to be ancient.

The huts were about as primitive as such rural dwellings could get. All of them had thatch roofs and wooden walls, which were plastered with wattle and daub. The edifices were about thirty feet long and half as wide. None of them had windows.

The villagers led them to one of the huts, which turned out to be uninhabited. Inside there was nothing but a small hearth at one end of the hut, with a chimney leading up to the roof. The floor was covered with straw.

Thankfully, the odor inside wasn't as bad as it would be in mid-summer. On the other hand, it would be cold tonight. The hearth was designed for cooking, not heating. There was no wood in it anyway. From the looks of things, the hut had been abandoned for some time. Months, maybe even a year. The people who'd lived there once had probably died. If not all of them, enough that the few survivors would have been taken in by other families. Villages like this were close-knit. Everyone who lived in it would be related to each other except for spouses who came from a nearby village—and they were probably related also, if not as closely.

The bigger of the two men, the one who seemed

to be in a position of some authority among the villagers, spoke to Barbeline. The girl translated.

"He says we can stay here tonight. Tomorrow night, too, if Litsa doesn't bring help from a town soon. After that, we'll have to pay more."

He did not offer any food or drink. Eva wasn't concerned about that, in itself. They still had some food left in their sacks and she wouldn't have wanted to drink the village's water anyway. Even without Missy's sometimes-ghastly admonitions, Eva had read enough about up-time medical practices to understand the danger of contaminated water. Fortunately, there'd been a stream not far from the meadow where she'd refilled all the canteens.

Still, the village headman's failure to offer food bothered her. The fare wouldn't have been much, to be sure: a small loaf of coarse rye bread, with perhaps one or two onions. But hospitality was something rural folk normally took quite a bit of pride in. At least, the ones where she'd grown up did. Perhaps customs were different here in Lorraine.

Then, finally, she realized what had been nagging at her.

"There aren't any dogs," she said. "They must have eaten them all."

Missy stared at her. "Which means..."

"They're desperate. That's why they haven't offered us any food. They don't have enough even for themselves—although that pig will keep them for a while."

Missy chewed on her lower lip for a few seconds. "If I'm interpreting that damn steely-calm demeanor of yours properly, what you're saying is that we're in trouble."

"Probably . . . yes."

"But . . . why did they help us at all? Why not just rob us right away—and kill us so there wouldn't be any witnesses."

Eva shook her head. "These villagers aren't criminals, Missy. Certainly not hardened ones. They're just desperate people, who needed time to work themselves up for something like this."

Missy leaned over to see how Matija was doing. He was asleep now.

"He's not going to be much help, I don't think. Not for days."

"Where's his pistol?"

"I have it in my bag."

"Give it to Barbeline."

Missy looked at the French girl, whose eyes were now very wide. "Why? She's only eight."

"Exactly. They won't see her as a danger."

"But—"

Eva shook her head. "Missy—*think*. We're not going to have a—what do you call it?—a 'shoot-out' with them." She glanced to the side of the hut, where Missy had propped her shotgun against the wall. "How many shells do you have left?"

"At least a dozen." The American suddenly looked both apprehensive and chagrinned. "Uh . . . well, there are two in the chambers. But the rest are still in the saddlebags."

Eva smiled. "Don't feel bad. I left my boar spear out there too."

They'd left their horses in a meadow just beyond the village limits, where the animals could graze.

Missy hurriedly started digging into her bag. As

she did so, she looked at the thick cloth covering the door. "Maybe..."

"If we're in trouble, it's already started. The horses won't be there any more. They'll have moved them somewhere else."

Missy found the pistol and brought it out. Then, checked the magazine. "It's full, looks like."

Eva shrugged. "And so what? We can keep them from charging into this hut, certainly. But we can't escape. Even a village as poor as this one will have some firearms. Old matchlocks, most likely. But at close range they'll be deadly enough if we try to escape"—she nodded toward the doorway—"and that's the only way out."

"It'll be a stand-off, then. At least..." Missy looked around the interior of the hut. "How easily does something like this burn?"

"The walls, not very easily. But unless it's rained recently, it won't be hard to set fire to the roof."

Missy made a face. "So what do we do?"

"Give the pistol to Barbeline."

"I don't know how to use it," the girl protested.

"I don't want *you* to use it. Just be ready to give it to someone when the time comes."

"How will I know that?"

"I'll tell you. Other than that, we just wait."

"For what?" asked Missy.

"For who, you should say. Someone will come looking for us."

"Harry Lefferts, you mean." Missy rolled her eyes. "That's likely to be a mixed blessing, you know."

Chapter 14

Early the next morning, Eva's apprehensions were confirmed. Just after sunrise, a woman's voice outside the hut called out something which Eva was able to translate without Barbeline's help.

"Hey, in there!"

She pulled back the cloth flap that served as a door and stuck her head out. One of the younger women was standing about twenty feet away from the hut. Off to the side, Eva could see the large man who seemed to be the leader of the small group of villagers crouching by the next hut over. He had a matchlock in his hands, with the fuse lit.

He looked unhappy but determined. The young woman—Eva thought she was his wife, but she wasn't certain—looked unhappy and scared. But . . . also determined.

"What do you want?" Eva asked. She motioned with her hand for Barbeline to come forward in case she needed translation—and Matija's pistol. Eva didn't think she could hit anything with the pistol, except by luck, but it was an up-time weapon. One of the ones they called an "automatic" pistol. The term meant that, whatever else, Eva could fire off several shots quickly if she needed to. That would probably be enough to scare off the villagers for a while.

Not for long, though, and they wouldn't run far. For all that Eva was angry at them for posing a threat, she also understood their situation and was even sympathetic. The problem was that she didn't see a good solution that would satisfy everyone.

The woman half-shouted something. Now crouched next to Eva, Barbeline whispered: "She said—"

"We have to give them all our money. I understood her." Eva had gotten familiar enough with the local dialect to be able to translate most of it into the court French she'd learned from a tutor.

"If it were only that simple..." she murmured. The problem was that the money they had on them wouldn't do more than tide the villagers over for a few weeks—two or three months, at most.

That wouldn't be enough. This little collection of huts wasn't even a village. There was no church, not even a building that could serve as a church. There was no linden tree, either, under which village council meetings could be held—although that German custom might not hold sway here in Lorraine. Eva wasn't sure.

What she was now sure of, however, was that this settlement had once been a hamlet attached to some village in the area, which had been abandoned. The people now living in it were themselves refugees from somewhere else. Squatters, not residents.

The legalities aside, what that almost certainly meant was that they had neither the tools nor the seed necessary to put in a harvest. So what good would it do them to be tided over the spring—even spring and summer? They'd just starve in the fall; they'd certainly not survive another winter. Several of the weaker ones and young children had probably died this past winter.

"Tell them we don't have enough for what they need," she said to Barbeline. Eva could have probably made herself clear, but this was no time to risk possible mistranslation.

After hearing what Barbeline shouted out, the woman's expression grew uncertain. She looked over to the man with the gun, obviously seeking guidance.

He wasn't the only one with a gun. Eva had been studying the area and had already spotted the other man who'd helped them the day before. He was crouched next to a hut on the other side and also had a gun with a lit fuse. From the looks of the thing, it was a relic from the Schmalkaldic Wars of the previous century.

Antique or not, the weapon looked deadly enough. It wouldn't be accurate beyond ten yards—if that—but the hut he was crouched next to was about that far away. In any event, she was more worried about the still younger man she could see—a teenager, from his appearance—who was crouched in the doorway of the same hut. He had a crossbow in his hands which would be more accurate than either of the firearms. If the boy knew how to use it, at any rate—which he probably didn't, at least not well, or they'd have been hunting game themselves.

But he didn't need to use it well. If Eva and Missy charged out of their hut blasting away with the shotgun and pistol, they'd certainly drive off their besiegers. And then what? Their horses would be hidden and Matija couldn't walk. If they tried to carry him on a litter they'd soon get exhausted—and, in any event, they'd be easy prey for ambushers. Barbeline was too little to carry one end of a litter, so she'd have to be their guard. And as determined and sometimes ferocious as the little girl was, the operative term was "little." She couldn't even fire the shotgun or the pistol, much less hit anything with them.

They could abandon Matija, true enough. But Eva wasn't willing to do that and she didn't think Missy would be either. Leaving everything else aside, by now Eva knew Harry Lefferts well enough to know that if she abandoned one of his companions under these circumstances, he wouldn't criticize her for it. But that would be the end of their relationship, too. And while Eva had no idea where that relationship was headed, what she was quite sure of was that she wanted to find out—and take plenty of time in the finding.

A siege, then. And they'd have to send for the captain. Eva didn't know how Harry could resolve the conflict, since he had no more money than they did. But she was confident that he'd find a way.

"Translate for me again, Barbeline. This is going to be more complicated and difficult."

The French girl nodded. "I can do it."

"Tell them that I am Eva Katherine von Anhalt-Dessau." She waited for Barbeline to shout out the sentence. The name itself wouldn't mean anything to the villagers, but the "von" part of it would.

"Now tell them that my brother—no, say it's my father—is the prince of Anhalt-Dessau."

Barbeline shouted out that sentence as well, in the local dialect. The German term *Fürst* did not mean exactly what the term "Prince" meant in English, and the French version of the title that Barbeline was using could mean several different things. But the fine distinctions didn't matter, certainly not to people as far down the social hierarchy as these peasants. All that mattered was that it sound very prestigious—and very rich.

"All right, Barbeline. Now tell them that my ransom will be very large, as long as—"

"What's a 'ransom'?"

Eva hadn't foreseen that problem. Would the villagers know the word, either? From the way the big man was holding his gun, Eva thought he probably had some military experience. If so, he'd certainly know the term. Capturing a wealthy officer and collecting his ransom was the surest way—almost the only way—for a common soldier to get rich.

"Just use the word the way I say it." She'd have to hope the local dialect wasn't too different. "Tell them that my ransom will be very large, as long as none of us is hurt. My father will be very angry if I'm hurt. Or any of my friends."

She waited for Barbeline to translate. And then waited while the villagers had time to digest the idea.

When she gauged the time was right, Eva rose to her feet. "You come with me, Barbeline. Missy, watch over me—no, you have another expression—"

"Cover me," Missy supplied. "Or 'I've got your back.'" She hefted the shotgun, looking very fierce. "Go ahead—and I sure hope you know what you're doing, girl."

Eva laid the pistol down next to Missy, swept aside the cloth and strode outside of the hut, doing her best to seem absolutely confident. Even a bit arrogant, although she didn't want to overdo it. Just enough to convince the villagers that she was really, really, really a princess with a really, really, really powerful and rich father.

She walked straight toward the big man. Seeing her come, he rose to his feet. She was relieved to see that he didn't aim the gun at her. He kept it in his hands but moved the barrel to one side.

His expression was still determined, but as she drew near it became shaded with some other emotion. Somewhere between shame and self-pity, she thought.

"I understand that you are desperate," she said. "But there is no need to do anything you will regret for the rest of your life."

Barbeline translated, but Eva thought the man already understood what she'd said. When the girl finished, he said something in response.

"He says that his mother already died, and his sister, and one of his children. He will not watch any more of his people die."

Eva nodded. "No reason he should. But tell him we need to send someone to find the captain—no, don't use that word, it'll scare—"

"What captain?" the man demanded, his hands tightening on the gun. "No soldiers!"

When he chose, it seemed the big man could speak fairly passable French, not just his local dialect. That confirmed for Eva that he'd had military experience at some point in his life. That was the usual reason that a man left his village for a time and ventured into the great world beyond.

Seeing no reason to continue with the pretense that the villager couldn't understand her without an interpreter, Eva now spoke to him directly. "The captain I am talking about is my personal guard, that's all. He will have no soldiers with him."

Of course, Harry could bring plenty of soldiers if he chose. But Eva thought doing so would be a mistake—and she could only hope that Harry would understand that.

The man looked hesitant.

Eva leaned forward and spoke to him softly. "What is your name?"

"Jules Chaboux."

"Jules, you have no choice. We need to do this quickly, for both our sakes."

"How do I know you're telling me the truth?"

"You don't. But what else are you going to do?" She turned and nodded toward Missy, who was half-hidden in the doorway—but whose shotgun was quite visible. "That is not the only weapon we have. If you charge us, several of you will die."

"We can starve you out. Or just burn down the hut."

"Yes, you can—in which case, you will get very little money. And when my captain arrives, he will take a terrible vengeance on you."

Now Jules looked very suspicious. "Alone? How? You said he had no soldiers."

"He doesn't. But he can certainly hire them."

The villager looked away for a moment. "Who will you send to find him?"

Again, Eva nodded at Missy. "Her. But she will need someone from your village to guide her. Someone who knows the way to Nancy. And it should be a woman."

Jules shook his head. "No. Two women, alone . . . too dangerous."

Eva chuckled, doing her best to make the sound seem very confident, very relaxed. "Not if one of them is my friend Missy. Not with that gun in her hands."

Jules peered at the shotgun. "It is . . . peculiar-looking."

Eva was tempted to say it was of up-time origin and that Missy herself was an up-timer. But it was quite possible that villagers as poor and isolated as these had never heard of the Ring of Fire, or had gotten a very garbled account if they had. The last thing she wanted was to have fears of witchcraft added to the mix.

"She's from Suhl. They have the world's best gun-makers there."

He'd probably never heard of Suhl, but it was the best she could manage.

"Decide, Jules. *Now.*"

There must have been something of the bite of a princess in that last command. The big man started slightly, and then lowered his gun and gestured to the woman.

"I agree we will send for the captain, and exchange you for a ransom. But I'm not letting any of you leave until we get the ransom." He nodded toward the woman, who was now standing next to him. "This is my wife Estiennette. She can find the way to Nancy. I'll send two of the men with her."

Estiennette herself didn't seem entirely confident she could do so. But Eva wasn't worried about that. Between Litsa and the village woman riding about trying to find Harry Lefferts, she didn't think there was much doubt they'd succeed. Or rather, that they'd make enough commotion that Harry would find them.

By noon, Jules' wife and her two companions were on their way. One of them was the boy with the crossbow, looking quite fierce. The other was a much older man; not the one with the other gun that Eva had seen, but someone whom she hadn't seen before. He was probably somewhere in his late forties or early fifties, although he looked positively ancient. The life of poor country folk was a hard one, and they aged quickly.

"And now we wait," she said. "How is Matija?"

From the gloom in the back of the hut, Matija himself provided the answer. "Feeling better. But this is a crazy plan. You should have just left me and made a run for it."

Eva smiled. "Is that what Captain Lefferts would have done?"

"No. Of course not."

"Well, then."

Chapter 15

Harry came into the hamlet two days later. He rode up in the middle of the afternoon, following the teenager with the crossbow. Behind him came Litsa, with Estiennette and the old man trailing at the end.

Harry dismounted in the middle of the little cluster of huts. He had a rifle in a saddle holster which Eva recognized. It was the lever-action type of up-time weapon which Harry called his "trusty Savage Model 99." Apparently it had been made for almost a century before the Ring of Fire, although his own was not that old.

She was relieved to see that Harry left the rifle in its holster. He alit on the ground carrying nothing but his pistol and Bowie knife—which still made him look quite threatening, especially the knife. People not familiar with up-time handguns were often dismissive of them, since they were considerably smaller than seventeenth-century wheel-lock pistols. Sometimes they didn't even recognize them as weapons at all, but thought they were some sort of odd-looking hammer.

She came out of the door entirely, so he could see

her—and see that she was unhurt. For good measure, she waved her hand as cheerily as she could manage.

He gave her his familiar grin. Then, transferred the grin to Jules Chaboux, who'd also come out of his hut. Chaboux was carrying his matchlock, with the fuse lit.

The moment Harry's grin fell on Chaboux, the man froze in place. And then, for all his size, took a step back as if he'd been struck.

And so, at last, Eva Katherine von Anhalt-Dessau finally met Captain Lefferts. Not the legend, not the witty charmer, not the passionate lover, but *the captain*. The ruthless killer who'd humbled two of Europe's kings and terrorized dozens of their agents. That was the same cold grin that would have been the last thing seen by Agnelli and the comte de Champcourt. It had no more humor in it than an open crevasse in a glacier.

She felt a spike of fear. She didn't want—

"Harry! Don't—"

He held out his hand to silence her. To Chaboux, he said: "What lies did my lady tell you? That I was her bodyguard? That her father is the richest prince in Germany?"

Harry's French had already acquired some of the cadence of the dialects of Lorraine, and even more of the idiom. There was no doubt that Jules understood him, without needing any translation. Mutely, the villager nodded.

Harry laughed. Like the grin, the sound had no humor in it at all. "Well, here's the truth. Her father died almost twenty years ago. Her brother is indeed a prince but they grow princes in Germany like weeds. He can afford to hunt and that's about it. And did she mention that she's the youngest of more than a dozen siblings? But that's not the worst of her lies. Here's the very worst one of them all."

He paused, for a moment. Not for a second had that killer's grin faded. "The worst lie is that I'm her bodyguard. The fact is, I'm her betrothed—and you are this close"—he held up his left hand with the tip of the thumb and forefinger less than an eighth of an inch apart—"to having really infuriated me."

He glanced at the matchlock in Jules' hands. "That's useless. So is the matchlock that he's got"—he pointed with his thumb over his shoulder at the man crouched against a wall of one of the huts—"and I'm not even going to bother talking about that kid with the silly crossbow. If there's any trouble, all three of you are dead within that many seconds."

He didn't even say that as if it were a threat. Just the same way he might have said that dark, looming clouds suggested rain was on the way.

Eva held her breath. If this exploded—

She was so tense Harry's next words startled her. "Did any of them hurt you, Eva?"

"No. No!"

"Did they hurt any of you?"

"No. Actually, they helped us... Harry—"

"Relax. As long as nobody's hurt, we're still in talking territory. Where's Missy?"

The American now emerged from the hut. Harry nodded toward her. "And that's the third lie my sweetheart told you. I swear, that woman should be ashamed of herself. She was protecting her friend by not telling you that she's the one who's *really* rich around here. Her husband owns about a third of Thuringia. Well, he would, if he bothered with land-grabbing."

Chaboux finally took his eyes off Harry and looked at Missy.

"So," Harry continued. "Here's how it's going to be." He seemed to settle back on his heels a little. That didn't bring much relaxation to the scene, though. Tigers settle back, too, just before springing.

"One of two things is going to happen," he said. "These are the only practical ways to handle the situation. The first—what's your name, big guy?"

Jules jerked his gaze back to Harry. "Jules. Jules Chaboux."

"Pleased to meet you. The first way it gets handled is that I kill you and your buddy and the kid with the crossbow. That's probably all it'll take to send the rest running off into the woods. Of course, they won't survive long, but that's their problem."

"Harry, you're an asshole!" said Missy angrily.

"I can be, no doubt about it." He shifted the grin to her, and it did not grow appreciably warmer. "Or we can handle it the second way, which you should have thought of right off the bat, Missy. And would have, if you could get yourself out of that idiot 'I'm-just-a-librarian' mindset."

"And what's that?"

"Hire 'em, for Chrissake. The whole lot, from Jules on down. I heard a baby cry on the way in so you might have to ease up on that one, even if they don't have any child labor laws in the here and now. But you can put the rest of them on your payroll."

From the blank expression on her face, it was obvious that Missy was still scrambling to catch up. "Hire them? To do what?"

"Whatever. That's *your* job, lady. You figure it out."

"But . . ." She looked at Jules, then at the others who were peering out from the various huts. "What do they know how to do?"

Harry's grin was gone, now. His expression was bleak. "Rich kids, I swear. They know how to *work*, Missy. What else do you need?"

Missy's mouth had been half-open. Now, it snapped shut.

"Okay," she said, glaring at Harry. "I'll hire them. Or tell Ron to do it. You're still an asshole."

He laughed, again—and now there was actual humor in his voice. He stepped forward a pace, moving a little slowly so as not to alarm the villager, and gave Jules a friendly slap on the shoulder. "Congratulations on your new job. If she doesn't pay you well enough, just let me know. I'm a union man, we'll straighten it out."

"Fuck you, Harry!" said Missy.

They waited until the next morning before setting out. Given the crowded conditions in the hut, Eva and Harry didn't do anything beyond cuddle. But it was still the best night she'd had in weeks.

"That was a clever ploy," she whispered. Her head was nestled on Harry's shoulder, very close to his ear. "Telling them we were betrothed."

He shook his head. "Wasn't a ploy. I was planning to ask you, I just wound up doing it sort of indirectly."

She thought about it, for a while.

Not very long, though. Less than half an hour. What made the decision so easy was that Harry didn't press her for an answer. Eva knew he would not have pressed her if she'd taken days—weeks, even months—instead of minutes. The man was able to see past the quiet, not just the scars.

"Yes," she said. "I have to caution you, however. My brother may be angry, when he hears about it, and deny me any dowry."

Harry shook his head again, more vigorously. "I don't give a fuck about the dowry."

She slapped his chest. "Silly! I know that. But I *do*. Not enough that I won't risk losing it, but I'd much rather not. How do you up-timers survive, you're so impractical?"

When she told Litsa, about an hour after they all set off for Nancy, her friend was ecstatic. She was practically bouncing up and down in the saddle.

"Oh! The scandal! But you have to let me write the story before anyone else! That's what they call 'getting the shovel.' I think."

Eva laughed. "Who's going to publish a story like that?"

"My new magazine. It'll be what they call a scandal sheet."

"You can't afford to publish a magazine."

"Missy will invest in it, once I tell her what the lead story will be. She is still furious with the captain."

Eva frowned. That didn't sound like Missy. "She's angry that Harry made her hire the villagers?"

"No, she's fine with that. It's that he made her feel stupid. Missy really hates feeling stupid."

Eva understood that feeling perfectly. She rarely felt stupid, which just made her detest the sensation all the more on the rare occasions when it happened.

"She's right," she said, nodding. "She should seek

vengeance. At all costs—well, at least the cost of financing a new magazine. What about *Simplicissimus*, though?"

Litsa waved her hand airily. "Oh, I'll still write for them. I'll have to, in order to maintain my cover."

"Your . . . *what*?"

"Cover. It's an up-time expression. It means my disguise, basically."

"What disguise?"

Litsa looked at her as if she really were stupid. "My cover as a respectable journalist. Eva, you *can't* write for a scandal sheet under your own name! I'd be *ruined*."

Eva tried to follow the logic and . . . managed. Barely.

"What pseudonym should I use? 'The Tattletale,' perhaps?"

"Or the 'Blow Fly.' Since you'll be everywhere there's something rotten."

"Don't be spiteful just because you're the subject of a scandal."

Once they reached Nancy, they went directly to the Ducal Palace. The palace had been built by René II, Duke of Lorraine, a century and a half earlier. As often happened with such palaces, it was expanded in the years that followed in a rather haphazard manner. One wing had eventually become vacant and Lefferts and his Spanish partner had gotten Duchess Nicole's permission to turn it into the domicile—officially, "the barracks"—of their newly formed militarized police force.

The company they were forming, even when it was fully fleshed out, would have room to spare in "the barracks." Harry figured that there would be plenty of room there for the villagers; and, at least for the time being, they could be set to work tending to the needs of the soldiers.

Temporarily, at least. The soldiers would already be gathering their own camp followers, who would eventually take over that work. But by then, the new enterprises being launched by Ron and Missy Stone should have plenty of employment opportunities even for semi-literate country folk.

Such was Harry's theory, at any rate. Missy had her doubts—but of one thing she was dead certain.

"Damned if I'm going to pay for your troops' cooks and laundresses, Harry. That's on your dime."

Harry looked mournful and began singing. "*Hard-headed woman, soft-hearted man, been the cause of trouble ever since the world began.*"

"Fuck you, Harry. And the pelvis you rode in on."

The timing was wrong, but Eva wasn't about to get stubborn on the subject. She was far too passionate herself, leaving aside whatever Harry might have wanted. The up-time term was "horny," which she thought was a bit grotesque.

To his credit, Harry had done his best to find a local variety of what he persisted in calling "rubbers" even if no one except up-timers and a few down-timers knew what rubber was. But, as he'd predicted, the devices were not especially reliable. One of them broke quite spectacularly in mid-use.

Besides, she disliked the things almost as much as he did. "Never mind," she finally said. "I'll take my chances for now. Next month we can do the right thing."

It sounded good, anyway.

❖   ❖   ❖

Vincente Jose-Maria de Castro y Papas returned to the barracks a week later, from a tour he'd done with twenty of his cavalrymen up the Meurthe River as far as the Vosges Mountains.

"No trouble worth talking about," he reported. "One small bandit gang was rumored to be in the area, but if they exist at all they're keeping very quiet. But what's this I hear that we're now a charitable organization? When did you become soft-hearted?"

Harry began crooning again. *"Hard-headed woman, soft-hearted man, been the cause of trouble ever since the world began."*

He shook his head. "What can I say? My betrothed insisted."

"My congratulations. To you. Where is Eva, by the way? I need to offer her my condolences."

"Ha. Ha. Ha. She and the Stone woman are having an audience with the duchess."

"About what?"

"You're asking me? Three women, together. It's bound to cause trouble. *Hard-headed woman, soft-hearted man, been the cause of trouble—*"

PART IV
Nancy, capital of the Duchy of Lorraine

Chapter 16

May 11, 1636

Ron Stone arrived in Nancy toward the middle of May. He would have rushed down immediately upon getting the news, but Missy made it clear in her letter that she was fine, the crisis was over, there wasn't anything for him to do, and he might as well finish up his business in Kassel first. Eva had already observed that while American marital and sexual relations inclined toward overwrought mysticism, Missy and Ron were almost as practical in that respect as level-headed down-timers.

Leaving aside the informality of the language, their undemonstrative greeting upon his arrival would have done any margrave and margravine proud.

"You okay, hon?" he asked, when he came into the big entry chamber that also served as a mess hall when all the troops were in the barracks. Missy was sitting at a table against one of the walls with Eva.

"Yeah, I'm fine," she said. "D'you get everything settled with the Hessians?"

"Much as we can for the time being. How're things shaping up down here?"

"Well enough—given that there's still not a lot we can do except help to settle things down. But that's mostly work for Harry and Vincente. You want to meet our new employees?"

"Maybe in a day or two. I'm still looking a little cross-eyed at their qualifications. 'Experienced at taking boss's wife hostage' isn't what you normally run across in a job application."

Missy smiled. "Especially since they flunked the qualifying exam. I admit that's mostly because of Harry." Her lips tightened a little. "Even if he's not my favorite person in the whole wide world."

"You aren't still pissed at him?"

"Like they say, that glass is half-empty. Or is it half-full? I can never remember."

She rose, gave her husband a kiss and an embrace, and then pointed at Eva. "She's still besotted with him, though, so I make allowances as best I can."

Ron nodded by way of a greeting, then asked, "What are you writing now?"

Eva looked down at the papers in front of her. "Just finishing the book. Or trying to, at least. I'm not happy yet with anything I've come up with for an ending."

"I suggested she end the book by saying 'and then I jumped his bones,'" said Missy. "But she thinks that's too crude."

Eva shook her head. "It's not the crudeness I object to, it's the violation of narrative distance. *The Adventures of Captain Lefferts, as told to Eva Katherine von Anhalt-Dessau* suggests a certain detachment on the part of the author. Hard to maintain that image when the reader knows that some of the tales were recorded while the author and her subject were nude, sweaty and entangled."

She smiled very cheerfully. "Which we have often been, of late."

✧   ✧   ✧

Litsa came charging into the room, holding several copies of a publication of the type that the French call a *bibliothèque bleue* and Germans called a *Volksbuch*. It was basically a broadside folded and cut so as to make an eight-page chapbook. The French typically used a cheap blue paper cover, but this one had a cover that seemed of somewhat better quality and was illustrated by the image of a peering eye. The image was clearly patterned after an Eye of Horus, but the artist had somehow managed to impart a vaguely leering aspect to it.

As Litsa came up to them, the title of the chapbook could be seen emblazoned across the top: THE NATIONAL OBSERVER. With a slogan inscribed in smaller letters just below:

Enquiring minds want to know!

"No," Ron groaned. "Please tell me that isn't what it looks like."

"The very first issue!" Litsa exclaimed happily. "It just came from the printer." She passed out copies to all of them. "The center story is mine. Not under my own name, of course."

Opening the chapbook, they saw the story headline. It was hard to miss.

CAPTAIN LEFFERTS AND
THE HOCHADEL VIXEN
By Agnetha

Eva burst into laughter. "By Agnetha! You are shameless, Litsa—shameless!"

Litsa grinned. "I thought it was—what is the American term?—'a nice touch,' I think."

Missy looked puzzled. "I don't get it."

"Agnetha is the German version of the Greek name Hagne," Eva explained. "The name is derived from the word *hagnos*, which means 'chaste.'"

She read through the first part of the story. "Which this article is anything but."

She read another few sentences. "That's not true at all!" Another few. "Oh! That's pure slander!"

And so it went, until she finished. Holding up the chapbook, she said: "This is a complete tissue of lies and fabrications, with just the occasional nugget of half-truths embedded in it."

But she was smiling when she said it.

"You're not offended?" Missy asked curiously. "Or worried this will give you a bad reputation?"

Eva dropped the chapbook onto the table and shrugged. "No, there's no clear description of this so-called 'Hochadel vixen.' Beyond generic nonsense like 'voluptuous' and 'slinky'—which is particularly silly because Litsa's using the root of the German word 'schleichen' which doesn't really mean the same thing at all. She'll probably get away with it, though, since this is written in Amideutsch. She just added a new bastard to that already illegitimate tongue."

She studied the cover of the chapbook for a moment, her lips pursed. "It's true that there are enough personal details about the 'vixen' that someone who knew me could figure it out, but not unless they knew me well. That's because of the critical detail that Litsa omitted."

Eva reached up and stroked her face. "There's no mention of the pox scars. Without those, no one will think of me. Well, my brother John Casimir, since he has a low mind, and one or two of my nosy sisters. But

I was going to tell my brother about Harry, anyway. Better he finds out directly from me than second-hand."

Ron had been reading the story himself. "I got to tell you, Litsa, the writing's pretty awful. I'd call it purple prose except it's more like ultra-violet. No, more like gamma ray prose."

Litsa grinned again. "I know I don't write well. That's a real problem when I'm working on a *Simplicissimus* story, but for this it's perfect. It makes the stuff seem authentic."

"Using the term 'authentic' creatively," mused Missy, who was also reading the article. "Kind of like saying that torture is the new massage."

"Yeah, I can hear the words shrieking," said Ron, wincing at a particularly tormented clause.

"None of this is helping me figure out a good ending for my book," Eva complained.

June 1, 1636

The solution to Eva's problem arrived the next month, in the person of one Baldur Norddahl, sometime Norwegian adventurer and currently the right-hand man of Prince Ulrik of Denmark.

He was looking for Captain Lefferts, but had to wait five days for Harry to return from one of his patrols. Norddahl didn't seem in the least bit impatient, however.

"I have no objection to lounging about in the luxury of what used to be the wing of a palace and still looks pretty much the same," he commented. "It's unfortunate that your plumbers haven't arrived yet to install the up-time toilet, of course."

Missy had *insisted* on that—and damn the cost. Her husband hadn't argued the point. He was no more fond of seventeenth-century toilet arrangements than she was.

"Still," Norddahl continued, "it's a great step up from my days as a slave for the Barbary pirates."

Litsa had been sitting in on the conservation. Her face now got the intense expression that always came to her when she spotted a possible story—all the more intense if it would be a story for *The National Observer* instead of *Simplicissimus.*

"Is it true that lascivious Moorish girls love to cavort with their slaves?" she demanded. "As a way of gaining some experience before they pass themselves off as virgins to their Moorish grooms. You always hear that."

The Norwegian laughed. "Not likely!"

"Wrong answer," she said, frowning.

"Well, there were stories, of course."

Litsa smiled. "Better answer. What were they?"

The next evening, when Eva, Ron and Missy met to discuss the business of the day, Litsa was absent.

"Where is she?" asked Ron. "I haven't noticed Baldur around anywhere, either."

Missy got a prim expression on her face. Eva pointed toward the upper floors. "Litsa's investigating the likelihood of Norddahl's improbable but not impossible tales. That part of it which can be investigated without going to Algiers or Salé, at least."

"They've been at it since late last night," Missy said. She gave Eva a very disapproving look. "Litsa's supposed to be a Calvinist like you, is that right?"

Eva nodded. "Yes, we both belong to the Reformed

church. There are not many Lutherans in our part of the Germanies."

"Huh!" Missy shook her head. "I swear, every illusion I ever had about Puritans has now been trampled flat. Completely flat. Squished-by-an-elephant flat."

Missy had once explained to the curious—and then appalled—princess of Anhalt-Dessau the history of the Puritans. At least, as interpreted by late twentieth-century Americans.

"I told you, that history made no sense at all. The teachings of the Reformed church can be quite stringent on theological matters, yes." Eva waved her hand dismissively. "But those issues involving sex that seem to preoccupy Americans so often—pfah. Didn't any of you ever read the Bible?"

Ron was now curious himself. "Yeah, I figured that out about Calvinists a while back. But you do take your creed very seriously about some issues. Like, for instance, Harry's a Catholic. What happens if your betrothal culminates in a marriage?"

"We discussed that already. Harry will convert, of course." Eva got a rather prim expression herself— something which came very rarely to the woman. "He has a properly dismissive attitude toward papistry. I admit, that comes more from a general indifference to theology than a truly suitable doctrinal stance. But I don't care that much and no parson—certainly not one employed by *my* family—will ask any awkward questions. The fact of the conversion will be enough."

"You're kidding," said Missy.

"No, not at all. Why would I?"

"Harry *Lefferts*? A born-again Calvinist? Oh, my aching brain."

June 6, 1636

When Harry came back to the barracks, his first words were: "I'd say we ought to celebrate D-Day a few centuries early, except that it'll never happen now."

Then, spotting the Norwegian in the small group that had gathered to meet him, his face became impassive. "Baldur Norddahl, in the very flesh. I haven't seen you since Copenhagen—what was that? More than two years ago. Am I right in assuming that I'm the reason you're here? And if so, why?"

Norddahl smiled thinly. "Yes, I came to see you. As to the reason... It will begin, I think, with another invasion of France. A quiet one, though. No guns will be needed."

Harry's responding smile was even thinner. "At the beginning, you mean."

The Norwegian nodded. "At the beginning. Later... Yes. If all goes well."

Ron shook his head. "You guys have a really screwed-up definition of 'if all goes well.' I'm thinking you don't need—or want, for that matter—anyone else involved in this discussion except Harry."

"That is correct," said Norddahl. "I mean no offense, but I would prefer to speak to Captain Lefferts privately."

"Believe me, none is taken. Come on, Missy. Loose lips sink ships and we don't want to hear this anyway."

"You got that right." His wife turned to follow. "Eva, Litsa, you coming?"

Harry placed a hand on Eva's shoulder, holding her in place. "She stays, Baldur. If that doesn't suit you, so be it. You know the way out."

"I'm staying too!" insisted Litsa. "There's a story here—don't try to lie to me, Baldur!"

He shook his head. "Yes, there's a story—but not one you'd be able to tell for quite a while. If ever."

"I'm very patient."

"Not in my experience," he said, grinning quickly. Then, sobering, he shrugged his shoulders.

"I don't really care if you stay—but if you do, you are sworn to silence until released from your oath. Which won't be sworn to me, but to the emperor."

That brought a measure of solemnity to everyone. Baldur waited until the Stone couple had left the room. Then he said to Harry:

"I assume you've heard the story about the Swedish queen's murder last October. And the assassination attempt on Princess Kristina and Prince Ulrik that was part of the plot."

Harry nodded. "The one that has Richelieu being behind the plot? Yes, I've heard it—but I stopped believing in fairy tales when I was about seven or so."

Norddahl cocked his head a bit. "You don't believe it, then?"

"No, of course not. It makes no sense."

"What do you think is a more likely explanation?"

This time, it was Lefferts who grinned quickly. "Why should I waste my time and effort explaining when it's obvious you're about to tell me? But if I was a betting man—which I am, now that I think about it—I'd put my money on the same Huguenot fanatics who tried to kill the pope."

"That is my theory as well. Mine and Prince Ulrik's, I should say. We discussed it at some length before I left Magdeburg."

Harry ran fingers through the short beard he favored. "You want me to work with you on it?"

"Yes." Norddahl patted his jacket. "I have a commission here signed by the emperor himself. There's a generous stipend, a bonus if we complete the mission successfully"—again, the quick grin appeared—"and a promotion to colonel. Also contingent upon success, of course. That would be a colonelship in the Swedish army, by the way. It wouldn't affect your rank in the USE's military."

Harry looked at Eva. "What do you think, hardheaded woman? Is a promotion likely to sway your brother on the dowry? And if so, is it worth being separated for a while?"

Eva shook her head. "No separation would be needed." She turned to Norddahl. "Am I right in assuming that you will begin this mission by visiting Henri de Rohan?"

"Yes. If there's anything happening among the Huguenots, the duke is almost certain to know something about it." Baldur shrugged. "Whether he will be willing to confide in us is uncertain."

Eva displayed her own quick grin. "How fortunate for you, then, that you will have me on the mission. Since I have something I can dangle under Duke Henri's nose by way of possible reward if he's cooperative."

Now, both Norddahl and Lefferts looked keenly interested. So did Litsa, of course.

"And what's that?" asked Harry.

"Everyone knows—well, everyone in the Reformed nobility—that the duke of Rohan is almost desperate to find a suitable husband for his daughter Marguerite, who is his only heir. And it so happens that another of my brothers, Georg Aribert, is close to the same age as Marguerite—not that that matters much, of course."

"He's still single?" asked Litsa. "I thought he was sniffing after that—I forget her name—?"

"He still is. But since that would have to be a morganatic marriage, my oldest brother John Casimir is not happy with the idea and would be delighted—no, *ecstatic*—if I could arrange a marriage between Georg and Marguerite de Rohan."

She spread her hands in a gesture of uncertainty. "There's no way to know if any of this would come to pass, of course. But it gives us a plausible reason to visit Rohan and would certainly incline him toward us favorably."

Norddahl was now looking at Eva much more intently than he had before. "Captain Lefferts, you do realize you're betrothed to a schemer? The Borgias and Medicis couldn't do any better."

"Yeah, isn't she something? All right, since Eva's okay with the idea, when do we leave? I just need a couple of days to square it with my partner Vincente. He should be back tomorrow from his patrol."

"The day after that, then. Unless you foresee a problem with this Vincente fellow."

Harry shook his head. "No, this has all become pretty routine. The key now is the anti-epidemic work, and that's mostly in Ron and Missy's corner from here on. I was already starting to feel a bit like a fifth wheel around here."

❖   ❖   ❖

That night, Eva finally finished the book.

> *And so, that is the last we will see of Captain Lefferts for a time. Departing on another mysterious mission, this one at the behest of Emperor Gustav Adolf himself.*
>
> *What mission? Where? That remains to be seen. Of one thing, however, we can all be sure. The day will come when all of Europe will hear about his newest exploit.*
>
> *No, one other matter is certain. Whenever that day comes, this author will be the one to tell the tale.*
>
> —*Eva Katherine von Anhalt-Dessau*

June 9, 1636

When they reached the outskirts of Nancy, they stopped for a moment to let the horses drink from a stream by the road. For the moment, Barbeline was riding in front of Eva.

Eva glanced at Baldur Norddahl and Donald Ohde, who were riding ahead of them, to make sure they were distant enough not to hear her. "I think I'm probably pregnant," she said. "Although I'm not sure yet."

"Okay," said Harry. "Let me know when you're sure so we can stop"—he glanced at the girl—"with that blasted, you know. Monthly stuff. Which looks like it didn't work anyway, so we wasted a lot of opportunity."

Barbeline frowned. "Make sure it's a girl, Maman. I want a sister. Boys are disgusting."

"I'll do my best," said Eva.

PART V

*Dessau, capital of the
principality of Anhalt-Dessau
Now part of the new province of Magdeburg*

Chapter 17

July 16, 1636

"You have to put a stop to it!" said Sibylle Christine, the countess of Hanau-Münzenberg. She had a chapbook clutched in her fist which she waved under the prince of Anhalt-Dessau's nose. "This is Eva Katherine in this disgraceful thing even if they don't name her! You know it is! And there are other stories about her too! It's not just this!"

John Casimir leaned back from his sister's spluttering outrage.

"Yes, I know it's her. What other young woman in the Hochadel would kill a rampaging boar to keep it from gutting her lover? And with a spear, just like Eva would!" He grinned. "There's bound to be some truth to that story, although I really doubt they were copulating when the pig came out of the brush. And it was probably a sow."

"It's not funny, Cas!" Sibylle Christine even went so far as to smack her older brother's head with the chapbook.

"Stop it, Sibbi. I knew about it anyway." He nodded toward the upper floor of the small palace, where his chambers were located. "I got a letter from Eva last week, letting me know about her betrothal. Of course, the letter didn't have any of the coarse details in that stupid chapbook."

Sibylle Christine's jaw sagged. "You already knew? Then why haven't you done something—?"

"Done *what*?" demanded the prince. "The only thing I can threaten her with is to withhold a dowry."

"Then do it! That'll bring her to heel!"

"Oh, don't be stupid. Just because Eva's quiet doesn't mean she's timid. You know what she's like when she gets stubborn about something. Besides, it would be a terrible idea anyway."

His sister's jaw sagged still further. "What are you talking about? Just because that silly child has let idiot American fantasies into her head is no reason for us to do so! Marriage is a serious business!"

John Casimir's indulgence was gone by now. "So it is, Countess. And perhaps you should start thinking seriously yourself. In case you haven't noticed, the emperor is back on his throne—quite functional, I assure you, even if he does have the occasional seizure—and he is none too pleased at the moment with Germany's aristocracy, especially the Hochadel, since most of them flocked to Oxenstierna and that blasted fool Wettin."

He glared down at her. "Or did you miss all those trivial events? The defeat of Banér by Stearns outside of Dresden. The killing of Oxenstierna—which they're now calling an execution, you might take note. Wettin's disgrace, although he's still in office. But he won't be when the new election is held. Either Piazza or Strigel will be the new prime minister. I'm hoping for Piazza myself, even if he is an up-timer."

The prince rubbed his face. "I had the good sense to keep my distance from Wettin this past year. And since I have the additional good fortune of being married to a half-sister of the former landgrave of Hesse-Kassel who got killed fighting the Poles, people associate me with his widow Amalie Elizabeth more than any other prominent figure in the Hochadel. So I am not under any suspicion personally.

"But—!" He held up an admonishing finger and wagged it in front of his sister's nose. "I have had to give up my campaign to get Anhalt-Dessau transferred from Magdeburg Province to Saxony."

Sibylle Christine looked blank-faced. "You did? But we all agreed..."

"That we'd be much better off as part of Saxony once John George was overthrown? For the love of—" John Casimir managed, barely, to refrain from blasphemy. "Did you miss *that* too, Sibbi? Saxony's in the clutches of Gretchen Richter, these days. Between her and those radicals in Magdeburg, I'll stay with Magdeburg, thank you very much."

"She's not—Ernst is still—"

He waved her down impatiently. "Yes, yes, yes. Ernst Wettin is still officially Saxony's administrator. He even gets along fairly well with Richter, he told me recently. But he also told me that he 'administers' Saxony—and Richter—the way a man administers the tide. He tells it to go out when it's going out, and tells it to come back when it's coming back.

"So, yes, let us be cold-blooded, practical and serious

about the marital prospects for our youngest sister. That would be the scarfaced one, remember, whom we all assumed would never get married at all. So what have we lost? Under the circumstances, I am not at all disturbed by the likelihood that we will soon be associated by marriage with a well-known up-timer."

"But he's absolutely notorious!"

"Yes, he is. All the better. Besides—"

The prince's good humor returned. "Little Eva! Who would have imagined she'd turn into such an adventuress? Whenever she returns with her new husband—which she will, since there will certainly be a sizeable dowry waiting for her—I can take her hunting and she can show me how she brought down that wild boar while she was stark naked."

"It's not funny, John Casimir!"

IF YOU LIKE...
YOU SHOULD TRY...

DAVID DRAKE
David Weber
Tony Daniel
John Lambshead

DAVID WEBER
John Ringo
Timothy Zahn
Linda Evans
Jane Lindskold
Sarah A. Hoyt

JOHN RINGO
Michael Z. Williamson
Tom Kratman
Larry Correia
Mike Kupari

ANNE MCCAFFREY
Mercedes Lackey
Lois McMaster Bujold
Liaden Universe® by Sharon Lee & Steve Miller
Sarah A. Hoyt
Mike Kupari

MERCEDES LACKEY
Wen Spencer
Andre Norton
James H. Schmitz

LARRY NIVEN
Tony Daniel
James P. Hogan
Travis S. Taylor
Brad Torgersen

ROBERT A. HEINLEIN
Jerry Pournelle
Lois McMaster Bujold
Michael Z. Williamson

HEINLEIN'S "JUVENILES"
Rats, Bats & Vats series by Eric Flint & Dave Freer
Brendan DuBois' *Dark Victory*
David Weber & Jane Lindskold's Star Kingdom
Series
Dean Ing's *It's Up to Charlie Hardin*
David Drake & Jim Kjelgaard's *The Hunter Returns*

HORATIO HORNBLOWER OR
PATRICK O'BRIAN
David Weber's Honor Harrington series
David Drake's RCN series
Alex Stewart's *Shooting the Rift*

HARRY POTTER
Mercedes Lackey's Urban Fantasy series

JIM BUTCHER
Larry Correia's The Grimnoir Chronicles
John Lambshead's *Wolf in Shadow*

TECHNOTHRILLERS
Larry Correia & Mike Kupari's Dead Six Series
Robert Conroy's *Stormfront*
Eric Stone's *Unforgettable*
Tom Kratman's Countdown Series

THE LORD OF THE RINGS
Elizabeth Moon's *The Deed of Paksenarrion*
Shattered Shields ed. by Schmidt and Brozek
P.C. Hodgell
Ryk E. Spoor's Phoenix Rising series

A GAME OF THRONES
Larry Correia's *Son of the Black Sword*
David Weber's fantasy novels
Sonia Orin Lyris' *The Seer*

H.P. LOVECRAFT
Larry Correia's Monster Hunter series
P.C. Hodgell's Kencyrath series
John Ringo's Special Circumstances Series

ZOMBIES
John Ringo's Black Tide Rising Series
Wm. Mark Simmons

GEORGETTE HEYER
Lois McMaster Bujold
Catherine Asaro
Liaden Universe® by Sharon Lee & Steve Miller
Dave Freer

DOCTOR WHO
Steve White's TRA Series
Michael Z. Williamson's *A Long Time Until Now*

HARD SCIENCE FICTION
Ben Bova
Les Johnson
Charles E. Gannon
Eric Flint & Ryk E. Spoor's Boundary Series
Mission: Tomorrow ed. by Bryan Thomas Schmidt

GREEK MYTHOLOGY
Pyramid Scheme by Eric Flint & Dave Freer
Forge of the Titans by Steve White
Blood of the Heroes by Steve White

NORSE MYTHOLOGY
Northworld Trilogy by David Drake
Pyramid Power by Eric Flint & Dave Freer

URBAN FANTASY
Mercedes Lackey's SERRAted Edge Series
Larry Correia's Monster Hunter International
Series
Sarah A. Hoyt's Shifter Series
Sharon Lee's Carousel Series
David B. Coe's Case Files of Justis Fearsson
The Wild Side ed. by Mark L. Van Name

DINOSAURS
David Drake's *Dinosaurs & a Dirigible*
David Drake & Tony Daniel's *The Heretic* and *The Savior*

HISTORY AND ALTERNATE HISTORY
Eric Flint's Ring of Fire Series
David Drake & Eric Flint's Belisarius Series
Robert Conroy
Harry Turtledove

HUMOR
Esther Friesner's *Chicks 'n Chainmail*
Rick Cook
Spider Robinson
Wm. Mark Simmons
Jody Lynn Nye

VAMPIRES & WEREWOLVES
Larry Correia
Wm. Mark Simmons
Ryk E. Spoor's *Paradigm's Lost*

WEBCOMICS
Sluggy Freelance... John Ringo's Posleen War Series
Schlock Mercenary...John Ringo's Troy Rising Series

NONFICTION
Hank Reinhardt
The Science Behind The Secret *by Travis Taylor*
Alien Invasion by Travis Taylor & Bob Boan
Going Interstellar ed. By Les Johnson